HER GUARDIANS SERIES

1-4

G. BAILEY

Her Guardians Series

1-4

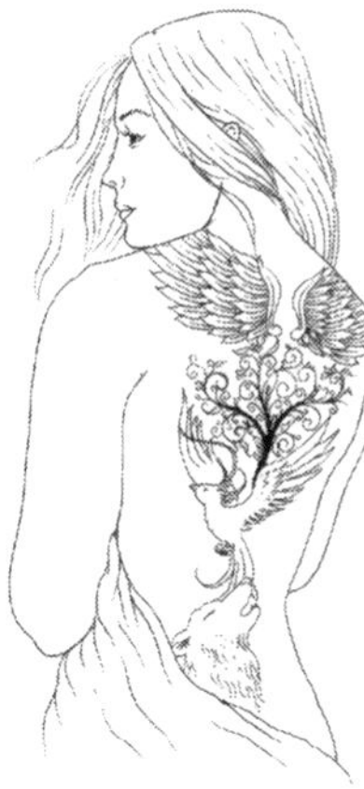

Wolf. Vampire. Witch. Angel. What happens when you're destined for all four?

When Winter started university with her best friend Alex, she didn't expect to find herself in the middle of a supernatural war. Who knew saving a stray wolf could earn you the alliance of the pack.
With danger, romance and old prophecy's ruling Winter's life, is love enough? Can Winter find the strength she needs when family secrets are revealed and threaten to destroy everything?

Two bonus epilogue chapters exclusive to this box set at the end!

WINTER'S GUARDIAN

Her Guardians Series

When Winter started university with her best friend Alex, she didn't expect to find herself in the middle of a supernatural war. Who knew saving a stray wolf could earn you the alliance of the pack. To make things more complicated, the broody and very attractive Jaxson is tasked with keeping her safe from the growing vampire threat in town. It's a shame he can't stand her and enjoys irritating the hell out of her. When she finds out her new boyfriend has his own secrets, can she trust anyone anymore?

What happens when you get yourself stuck in the middle of a war?

Reverse Harem

PROLOGUE

The blue-sided human will choose a side.
When four princes are born on the same day, they will rule true.
Her saviour will die when the choice is made.
If she chooses wrong, she will fall.
If she chooses right, then she will rule.
Only her mates can stop her from the destruction of all.
If the fates allow, no one need fall.
For only the true kings hold her fate, and they will be her mates.

"The prophecy has come true. I found out that the vampire, angel, and witches' royal sons were born yesterday," my sister says to me, a look of worry on her faultless face as I hold my little baby closer to me.

I look down at the sweet, little boy in my arms. The new shifter prince, my son and the last royal male wolf. His green eyes are glowing as he looks up at me like he holds the entire earth in his sweet eyes. I know the goddess will protect him.

"Then it's true. The goddess planned this all," I whisper.

"We must make sure they are close. Despite our wars and disagreements, the children should grow up together," she tells me and I know she is right.

"We have a lot of planning to do, sister." I stare down at my little boy as I speak to her, "You are right, if they have any chance of winning the human's heart, they must be united."

"Yes, my queen." My sister bows her head at me and leaves the room. If only I could protect my child from the responsibility he now has on his tiny shoulders.

The responsibility of saving the whole world.

1

WINTER

"So, class, please start by reading page thirty-two in your books," the professor goes on, as my class starts after he walks in. The professor looks as ancient as the old room we are all sat in, with his brown hair and beard, and very dated clothes that look like he hasn't washed them in a while. I push my own out-of-control, wavy brown hair over my shoulder, wishing I had tied it up this morning. It's a hot day, and the room is stuffy because of the lack of opened windows, making my hair stick the back of my head. I glance over at my best friend, Alex, who has her head on her desk, lightly snoring. I chuckle before kicking her leg and waking her up. She moves her waist-length, straight, red hair off her face to glare at me. "I was resting, Win," she mutters, hiding her eyes with her arm and huffing at me.

"The professor is here," I giggle, trying to whisper to her as she nearly falls off the side of the desk, while half asleep.

"Oh, what page?" She yawns, looking like she is going to drop back off to sleep already. I sigh, remembering how she actually has a boyfriend to keep her up all night. I, on the other hand, can't find a good one. The last time I had a boyfriend was over a year ago, and I found out he had a bad habit of sleeping around at parties. The unfortunate way I found this out was when I walked into his bedroom at his party, to find him in bed with two other girls. Let's just say he has put me off men for life, or at least for a while.

"Thirty-two," I roll my eyes at her grin.

"I might nap instead, I had a long night," she winks.

"Don't rub it in," I groan.

"Well, you're coming to Drake's party this weekend, and no, you don't have a choice. I bought you a dress, and I found you a date," she grins. I don't know which one was worse about that sentence. The fact she has bought me a dress, which I know will be way too slutty for my style, or the unlucky guy she has found for me. I decide to go with the second problem first.

"A date? You know I don't date," I hiss, while she continues to grin.

"Hey, you can't judge every man because of one. This guy is nice, a friend of Drake's." She makes that annoying face she knows I haven't ever been able to say no to since we were eight. I will never forget when I first met Alex. My mum had taken me to get an ice cream from the local ice cream van. Alex had just gotten hers in front of me, and I decided to get the same because her ice cream looked good. When the truck left, Alex tripped and dropped hers. My mum and I rushed over as she cried her eyes out over her ice cream. I offered to share mine and then, when I saw her at school the next day, we were inseparable.

"Fine, but if this doesn't go well I'm blaming you," I laugh.

"Winter Masters, is there something wrong?" My

professor asks, causing the whole class to look at me. I can hear Alex's quiet snort as I answer.

"No, sir. We were just discussing the work," I say with red cheeks. The professor raises his bushy eyebrows at me. I know he doesn't believe me. Damn, I wouldn't believe me, either. *I'm a terrible liar.*

"Well, discuss it more quietly next time, I'm sure the whole class doesn't want to know about your dating life," he replies. I hold in the urge to hide under the table at his blunt reply. A guy about my age puts his hand up at the front, drawing the whole room's attention to him. The boy has messy, brown hair that's covered up with a backwards cap. He is quite muscular under his top and shorts from what I can see. I've heard a few comments about how attractive he is, which he definitely is, but I can't remember his name.

"I would like to know, sir," he says loudly before winking at me over his shoulder. I know I'm redder than a tomato now, and one glance at Alex shows how funny she thinks this is. I'm leaving her to sleep through the class next time.

"That's enough, Harris. All of you get back to work. I am running tests on this next week." He picks up a large pile of papers, most likely the tests he made us do last week, and hasn't bothered to mark yet. I watch as he goes to his desk and pulls out his phone. I'm sure he is playing some game by the way he is typing, but he definitely isn't marking the tests.

"Also, while I remember, you need to find work experience in the next week or you'll be helping me sort out the university lost and found…for four weeks." I swear the old professor even smirked but I didn't see him do it. I bet they would be getting him more coffees than they would be doing anything else.

"Have you heard back from the local vets yet?" Alex asks, opening her book as everyone else starts reading quietly.

"Yes, they called yesterday, and I'm all sorted." I grin, remembering jumping up and down in happiness after the call. I had applied months ago, and no one from our course was accepted, but I held out hope as I hadn't been rejected. My back-up was to work at a local farm, with half our class. Studying to become a vet is hard work, and there isn't much work experience available. This is an English class, and we have to pass it to stay at the university. That's why Alex, who is a music student, is taking this class with me.

"That's great," she smiles widely, making a few guys next to us turn to look at her. Alex is that very pretty girl you always wanted to be. She is tall with boobs and hips that are perfect no matter what she eats. I look at a McDonald's meal, and my ass gets bigger. I've been told I'm pretty, but I like my food too much. So I have curves, unlike my skinny-ass best friend. My best qualities are my shiny, brown hair and blue eyes, which I have to admit, suit my golden complexion. We don't say any more and get on with our work. At the end of class, I hand in my permission forms for the work experience, before finding Alex with her boyfriend, Drake, outside class.

"Hey, do you still need a lift?" I ask when I get close to them.

"Nope, thanks, honey. I'm going to Drake's, but I will see you tomorrow to get ready for the party." She winks, leaning against Drake. Drake is a good-looking guy, but is kind of strange-looking, and I can't put my finger on why. Honestly, he looks like a typical, scary-ass man all the time. I don't think he has a none serious expression. He has dark, nearly black eyes and black hair that's cut in a buzz cut, but he makes it work. It's the eyes that give him the strangeness, they are too dark, darker than I have ever seen anyone's. I always thought that he must spend a lot of time in a gym or something because he is all muscles, wearing expensive clothes. Alex has told me he is well off, but I knew that anyway from the car he drives and the designer clothes he wears. It's not just the looks and money, it's more how much older he acts, when he must be around twenty, like us. Alex doesn't answer many questions about him, but they have dated a while, so I'm guessing she really likes him.

"My friend is looking forward to your date," Drake says coldly in a slight Russian accent. Alex says he not actually from there, but his parents were, apparently.

"Me, too," I lie and frown at Alex's chuckle.

"I love you, Win, never change," she says to me, as she gives me a hug before we wave goodbye. Drake doesn't say anything else but that's normal.

I click my old, red Rover open before sliding in. My mum bought it for me as a going away present, and I love the old car, though maybe not the unusual stain on the driver seat I can't seem to get rid of; I think it's red pen. *Well, I'm hoping it is anyway.* We never had a lot of money growing up as it was just me and mum. As I drive home, I try to think about ways to get out of this date, but eventually come to the conclusion that it couldn't go that badly. *Right?*

2

WINTER

"You're joking, right? I can't wear this." I gesture to the tight, red dress I'm wearing. My hair is up in a messy bun with a few wavy strands around my face. My makeup is perfectly done, thanks to Alex, but I have to admit I don't look anything like myself.

"You look hot, Win," she says, pretending to cool herself down by waving her hand at her face. I look back to the mirror and glance down at the dress. It stops around mid-thigh and has a slit down the middle at the front, stopping just before my underwear, and making it impossible to wear a bra. Not that I'm worried, I'm not big chested enough to really have an issue.

"He is going to think I'm easy if I'm wearing this," I say, sighing and turning around with my arms around my waist.

"No, he is going to think he is a lucky fucker," she laughs before straightening her own dress. Alex is wearing her little, black dress, which is a little too little but looks nice.

"Alright. But again, I'm blaming you if anything goes

wrong." I laugh to myself, knowing this could only go wrong. I shut the door to my bedroom before leaving our apartment. Alex and I have a two-bedroom apartment near the university, which we rent together. It's cheap enough, and the area isn't too bad, but we still make sure we lock up.

"So, what's my date's name?" I ask as we wait outside for Drake to turn up. We are lucky the weather has been so good recently. Welsh weather is known for its constant rain, and our town is right in the middle of the mountains. Calroh is a small town but has a great university, and that's why we chose it, also the cheap apartments to rent helped. It's right in the middle of two large mountains and surrounded by a large forest. There's only one road out of town, but the town is well-stocked enough to look after itself with many large superstores.

"Wyatt. I haven't met him, but Drake speaks highly of him," she winks at me.

I think of his name for a second trying to imagine the guy. "So, is it getting serious between you and Drake?" I ask gently, knowing Alex doesn't like to speak about relationships. Not her own at least.

"I don't know. He is so secretive that I–" she stops talking as Drake's car pulls in front us. I glance at her, and I am wondering what the end of that sentence was, but she shakes her head, smiling before opening her door. I do the same sliding into the back.

"Hey, Drake," I say as I get in, and Alex pulls back from kissing Drake hello.

"I thought Wyatt was coming with us?" Alex asks, noticing the empty seat by me. I smile widely, hoping he is ill or isn't coming.

"He is meeting us there," Drake says bluntly before driving off.

There goes my dream of taking off this dress and changing into my PJ's, with a bottle of wine.

I don't say anything, growing a little more nervous the nearer we get to Drake's apartment.

As we pull into the expensive apartment building, we can see the party has started. The music is loud, and there are cars everywhere. I mentally tell myself that going to a party at twenty years old is normal, and I should smile before getting out of the car. I walk next to Alex as Drake puts his arm around her shoulders. Just as we walk in, and the loud music fills my ears, I see a blond man leaning against the wall next to the door of Drake's apartment. I can't help but stare a little at his muscular frame and his strong-looking face that I have to admit is a little scary. He seems to notice me staring and looks right at me. I first notice his eyes are that nearly black in colour or maybe just a dark-brown like Drake's. I look around quickly noticing that nearly every girl nearby is watching the breath-taking guy like I am. My eyes draw back to his, noticing how powerful he looks. He can't be more than twenty-five but looks like he owns the very street he is standing on. The guy's eyes never leave mine as I look him over, and I shiver from the anger I feel in his eyes. *How can someone look so serious and cold at our age?* I continue walking with Alex until we stop in front of the guy, and I want to get to know him or hear him speak. My mind and body feel drawn to him, and I don't like it.

"Drake, this must be my date," the man says in a dark, underwear-dropping voice, nodding at Drake before looking back at me. I feel myself blush as his gaze takes in all of me slowly. I do the same, noticing for the first time that he is wearing a black jumper with black jeans, which look like they were custom-made for him; they possibly were.

"Wyatt. It's nice to meet you, Winter," he offers his hand. I take his cold hand, and he shocks me by bringing it up to his mouth and placing a kiss on the back. His lips feel cold on my hand, but I feel a strange shock when his lips meet my skin. It takes everything in me not to pull my hand away and run in the other direction like my body is screaming for me to do. For some reason, I don't feel safe with him.

"Nice to meet you, too," I mutter a slight lie, pulling back my hand.

Wyatt just flashes me a knowing look before saying to Drake, "There was a problem tonight, they are getting braver," his deep voice gets stronger about whatever they are discussing. It's almost like his voice draws you in and demands that you listen.

"Just a few newbies chasing a pup, it's being dealt with," Drake smiles with a cold look in my direction.

"Good. Now, can I get you a drink?" Wyatt asks looking back at me. It's strange to see how Wyatt spoke to Drake then. It was like a boss ordering around an employee, and worse, I had no idea what they were speaking about. *What's a pup?* Maybe it's a kind of business talk, I doubt they mean a puppy.

"Sure," I say taking his open arm and letting him guide me through the house. I can feel how cold he is even through his jacket. I look back to see Alex, who has disappeared with Drake. Knowing Alex, they might have already left, thinking Wyatt seems nice. While I don't feel that he is at all; he seems too haunted to be described as nice. Seeing how he spoke to Drake just then, makes me more distrusting of him.

"Are you cold?" I ask noticing that's it's a hot summer day in May. I'm even warm, in a little dress, and he is cold in a jumper.

"Just cold-blooded," he winks at me. I can't help but blush a little, but who wouldn't when a very hot guy flirts with you. I know I need to act normal for a bit, before making an excuse and leaving. We weave through the hallways of the building and up two floors in the elevator, which is filled with couples making out. I watch as they stop and stare at Wyatt like he is a god and ignore me completely. It's all very odd.

"So, tell me, what do you study?" he asks as we enter the kitchen. It's a modern kitchen with many cabinets that don't look used, and there's even a bar on the one side next to an impressive window. There are a few people around, but it's quiet enough in here to not have to talk too loudly. Wherever the loud music is coming from, it's not nearby.

"I'm studying to become a vet. What about you?" I look over the view of the nearby forest and mountains as he hands me an opened beer. I don't like beer, but I'm not telling him that, so I pretend to drink it.

"The family business," he says still looking at me. He moves closer, so I have to lift my head up to look at him.

Being so short can be really an annoying at times, I think to myself. This guy has at least a foot on me, and I feel small around him. Now that he is closer, I can see that his eyes are definitely black with little silver sparks in them. I've never seen eyes like his, and they are really stunning. I clear my throat before asking, "Have you known Drake long?"

"Yes, it feels like I've known Drake forever, sometimes," he grins at me like I'm missing a joke.

"I feel like that with Alex, sometimes," I say, looking away because his eyes are so stunning that they draw you in. The other door in the room opens as a drunken man stumbles in, he quickly leaves again when he sees Wyatt but leaves the door open. I can see the living room, well it's more a dance room. The dancing bodies are pushed so closely together that you can't see their faces. The music is beating hard and fast compared to the slow-moving young people swaying around. I turn back to see Wyatt watching me closely.

"Dance with me? You seem like you need to relax," he asks. I lift my head to stare into his eyes, and I feel the need to dance with him, to do anything he wants. I stare at his eyes as he smirks, moving closer to me. I could have sworn his eyes had silver sparks, nothing like the empty, black pits I'm staring into now.

I shake my head, stepping back. "No thanks, I don't dance," I say to Wyatt's cold gaze. This time, his face converts into confusion, and he steps closer to me than before. We are almost touching with how close he is.

"Dance with me, Winter," he says looking into my eyes again, his eyes glowing far brighter than they should. I yelp when he grabs my arm roughly. I take a step away. His grip is strong, but I realise he isn't trying to hurt me. I don't dare look away from him as the black, glowing eyes stare into me, like he is looking into my soul.

"No, let go, Wyatt," I say firmly, challenging his grip by struggling away. I don't know what changes, but he lets me go with an utterly confused and shocked look marking his handsome face.

"How is that possible?" he mutters to himself, running his hands through his hair, and stepping away from me. I take the chance he gives me to run out the door, not caring who is looking. I have a feeling challenging a scary man like that is not a good idea. I don't think running from him is a good idea either, but, hey, it's all I have right now. *I couldn't have seen glowing eyes, right?* I mean that doesn't even make sense to me, it must have been a trick of the light or something. I eventually make my way outside. I can't believe my luck when I spot the guy from class, Harris, opening his car door for a young girl to get in. I'm glad I remembered his name now.

"Wait, Harris!" I shout from the door, and he turns to me, looking a little shocked, but more worried than anything else.

"Are you alright?" he asks none too gently as he grabs my shoulders, pulling me closer, and looking me up and down.

"Yes, but I could use a lift home," I say gently as I pull away from him a little, enough that he drops his warm hands.

"Sure, I was just taking my sister home. My parents are going to kill her for sneaking out tonight. So, I'm sure she needs some extra time to come up with a decent excuse," he laughs, opening the back door for me.

As I get in, I look behind me to see Wyatt watching me from the door. I swear I'll never forget the look he has on his face as watches me get into the car. He is looking at me like he is a starving man, and I am his meal. I gasp before slamming the door shut and closing my eyes for a second, resting my head against the cold leather.

"So, what's your name?" the girl in the front asks the minute I get in. I smile as I hear her draw out the sentence. I open my eyes to see a pair of light-blue ones sparkling at me.

"I'm Winter, and you are?" I put on my seat belt as Harris gets in.

"I'm Katy. How do you know my brother?" she smiles, but it looks cheeky.

"You should be thinking of excuses to help yourself, and not asking questions," Harris answers her question as he looks at me in the rear-view mirror. I smirk at him when I see he is trying not to laugh, and he winks at me.

"They are going to ground me for life, anyway," she

says to Harris with a huff and looks back at me, "so, do you have a boyfriend?" she asks, clearly not concerned about her parents, and I look her over now. She has the same light-brown hair as Harris and matching blue eyes, that are lighter than most. I would guess she is around sixteen, making her way too young to be here. She is wearing a purple dress that is as short as mine but makes her look a hell of a lot older than she is. I can see why Harris' parents are going to be mad. I'm guessing the amount of makeup she has on isn't going to help her case. She doesn't need it, though, I can see under it all that she is very pretty.

"No. I'm escaping a bad date, actually," I mutter as she laughs.

"Harris should ask you out, he wouldn't be a bad date," she winks, and I see Harris blush.

"I'm not dating anymore, but if I was, Harris would be a good choice," I say gently, letting them both down easily.

"You should change your mind. You're really pretty." She sighs, finally turning around. Harris asks for the address, so I give it to him before opening my phone. I'm surprised not to see any messages from Alex, I send her a quick one:

Date was awful, shame the hot ones are always crazy. I got a lift home. I will see you tomorrow. Love you xx

I missed out on the start of the argument, as I was texting, but from Harris's angry face he isn't happy.

"There are loads of them around right now, Katy. I don't want to find you sneaking out again." He shouts leaving me to wonder what he is talking about. Katy is looking tense in her seat at whatever it is.

"I know. But, I never get to leave the pack," she says looking out the window with a long sigh. I'm sure that I see tears in her eyes as she picks her nails, looking worried.

"It won't always be like this, but please, for me, don't leave again without one of us." He stares at her through the mirror, and I see her lower her gaze quickly.

"I promise," Katy says with a frown, and Harris nods, looking back at the empty road. I watch as he turns to look at me, and a grin lights up his face when he sees what I'm wearing. Typical guy, but at least he has the common sense to look back at the road after a second, not voicing his opinion.

"What's a pack?" I ask clearing my throat and hopefully my red cheeks from Harris's stare. I remember reading about packs of wolves in class, but I don't think they are talking about that. Maybe it's some kind of gang or a name of a house, I don't want to guess because I'm sure I'm going to come up with something worse than what it actually is. I glance at Harris who isn't answering my question, so I repeat myself.

"Oh, it's nothing important," Harris says quickly, all the while he is glaring at Katy like a parent whose kid just told someone a big secret of theirs. I glance back at Katy, who looks very guilty, as she shrugs at me, and avoids looking at Harris at all. This night is proving to be all kinds of confusing, and I'm pretty sure forgetting it is the easier way. No one says anything else while we drive home, and a tense silence descends on the car.

"Are you going to be okay to walk in? I don't think I can get in the car park with the gate down," Harris looks at me, as he stops on the road outside my building. The whole building is close to the university, so it has to be on lock down after a certain time, and you can only walk in, past a locked gate. I'm lucky the gate's broken, so you don't need a key to get in. Well, unlucky in certain ways because it means anyone can get in.

"Yeah, I'll walk in. The gate is open," I say to Harris, and he nods, watching me closely like he wants to say something, but I get out of the car before he can.

"Bye Katy, and good luck with your parents," I say through the open window, and I laugh, hearing her grumble before I move away from the car. I wave them both off before opening the broken gate to the locked car park, the door is slightly open anyway from our neighbours. The car park is almost as big as the building in length, and you have to walk across the whole thing to get to my building. My building has three flats, on three levels, and we have the bottom one. The car park is empty, besides my car and one other. I walk slowly; only the dim lights of the street lamps near the building are lighting my path, showing me where I'm going. In the distance, I notice a big, dark shape lying next to my car, near the door to my building. I run over quickly, my footsteps being the only noise in the dark night. I'm hoping the person is okay and pull my phone out of my bag as I run, to call an ambulance, but as I get closer I see it's a wolf.

Could my night get any more weird?

3

WINTER

I slowly move forward to get a closer look, slipping my phone back in my bag. I'm a little relieved to see it's not a big wolf. The wolf is the size of a small child and has light-brown fur or it could be black, but I can't tell in the dim light. The light catches against the large dagger, stuck in its back leg. I hear him whine as he looks up at me with dark eyes, I don't feel like he could attack me if he tried, so I carefully move closer. I know how dangerous it is, and Alex would kill me for this, but there's a reason I wanted to be a vet. I love helping animals, I've been helping injured animals since I was a little girl, and I brought home a cat that had been run over. So, there's no way I can leave this wolf now, no matter how foolish it might seem.

"Hey you, look I'm a vet," I say in a calm, soothing voice and then think to myself that I should leave out the in-training part.

"I can help you, but you can't hurt me, or I will have to leave you alone, alright?" I say gently, hoping my calming tone of my voice soothes him enough that he will trust me.

The wolf must be smart because I swear he is listening to every word and hasn't growled at me once yet. He might be someone's pet, as he doesn't seem to be scared of me like most wild animals are of humans. I don't know why I'm suddenly calling this wolf he, it might be a girl for all I know.

The wolf whines at me, so I take that as a yes. I know I can't take him to a vet, or they might put him down. Even if he is tame, most vets won't help him. The wolf is a wild animal that is usually hunted in other countries, but I can't just do nothing. My mum would be going mad right now; like the time I brought home another injured cat, that was a local stray, and it chased me around the house when it woke up, trying to bite me. That cat was not thankful for my help.

I crouch down on my knees, carefully turning my phone light on to look closer. The wolf is nearly all black, as I run a hand over his fur and pull it back because he is mostly covered in blood. I know I need to pull this dagger out and then get him inside to stitch it up. I'm lucky I have some stuff in my emergency medical box that I can use.

"Alright, handsome wolf, I'm going to pull this out and then get you inside to my apartment. I can stitch this up for you," I say to him. I swear that he actually blinks at me as an answer.

"Please don't hurt me for this," I mutter and quickly pull it out with a shaky hand, and he yelps loudly. I'm surprised when he doesn't growl at me, and I could swear little tears are coming out of his eyes as he crashes to the ground.

"Shush, I'm so sorry, little wolf," I say gently as I stroke his neck. He passes out after a few minutes, which is likely from all the blood loss. I'm hoping he is strong enough to make it through this because I have no idea how much blood he could have lost just getting here. I stand up, looking down at the wolf and think through my options quickly. I know with him unconscious, I can get him back to my flat without making too much noise, or distressing the poor creature. I look at the knife in my hand, it's heavy, and I think it's real silver as it shines in the moonlight, the blood dripping off it looking unnatural and scary. It has unusual drawings all over it, that I don't recognise, but they look very much like crowns. I put it in my handbag with my phone, shutting off the light. I'm lucky I'm kind of strong because half carrying the large wolf the short walk to my ground floor apartment is almost killing me. I eventually get to my door, opening it before carrying the wolf into my lounge. I lean against the wall, getting my breath back and look down at my red dress, now covered in blood and stuck to me with sweat. I put the lights on and walk out to grab the first aid box out in the kitchen. When I come back in, I scream.

I must be going crazy because where I left the wolf, there is now a young boy around eight or so, curled up in a ball, with a mop of black hair with blond tips covering his face, and he's naked. I rush over to him, seeing how pale he is and looking around for the wolf in my small lounge. The front door is shut, so I know he didn't get out, but as soon as I'm close to the boy, his body shakes before he shifts back into the black wolf.

I scream again, dropping the box on the floor and just stare at the passed- out little wolf.

What the hell? I know I'm having a really bad night, but I really didn't think I had gone completely mad. I slide to the floor staring at the wolf, and I remember some weird things. Like all the books I read as a teenager about werewolves, and now there is a real one in my living room. Who knew they were actually real? *Should I be running out of the room screaming?* The image of the small boy appears in my mind as I look at the wolf, and I realise that I don't care what he is, he needs my help.

I eventually calm myself down, knowing that the wolf is only a child and needs help, no matter what he is, helps me do that. I go closer to see the stab wound, and I'm surprised it is looking better, as it's nearly all sealed up. I decide to grab a blanket from my room and cover the wolf up to the neck, just in case he turns again. I'm guessing the fast healing must be a wolf thing. I do eventually think of the downside of having a supernatural creature in my house, what if others that are like him, come looking for the child and think I hurt him? I should run, but I don't because I can't leave a child, without knowing for certain he is okay.

I've always been the type to do a massive cleaning when I'm stressed. Alex is the kind that cooks everything, like my mum does, but Alex doesn't make anything edible or without a high risk of food poisoning. I get some bleach and water then start scrubbing the floor up to the door, where there is blood and outside my door too, before locking it.

I check on the wolf, and I'm not that surprised to see it's the boy again but it still looks like he is sleeping. I go to my room, taking off the now blood- covered dress and putting on some casual clothes. I avoid looking at myself in the mirror because that would make this night way too real for me, and I want some answers from the boy before I do that.

I get a wash cloth out of my bathroom, getting it a little wet before going to the boy.

"Hey, I'm just going to clean you up a little," I say to him, even if he isn't awake, I'm hoping he can hear me. I can still hear his yelp when I pulled that dagger out, who would hurt a little child like that?

I clean his face and then his shoulders. I lift the blanket to look at the dagger wound on his lower leg. It's nearly all healed, so I clean it up carefully and put a bandage on it before covering his leg up again.

I sit down on the couch, looking at the boy, wondering what the hell to do now. It's not like I can call a doctor to explain I have a boy that changes into a wolf sometimes. Or would I call a vet? I eventually lie down on my couch and drift off to sleep.

4

WYATT

"Atti, I know it's her for fuck's sake," I mutter down the phone. Atti is a witch and general pain in the ass, but I need him to know about this.

"Hold on a sec," he says to someone else and puts the phone down on me. I'm the prince of the fucking vampires, and he puts the phone down on me like he couldn't give two shits. *Typical.*

"I've cleared the apartment, now tell me what's going on?" Drake says, coming into the living room.

"It's Winter, the girl we have all been waiting for. She's been your mate's best friend all this time," I tell him harshly, and he tries to hide his shock.

"I can't believe it," he eventually mutters. Drake paces by the door, and I just watch him as he tries to process this. Drake has been my protector since I was born. I think he is around a hundred years old and never took a mate. When he told me he was mating with a human girl he had met, I was a little taken back. Drake basically brought me up and yet is never nice to anyone other than me.

"Baby, are you in here?" Alex's voice comes from the other side of the door. Drake opens the door and takes her hand gently.

"We will discuss this another time," he tells me, and I nod at him.

"Wait. How did your date go?" Alex asks pushing around Drake. Alex has known about us for over a year. She met him in a local pub, and she let Drake feed on her. From the first time he saw her, he told me he didn't want to leave her and had to get to know her. I have no idea why she thought setting her best friend up on a date with a vampire was a good idea, but she did.

"I may have messed it up a little," I say to her.

"If you upset her, I swear I'll find a way to stake your ass," she says with a glare, trying to move towards me, but Drake lifts her over his shoulder.

"Winter may have left the date after an argument," I say.

"Drake put me down and help me find a stake!" she tells him, loudly.

"Stakes don't work Alex, and I didn't upset her too much," I tell her, as Drake whispers something to her, I could listen in, but I don't.

"Fine, we can talk about this in the morning, and I know stakes don't work. But, I bet it would hurt." She grins at me, and I hear Drake's chuckle as he walks her out.

A few minutes later, as I walk aimlessly around my apartment, Atti appears in the room. Witches can travel anywhere they have been before. Atti is their soon-to-be leader, their prince, and is the most powerful witch around.

"You're sure? Like completely, not fucking around with me right now?" he asks in my mind. Another annoying habit of his, forgetting to actually talk out loud, when he knows it gives me a headache.

"Yes, I tried to make her dance with me, and she resisted like it was nothing. No one has ever been able to stop me, other than my father and some witches. It's also how drawn I was to her; like she was all I could see," I tell him out loud. I sit in my chair by my fireplace, thinking about Winter.

"Don't forget me, D, and Jax. Your powers never work on us, it does make me laugh, though," He laughs out loud, and I fold in my fists. I know how much Atti likes to fuck with me.

"Tell me about her?" Atti asks, thankfully out loud, as he takes the seat opposite me.

"She has long, brown hair, light-blue eyes, a body that could outdo an angel's, and from the little I spoke to her, she seemed good," I tell him.

"Of course, she is good. Man, I love brunettes." Atti sighs, rubbing his tired face.

"I have to tell Dabriel," I tell him.

"And Jax," Atti tells me with a stern look on his face.

"No, he made it clear that he didn't want anything to do with us after what happened. We haven't seen him in seven years," I remind Atti. It's difficult to even talk about him, he was like a brother to me.

"That was in the past and nothing to do with Winter," Atti says. A sad look crosses his face, as I know he feels sorry for me. I have to remind myself not to punch him. He, too, is like a brother to me; plus I don't want to destroy my apartment by fighting with him.

"Doesn't matter. He would kill her first and ask questions later," I tell him.

"Fine. Just for now, until we tell Winter who she is, but you know D likely knows about her by now," Atti says. Dabriel is an angel and a prince. Angels have the power to tell the future, among other things.

"He doesn't see everything, and his council won't let him go near her, anyway," I remind Atti again about all the stupid, fucking rules.

"The prophecy says–" Atti starts, but I cut him off.

"It says a hell of a lot, but no one believes it anymore. Our births were deemed as miracles and not the work of the goddess. We are on our own, and it's best we keep this a secret. I don't want my father finding out about Winter," I tell him and he nods.

"It's best my coven doesn't find out yet, they are still planning this stupid marriage between me and the leader of the dark witches," Atti says, his face looking like he is sucking lemons.

"Then we are in agreement. I'll get to know her and eventually introduce you," I tell him. I may have to get Alex to help me. I think I was a bit rude and maybe scary tonight. It just took me by surprise to see her there. I expected a pretty girl for the night, and instead, this stunning girl walks up to me, looking perfect and smelling like sin. I just wanted to taste her right then. I had to drink four bags of blood tonight to stop myself from chasing after her.

"I can't see her for a few weeks, there's a meeting between our kind, and I have to be there constantly. The amount of stupid fights I'll have to break up in the next two weeks is bloody stupid," Atti grumbles.

"That's what happens when all your council are women, and you're the only male allowed in." I tell him. I don't want to swap places with him when he has to deal with their cat fights. Atti once told me that he had to put ten women to sleep when a fight broke out over him. Every woman in his coven would die for a chance to mate with him. He is lucky his mother still protects him, and as Queen, most of them are terrified of her. They should be.

"I had to be the first royal, male witch born in thousands of years," Atti grumbles.

"Yes, you unlucky fucker, hordes of hot witches throwing themselves at you," I smirk at him.

"Well, I'm going to be without a bed mate for a long time, now that we have found her," he tells me.

"Aren't we all? Honestly, after seeing her, I couldn't touch anyone else," I look away as I speak.

"She must be something." Atti stands. I don't want to admit how much of a something she is. She is the first girl I've felt anything for since I lost Demi. Demi was my childhood friend, and we only had a year together, romantically, before she was killed. I thought I'd never get over her, but I always knew she wasn't meant to be my mate. I knew since I was a child that another was destined for me, but I was young and stubborn. I never tried to mate with her, and she never asked me to. She knew I was meant for another, but she said she wanted what little time she could have. I try to ignore the sharp pain of guilt in my heart at the fact I'm moving on.

"I can't stay. A word of warning for a friend, your father has met with my mother, he wants her help for something, but she won't tell me what it is. Do you think he knows where the pack is?" Atti asks.

"No, I keep them safe. That's why I still stay around this small town," I don't mean it to sound as hostile as it comes out. Atti ignores it or is used to my curt tone, because he doesn't show any response.

"Something is changing. The witches are feeling it, be careful, brother." Atti pats my shoulder as he passes.

"I will," I reply, watching the fireplace.

"Keep her safe and no sleeping with her. Not yet," Atti tells me.

I try to keep the grin from my face, "No promises. She is going to be my mate, after all."

"Mine, too." Atti says before he disappears.

5

WINTER

"Hey, lady, wake up," a voice says as I groan mentally. I open my eyes to see the boy from last night kneeling in front of the sofa with his face close to mine. With his eyes open, I can see they are a very bright shade of brown, and I quickly sit up as he leans back holding the blanket tight around his waist.

"Hi," I feel awkward as I look him over. I was right thinking he can't be more than eight. He has a young face, messy black hair with what looks like dyed-blond tips, and a skinny frame.

"Thanks for helping me. I would be dead now, if you hadn't," he tells me, looking down at the floor, and I just stare in silence.

"I'm guessing you know I'm a shifter. My uncle J is going to go ape when he finds me with a human." The boy drops his head down into his one hand, and I hear a few sobs as he wipes away his tears.

"Hey, don't get upset. Look, what's your name?" He looks up at me in confusion and I can see how truly upset he is. I have no idea if he has rules about telling humans, I mean me, about shifters.

"Freddy. You?" he says carefully, like I'm going to start screaming or attacking him like a crazy person. I guess a normal person might have that reaction to a shifter, but, honestly, I'm not that shocked that's there's more than humans on earth.

"Winter. Right wolf-boy or not, you need some clothes and food." I get up, moving around him to my room while he watches me. I grab my old boyfriend's shorts and top that I was going to throw out. I know they are going to be too big for him, but the shorts have strings that he can tie up.

"Here, change into these while I cook. Are bacon and eggs alright?" I ask coming back into the room and handing him the clothes as he watches me carefully.

"Yes," he mutters, blushing a little, which makes me smile.

"How's the leg by the way? It looked almost fully healed last night." I comment, waving a hand towards the boy's leg.

"It's all healed, look." He shows me his leg quickly. I watch in mild curiosity as he pulls the bandage off and shows me his unharmed leg. My mouth must have dropped open because Freddy laughs.

"I can tell you some cool stuff about wolves, if you want, like healing. I'm a little different because I can heal quicker than most wolves, and I am immune to silver, so I won't get ill," he tells me, looking very proud of that fact. I can't help the little smile I give him. I have to admit the kid is cute, and I bet he is used to being spoilt.

"Why would you have died, if you can heal like that?" I ask, a little confused about last night.

"Silver is poisonous to us, and I would be dead if I

didn't have the immunity, the longer we are in contact with it, the more it poisons us. With the dagger inside my leg, I would have just bled out. My wolf won't let me shift back when I'm in danger, and I couldn't run home," he comments with a pained look.

"Right, that's interesting, and a lot to take in. I'm going to go cook, then we can call someone to come and get you," I tell him, feeling tired. The clock in the room says it's only four in the morning, so I didn't get much sleep.

"My pack will find me soon, anyway, don't worry." He grins back at me, as he carries the blanket and clothes into my room. I must stand staring at the closed bedroom door for a few minutes, as I think about what he just said. *What will his pack think when they find him here with me?* I don't get the impression they will hurt me for knowing about shifters because Freddy seems so relaxed. I mentally sigh to myself. I go into the kitchen and start pulling out food from the fridge.

I'm half-way through cooking when my front door is banged loudly three times, followed by a man's voice, with a slight Scottish accent, shouting, "I know you're in there, lad, and you have some explaining to do." The voice sounds gruff and deep, enough for me to know it's an older man.

I turn off the cooker with slightly shaking hands, before opening the door to a much younger man than I expected. The only thought that comes to mind is how good-looking he is. I look down at his leather boots, black jeans, leather jacket that's stretched across his impressive chest and finally to his frowning face. He is freshly shaven with dark-brown hair cut short on the sides and bits of it falling on his forehead at the top. His bright green eyes, as bright as Freddy's brown ones, are glaring at me. He maybe attractive but he is clearly not friendly. I just smile back, and that seems to confuse him.

"Where's my nephew, and why the hell can I smell his blood, lass? Don't make me hurt you to find out," he says in a growling voice, which makes me shiver, and want to tell him anything he wants out of fear. I shiver a little, as he moves closer and looks at me. I don't lose eye contact, as we both stare at each other. I don't say anything because I can't back down, and I try to ignore the fact that he smells amazing this close. The man looks like he wants to kill me, and I'm focusing on what he smells like and not telling him his nephew is fine. What is wrong with me?

"Don't you dare hurt her, I owe her my life, uncle Jaxson." Freddy's voice comes from right behind me. I feel his hand press onto my shoulder in comfort, and that finally makes me look away from Jaxson, who is now growling at me with glowing green eyes. The man looks close to killing me, but he seems annoyed that he can't. So, his name is Jaxson, it kind of suits him.

"Why don't you come in, and less of the growling, please?" I tut at him in a nervous voice and walk past Freddy, who follows me into the kitchen. I can hear Jaxson's loud boots as he walks in. The slam of the door tells me he is not happy.

"Now you go and sit back down. Your uncle won't hurt me, and I will finish your food while I explain last night to him," I tell Freddy as I lay a hand on his shoulder. He looks so worried that I want to protect him, even from his uncle. I don't care who the hot guy is, Freddy has had a rough night and needs to rest. Wolf-boy or not.

"No, Freddy will explain it to me, not some human." He gives a disgusted look at my hand on Freddy's shoulder. What bugs me more is how he talks like it's a fact, no discussion is going to be had. He has another think coming if he thinks I'm going to be spoken to like that, before I've even had a coffee this morning.

"No, he won't. He is a child and has had a long night. I don't care who you are, Wolfman, but Freddy needs to rest. So, shut it," I tell him, and I try to ignore the loud growling that I hear. I turn to look at Freddy, who is looking at us both, smiling like he has won a prize.

"Go and sit," I say waving towards the lounge, and he nods, walking off. I don't bother to turn and look at Jaxson as I go back to my cooking. I finish off the bacon and eggs and put them on a plate in the weird silence of the kitchen. He may not say anything, but I can feel his hot gaze on me as I move around the kitchen. After I make myself a coffee, not bothering to offer him one, I turn to him.

"Come on, Wolfman, let's have a long chat," I tell him. I hear him mutter something under his breath, but I can't hear what he said.

"Fair warning, if you try to hurt me you will regret it." I turn to glare at him, and he smirks at me as he crosses his arms and nods. I know what he could shift into, but I won't go down quietly. My mum always taught me how to look after myself and made me go to self-defence lessons for years. Jaxson hasn't moved from the middle of the kitchen and has been silent, watching me cook until he comes to stand in front of me, way too close, and blocking me in between the counter and him. Jaxson is much taller than me and causes me to look way up, just so I can see him, I watch as his eyes lower to my neck before moving up to my eyes.

"Aye lass, now how will you do that? If you hurt my nephew you will pay for it." He whispers the end part in my ear, before sniffing my hair, I think.

"Back off!" I shout at him with a shove to his shoulders, and his eyebrows rise, before he backs away with a smirk.

He is clearly a class 'A' jerk.

"I have a call to make to my pack, feed him." He points at the lounge where Freddy is. I have every urge to throw the food in his face, but I take a deep breath and swallow back the need to. No point poking the beast.

"Fine." I say through gritted teeth, and walk past the annoying man.

I walk into my lounge to see Freddy in the oversized clothes, the shirt arms are rolled up, and the shirt is tucked into the shorts that aren't too big on him. I smile a little inside at the fact that he has covered the blood stain on the floor up with a spare blanket. The little gesture makes me want to hug him.

"Here you go." I pass him the plate, and sit next to him with my coffee. I take a deep drink before putting it on the small, wooden table next to sofa.

"Thanks, this looks awesome." He smiles happily as he digs into the food. The Wolfman walks back in a few minutes later and sits on the edge of my coffee table, right in front of me. What is with this guy and personal space? To be honest with myself, I feel like drooling over him, and most girls would die to be close to a hot guy like him. What's worse, is that I like him being close because what girl wouldn't. But, then he opens his mouth, ruining my good thoughts about him.

"So, what the fuck happened last night?" He glares at me, crossing his muscular arms across his large chest.

"I found Freddy in the car park, with a dagger in his lower leg. He was a wolf at the start, and I couldn't leave him. Once I got him inside, he turned into the boy next to me and back again. I have the dagger in my bag, if you want it." I tell him calmly, noticing how his face tightens and goes a little pale as he releases a breath.

"Freddy, what happened?" he asks, clearly trying to stay calm as he tightens his fists. I can see how tense he is from how he looks like he wants to kill something. I'm glad he isn't looking at me now.

"A group of young vamps hunted me when I went to the shops. I ran, but there were around five, and they were fast. Someone stopped them from following me but not before the dagger got me. I'm sorry, I know I shouldn't have been out late, but I wanted to get away for a bit," he explains as he stops eating, putting the plate to the side. Jax releases a long growl, and I watch as Freddy does a weird turn with his head, showing his uncle his neck before looking down.

"We will talk about how you're going to fix this later, but I'm glad you're alive," he tells Freddy who nods, looking sad.

"You do realise your wolf owes this woman its life, and as your guardian, I have to take the responsibility. I'll have to tell the alpha, and she will have to be looked after." Jax says getting up to pace near my window. I can tell he isn't happy by the idea of owing me anything by the way he spits out the sentence.

"I'm sorry, uncle Jax. I like her. She won't tell anyone and didn't freak out. It's not like she is going to get herself in a life or death situation anytime soon." Freddy rolls his eyes at me, and I can't help but smile at the cheeky lad.

"Don't encourage him." I hear the growl of the words from Jaxson by the window.

"What's your name?" he asks in a rude, snapping voice. I ignore my need to give him a sarcastic answer. I decide not to answer instead because I might shout at him.

"Well, I'm Jaxson, what's yours, lass?" he asks in a tired,

but more polite voice as he comes to stand next to the sofa and looks down at Freddy.

"Winter, its nice meeting both of you. Well maybe not you, Wolfman." I point at him, and he smirks back, it's not even funny that I seem to be amusing him.

"I want to get some sleep, so you should leave," I say as I wave my hand to the door of the lounge.

I jump when Freddy turns into his wolf, ripping all the clothes, and then trots happily over to me nudging my hand with his wet nose. I don't know what to do other than back away a little, but he just follows, nudging my hand again.

"Alright, one stroke," I mutter, stroking his head.

"Freddy's wolf doesn't want to leave you because he thinks you're in some kind of danger, and he thinks you are part of his pack now." Jaxson growls and shakes his head at Freddy, who is pushed closely to my side.

"His wolf won't leave you in any potential danger, and I won't make him, I'm not his alpha. You're going to have to come back to the pack with me." He groans, looking like it's the worst thing that could happen. Freddy nods his head up and down in happiness.

"I'm not happy with you Fred, the pack won't like having a human in it," Jax says to Freddy gently.

"There is no way I am going with you. I had a bad night and then came home to carry a heavy wolf into my apartment. I got maybe two hours sleep," I tell Jax who watches me as I carry on talking and move to stand in front of him.

"I'm tired, so you can leave. Freddy is welcome. You are not," I say poking my finger into his hard chest.

"You are one annoying female, lass," he says.

"My name is Winter, W-I-N-T-E-R, not 'lass'," I nearly shout, poking him again.

"Winter, you're coming back to my pack with us. I don't care if you want to, but it's safer for Freddy," he says as he tries to guilt trip me.

"No," I tell him firmly and cross my arms as I glare up at him.

"Fine, you can have a wolf follow you everywhere you go. It will save me feeding him." Jaxson smirks, and I have a strange urge to hit him.

"Fine, but I'm having a shower, and then we can go," I stomp off to my room hearing his chuckle as I go. Freddy's wolf sits outside my room as guard, which makes me smile. I take a deep breath in the shower as the reality hits me; I'm going to meet a lot of wolves soon.

6

WINTER

I run my fingers through Freddy's black fur as I sit in the back of Jaxson's large jeep. To say Jaxson isn't a good driver would be an understatement. I'm hoping the drive doesn't last too much longer or I'm going to throw up. At least I can let go of my seat now that we are out of town, and there aren't that many turns. Jaxson drives us straight towards the large mountain to the left of the town and into the massive forest that lies before it. We hit the start of the trees, and then the roads all look the same for around half an hour. So far, it's taken at least an hour to get to this point.

"Why do I need to come back to your house?" I ask the now silent Wolfman, who is driving slowly down the empty road. There are tall trees lining the sides of the road, and they hang above us, enough that it could be mistaken for night instead of early morning. I don't think he will reply, but he does, in a gruff voice,

"The alpha can make you a pack member, and then Freddy will chill out. Freddy is blood bound to him, so he will feel connected to you then," he tells me.

"What's an alpha? And, blood bound means what?" I ask a little nervously as my palms start sweating, I'm hoping they don't mean the literal sense of using blood to bind people.

He sighs like I'm wasting his time before answering, "The alpha is the leader of our pack, lass. He is one of the strongest wolves, so he became alpha when it was needed."

"Right, so why are you the guardian of Freddy?" I ask wondering because he looks around twenty-five and that's young to be looking after an eight-year-old.

"When my sister died, she made me promise to keep him safe. So, I do," he mutters, showing the pain on his face before he turns away from me. Freddy whines slowly next to me, and I see Jaxson look back with a look of pure sorrow for his lost sister. I couldn't imagine losing Alex, she is like a sister to me, and I would be heartbroken.

"I'm sorry for your loss." I stroke Freddy's head, when he whines gently again and puts his head on my lap. Jaxson watches Freddy with a strange expression before commenting,

"I can't believe his wolf lets you so near. Wolves hate humans, even ones they are protecting." He looks back at me in the mirror, trying to find a reason.

"Animals become calm around me. They always have. That's one of the reasons why I want to be a vet," I tell him before looking away at the passing trees. I swear I see a few glimpses of animals watching us as we pass. We don't say anything more, but I'm aware every time Jaxson watches me in his mirror, like he is trying to work something out about me. We take too many turns for me to remember until we come to a line of trees.

"It will feel weird for you to pass, but hold onto Freddy and don't let go," Jaxson warns me, I go to reply but stop as Jaxson drives through the trees, they part for him as he gets close. A warm sensation covers my body, and my grip on Freddy tightens as I fight a wave of sickness that causes me to close my eyes. When I finally open my eyes, I see we are driving up on a long road with many cabins on each side. There are several people walking around, and I see around twenty cabins. There are small dirt roads leading off the main one to other cabins in the distance. We eventually pull up to one of the larger cabins that stands out from the rest. It looks around three stories, with old-style, wooden windows. The cabin itself has a wraparound porch on the lower level, and many potted plants line the ground near the house. There's a large garage at the side with enough room for at least five cars with a few parked outside. I look back at the large, wooden door that has two large wolves facing each other carved into the wood, I can't miss it even from the car. I also notice the two really large wolves standing by the front door, one is a cream colour with brown patches, and the other is a light-brown. I'm guessing this is the alpha's house.

I climb out of the car with Freddy following close behind me.

Jaxson doesn't wait for us and barges past the wolves, not even looking at them, before opening the large, front door like it's made of paper and not solid wood. The wolves growl at me as I walk past, but Freddy growls louder, and they both stop. I stop in fear as one wolf moves closer to me, blocking the door.

"Let the lass go past, Joe, unless you want to try that shit with me." Jaxson's voice comes from inside the house, and as if a button is pressed, the wolf called Joe backs away. They both go back to staring behind me at the road like I'm not here, and a nudge from Freddy on the back of my legs reminds me to keep moving.

I walk into the cabin, straight into a massive open-planned living room. It has hardwood floors that match the wooden walls giving the place a cosy feel. In the centre of the room, is a square fireplace that goes up through the ceiling with a middle part that's open with surrounding glass. There's a fire going in it, and it lights the room up as well as the open curtains. There are four brown leather sofas around the fireplace, and a bar on one wall. There are a few pictures on the walls, mainly of sea sides and I'm guessing some family, but I don't move closer to have a look.

"Take a seat," Jaxson says, while he leans against the wall by the door. I try not to jump at his voice, but I fail, and he chuckles. I huff at him and take a seat on one of the sofas, with Freddy sitting by my feet.

"Someone's got a lot to explain to me. Including why there is a human here," a deep voice, much like Jaxson's says from right behind me. I turn on the sofa to see an impressive guy walking in the room. I would guess he is in his early twenties, but something about him makes me think he could be older than me. The man looks like Jaxson, with the same dark, nearly black hair, but his is longer, tied with a band at the back of his head. His dark-brown eyes pierce through me, and I look away before I start a staring contest like I did with Jaxson. The one thing that is clear is that this man is powerful, and even I can sense that. Dressed in only denim jeans with no shirt, he is showing off a largely muscled chest that would make any girl swoon. Surprisingly, my eyes flutter back to Jaxson. I bet his chest is nicer. He stares at me for a second before shifting his gaze to Freddy with a massive frown.

"Shift back, pup!" he shouts at Freddy, his tone downright scares me, but the change is almost instant for Freddy. I look away as he grabs a blanket off the sofa wrapping it around himself.

"Explain, Jax," the man asks, never taking his eyes off me as he sits on the edge of another sofa.

"This is Winter, and, Winter, this is my brother, Fergus," Jaxson says as he leans against the wall.

"I didn't mean names," Fergus says with a dirty look in Jaxson's direction. I notice he doesn't have a Scottish accent like Jaxson, but they are brothers. I can see there are a lot of differences between them, including the fact Jaxson has bright green eyes and Fergus doesn't.

Jaxson goes on to explain everything that happened, while Freddy goes to get some clothes on. The whole time Fergus watches me as Jaxson talks, and I can see he seems shocked by everything.

"That boy is going to be in training every day, before and after school, for a month for this. He is lucky he is my nephew, or it would be worse punishment." Fergus growls loudly, and I know it's so Freddy can hear, I'm guessing the wolves have sensitive hearing.

"Right, well, I guess I owe you a 'thank you' for saving one of my wolves' lives," Fergus says to me, without a hint of a smile. I have a feeling he doesn't like me.

"No need to thank me, but I should be leaving," I say, getting to my feet.

"Hold on, I'm taking you into the pack. It's an old law, but one that cannot be ignored. Not many humans would save an animal these days, so the likelihood of this happening is rare." Fergus tells me and Jaxson nods his agreement.

"Humans aren't all bad, I know several people who would have tried to help," I tell him, well maybe they would have called a vet instead.

"I doubt it, humans have hunted us many times over the years. We now have to keep our pack hidden from your kind, but enough about that." Fergus cuts off my argument and turns to Jaxson.

"You will bind her to you, and I will bind her to the pack. She is your responsibility when she is away from the pack," he tells Jaxson, his voice firm and strong.

"No, I'm not doing that with her," Jaxson growls.

"I'm not asking Jax, you wanted custody of Freddy, and I let you have him, so this is your problem. I would do it myself or make one of my betas do it, but I can't leave to help her. None of my betas would take her seriously because they hate humans more than you do."

Jaxson stares at me for a second before he nods.

"Good, Winter, being brought into the pack is simple. Usually, we would share blood, and you would feel a link to us, but as you're human, you only have to link to one wolf in the pack to feel the link. Jaxson will be the best option for you. Jaxson is the only wolf who works outside the pack and, therefore, can check up on you." Fergus tells me, getting my attention.

"Right, what if I don't want this?" I ask.

"Then Freddy will keep coming to you. Being part of this pack is just for protection purposes, we could teach you how to protect yourself from our kind who have gone rogue, and other supernatural beings that could be a danger to you," he tells me firmly. I don't want to even know in this moment what other kinds of beings there are, but I don't want Freddy to suffer because of some link between us.

"Why would they be a danger to me?" I finally ask after thinking quietly for a while.

"The whole town is full of them, you don't have to learn, just an offer," Fergus says like he couldn't give a damn if I do or don't.

“She wouldn’t be able to protect herself, even if I taught her myself,” Jaxson scoffs.

“You’re a real asshole, you know that?” I tell him, and he just shrugs.

“Jax, you’ll need to check on her often anyway, so why don’t you teach her?” Fergus says with a small smile. I have a feeling he is testing Jaxson in some way, and I have no idea why.

“Fine, let’s get this done,” Jaxson growls and stomps over to me. I watch as Jaxson slides out a silver dagger from his boot. The dagger is small but looks like one of those throwing daggers I’ve seen in movies.

“Your finger.” He holds out his hand, and I slide my hand into his. I watch as he carefully hands the knife to Fergus with a nod. Jaxson holds my finger up to Fergus who makes a small cut, and I hold back a squeak of pain. I watch as Fergus cuts Jaxson’s finger, and then pushes it into mine. For a second, all I see is Jaxson’s green eyes as they glow, looking straight through me before he pulls away and walks back to the wall where he was standing.

“All done, welcome to the pack,” Fergus says, and I hold my finger with my other hand to stop the bleeding. I don’t feel any different, except for a warm sensation on the back of my neck.

“I should go, I’ve had a long night,” I tell Fergus who nods, and Jaxson turns to me from his spot near the wall.

"You’re under my protection now, lass, so you'll have to come here sometimes to please my wolf," he tells me. I can’t make out his expression, but I’m sure it’s not happy.

"Who says I want to please you?" I glare at him.

"You sure you don't?" He winks at me, making me blush a bright shade of red and look away at the fireplace.

"Jaxy, I heard all about Freddy, I'm glad he is okay," says a very pretty dark-haired girl, about my age, as she comes into the room. She stops at Jaxson's side taking his hand, and he doesn't even respond to her as he watches me. I can't help but notice how she looks like a super-model with long legs, perfect figure, a baby face, and shiny hair.

"Aye, he is fine now, Esta." Jaxson finally responds, breaking the tense silence. I notice he looks at me for a second before turning away from Esta and me, to stare out a window.

"I would say it's nice to meet you, but you're a human. I'm Esta." The girl smiles at me, but her tone that suggests she feels sorry for me.

"What's wrong with being human? You know what, I don't care what your answer is," I tell Esta before turning to face Jaxson

"Can you take me home now?" I ask again, and he doesn't reply. I grit my teeth together.

Just as Esta goes to talk, Fergus says, "Take the girl home, Jax, but I want a word first, alone."

Jaxson nods, leaving the room. Esta looks me up and down before coming to stand in front of me.

"Keep those dirty eyes and hands to yourself, little human. Jaxson is mine," she growls at me. I raise one eyebrow. I don't know what comes over me, but I move closer, we are nearly the same height, and for some reason, I can't back down.

"I don't like being threatened," I say calmly and then back away when her dark-green eyes start glowing.

"He is my mate," she says, but it comes out more of a growl.

"No, my uncle isn't yet. Just because your parents set the mating up, doesn't mean he is yours, Esta. Winter is under Jaxson's protection, I don't think he would take it well if you tried to hurt her," Freddy says coming into the room. I smirk at the Harry Potter top he is wearing, and I want to tell him I have one just like it at home.

"Back off, Freddy," Esta growls, but it's lost its dangerous tone. So much for caring if Freddy is okay. She could have asked him by now. It's clear she is only interested in Jaxson, and, for some reason, I'm finding myself protective of them both.

"Make me," Freddy growls seeming more than the sweet eight-year-old I have gotten to know. I really feel the wave of power he admits before Esta whines, I watch as she shows Freddy her neck, and then she stomps out of the room.

"Sorry, it's a wolf thing," he mutters with a grin.

"Freddy, where have you been? You're a giant pain in the ass, but I want to see if you're okay," a voice I recognise comes from the doorway a minute before Katy appears. She looks at Freddy with a big grin before seeing me and running over to give me a hug.

"What are you doing here, Winter?" She smiles and pulls away. Katy looks much better tonight in casual clothes and no intense makeup.

"How do you know each other?" Jaxson asks, walking back in the room, his voice dripping with suspicion.

"She's my brother's girlfriend," Katy says with a grin at my shocked face. I go to respond, but Jaxson beats me to it.

"What?" Jaxson growls, and Katy looks as confused as I am at his anger.

"Girl-friend as in a girl he knows from uni," she says as she rolls her eyes, and I notice Jaxson seems to relax. I narrow my eyes at him, which seems to have the effect of making him smirk.

"Right, lass, I'll take you home, but a few days a week, you're here for an hour, to please my wolf, and we will be doing self-defence classes, so I can put up with you." He mutters the end part to himself but doesn't make his voice quiet enough that I don't hear. I kind of think that's the point.

"We, as in both of us?" I laugh at the idea of him needing self-defence. I have a feeling he doesn't need to learn anything about fighting from anyone else.

"Yes, I will be teaching you. It will help please me, and my wolf, to know you can defend yourself," he tells me, and Katy's jaw drops open as she stares between us.

"Hold on, can someone tell me what's going on?" Katy finally asks with a small voice.

"Freddy, find Anna to escort Katy back to her cabin," he tells Freddy.

"Why can't I take her?" he asks, crossing his arms and standing taller.

"Don't you think you're going to be busy? I know Fergus has some training for you, I'm sure I can persuade Anna to find something for you to clean as well if you have the time," Jaxson says, and Freddy deflates with a grumble.

"Katy, I believe you're grounded, and your parents aren't going to be happy you're here. Tell Harris to come and see me." Jaxson tells her, and she rolls her eyes at him.

"Why?" she responds.

"Just do it, Katy." Jaxson exhales, looking beyond frustrated at all the questions.

"Well, I will see you soon." Katy hugs me once more, before dragging a waving Freddy out the door.

"She's just a little nuts," I mumble, which makes Jaxson smile at me. It takes my breath away how handsome he is when he smiles. I nearly do the whole swoon thing that I've heard girls do. I've never been that kind of girl who was overly interested in guys. I mean I had boyfriends, but they were all average and quite boring guys. Jaxson is not the type of guy I would have even looked at before today. He is beyond hot, and his voice sends shivers through me. No, I would have run in the opposite direction because a guy like Jaxson could break me.

"My cousin is like that," he laughs, snapping me out of my thoughts.

"Oh, so do all your close family live in this pack?" I ask trying to get an understanding of what it's like around here.

"Not exactly, but this pack is family to us, and you have our protection, lass," he says, not looking happy about it.

"Oh well, thanks, and I already know a lot of self-defence. My mum made me go to a local class two times a week for years, until I left for uni," I tell him crossing my arms.

"Great, at least you know the basics. Let's go," he smirks at me before walking out.

"Doesn't anyone say 'ladies first', anymore?" I shout at his back, and I hear his laugh. Freddy comes through the door that Jaxson opens and leaves to shut behind him.

"Jackass," I mutter to myself.

"I guess I will see you around, Freddy." I smile at the boy who looks worried, as he runs up to me in the lounge.

"This is my fault entirely, and I'm sorry I got you into this." He looks down, and I walk over to him and put my hand on his shoulder.

"I wouldn't change a thing. Well, maybe you getting hurt in the first place," I say, and he finally looks up at me.

"You're okay, and that's all that matters," I tell him, holding eye contact, and I know I mean that. I may not be happy with being stuck with a grumpy wolf as a guardian and learning all about werewolves/shifters, but I am happy that Freddy is safe. Honestly, I'm surprised I'm not more freaked out right now, but I know there isn't much point in freaking out.

"Hurry up, Winter, or he will only get worse," Freddy laughs as he smiles at me before walking off.

I hear the horn beeping from the car three times before I walk out, huffing to myself. I walk past the wolves, who don't growl at me this time, but I still move quickly back to Jaxson's car just in case.

"You took your time," he grumbles at me the minute I get in. I don't even want to tell him I know that he could have heard my conversation with Freddy, so he knows why I was delayed.

"I'm sorry, but have I done something to piss you off? I get the feeling you don't like me." I ask him as I pull my seatbelt on.

Jaxson looks at me for a while, and I get the feeling he is trying to come up with an answer, but he shakes his head and just starts driving.

"Right, no answer," I murmur under my breath. I know he heard me by the twitch of his lips.

"I can pick you up on Monday at four, give me your phone?" he asks holding out his hand.

"No," I say.

"No?" he questions with a quick glare at me before looking back at the road.

"You do know what 'no' means, right? You're not having my number unless you ask nicely because so far all you have done is demand stuff," I tell him and cross my arms staring him down as he drives.

"You are unbelievable, lass. I don't ask for anything nicely, but fine," he groans before saying tensely, "Please, may I have your number?" His hands clench the steering wheel so tightly, I'm afraid he might break it. I can't help but laugh my head off at how tense he sounds, which even makes him smile then eventually laugh with me.

"Sure," I say wiping my tears away, and smiling back at him.

"You should smile more, lass, you look lovely when you do." I blush under his gaze before turning to look out the window. I watch as he puts his number on my phone while still driving like a crazy person down, thankfully, empty roads. We don't talk for the rest of the drive, and I find myself drifting off to sleep as we pass lots of trees.

"We're here." Jaxson's voice drifts through my mind, and a large hand is shaking me gently by my shoulder to wake me up. I open my eyes to see his close to mine. He has really bright eyes that draw you in. I find it hard to look away as I wake up.

"I don't have to go over the whole 'you can't tell anyone about us' thing, right?" He asks with a small grin at me as he hands me my phone. I notice how it really suits him, looking less angry and happier for once.

"Yeah, I get it, plus anyone would think I'm mad." I laugh and hop out of the car before I shut the door, "You look nice when you smile, too, Jaxson."

I see his shocked face before I turn and walk back to my apartment that seems really empty without that annoying wolf around.

7

JAXSON

"Another one." I hold up my empty beer glass, and the bartender, a very hot, blonde human, winks at me as she goes to fill it up. The pub is full tonight of unsuspecting humans, humans I don't usually like to be around, but I don't have a choice. *Fucking Dabriel.* Angels are all the same, all high and mighty. Dabriel used to be my friend, but he isn't now. If things were different then....

My phone rings, stopping the thought, I pull my gaze from the bartender as I answer.

"Uncle J, when you coming home? Anna is being annoying." Freddy's voice fills my phone, and I hold back a grin. I hate the uncle J nickname, but I love Freddy. I have to admit taking on a young child wasn't easy, but we made it work with the help of my brother's mate.

"Why? What is she doing?" I ask.

"Just making me clean my room, it's not that bad as she is making it out to be. I think she said it looked like mini demons had trashed the place and had an after party," he mutters. I can hear the annoyance in his voice. I try not to laugh at my sister-in-law's use of words, but she isn't far from the truth. Mini demons do love to make a mess, I mean huge fucking messes that take days to clean. We had them once, and, thankfully, they left after they had their fun.

"How about I bring you a pizza back? You know that hot one from Pizza Hut?" I ask, knowing it's his favourite, and I feel bad for him. The last few days he has had more training than he has ever had, but he needs it. My chest still feels tight at the thought of how close I came to losing him. When I came back from my job to find he wasn't home, I alerted the pack, and we searched everywhere. I finally tracked his scent into town and, thankfully, found him alive. I took the dagger from Winter's kitchen, and I plan to return it into whichever fucking vampires hurt my nephew. I feel the hard, silver dagger in my boot, and the thought makes me relax, a tad.

"With a bottle of Coke and brownies?" he finally replies after thinking about it.

"Yes, but the second box of brownies is mine. No trying to eat them like last time," I tell him, and I hear his chuckle.

"Deal," Freddy says, and I can hear the smile this time.

"Make sure the room is tidy. Anna is right, the room looked like a bomb went off the last time I was in there," I tell him, and I hear his groan.

"Fine, you're getting old and boring uncle J. You won't get a girl like Winter, if you act old," he tells me, like I need dating advice from an eight-year-old. Not that I would ever touch Winter, she is a human.

"I'm not old, and Winter isn't my type. I prefer blondes," I tell him, only slightly lying. The blonde bartender is my type, and I could easily take her home tonight, but something is stopping me. A beautiful brown-haired girl with sparkling blue eyes is the cause of my issues tonight.

"Whatever. You were following her around like a puppy. She is pretty, shame I'm not older. Hey, did she mention any sisters?" he asks. When did he start liking girls, I swear it was only five minutes ago that he was playing with action figures.

"No sisters. I've got to go. I'll be back in an hour," I tell him.

"Cool, I'll get the Harry Potter movies out for us. Also, I saw this new Harry Potter mug that when you add hot water, the Marauder's map appears. Totally cool," he mumbles on excitedly.

"Why do I need to watch those again? And, why did I need to hear about the mug?" I ask, mentally thinking of a way to get out of film night. I don't enjoy those films, but I've watched them ten times now, over the years. Thank god, the last one finally came out, I'd hoped he would move on from the series by now, but he hasn't.

"You like them Uncle J, although they got witches wrong. They don't have wands, but it would be so cool if they did," he tells me, and I try not to think about Atti. I haven't seen him, or any of my friends, in years. I'm about to see Dabriel for the first time in seven years, and not for a good reason.

"Oh, and it's my birthday soon. Just dropping some hints." He laughs, and I'll have to remember to order that mug now.

"Fine. Later, Freds," I say to him.

"Later Uncle J," he says and puts the phone down.

"Getting drunk? Doesn't suit you, Jax." Dabriel takes a seat next to me. A few people turn to stare at him. He ignores them, but he would stand out anywhere. His long, white hair and massive build kind of attract attention.

"I want to know," I tell him, cutting straight to the point.

"You already know, I've seen it. I've seen you and her." He smirks, leaning back on the bar. The bartender hands me my drink, but I don't find it the slight bit interesting.

"Why the fuck didn't you warn me? Keep her the fuck away from me? I came close to killing her," I shout at him, and he just smiles back at me. A few humans stop to watch us. My wolf growls in my mind, *he is challenging you, you should bite him*. I don't listen, thankfully. The fact that my wolf isn't trying to kill him is annoying me. My wolf loves him like a brother, and, despite everything, I still think of him as one.

"This was always going to happen. Don't pretend you didn't feel it. I haven't met her yet, but I am watching," he tells me.

"Yeah, but you can't get involved, right?" I smirk at him when he tenses.

"I would have stopped her death, if I could. No matter what I did, the ending didn't change," he says calmly, and I lose it. I grab him by the neck and throw him across the bar. The bottles smash into pieces as people scream, scrambling to get out. I jump over the bar and walk over to him, as he gets up. The cuts on his face are already healing.

"Don't fucking pretend you couldn't have saved my sister. I don't want anything to do with the prophecy, and no human girl is going to change my mind," I warn him. I try to ignore my wolf's whine at the thought of Winter. I've been with girls, countless one-night-stands, but Winter calls to my wolf more than anyone else ever has. I've tried to listen to the witches and mate with Esta, but my wolf is just as turned off by her as I am. Winter has the perfect fucking body, a body that I could spend hours with, but her sassy mouth was what turned me on the most. She didn't seem to give two fucks about how I spoke to her, and my general dislike for her. I can't even walk away from her now. I feel her in my blood, and my wolf knows she is pack.

"I would have saved her. Wyatt would have, too," he says, holding up his hands, the runes of angel language appearing on his skin. They are for protection, among other things, and the more an angel has, the more powerful they are. When Dabriel is showing his, there's not an inch of his body that doesn't have them. Not that I've checked, but the fucker likes to brag.

"Like fuck you would have, we were friends all our lives. You were my pack. I don't want anything to do with this. Or her." I slam my hand on the bar, trying to control my anger.

"Isn't it too late? She is yours to protect now, and I know she will need it soon." Dabriel tells me, taking a step closer.

"Are you going to let her die, too?" I mutter, and he punches me. I don't lose my footing but it's close, he can fire a heavy blow when he wants.

"You don't deserve her, Jax," Dabriel says and jumps over the bar. I watch him leave as I grab a bottle of whisky off the floor. I leave a wad of cash on the side of the bar before I leave, taking a deep drink. I need to find a way to get rid of Winter, and I need to do it fast. I can't let her close because I can't be who she needs. I'm too fucked up, I'm too broken, and I need to be alone. Pulling the dagger out of my boot and I grin. I know a perfect way to get rid of some anger.

8

WINTER

My only thought when I know I'm dreaming is how real these dreams are. They don't happen very often, but they scare me all the same. I open my eyes to see the same girl sitting on the floor with her legs crossed. We are in the middle of some woods I don't recognise, and she is wearing the same simple, white dress she always is. It's the middle of the night, and the only light is the fire burning in front of her, and the moon and stars shining high in the sky.

"There will be a time, a time you will understand," she says in a whisper to the raging fire in front of her, her voice sounds like heaven, making me feel safe. The girl who looks around my age stands, turning towards me, her glowing, blue eyes staring at me. It always shocks me how beautiful she is, how innocent. I always feel safe, yet scared of her at the same time. I try to move away, but I can't, I never can, as she walks over to stand right in front of me, her bright, shining eyes locked with mine.

The girl's long, black hair flows with the wind, as she says in a deep whisper that fills my head instead of coming from her lips.

"There will be a time, a time you will understand." her hand reaches for me, as I feel the darkness creeping in.

"Sexy cake, where are you?" Alex shouts through the apartment as I hear the door slam shut. I groan to myself at her happy tone, after a long day and a night of little sleep, I'm feeling tired. I keep running over everything that happened with the wolves in my head, the dream is the last thing I need now. The one person I couldn't get out of my thoughts was Jaxson, and then, when I did fall asleep, I had one of those weird dreams again. My thoughts flutter back to Jaxson again, as I remember everything about him that draws me in, and at the same time, I want to run away from him. My door is slammed open by a pale-looking Alex, who is wearing a tight, green maxi dress with her long, red hair up in a high ponytail.

"Was it a long night again?" I ask. Seeing my kindle open on my pillow, I shut it off. I must have fallen asleep reading, annoyingly as I was getting to a good part in a romance. Although, it only had me thinking of Jaxson's hard body and not the characters'.

"Something like that, but we are going out for dinner. There's this new place called Ladino that's opened in town, and we have to go," she smirks leaning against the doorway. I have a feeling like I'm falling into one of her traps, but I relent saying, "Sure, but you can pay. You owe me for that horrible date," I tell her with a slight glare, as I get out of bed and start stretching.

Alex raises her perfect eyebrows at me, "What happened? Wyatt said he had a good night with you, but he is an idiot, apparently," she replies as she jumps on my bed and gets comfy. I shake my head at her and how relaxed she is.

"He is weird, and he scared me, Alex. I'm not seeing

him again," I tell her and go through my clothes for something to wear.

"He isn't that bad, maybe you just got off on the wrong foot. Drake said he is having a hard time with his father at the moment," she says.

I want to listen, but all I can remember is how he demanded I dance with him. I know when I'm around him, I feel wrong and scared. No matter how hot someone is, you can't ignore feelings like that.

"I don't think so. No more blind dates." I wag a finger at her, and she laughs.

"You have to admit that he is hot, and if he is anything like Drake in bed, then wow," she winks at me with a laugh, and I can't help but laugh a little with her.

"Give me an hour to shower and dress," I say getting up, and Alex nods, shutting my door on her way out. My phone rings as I'm choosing my jeans and a purple halter top.

"Hey, Mum," I answer, actually looking forward to hearing her voice. It reminds me that some things can be normal in my life.

"Hey, Honey. How is everything going?" she asks in her usual bright and cheery voice. You wouldn't ever guess that Daniella is my mum, with her white-blonde hair and sparkling, brown eyes. She always told me I look more like my dad, but I have a little of her personality. My mum is constantly like a ray of sunshine and is worse than I am at helping everyone she meets. My mum runs a local food bank and helps out at many charities in her spare time, Alex and I have always agreed that you couldn't find anyone better than her for a mum.

"It's all good, but I miss you and your cooking," I smile when I hear her laughter.

"You are eating okay, right? I can send more money if you need it," she says in her worried-mum tone.

"Yes, we're eating fine, but nothing beats your home cooking Mum," I say with a big smile.

"Okay, I'll leave you be. So, any plans for tonight?" she asks.

"Alex and I are going out for dinner," I tell her, and she laughs again.

"Well, honey, I did try and teach you how to cook before you left for university. You'll be home in two months, right?" she asks referring to the summer holidays coming up.

"Yes, and I honestly can't wait." I need the normality of waking up to my mum's cooking, and Alex is hoping for a hot summer to sunbathe on the local beach. My mum lives in Cornwall where the beaches are lovely, if you can find the ones without all the tourists around.

"Well, have fun tonight, Honey, I just wanted to check on you," she says.

"I will," I twist my wavy, brown hair around my finger, wishing I did inherit her blonde hair. Mine is such a dull brown, and I don't want to dye it. She used to dye her hair brown when she was in college, she told me once, but now she just adds highlights to her natural blonde.

"I love you, and tell Alex I love her too, and to answer her phone," she chuckles.

"She has a new boyfriend, so I'll remind her to when I see her," I chuckle back. My mum loves Alex as much as me. Alex doesn't have good parents and was always around my mums house for a cooked meal. Her own parents were too busy getting drunk to notice she was even missing.

"Ah that explains it, talk to you next week, Honey, bye," she says, hanging up after I say bye. I leave my things on my bed and walk into my bathroom. It's the typical whitewashed wet room. I make quick work of showering and drying my hair. I plait it tightly down my back, leaving a few curls to shape my face before getting changed. It's warm enough not to need a coat, so I head to the lounge.

"Hey, you ready, Win?" Alex asks sitting on the couch and looking at my outfit, as I find my purse and phone, putting them in a small bag. I watch as she nods her head at what I'm wearing. She should like it, considering she bought it for me. She quickly does something on her phone before getting up. We were lucky that my father left me a large amount of money for college. My mum refused to use it, so I used it to pay for my and Alex's college. We have enough left over for rent and bills for the next few years. Alex swears she is paying me back, but I won't let her.

"Sure," I follow her out. We take Alex's red Volvo to the restaurant, chatting about the university on the way. I ask what I really want to know, "How serious are you and Drake? I mean I've never seen you date anyone this long before." I watch how her face lights up at his name.

"I love him, Win," she sighs with her cheeks blushing.

"Wow, that's great, Alex," I say honestly. I have never seen Alex this happy before. Even if he seems quiet and strange, he makes her smile. That's all I could want for her. I ignore the slight jealously of her having someone when I don't. My best friend being in love is something to be happy about, not envious.

"He told me he loves me, too. I can't get enough of him, and I don't just mean the sex. I love talking to him and," she stops, mumbling and blushing more when I smile at her. She turns back to the road, tapping her fingers on the wheel.

"I get it," I say softly, causing us both to start laughing.

"I didn't plan on a serious relationship while I'm still at uni, but I feel like he's the one, you know?" she tells me.

My thoughts go to Jaxson for a second, before I mentally shake myself and answer her. "I don't, but I'm really happy for you."

She reaches over to squeeze my hand, "It will happen for you, one day you'll just know, and there'll be no going back."

"It won't. I have bad luck with guys, and I just don't want anything now." I ignore how my thoughts betray me by thinking of Jaxson.

We don't talk much more, and about twenty minutes later we pull up at the restaurant. It's really cute, the outside looking like an old, English pub, but it's been redone to give it a more rustic theme. There's a large, glowing sign with the name on it above the door. We walk in, and I don't hear what Alex says, as the man asks if we need a table, because my eyes are drawn to Drake and Wyatt sitting at a table in the corner. My eyes don't leave Wyatt's as he turns, somehow noticing me come in. We enter a silent staring contest, while my anger rises, with neither one of us giving in. His lips pull up into a smile as Alex pulls me away, linking my arm with hers and whispering,

"One more chance, please don't be mad at me."

I all but snarl at her in response, but I let her lead to me the table. I now know why she wanted to drive tonight, I should have seen this coming. Alex isn't going to give up the idea of us dating these best friends together, easily. Drake gets up, kissing Alex on the cheek, and Wyatt smiles at me as he stands to hold out an open chair in front of him. I keep my best 'I'm not impressed' look, as my eyes take him in. Wyatt is wearing a tight, black suit; his jacket is off and his white shirt rolled up. A blue tie is loose around his neck, and one glance at Drake in the same kind of suit, makes me think they must have come from work. I can't help but gaze at his wavy, blond hair that is styled to show his dark eyes, which look over me with far too much interest.

"You look beautiful, Winter," he says in that dark, seductive voice. I'd somehow forgotten how enticing it is. I have to admit it's actually nice to hear when he isn't angry or being a dick. I take the seat he offers, and he sits down next to me, close enough that his arm brushes mine.

"Thanks," I mutter, pulling my menu out and holding it in front of my face like a weapon. Alex glances at me in the middle of her conversation with Drake, and the little shit is trying not to laugh at my flustered face. I put the menu down as the waitress comes over.

"What can I get you, handsome boys?" she asks while adjusting her top. Well, more pulling it down and leaning over the table so the 'boys' can have a good view. What a slut. I don't care if she gets Wyatt's attention; well I keep telling myself that.

"The lobster and a beer," Drake says, while Wyatt's eyes never leave mine as he orders, as does Alex. I ask for the half roast chicken and a glass of wine, as I'm going to need it.

"If you need anything, just call," she says while running her fingers over Wyatt's shoulder. He doesn't even glance her way, his gaze never leaving mine. I have to admit it's nice that he doesn't look at her, he seems to think he has won something because he smiles. It highlights the high cheekbones of his face and his dark eyelashes. Under the dim lights of the restaurant, the effect is sexy as sin.

"How was your day?" I ask Wyatt, trying to be polite.

"Better, now that I'm on a date with you," he tells me honestly. I have to admit I'm not that shocked he has found a way to get a date with me, the way he stared at me as I left him at the party is still strong in my mind.

"This isn't a date, I never agreed to it," I glare at him.

Wyatt leans back with a frown, as Drake surprises me by laughing. Alex grins in my direction.

"That's the first time anyone has actually said they didn't want a date with him. You're going to hurt his ego." Drake says, calming himself down from laughing. Drake smiles at my shocked face, I'm not shocked that Wyatt isn't turned down very often, but I am that Drake actually smiled at me.

"I'm sure he will survive," I say dryly. Alex nudges me with her leg under the table, and I just lean back in my chair looking out the window. Our drinks arrive with the flirty waitress, who again tries to get Wyatt's attention, but he looks like he is trying to solve a puzzle while staring at me.

"I'm using the bathroom," Alex says getting up.

"Me too," Drake says watching her, and I hear their giggles as they walk away. I can't help the smile that appears on my face for my best friend.

"I like it when you smile," Wyatt says, and I look back to him seeing him resting his head on his joined hands.

"You've not seen much of it. Not that you've given me a reason to smile around you," I state, crossing my arms.

"I'm sorry, my approach to you was rude. Drake was right, I've never had to do much. You were a welcome surprise," he says, flashing me a cheeky smile.

"I'm sure you can find someone easy again, hell the waitress would take you home in a second," I say, realising quickly how jealous I sound.

Wyatt never misses a beat as he grins, making my heart bounce in my chest at how breathtakingly handsome he is.

"Can you give me a fresh start?" he asks taking my

hand in his cold one. It's oddly comforting. Instead of feeling scared around him, I'm starting to feel safe like when I'm with Jaxson. I push thoughts of Jaxson away, he wouldn't want anything to do with me, but this conversation reminds me of his compliment about my smile.

"Alright. Hi, I'm Winter, I'm studying to be a vet, and I have a weakness for any kind of fast food." I hold out my hand which he takes and places a sweet kiss on it.

"I'm Wyatt, I'm working in my family's business, and my favourite food is a secret, but I might tell you one day," he jokes with a big grin. I can't help but smile back, wondering what the hell it is that he doesn't want to say. It's going to be something weird, like liver, who actually eats that stuff?

Wyatt and I chat for a while about the weather and other things before the food arrives. Alex and Drake turn up just after, with Alex looking a little dishevelled with messy hair, and she is straightening her clothes.

"Did you guys get lost?" I ask with a wink. Alex laughs, not embarrassed at all about her appearance, and Drake just slides into his seat ignoring everything other than his food.

"No, but I can tell you how many times I–," she says before Drake kisses her, effectively shutting her up and making me chuckle.

We all eat our food, which is amazing, and then we go to the bar to order a few drinks. There are a few sofas around the room to sit on, and Wyatt takes my free hand, tugging me down on one right next to him. I can't help but feel his slightly cold leg pushed against mine or his hand resting lightly against my shoulder. His amazing smell surrounds me making me want to lean into him. Wyatt smells like fire, a bonfire on a cold, autumn night that we used to have to get rid of leaves. I look up to see him staring down at me. I know I shouldn't, but my gaze goes to his perfect lips before wetting my own with my tongue. The spell I'm under is snapped when Alex starts talking from the other sofa, right in front of me. I didn't even notice her sitting down, I really need to stop staring at Wyatt.

"I'm not feeling well, so Drake is taking me home. Can you take Winter home, Wyatt? Drake can drive my car," she winks at me when no one is looking.

Wyatt nods, and I want to kick her, knowing she did this on purpose. Alex smirks at me, before kissing my cheek, and waving goodbye. Drake nods his goodbye and follows Alex, who I'm sure is grinning ear to ear.

"We can leave if you want. I don't want to force you to spend time with me." Wyatt tells me, and I glance up at him, trying to read his locked-up expression.

"No, we can stay. Tell me about yourself," I ask, keeping my responses on neutral ground and not confirming anything to him. I don't want to admit that I want to stay to talk to him, or just be around him.

"Well, I live in an apartment I share with Drake. I work a lot, so I can take over from my father, eventually. There isn't much else to tell," he says looking a little tense.

"I'm sure there's more, any sisters or brothers?" I ask.

"No, but Drake has been around me since we were both children, so I consider him a brother to me." He smiles down at me, and I feel his fingers rubbing circles into my shoulder. I don't think he knows he is doing it.

"I see that. He seems close to you. What's your dad, and mum, like?" I ask and regret it a little as Wyatt's closed expression drops, and I see the sadness etched into his handsome face.

"My mother passed when I was born, and my father is difficult." He emphasises the word 'difficult'.

"I'm sorry, Wyatt," I say placing my hand over his, he turns his hand, so ours are locked together as he entwines our fingers. My small hand seems tiny in his.

"Don't be, it is what it is. Tell me about your parents," he changes the subject quickly.

"Only my mum is around. She is a good mum, and I'm close with her. My dad passed away when I was around four. I don't remember him. My mum never really recovered from his death," I tell him.

“How did he pass? If you don’t mind me asking,” he asks.

“A bad car accident, I was in the car, but I wasn’t hurt. I was lucky,” I try to ignore the grief I feel at the memory.

"I'm sorry for your loss. I'm sure your father would be proud of the woman you are now," he says quietly, making me blush.

"Well, I hope so. I have no brothers or sisters, but Alex moved into our home when I was twelve. She was staying at our house all the time because of her issues at home, and we were very close. So, when social services finally got custody of Alex, it was like it was meant to be. My mum adopted her, so in most ways, I always had a sister," I tell him with a small smile. The day Alex moved in, our mum took us camping, and we had a great night roasting marshmallows and telling silly, scary stories. We didn’t even care that it rained all the rest of the weekend.

"She talks highly of you," Wyatt comments.

"She means a lot to me, so I hope she does," I say back with a chuckle.

Wyatt leans into me more, tucking a piece of hair behind my ear.

"Can I persuade you to let me take you on a date next weekend?" he asks in a careless whisper. His finger glides down my cheek as he looks into my eyes. I feel like I'm trapped in his gaze as I nod.

"I would like that," I say, in case he didn't get it.

"Me, too," he comments before he shocks me by kissing me briefly. His lips feel soft but strong as they brush mine. He pulls back so quickly, that I didn't get to know how he tastes. I want to push my lips back to him, but he stands up, pulling me up with him in my state of shock and desire.

"I should take you home. Alex said you have an early start," he says picking his jacket up.

"Yeah, I have an exam. I'm dreading it." I laugh, and he smiles at me. Wyatt looks tense, and I'm not sure why. I wonder if he didn't like the kiss. Well, I might not be getting another date in that case.

"Come on." He seems a little rushed as he walks us out, and we get into his expensive, red convertible that's parked right outside.

As I strap myself in I say to him, "You know, this is exactly the car I expected you to drive."

Wyatt doesn't say anything, but I see his lip twitch in laughter. His phone rings several times as we drive, and every time his hands tighten on the steering wheel until, eventually, I can't take it.

"You can answer that," I say gently and he gives me a tight-lipped look before responding

"No, it's work or my father. They both can wait." He glances at me again, but we don't talk anymore as he drives me home. I don't think to ask how he knows where I live; it's too tense in the car to ask him anything, anyway.

Wyatt walks me to my door, like a gentleman. I don't know why it surprises me a little. He stops me before I find my keys in my bag.

"Thank you for giving me a second chance," he says,

pushing a curl behind my ear, while I see his impossibly dark eyes get darker as he stares at me.

"Don't ruin it, please," I say with a sigh, before leaning forward and kissing his cheek. "Bye, Wyatt," I tell him, moving away and getting my keys out as he watches.

"Bye, Winter, until next time," he says as his phone rings again, and he walks away. I watch him until I can't see him anymore. It's like I can breathe again when he isn't near. Being around him is like sinking in mud. I know I'm in way too deep, as I let myself into the apartment, locking the door behind me.

I check my phone, seeing no messages, and it annoys me how much I was hoping to see one from a certain Wolfman.

I hardly believe my own life anymore.

9

WINTER

"Did you understand a word he just said? I swear that man talks in riddles," Alex says, picking up her books off the desk next to mine. Honestly, I wasn't paying much attention today. My thoughts were on seeing Jaxson and then watching Harris. I grab my stuff quickly, ignoring Alex and run down the steps towards Harris just as he's leaving. I tried to get his attention throughout the class, but he never looked my way.

"Harris," I shout, and a few people glance at me. Harris clearly heard me as he stops, waiting for me by the door. Harris watches me a little warily, as I get close.

"Hey, what's up?" he asks when I get to him.

"Can we talk? Alone," I ask, shifting my heavy bag onto my other arm.

"Here, give me that. How about we get lunch?" he asks as I hand my bag over to him. I watch as he throws it over his shoulder like it weighs nothing, and it's a sharp reminder that Harris isn't just a college kid, he is a wolf with superhuman strength. I go to comment, but Alex's voice behind me stops that.

"Jesus, Win, don't run like that, some of us can't run like a horse whose ass is on fire," she says, completely breathless.

I snort in laughter, and Harris chuckles, running his hand through his spiked hair.

"Sorry, Alex. Alex, this is Harris." I point at him, introducing them both.

"Nice to meet you," Alex says looking him over and, apparently, liking what she sees as she winks at me. I go to tell her it isn't anything like that, but I can't in front of Harris without sounding like a bitch.

"Shoot I have to go, see you tonight," she says before kissing my cheek and jogging out the room. I shake my head at her antics. Harris and I start walking out of class now that the classroom has emptied out a little. We cross over the field, not talking, and into the university café.

Harris leads me to a table away from other people, and orders two teas for us. We both order some sandwiches, too.

"So, what did you want to chat about?" he asks, leaning back in his seat.

"I have a list," I say, pulling out my phone and finding the list I wrote in bed last night. Harris chuckles at me but offers me a head nod in acceptance. I wasn't sure if he would answer anything, but seeing as I'm pack now, I thought he might do. Harris seems more laid back than Jaxson. I couldn't ask him any questions without getting my head bitten off.

"Go on then," he chuckles.

"Can you shift whenever you want?" I ask.

"Yes, for adults. The younger pups, like my sister Katy, have trouble shifting back without an alpha command, and they can shift uncontrollably when they have high emotions," he tells me. It explains a lot about why Freddy only shifted when Fergus told him to.

"Is Fergus the only alpha?" I ask, although it's not one of my questions.

"No, well, yes. It's complicated," he mutters.

"Who else is then?" I ask. The waitress chooses that time to bring us our tea, and I put my phone down to pour milk in mine from those silly, little cups. Hell, I need like four before it even looks like I added milk. Harris doesn't seem to have my problem, only adding one cup and four sugars. Our sandwiches are brought over, and we both dig into our food as I wait for him to answer me. I raise my eyebrows at him when he looks at me. He groans, I think he hoped I would have forgotten my question because of the distraction.

"I can't answer that. I'm bound, in a way," he looks very uncomfortable.

"Explain?" I ask gently.

"Well, when you choose a pack, you have to share your blood with your alpha like you did with Jaxson. They can then command you to shift or order you not to do certain things," he tells me.

"Like telling me who the other alphas are in your pack?" I say, coming to the conclusion myself. That must be bad if they have a cruel alpha because they could order them to do anything. I wonder how many packs there are out there or if there are different types of shifters. The more I've thought about the supernatural world, the more I don't feel scared of it. I'm just interested to know more.

"Exactly," he answers.

"So, does that make Jaxson my alpha?" I ask. A flutter of desire runs through me at the thought of him ordering me around.

There is seriously something wrong with me.

“Yes, but you’re not a wolf, so he doesn’t have any control over you. If you were seriously hurt, he would know, and his wolf would demand he protect you. Alphas can tell when anyone in their pack is hurt or close to death,” he tells me. I think over his words and eat some more of my sandwich. I guess it’s not awful having someone who would know if I needed them at any time.

“Any other questions?" Harris asks with a smile.

"What do you eat? I mean do you hunt animals?" I ask. I want to ask if they hunt humans, but I have a feeling they don't. They don’t seem like crazy murderers.

"We need a lot of normal fatty foods, as we burn a lot more than humans by shifting. I eat around six meals a day, as well as snacks. Yes, we do hunt in our wolf form but not often. Some prefer to hunt, I don't look good covered in blood and fur," he jokes with a grin.

"Where did werewolves come from? I mean do you have a God?" I ask him.

"It's a long story, and I don't know all of it. You ready for a real life fairy-tale?" he laughs.

"Is it a good kind?" I joke, and Harris grins.

"Only the best," he says, and I nod. Harris drinks a sip of tea before starting.

"Well, there was once, and I'm talking thousands of years ago, a human who saved the life of the Goddess called Demtra. Demtra held the dying man, and he wished that his four sons would have her blessing,” he stops as I lean forward, extremely interested in his story.

“Demtra swore she would give them long lives, and they would be like her own children."

Harris pauses before continuing as I stare wide-eyed at him.

"By the time she found the two twin sons, one had passed away from an illness, and another was gravely injured. The one son had only just died, so she breathed life into the man, and he came back as what are known as vampires. The other son, she pushed earthly powers into, and he became a wolf as he healed. The twins both lived longer lives than a human, and it's said that is where we come from," he stops as he notices my jaw hanging open.

"Vampires are real?" I whisper harshly.

"Yes. Are you that shocked?" he laughs

"What about the other two sons?"

"Well, I don't know the whole story, just rumours, but they started the witch and angel races."

"Witches? Angels? They are real too?" I sit back.

"Yep," he tells me.

"Fairies? Dragons? Oh, I've always wanted to see a unicorn," I ask smiling widely, and Harris starts laughing.

"Who knows? I don't think they're real, but my mother always warned me that fairies would come and steal me if I was a bad child." He laughs with me, and soon people are staring at the mad couple in the corner wiping tears from our eyes.

"Honestly, there are sub-demons. I don't know if demons are real, but their pests are. The sub-demons glamour themselves to look like rodents. They mainly do this for humans, so they don't get killed or found out. Witches have familiar, sub-demons that can look like normal pets," he says.

"This would be hard to believe if I hadn't seen it. How many of you are there? I mean supernaturals," I ask.

"Well, that's a complicated question. No one really knows because of the wars between our kinds," he says quietly.

"What wars?" I say just as quietly because some people walk past our table.

"I can't tell you. You're human, but let's say vampires are not like us, witches are neutral and help whoever pays. The angels are–well, they're dicks–but they hate witches," he says.

"Why are vampires not like us?" I ask.

"They feed on humans, Winter. They need you to survive," he says in a scary tone. The café is strangely quiet as if his words scared more than just me.

“So, how long do you live for? Are you immortal?” I ask.

“We live for around two hundred years or so. All the supernaturals have the same life span,” He tells me.

My phone rings as Harris finishes his sandwich like it's just a normal lunch, and he hasn't just shared the secrets of his world with me.

"Hey," I answer without looking.

"I'm picking you up at five tonight." Jaxson's growly voice says down the phone.

"Alright," I answer, but the bastard has hung up on me.

"Jax, I'm guessing?" Harris laughs as he asks.

"He is one rude asshole," I tell Harris.

"Nah he just, well, he doesn't let people close, and he dislikes humans. It's not personal," he tells me.

"Right," I mutter, not wanting Harris to see how that affected me. I stand up grabbing my bag.

"He is picking me up at five, and I have an essay to finish tonight, so I have to go," I tell him as he stands too.

Harris shocks me by pulling me into a tight hug.

"We shifters can smell your strong emotions. Don't let Jax upset you because I have a feeling you're going to change his stubborn mind," Harris whispers before letting me go.

"Shoot, I forgot about the rest of my questions," I say as I put our rubbish in the bin by the door.

"Another time." He laughs before we both walk out. I shoot a wave at Harris before turning and walking to my car and going home quickly to get some work done.

The sound of my door being knocked on distracts my attention from my laptop a few hours later. Alex walks into my room looking like someone just pushed her out of bed, yet she still manages to look great.

"There is a seriously hot guy waiting for you in the lounge, want to explain?" Alex says raising an eyebrow at me. I almost laugh at her annoyed face in her fluffy pink PJ's that she would never let a guy see her in.

"Who is he? You've been holding out on me. First, it's that hot guy in class and now this one," she crosses her arms with her face in a pout.

"First off, it's not like that with Harris," I tell her truthfully, he's already starting to be too much of a good friend to be anything more.

"Second, the mildly attractive asshole out there is my new self-defence teacher. He lives near here, and we are carpooling to class," I say. I don't even want to admit the number of lies in that sentence to myself.

I hate lying to her, but at least some of it is true, we are doing self-defence because it's the only way he could persuade me to spend time with the pack. Honestly, I loved learning how to defend myself growing up, I was always top of my class, and I won a lot of awards. After what Harris said today about all the different supernaturals out there, I want to see if they have weaknesses that I can use to defend myself.

"Sure, that's why he is giving you a lift. For a smart girl, you're so clueless," she shakes her head at me.

"Honestly, he doesn't see me like that. I agreed to a date with Wyatt," I tell her and enjoy watching her whole face light up. I can see she is planning double weddings at this point, knowing my best friend as I do. That thought alone makes me want to run for the hills.

"That's amazing," she squeals. I grab my bag off the side of my bed laughing and walk out of my room with Alex following. I changed earlier into yoga pants and a tight-fitting tank top, knowing I would need to be able to move. My hair is up an in a tight bun, so it's out of the way. This is how I've always dressed when I go to class, but, as soon as I see Jaxson, I'm aware that I have too much skin on show.

Jaxson is looking at a picture of me and Alex at a fun fair that's sitting on the fireplace in the living room. We must have been around ten in the picture. I smile, remembering how happy I was that day.

"Are you ready?" Jaxson asks turning away from the picture to look me in the eye. I can't help but feel a flush of heat looking at him dressed in black sweats with a tight, black shirt showing off his impressive chest. My breath catches as I see him eyeing my outfit in the same way I'm checking him out, but as if he hears my inner thoughts he decides to glare at me. It should be scary to have him glaring at me, but it isn't. Oh no, it has a different kind of effect altogether.

"Are you going to answer? Or have you forgotten the English language since we last met, lass?" he asks.

"Don't be a jackass already, let's go," I say, watching as he laughs deeply as he replies.

"No one's called me a jackass in a long time. It almost

seems comical coming from someone like you." My anger burns as he continues to laugh, and Alex clears her throat behind me.

"Jaxson, this is Alex," I introduce her through gritted teeth, while he turns on a charming smile.

"Hello Alex, it's nice to meet you," he says politely, no sign of the previously rude Jaxson. My jaw drops open before I grit my teeth in annoyance. Alex, he is nice to?

"Likewise," Alex says winking at me.

"Let's go," I repeat as I walk past Alex, who pulls me into a hug before I can escape.

"There is no way that man doesn't want to do naughty things to you," she whispers.

I shake my head at her as she lets go of me, and I follow Jaxson out to his car.

"So, how's Freddy?" I ask when he starts driving.

"Being Freddy. He talks about you a lot. I think you have an admirer," Jaxson smirks at me.

"He is a sweet boy." I smile thinking of the little wolf.

"Yes, but slowly becoming a handful. This interest in girls is a new one." He laughs, and I can't help but join in.

"I think that's normal for his age," I say.

"So, tell me, lass, are you looking forward to me showing you how to protect yourself?" he asks me.

"I already know how to. So, no, this is a waste of time."

"No, it's not. You've put yourself in a dangerous world. I promised Freddy I would make sure you are safe, so here we are," he says, acting like it's the worst thing in the world. I cross my arms, ignoring him to look out the window. For one moment, I thought we could get along, then he ruins it.

Jaxson doesn't stop the car when we come to the wall

of trees but drives right through them. I feel a slight wave of some kind of energy, but it is nowhere near as bad as last time.

“How does that work?” I ask Jaxson.

“A witch created the barrier, as long as the alpha is alive, no one can enter unless invited by a wolf or pack,” he tells me. I should have guessed it was some kind of magic.

We don't speak as we drive past the cabins where people, as well as a few wolves, watch our car. A lot of people stop what they are doing to stare at us. It's a little unnerving. The only good thing is the few children I see running through the cabins playing ball. The wolves all look like normal people of different ages and wearing modern clothes. I don’t know what I expected them to be like, but this wasn’t it. You couldn’t tell there was anything different about them, other than they all seem better looking than most people. I wonder if that’s a wolf thing.

I wave back when a little boy about six starts jumping up and down, waving at me.

"Don't worry, lass, they haven't seen a human on pack lands in a little while," he tells me.

"Why?" I ask still watching the people. They weren’t outside the last time we came, and I wonder if it’s because I was coming, and they didn’t know what to expect.

"Humans and wolves don't mix," he looks at me in a strange way as he talks like he is reminding himself of that fact. I want to reply, but he makes it clear the conversation is off-limits by stopping the car and getting out.

The slam of his door snaps me out of my internal thoughts, and I jump out of my side of the car. He leads us around the main cabin and towards a large ground-floor cabin. The outside yard is empty, and the building hasn’t many windows.

Jaxson opens the door for me. As I walk in he says, "This is our training room." I watch as he moves away from me and flips a switch on the wall.

My jaw drops as the massive room comes into view. It's fitted with grey, plain walls and matching soft, tile flooring. There is one wall full of weaponry, kinds you can only imagine, and all of them shine silver as the lights hit them. The other wall has ropes and benches lined up, with mats against the wall.

"There isn't anyone here," I comment as Jaxson pulls out two mats and chucks them to the floor like they weigh nothing. My ears ring as they slam to the ground.

"No, I asked for it to be empty for a few hours," he says, "or else everyone would want to talk to you."

"Did you ask them nicely, and did you say please?" I inquire with a chuckle, and he doesn't answer, but I see the small smile he tries to hide.

"Right, smartass, we will start with stretches, and then I want you to run on the treadmill for thirty minutes." he tells me.

"You're joking, right?" I ask, and he puts his hands on his hips as he glares at me.

"We will do hand-to-hand combat when you're in shape," he states.

"I am in shape!" I tell him.

"I can see that," he looks down my body, surprisingly it didn't sound like an insult. More like a fact he is aware of but doesn't want to be. Or he could just be a jackass.

"Fine, let's get this over with," I mutter, knowing there isn't much point fighting him on this.

Half an hour later, I practically fall off the treadmill, which he set to a super-fast speed to piss me off–I'm sure of it. I walk over to a happy-looking Jaxson, who is lifting some weights. Each weight looks the size of me, and it's a little concerning how turned on I am at the sight of his straining muscles.

"Does my suffering make you happy?" I ask, and he laughs. I'm a little caught off guard at how sexy he sounds.

"No, lass, but we will be doing this three times a week, and I thought thirty minutes instead of a normal hour was me being nice." He is still laughing at me as he speaks.

"Fuck. You," I say slowly, crossing my arms, and he laughs more. He coaxes me over to the mat by waggling a finger at me.

"Well, you apparently know the basics, so I'm just going to attack you, and you try to stop me," he shrugs.

"Right, that's not fair, your shifter stuff makes you a hell of a lot stronger than me," I point out, but I still lower myself into a defensive position as he smirks at me.

"I will go easy, lass," he chuckles like this is all a joke to him. Then, before I can blink, he is in front of me. It takes him less than a second to knock my legs from under me, and all my previous training flies out the window. I blink for a few seconds, then glare up at him.

"Come on, lass, you're better than that," he taunts me.

I jump up and attack him, this time my muscles are remembering my classes. We go over the basics as he defends himself from me. The problem is the man is a wall, and no matter what I'm doing, he's still smirking at me.

I somehow twist around him, as he grabs me, and I elbow him in the back, before backing away again.

"You're fast, good," he comments as we circle each other. For the next hour, he knocks me on my back a million times, but I manage to get a few decent hits in. My body feels like it's on fire, but he hasn't hurt me enough to have any bruises after this.

"Last time," he says still smirking, as I wipe the sweat off my head. I look at the clock on the wall. It's nearly seven, and it's still very light outside. I try not to look at Jaxson as he drinks some water, a few drops slip down his chin and down his throat. I find myself wishing I could lick the water off him. I shake my head as he puts the water down and faces me.

This time, he doesn't let me prepare for him, and he knocks me to the ground straight away, shifting us both mid-air, so he takes the brunt of the landing, and I've fallen smack on top of him.

We both stare at each other, with our bodies pushed closely together, he rolls us over after a second. I shiver when he is on top of me but somehow not resting all his weight on me. I feel deliciously trapped between his muscled arms as he lifts a hand to push one of my always escaping brown hairs out of my eyes, and his finger traces down my face.

My breath catches as my eyes flutter to his perfect lips, as his eyes seem to be doing the same to mine. For one second, I'm sure he is going to kiss me before he shuts down, pushing himself off me and stalking out. The door slams, shaking the cabin with his anger.

What the hell was I thinking to let him get that close anyway? It's clear he doesn't like me, I sit up looking around at the empty room before the door opens again. Freddy walks in with a big smile.

"Winter!" he shouts running over to me as I stand, and soon I'm pulled into a big hug from a stronger-than-he-looks little boy.

"Freddy...can't...breathe," I push out as Freddy lets me go, laughing.

"Whoops sorry, I kind of forgot you're human," he says

it like it was a little bit of an insult to be human, and I try not to take offense.

"Right. How are you? No more sneaking out, I hope?" I ask.

"No. I'm still grounded, but it's alright. Do you want dinner? Fergus and his mate, Anna, are cooking," he asks quickly, looking far too excited.

I look towards the door where Jaxson left, and I know he wouldn't want me there.

"No, I don't think I should come to dinner, Freddy. As much as I want to see you, I think it would be a bad idea," I say placing my hand on his shoulder.

"Please," he says with actual puppy dog eyes.

"Come on, don't make him start his fake tears to convince you," Fergus says from the doorway with a smirk, very much like Jaxson's, fixed on his face.

"Would the tears work? I mean, it works on Anna." Freddy smiles up at me, clearly proud of his work.

"No need for dramatics, I will eat with you, if that's okay, Fergus?" I ask, glancing at the huge alpha. If it's possible he looks bigger now than when I first saw him. Despite the fact he is just wearing worn jeans and a blue shirt, he seems to command the room. His brown hair, shorter than Jaxson's, is windswept. Even I have to admit he is attractive, looking like he should be cutting wood in a magazine or something. Maybe it's just the resemblance to Jaxson, whom I do have a crush on. Well, I can acknowledge it to myself, just not out loud.

"We would be honoured for you to join us for dinner, Winter," he says politely, showing a little of his sharp teeth, and I smile a little, even if he intimidates the hell out me.

"I'm not dressed for dinner," I comment, feeling my sweat-filled clothes sticking to me, as Freddy and I walk over to Fergus.

"My mate will find you something to borrow, and you can get a shower. You look around the same size," he says before turning, and we follow him out. Freddy slips his small hand into mine, and I give it a little squeeze.

"So, do you go to school, Freddy?" I ask wondering about it now. If they don't see humans, then they can't be going to any of the schools around here. I guess it would be hard for them to hide their wolves when they lose their temper. I remember Harris telling me they can't control themselves until they're adults.

"Nope, we're home-schooled. Anna is our teacher, actually. It's safer this way. No humans because of the w–"

Freddy is cut off by Fergus' loud growl. "No speaking of that," he says turning to give a warning look to Freddy, who looks down quickly.

"So, do you have a small class? If Anna is the only teacher," I ask.

"Children are rare for wolves because we don't have many females, and we don't mix with other species," Fergus tells me, and Freddy nods.

"Why not?" I ask.

"True mates are only found between the same species; the Goddess won't allow half-breeds to be born and mix our races. There are couples who ignored this rule, but no children ever came from it, that we know of. There is one exception, but I'm not too concerned that it's anything other than a fairy tale," he tells me, a distant look in his eyes.

I don't say anything else as we walk to the house, entering through a back door with a wolf sitting outside. This one has a creamy coat, and is a little smaller than the others I've seen. I'm guessing that it's a she-wolf, not a male. The wolf seems to stare at me for a long time before looking back towards the forest behind me. We come straight into a large kitchen with light wooden cabinets and matching appliances littered around. There is a big fireplace in the room which makes it seem homely. A small woman is in the fridge, pushing things around, and turns to see us come in. Her blonde hair is in a bun, and she looks to be in her early thirties. She is wearing a pretty, pink sundress with a little white cardigan over the top.

"I finally get to meet the famous Winter," she says kindly as her face lights up, "Hello." She drops the food on one of the side tables and walks over to me. I'm surprised when she pulls me into a strong hug, and when she pulls away I see the small bump of her stomach. Fergus kisses her cheek as he walks past. I watch in amusement as he tries to take a cookie off the plate on the side. "None of that, dinner is nearly ready." Anna scolds and Fergus looks at her for a second before putting the cookie back with a long sigh.

"Hello. You must be Anna," I say with a friendly smile, her attention back on me. It doesn't escape my notice that there is an age gap between Anna and Fergus, but one look at Fergus' face as he watches Anna, tells me they are so much in love that it doesn't matter.

"I am, and you're far more beautiful than Jaxson, let me believe. Now are you joining us for dinner?" she asks.

"If that's alright?" I ask her.

"It's perfect," she beams, and I find myself instantly liking her. She reminds me of my mum.

"Come on, we'll find you some clothes," she says, linking her arm with mine.

"I can check on the food for you," Fergus says happily behind me, as we leave.

"You keep your grubby hands away from our dinner, Fergus! Alpha or not, you don't get to touch it," she shouts over her shoulder, and I hear the loud laughter float in from the kitchen.

She looks at me. "He thinks I'm joking," she laughs, and I can't help but join in.

"Anyway, how are you? It must be a lot to handle finding out about all this," she waves a hand around the empty hallway we walk down, after she leads me up the stairs, past the living room I saw before. The stairs are in the back of the house, and there's another empty corridor at the top of them with stairs at the end, leading to the third floor, I imagine.

"I'm dealing. Honestly, it doesn't shock me as much as it should. I feel safe around Jaxson and Freddy," I tell her, and she gives me a slightly wide-eyed look.

"That's unusual," she finally says, looking over at me before opening a door to a large bedroom.

"Why?" I ask, as she shuts the door.

"Most humans can't cope with the fact that there is so much out there," she says.

"I read a lot of books, I always thought that maybe some of it was true. I guess I might be a little stupid for not caring," I mutter.

"Not stupid, I think you're pretty incredible, actually," she says and gives me a side hug.

"This is the room I share with Fergus. I will get you a dress, I have lots of pre-pregnancy dresses that I won't be able to wear for a long time. They should fit you," she comments in a friendly manner.

"Thanks. Congratulations, how far gone are you?" I ask.

"About five months. This is my first and an alpha, too. Fergus has practically locked me in the house since he scented the pregnancy, so I'm glad to have someone else to talk to." She beams as she rubs her little bump.

"Scented?" I ask loudly so she can hear me, as she goes through her wardrobe.

"Oh, wolves have heightened smells, fears, desires, a new baby isn't anything to us," she comments. I sit in the small, red chair in the corner of the room. "Found it!" she shouts before coming back to me with a tight-looking, pale-nude dress. It has a sweetheart neckline, and it looks way too expensive for me to be okay with wearing it.

"I can't borrow this, it's too much," I shake my head. I look over the room; it has another large fireplace and a huge four-poster bed made of dark wood. The bed sheets match the red curtains. There are two paintings of packs of wolves on the walls. There are wild flowers on the windowsill and chest of drawers, along with many other little bottles of things.

"You can, and you will," Anna states, I recognise her mother-like tone. It's one where you know you won't win the argument, so it's best to just nod, and I give in.

"There's a shower in there if you want to clean up." she says with a smile. "Come down when you're ready."

I wave goodbye to her before going into the bathroom. I keep my hair out of the water, as I quickly shower and dry off. I slip on the dress and let my hair down, running my fingers through it a few times. It's little better than a frizzy mess.

I leave my pile of clothes in a neat pile on the counter. I'll change back into them before I leave tonight. I slip my trainers back on; I'm lucky they are small and black, so they don't look too weird.

I shut the bedroom door behind me as I leave, making a mental note to thank Anna again when I see my outfit in the full-length mirror in the hallway. The dress hugs my curves and pushes up my chest, making me look a lot hotter than I am. I shake my head at myself as I walk down the corridor. It's an empty corridor with about five doors leading off it, there are a few pictures on the walls of people I don't know.

I stop when the door in front of me opens, and a freshly-showered Jaxson walks out. His eyes widen as he looks at me, his eyes go from the bottom of my legs to my eyes before moving to shut the door behind him.

"You look, beautiful, lass," he says like a dark warning, as he walks towards me. I feel like I'm the prey, and he is a hunter as my heartbeat picks up. My back hits a wall as he cages me in, with his face hovering close to mine.

Jaxson moves my hair to the side, as he starts running his hand down my neck. I move my head to the side to give him more access, and he growls at me. I don't move as he lowers his head to land a kiss on my neck, the feel of his lips on my neck makes me feel weak at the knees. His hot breath and soft lips make me release a soft sigh as his lips move slowly up my neck. Jaxson's chest makes a louder growl, before he sniffs me. I mean, I really kind of forgot about his wolf side until then.

"Jesus, Winter, I need to go," he says in a deep, growling voice, as he quickly pushes away from me and starts storming down the corridor. The muscles in his back look tight, and I just watch him as he leaves.

I rest my head back on the wall for a second, wondering what I'm feeling for the Wolfman. My thoughts flash to Wyatt for a second, but my mind doesn't have the ability to stay away from Jaxson for long after being so close to him. I run my hand to my neck where he kissed me. I don't think I've ever felt anything that amazing. Well, maybe when Wyatt kissed me, that kiss was something else, too. How bad does that make me sound?

"Winter, are you ready?" Anna's voice floats from the

nearby kitchen, shaking me out of my thoughts. I walk in a daze until I find her in the kitchen, running around.

"Do you want any help?" I ask.

"Wow, you look amazing, you're keeping that dress. It never suited me like it does you," she tells me as she waves a spoon around.

I go to reply, but she cuts me off, clearly not to be argued with.

"Can you take that dish of vegetables to the table? It's just through there. You can sit, we'll all be in soon," she says with a small smile, pointing to the door next to the fireplace.

"Sure," I say taking the dish she points at, before using one arm to open the door and let myself into the dining room.

It's a simple room with dark-brown walls and a huge fireplace with red brickwork. It looks old and makes me wonder if it was the oldest thing in the house. The table is massive with ten, dark wooden chairs. There is a wolf statue in the middle of the table. It's made of wood and stone. It looks beautiful, the wolf looking like it's howling at the moon.

"My great-grandfather made it; I like it, do you?" Fergus asks, startling me a little as he sits at the head of the table. I notice he is carrying two bowls of potatoes, which he puts down. The table is already set with glasses and plates.

I place the vegetables down next the statue in the middle before taking a seat next to Fergus on his right.

"Is it okay to sit here?" I ask before actually sitting down.

"Yes," he comments waving a hand.

"The statue is lovely," I say, in answer to his question.

"We don't like to hide who we are here, that why there

are wolves all around," he says looking away from me at the table.

"I don't see anything wrong with that," I tell him.

"Would you like a drink? We have wine or water," he asks, not replying to what I said.

"Wine would be lovely," I say, and Fergus pours two glasses. Jaxson comes into the room followed by Freddy.

Jaxson scowls at Fergus a second before taking the seat next to me. Freddy takes the one opposite leaving the space in front of me for Anna.

"Hello," I say with a smile, trying to not stare at Jaxson's lips.

"Hello, Winter," Freddy says with such happiness in his voice, I can't help but smile at him.

Anna comes in with a dish with a large cooked piece of beef on it. She places it in front of Fergus before kissing his cheek and sitting in front of me.

"Dig in before it gets cold," Anna says, passing me a spoon for the potatoes in front of me.

We all share the food around before starting to eat.

"Tell us about your family, Winter?" Fergus asks. Jaxson's hand tightens on his fork in reaction.

"She doesn't have to answer any questions." Jaxson says warningly.

"I'm only being friendly, brother," Fergus says as I see Jaxson's whole body tense up. I decide to intervene before this ends badly.

"It's alright, I grew up with my mother and best friend Alex. I now share an apartment with her."

"No siblings or father around?" Fergus asks as I tense a little.

"Nope," I draw out the word as I take a sip of my wine, needing it.

"A boyfriend?" he asks a little rudely, but I ignore it.

"No again," I say, and I can't help but flicker to Wyatt in my head. He isn't my boyfriend, but somehow it feels wrong to say I'm not involved with anyone.

"You're lying, well slightly," Fergus comments.

"She doesn't have to answer everything you ask, brother. She isn't one of your wolves," Jaxson growls.

"I guess I did lie a little. How did you know?" I ask.

"It is a gift from the Goddess," Fergus answers.

"It's like Uncle J's ability to control the earth or Anna's ability to see relationships between people. Some of us have extra gifts, but I don't know if I'll have any. They don't show until you get older," Freddy tells me.

Fergus looks annoyed. I smile at him.

"You can control the earth?" I ask turning to Jaxson with wide eyes.

"Are you asking me or requesting I show you? I won't do either for someone like you. So, don't waste your time asking." Jaxson replies curtly.

"Jax," Anna scolds, but he ignores her as his eyes lock with mine. The pressure to turn and run out of the room is overwhelming, but I can't back away. You can thank my mother for my stubbornness.

"You would be better off leaving with me and going back to your human life. You're not wanted here," Jaxson says coldly, it's like a wall has gone up, and he is back to the asshole I know.

"Freddy, go and get me a drink, would you?" Anna asks, and Freddy nods. I wait until he has left before I say anything.

"You're a total bastard at times, you know that, right?" I tell him.

"No, I'm just honest about unfortunate truths," he replies with cold eyes.

"Just a cold jackass then. What flew up your ass

today?" I ask, and I hear Anna's little laugh in the background.

"You can call me whatever, lass, not like it matters in the long run. Your opinion of me, that is," he says with a shrug.

"No, because the great Jaxson wouldn't care what a stupid, silly, little human thinks, huh? You know what, stay the fuck away from me," I shout at him as I slam my hands on the table. I push my chair away and walk out of the room before I end up throwing the wolf statue at his head. I don't know why he affects me so much, but something has cracked, and I can't fix it.

I stop in the living room, realising that I can't even get home on my own, as he brought me here. Maybe I can find Harris and Katy's cabin, and then I can get them to take me home. The two wolves at the door growl at me as I walk past. I actually growl back.

"Fucking bite me, if you're going to, I literally don't give a crap," I say to them, and start walking away. I don't have it in me to care anymore if they follow. I feel like I have a heavy weight on my heart, and I don't know how to remove it. The trees and paths blur as I jog though the woods. I pass a few cabins, but from the look at the cars outside, I know they're not Harris's home. A few people stop to stare at me, but I ignore them. I know it would be smart to ask for help, but I feel so angry, I'm scared I'll just burst into tears.

"Lass, wait," Jaxson shouts behind me. The sound of his heavy boots slamming across the leaves is the only sound I hear as I run away. Some part of me knows running is pointless when he is a lot faster than I am.

"No, I will find Harris and beg for a lift home. I meant what I said. Stay away from me," I shout over my shoulder, as I run faster through the trees. I see another cabin coming up, and I'm sure that it's Harris's truck outside.

A hand snakes around my waist before I'm pulled over a shoulder. I smack my wrists against his back and try to wriggle off. The mountain of a man just chuckles and wraps an arm around the back of my legs to stop me from kicking him.

"Put me down now, Jaxson!" I shout in a frustrated growl.

"Fine, but hear me out."

I kick him one last one time before muttering, "Fine," and I hear him chuckle, but at least he is smart enough to not outright laugh at me.

Jaxson puts me down gently before standing close to me. The freshly cut wood scent of him surrounds me as I look up into his bright-green eyes. His hair is slightly messy on top, where he has been running his fingers through it, and his shirt has mud from my trainers all over it. I want to say the messy look doesn't suit him, but it does–it does way too much.

"I'm sorry, look, things are complicated, and it's not your fault," he tells me gently. I've never heard him be gentle with me, it throws me off my game for a second.

"I've never met anyone like you. I don't like humans and–," he says, and I cut him off.

"I want to leave." I cross my arms and back away from him a little. Jaxson raises his eyes to look at me, and we stare at each other, something changing in his gaze. There's a vulnerability I thought I'd never see in his eyes. I've never been good at hiding my feelings, I'm sure he is reading me like a book now.

"Can I show you something, first?" he asks carefully, holding out his hand for me to take.

"Why?" I ask, eyeing his hand.

"Because for some reason, I need to show you I'm not a jackass all the time," he says looking down to the ground like it holds all the answers.

Against my better judgment, I whisper, "Okay."

Jaxson's head snaps up with his beautiful eyes lit up like a green forest, a small smile on the corner of his lips.

"Let's go, lass," he extends his hand towards me further, and I hesitate a little, before slipping my hand in his. Jaxson interlaces our fingers, not looking my way as he leads me back to the house and around the back. We walk past the training cabin into the woods behind. I try to ignore the rough feel of his fingers against mine or the way my tiny hand seems to fit into his perfectly.

"Can I ask you something?" I ask, pushing my luck a little, while he is in a good mood.

"You can ask me anything you like, I may not choose to answer you, but go on." He squeezes my hand gently. I guess it's the best I can ask for.

"Why do you have a slight Scottish accent, but Fergus and Freddy don't?" I ask him carefully, Jaxson tenses slightly at my question, but he exhales before answering.

"Fergus is my half-brother. We have different mothers, and Freddy's mum was my half-sister, too," he tells me.

"Oh," is all I say, as I process it.

"My father was...he was broken when my mother died. He had relationships with a lot of women before his death a few years ago. I grew up with my mother's family in Scotland, and Fergus was sent to us when he was fourteen after his own mother passed away." He explains as we go around a large rock. There is a small dirt path that wasn't here before, and we walk up to it. I'm glad it's not too cold because wearing this dress is not ideal for a late- night walk. The sun is just setting in the sky, and the large trees are starting to look a little scary now as they cast shadows.

"And your sister?" I ask, keeping my eyes on Jaxson instead of where we are.

"I didn't know about her until about nine years ago lass, and she wasn't in a good place," he says sadly.

"What happened?" I ask quietly, the forest seems silent as it waits for an answer with me.

"Someone saved her and Freddy, who she was pregnant with at the time. Her own mother had sold her, and she basically lived her whole life as a slave for vampires. I owe one vampire a debt because he found a way to get her out," he says, a brief flicker of pain crosses his features.

"What was she like?" I ask him.

"Striking. She was also very feisty, somehow, even after all those years. She lived for Freddy, and once she got to know me and Fergus, she was happy." He smiles as he talks.

"How did she die?" I ask. I see how hard it is for him to talk to me about her, but, to my shock, he does answer.

"She went out, she didn't tell anyone, and by the time we found her, it was too late. The vampires took her life," he growls.

"When did your mother pass away?" I ask gently, after we walk in silence for a while. Both of us are walking slowly. I'm enjoying just being near him, and I hope he is feeling the same way.

"I was about one, or so I've been told. I don't remember her, but everyone told me she had a kind soul," he says.

"I think somewhere hidden in pain, is a kind soul inside of you too," I comment my inner thoughts on Jaxson.

Jaxson stops walking to stare at me, before shaking his head. He tugs on my hand, so we keep walking.

"How long have you been Freddy's guardian?" I ask.

"About seven years," he says.

"Can I be rude and ask about his father?" I ask.

"It's not a nice story lass, I'll share it with you one day but not today." He says darkly, lost in his own memories.

"Okay." I squeeze his hand in comfort. My gaze goes forward to a cliff we are coming up to. It's hanging over the woods, a few steps ahead of us. To the right, the view over the town is amazing, lit up with its lights as it is and to the left, more woods. But what really gets your attention, is the dim-lit summer sky. The summer nights here don't get dark until at least ten, and even then, they aren't truly dark.

"I've never done this with anyone, so you'll have to hold on tight." He says before walking over to the edge of the cliff and standing on a large flat rock.

"What are you talking about?" I ask as I walk over to him. I step onto the rock and move closer to him.

"Trust me?" he whispers in my ear, as his arm twists around my waist, pulling me to his hard body.

"Yes," I whisper as my body melts into his. I don't notice the rock move at first but my eyes widen as the large rock lifts off the ground.

"Jaxson." I whisper in shock, as we float over the cliff, and I nearly scream at the height. I hold onto Jaxson tightly as we float on the rock, down the cliff. My gaze goes to him, when I finally am brave enough to look up. His eyes are glowing green, making all the features in his face look more like the supernatural wolf I know he is. The smack of the rock hitting the ground shakes me from my gaze as I wobble on the rock with Jaxson's arms still wrapped around me. I look away from his glowing eyes to see he has landed us inside a cavern in the cliff. There is a small waterfall in the corner, and I let go and walk over. It pours down the side of the cavern wall, I run my hand in the water watching as it flows around my hand.

"I found this place when I was about ten, I was a troublesome child, always running off into the woods and testing my new-found powers. My auntie used to bring me here every summer to meet the pack as she trained me to be Alpha," he tells me.

"You were meant to be Alpha?" I whisper, turning to face Jaxson, who is sitting on the edge of the cavern looking out. I walk over and sit next to him, close enough that our thighs touched.

"Fergus is the better alpha. When my sister was killed, and I couldn't save her...," his voice cracks a little, my heart breaks for the kind man hidden in grief. I lean my shoulder on his. Jaxson's arm falls around my waist as he continues to tell me.

"I was too late, lass, he killed her, and I wasn't there for her like I should have been, like an alpha would have been. Because I was rejecting whom I'm meant to be," he says, his voice echoing around the cavern.

"I don't believe that," I whisper.

"Why?" he asks quietly back.

"You're kind, Jaxson. And, the way Freddy looks up to you, shows me you're more designed to look after people than you think. You didn't kill your sister, it wasn't your fault," I tell him.

"I should have been there. I wasn't protecting her when I was meant to because I went out to find a vampire I had a tip on," he tells me.

"Did you find him?" I ask gently.

"No, it was a distraction. He wanted her alone and he," he stops talking, looking away from me and out at the woods.

"I'm sorry. Was it a vampire she knew then?" I ask.

"Yes, and when I find the bastard. I will kill him," he vows the words; some words are filled with the power of a promise, and you can't miss it.

"I know you will," I echo as the stars start showing themselves, and the moon hovers in the sky. "Thank you for showing me this, it's really something beautiful," I tell him.

"Much like you," he says as he turns my face to look at him. Our mouths are a breath away as he sighs, pulling back from me.

"I want to kiss you, lass, more than anything, but I won't. You don't deserve that. I can't be more than your friend," he says, looking as frustrated as I feel. I push down the massive pain that crosses my heart and nod at him as I turn away. I don't trust myself to speak.

"I'm kind of seeing someone too, you're right. We should just be friends." I tell him when I get my voice back, and his fists clench. That's the only response I get. We both sit in silence for a while, just listening to the waterfall, like it could wash away all my feelings for him.

"You said you had your powers as a child, but Freddy said he wouldn't get them until he was older," I ask, desperate to get back to being friends.

"I'm different. The day I was born, I got my powers. The trees sang to all the wolves, putting them into a daze and vines from the ground wrapped around my cot as they howled. The vines covered me, my whole body. When they let go, they say my eyes were glowing green." He tells me, his voice lost in a memory.

"Will you ever be alpha?" I ask. I don't reply to his story because it sounds like he resents his powers. I imagine the pressure of being alpha when you grow up, and being a special baby with strong powers is a lot of pressure.

"No, I gave it up to Fergus, and I won't take it, for any reason. I will always support my brother," he says, and let's go of my hand.

"Is he your alpha?" I ask as he stands and looks down at me.

"No, I've never knelt to anyone, and I never will," he tells me firmly before walking away to the rock.

With those words haunting my mind, I walk over and wrap my arms around him as his eyes start glowing. I squeeze him in a tight hug before I have to let go and his arms tighten around mine. I swear it's like he doesn't want me to let go.

10

WINTER

"There you are," a strong male voice shouts out, as I open my eyes into another dream. Shock fills me when I see it isn't the normal one I have had for years, but it feels just as real. The same girl is here but different, older maybe. She is sitting with her hair in a tight bun, filled with braids. It must have taken forever to get her hair just like that. I notice straight away that she is wearing odd clothes, which I don't recognise. They just about cover her. It's done in layers of purple satin that are wrapped around her body and flow out into a big skirt at the bottom. There's a beautiful crown, which lies on her head, made of little gold flowers and vines. There is a large, white, oval stone in the middle, and it glitters from the streams of light coming through the thin curtains in the room. Am I dreaming about a queen?

"Leo," she exhales, her face filling with joy at the male outside the room. I grimace to myself as I look around the room we are in, it's nothing like I've ever seen, and I'm not sure how I've made it up. There is a massive, white bed in the middle of the room, on a kind of altar. And, there are several archways to the outside, with thin, white curtains that sway in the breeze. The floor is white marble, and there

isn't anything else in the room to help me know where I am. All I see is white. My thoughts are distracted as a man pushes though the curtains, and my jaw drops when I look at him. He looks just like Jaxson, the same black hair, but his eyes are light-blue, and there is a little difference in his face that shows me it's not him. His face looks older than Jaxson's and full of love for the woman in front of him. He is wearing a black toga with a badge in gold in the middle, with some kind of symbol on it that I can't see from where I am.

"Elissa, are you okay?" he asks the woman. Ah ha, at least I know her name. I'm not sure if that makes me crazier, the fact I'm happy my made-up, dream woman has a name or the fact I have these dreams in the first place. Elissa makes no move to go near him, she stands in the middle of the room, facing an empty door.

"I keep seeing her, the war, all of it," she whispers inside my head, the same way she talked to me in the other dreams. The feeling is peaceful and tranquil just like she is.

Leo's face fills with sympathy as he walks over and pulls her into an embrace that she doesn't resist.

"What have you learnt?" he asks gently. It's clear this man loves her dearly.

Elissa pushes him away and starts to pace right in front of me, so close I can almost touch her, but I can't move as usual.

"He will find me, find us. The end is near, and her future isn't safe. He will hunt her, and all of them, until the prophecy is no more," she mutters as her eyes start to glow a bright blue.

"She is safe, I have made sure of it," the man states.

"Our deaths will guard her and her children. I can't change it. I can't save you," she wails, falling to the ground.

The man falls to his knees in front of her, pulling her to his chest. The man gently rocks her as she cries.

"I wouldn't change anything. I love you," he says.

"And I you," she whispers to him, before she looks up, over Leo's shoulder, directly at me.

"There will be a time, a time you will understand, and it is closer than it has ever been now," she whispers in my mind.

I gasp, waking up with a start, feeling myself covered in sweat.

The thoughts of Elissa and Leo run through my mind, as I look at my phone and see it's midday. I must have slept a hell of a lot longer than I wanted, but thank god, it's the weekend.

How can these dreams be so real? It's like I was there next to her as she cried. My heart goes out to her, like the women in the romantic movies I used to watch. Maybe that's where I'm getting my strong imagination from.

I flick though my phone for a minute before seeing a text from Wyatt:

I will pick you up at 7. Can't wait to see you. X

I lie back in my bed, staring at the white ceiling. Why do I feel guilty for going on a date with Wyatt when Jaxson has made it clear nothing can happen between us? My feelings for Wyatt aren't as strong, but I haven't really gotten to know him. I know from the kiss that there could be a good thing between us.

I want Jaxson just as much as I want Wyatt. I know having dreams about a romance that's clearly not allowed is my mind trying to tell me something. That's why I need to give Wyatt a chance. He is a nice guy, a little intimating and scary, but there is something about him.

I text Wyatt back saying okay, and take a shower.

When I come out my room with my sweats on and a tank top, I find a note on the fridge from Alex, saying she is staying at Drake's for the weekend.

Lucky girl, I smile to myself at the thought of how

happy she is. She never let anyone close, other than me and my mum growing up, so no boy had a chance. Until this one.

I spend the rest of the day painting my toes and nails red, and then watching silly movies. By the time seven comes around and there's a knock at the door, I've gotten myself into a black, skater dress with black, high heels. Grabbing my purse and keys, I open the door to Wyatt and see him leaning against the door frame, looking way too attractive for his own good. His blond hair has been styled lightly, making it look softer than usual. I take my time to look at him, he's wearing stylish, black trousers and a button-down, dark-blue shirt. His dark-brown eyes regard me with humour, knowing I'm checking him out, when I meet them eventually.

"You look beautiful as always, sweetheart," he comments, checking out my outfit before stepping into my personal space.

"I like your hair like this, it suits you," he says as he runs his hand through my straight hair. The top part is put up in two plaits that join in the middle, and the rest falls gently over my shoulders.

"Thanks," I say, feeling my throat going dry at the enticing smell of him.

"Shall we?" he asks, holding out a hand, which I accept with a shy nod. I lock the door while he waits, and then he leads me to his car. Once I'm seated, he starts to drive and tells me, "It's a bit of a drive, but the place is worth it."

"I don't mind." I'm looking out at the woods. My thoughts flicker to Jaxson holding me in that cave with his glowing eyes, and the need for him to kiss me. It hurts thinking of the reasons why he didn't. My gaze goes to the extremely attractive guy I'm on a date with, and guilt fills me. Is it wrong that I want them both, two people who don't know each other and most likely would hate each other? Jaxson hates humans, I doubt he would be okay with me kissing one. The bad problem is that I couldn't give either one of them up.

"Are you okay?" Wyatt asks, like he can actually feel my guilt.

"Mm. So, what have you been up to this week?" I ask to change the subject. Wyatt frowns at me before letting it go and answering.

"I've been working with my father, and Drake has been helping. There is some new information that's come to light, and we are planning a take-over," he tells me, his jaw is clicking as he talks, and I get the impression it's not what he wants.

"A take-over? Like acquiring a new business or something?" I ask.

"No, we will take it apart, so it can't hurt anyone else. The group is going to do something terrible. I might get in trouble for stopping them, but it's the right thing to do," he says, and I get the feeling he didn't mean to tell me that when he looks at me. I've always had the feeling Wyatt isn't telling me something, but I'm not sure how to ask him about it.

"Why?" I ask.

"It's not us being evil, Winter. They would do the same to us without a second thought, and it's better to take out the threat before they become a bigger one," he says without a hint of emotion, one of his pale hands reaches over and takes mine. I let him hold my hand for a while, neither of us saying a word.

"Doesn't make it right," I say finally, as he looks at me oddly.

"You're right, it doesn't, but we don't all have a choice.

Sometimes a wrong can make a right." He smiles with a sadness that I don't understand.

I yawn, feeling how tired I am from last night. When I have nightmares, I don't get any sleep and usually feel more tired than usual. They started when I was ten, and I used to wake up screaming. My mum took me to the doctors after I started getting one every month, but they didn't help. I eventually learnt that they aren't that scary, they just feel very real. I told my mum I didn't get them anymore, when I couldn't stand her looking at me with concern all the time. Alex knows and usually would help me, but the dreams aren't all always the same. Sometimes I dream of fire-covered demons and beautiful people who glow different colours, but some of them are so awful that they scare me into not sleeping for days. Thankfully, I only seem to get those dreams once a year now.

"You look tired, a rough night?" he asks, watching me from the corner of his eye.

"Just bad dreams keeping me awake," I tell him honestly.

"What were they about?" he asks gently.

"Oh, the usual, strange people, I don't know, arguing and wearing weird clothes. It wasn't a nightmare, but it didn't feel good. It doesn't matter." I mumble looking away. I can't tell him how I think it's my subconscious trying to tell me I have feelings for someone who is just a friend.

"Maybe you need a strong, blond man in your bed, to protect you from bad dreams," he says, I giggle when I see the small twitch in his lips.

"You need to work on your chat-up lines, buddy," I grin. This makes us both start laughing.

"I don't usually need them, but, I agree, that was bad," he chuckles as he takes my hand and brings it to his mouth.

Wyatt places a gentle kiss on the back of it before letting go to change the gear.

"We're here," he says, and I can see how excited he is from his eyes. I get out of his car to see we are parked outside a very small restaurant. It looks like a cottage in the middle of nowhere with a few lanterns in the windows. I look at Wyatt in confusion.

"You should never judge a book by its cover, hasn't anyone ever told you that?" He chuckles when I don't reply, and he comes over, taking my hand. Wyatt leads me to the entrance, and a man opens the door, nodding to Wyatt as he leads me in. The room is practically empty, except for a staircase lit up by fairy lights on the big banisters. The staircase leads down into the ground, and I can't see where it goes. There were a few cars parked outside, so there must be other people down here.

"After you, sweetheart," Wyatt whispers in my ear, as he pushes my hair over my shoulder. I smile, walking down the staircase, then my jaw drops open.

There is a massive room under the small restaurant, with tables in the middle. The ceiling has hundreds of different lights, and the walls are filled with bottles of wine on a display. Wyatt gently nudges me down the staircase with his hand, and the man at the end dressed all in black smiles at us. The staircase looks like it's been carved out of one piece of wood, and little twirls are carved into it. It makes me wonder how the hell they got the staircase into here. It must have been a hell of a job.

"Sir, you and your lovely guest are very welcome here, tonight. It's been such a long time since I have seen you. The usual table?" he asks with a small bow. The man is dressed all in black, a small red crown is stitched into the pocket on his chest.

"Please, Albert," Wyatt answers. I scowl a little inside,

as we are led to a nice table in the corner, thinking about how many girls he has brought here. A wave of jealously hits me as I imagine Wyatt with anyone else, but I push it away as Wyatt looks through the drinks menu. I can't be jealous of people who came before me, but, for some reason, I know I am. The way Wyatt looks at me, suggests that he isn't seeing anyone else, so I should relax.

"I will have my usual red wine, and what would you like?" he asks me, and I ask for a glass of any white wine.

"That's no problem. I can choose something for you," Albert nods before leaving.

"The lobster is really tasty here, it's a favourite of mine, but anything here is. The chef is known around the world for his cooking talents, and has won many awards. I wouldn't stop eating if that man cooked for me all the time," Wyatt says as I skim though the menu.

"It sounds really good," I reply, vaguely wondering how expensive the food must be here. The menu doesn't have any prices, which makes it beyond expensive. I don't know if I like Wyatt spending that much money on me. I know he must be well off because of his car; it's still something I'm not sure how to get used to. We weren't poor by any means growing up, we had a lovely two-bedroom house in a nice neighbourhood, and my mum found enough to take us on a few holidays over the years. I've just never been to a place as expensive as this, and, honestly, I think I'm a little intimidated by it all. I don't want to ruin tonight, so I force myself to act comfortable.

I decide on the mixed fish food plate, and as the waiter brings us our drinks, I order my food and Wyatt has the same as me.

"How did you find this place, it's almost magical?" I inquire as I look around. The walls look like they are polished, brown stone, and there are a few couples at the other tables who look more interested in the room than their partners. The thoughts of what Harris said about other supernaturals flutters to my mind as I look around the place. It's really a very magical place with the lights looking like they are hovering above us, too bright for me to make out. The table even has a rose which looks too perfect to be real.

"This place was created by my mother. I actually own it now, but it always feels like hers. My mother was just like this place, unique and stunning," he looks around the room as he talks, his eyes are distant with a lost memory.

"Your mother had beautiful taste in things," I comment.

"She did. She was a magical person inside and out, you could say," he smiles, and I'm reminded how handsome he is when he does. We chat about normal things until our food arrives and Wyatt was right, the lobster was amazing, as it all was.

"Would you like dessert, sir?" Albert asks when we have finished.

"A chocolate pudding to share please," he says, and Albert nods before he leaves.

"How did you know I wanted dessert?" I ask with a slight smile when he grins at me.

"Well, a little bird told me of your weak spot for chocolate," he says with a wink.

"Alex," I groan, and he laughs. She is right, I have a serious addiction to chocolate. I really believe the stuff should be banned because it's the main problem for my hips and ass. Actually, I don't want it banned, I would have to buy it illegally and then end up in prison.

"What else did she say?" I ask, feeling my cheeks going red.

"I'm afraid we discussed your running around the

house naked phase at nine, and my favourite is the time you tried to save a cat in a tall tree and got stuck for a whole night, while everyone searched for you." He laughs with me as I chuckle. I put my hands on my red cheeks trying to hide them.

"The damn cat betrayed me," I say with a pout as Wyatt laughs.

"How did the cat betray you?" he manages to ask between laughter.

"The cat climbed down, once I got up and walked off. I had to have firefighters use their truck ladders to get me down." Wyatt laughs harder as I add, "The whole neighbourhood had to watch as I was thrown over one of the men's shoulders, and my skirt flew up, flashing everyone my kitten knickers," I say with a slight grumble that makes Wyatt laugh more.

I can't help but laugh with him, as I plan ways to get back at my revealing friend later.

The waiter smiles as he hands us the chocolate pudding with only one spoon.

Wyatt calms down enough to break off a bit of mouth-watering pudding, and smirks at me.

"Try this," he whispers as he leads the spoon to my mouth, and slowly feeds me it. I can't help the small moan that escapes my lips as I taste the amazing flavour of the pudding.

I look up to see Wyatt's eyes almost glowing black before he looks away.

"You can have the rest if you want," he says gently.

"We can share," I say, and we take turns feeding each other. It becomes way too much of a turn on every time he licks the spoon, so I have to go to the toilet to calm down and get away from him for a second before I do or say something embarrassing. I finish in the bathroom, and when I come back to the table, there is a man in my seat.

I can only see his back and that he has a lot of shiny, white hair that's tied loosely at the nape of his neck in braids and goes down to his middle back. There are odd bits of silver in it, and I think it must be a really expensive dye job. When I get to the table, both the men stop talking, and Wyatt looks up at me with a slight smile. The white-haired man is even more impressive from the front. He has a handsome, baby face, with white eyebrows that I wouldn't think could look hot on a guy, but it does for him. His purple eyes are big and bright as he stares at me, I notice he is wearing some kind of white tunic with what looks like white trousers underneath that showcase his massive build. I would guess he as big as Jaxson, or just a tad bigger than Wyatt, but who knows? When he smiles at me, two perfectly placed dimples appear.

"Wyatt, where have you been hiding this gorgeous one?" he asks, and I watch in slight curiosity as he stands and offers me my chair back. I was wrong about his height, he towers over me, and I feel tiny next to him. I take the chair and feel his large fingers slide across my back as he tucks me in.

"Dabriel, this is Winter," Wyatt introduces me with a friendly smile on his lips. I'm a little surprised he didn't take offence to this guy calling me gorgeous, but maybe they are just good friends.

"Nice to meet you, that's an unusual name you have," I comment and smile up at him from my seat. I watch as Dabriel gets another chair from a nearby table and moves it next to ours.

"So is Winter. Were you born in winter by any chance?" Dabriel winks at me, and I laugh.

"Nope, my birthday is in May. I asked my mum about

it once, and she said she just loves winter. It's odd, actually, because when it's cold at home, she hates it," I say, and we all laugh a little.

"How do you guys know each other?" I ask, Dabriel looks the same age as Wyatt, so maybe they grew up together.

"We have been friends for a long time. Atti will want to meet you; he is our other friend. It's a shame that Jax won't speak to us still." Dabriel says, and I briefly panic before deciding that they couldn't mean Jaxson. That would be impossible. I couldn't imagine the big, bad wolf having friends that are human. It must just be a coincidence.

"I bet he would, and one day, Jax will stop being an idiot." Wyatt shakes his head.

"Yeah, that's not happening." Dabriel laughs.

"Can I call you Dab? I like it." I say randomly.

"You can call me whatever, hot stuff." Dabriel winks,

"That was bad. Winter said I was bad at hitting on her, but come on, he is worse," Wyatt waves a hand at a laughing Dabriel.

"Okay, I'll admit you're both bad. How do you get dates?" I laugh at their pouting faces. "Must be the good looks." I think and realise too late that I've said it out loud. Both of them grin at me.

Men and their egos.

"I have to leave, but I will see you again, Winter," Dabriel says as he gets to his feet.

"Dabriel," Wyatt warns in a low voice.

"It's true, it's not the right time but soon." Dabriel tells Wyatt, and they both stare each other down before Wyatt nods. He looks at me and eventually smiles.

"Soon, Winter." Dabriel says before walking off. I watch until he leaves the restaurant.

"Sorry about Dabriel, he is, different and, well, not

usually this friendly. Honestly, I've never seen him come out with such terrible pickup lines before." Wyatt apologises.

"I thought he was nice," I say, not wanting to tell him that I actually thought he was hot as sin, wrapped up in a tight package. I wonder what colour his eyes are usually, I think he must have worn some cool contacts. I remember when Alex bought some pink, ones and she looked really creepy for a while. It kind of suits Dabriel.

"Nice is a word I'm sure Dabriel has never been called." Wyatt chuckles to himself, his dark eyes meeting mine.

"How did you meet him?" I ask, breaking the building tension between us.

"Our fathers all hated each other, when they were all alive at least. We all protested against them by being secret friends as kids. Atti was the first to come to us all, he found a way without anyone knowing, and then we all used to meet once a week. As we got older, they became like brothers to me. We all have our own family issues, and it was great way to escape," he says.

"Sounds like most kids, tell them not to do something, and they will go straight ahead and do it," I chuckle.

"I enjoyed tonight, spending time with you is relaxing," Wyatt tells me.

"Me too," I whisper with blushing cheeks, and he runs his fingers across my hand on the table. We leave not long after. On the way home, I look over at Wyatt. "Thank you for tonight, I had a really good time," I say, and I mean it. Being with Wyatt has become relaxing. Jaxson is so intense that I feel like I'm going to kill him half the time, whereas being with Wyatt is fun.

"How about next week, same time? I'm free Friday if you are, and I could invite Atti to meet you," he asks.

"I would like that. I like getting to know you and meeting your friends," I say gently, placing my hand on his arm.

Wyatt stops the car on the side of the road, ignoring my questioning gaze. I let him undo my seatbelt and pull me onto his lap.

"It's so hard to be around you all night, and not beg you for a kiss," he says before his hands cup my face, and his cold lips meet mine. My hands curl around his neck and into his hair, as he kisses his way down my jaw and to my neck. I lean my head back to give him more access, but he pulls away looking at me, his hands tightly holding my waist.

"You're beyond temptation, you know that?" he groans, kissing my forehead before lifting me and clipping me back in my seat.

"Am I?" I flirt a little, as I check him out with his messy hair from my hands. I like the relaxed look on him.

"If you keep looking at me like that, sweetheart, I will end up showing you in my car how much of temptation you are," he says as smirks at me.

Wyatt drops me off home with a sweet kiss, not letting the kiss go any further as I scowl at him.

"I don't want to rush this…us. There are things I haven't told you, and I need you to know before we become serious," he says rubbing my arms, as he pulls me into his chest for a hug. I wonder what he needs to tell me. I mean I have the feeling he is a good guy, well I hope he is. My thoughts go back to when we first met, how scary he was to me and how much I wanted to run. I can't understand what changed my mind other than he seems like a different person to who he was when we first met. He seems warmer.

"No rush," I whisper back confirming his thoughts. My

feelings rush to Jaxson and how different it feels to be held by him. Wyatt feels relaxed and safe in a way. Jaxson feels wild and untamed but safe in the same kind of way.

"Goodnight, Winter," he whispers as he kisses the top of my head. I walk into my apartment, locking the door behind me with a large grin on my face.

11

DABRIEL

The prophecy said she would be the one for me, but I didn't expect to like her the moment I met her. I had been warned about a human girl all my life, but my visions never warned me about how it would feel. I saw myself meeting her tonight, I saw how happy I was. For once in my life, I actually felt at peace when I walked into that restaurant, my powers weren't pressing me to heal everyone in the room, anything from a paper cut to cancer.

My mind and eyes couldn't look away from her. Winter has an aura like no other, like a glowing, blue beacon, and it's beautiful, much like her. Her dark-brown hair looks softer than fairy wings, and her body was made to make angels fall. I can't actually fall by mating with humans because that's just a human rumour. We angels are born either light or dark, two light angels can have a dark angel child, much like two dark angels can have a light child. We don't mix our races, yet somehow the Goddess always chooses who we belong too.

"We have a problem," I say to Wyatt, flying down next

to his car outside Winter's apartment. I flew behind them, watching as he kissed her. I can't say I'm not a little jealous, but I'm trying not to be.

"Yeah, what?" he asks as he watches my wings. Supernaturals are always fascinated with our wings. We hide them from humans most of the time, and I was a little surprised that Winter didn't see through my glamour tonight at the restaurant. Her powers are coming through, but I'm not sure what they are, what she is.

"Jax is protecting her. Our little wildfire is tangling with the wolves," I tell Wyatt who looks over at me in shock.

"How?" he asks finally.

"Jax didn't tell me. All I know is that he hasn't killed her, and they have swapped blood. He thinks of her as his pack. I didn't see it in a vision until after it happened or I would have stopped it," I tell Wyatt, who nods.

"We always knew she would find us all. I'm more surprised that Jax didn't try to kill her. I smelt a faint wolf on her, but I assumed she had a friend at school," Wyatt says, and I nod.

"My visions aren't clear about her. There is one, but I'm only getting a part and a bad feeling," I tell him.

"You need to work on that, brother," he smirks.

"I don't like it. I've never been stopped from seeing something important before. Winter's future is lost to me, all I see is death and love," I say tensely. My visions have never been something I've feared, but now they scare me.

"What can we do? We have to be here for her and lead her along her path," Wyatt tells me. Like I don't already know this.

"What is your father up to? My council has told me he has called us three times. Each time he wants us to stay out of something. I haven't seen any visions about him in a long time, enough time that I believe he is blocking me somehow," I tell Wyatt. A worried look clouds his face as he thinks. His father is pure evil; and anything he does, everyone needs to be aware of. He won't risk a war with the angels or witches. As far as I know, we are both still neutral, the witches are siding more and more with the wolves, and I bet Wyatt's dad knows this.

"How could he block you?" he asks me.

"No clue, man," I tell him, I don't know of any power that could block us. I look over at Winter's simple apartment. It's a grey building like many others in this town. It's nothing remarkable, and neither is our university, so why did Winter turn up here? I think someone must have known about her and sent her to the town with the most supernaturals. The only place she could have met all of us.

"I'm doing a protective ward on her building, Atti is going to come tonight and put another layer of protection on it," I tell Wyatt.

"Make sure the wolves can enter," he says while watching the apartment.

"Aren't you worried Jax will hurt her?" I ask. I'm half tempted to tell Wyatt, no. I don't want Jax near her when he is like this. The brother I grew up with, one of my best friends is lost because of his sister's death. A death I saw way too late.

"If he does, I will beat the shit out of him," Wyatt says bluntly. I have no doubt he would. Jax only hates me and Atti because we sided with Wyatt when he needed us. There was no right or wrong person, but Jax didn't see that. That wolf is as stubborn as the rest of us.

"So, would I. I'm more worried about her heart," I tell Wyatt.

"She will fall for me instead," he laughs, messing with his wavy, blond hair.

"I'll be around." I narrow my eyes at him, and he smirks at me.

"I'm sure you won't go far," he replies, a slight challenge in his gaze. There isn't the normal jealously you would expect to find when I think about sharing Winter. I know if I had to share her with anyone else, I would lose it. My best friends are different, I guess it helps that I've always known I would have to share her. Sharing mates is not unheard of with many of our kinds, with our races not bringing out an even number of females and males. The slight problem with us sharing is that it's never happened between separate races before. I know all our families would lose their shit over this, I have enough problems with my two younger brothers as it is. They highly dislike me and want the throne I will inherit from my council in a year. The problem is, I have to follow every one of the council's rules, or they will give my throne to one of my brothers. They dislike me as much as I dislike them; a bunch of very old angels who believe their word is law, and we shouldn't help others.

"I researched her family," he tells me, shaking me from my own issues. Winter is all that matters now.

"And?"

"One mother, no other family, but there isn't a birth certificate for Winter's birth. There's a fake one, but it was made when Winter was at least two years old. I want to meet her mother and ask some questions," he tells me. I have a big suspicion that Winter isn't human, maybe a half of something. Purely because I've never seen humans have such a strong aura. Or a blue one for that matter.

Vampires have a black aura, angels are yellow, witches are purple, and shifters are green. Humans are gold.

"Her father?" I ask.

"None around, her mother grew up in the small town

she lives in. She moved into her family home when her parents passed away. I saw that she went to university a few years before Winter was born but nothing else," he says.

"It's odd. I expected her parents to protect her from us, not send her straight to us," I tell him. I knew we would meet her eventually, but I expected her to have protective parents. I know she isn't all human because a seer told us that she would have strong parents. That was over a hundred years ago, way before any of us were born, so who knows? It could all be hearsay.

"Me, too. Something is going on, and I'm not sure what. From the pictures, I have of Winter's mother, they do look kind of alike, so I doubt she isn't really Winter's mother," Wyatt says.

"I'll look into it, I wish I knew a dark angel who didn't like their queen," I joke. Dark angels can see the past and have visions of it, unlike light angels who can only see the near future.

"I don't know any. I bet my father does, but I'm not telling him about Winter, he would expect me to turn her," Wyatt says.

"I'll ask Atti," I reply, with a slight grimace at his father being mentioned. The King of the vampires isn't a good man, and I want Winter as far away from him as possible.

"Got to go, I'm hungry," he grins at me.

"Later, Vampire." I laugh and walk towards Winter's home. I whisper the protection ward, linking it to my powers, it will hold until I die. I will feel everyone that enters her home with bad intentions, it's a power meant to protect our young, and our mates.

I watch from the shadows as Wyatt drives off before letting my bright-white wings out. I'm flying home when a vision hits me.

12

WINTER

"I can only say sorry in advance for Atti. The guy knows no boundaries and says whatever he thinks," Wyatt tells me, a small, affectionate smile on his face. We are driving towards our restaurant. Atti, which I've learnt is short for Atticus, is meeting us there.

"No problem, Alex can be the same, and she is my best friend," I tell him, and he laughs.

"She has nothing on Atti, trust me," he mutters.

"Alright, I will believe you," I say.

"When we were kids, about eight, Atti decided that he thought it was funny to hide my things in random places. I'm not a control freak, but I don't and didn't like things in my room being moved. Anyway, he started off with little things, books, clothes, and then moved onto bigger stuff. The worse one I can remember is when we were fourteen. I liked this girl and invited her back to my room. I was hoping to get my first kiss, it didn't work out like that," he grins at me.

"Atti had hidden my shaving cream bottle under my pillow on my bed, so when I sat on my bed and laid back, the can exploded all over my back and into my hair," he chuckles.

"I bet you weren't happy with him," I giggle.

"No, the prettiest girl in class told all her friends. Let just say I was uncool for a month or so. I never did get that kiss until I was fifteen. It helped that I had a massive growth spurt at fifteen."

He just chuckles at me for a reply. I laugh as I think whomever that girl was that got his first kiss, was lucky.

Wyatt is dressed like a supermodel tonight, making my mouth water every time I look at him. He has a white shirt and black blazer over black trousers. His hair is styled away from face, and his jaw is freshly shaven. It doesn't help that he smells amazing, too, so even when I'm not looking at him, I'm forced to remember how hot he is.

"Tell me a hobby of yours," I ask. He seems to think about it for a while before he answers.

"I play the piano, I enjoy making new music too," he tells me.

"I would love to hear you play sometime." I look over at him.

"One day. What about you?" he asks, directing the conversation away. A sad look passing on his face.

"I can sing, I don't like to, but I've been told I'm good at it," I say quietly.

"I could play, and you could sing for me," he smiles at me. The sadness slips from his face slowly. The drive ends too soon as we pull up at the restaurant. We walk straight in, with Wyatt's hand on my waist.

"Hello, Albert." I smile at the waiter. He smiles back, a true friendly smile.

"We will have our old table, is Atticus here yet?"

"No, he is not. This way." He nods to Wyatt, and we both follow him to our table. The restaurant is full again, mainly couples, but one table has a few children with them who are staring around the room.

Wyatt pulls my chair out for me, and we both sit. We both order our drinks while we wait for Atti.

A kiss is placed on my cheek as I feel a warm body lean over the back of my chair. I move my head, and I'm faced with the palest grey eyes I've ever seen. The very attractive man winks before moving back, and my eyes widen at how hot he is. This guy has blond hair, much like Wyatt's but darker, and it's long but tied up in a bob on top of his head. He has a big build, towering over me and the table. The guy must be six-foot-eight, with large, muscular arms that look like he works out all the time. The man is wearing a black t-shirt that says 'you know you want me' in fancy writing across his chest. He is wearing black jeans and has on glasses that make him look like a hot geek.

"This is Atti. Atti this is Winter Masters," Wyatt interrupts my staring at his friend, and I suddenly look away at Wyatt who is just grinning at Atti, both of them are looking like they are having some kind of silent conversation.

"Everything alright?" I ask after the silence becomes deafening, and they are still staring at each other. They don't look angry, in fact, Wyatt looks like he won some kind of bet.

"Sorry, pretty lady, I'm just surprised," Atti says.

"What about?" I ask him.

"Wyatt told me he had met a beautiful woman. He told me I had to meet her. He forgot to mention how sexy and completely, fucking stunning you are." He says as he waves a hand at me, and I'm sure I'm blushing five different shades of red.

"If I had told you that, you would have demanded to meet her sooner," Wyatt says with a small chuckle.

"Anyhow," I clear my throat, desperate to change the subject. "Tell me about yourself, Atti."

"Well, I make gaming software for a living. I have two cats, both of which are crazy. I'm single and like brown-haired girls, that like to wear purple dresses." He winks at me. Yes, I'm wearing a purple dress.

"What are your cats called?" I ask.

"One is called Mags because I found her in a box of magazines in a bin one day. She was only a few weeks old, and it was touch and go for a while. I kept the name Mags because she likes to sleep on them, even now that she's eight years old," He tells me.

"Aw, poor thing," I say, feeling terrible for the little kitten, and I try to ignore how much of a turn on it is for him to like to rescue animals.

"Tell her about Jewels." Wyatt laughs, and Atti narrows his eyes at him.

"Jewels is my other cat, only three, and I've had her a year. My friend runs a cattery, and Jewels had been returned five times. She was going to be put down, so I offered to give her a home. Little did I know that she got her name from her obsession with stealing people's jewellery and swallowing it. Sometimes she puts her findings in her bed but not often," he smirks.

"I can't imagine you have a lot of jewellery." I laugh imagining a cat wearing a shiny necklace.

"Oh, not mine, only all the neighbours for a ten-mile stretch, she has robbed at least once," he says with a slight blush on his golden cheeks.

"It's so fucking funny when he calls to say he has to go through her shit again," Wyatt chuckles as Atti punches him on the arm.

"At least she does it in only one place in the garden," Atti shivers, a grim look on his face as Wyatt and I laugh.

"Doesn't it ever get stuck?" I wonder.

"No, the vets think she is some kind of wonder. She is some kind of pain in the ass instead." He winks at me.

"Why don't you keep her in, a house cat?" I ask.

"She can open doors," he says dryly. A slight annoyance is clear on his face.

"Sounds like a smart kitty," I reply.

"They rule the house," he laughs.

We all order food while we chat, and Atti never takes his eyes off me, as I tell him about my childhood.

"What about you? Siblings?" I ask him.

"Nope, I am an only child like Wyatt. Dabriel's an unlucky fucker with two real half-brothers," he says.

"Are you all the same age?" I ask.

"Yes, we were all born on the same day. Strange, huh?" He says.

"Yes very, very strange," I mutter. I'm sure I've seen similar things happening into those magazines you can buy in nearly every shop.

"So, tell me, are you sleeping with anyone? I know dumbass over here hasn't got you into bed, but I'm curious." He points a thumb in Wyatt's direction.

"That's a rude question," I say. I'm not exactly annoyed by his question, but it doesn't mean I want to answer him.

"I'm a bad boy, what can I say? Do I get an answer?" he asks.

"You don't have to answer, Winter," Wyatt tells me and shoots daggers at Atti, who ignores him.

"No, I'm not," I say with my arms crossed.

"Do you want to be?" He winks, and Wyatt whacks him on the back of the head.

"Enough, I am sorry, sweetheart. I forgot to tell you that he can't be taken out in public." Wyatt says, shaking his head.

"You wanted that answer as much as me, I just have the balls to ask," Atti replies and calls the waiter over.

"We will have three chocolate puddings, I heard someone is a fan." Atti winks at me.

"Don't tell me, you've met Alex?" I say.

"Yep, I like her. Drake is a lucky guy," he tells me.

"He is," I comment back, a small smile on my face.

"Although, Wyatt told me the most about you, I have to ask, do you still own that kitten underwear?" Atti asks, and Wyatt tries to hold in a chuckle when I glare at him.

"No, I've out-grown them. Thankfully," I say to Atti.

"Oh, I don't know. You already know I like kitties." He grins as he rests his head on his hands on the table.

"I imagine you don't have any trouble finding another kitty to play with," I say, empathizing the word, and Atti throws his head back, laughing. Wyatt is laughing too as I grin.

"No, I don't, but I think Wyatt has found the best kitty yet. I'll let you know when I find out how sweet she really is," he says, and I shake my head as my cheeks go red. I don't have a comeback for that, and I have the feeling not a lot of people can spar words with Atti. Hell, the man looks like a giant, so I doubt a lot of people would beat him in a fight either. I'm trying to ignore the underlying attraction I'm feeling towards him, it feels wrong when I'm sort of dating Wyatt. Wyatt doesn't seem remotely concerned about me and Atti flirting, I want to ask him why. He seems like the jealous type, so this isn't making any sense.

"So, tell me about you?" he asks, leaning on his hands on the table.

"Not much to tell, I am studying to be a vet, and I live with Alex. I'm going back home soon for a couple of weeks at my mum's," I say smiling.

"No dad around?" Atti asks.

"Nope, but my mum is better than two parents put together," I tell him.

"My mum is the same, she never needed anyone," he chuckles.

"We have that in common," I laugh.

"Maybe I can get you to come to my house to see my cats?" he winks.

"No, Atti. I'm sure she doesn't want to meet your cats. I can tell you now that's not how you're getting her back to your place." Wyatt glares at him.

"Not yet," Atti smirks at Wyatt, who looks ready to start throwing things at him.

We chat for a while, Atti tells me what Wyatt was like as a child, and Wyatt tries not to inflict bodily harm on Atti, if looks are anything to go by.

Atti walks out with us, and I see a bright-yellow convertible parked next to us.

"I'm guessing that's yours?" I ask, laughing because it doesn't surprise me.

"Yep, you're more than welcome for a ride," he jokes. Just as we get to the cars, he leans close to my ear. "I didn't just mean a ride in my car," he whispers in a very seductive tone, a tone I'm sure has brought many women to their knees.

I cough when I get his meaning, and I'm sure I'm turning redder than is attractive.

"Don't I get a hug goodbye?" Atti asks as Wyatt unlocks his car. Wyatt gets in after opening my door and putting up a middle finger at Atti, who can't stop laughing.

"I'm sorry, I think I've put him in a bad mood for your drive home," Atti says as he moves closer.

"It's fine," I say trying not to look up into his eyes.

"So, about that hug goodbye? I'm a hugger, so I'm not leaving without one," he grins.

I move the last step closer and go to wrap my arms around him when he shocks me by picking me up around my waist. He pulls me to his chest, and I rest my head on his large shoulder as he cuddles me.

"You smell amazing," he mutters, and then he kisses my cheek. Unlike the first unexpected time, his lips stay longer. I feel the firmness of them, and his scent overwhelms me. He smells like flowers, extremely sweet, but it somehow doesn't take away from his manliness.

"I can't wait," he says before he pulls away, I look up at him in confusion as he puts me down, and he just grins.

"Wyatt look after our girl," Atti shouts, and I don't hear Wyatt's mumble as I get in his car.

"I swear that guy was made to piss me off. It's a shame I can't kill him," Wyatt mumbles as he drives, and I just laugh.

"He is different, but harmless. I think." I smile at Wyatt as he puts a hand on my knee.

"Atti isn't harmless, trust me. But, he wouldn't ever hurt you," he tells me. A look I don't understand is on his face.

Wyatt drives me home with another one of those teasing kisses by my door.

My dreams are filled with a cheeky face and floating flowers.

13

WINTER

"Can we try something new today?" I breathlessly ask Jaxson after he knocks me on my back again. I groan as I roll on my side and get up. The bastard is standing near me, with his arms crossed and an amused look on his smug face. I know he enjoys watching me suffer. It was also not funny when I got lost on my drive here, his directions do not make sense. I must have taken five wrong turns before I got here.

"Like what, lass?" he finally asks. I ignore him and walk over to the wall of weapons. There is every type you can think of hung on the wall and several that I have no idea what they do. The crossbow catches my eye, and I walk towards it without knowing why.

"Careful, why do you want to learn this?" Jaxson asks as I touch the wooden crossbow. It's silver in the middle with a wooden base and leather around the handle.

"I just do, can I have a try? If I'm terrible then I won't ask again, and I'll get you a bag of brownies from the café at uni," I say.

"How did you find out I like brownies?" he asks me.

"Freddy texts me now. It came up." I laugh when Jaxson frowns.

"I didn't know he had a phone," he replies, and I fail at holding in a louder giggle.

"So?" I ask as he pulls the crossbow off the wall and gets a bag of wooden arrows out of the closet.

"Come on," he answers me with a wave over his shoulder. I guess I should bribe him with brownies more often.

"Why don't we use those arrows?" I point to the small bag hanging on the wall by the crossbow.

"They are silver tipped, I don't want you shooting me with them," he answers, not looking back at me.

"Why silver?" I ask as I follow him out the training room. We walk around the training building, and at the back are five dummies with targets on their chests. We walk a good distance away before Jaxson answers me.

"Silver is poisonous to most of our kind, some of us are immune, like Freddy. But nearly every type of supernatural will die if you hit them in the heart with silver," he tells me.

"How did you find out Freddy is immune?" I ask. I don't think that Jaxson would have tested it on him.

"Let's just say that Freddy is a nosy child. I nearly lost it when he was five and came into the lounge holding two silver swords that he found. Both of his hands were cut, and he didn't get ill from it. Freddy kept those swords and practises every day with them, he is pretty good now," he tells me and hands me the crossbow.

I lift it up slowly because it's heavier than it looks, and Jaxson shows me how to hold it right. I try to ignore how good it feels when his large hands cover my hips and turn my body slightly to the side. I let Jaxson load an arrow as I watch how to do it and then get into position.

"Right, try to aim at the target, when you're ready, you fire the arrow like a gun," he tells me, showing me where to press the button. I breathe in Jaxson's wood scent to calm myself before he moves away. The first three times I shoot, I miss the target altogether, and I hear Jaxson's chuckle.

"No worries, lass, I still get my brownies for this wasted time," he says as I load another three arrows. I ignore him, or try to, as my anger builds. I close my eyes this time, just listening to the forest and then move my body. I don't know what happens, but I feel a peace fall over me as I fire the next shot. I fire all three before I realised I've done it, and Jaxson's deep voice snaps me out of my dream-like state.

"Winter, how the hell did you do that?" he asks, wonder filling his tone. I look back at him as he looks around the empty training yard. I blink in confusion when I see all my arrows have hit the target. Dead centre.

"I don't know," I mumble as I put the crossbow down.

"I think I do, hold on, I have another idea," Jaxson says and runs back around the training building. I pull my arrows out of the targets as I wait for him to come back. When he does, he has two small daggers in his hands.

"Come here, Winter," he tells me. I don't bother arguing with him and move to stand next to him, about a hundred yards away from the targets. I watch in fascination as Jaxson throws the daggers, and they hit the targets, a perfect hit in the middle as well.

"Do it slower," I tell him, understanding that he wants me to throw them like him. He nods and gets the daggers and repeats what he did. Slowing his arm movements down, so I can see how he throws them.

"Your turn." Jaxson hands me the daggers when he comes back.

"You're good at this," I comment as I take the daggers.

"I'm more than just good at many weapons, my sword is my most preferred choice of weapon," he tells me.

"Can I see your sword?" I ask him, trying to keep the dirty thoughts from that sentence.

"I would love to show you my sword anytime, it's in my bedroom," he winks at me

My jaw drops open at his flirting, and I stutter, "Err, I don't know."

"I'm messing with you, Winter, now throw them," he tells me, a smirk on his face at my red cheeks. I try to ignore him as I take his place and get ready to throw the daggers. I remember the calm I felt and again, I hit both the targets. Dead in the centre of them.

"I know what we are practising next time," Jaxson tells me as he fetches the daggers.

"How is it possible?" I ask him, and he looks away from me.

"Lessons are over. See you around." Jaxson walks off, and just before he steps out of sight he stops and turns, "Don't forget my brownies, lass." Then he walks away.

14

ATTICUS

"You have three months until the wedding, Atticus." My mother's voice rings across the throne room, seconds after I travel into the cold, empty room. A shimmer of air next to my leg, tells me that one of my familiars has followed me back. I look down at Mags' grey eyes and run a hand over her head.

"Excuse me? You're joking, right?" I ask her. Mags pushes against my side in comfort. I look down at Mags, currently in her true form. Mags looks kind of like a white tiger but with two large pronounced teeth that drop from her mouth and a tail full of spikes. I remember telling Winter about my two cats, they do look like big cats when they are wearing their glamors. All powerful witches have a familiar, I'm the first to have two. I didn't lie about how I found Mags, she really was dumped into a load of magazines as a new-born. Familiars are a type of sub-demon and come out of the underworld when they sense their owner needs them.

"I'm not marrying anyone, I found the girl. The girl from the–"

She cuts me off and shouts, "I don't believe that rubbish, where was the Goddess when all the new-born, royal males died in our arms until you? Where was the Goddess when the angels attacked us?"

"We have a truce with them now, and she cannot change everything," I mutter.

"A truce I made! Not her! Your Goddess didn't save your father's life when an angel took his head," she says, and I see the tears this time. With a sigh, I go over to her and pull her into a hug.

"I know you don't believe in her anymore, but I do, and marrying someone else won't give us a true future," I tell her as she sobs. My mother is a powerful woman who rules on her own. When my father died, they expected her to stand down and let one of my male, second cousins take the throne until I was of age. They have no royal blood, but they are married into our family, so they could have been accepted. My mother scoffed at the idea and held an arena fight. I was only one at the time, and she fought twenty heirs to keep the throne. No one challenged her again, and when she formed a truce with the angels, the witches respected her. My mother never remarried, despite our council trying to demand that she did, I know she doesn't because of her love for my father. They were the couple that stories are written about.

"It's just a marriage, the dark witch's Queen is young and very beautiful. You can still mate permanently with someone else," she says, offering a different deal.

"I don't want that, mother. I love you but don't make me choose," I tell her.

"I can delay the wedding, but I can't stop it. The witches want us to all work together. Having two different leaders isn't working anymore. We share this earth, we can't risk a war against our own kind," she tells me.

She pulls away from my hug and walks to one of the large windows, which overlook our secret city. My mother looks every bit the queen in her long, green dress and circular, black crown on her head of blonde hair. Surprisingly, the dark witches have a white crown that they made, as well as a fake queen to wear it. The crown my mother wears was rumoured to have been made for the witches by the Goddess. The vampires, angels, and wolves also have crowns that make the true owner stronger. I've only ever seen my mother's and the vampire King's crowns. They look similar, but ours has twirls that hold up the four black stones around the crown. The vampire King's is a dark red colour and has deep red stones instead. Their crown is made of thorns.

"I do everything I can to protect you, Atticus. I fear there is something far worse coming for our kind. We won't make it out of this new threat without being united. I won't lose you, my son" she says.

"Is it the vampire King?" I ask her, moving closer to her side.

"Yes, he has started something he can't stop. He is a foolish, evil man and he will regret his actions in the end," she whispers to the window.

"What has he done?" I demand.

"I cannot tell you," she tells me firmly and walks towards the doors that open for her without being touched.

"I have a wedding to postpone, I believe you have a mate to chase. If there is a Goddess around, we need her help for what will come. I don't wish you to be unhappy, son," she says, her words echoing around the throne room before she walks out. I stand next to the two gold thrones in the empty room for a long time. The wide windows don't feel as open as they did when I got here, in fact, I feel like someone is trying to suffocate me. I call my power and imagine Wyatt's living room, it takes a second for me to feel my body disappearing and reappearing in front of the fake fireplace.

"Oh god, Drake," I hear from behind me, and I turn to see Drake, thankfully fully clothed, feeding on Alex's neck on the sofa. Alex's eyes meet mine, and she screams.

"Shit I didn't mean to interrupt, I swear I'm not into watching people," I say and close my eyes.

"Get out," Drake says, and I open my eyes to see them both sitting up on the sofa. Alex is bright red, and I'm trying not to laugh.

"No can do. As much as Drake doesn't turn me on, I need to stay and see Wyatt," I say, and Alex chuckles into Drake's shoulder as she holds him back from trying to hit me.

"Wyatt is feeding in the kitchen," Drake growls, and I laugh. I walk out before he decides to actually hit me.

Wyatt's apartment is one of those new, shiny places that he is anal about keeping clean. I don't like things being messy, but every time I'm here I can't help myself from moving stuff around. I chuckle when I see his bedroom, and I slip inside.

I find his box of stupidly expensive watches that he loves, and I move them into his bathroom. I use my magic to hang each one on the curtain rail. After a chuckle, I leave to find Wyatt. The small things really piss him off, like the time that it took him a month to find his expensive wine collection. I moved them all into his garage, and he said they were all one of a kind. I left them inside his spare car, and I really didn't think it would take him so long to find them. It was a funny month of him trying to kill me.

Wyatt is drinking a bag of blood when I come in, his eyes doing that weird thing where they turn all silver.

"The silver is creepy, dude," I tell him as I open his

fridge, grabbing a bottle of orange juice out and drinking it. Most vampires' eyes are dark brown all the time and change to red when they feed. Wyatt is weird.

"Atti, what do I owe the pleasure?" he asks when he is finished and throws the empty bag in the bin. I ignore him to go through his cupboards until I find his Oreos.

"Don't be a prick, not those," Wyatt says behind me, and I watch in amusement as he knocks me out of the way and takes his Oreos back.

"You're holding them like they're your babies, you have a problem, Wyatt," I tell him.

"Whatever." He glares at me and punches me on the arm as he puts his Oreos back and stands in front of the cupboard.

"Mother is planning my wedding, she said she would postpone it, but I think we need to tell Winter everything. I need a mate to get out of this or at least take Winter to my city and–"

"I know, believe me, I get it. But, she isn't ready to hear everything yet," he interrupts.

"I can't marry a dark witch. I think it's stupid to keep her in the dark about us. About what she is," I tell him, trying to make him see.

"Soon, Atti, I will tell her soon about me and then sort everything else. I know she has been around wolves a lot recently. I want to see if she can change Jaxson's mind," Wyatt says.

"I think she already has. He hasn't hurt her," I tell him.

"Not yet," Wyatt replies gently.

"I heard from a little birdy that he is still planning his mating with that wolf," I tell Wyatt.

"It was one of your witches that said they should be together," he replies with a slightly distasteful look in my direction.

"It's a load of bull. That wolf's parents must have paid a pretty penny for them to say that. Mating with Jaxson would be most wolves' dream come true for their child," I tell him.

"Let's hope he realises what he is doing, sooner rather than later," he says.

"He will," I say.

15

WINTER

The next two weeks pass uneventfully, as I train with Jaxson three times a week, and I go on dates with Wyatt on the weekends. I've seen Atti twice, after the first time we met, once when he turned up at the café where I was having lunch. The other time was when he invited himself to dinner with me and Wyatt. Wyatt doesn't seem to mind his light personality and carefree attitude, even with the long hugs goodbye.

My classes are ending this week, and I'll finally get to go home. A whole two weeks of mum's cooking and relaxing, with no boys. No worrying about the fact I'm crushing on four guys. At least Atti and Dabriel aren't hanging out with me all the time. Wyatt's little kisses have become beyond frustrating, but I understand that he wants us to go slow.

My training with Jaxson has become so tense. I can hardly stand to go except for the fact that he believes he owes me and wants to train me. I remember last week, as he took off his shirt since it was wet with sweat, and I nearly drooled all over his rock-hard abs. He has that amazing v that goes down to a little patch of hair I saw....

I slam into a rock wall as I am walking out of class not looking where I'm going. I lift my gaze to see that I bumped into Harris, not an actual wall. Although, he felt like it.

"Whoa, look out," he laughs, holding my shoulders and pushing me away from his chest. I laugh, too.

"Sorry, I was thinking about going home next week," I say slightly lying, but Harris doesn't know that.

"Cool, but it's only Monday, you have a while yet. Oh, we have a sort of party this weekend. I don't know if you're going, but I could give you a ride." He stumbles a little and blushes.

"I will ask Jaxson if I can come, and if he says yes, then I will. I don't want to over stay my welcome with your pack," I whisper the end part as some people pass us.

"You saved one of our pups, you won't over stay your welcome anytime soon, Winter, and you are pack to us," he mutters to me with a look.

"Alright, but I'm still checking," I say with a smile at him, while he shakes his head with a bigger smile. I give Harris a small hug before saying goodbye and driving back to my apartment.

"Alex, can I come in?" I ask, knocking her door, she has been ill for a few days. She didn't come to class today, and I'm getting worried about her.

Drake opens the door with his usual cold, stone face, but he looks tired.

"She is feeling better, it's just a nasty bug," he tells me with a hand waving me into her room. She does look better, as she eats a sandwich, sitting in the middle of her bed. Alex's room is covered in everything purple you could think of, and she has always been like this. I smile as I sit on the purple bed sheets of her metal-framed bed. She looks like a purple princess, as she leans back on big, glittery, purple cushions. She is wrapped in a bright-purple dressing gown, and the hood is up.

"How are you feeling?" I ask as she smiles at me and takes the hood down. She does look better; honestly, she looks better than usual. Her red hair looks shinier, and her skin looks golden. I want to ask if she is wearing makeup because her eyelashes look longer, and her lips look like she has on a pale lipstick.

"Better, sorry if I worried you." She picks up my hand and gives it a squeeze. Her eyes flash black for a second before she looks at Drake at the door. When she looks back at me, they are their normal brown colour. I must be seeing things.

"No problem," I say hugging her slightly before letting her finish eating in peace.

Drake stands just at the door like he can't stand to leave her when I walk out.

"Thanks for looking after her," I say to him, trying to ignore the slightly distasteful look he gives me.

"I will always look after her, you need not worry, Winter," he says like he expects me to agree with him.

"You best do, or I will hunt your ass down." I point a finger at him as he smirks at me. A low chuckle fills his mouth before he holds it in.

"I have no doubt," the bastard says while he is trying not to laugh.

My phone rings as Drake walks into Alex's bedroom, and I go to my own to answer it.

"Hey," I answer, I really should start looking at who it is ringing me before I just swipe it open.

"It's me, training in about an hour? I have to do something tomorrow. So, I can't do our usual day," Jaxson's gruff voice says down the phone.

"That's fine, I was only finishing some grade work that I can do tomorrow instead," I tell him. "Why don't you just text?" I ask.

"I don't like using phones at all. I don't text," he says seriously, and I try not to giggle, but I'm sure he heard me.

"Can you drive out here? My truck is playing up, I can borrow someone else's if you want," he says in a clipped tone. I must have pissed him off; the thought only makes me want to laugh a little more.

"No, I will drive, it's cool," I say.

"See you, Winter," he says in a more annoyed tone before putting the phone down. I chuckle thinking I've at least improved in his mind from just putting the phone down, I now get a 'see you'.

I put on my black yoga pants and just a sports bra today because it's boiling outside. The weather forecast, a heat wave, in England is rare but welcome. It's a shame I can't just sunbathe all day.

I decide to pull into a local bakery on the way, and I walk in to look at the selection. I choose some brownies and blueberry muffins. I get a few of each so I can give everyone some when I give Jaxson his brownies. Hopefully, chocolate will make him forgive me for laughing. I know I would accept chocolate as a sorry. Hell, Jaxson would probably like chocolate-covered daggers, but I don't think I can find them in a few minutes. A warm hand on my back stops my inner rambling, and I turn around in the queue. Dabriel is standing behind me, looking like a normal college kid. His lovely hair is covered up with a cap he has on backwards, and he is wearing a normal top and jeans. I can't believe how much hotter he looks like this; my eyes literally can't stop looking over his body. His arms are out and there are weird white symbols tattooed like bracelets around his wrists. I swear that they are glowing white for a second, but a quick shake of my head, and they disappear altogether. I really think I need some more sleep today.

"Winter, you are looking as stunning as ever," he tells me.

"Dab," I smile at him, and he pulls me into a hug, as he whispers in my ear.

"I'm not allowed to be here, to warn you, but you need to trust me. You cannot go to the party. I don't know which party, but death is chasing you. Be safe for me, Winter," he says and lets go. I watch in confusion as he walks away.

"Dab, what are you talking about?" I shout. He doesn't look back as he walks out. A few people stare at me, but it's like they didn't notice Dab was here. You couldn't miss a guy like that. My palms sweat as I wonder what he was talking about. The only party I can think of is the wolf one, and I don't think I'm invited anyway. What the hell was he talking about, death is chasing me?

I'm half-tempted to call Wyatt and ask if Dabriel is crazy, but it's my turn to get my cakes, and I decide to leave it.

Dead on an hour later, I pull up at the main house. A few young boys with their mother walk past my car, looking in interest before their mother shouts at them, "We don't stare at human girls, let's go."

"Why not?" the first boy asks. All the times I've been here, I haven't seen any girl children running around. A lot of boys like these ones but not girls. It's really strange to see.

"It's not allowed, she shouldn't be here," the mother says, looking directly at me now. It's clear she knows my windows are down, and I can hear every word she says.

The boys look down and follow their mum, walking away into the woods.

I lock my car before walking up to the two 'guard' wolves at the front door. I'm just about to knock, when the door is opened for me by Freddy, who pulls me into a strong hug.

"Hey, little wolf," I say.

"Hey, I'm not little, I missed seeing you around the pack, Winter. Uncle J wouldn't let me come to see you after the meal. He made Anna watch me when you were here, so I wouldn't be able to sneak in," he says with a little blush, and I mess up his hair as I speak.

"That sucks, but I'm okay, I promise," I tell him.

"Good. I don't want you to leave us," he says, his eyes filled with emotions, and I just want to hug him and say I'm never leaving.

"That's enough, Freddy," Fergus says sternly, coming to join us on the porch which now feels very small.

"Jaxson is waiting for you in the training cabin," Fergus tells me as he lays a hand on Freddy's shoulder, a kind smile on his face as he looks at Freddy.

"Right, well I'll see you around, Freddy," I mutter to him and gently hug him under the watchful stare of Fergus before walking away. I forgot the cakes, so I quickly get them out of the car before walking to the training cabin.

I find Jaxson hitting the shit out of a punching bag as I walk in. His back goes stiff as he notices me in the room, even if I didn't make any sound.

"Winter," he says as a welcome as he wipes the sweat off his head and stares at me. His gaze dips down my body as his eyes darken.

"I brought you a sorry gift, well, one. The rest are for your family," I say holding up the bag. Jaxson takes the bag, and he chuckles as he sees the food. He eats two of the brownies, while I put my phone on the side and tie my hair up in a ponytail. I watch as he puts the bag of food on a bench and walks back to me. *I suppose I'm not getting a thank you for those.*

"So, what have you got planned today, Wolfman?" I joke using the nickname he hates, as I try to ignore the building tension in the room between us.

"Hand-to-hand combat only today, after you warm up," he says, looking away from me, as I start stretching.

"Come on then, Teach." I taunt him, as I step onto the mats he has laid out for us.

"Sure." He growls, running at me, and I feint left before sharply turning right to avoid him hitting me. Not that he ever has, he always stops seconds away from me, like he couldn't hurt me.

"Good, but faster," he says as he catches me around the waist, and I slip under his arm, and out of his reach. We avoid each other a few more times before I see him move more to my right. I go to hit his midsection, but I miss, and he flips me effortlessly onto my back. I swing my legs out as he grins, and he lands with a bang on the mat next to me.

Jaxson rolls on top of me, holding my hands above my head as he smiles.

"That was good." He breathes heavily, and a wave of arousal hits me as I feel all of him pressed tightly against me.

Jaxson growls before he kisses me, a kiss I wasn't expecting, and I don't have the power to stop. The man kisses me like a man possessed, and I can do nothing but accept him. My mind goes hazy, as he tastes amazing and his kisses are perfection. A few seconds or, hell, years later, I don't know, Jaxson jumps off me and walks away swearing under his breath.

"Shit, I'm sorry I shouldn't have done that." He slams a

hand into the wall. The wooden cabin shakes, and the floor starts lightly shaking. I catch a glimpse of his glowing, green eyes, and I know he is close to losing it. I don't think as I reply to him.

"You're sorry? You going to tell me I'm a mistake next?" I ask tensely.

"You should be sorry, fuck I don't want this. This stupid, fucking prophecy, I…," he frowns, running his hand through his hair as he stops talking, and the ground stops shaking. The door to the training room slams open, and Fergus comes in with a frown on his face as he looks at us both. I'm sure with my swollen lips and Jaxson's angry face, he can tell what has happened. I don't forget the extra sense of smell wolves have, either.

"I need a word, now, Jax." He walks out.

"Come on, you can wait in the house while we chat," Jaxson says, walking away from me, as my hand finds its way to my lips. I shake away the ground-breaking kiss and follow a very tense-looking Jax into the house. He leaves me in the massive living room as he goes into another room in the hallway. After a minute, I know I need to use the bathroom, so I go to the door I saw Jax go into and lift my hand to knock, but then I hear them.

"You could smell the arousal from both of you a mile away, Jax. Have you forgotten you're soon to be mated?" Fergus shouts, and Jax doesn't say anything as Fergus continues, "She is human! The prophecy makes it damn clear what will happen, and it could be her, and for what? A good fuck?"

"Don't speak about her like that, brother. She doesn't have anything to do with the prophecy," Jax shouts causing me to flinch. A loud growl fills the house.

"She could destroy us all!" Fergus bellows in a loud growl. "Do I have to remind you who your mother was?

No one but me knows, and, you of all people, shouldn't be around a human. You need to kill her. I'm certain it's her, and the others will find her. If they haven't already," Fergus says, muttering the end part. I hear the growling getting louder.

"No one will harm her!" Jaxson shouts, and I hear a large something or someone slam into the wall by the door, making me jump back.

"Put me down, it's too late. You're already protecting her, and you know it's her, don't you? I can kill her for you. It needs to be done before it's too late," Fergus' weak voice says like someone is cutting off his oxygen supply. I have a good idea who is.

I back away not wanting to hear anymore and run to the training room to get my bag. What the hell do they think I am? What is the prophecy about, that makes them want to kill me? I wouldn't harm anyone, let alone destroy them.

I grab my bag and turn to see Esta, shutting the training room door behind her.

"I'm leaving, I can't deal with you right now," I say to her and go to walk past her when she shocks me by pushing me hard. I fly across the room, hitting my side on the floor. Fuck that hurt. My head bangs off the floor, and the room spins as I hear her boots clicking on the floor as Esta walks over to me.

"You think you can have my mate?" she screeches, as she paces in front of me. I lean up on an elbow feeling pain radiate through my side. *That is going to bruise*, I think or maybe it's a broken rib or two. She rants on before I start listening to what she is saying.

"If I kill you, I can say you attacked me. They would believe me." She says to herself, as she pulls off her coat.

"I'm leaving, and you won't kill me because you don't

even believe your own words. You know they won't believe you, they will know you acted in jealously. Is Jaxson even worth this, killing me? Risking your own life?" I ask, getting to my feet and walking around her as fast as I can.

"Wait," she says too sweetly, and I turn in time to see her body convulse before turning into a grey wolf, as pieces of her clothing go flying in every direction. The wolf growls loudly at me as it lowers its head and stretches its paws out, looking ready to jump on me. If she wasn't trying to kill me, and I wasn't shaking so hard, I would say her grey wolf is really a beautiful sight.

By the time I realise I'm being stupid by just standing here, I scream out for Jaxson and run to the door. I see Esta jump, and I fall to the left as she slams into the wall by the door, knocking her head. I run the final few steps and pull the door open. I run fast as I can outside. I realise straight away how stupid it was to leave the room full of weapons for an open field.

"Jaxson!" I scream again, as I run toward the main house. The loud growl behind me is all the warning I get before something strong knocks me to the ground. I roll over after I fall, to see a jaw full of large teeth growling at me. I hear noises around me, but everything goes blank as she leans back to bite my neck and finish my life. Then the ground starts shaking underneath me, and Esta stops for a second, her eyes meeting mine, and the fear is clear throughout them. I close my eyes when I see her mind is made up.

A whoosh of air hits my face, as I open my eyes and look over to see Esta over by the tree on my left. I watch as she shifts back, and I turn my gaze to the massive, black wolf standing in front of me. The wolf is huge, maybe four times as big as me, and his massive face turns to me. I shake as he comes over and nudges me gently with his mouth full of sharp-looking teeth. I look up into his eyes recognising Jaxson, and I sigh. Just being near him is relaxing me. The ground stops shaking, and Jaxson licks my neck, I can't help the little chuckle that comes out of me as I stroke his face. Despite being terrified, being around Jaxson is like a false sense of safety. I should be scared of him after what I heard, but I'm not. I know he would defend me, but I'm not sure if I want him to. What if he gets hurt trying?

"Jaxson, she is dangerous. Let me kill her!" Esta screams as I tense up. Jaxson's wolf shimmers slightly before a very naked Jaxson is sitting in front of me, with a worried face. My face turns red as I try not to look down at him, as he turns to face Esta, who is annoyingly perfect in her naked, human form. I do sneak a look at Jaxson's perfect ass before looking away.

"She is my pack. I protect her, and you won't hurt her, Esta," he warns, a low growl coming out of his mouth.

"She isn't yours. I'm to be your mate, not some human!" she shouts, her words causing a pain in my heart like no other.

"I don't have to explain myself to you. Don't cross me again, Esta, you won't like it," he replies, not denying that he is still going to mate with her. Her eyes meet mine across the grass. Sorrow and pain are written in her eyes, as well as a lot of heartbreak. It's never really crossed my mind that Esta really might love Jaxson. The thought doesn't sit well with me. I never wanted to hurt anyone by falling for Jaxson, but it looks like I have.

Esta shifts fluidly into her wolf, she whines at us once before running through the woods, away from us. Jaxson thanks Anna, who comes running over with some jeans and a top for Jaxson. As he changes, she rushes to me, helping me up.

"Are you alright? Do you need a hospital?" she asks quickly while checking me over for injuries.

"No, I'm just going home," I say, looking away from them both, as I remember Jaxson and his brother talking. I should stay away, no matter what I feel for Jaxson. I can't be around him knowing that they think I'm someone I'm not. Jaxson stares at me and I at him. We don't talk as he opens his mouth a few times to speak, but no one voices any words. I turn and leave, my heart breaking as I know I have to leave him. He won't be happy with me around, and he can't be with me. I don't want to hurt Esta. It's different for her, and at the end of the day, I'm just a human.

"Wait, Winter," Jaxson shouts as I get into my car. Not wanting to talk, I lift my eyes to see his as he runs over to me. I start my car and drive off. The tears fall, as my heart breaks, the thought that one kiss will never be enough runs through my mind. I try to stop it, I have to remember that he isn't mine. Jaxson never will be.

16

WINTER

"Where is she?" a man cries, making me flinch. I open my eyes to the chaos before me. Elissa is in the tight grip of a brown-haired man, he is tall and built like a guy that loves the gym. They are both wearing the strange clothing from before, but he has a crown on his head. The crown is the matching one to the one Elissa wears, but it's a dark-blue colour. I can't see his face from where I am, but it's clear he is older than me. It's the same bedroom as before but everything is ruined, smoke fills the room from the empty archways. The sounds of screams fill the air as I glance back at the large man. He is covered in blood and shaking Elissa, who looks defeated but not scared.

"You'll never find her, she is safe from you. The prophecy will come true because of you." She smiles gently at him.

Prophecy. It can't be the same one Jaxson was talking about, right? These can't be real. Can they?

The man growls loudly, the sound filling the room, joining the smoke from the archways. I spot a wolf running past in the corridor, covered in blood.

"She is my child, mine! You are my queen and my mate, but I will kill you if you don't give her back to me," he shouts into her

face. Elissa is far braver than I ever thought, as she doesn't back down, in fact, his words make her face harden.

"I have seen it all, you would kill her and me, regardless. I will save my child," she whispers as the man lifts the large sword at his side.

"Then rot in death, Goddess, and know that I'm the last God on this earth. She will be mine, and we will rule," he says before pushing the sword through her stomach. I watch in horror as he slowly pulls the sword out, holding it high at his side as her blood drips onto the floor from his hand. The man lets her drop to the floor, before walking out, not looking back once at the beautiful woman he just killed.

I never get to see his face.

I try to push against the hold on me, I have to get to her, for some reason I'm desperate to not let this stranger die alone. It doesn't work. I watch the blood pour out of the woman onto the cold, white flooring.

Her eyes meet mine as we stare at each over the room, and her voice fills my head.

"She is safe," her voice fills with happiness as she stares at me before her eyes empty, I feel her soul leave the room.

Then I start to scream.

I wake up, screaming and battling my quilt off me. My door slams open, and, to my surprise, Wyatt runs in with Alex at his heels.

"Are you okay?" he asks, looking around my room for danger.

"Sorry, yeah. Just, a bad dream," I say trying to calm myself down. He comes over and gives me a look then kisses my forehead.

"Oh, honey, they have never been this bad before," Alex says, coming over to give me a little hug.

"I know, but I'm really okay," I whisper to her, and she gives me a nod.

A ringing noise beeps in the background, sounding

worrying like the fire alarm, as Alex runs out the room shouting, "Shoot, I forgot the pancakes!"

I shake my head at the thought of my best friend attempting to cook anything edible. She and I are the reason takeaways make so much money. I suddenly remember Wyatt is here in my apartment, and I smile at him.

"So, what are you doing here? I have class in," I check my clock on the wall. "Two hours," I cringe at the fact I'm wearing an old, tatty shirt that is stuck to me with sweat. I pull my covers closer around me, and Wyatt just smirks like he can read my mind. Wyatt looks good today in black shorts and a black shirt, his sunglasses slipped in the top.

"I was invited to breakfast, but I think I might pass now." He laughs and I enjoy the sound. I get out of my bed and flinch at the pain of my ribs, from where I was thrown yesterday. Wyatt, never missing anything about me, strides over with a worried face.

"Lift your top," he demands. I raise an eyebrow at his demand, not sure how to take this serious Wyatt. I am way too aware I don't have any bottoms on, and if I did what he asked, I would be showing him my terrible, yellow knickers.

"Just so I can see where you're in pain," he chuckles.

"I fell in self-defence class last night, it's nothing," I mutter.

"I'm not leaving until I see how bad it is." Wyatt crosses his arms.

"I'm not showing you my knickers." I glare at him. I suppose I could just put some trousers on, but I really don't want to be moving right now.

"I won't look at those until you invite me to take them off, trust me." He says, moving closer and gently running a hand down my arm. The thought of him taking my knickers off has me blushing redder than a tomato.

I sigh watching his stubborn face before pulling my shirt up, and he takes a long intake of breath.

"Winter, fuck, you look like you've broken a rib," he says. I don't look up at him as I pull my top down.

"I'm fine." I wave him off, as he looks at me with a slightly angry expression.

"You're not, I have some cream that works wonders on bruises. I'll bring you some from home," he tells me, and I nod.

"Your phone has been ringing like mad, some people called Jackass and Harris. I picked it up to bring it to you before you screamed." He offers me the phone. I don't answer his unsaid question about the 'Jackass' number. I can't tell him I put that in there for Jaxson, before I got to know him. I should really change it back before he sees it. I'll end up having to buy him more than a couple of brownies for forgiveness. My heart contracts as I remember that I can't see him anymore. I honestly forgot about everything that happened. These dreams are doing a number on me. And, intensely hot guys coming into my room first thing in the morning. That doesn't help.

"Thanks, Wyatt," I say.

I accept my phone from him to see there are a ton of missed calls and voice messages from both Harris and Jaxson. I don't want to listen to them because I can't hear his voice, no matter what he has to say.

"They are some guys from my class, it's likely they haven't done the paper due tomorrow," I say, trying to keep my eyes on the floor. When I look up, Wyatt's eyes narrow at my lie, but he just groans shaking his head.

"I'm going to help your friend." He walks away looking dejected.

"Are you okay?" I ask reaching out to stop him leaving.

"I don't do relationships, but I'm incredibly jealous at the moment. I've only felt this way once, and I don't know how to be around you, Winter." He pulls me gently into his arms and places a kiss on my head.

"Who was the other person?" I ask being nosy, but at the same time, I don't know what to say to him about feeling jealous. We aren't in a relationship, and he hasn't asked me for anything other than a few kisses yet. It was he that suggested we take things slow.

"My childhood friend turned girlfriend for a short while. She passed away a while ago." He says, looking so sad that I go to him. I wrap my arms around his waist and rest my head on his chest. His arms tighten around me.

"I'm sorry," I say, squeezing him tightly.

"I put her in danger. Hell, being near me is dangerous for you, but I don't know how to push you away," he says with a frown.

"What do you mean?" I ask looking up at him in confusion.

"Hey guys, we are going to the café in town for breakfast. I'm not trying to cook again." Alex shouts down the hallway before she gets to my door. She smiles fondly at me from the doorway. I try not to chuckle at the black ash on her cheek. Her hair is all over the place, and she looks flustered.

"Babe, you could have let me help," Drake says coming behind her and wrapping her in his arms. She melts against him, reminding me how I'm in Wyatt's arms, and I somehow forgot because it feels right.

"Shush, you," she mutters to him. I watch as he wipes her cheek clean, and she looks up at him in adoration. They both seem to have forgotten we are here. I read about this kind of love, a love that makes you forget anything else in the world. A love that can stop time for you and them. I feel lucky just to be able to see it.

"Sounds good, we can meet you there. I'm sure Winter needs to get ready," Wyatt says, his warm breath moving my hair. I look up at Wyatt as he talks, everything about him draws me in. I know I'm falling for him, even if I don't want to, I don't want to be vulnerable. I finally pull my gaze from Wyatt to Alex and Drake.

"I won't be long," I say, narrowing my eyes at her wagging eyebrows. I know she loves finding me hugging Wyatt, it's like her grand scheming has finally panned out.

I quickly shower before drying my hair and dressing in three-quarter length jeans, and a Batman top. I am a huge fan of the muscular, deep-speaking man; I don't care who judges me for it. I find Wyatt sitting on my sofa, typing on his phone, looking like a hot model in a photo shoot. His blond hair is a little longer than when we first met and falls down his forehead. Wyatt looks up, reminding me so much of how my feelings for him are as strong as they are for Jaxson. Should I tell Wyatt I let someone else kiss me?

His dark eyes lift taking me in, a slight lift of his lips at the Batman symbol.

"Beautiful as always Winter. I believe I've seen Atti in a terrible shirt like yours," he says looking away from me as a shimmer of pain hits his handsome face.

"What was she like?" I ask, calmly going to sit next to him. I can't explain it, but I feel like he needs to talk to me about her. To be honest, I feel like he is hiding so much of himself from me. I want him to let me in, I need him too.

"She was a wild cat. I can't explain her, no one could really but she didn't deserve her ending, and I would do anything to change it." He drops his head as he speaks.

"It's not your fault." I remind him, I take his hand wanting to comfort him.

"Let's go." Wyatt stands, his whole body tenses. He pushes my hand away.

"Sorry, I didn't mean to–"

He cuts me off, "You don't know a thing, Winter." He walks out, expecting me to follow. I take my time getting my stuff and locking the door, so he has time to calm down. How did she die, and what was her name?

Why do I have a bad feeling that Wyatt feels responsible for her death?

Wyatt is sitting inside his car when I come out, and I go to the passenger side to open the door.

Sliding into the seat, I do up my seatbelt up as he drives, his hands grip the steering wheel so hard I'm worried he will break it. The tension is strong as he drives us to the cafe.

I go to get out of the car and Wyatt finally says, "I'm sorry, I just feel guilty for the way I'm looking at you; the way I looked at Demi," he speaks her name softly. A brief glimmer of jealously ripples through me before I realise I'm getting jealous of a dead woman.

"She wouldn't want that if she loved you," I say. I let myself out of the car not waiting for him. Honestly, I'm not sure what I'm doing. There are too many secrets between us, and I can't be like the girl he is clearly remembering.

"Winter, please wait," Wyatt shouts behind me, and I jump when he is suddenly in front of me. A brief whoosh of wind is the only sound that I heard in my ears.

"How did you?" I ask, backing away from him, a little worried now. I know Harris told me about other supernaturals, but could I have been dating one the entire time? Is that why I feel like he is different. I look at Wyatt, seeing him with new eyes as everything comes together. I'm so stupid, of course, he is a supernatural, and I know which one. It's clear he's a vampire. The coldness of him, the fast speed, and how he seems to struggle to be close to me, I imagine it's hard to date your food source. Although, I could imagine dating chocolate, yep that sounds good.

"Shit, sorry I didn't mean to–" he stops talking suddenly, and grabs my arm, pushing me behind him.

"Your father wants to see you," a gravelly dark voice says behind me. Wyatt tenses as he looks over my shoulder. He moves around me, a quiet warning in his eyes as he looks at me once.

"Fine, let me take–" Wyatt starts talking, but the gravely speaking man speaks again.

"Let's see the pretty food you have there," the man interrupts Wyatt.

"You will forget that you've ever seen her," Wyatt says, his voice dripping with power. The force of his words blasts against my mind, making me want to do what he says. I let out a strangled gasp as I push him out of my head. Wyatt turns to look at me, fear ripping through his expression before I shake my head, and he looks away.

"The King has sent me for her, and we have your blood in us. Don't bother with your tricks, little Prince," the man says. I move slightly around Wyatt to have a look at the man. The man is very tanned and huge, with a bald head that has a red crown tattooed on the side. He is wearing an all-black outfit that has a circle in red on the shirt pocket. I'm too far away to see what it is but it looks like a red crown, like his tattoo. His look is pure evil as he sneers at me and licks his lips.

"She isn't going anywhere," Wyatt says, his words dripping with a silent warning and crippling power.

The man laughs at Wyatt's dark words, and before I know what's happening Wyatt has left me to punch the massive guy in the head. The force makes him slam back into a nearby car, sounding the alarm. The other man, who I now can see, is a smaller white guy with greasy, black hair. His beady eyes lock onto me and with a speed, I've not seen before, rushes at me. I hold in a very girly squeal as just before he grabs me, he is pulled from behind and thrown in the same direction as the other guy by Wyatt.

"Winter trust me, alright?" Wyatt says, as he throws me over his shoulder and everything goes blurry. I must have blacked out because the next thing I'm aware of is a soft hand stroking my hair and loud voices.

"How on earth are we going to explain all of this to her? She will think we are all crazy," Alex says as I become aware it's she is stroking my hair.

"I can't stay away from her, I want to, but I can't now. He will send someone else, and I will have to take her to him. He must think I've found my mate or I'm going to turn her," Wyatt says from not far away.

"Great," Alex says in a tense voice.

"Who will?" I ask, opening my eyes and sitting up on my bed. Alex is sitting next to me, and Wyatt is standing by the door.

My eyes lock with his as he says, "My father, he will know you mean something to me now, and he will want to know about you."

"Why would he hurt me?" I ask pulling my arm away from Alex, when she tries to hold me back from getting off the bed.

"Because you're human, and humans are literal chew toys for him, sweetheart," he says with a cold gaze. I feel like I'm under some kind of test as he watches me.

"And, what are you?" I ask, wanting him to tell me. I know the answer, and I'm sure he knows I do.

"A vampire," he answers bluntly and crosses his arms.

He has a look like he expects me to start screaming, and I raise my eyebrows at him.

"Hell, you don't even sparkle," I mutter, and Alex snorts in laughter behind me. I even see a small smile on Wyatt's face.

"No, I don't," he says with a slightly confused look at me.

"Can you keep me safe?" I ask him. We watch each other for a while before he answers. I repeat all the warnings Harris gave me about vampires being dangerous in my head, but I know Wyatt. I know he is dangerous, only a fool wouldn't pick up on that but not to me. I don't think he is evil, and that's all that matters. I might have to avoid the family dinners, though.

"You should be asking if you're safe from me," he finally replies with a small smile on his lips.

"I know I am," I say firmly. I trust him even if that makes me a fool.

Wyatt tilts his head to the side before nodding at me. I stay still as he moves closer, his cold hand winding into my hair, and he pulls us together until our lips meet. We both sigh at the close contact before he moves away, stopping the kiss.

"You are," he whispers. The words go through me, with the promise his voice holds.

"It makes a lot of sense," I laugh to myself.

"Sorry, why aren't you freaking out? I freaked out when Drake told me. You just believe him?" Alex questions me, standing off the bed to face me.

"He's not the first supernatural I've met." I wink at her, and she frowns.

"Who?" she asks, but I think she's lying. I don't know how I know that, but it's a sister thing. I know Alex better than I know myself.

"Yes, Winter, who? Or what?" Wyatt asks, a protective quality to his tone.

"Would they be safe from you, if I told you?" I ask him.

"I can't promise you that," he replies, a grim look on his face as he realises I won't tell him.

"Then I'm not saying a word. Why was I passed out by the way?" I quickly change the subject as his eyes darken.

"Who, Winter?" he asks again, ignoring my question.

"No," I say holding my chin up high as his eyes start glowing in a similar way that Jaxson's does, but they're so dark instead, almost black like the night. Jaxson's glow like the earth, so bright that you wish you could walk into them. Wyatt's are dark and almost like you could lose yourself in them if you attempted to get close.

Wyatt moves so quickly, like a bullet, until he is standing right in front of me again. I take a deep breath to calm myself as his smell surrounds me. I get angry that he is pushing this out of me as his stubborn gaze meets mine.

"I can't make you tell me, but I wish you would trust me. I need you to trust me because you're mine." He strokes the side of my cheek.

"I'm not yours, Wyatt," I whisper.

"Not yet, but you won't just belong to me, will you sweetheart?" he whispers back. I have no idea what he is talking about, but he just smiles down at me.

"They are gone, they will be back. I don't think they got Winter's scent. If they did, we would know. If your dad wants to meet her, you can't fight him on this alone," Drake says as he comes in the room, stopping close to Alex but speaking to directly to Wyatt.

"Thanks, Drake," Wyatt says, finally looking away. I move back next to Alex, who is looking at me with wide eyes.

"So, your boyfriend is a vampire," I try to joke and she

laughs.

"Actually, her mate is." Drake corrects, coming over to kiss her forehead.

"You're mated? Like married?" I ask, a little shocked.

"Yes, I wanted to tell you, but how could I explain it?" she says, looking guilty.

"I understand." I grab her hand, holding it tight. I do understand there would have been no way to explain this all to me unless I had seen it. I'm sad that I didn't get to celebrate with her, but I can't change the past.

"How does that work? I mean you're not a vampire, are you?" I ask Alex. I mean I would have to be a fool not to notice some of her changes. She has always been beautiful, but now Alex looks unreal. Everything about her looks shinier, and her eyes are brighter. All the supernaturals I've met look different; better looking than normal humans. Even the two guys that just tried to attack me still had those unique qualities. I end up thinking about Dab and Atti. They never looked human, but I ignored it, they must be vampires too. It makes sense if they are friends of Wyatt.

"Alex shares my abilities and lifespan, but is still human in some ways. She has to drink blood from me to survive, but only needs a little," Drake tells me as Alex leans onto his side.

“But you all eat human food. I've seen you eat normal food,” I inquire to Wyatt, who smiles.

“We can eat both, but we would die without a few bags of blood a week,” he tells me.

"So, you'll live a long time," I say, looking back at Alex, feeling a little sad that she will outlive me.

"You might, too," she whispers to me as she pulls me into a tight hug. I shake my head next to hers.

"Too tight." I choke out as she squeezes me.

“That’s what she said,” Wyatt says. I’m so shocked at his joke that I can’t laugh, but everyone else does.

"Shoot, sorry." Alex lets go, blushing slightly.

“You’ve been spending way too much time with Atti, if you’re coming out with that kind of joke,” Drake says, I can hear the smile in his voice.

"So, do you drink blood from people?" I ask. I remember Harris saying something about a war, and if they are against each other then what am I doing in the middle? The big fact is, that they are all fighting, and I am human. Shit, this isn't good, I should really stay away from Jaxson. If I just tell him I can't be around him, hopefully then he will leave me alone, and no one has to get hurt. Except me. When I think of not seeing Jaxson again, I feel like being sick.

"Yes," Wyatt answers staring at me while trying to pick my thoughts apart.

"Do you kill people?" I ask and Wyatt goes tense.

"Not to feed, there are blood banks these days, but all of my kind don’t have the same morals,” he tells me. A shiver flutters through me as I remember the guy that attacked me, I remember him calling me food.

"Do you kill shifters?" I ask, and Wyatt moves into my face again.

“I'm not a good person, Winter, not since Demi. But I’m not a monster. I don’t kill unless I have to, and the shifter war isn’t my war, it’s my father’s," He tells me. I wrap my arms around his waist and press my head into his chest.

"There's a war, I get it. Please don't kill anyone else that doesn’t deserve it. That is the only thing I can’t forgive you for," I tell him. I can’t blame him for his past, but I would blame him for anything else that happens now.

"I won’t unless I have to, Winter,” he tells me. His lips

brush against mine softly.

"Thank you," I say against his cheek as I move so my head is on his chest.

"Who are you scared I'm going to kill?" he asks, running his hands up and down my back, in a soothing motion.

"My friends," I tell him.

"They would try to kill me first if they are supernaturals. I imagine the Prince of vampires would be good bait for my father," he tells me.

I can't help the chuckles that come out. "Prince of vampires, I like that, it's funny," I say.

“I agree, it sounds like something out of a porno. ‘The Prince of the Vampires and the Sexy Human, Part One’,” Alex says with a laugh, and I laugh with her.

"You’re seriously crazy," Wyatt grins down at me.

"Maybe, but you like me." I shrug.

"You’re right I do, I have to go and talk to my father. I might be able to persuade him to leave you alone," he tells me.

"What would he ask from you to do that?" I ask, worried about what Wyatt would do to keep me safe.

"I don't know," he says, pulling away from me.

"Please stay in today, the place is guarded against my kind. I need to take Drake with me, and Alex should come, too. I'll have to Skype him at home, and he will want to ask them about you," Wyatt tells me. I hold in the chuckle at the idea of the King of vampires on a video chat.

"I will stay here and wait for you to come back." I smile at him.

"Promise me?" he asks, watching me closely. I don’t know why he is asking me, he looks so serious.

"I don’t have anywhere to go as I’ve missed class," I say, having the feeling I shouldn’t promise him anything.

Wyatt's eyes glow before he walks out. I hear Alex follow, with Drake not far behind them. They shout bye to me as the door slams shut.

My phone rings again as I groan, falling to the sofa. What the hell have I gotten myself into?

There are two loud knocks on my door, which instantly makes me tense up, expecting the door to be slammed open. I remember Wyatt's words about the place being protected and take a deep breath. The men from earlier can't get in here. I probably don't want to know about how it's protected.

"It's Katy and Harris. We're not going to hurt you. Not like some crazy ass bitch we know!" she shouts through the door, and I pray my neighbours didn't hear the teen shout that.

I swing open the door, to two worried faces before I get a face full of brown hair as Katy hugs me.

"I heard what that skank did to you. Don't worry, Jaxson will deal with her. There's no way he would let her get away with trying to kill you," she says into my ear.

"Are you okay?" Harris asks from behind her.

"Yeah, come in." I nod, looking away from him. Should I tell them to stay away as well? I don't think I can choose between Wyatt and the wolves who all feel like family to me now. Katy lets me go to walk into my kitchen, and straight to the fridge.

"Ohh, you have the good stuff. Our mother is on a silly diet, and our dads just agree to everything she says." She pulls out Alex's chocolate milkshake and some lemon drizzle cake, I made earlier this week.

"Katy, you can't just walk into people's houses and eat their food," Harris starts shaking his head as he sits on my sofa.

"It's alright," I smirk at Katy.

"She isn't anyone, she is pack," Katy says, with a mouth full of cake.

"Katy, at least try to be a girl for once. You have cake on your dress," Harris groans.

"What are you here for? Not that I mind seeing you," I change the subject as Katy glares at Harris.

"You weren't in class, and I was worried," he takes my hand and gently squeezes it.

"This one hid in my back seat, hiding her scent. That's an annoying trick she has," Harris mutters.

"It's cool, and you know it. I'm the master at hide and seek in the pack since I got my powers last year." Katy laughs.

"How did you know I was coming? I didn't tell anyone," he asks Katy.

"Well, I overheard you were going to see Winter, when you were shouting at Jaxson," Katy admits.

"Why were you shouting?" I ask, and Harris blushes a little.

"I felt he should have protected you better, we all see how he looks at you, and you at him," he tells me. I go to correct him, but he shakes his head.

"It's obvious you guys want to be doing the horizontal tango." Katy winks at me, as she hangs her legs over the side of my chair in the lounge.

"Katy, God, you shouldn't even know about that stuff," Harris groans at her.

"I'm fifteen, not ten." Katy rolls her eyes at his horrified face.

"Still, just no." Harris shakes his head.

"I'm the only teenaged girl in our pack. There are five teenaged boys my age. What do you think they talk to me about?" Katy laughs as she winds her brother up.

"I'll tell our dads, they will help me sort that problem

out," Harris says.

"Fine, whatever." Katy waves a hand at him, a faint blush on her cheeks.

"Do you have different dads then?" I ask.

"Well, maybe, we don't know. My mum has five mates, and they are all our dads. I told you we have a low rate of girls being born. There are ten girls in our pack and forty-eight guys. Not all of them are mated, but most share one mate," he says, I've never even thought about being with more than one guy but mating five. That's a new thought, a damn scary one.

"Okay, I'm not judging, but how does it work?" I ask.

"They all love my mum, and she is the boss of them. I've never seen them argue, and they were all friends for years before they started dating my mum," Katy tells me.

"It works," Harris shrugs.

"So, how were Jaxson and Esta chosen to be mates?" I ask.

"This is where it gets complicated, you explain. I need to eat more. The sugar in this place and I need to get to know each other," Katy tells Harris seriously as she opens a bag of strawberry laces. Harris just shakes his head as she continues to eat her cake and laces at the same time.

"Alphas aren't known to share. In my mum's group, there isn't a leader. They are all the same level of dominance or close to it, anyway. An alpha would control any other mates and would see them as a constant challenge. If his mate took another mate, he might kill him, so it has never worked. The other mate would have to be as strong as Jaxson and therefore Esta was chosen just for him. She agreed not to take any other mates," he tells me.

"What's the prophecy?" I ask remembering the argument Fergus had with Jaxson. It seems it's the reason I'm told to stay away from them.

"How did you hear about that?" Harris' normally pale skin goes paler. Katy looks up, with a strawberry lace hanging out of her mouth.

"I overheard Jaxson and Fergus arguing," I tell them both.

"We can't tell you, the alpha has us all under an oath," Katy says looking pale as she eats her food. For all our sakes, I change the subject, even if it pisses me off.

"Back to Jaxson, he couldn't have known Esta would attack me," I tell them both, it's not like we planned that kiss.

"Yeah, he should have. Esta is his intended mate, and he isn't meant to want anyone else. They should have mated years ago, but he just strings her along," Harris growls. I widen my eyes at the jealously on his face before realising that maybe Harris likes Esta. I guess it's possible with so little women in the pack. Harris must have grown up with Esta. I don't know her well enough to know why he would like her. My experiences of her are all shadowed by jealously.

"What does that exactly mean?" I ask.

"They were chosen for each other when they were born, by a local witch," he says making my stomach feel sick.

"So, they are soul mates," I finish for him.

"Not always, the witch isn't always right, and I know she was friends with Esta's parents. I think they paid her to make that choice," Katy says, frowning at my heartbroken face.

"But, sometimes she is right. I could have been getting in the way of something that's meant to be," I mumble. I remember Esta's heartbroken face, and something I haven't felt much of before appears, guilt.

"No, Winter. Jaxson could have mated her when they

both turned eighteen. Jaxson is twenty-four now, and he still hasn't even tried a relationship with her. If that's destined to be together, I call bullshit," Katy says.

"I still can't ever be with him, can I?" I ask them, looking out the window as I do because I can't see anyone's face when they tell me the answer.

"No, you can't. A human wouldn't survive a mating, and his wolf would be too jealous to live without trying to mate you. Vampires, witches, and angels can mate with humans, but we can't. Trust me, it's been tried, but it always kills the human. If they don't mate, the wolf will go crazy and try to kill anyone that looks at their human," Harris says before Katy can say anything more. Not wanting them to see how hurt I am, I stand up, moving some blankets around and picking up some cups. I should send them away before Wyatt finds out and makes them stay away. They both watch me as I take the cups to the kitchen and come back.

"I should stay away from the pack, I think it's for the best. I'll tell Jaxson, but I think you should leave," I tell them. Katy's face drops at my words.

"You're still pack. Jaxson will mate fully with Esta soon, and then it will be okay." Harris sounds as heartbroken as I feel. One look at his face shows me how much he struggled with those words.

"Leave, Harris, please." I choke on the last words of my sentence. I can see it's hard for him, but this whole night is feeling like someone is banging a hammer against my heart.

"Winter," Katy tries to come to me, but I shake my head. I see from the corner of my eye Harris pulling her out of my apartment. The shutting of the door slams the final nail in the coffin, and I burst into tears, sliding down onto the floor.

17

WINTER

The rest of the night, I spend half sleeping on the sofa and half crying. My phone rings a few times from Jaxson and Wyatt. I can't make myself answer either of them. When the morning sun lights up the room, it burns my dry eyes. I know I need to go to university today, I only have two days left, and I missed all of yesterday. I pick up my phone and read the messages from Wyatt, saying that he is picking me up in an hour for class and to call him. I don't call, but I force myself off the sofa, leaving my misery behind to shower and change. Once I'm dressed in a turtleneck sweater dress and black knee-high boots, I throw my laptop and class work into my bag. Wyatt doesn't knock, so I'm in the kitchen eating a breakfast bar as he strolls in. His gaze descends my whole body before meeting my eyes, and I can almost taste his anger.

"You had a wolf here, I have smelt a wolf around you for ages, but not in your home. Don't you know not to invite the big, bad wolf into your home?" He remarks, his fists tightly clenched as he strolls forward. I almost feel the anger in each forceful step until he is standing in front of me, forcing my gaze to look up at him.

"Do you have any idea how worried I was when you didn't answer?" His gaze is trying to hide the pain that is clearly etched on his face.

"I'm sorry." I place my hand on his rough stubble on his cheek, and he leans into my touch.

"Sweetheart." He sighs before leaning down and kissing my forehead. "I'm scared that he will hurt you again. I don't want to see your bruises anymore. I brought this cream for you." He passes me a white tub. My ribs aren't too sore, I must not have hurt them as bad as I thought. I've always healed quickly growing up, so I'm not worried.

"Thanks, but none of my friends did this to me. That I promise you, they wouldn't hurt me, Wyatt." I say and pull my shirt up. Wyatt takes a seat, watching me as I rub the green-looking cream into my skin. My skin tingles for a second, and I watch as a slight glow comes from where my bruises are.

"What is that?" I ask.

"It's from Dabriel. He is good at making things for healing. I don't know what's in it, but it heals anything very quickly," Wyatt tells me.

"It's magic?" I ask, and Wyatt nods for an answer. I pull my shirt down and offer him the tub back.

"Keep it," he says, and I put in on my coffee table.

"What did your father ask of you?" I ask him.

Wyatt moves quickly away from me, and stands next to the door. "You're safe for now, that's all that matters," he says in a cold tone. The Wyatt I know is lost now, and he is cutting me off.

"Wyatt," I warn.

"I was going to drive you, but I have something else to

do," he says, his eyes meet mine for a second, long enough for me to see the guilt in them.

"Wyatt!" I all but shout into the wind, as he disappears out the open door. My worry hits an all-time high as I make my way to class and sit in my seat. Harris waves as he comes in, and I wave back, looking around for Alex. She doesn't come to class, which makes me worry more, I try to send a message to her, but she doesn't reply by the end of my classes. I walk out, not really looking where I'm going and bump into Harris who clearly wants to talk to me.

"Hey Winter, or should I call you the girl that likes to bump into me a lot. I know he is an ass, but Jaxson said—"

I stop him with a raised hand. "Honestly, I don't want to know. I have other problems now. I can't deal with him," I say, moving around him and ignoring the second voice in my head saying I desperately want to know.

"Winter, wait," he says behind me, as I walk faster away and finally get to my car.

"Winter." I hear the faint growl in his voice, but I ignore him all the same. He must have known he had upset me yesterday, and why do I have the feeling he did it on purpose?

I drive away, while Harris watches with his blue eyes almost glowing. It once scared me to see them do that, but now I really don't care. I feel like part of me has been cut off, and I'm not sure how to get it back.

When I pull into my apartment car park, I spend way too long staring at the place I found Freddy. It was the same night I met Wyatt, and I think how complicated that whole night seemed to be. There are too many questions and fewer answers to be found in my mind, without any help. Would I change anything? I don't think I would. Wyatt is winning my heart, but I'm so scared he's going to do something stupid to protect me. Jaxson has my heart already, but he doesn't want it. Maybe I should just stick with my love for Freddy, the boy I'm getting so protective of. I have to remind myself to message him back. He keeps sending me funny Harry Potter memes.

"Why are you sitting in your car?" Jaxson asks, opening my passenger door and making me jump. His green eyes hold amusement as he slides into my small car, which seems far smaller with him inside.

"I don't know, I was thinking of Freddy," I say honestly.

Jaxson regards me for a second, looking at the empty parking lot with me. The sun is almost shining through the dark clouds, but the place makes me feel alone with all my worries.

"He misses you," he says finally, and I have a feeling he isn't the only one with the way Jaxson is looking at me. He reaches out brushing away a stray bit of hair from my face.

"Please don't. Don't make this harder," I whisper, unable to pull away as his finger traces my cheek to my lips.

"Winter, I can't stay away. I need to tell you something," he says, a cold, cocky tone coming back into his voice. It's like he needs to put up a mental barrier before trying to talk to me. I watch as he pulls away from me, with his whole body going tense.

"I came to tell you I can't train you anymore. It's not fair to Esta. Harris will, instead, if you wish," he says. His hands tighten on his thighs, and I notice for the first time how conflicted he looks.

"Okay, just leave, Jaxson," I say, losing any energy to fight him on this. He has already given up on us.

"I want this to be different, but I can't pull you into my world," he tells me, looking out the window of the car. The muscles in his neck are looking tight, and the unshaved scruff on his face is begging me to tell him how I won't leave him. The words never come out as I harden my face into a neutral expression.

"Leave, Jaxson, I can't be around you, and I need to see you walk away from me," I say, meeting his eyes. The green in his eyes is starting to glow as my heart breaks. I realise that I'm completely in love with him.

"Winter, I–" he starts, reaching for me.

"Don't," I croak out, before getting out of the car as quickly as I can. For some time, I've known I've been falling for him, but I can't believe I realised it when he is leaving me for someone else. I can't hear what he has to say because the need to beg him to stay is too strong, and I'm not that kind of girl. No girl should have to beg a man to stay in her life. If he loved me, he would fight for us.

When I turn around, I know Jaxson is gone. I have the feeling eyes are watching me. I turn to see the massive, black wolf sitting on the edge of the car park. It whines at me gently before bowing its head. I don't move as Jaxson's wolf turns and runs down a nearby alley toward the woods. A long howl fills the air, and everything stills with the pain I feel in it.

Despite wanting to spend the night suffering in misery and eating junk food, Alex and Drake come home around seven with bags of Chinese food.

"I'm here to cheer you up. We need a sister night," she announces with a cheery grin. One she loses when she sees me on the sofa. I must look terrible with tissues all around and puffy eyes.

"See you later, hot stuff," she says to Drake, before giving him a very long kiss and shoving him towards the door.

"Goodbye," he says formally to me, making Alex laugh.

"I forget how much older you are than me," she says.

"Careful," he purrs, winking at her and making her giggle. I am shocked at this playful side of him that I've never seen.

"Bye!" she shouts as she shuts the door when he leaves. Alex puts a comedy on and then we eat out of the boxes as we chat.

"So, which one are you more upset about?" she asks, a raised eyebrow in my direction.

"What?" I say, shoving more egg fried rice into my mouth. I really need chocolate, but this will do.

"Well, Wyatt is hot, but Jaxson has this whole brooding thing going on. Plus, how hot would a werewolf be in bed? Drake is amazing, but I'm guessing all supernaturals are," She tells me as my jaw drops open.

"You know about Jaxson being a wolf?" I ask dropping my fork onto the sofa in shock. I pick it up as she says,

"Well, yeah, when I met him. The whole overwhelming smell of woods isn't a human thing. You forget I'm mated, extra abilities." She taps her nose.

"Did you?" I'm cut off by her huff.

"No, Drake would lose his shit, but you weren't in danger. Well, maybe your virtue was, but that doesn't count." She winks at me, causing me to laugh for the first time in a while.

"So?" she questions.

"Wyatt feels like being close to the sun, keeps you hot all the time, but I'm scared I'm going to get burnt. I feel like he is so haunted, that I can't get close to him. He's also a vampire prince, I'm not sure his dad is going to be cool with him dating a human," I tell her.

"He lost his girlfriend, who he wanted to mate with

eventually. Drake said it almost destroyed him, but around you he can be different, happy almost," she replies.

"I know, I get that. I want him to let me in more, but I'm scared how much more I would fall for him if I did," I reply.

"That silly man is in love with you, you know that, and I've seen the way you look at him. It may be too late for that," she tells me, and I try not to think about her words. I love seeing Wyatt; the playful side he has with Atti and the passionate way he can be. I love hearing him tell me about his love for music and his promises to show me how he plays sometime. I just can't admit I love him, yet.

"Jaxson?" she asks, and my smile fades.

"When I'm around him, it's like I can't breathe, and he is the air I damn well need but can't have. One kiss with him, and I know I'd do anything for him, even if I end up getting hurt," I tell her, trying to ignore how much it hurts to say that.

"You love him," she says in awe a little.

"He is going to be mated to someone else, her name is Esta. Her wolf tried to kill me a few days ago because Jaxson kissed me," I say sadly, and my eyes widen as Alex's normal, brown eyes start glowing.

"I'm going to kill that wolf bitch," she states.

"I want the same, but she is meant for Jaxson. Harris said a witch fated them to be together. I can understand her point of view. I'm a human who has just appeared in Jaxson's life and kissed the wolf she has been told her whole life that is meant for her. You should have seen her face after Jaxson shouted at her. She was heartbroken, she really cares for him, and I felt bad for her," I tell Alex.

"Witches are wrong all the time. Drake said that once to Wyatt," she tells me.

"I won't make him choose between his pack and me. I

don't think he feels the same, anyway. He walked away from me today, knowing it would break me," I say. I finally sob into my hands before wiping the tears away.

"Oh, Winter," she pulls me to her and lets me cry it out.

"I'm sorry for being a baby." I pull back.

"Don't be, what are sisters for?" She winks at me.

"How about more junk food and more funny movies?" I ask.

"Perfect," she laughs. We spend a night being lazy and having fun. I force myself to forget about everything else. It was just what I needed.

18

WINTER

The last day of university went well. Harris didn't turn up, but Alex stayed with me. I clearly worried her last night when I opened up about nearly everything. Although, I still haven't told her about the eerie life-like dream. I don't know how to bring up the fact that the woman in my dreams talked about a prophecy, and that everyone seems to think I have something to do with it. I would be stupid to bring it up to any wolves. They might kill me on the spot. I don't know if I should tell Wyatt. Currently, I'm replying to Atti, who somehow got my number, he has sent me pictures of his cats. They are far bigger than I expected, but I have a really funny one of his cat, Mags, asleep on a porno magazine. Atti said that the magazine belongs to Dabriel. I highly doubt that is true. I am happy he got my number, his funny messages and pictures have kept me smiling all day.

My phone rings, my smile growing when I see it's my mum.

"Hey, Mum." I'm relieved to talk to her.

"Hey, Baby, just one day until I get a hug," she squeals down the phone, and I chuckle.

"I'm just packing now," I tell her, knowing it will make her happy.

"Only just packing now, oh Winter, that is last minute. I've bought all your favourite food for when you're home." She changes the subject. I know she will take everything out of my bag when I get home, anyway, and wash it all. That's my mum for you.

"The local shop's chocolate fudge pie?" I inquire as my mouth waters.

"Yes, two of them," she chuckles.

"I love you," I state, grinning widely when I hear her laugh.

"I will let you pack, I only wanted to check up on you. I'm calling Alex next," she tells me.

"Bye, Mum," I say smiling.

"Bye, Baby," she replies and puts the phone down. I finish chucking my spare shoes in my bag with the rest of my stuff. Sitting on my suitcase to shut it, I smile when I finally get the zip done up. My phone rings again, and guessing it's my mum, I don't look as I answer.

"Winter?" Freddy's voice says into the phone.

"Freddy, how are you?" I'm surprised how nice it is to hear his voice.

"All good, but I want to see you, I'm coming with Harris and Katy to pick you up," he says like the excited voice of a child on lots of sugar.

"Oh, and why are they picking me up?" I ask him.

"We all miss you." Katy takes the phone off Freddy, and I hear his grumbling in the background.

"Where are we going?" I ask her.

"To a party, so dress up. One hour." She puts the phone down before I can reply. I smack my head with my hand, intending to kill Harris when he gets here for letting them call me. I stop half-way to my wardrobe when I remember Dabriel's words. He told me not to go to a party and something about death. I forgot to ask Wyatt about that. But, one party can't hurt.

I open my wardrobe and find a long, purple, maxi dress, it has purple beads in a halter style that holds it up. Slipping it on and letting my dark brown hair fall down my back, wavy from the bun it was in. I'm surprised how good it looks in wavy curls and not a big ball of frizz, for once. I put a little makeup on before finding my bag and stuffing my phone in it. The doorbell rings, as I finish locking my room.

I open the door to a grinning Freddy, he is wearing a white shirt and black trousers, looking very smart. I try to ignore the way he looks too much like Jaxson, but it hurts a little to look at him for a second. Freddy's short hair is dark-brown with blond tips. The dark-brown is clearly from Jaxson's side of the family. I wonder if his mum or dad was blonde.

"Winter!" he grins widely pulling me into a strong hug. So strong that I have to get my breath back when he lets go.

"Come on, we have to go," he says with such a huge grin I can't say no. Damn Katy, she knew sending him up here would work. I lock the doors with a smile and let Freddy grab my hand, pulling me outside. Harris looks guilty as I pass him and sit in the back seat. Freddy gets into the other side. Katy beams when she sees me.

"You look so totally hot." She pulls on Harris' arm so he looks back at me. I smile in a friendly way, that I hope shows I'm not mad at him.

"You look lovely, Winter," he says with a roll of his eyes at Katy and a small smile for me.

"Where's the party?" I ask.

"It's a mating party, there are three wolves being mated tonight," Harris answers.

"At the pack?" I ask, a little nervous for his answer. I know the answer, but I need to hear him say it.

"Yes," Freddy smirks, and Harris starts driving.

"You can't avoid us. Jaxson is well, whatever, but you're my friend," Freddy says with those damn, puppy dog eyes.

"Fine one hour, and then Harris is driving me home," I demand, and Harris nods with a small smile.

"I'm sorry if we upset you the other day," Katy says awkwardly.

"I get it, you were being honest and didn't want me getting hurt," I tell her, and she looks relieved.

She nods sadly before turning back to the front. The rest of the drive, Freddy tells me about his school work and how Anna made him homemade, strawberry ice cream. It's funny to see how happy it makes him. My body tenses as we pull into the pack lands, there are two wolves by the entrance to the long path, and they nod at Harris as he turns. We stop at a small cabin further away from the main house I'm used to, and we all get out.

"So, how good are you at dancing?" Katy asks as I follow a tense Harris up the main path towards the main house. All the cabins have green lanterns outside. I've been here at night, but I've never seen that. It must be a wedding thing.

"Terrible." I laugh, and Katy grins evilly.

"I can't wait to see that," she chuckles.

"You won't," I warn.

"But, you have to dance with me," Freddy says, coming up next to me, it's only then I notice Harris is wearing the same white shirt and black trousers, while Katy is dressed in a blue skater dress. It's simple, but it suits her figure making her seem older than her fifteen years. Katy is really stunning tonight, and I know she will be a handful for some guy when she is older.

"Don't do the eyes." I look away from Freddy, and he chuckles.

"I will get her to dance," Freddy whispers to Katy, and Katy laughs as they fall behind me to conspire. I catch up to Harris, and I'm about to say something, but I forget when I see the sight in front of me.

The trees around the main house are filled with green lanterns that give an earthly effect to the white tables lined out in front of the house. There is a stage made up with a band playing gentle music as a couple dances with everyone watching them. My eyes are drawn to them as they sway to the music, and the man spins the girl, her long, brown, braided hair floating around her. Her light-green dress is low at the back, so I can see all the way up her spine. She has a tattoo like I've never seen. It looks like vines, but it clearly makes a symbol I don't understand. There are also three wolves tattooed to look real, the closer we get the more real they become. I look over to see two other men, watching the couple dance, but they are only watching her. There's no jealously on their faces. I realise they are her other mates. The song ends. The couple walks over to them, and one of the other guys pulls her into a passionate kiss. The others don't look away, and it's strange to see. Not a bad strange, but, still, it's something else.

"That's a mating mark. Whatever our mates are born with on them, we get an equal one that appears once a mating is completed," Katy whispers.

"It looks beautiful." I gaze out at the couple, they look so happy. More couples join the dance, and I see Fergus, leading Anna to dance. Her stomach is wider now, and she is wearing a similar blue dress to mine that shows off her bump. I have to admit that baby is going to beautiful with parents like them. I hope I get to see the baby at least once, I will get them a lovely gift for when the baby comes. Fergus and Anna look so relaxed as they sway to the music. My gaze shifts when I spot Jaxson. My heart stops as I see him wearing a spotless white shirt that shows off all the muscles on his chest. The black trousers and his nearly black hair reflect the soft-green, fairy lights. Two hands appear on his chest as he puts his hands on Esta's small waist as they dance. She looks up at him in adoration, as stunning as ever in a tight, yellow dress. She wraps her arms around his neck leaning up over his shoulder as they move, and her dark eyes lock onto me with a big smirk. I don't move as she leans up and kisses Jaxson. Jaxson doesn't move to stop the kiss, as my heart feels like it's stopped moving. My feet move on their own, as I turn away from the voices that shout my name and towards the training room at the back of the house to catch my breath. I lean against the door, as I wipe the stupid tears that fall on my face.

"Winter," Katy says coming to my side and hugging me. The building is lit up from outdoor lights, so she can see me clearly.

"Go back to the party. I will just wait in Harris' car. You'll know when I've calmed down enough to move," I tell her, not wanting to ruin her fun.

"I didn't know, I swear none of us would have brought you to cause you any pain." She hugs me and pulls back. She holds my hand as I stare into the trees. We don't say anything for a long time as I cry silent tears and try to pull myself together.

A loud scream fills the air, as well as a whoosh of something flying through the air. Katy knocks me to the ground, covering my body with hers.

Katy rolls away from me, laying on her back as I look at her in shock.

"Katy!" I scream, shaking her as she blinks up at me, holding her side. I pull her hand away to see it stained red.

"The alpha is dead, that must be how they got in. Run, Winter," she mutters before passing out. Screams fill the air from the front of the house, and I hear growls in the background too. The ground starts shaking madly, and it's hard to stand up. I know what I have to do. I can't leave Freddy to fight anyone. I don't know who we are fighting, but I have an idea it's the vampires. I know I can leave Katy when I see the little silver bullet on the floor. It would only kill her if it was still inside her.

I drag Katy into the training room, before grabbing the crossbow off the wall and slipping some arrows in a bag on my shoulder. I load a couple of arrows quickly before locking the training room door. I hope Katy is safe, but I can't help her now. I can't think straight as I run across the grass, scared out of my mind about Jaxson and Freddy. If they got to Fergus and killed him, they could have hurt them, too. I think Jaxson is okay by the shaking ground and the sound of trees being ripped out in the background.

I run around the house and pause for a second at the horrible sight, blood pours out the mouth of a sandy wolf at my feet. I look up to see a man coming towards me, wearing all black and moving at a leisured pace like this is a game for him. His eyes are glowing a dangerous red, and there's a smirk on his face which dies when I shoot him in the heart. I watch as he falls to the ground holding the arrow. The man, or vampire I'm guessing by the teeth, turns black all over and crumbles into black dust. *Because that's not creepy at all.* A loud scream nearby directs my attention from the dust. My eyes widen as I see Esta shift quickly and start fighting two men in her wolf form, and

Anna is hiding behind her. I shoot one of the men she is fighting in the neck, and as he falls, I fire another into his chest finishing him. Esta's wolf takes the chance and kills the other vampire by tearing his head off. She nods in my direction before putting Anna on her back and making a run into the forest. I look around for Jaxson, and I can't see him. I go to move towards the fighting when I feel the pain.

I cough and raise my hand to my mouth, pulling it away to see blood. I look down in slow motion, seeing the dagger in my heart. I don't feel myself fall.

My eyes stay open, as I stare up at the night sky filled with stars.

"Winter, no, no! What are you doing here?" A voice floats around my brain, as my head is pulled into a lap. The arms surrounding me feel cold but my mind won't tell me who it is. My vision blurs, so I can only see the outline of a man and the stars behind him.

"Not yet, I'm sorry for this. I can't lose you, it's not your time, Winter," A familiar male voice says in a whisper, as I hear a crunching sound before my mouth is filled with a thick water. I choke on it, or my blood, once more before blackness creeps into my eyes. I feel my body being lifted. I'm sure just as the trees fade into blackness that I hear a heart-wrenching scream from the wolf I love,

"Winter!"

EPILOGUE

Wyatt

"I don't fucking know what she was doing there," I tell Dabriel as he holds his glowing hands over Winter's body. His whole body is glowing like a Christmas tree as he speeds up Winter's recovery.

"This isn't right," he says to Winter with a shake of his head.

"I didn't have a choice," I say to him. I watch as he gets up, his white symbols stop glowing on his skin, and he walks out the room. I follow him as I wait for him to tell me if she is going to make it. *What if I was too late?*

"She isn't a vampire," he tells me.

"That's impossible," I say firmly. I can already feel our bond, the connection we will have because she shares my blood.

"She isn't. I can tell. She still appears human but she is more. She is changing into something else," he tells me.

We both look through the door as we both hear something that we shouldn't.

A heartbeat.
Vampire's hearts don't beat.

WINTER'S KISS

When love and old prophecy's control your life, who can you trust?

Winter's life has been turned upside down since finding out that all the fairy tales exist and she doesn't know who to turn to. When everything is against her, can the men who love her keep her alive?

The rules are changing and Winter needs to fight to protect what is hers and avoid the destruction of everyone she has come to love.

What happens when you want to stop a prophecy before it's too late?

18+ due to violence, sexual scenes and language

This is a Reverse Harem Series

19

WINTER

"Winter, Winter, Winter understands at last, the war is coming, the war is death," a sweet, childlike voice sings into the cold air. The song is repeated again and again until I can no longer understand the words.

Everywhere is white as I look around, snow is falling as I stand in the middle of a white field. My hands tremble, and I lift my hand in front of my face as snowflakes float around me. The snowflakes slow down, so slow I can reach out to touch one.

"Finally, we meet, child of my blood," a soft voice behind me causes me to spin around. Standing directly in front of me is Elissa, or at least I think it is her. The woman I always dream of. I didn't know her name until recently. Her short, black hair floats in the wind, mixing with the falling snow as her bright-green eyes stare at me in a way I don't understand. Elissa has never had short hair before.

"Elissa," I say.

"Not quite, but you are ready. It's time," she says. The song is still being sung all around me, the tune haunting and familiar, but the words are blurred. Just the sweet voice is humming along.

"You knew this would happen?" I ask, referring to the fact I'm dead after being stabbed in the heart. My hand falls to my chest

feeling for a mark that isn't there. I look down and see I'm wearing the same white dress that she is. It's straightforward and long as it floats in the wind around my legs.

"It's time to wake up, child. It's time to finish what I couldn't," she says.

"Stop talking in riddles. I'm dead like you, there isn't any waking up," I whisper as I *wave my hands out at her.*

"No, Winter, they all need you. Now, go and choose wisely."

"Choose what wisely?" I ask as I feel myself falling away from her.

"Who to trust," she smiles sadly at me as her face floats away into darkness.

I wake up with a gasp, feeling air rushing into my lungs, and my vision is very blurry as I struggle to see where I am. I can smell something comforting like vanilla ice cream, and I swear I can also smell something incredibly sweet. When the room slowly comes into focus, I first see I'm in a dark-red bedroom. The room is unfamiliar. There's a big bed, which I'm currently sitting in the middle of. Other than that, there are two double wardrobes and a large fireplace in the room. There's a large mirror opposite the bed, and once I see myself, I can't look away.

I don't look healthy. Well, I look like me, but my hair is longer, almost hitting my waist, and my eyes are glowing blue. They look like, well like Jaxson's but not green. I'm dressed in a black, silk nightie and little else. I feel around my chest, as everything hits me.

I was stabbed.

I should be dead, and yet, I'm alone in a large bedroom.

The door opens to my left, and a very dishevelled-looking Wyatt is suddenly standing there watching me. His jaw is unshaven, and his clothes have seen better days. The man looks nothing like my Wyatt.

"Winter," he whispers and walks quickly over to me. His hand goes straight into my hair, and he leans his head down to mine. Our lips meet in a passionate kiss. The second I taste him, I can't get enough. I pull him onto to the bed, and he happily holds his body over mine. The kiss deepens until he pulls away.

"As much as this is a slight turn on, don't you think we need to talk to Winter?"

Wyatt moves off me quickly, with a speed I've never been able to see, until now. It's like the room's gone into slow motion, and I could see what he did. I shake my head and turn to see Atti standing at the door. He grins at me, but it's lost all the usual humour in his eyes. He looks terrible, with big shadows under his eyes, and his hair is down. I've never seen him with his hair like this, it stops at his shoulders and shapes his face. It makes him look so handsome.

"Do I get a hug? I've been waiting a month for you to wake up," he tells me. Wyatt sits on the end of my bed as I nod at Atti. My mind takes a minute to process what he said.

"A month?" I ask him, and he nods. Atti comes over and pulls me into his arms.

"I missed you," he whispers into my ear. His arms wrapped tightly around me. I love his hugs. Atti gives the best hugs.

"Explain what happened," I say when Atti lets go of me. He stays close, sitting right next to me on the bed.

"You nearly died, Winter. What the hell were you thinking?"

“I don’t–” I get out, but apparently Wyatt isn’t done with his rant at me.

“Do you know how crazy you were, running head first into a supernatural battle like that?" Wyatt says, well more shouts at me. I watch as he gets up to pace the bedroom. Atti links his fingers in mine.

"I love those wolves, they were in danger, and I knew I could help. I'm no coward. I won't hide when my friends are dying," I tell him honestly. I knew the massive amount of danger I was in when I picked up the crossbow.

"You stood no chance, Winter. If I wasn't there. . .," Wyatt says as he stops at the end of the bed. The scary look on his face makes me scoot closer to Atti.

"How am I alive?" I ask him. Wyatt finally turns to look at me.

"I gave you my blood, I tried to turn you into a vampire and make you my mate," he says, and my skin turns cold. Is that why I look different? I don't feel different.

"Tried?" I ask Wyatt.

"We don't know what you are, you have a heartbeat. Winter, vampires don't have heartbeats, and your eyes are blue. All vampires' eyes are black or very dark-brown," Atti answers as I hold Wyatt's gaze. I feel more drawn to him than ever before, and I swear I can even feel his anger and how scared he is, in my chest. It's like I can feel what he is feeling.

"Why do I feel like I need to be near you?" I ask him, and he looks away from me.

"We are mated, you wear my mark now, and the urge to be close is something you will get used to. I've always felt that way around you," Wyatt admits.

"Mark?" I ask, and Atti grins when I look up at him.

"It's on the bottom of your back, you would have to lose some clothes to see it," Atti says with a waggle of his eyebrows that makes me blush.

"I will wait then," I say with a nervous laugh as Atti

looks at me differently. There was always some boundary before, and it doesn't feel that way anymore.

"So, we are mated now?" I ask Wyatt.

"Yes. I didn't want it to be like this," he says sharply.

I watch as he walks out the room, and the door slams shut. I know he didn't mean to hurt me, but the reaction still hurts my heart. I feel myself rubbing my chest without thinking.

"We have a lot to talk about, Love," Atti tells me and pulls me to his chest. I rest my hand on his chest, noticing that my nails are longer and look like I've had a manicure.

"How did Wyatt and I mate?" I ask him.

"Vampires have to give their blood to a human or vampire, seconds before they will die." Atti says, the shadows under his eyes seem darker as he moves a little closer to me.

"Oh," I say, a little dazed.

"Don't be mad at him, I would have done the same in his situation. I would have done anything in my power to save you and fuck the consequences," he says, and my cheeks warm up. I wrap my arms around his chest, and he holds me close.

"What are you then?" I ask him. I know he isn't a vampire because I can hear his heartbeat under my cheek. He smells so good, and all I want to do is push myself closer to him.

"A witch."

"Not a wizard, then, because witches remind me of women in corsets and spiky hats?" I ask him

He laughs, "No, there are no such things as wizards. Witches are the term for male and female witches."

"Can you fly on a broom?" I ask, and he laughs louder.

"No, but I can do this," he talks in my head, and I jump.

"You can hear my thoughts?" I ask a little worried. Ok, a lot worried.

"No, but I would like to," he says in my mind again, and I can see his grinning face.

"What else can witches do?" I ask him.

"We have high connections with the elements, we can move things with our minds, and talk to people in our heads. I can boost individual angel powers, and the best one is, I can make myself and others move to wherever I have been before. I can also go directly to someone if I know them well," he says, and I watch as he disappears, causing me to fall onto the bed. I turn to see him reappear by another door in the room. He opens it, while I look at him like a gaping fish. Well, I guess that's what I look like.

"Why don't you have a shower, and I will get you some clothes? I will leave them in here for you," he says, and I get off the bed.

"What is that smell?" I ask when I get closer to him. I smelt it before, but it smells better now.

"Winter, your eyes," he watches me as I move closer. I know it's him that feels nice, and I press my face into his neck.

"You smell like chocolate," I mumble, and I hear his chuckle as I realize what I've just said. My cheeks are feeling warm.

"Winter your eyes are silver, like Wyatt's when he feeds, but it's not creepy as fuck. In fact, it's hot. Maybe you need to feed as he does," Atti tells me, and I snap out of whatever I was doing by moving away.

"No, that's just, well, no," I say quickly and run into the bathroom, slamming the door behind me.

20

WINTER

I rest my head against the cold bathroom door, as I calm myself down. I risk a quick glance at myself in the full-length mirror next to the shower, and I push myself as close to the cold door as I can.

My eyes are silver in the middle, bright silver. It's so strange, I watch as my eyes turn back to a bright blue that is more familiar. I look wild and out of control with my long hair and panicked face. I have to close my eyes for a while to get my head around everything. I'm mated to Wyatt. That seems like a long-term kind of thing, with a man who is haunted, and I'm not sure I'm in love with. I've been sleeping a month, and my mother most likely has no idea where I am.

How did this all happen?

My tears fall faster than I can stop them as I slide to the floor and wrap my arms around my knees. I have to remind myself that I'm stronger than this. I eventually get up and run the shower. It's one of those small ones with glass walls all around it and a glass door.

I pull the silk nightie off me and just stare at myself in

the mirror. I'm still curvy as I have always been. I have the same pale skin and dark-brown hair, but it all looks different. For one, my hair is longer, much longer than I've ever had it, and it looks softer. I feel different, I feel stronger.

I sound like a superhero out of a comic when he first gets his powers. *My thoughts are lame.*

I turn, so I can see my back in the mirror, remembering what Wyatt said about his mark. Right in the middle of my back is a black tattoo about the size of a fist. Holy crap I have a tattoo, as I look closer at it, it glows too. That's cool.

It's a phoenix, with a small body in the middle and the wings are taking off. The wings gently move as I watch and its tail is long, full of swirls. It is strong and elegant. It reminds me of Wyatt in a way. It could pass as an ordinary tattoo like most normal girls get.

Hell, who am I kidding, none of this can be classified as normal. I force myself into the shower, I use the men's shampoo I find and a razor to clean myself up. I come out of the bathroom a little later just in a towel. Alex is sitting on my bed, a pile of clothes next to her, and she is playing on her phone. Her eyes widen when she sees me. Alex looks as awful as Wyatt and Atti did. Her skinny frame is covered in sweatpants and a baggy jumper. Her eyes look red from crying, and her hair is in a messy bun that looks slept on. I have never seen Alex look this tired.

"Win," she cracks out as she stands, dropping her phone on the bed. "I heard sleeping beauty finally woke up. You scared the crap out of me. I thought I'd lost you, and I couldn't cope. Come and hug me already." Alex is in tears as she opens her arms. I walk over, and we hug for a long time as she cries. I couldn't imagine losing Alex, so I have an idea of how scared she is.

"What does mum think?" I ask her.

"That you and I are on a trip. She doesn't believe it, but I have been messaging her off your phone pretending to be you. I have spoken to her a few times, and she's worried," she tells me, and I'm filled with relief. Well, sort of, my mum isn't stupid, and I'm going to get an ear full when I speak to her.

"I bet she is. I can call her tonight," I say quietly.

"Yes, you should. She'll go mad at you because she thinks you're too busy to talk to her. I couldn't exactly say that her daughter was stabbed, and her vampire boyfriend turned her into a weird version of a vampire. She would have me committed," Alex lightly chuckles.

"I love you, you know that, right?" I tell her as I pick up the pile of clothes.

"I know," she says.

"Let me get dressed, and then you can catch me up on what I've missed," I tell her, and she nods as she wipes her eyes. I get changed in the bathroom into a tight, yellow top and skinny, black jeans. I don't think too long about how my underwear got here, the other clothes aren't mine but fit well. They can't be Alex's because she is at least two sizes smaller than me. Lucky cow.

My hair looks like I've spent hours with a curler on it and has dried on its own. I don't bother trying to find a hair band, but I do look at my face in the mirror.

I don't know how to feel about all this. I force myself not to think about Jaxson and the pack. The pain of Fergus's loss is heavy in my heart already. I didn't know him well, but I know he loved his pack. Poor Anna, and she is pregnant. I can't imagine how she is feeling. I remember seeing her terrified, pain-filled look just before Esta took her away. I wonder if Anna couldn't shift because she was pregnant. I doubt she was stronger in her usual form.

When I finally have the courage to walk out, Alex is waiting by the open bedroom door.

"Come on, you have three hot guys waiting to talk to you," she says, and I walk to the door. "You're such a lucky bitch, we need to chat about that," she shouts, and I hear a chuckle in the other room.

"Alex," I groan, and she chuckles as I walk past. I let my hearing lead me down the small hallway and into a living room. There are two leather chairs facing a large, fake fireplace and a leather sofa against the wall by the door. There's also a large bookcase filled with books in the one corner. I see Dabriel first, and I nearly fall over in shock. I take a step back as I see his big white wings on his back. I can only see his wings and his white hair as he's looking out the window, but I would recognise him anywhere. He turns at my small gasp, and his purple eyes find mine. I just stare as he realises I'm looking at his wings, he's dressed in a white shirt and black trousers. Looking like a sexy angel straight from heaven.

"You look stunning, you always were something else, but now, I've never seen anyone as lovely as you, Winter," he says and comes over to me. I let him pull me into a massive hug, lifting me off the ground as he does. The overwhelming scent of Dabriel hits me stronger than it ever has before, like vanilla and something else.

"You're still in a slight bit of pain, what's wrong?" he asks me as he puts me down. I watch as his hands glow and white symbols appear on them. The light is so bright I can't make out what they are, but as he puts his hands on my cheeks, I feel the warmth of them.

"You need to feed, like a vampire," he tells me and lets go. I instantly miss the sensation, and I almost go to grab his hands before remembering how weird that would be.

Try to act cool, Winter, I tell myself, especially in front of one the hottest guys you know.

"I can help you with that," he grins as he points at his neck, and I shake my head wondering what he is talking about.

"She shouldn't have angel blood for a starter, she wouldn't be able to stop," Wyatt says, drawing my attention to him. I knew he was in the room, but he hasn't moved or said a word until now.

"So, you're suggesting you feed her?" Dabriel says moving away from me slightly.

"Shouldn't it be Winter's choice?" Atti asks from the doorway. Atti and Wyatt start staring each other down as I watch. I move in the middle of the three, drawing all their gazes to me.

"Guys, enough! Don't you think I can talk for myself? I don't want to feed on anyone, just an ordinary sandwich will be alright," I say. I do feel hungry.

"Winter, it won't be enough," Dabriel starts, and I shake my head.

"I want to know what happened the night I almost died," I say. They all go silent, and I take a seat on one of the chairs by the fireplace as Alex sits on the arm of the chair.

"You all were told. Very sexy teacher attitude you've got going there, Win," Alex says into the silence, making me laugh, and a few of the guys chuckle.

"You can be my teacher any day, I think I like being told off by you," Atti says and grins at me.

Wyatt takes the seat opposite me, and everyone else finds seats as the joke stops the tension. I feel Atti standing behind me like he needs to be close.

"I'll make you a sandwich, I want to call Drake and see what's going on, anyway," Alex says, and leaves the room when I smile at her. I hope she doesn't try to cook anything, I'm sure we don't need a fire right now. You'd think a sandwich was a safe thing to have her make you, it's not.

"First off, you did die, Winter. Your heart didn't beat for the longest day of my life," Wyatt tells me, his face colder than ever as he talks to me. I don't believe it's aimed at me but hurts all the same.

"How am I alive now, then?"

"When I got to the pack, I was too late to stop the newly turned vampires from attacking them, but I tried to help. My father didn't tell me about the attack, but I have friends in his court that let me know. I saw you straight away. You were so close to death when I got to you, I gave you my blood, and you died," he says, and I suddenly feel the chill in the air.

"Then you came back, with a heartbeat and normal eyes. You do smell like a vampire but slightly different," Atti finishes.

"The pack, did many of them die? Are they okay?" I ask quickly. My heart feels in pieces at the thought that any of them are dead. Jaxson is my primary thought, I hold back the urge to be sick at the idea he isn't okay.

"I don't know, none of us have left this apartment for more than an hour since I brought you back," Wyatt says.

"I have to go back to my apartment and then to the pack," I stand up, and Atti's hand stops me.

"There is more we need to tell you, and then we will all take you back to see them," Atti says, and I sit down.

"What now?" I ask.

"My father knows I turned you because some of the vampires saw me feed you, and they escaped. You're expected at court to be introduced as my new mate in a week. We will have to travel to France and go to my old home. Atti will spell you so your eyes and heartbeat can't be detected. My court won't accept Atti or Dabriel to come with us, but they can visit if need be."

"But, Alex's eyes haven't changed, so why do mine have to?" I ask.

"Alex isn't meant to be a full vampire. She shares blood with Drake regularly, and that's how she mated with him. She never died, and you did, in front of a lot of vampires who told my father. If Alex died then, Drake would entirely turn her, but there are risks. Most don't survive, I never expected you to," Wyatt's sentences drift off, and I feel a slight pain in my chest. I'm pretty sure it's his emotion and not mine. I will have to ask him about that, alone maybe.

"So, Alex could be human again if she stopped feeding with Drake?" I ask, not because I want her to, but I'm curious how this all works.

"No, she would die, she is a half-mate. That's what we call them, humans like Alex. She already is marked and needs vampire blood but not a lot of it. Most people don't survive losing their mates anyway," Wyatt answers.

"So, your father expects me to be a full vampire?" I ask him.

"Yes, the fact you were human will annoy him, but he will get over it," he says, his voice sounding tired.

"Do I have a choice? Is it safe?" I ask Wyatt.

His grim look is the answer I need, but he responds anyway, "No, you don't have a choice, but I promised I would keep you safe. I will protect you."

"Fine, but I want to see the pack first," I say crossing my arms. I need to see Jaxson. I watch as Wyatt and Atti have a silent conversation.

"Winter we need to tell you something—" Wyatt starts.

Alex comes into the room shouting, "I found chocolate

that was hidden, that should stop your need to snack on us."

"Thanks." I smile, accepting the food. I devour it all quickly as everyone watches, it's a little weird. I'm so happy Alex found chocolate, it turned out to be Malteasers. Oh, how I love her.

"Can I have one?" Atti reaches his hand over the chair for a Malteaser.

"Not that I don't like you, but I will bite you if you try to take this chocolate from me. Fair warning." I grin up at him, and his hand moves away.

"You can bite me whenever you like, Love," he winks.

I can't stop staring at Atti, I've always known how attractive he is, but I don't know why he seems more now. Atti's light-blond hair shapes his face as it falls on his shoulders and is parted at the top. The slight beard he is growing suits him. It's like a glimpse into what an older Atti will look like. His grey eyes meet mine, as he gently strokes my cheek.

"You will need to feed soon Winter, I can feel you fading," Dabriel says breaking up our moment, and I blink seeing that he is standing next to my chair.

"I'll sort it out," Wyatt says. I want to know how he plans to make me eat anything. If his mind power didn't work on me as a human, it sure won't now.

"Fine," Dabriel says tensely to Wyatt but pats his shoulder.

"I'm hungry, are there any Oreos in the cupboard, Alex?" Atti asks her.

"Yes, but–" she answers, and is cut off by Wyatt.

"Don't be a little shit," Wyatt says tensely as he stands.

Atti laughs as he jumps up from his seat and walks out of the room. Wyatt moves quickly to catch up with him, and the two of them crash into the door. Atti disappears altogether into thin air.

"You're such a fucker, using your powers," Wyatt swears before stomping out of the room.

"Should I even ask?" I ask Dabriel, who just leans against the wall by the fireplace.

"No," he says with a small smile.

"Right…when are we leaving?" I ask instead.

21

WINTER

"Are you sure you want to do this?" Wyatt asks me again. We're travelling to my apartment after a long discussion with my mother over the phone. She is furious that Alex and I dropped out of university to go travelling. She was even madder that I didn't have time or signal to call her. I'm so glad my mum doesn't understand technology, or she would have seen straight through that massive lie. Eventually, I managed to get her to let me go after I said I just needed to explore before settling down. I still don't think she believes me but isn't pressuring me into it. I believe she was glad to speak to me. Alex said she told mum that I had a bad break up with someone and needed some time away. My university course is on hold, for the considerable future. I'm not sure when I can go back, and it makes me sad. I worked so bloody hard to get into that university, and it's all useless. I guess it's nothing in perspective of what Jaxson and his pack must be going through. If he survived.

I'm sure he must be alpha now, and I wonder if he mated with Esta. Did he look for me at all? My heart breaks at the idea, and I know why. I love him, and it's hard not to burst into tears every time I think of him. I'm so mad at him for letting Esta kiss him, and I'm mad at him for not loving me back. Jaxson had never been a coward before, but he was when he walked away from me.

"Yes, I need to see him. I need to know he is alive. I met someone called Jaxson, and I have to know." I tell Wyatt who nods at me with a tense look. Atti and Dabriel are in the car behind us because Wyatt's convertible won't fit more than two, and Wyatt refused to drive anything else. I wouldn't let Atti use his power because if Jaxson is here, popping in with a witch wouldn't get a great reaction from him. It just wasn't worth the possible argument. I cover Wyatt's hand on the steering wheel as we pull up outside my apartment. Alex told me that Atti got clothes for me but didn't stay long and that no one had gone back. I cringe, thinking of Atti going through my underwear. I'm glad that he only packed the sweet things. Not my granny panties I use for my period. I think I would die of embarrassment if he saw those.

"Are you coming?" I ask a tense Wyatt, who nods at me.

We both get out of his car as Atti pulls up in his, and they both get out. They walk with me in the middle to my apartment until I push them out of the way.

"I'm walking in first," I mutter.

"I have the keys, Love." Atti holds the keys up in the air, and I hold my hand out. After he makes me jump a little, he gives them to me, and I let myself in.

I stare in shock as I see Harris sleeping on my sofa. He's wearing just jeans, and his hair is all messed up. He must have heard us move into the room, and I walk over, dropping to my knees in front of him.

"You're alive," Harris says in a whisper as he opens his

eyes to face me. I laugh as he pulls me to his naked chest, and I hear three very thunderous-like noises behind me before someone pulls me away from Harris.

"Get a shirt on, wolf and call your alpha," Atti says, his mouth close to my ear, and his arm sliding around my waist. I hear the threat laced into his words, and it pisses me off. I'm not used to Atti acting all alpha male on me.

"Who the fuck are you?" Harris stands up off the sofa.

"The fucking prince of the witches. In fact, you're with all the princes, and we need Jaxson."

Harris' mouth drops open, and I turn to glare at all three of them.

"You know Jaxson? Is he alive? Does he know I am?" I ask all these questions quickly, and none of them answer me because they are staring at the door.

"I didn't know you were alive, but I never gave up. Not for one second," Jaxson says from the open door. I push my guys out of the way and run to Jaxson. I throw myself into his open arms, and he squeezes me tightly to him.

"Jaxson, I–" I start, but he stops me with a kiss. I didn't expect the kiss, but I don't stop it as he pulls my head closer and takes control of the kiss as his tongue slips inside my mouth.

I'm pulled away from Jaxson by strong arms, and I know it's Dabriel by his smell.

"You don't fucking deserve her! You nearly got her killed, and I won't watch you hurt her like this," Wyatt says and punches Jaxson. I'm surprised that Jaxson doesn't stop the punch as his head swings to the side. Jaxson just nods his head at Wyatt. They both stare each other down.

"Leave, Harris," he tells Harris who nods before walking out the door and shutting it behind him.

"One, you get because I should have protected her. Try

it again, and you'll start something you can't fucking finish, Wyatt," Jaxson warns.

Wyatt just laughs darkly before tackling Jaxson, and they both fly through the wall of my apartment and into the living room.

Hell, there goes my deposit in this place. I run around the massive hole in the wall to see Jaxson throw a punch at Wyatt.

"Stop!" I shout and feel a pressure inside my head. I hold my head and close my eyes as the feeling leaves me. When I open my eyes, all four of the guys are on the floor. The furniture is all over the place, and four pairs of worried eyes are staring at me.

"Stop it, both of you! You all have a lot of explaining to do!" I shout at them, and they are still silent. All of them are on the ground near the walls, and it just hits me that I don't know how they got here.

"J, did you see her glow blue?" Atti asks Jaxson, who nods.

"She is definitely not human," Dabriel says as he stands up. The familiar look he gives Jaxson makes me confused.

"First off, I need to talk to Jaxson, alone," I say when Dabriel goes to say something, but I interrupt him.

"Then you guys are going to explain how the fuck you all know each other," I say, and they all look at each other like they're seeing who is brave enough to tell me.

"What the fuck did you do to her?" Jaxson asks Wyatt, and he never takes his eyes off me.

"No fucking idea, the glowing silver eyes are clearly from me, but mine only turn when I'm feeding, as you know," he replies.

"They are pretty," Dabriel says.

"Winter is hot when she's mad," Atti agrees, nodding his head at Dabriel.

"What the hell are you guys muttering about?" I ask with my hands on my hips.

"Your eyes are silver, lass," Jaxson says with an amused look.

"Oh, again?" I say and walk away from them all and into my bedroom. The second I see myself in the mirror, I hold in the urge to jump backward. I don't think I will ever get used to seeing myself like this.

"It must be a side effect of Wyatt turning you, he hasn't turned anyone before," Jaxson says from the door to my bedroom, and he comes in, shutting the door behind him.

"It's weird," I move away from my mirror and sit on the end of my bed. I don't mean just my eyes or being alone with Jaxson. Everything has changed, and the secret world I've just been introduced to, I have somehow become part of. I remember the last day of university and how happy I was to go home. Just the thought of my mother sitting alone, worrying about Alex and me is enough to make me want to break down. I glance up at Jaxson, his arms crossed as he stands to watch me. Jaxson looks impressive as always, but something is different. I can see it in his eyes as he looks at me, I feel like something massive has changed between us. Jaxson is wearing worn jeans and a tight, white shirt that leaves his muscular arms for all to see. The green eyes that make his face seem more attractive than he already is, watches me with the same interest. There has always been this attraction between us, even when he was breaking my heart.

"Is everyone okay? Freddy and Katy? Anna?" I ask him as he sits on the bed next to me.

"Yes, Katy was touch-and-go for a little while, but she

made it and is back to herself now. Fergus is," he stops, clearing his throat, and I cover his hand with mine.

"I am so sorry for your loss. Fergus was a good man and a real alpha." I say, and he nods, looking at the ground.

"He was. I found his body, someone in the pack killed him," he tells me, and I lean back a little shocked. From what I saw and heard, they loved their alpha. I don't understand why anyone would kill him and let vampires in. It must have been pre-planned because of how it happened. There is no way it was a coincidence.

"That night, I know you saw Esta kiss me." He starts, and I try to move off the bed, but his large arm stops me. Jaxson turns me to face him; so I have to look into his eyes as he talks. I hold back my emotions because I don't want him to see how I feel. All I want to do is run from this conversation. Hearing him talk of Esta, who could be his mate by now, will destroy the little grip I have on the sanity that I have left.

"I ended the mating before the party, she surprised me by that kiss, and she has never tried to kiss me before. I didn't kiss her back, Winter. I told her how I only see her as a friend," he tells me. I can't hide my shock as Jaxson smiles a little and moves closer to me on the bed. His face is inches away from mine as he speaks.

"I knew from the moment I met you, it was you for me. But I didn't, and still don't, know how to keep you safe in my world," he tells me, and I watch as he slides off my bed and kneels in front of me. Jaxson stares up at me, eyes full of emotion that is squeezing my heart. I wipe my tears away as I look down at him on his knees. I remember a time when he said he would never kneel for anyone, yet here he is.

"I know there is a lot we have to face before there's

even a chance of a happy ending for us, but I need you to know I love you, and I will do anything to keep you safe. I never thought I'd fall in love with a human, a human who can make me laugh and be the sexiest women I've ever seen without even realising it. My world is full of danger, and not everyone will accept you, but I will be there. I will be at your side," he says.

My heart beats fast, and I blurt out, "I want you at my side, when I met you I thought you were a jackass."

He chuckles, "I think I'm the more romantic one if that's all you've got to say, lass."

I laugh, "Despite how much you tried to keep me at a distance, I fell for you. I fell for the playfulness, the sarcastic remarks, the loving nature you gave Freddy and most of all how you looked at me sometimes."

"How did I look at you?" he asks.

"Like you wanted to kill me and kiss me at the same time. I love you Jaxson," I tell him.

His face lights up in a grin, and he stands up, pulling me with him and presses a gentle kiss on my lips. We hold each other for what feels like a lifetime before he lets me go.

"We have a lot to tell you, come on, lass," he says pulling me out of the room.

I stop to shut my door and ask him, "Like how you guys know each other?"

"Yes, and I know you're not going to like it," he mutters with a little grimace at me. I raise my eyebrows, but I don't reply, and instead, I walk in front of him.

22

WINTER

When I come into my lounge, it's to the sight of three incredibly hot guys sitting on my couches looking equally worried and looking like they could be selling the sofa with how attractive they are. All their faces light up when they see me.

Atti shouts, "Come sit next to me, Love." I let go of Jaxson's hand and take the seat on the sofa, next to him. Wyatt and Dabriel are on the other sofa, and Jaxson leans against the wall. All their eyes are on me.

"Start talking," I say firmly.

Wyatt looks around before groaning, "I guess I'm telling her?"

"Yes." Dabriel answers, and I jump a little as Atti moves closer to me, putting his arm around my shoulders. I swallow the urge to lay my head on his shoulder. It's unfair that I'm so attracted to them all. Jaxson is the stern one. Wyatt is more passionate, as much as Atti is playful. Dabriel comes across as protective and sweet at times. All of them are the perfect guys.

"We have known Jax our whole lives. You know I said

we were all friends growing up. Jax was with us until we fell out." Wyatt says, and Jaxson growls loudly.

"Winter, we always knew that we would find a human. A unique person that could be our mate to share. Most of us didn't believe we would find you alive or find you at all," Wyatt says, and I have to force myself to answer him and not focus on the shared part.

"The prophecy?" I ask, and Wyatt nods, looking impressed that I figured that out.

"We don't know if it's true, but our births were the first proof in hundreds of years," Dabriel says, and I nod remembering Atti telling me that they were all born on the same day. I wonder if Jax was too.

"Someone best tell me the damn thing, then," I reply, and Atti snorts in laughter.

"You could say please, lass," Jaxson says, and I smirk at him.

"Nope," I draw out the word.

He laughs at me while everyone else looks a little confused.

"I will tell you," Dabriel says and starts the prophecy.

The blue-sided human will choose a side.
When four princes are born, on the same day, they will rule true.
Her saviour will die when the choice is made.
If she chooses wrong, she will fall.
If she chooses right, then she will rule.
Only her mates can stop her from the destruction of all.
If the fates allow, no one need fall.
For the true kings only hold her fate, and they will be her mates.

Dabriel repeats the prophecy again, but all I can hear is the end part. They will be your mates. I know sharing a female is normal for wolves, but is it for all of them? They don't even get along. It's not something I ever considered, and I admit it's freaking me out a little as they all stare at me. One problem at a time, it's not like they expect me to just mate with them all now. At least, I hope they don't.

"Hold on. You're all princes, and if Jaxson was born on the same day as all of you," I stop when Wyatt nods at me.

"You think I'm your mate? All of you?" I ask.

Atti answers, "We know, even stubborn ass over there knew when he met you." He waves a hand towards Jaxson. Jaxson just glowers at him, but I see the tiny twitch of his lips.

"I can't deal with this right now. It's too much, I'm only human and," I blurt out. I can't be with all of them, I don't even know how to process that. I love Jaxson, and maybe my feelings for Wyatt are strong. I don't know Atti and Dabriel that well, but there has always been a connection. I've always felt safe with them and lost when I was away from them. Each one of them feels like home to me, and it's scary.

"I know humans don't share, and it's something you have to get used to, but. . . ." Atti says.

"No. This isn't an easy decision, and I need to think about it. I'm not saying no, it's just a lot," I say, waving a hand at them all.

"Could you walk away from any of us, lass?" Jaxson asks me.

"I'm human, Jaxson. Wolves share, and that's cool. But, that's not how I was brought up," I say, and he nods.

"We will discuss this another time, it's been a long week

for Winter to have to make any decisions," Wyatt says. The rest of them look at me, but they seem to let it go for now as Wyatt suggested.

"You have never been only human, and you certainly aren't now. I knew when I saw you. All people have auras, and yours is like nothing I've ever seen before," Dabriel tells me firmly. His words slow my panicking down a little.

"What is mine like, then?" I ask, a little curious.

"It's so blue, bright and yet stunning," he says.

"The blue-sided human?" I ask, and they all nod at me. "What does it mean?" I ask.

"We don't know," Atti answers.

"Why did you two fall out?" I ask Jaxson and Wyatt. Both of them go tense.

"You know. I told you about Demi. Demi was Jaxson's sister," Wyatt tells me. I can't process everything as I turn wide-eyed to a tense Jaxson by the door.

"What about Fr-," I go to say, but Jaxson's shake of his head stops me from saying Freddy's name. Oh my god. Freddy is Wyatt's son.

Freddy is half wolf and half vampire. Why didn't I see it before? It all makes sense. Now that I think of the little boy, I know it. The blond tips of his hair, the smirk he gives when he's cheeky is just like Wyatt's. I always thought he looked so familiar, and I blamed it on him being like Jaxson, but it wasn't. It never was. How long has Jaxson kept this secret? I'm taking a wild guess that Dab and Atti don't know.

"I would have saved her if I could have, Jax," Wyatt says tensely, holding the arms of my sofa like he is close to ripping it apart.

Jaxson doesn't say anything, I watch as Jaxson and Wyatt just stare at each other for a long time before Jaxson nods.

"For Winter. I can't forget everything that's happened between us, but Demi wouldn't want this. You're my brother," Jaxson says.

"For Winter," he responds with a nod of his head.

"Can we all hug now? I like group hugs." Atti says, and Dabriel whacks him on the arm. The tension leaves the room as everyone laughs.

"We have to leave tonight, Winter," Wyatt says, and Jaxson tenses up.

"No, I've just gotten her back, and she is coming back, to my pack with me for the night."

"My father, "Wyatt replies as he stands.

"Can wait. I need to see the pack," I tell Wyatt, who tensely nods. I know he doesn't like the idea, but he seems to be giving me time.

"I have friends I need to see in the pack before we leave, is that okay?" I ask Wyatt as he watches me tensely. I walk over and wrap my arms around his waist and hug him. He hesitates a little before kissing the top of my head and pulls me closer.

"Yes, but Dabriel and Atti are going with you. They can bring you to me if you need to feed."

"I don't need to," I start, but Jax puts his hand on my shoulder.

"You are all welcome in my pack," he tells them.

"Sorted, now who is cooking dinner at your pack these days?" Atti asks, looking excited as I turn and I smile at him as he winks at me.

23

WINTER

The drive to the pack was a little awkward and partly scary because Jaxson was driving. The guys just didn't know how to speak to each other after years of no talking. Or at least that's what I think has happened. I can see them being friends once, brothers even.

"So, is it cool being alpha now?" Atti asks, and Jaxson looks back at him for a second. I hold the handle of the door as Jaxson swerves out of the way of a car. I take it back, I don't want them to talk because Jaxson apparently can't drive and talk without nearly killing us.

"Not exactly. The war has been going on so long, since my sister's death and the deaths of many other wolves at the vampire king's hand. When the war was declared, the pack got used to losing people, but now they are losing hope. Things are changing. The pack lost eight wolves in the battle, and we still don't know who killed Fergus in the first place. The pack is grieving and feeling lost," Jaxson replies. I put my hand on his arm.

"I liked Fergus, he never told on us when he caught us meeting up," Atti says.

"That's because he wanted to come with us. We were seventeen and going to find girls. Fergus was younger and couldn't talk to girls," Jaxson says.

"Yeah, that would've been a problem, not that we were very good at getting girls anyway," Atti says with a little laugh.

"If your chat-up lines are anything like they are now, then I can see the problem," I say, and they laugh.

"I always had to speak for them, they never got girls," Jaxson says with a smirk.

"Come on, we are not that bad." Atti whacks Jaxson's arm, and he laughs.

"You once told a girl that you thought her mouth looked big. That was the first thing you said to her, she threw her drink at you as a response," Dabriel replies dryly. I turn to him, and he flashes me a little smile.

"Okay, that was a bad day, but it was the only thing nice about her," Atti admits.

"That's terrible," I laugh.

"I know this is going to sound bad, but how many people have you guys slept with?" I ask. I probably don't want the answer, but it's a little annoying that they seem far more experienced than I am. I've slept with two guys. One was a guy from school and my first time, but we didn't work well together, so we broke up. The second was my asshole of an ex, who liked to sleep with other girls. It was different with him because he was good in bed, but I guess it was his experience with other girls that taught him how to be good.

"I don't want to answer that," Jaxson says looking away.

"Only a few," Atti says, and I turn to see him looking away.

"Dab?"

"No one. Angels can only sleep with their mate, I always intended that to be you," he replies, and I look at him in shock.

"Show off," Jaxson mutters as I blush.

"Why didn't you wait? Not that I'm mad or jealous," I say, knowing it does sound jealous.

"For wolves, it's difficult not to have a sexual relationship sometimes for a release. I didn't want to go mad and end up mating with Esta. Nonetheless, the prophecy was ancient, and who knew if you actually existed?"

"Yeah, what if we met you, and you had a husband and two kids?" Atti asks. I sense the guilt when I turn slightly to face him.

"I see your point. I don't think I could put my whole life on hold for a story," I tell him. None of them reply, but I do get it. I can't say I'm not a little jealous that anyone got to be with my hot men first. Wait, they aren't all mine, or are they?

We soon get to the line of trees that marks the perimeter of the pack, and Jaxson drives us through after giving permission for Dab and Atti to come in. The pack doesn't look any different, the same cabins and the same paths. The main difference is that there are no kids running around, and the people smile sadly at us as we drive past. Jaxson drives the car in front of the main cabin, and we all get out. I let Jaxson take my hand and lead me to the front door. It's weird to think that he is alpha now. There are two wolves, standing guard outside like before. One of them is black and the other is slightly smaller and brown. They nod at Jaxson as he walks us past, Atti, and Dabriel following closely behind us. We walk into the lounge, and I see Anna standing next to the fire. She is watching it and doesn't seem to notice us come in.

"Anna," I say gently, and she turns to face me. Her face is red from crying, and her bump is so much bigger than when I last saw her. It hurts my chest to see her looking so vulnerable and lost.

"Winter, oh god," she says with a shocked smile, and I let go of Jaxson to run over to her. She pulls me into a big hug the second I'm close enough, and we embrace for a long time. I even feel her baby kick my stomach.

"I shouldn't have let Esta take me away that night. I should have saved you," she says.

"I'm okay, Anna, are you?" I ask her.

"Some days, not always. I have a few months left before this baby comes, and I have to be prepared," she says softly, a little crack in her words is all that I can hear to suggest it's hard for her to say.

"Fergus would be proud of you, he was a good man," I say, echoing the words that I told Jaxson earlier.

"Winter?" I hear being shouted behind me and Anna lets go of me. I turn to see Freddy jump over a sofa and crush me to him. Damn, did he get bigger? He's almost as tall as me now. I kiss the top of his head of brown hair, the blond tips reminding me who he is. Freddy smells so much like Jaxson, but there's a hint of something else. I can't explain it, but I couldn't tell before. It must be a weird new vampire thing. Can I even call myself a vampire? I'm not really, I'm just different, and like Freddy, I guess.

"I was so scared that Uncle J was wrong, and you weren't alive. I tried to find you in the fight, but I had to get rid of a vampire in the house who wanted to kill me. I did find my swords, and I saw you out the window. I saw that stupid, big vampire take you away. I missed you," he says, crying into my shoulder. I hold him close to me, feeling more than a little sad that the first time he saw his father was when he was carrying me away, he doesn't even understand what happened.

"Oh, Freddy. I'm so sorry I scared you. You know I wouldn't leave you if I didn't have to. I was having a long sleep because the vampire you saw saved me, and I couldn't come back to you," I tell him.

I hear a muffled reply, "You're not leaving now, are you?"

I look over at Jaxson with pleading eyes. I can't tell him I have to leave for a while again. Dabriel and Atti are staring at Freddy, and I know that they won't let this go.

"Freddy, let Winter sit down. It's been a long day," Jaxson's deep voice says. Freddy does and takes my hand in his. I sit on the sofa, and Freddy sits as close to me as possible, without getting in my lap. Jaxson seems to find this funny because he is openly smirking.

"Uncle J?" Atti questions Jaxson who nods as an answer.

"I didn't realise you had a child, Anna."

"Freddy is Demi's son. Jaxson has brought him up."

"I didn't know she had a child."

"Yes, when she came back from the vampires she was pregnant. She told us she had a relationship with another wolf that was kept there, but he died."

"Interesting, and I'm sorry for your losses, Freddy," Dabriel says to Freddy, who stares at him.

"Uncle J was like a dad, anyway," he replies, and Dabriel tenses. Atti is looking at us in apparent shock but quickly hides his reaction as I shake my head at him. The room goes into a very uncomfortable silence.

"We need a private chat," Dabriel says darkly, and Jaxson glares at him.

"Freddy, go and get Katy and Harris."

"I'll go and cook something for us all," Anna says, walking from the room. Her usually happy self is gone, and I'm scared I won't see it again.

"You'll be here when I get back?" Freddy asks me, and I nod. He moves away and goes out the door. Everyone watches him leave.

"Is that Wyatt's son?" Atti asks loudly when it's been a few minutes since Freddy left, and there's no chance of him over hearing us.

"Yes, "Jaxson replies. The one-word answer floats around the room, and none of us know how to respond.

"Are you going to bother explaining why Wyatt doesn't know? How a half-breed is even possible?" Dabriel asks, moving to stand in front of Jaxson. I've never seen Dabriel angry before, his wings flutter behind him, and his skin is faintly showing symbols. Both of them start staring each other down, as they are the same height. When I see Dabriel's wings starting to spread out, and Jaxson's eyes start glowing, I know I have to intervene. I move in between them as the power in the room becomes frightening. I see Atti moving closer, most likely to stop this if it goes too far. It's a tight fit with Jaxson at my front, our bodies pressed tightly together. Dabriel's hard body is pressed against my back, and it's hard for me to even focus on what we were arguing about: Freddy, Wyatt's son.

"Jaxson, I know you didn't hide Freddy from Wyatt because of anger. I know because you love him like your child, and you wouldn't ever hurt him like that. They just want to know and help you. Dabriel is worried about Wyatt," I tell Jaxson who looks down at me. His eyes slowly return to their normal green, and he nods. I take a deep breath, I was worried he wouldn't listen to me.

I hug him carefully and let him keep me in his arms as I turn around. Dabriel is looking down at me, I'm surprised there is so much passion in his eyes. My breath catches as I'm sure I can smell how much he wants to kiss me right now. As much as I want to kiss him. I've always felt this desire for him, it's overwhelming and sucks you in.

"How is he alive?" Atti asks breaking the eye connection between Dabriel and me. Dabriel moves away, his arms crossed tightly across his chest as he stares at Jaxson above me. Jaxson keeps his arm around my waist as he talks.

"I don't know. When he was born, we didn't know what to expect. I was sure he would die. He didn't."

"He smells and looks just like a wolf. The only giveaway is his aura. I guess you've never let an angel see him," Dabriel says.

"He hasn't left the pack. He is a regular wolf. In fact, he's stronger than all the wolves near his age, he has immunity to silver, and can heal super-fast," he tells them, and they look a little shocked.

"Why did you hide him from us? We would have helped you, brother," Atti asks eventually, as he sits on the sofa. He rubs his face with his hands, looking stressed.

"Demi made me swear not to tell Wyatt. When she first came here, she was so scared of his father. She would wake up screaming, refuse to eat, and she wouldn't leave the house. She told me she would leave with Freddy if I didn't do a blood oath. I wanted to refuse, but I couldn't. She wasn't right in her head at that time, and I knew she would run. I swore not to tell anyone that could tell Wyatt," Jaxson says, and they both nod their heads.

"He needs to know," I say to Jaxson.

"He won't take it well, lass," he replies. I can just imagine how badly that could go. I am his mate, so shouldn't I tell him? Maybe he'll listen to me for a second before going to punch and likely try to kill Jaxson.

"I'll tell him. When the time is right, I can tell him for you," I tell Jaxson. He nods down at me, in agreement.

"Winter!" Katy shouts from the doorway. She knocks Dabriel out of the way as she gets to me and pulls me into a hug. I remember how painful their hugs could be before, and now it's not as bad. I wonder if I'm stronger than before. Katy pulls back and looks at me. I look her over, too, she seems older than when I last saw her, just like Freddy. I think losing Fergus, and the other wolves have had a bad effect on the pack. Katy is wearing jeans and a pink top, she looks okay considering the last time I saw her is when I dragged her into the training room, and she had been shot. I notice her hair is shorter, but it's tied back, so I can't see how short.

"What happened to you? You look like you've just come from an intensive makeover trip like they do on TV for ugly humans. Not that you weren't hot before, but wow," she says, and I laugh.

"Long story, but it wasn't a trip," I say, and she nods. Katy takes my hand and gives it a squeeze.

"You saved my life," I say, as I held onto her hand. I remember her jumping in front of me and knocking me down. I have no doubt I would have died there and then from that bullet. I was lucky in a way that I died closer to the main action, where Wyatt saw me and managed to save me.

"You likely saved mine too, by moving me. You're pack to me," she shrugs, and I give her another quick hug. I'm so happy to see her okay.

"So, who invited the witch and the angel?" Katy asks as she looks around and then laughs. "That sounded like the start of a lame joke," she says, and I laugh.

"This is Atti and Dabriel. They're friends of mine," I introduce them, and they both nod for a hello.

"How do you always find the hot guys?" she whispers to me, and I smile.

"Don't know," I say, looking at them. I don't know how to believe they are my destined mates. I would thank the goddess for sending me them if I was sure she was real.

"Let's go and help Anna," I say to Katy who nods. I leave the boys with a warning look and say, "Behave and no fights."

"Yes, madam." Atti winks, and Dabriel whacks him on the back of his head as I laugh.

"How the hell did you get those guys to listen to you?" Katy asks as we walk out.

"I didn't. I'm just friends with them," I say honestly, well not that honest, but I don't want to explain the whole situation to her. At the moment, Atti and Dabriel are just friends. They have suggested they like me, but how much of it is the prophecy and how much is how they feel?

"Friends . . . right." Katy laughs. Anna is sliding around the kitchen when we come in, and she stops when she sees me.

"We've come to help," I say with a smile. Anna smiles back a little, but it seems forced. I want to tell her that I don't think she should be cooking a meal for so many people while she is heavily pregnant, but that will just upset her. I can see she is trying to keep herself busy and help in any way she can.

"I'm just making pasta. Light and easy to make. You could help me serve it up," she says, and we all get to work sorting the food out.

When it's all on the table, Anna shouts, "Food's ready." And, I'm surprised how loud she can be.

"How's the baby?" I ask as we sit down. Anna waits to answer as Jaxson takes the seat to the left of me and Dabriel sits on my other side. Atti grumbles but takes the seat next to Anna in front of me. Katy and Freddy sit on the ends.

"Healthy. I'm trying to stay happy for my child. It's not easy when I miss him," she says and puts down her fork.

"When he's born, you will have a piece of Fergus, Anna. He would want you to be happy," I tell her, and she nods at me and starts eating. I don't know how to sympathise with her.

We all eat while everyone chats. Atti seems to like Freddy as he shows him something funny on his phone.

"That's the first time I've seen Anna eat a real meal in a month. Thank you," Jaxson whispers in my ear. His hand slides under the table and rests on my knee.

"No problem," I mutter as I start feeling dizzy as he rubs my thigh. I try to eat the pasta, but it doesn't taste right. Everything is going blurry, and my hands are shaking. I don't know what's happening to me, but as I run my tongue over my teeth as they ache, I feel two small, sharp points. Fucking hell, I'm a vampire. It hasn't hit home until now, and all I can focus on is how the food in front of me looks terrible. All I can smell is Dabriel next to me, Jaxson and Atti smell good too, but Dabriel smells like a chocolate sundae right now.

"My little wildfire needs to eat," Dabriel whispers in my other ear. Jaxson and Atti hear because they both look at me.

"My room," Jaxson says, he takes my hand and leads me out the room as everything gets blurrier. I hear Atti explaining to the others what we are doing, but everything else drones out. When we get to the stairs, I stop as everything blurs but the smell of Dabriel and Jaxson. I try to get to Dabriel, but he moves away, and Jaxson steps in front of him. Jaxson lifts me into a hug, not an ounce of fear in his eyes.

My body seems to know what to do as I go to kiss his neck. I don't think, I only feel my teeth painfully screaming at me, and I sink my teeth into his neck. The taste of Jaxson is amazing, I feel myself being moved as I drink, the revulsion I expected to feel isn't there. I wrap my legs around his waist as my hands go into his hair. I can't help the loud moan that escapes my lips as I rock my body against Jaxson. I pull my mouth away, and look up at him. Our faces are inches apart, and my body is desperate for him. Jaxson takes my mouth in a passionate kiss. A kiss meant for a dying person, a kiss that is so passionate that I can't comprehend it.

"Winter," he mumbles against my lips, and his lips go down my neck. My neck falls back in pleasure, the need to be with him is ruling every thought.

"Guys, you have an audience," Atti's voice comes through the haze. Jaxson tenses up but removes his lips from my neck. A little growl fills the air from Jaxson. It's not so much threatening as it is a warning.

"J, she isn't herself. She's jacked up on sex hormones. You don't want your first time to be like this," Atti says, my mind clears a little, and I know he is right. I glance up at Jaxson, and his eyes are still glowing a threatening green.

"You've already swapped enough blood, sex would make you mates forever, and Winter needs to choose that," Dabriel says, coming into the room, and I hear the door slam shut.

"Dab?" I ask. Everything hits me quickly. My hand falls to my now normal teeth.

"Jaxson, I'm so sorry. I don't know what happened. I just," I blurt out quickly, Jaxson stops me with a small kiss.

"Don't over-think this. You're part vampire now or a full one. Who knows? But if you need blood, I'm here," he says as he kisses my nose. The little gesture makes me smile.

"Me too, if I get that display," Atti says, and it makes me laugh.

Jaxson slides me painfully slowly down his body until my feet touch the floor.

"I feel better, all day I've been tired and a little stressed, but now," I say, and they all smile at me. It must be a regular thing for a vampire.

“Whose room is this?” I look around, there’s a massive sword on the wall over the dresser. The handle is green and brown. As I look closer, I can see the sword has wolves running down the middle of it. It’s so big I would be worried I’d fall over if I tried to pick it up.

“I finally get to see your sword, you weren’t joking when you said it was in your room,” I say.

“He didn’t mean that sword, I’m sure he meant his cock,” Atti says and Dabriel whacks the back of his head, again.

“Stop doing that shit,” Atti says, rubbing his head.

“You’re an idiot,” Dabriel says, and Atti grins as he replies, “Takes one to know one.”

“Make that a child as well,” Jaxson says, and Atti just laughs.

"I’ll go tell Wyatt about your feeding, and keep him up to date. I need to visit my mother too, so I'll be a while," Atti says and comes over to me. He gently kisses my cheek and then disappears.

"That's creepy," I say looking at where he just stood.

"Can I have a word with Winter alone, Jax?" Dabriel asks us both. He’s leaning against the closed door. His purple eyes are watching me carefully.

"Yes." Jaxson nods at Dabriel. "We’ll stay in here

tonight," he says to me, and his hand brushes mine as he walks to the door that Dabriel opens.

"I'm going to help Anna clean up and get Freddy to bed. Call me if you need me," Jax says by the door. Dabriel and he stare at each other for a second, and Jaxson nods.

"Good luck with that." I smile at him. He chuckles as he walks out, and Dabriel shuts the door behind him.

"Come here," he says, holding his arms open for me. I don't think as I practically run to him. He holds me tightly to his chest, and we both don't move for a while. I breathe in his scent, he smells like the sweetest thing I've ever smelt, and I feel my teeth getting longer.

"You smell like, well I guess an angel," I say, and he laughs.

"Well, that's what I am. I didn't want you to feed on me first, angel blood is a lot stronger than other kinds. I can't always be around in the next few weeks, and you will need someone else. Don't think I don't want you, never believe that for a second," he says and looks down at me.

"You sure you don't just like me because of the prophecy?" I ask him.

"I know we haven't spent much time together, but one of my powers is to see the future. I cannot see yours well, only little things here and there, but the day I met you I had a big vision."

"What of?" I ask into his chest.

"All of us. We were at a lake, Jax and Wyatt were in the water playing ball with Freddy. You were lying on my chest, and Atti was cooking some food on a barbecue. I never knew who Freddy was, but he was much older in my vision. He looked around eighteen."

"And, you like me because of that?" I ask a little confused.

"No, for the peace and love I felt. The completion. The

way you looked at me and how I felt for you. The vision showed me what I had already guessed. You are my future, Winter."

"Dab," I say as I look up, his skin is faintly glowing, and the effect is remarkable.

"You are so beautiful, Winter. I could spend the rest of my life staring into your eyes and never wanting to be anywhere else," he whispers. I don't say anything as I feel my heart pounding, for most guys that would sound cheesy but not him.

Dabriel is sweet, caring, and to me, he seems too romantic. I lift my head, sighing and press my lips to his.

The first brush of our lips is all me until Dabriel takes over. His mouth widens, and our lips crash together in a strong passion. He moans as he lifts me higher, and I feel him moving us.

We don't break our kiss as he lays me back on the bed and hovers over me as he deepens the kiss.

"Dabriel," I whisper as his body brushes against mine.

"Why do I feel like I'm always missing something?" Atti's voice says from right next to us. Our lips freeze, and Dab lifts his head to stare at Atti. My eyes widen when I see his massive wings. They are full out behind his head, and I reach one hand up to stroke across his wing.

"It's because you have terrible timing, Atti," Dabriel answers with a shiver. His purple eyes look down at me, and he moves his body off of mine. I sit up, and Dabriel sits firmly next to me, his hand on my lower back.

"Wyatt is a little angry that you lost control, but at least it was Jaxson you decided to make a meal of," Atti sits on the bed on the other side of me. I feel like I'm in a perfect place, a place a lot of girls would sell everything they own to be in.

"Anyway, Wyatt and I think it's safer if I spell you now

and then see my mother later. I'll spell you to have brown eyes and hide your scent, but it won't work if you lose control and go all silver-eyed."

I turn to look at him on the bed as he takes my hand. "So, no getting angry?" I ask.

"No, Love," he answers seriously. I don't like seeing Atti being serious, it's weird.

"I need to return to my kind. I've been away too much, and my council is getting suspicious," Dabriel says, and I nod in understanding.

"Okay, I will see you soon, right?" I ask.

"Yes, and the next time we meet, I know our kiss won't be interrupted," he grins and stands up.

"How do you know that?" I ask.

"The same way I told you not to go to the party. You still ignored me," he says with a slight bit of anger in his gaze.

"I paid the price for that," I say, regretting my actions.

"We all did, and I should have been there, I won't let you fall again, Winter."

"He is good at the romantic shit," Atti comments.

I laugh, "You're right."

"Atti, I need a lift," he says, and Atti nods.

"Be right back," Atti says and kisses my head. I watch them both disappear before lying back on the very comfy bed.

24

WINTER

"She was born in the winter, Winter is her name, oh she brings the time of change, change that's needed and a change that is planned," the childlike, female voice sings in the background of the cold room I'm in. What's with the weird songs? I look around, and I can't see the person who is singing, the song is just a hum in the background as it fades away. The room is empty, it looks like an apothecary with dozens of herbs in little bottles on a bench. There are many shelves all around, all of them are littered with glowing stones and jars of things I don't recognise.

"Why him?" a man shouts as he slams the door open on the room I'm in. His figure is massive, and large, black wings are fluttering behind him. They have white tips making me wonder what kind of angel he is. Elissa walks in after him and shuts the door. The man is tall with long, white hair that touches the floor, his purple eyes are the first thing I see, and I wonder if he is related to Dabriel. He looks so much like him, but this man is older, the grey in his hair coming out. He looks around the empty room with anger. Elissa places a hand on his shoulder, but he steps away, and I can see Elissa for the first time. She looks older than I usually see her, I can tell from one look at her. She looks closer to the age when I saw her die, and with the man Leo.

Her black hair is piled in dozens of braids on her head, and she is wearing a green dress. The dress is far too revealing, and the man is just dressed in a black toga skirt. The man's chest is hard not to look at, he is extremely muscular and tanned like he is out in the sun all day.

"Nicolas, I love him as much as I love you. This was never a competition between us all," Elissa says sadly.

"No, because he had you first, and he left you. Now he walks back into our lives, and you claim to want us still. He is the king of the demons, and even your sister doesn't trust him," he spits out and turns to face her.

"Plenty of women had all of you first, and you don't see me upset when you hold your children or grandchildren," she replies, I watch her face carefully, and I feel she regrets saying that.

"That was before I saw you and before I loved you. I love my children and you equally," he replies, but his words are full of anger.

"Then can you see how I love him equally to you all?" she asks, using his words against him.

"This is a mistake, Elissa, but I won't leave you for it. Love makes even the goddesses fall, apparently," he says, and she moves to stand close to him. He kisses her lightly and pulls away.

"No more secrets, Elissa, I mean it," he says, holding her chin with his fingers.

"No more," she says carefully, and he lets go. She turns to look at me in the corner of the room, and her face lights up in happiness.

"We need to get up, lass," A deep voice drifts into my tired mind and pulls me out of the dream. I snuggle myself deeper into the warm pillow I'm lying on. I'm comfy as my mind replays everything in that dream. Elissa loved a demon king and an angel, I think. The man I saw her with before, Leo, looked too much like Jaxson not to be related to him, so he must have been a wolf. I don't get why I'm having these dreams of her, what's the point of them?

"Winter," the same voice repeats and a big hand slides down my face. I open my eyes to a golden chest.

I look up to see that I'm lying on top of Jaxson. My body is wrapped around his, and he's lying on some pillows. A quilt is wrapped around me, and I note quickly that I'm still in my clothes from yesterday. I move a little and feel something very hard pressing into my thigh.

"It's not every day you wake up with a beautiful woman in your arms," Jaxson says as a response, and I look up at him.

"No, I guess not, but I think you must be mistaking me for someone else. I can't look good with morning hair and bad breath," I mutter, and he laughs. He pulls me up to him and presses his lips to mine. A sweet kiss that starts an inferno and soon I'm on my back, and Jaxson is on top of me. His tongue slips inside my mouth as he presses himself between my jean-covered legs.

His one hand moves slowly down my body, and just before his hand goes up my shirt a knock on the door stops us.

"I want to see Winter before she leaves for the vampire den!" Freddy shouts.

"It's a castle, not a den," Atti shouts down the corridor.

"Whatever! I still want to see Winter, but I'm not stupid enough to walk into that room without knocking," Freddy says with a hint of sarcasm. The little wolf is brave, I'll give him that.

"I can go in," Atti says.

I laugh into Jaxson's neck as he shouts, "You all need to bugger off."

"Only because you don't want to leave Winter," Freddy shouts back, and we hear him high-five Atti outside the room. We listen to their footsteps as I'm sure Atti is distracting him for a little bit.

"God, I'm going to kill Atti, he is a bad influence on Freddy," Jaxson says, and I laugh more.

"I think Atti is a bad influence on most people." I smile.

"I can't see you for at least a week because my aunt's pack is moving here. My aunt and her four mates run the biggest pack in Europe, and it's in Scotland, so they won't be long. There are four other packs travelling this way, too," Jaxson says and then kisses me gently.

"They want you as their alpha?" I ask him.

"Yes," Jaxson replies quietly. He looks so stressed as he leans over me. I just notice that he must have shaved and showered as his face is smooth. I guess I was exhausted to have missed that. Jaxson's hair is still longer than usual, he has to brush it out of the way as it falls into his eyes at the front. It makes him look wilder, more like a wolf.

"I'll miss you, too," I tell him.

"I can't protect you there. I trust Wyatt, but his family is a different matter."

"Wyatt will keep me safe. You can trust me with him at my side, hopefully, we won't stay long, anyway."

"I still worry about you, I lost you once, and it shattered me, Winter. This is my second chance from the goddess," he tells me, and my stomach interrupts him by growling loudly.

"I'll be right back. I'm going to get you some breakfast before your stomach decides to try and eat me," he says with a wink, and I laugh as my stomach rumbles again. He slides out of bed, and I see that he's only wearing jeans.

His naked chest looks better than it feels. The dips on the sides that go into a very nice V shape I want to touch. Unfortunately, Jaxson picks up a shirt off the end of the bed and pulls it on. Damn, it's like watching a reverse strip tease. Why did I sleep with him pulling that shirt off in the first place? Some things have to come before sleep, like watching Jaxson undress.

Jaxson pulls the door open as I sit up, and Freddy is waiting on the other side. I'm sure Atti couldn't keep him away any longer.

"Go on then," he waves a hand towards me, and Freddy grins. He jumps onto the bed, making me nearly bounce off.

"Winter, it was my birthday last week, and Anna got me this top. Do you like it?" He shows me his Harry Potter top that has 'Expecto Patronum' and a wand lighting up at the end.

"That's wicked." I grin, and he laughs.

"So, you and my uncle? Does that make you my auntie? Auntie Win?" he asks.

"Err, I guess." I smile.

"Cool, I like it. Anyway, Atti is a witch, and that Dabriel is an angel. How cool is that?" he tells me, and I nod with a laugh.

Looking at Freddy now, I don't know how I missed that he's Wyatt's son. They look so similar in their faces, the same nose, and same grin. The eyes are his mother's, and the blond tips on his hair must be from his dad.

"You okay? You looked at me weird," Freddy says.

"Sorry, just a long day ahead."

"My new, little buddy, I need to spell Winter, and you have training," Atti says from the doorway.

"Okay." He drags out the word and hugs me.

"He has the same moody attitude as someone else," Atti says once Freddy leaves.

"I knew I recognised it from somewhere." I chuckle.

"I made this for you, it will keep the spell on you as long as you keep it on and no silver eyes. It will make them look brown to everyone and mask your scent, so you just smell like a vampire."

Atti holds up a long necklace with a pink crystal on end.

"What kind of crystal is it?" I ask. It looks nothing like I've seen before, the inside of the stone has dozens of little pink things moving, and the outside is translucent.

"None that humans have ever seen or heard of. They are called Rose hearts. We grow them with our magic. We grow a lot of different crystal trees in our city. They all do different things, most are used to contain magic. Like Jaxson's ward, there's a large glass in the house somewhere that links his blood to it and keeps the department up. I'll have to ask him who did it for him. I did the last one for Fergus," he says with a little hint of sadness.

"This crystal keeps magic inside it. A little of mine is in it, and it will make sure my spell doesn't wear off," he says as he walks over to me.

"Also, don't let anyone see it, witch stones are well known to hold spells," Atti tells me seriously.

"Okay, let's get this done," I say getting off the bed and walking over to him. He puts the necklace over my head. His grey eyes start glowing as he speaks some words I can't understand or hear. A warm glow fills my chest by the necklace, and I look down to see it glowing before it stops.

"It's worked." Atti grins, and I smile back. Atti is so handsome when he's this close. From a distance, he looks scary with his massive build and huge hands that look like he could squash you in two. It's when you get close and see the playfulness in his eyes that the giant suddenly becomes something else. He's handsome and perfect, every part of his face is free of any imperfections. He doesn't have the stress or grief that follows Jaxson and Wyatt. Well, if he does, he hides it well. Dabriel is very dangerous, and I think that's something to do with the responsibility he has in his life. Atti has been sheltered from that, but I wonder when he takes his throne, will he change? I don't think I want him to.

"Here, I brought you some normal food," Jaxson says coming into the room. I realise I've just been staring at Atti, and I move around him. I smile at Jaxson as I accept the bacon sandwich he made me.

I finish the food and freshen up in the bathroom. Atti gave me some of my clothes, and I change into a cream, turtle-neck dress and black leggings. I slip the coat on and my knee-high black boots. My hair I leave down, and the necklace is hidden well under my clothes. I didn't even need to do anything to my hair. It still looks like I've just walked out of a salon. Most girls would love this magic hair shit.

"Looking hot, Winter," Atti says with a whistle. Jaxson looks me over and nods at me. I know he likes it, but he doesn't have to say it.

"We need to leave," Atti says gently. Jaxson moves towards me and pulls me to him for a long kiss.

"Soon," he whispers as he lets go. I know it's only going to be awhile, but it doesn't feel right leaving Jaxson. Half of me wants to stay with him, but I know I need to be stronger. I need to be the kind of girl he has at his side and not an emotional wreck.

I move towards Atti, who pulls me to his chest when I get near.

"It feels weird, but just hold your breath. It helps. The first time is always the worst," he tells me before I feel myself disappearing. I can't look back at Jaxson as I have to leave him, so I close my eyes and hold my breath as Atti said. A hot sensation fills my whole body until it feels like

I'm going to explode, and then my feet hit the ground. My arms are clenched around Atti.

"Winter, you're here," Atti whispers into my ear, and I finally find the strength to let go of him. The cold temperature is the first thing I notice. The second is that we are in the middle of snow-covered woods. High trees, covered in snow, line the sky, and the ground has several layers of snow on it. The temperature is freezing, but my coat helps a little. I'm not as cold as I think I should be. It must be another new thing to add to the 'Winter's weird shit she can make' list.

"Where are we?" I ask Atti.

"Wyatt will meet us here in a bit. I have to leave and come back as an official guest. I can't come as your friend or Wyatt's. The vampire king is doing business with my mother, and I want to find out what it is. This trip works both ways, I can look after you and find out what's going on that scares my mother," he tells me, and I nod in understanding.

"Winter, I–" he starts, but the sound of loud horses behind me makes me turn back, and I can see a few horses coming towards us.

"Horses? Where the hell are the cars?" I mutter, and Atti chuckles.

"You can't get a car up here. It's about another half an hour on horseback to get to the castle," he tells me.

"This sounds like a fucked-up fairy tale," I mumble, but Atti hears.

"Here comes your knight in shining armour, "Atti says as he takes my hand, and I see Wyatt riding towards me on a white horse.

Wyatt looks like a real knight on a white horse, he even has a silver sword strapped to the side of the horse. I didn't know he could use a sword, but it makes sense. How strange is my life?

Behind Wyatt, are Drake and Alex on tall, brown horses. A grey horse with a young girl riding it is following them. The girl looks younger than me–around eighteen, if I had to guess. She's pretty under her hood from what I can see, and I can just see the ends of her long, black hair. Her nearly black eyes meet mine like she knows I'm watching her. Alex and the girl are wearing big, black cloaks that cover them, and Drake has a long, black coat on. They both look snow covered, I wonder how long they've been riding.

"Hey," I say when Wyatt stops in front of me. The white horse is huge this close up. She or he has a long, silver mane, and its very intelligent eyes watch me. I gently stroke my hand up the horse's nose and the horse whinnies a little.

"Come, we need to leave, Winter," Wyatt says tensely, looking around where we are.

"Thanks for the lift, I suppose I will see you in a bit," I turn to Atti.

"Remember, I'm not your friend in court. I don't want to ignore you, but I must in public. Bye, Love," he says and disappears once I step away.

"Hey, girl, it's bloody freezing," Alex shouts, and I smile over at her.

"I agree," I laugh.

Wyatt holds a hand out to me, and once I put my hand in his, he pulls me up in front of him with surprising speed. I manage to get my other leg over the horse as Wyatt holds my waist with both of his hands. He pulls me back to him, so I can rest on him as he holds the reins in front of me. Drake's and Alex's horses ride ahead, and the other girl nods at me as she passes to follow.

"How are you?" he asks once we set off. It takes a minute for me to get used to the feeling of riding, I hadn't ridden a horse before but did use to ride donkeys at the beach in the summer, when I was a child. They would get them out for the tourists, but Alex and I would save up our pocket money to have a go once a week. I guess it's not too different, but Wyatt is in charge, and I'm just holding on to him.

"A little overwhelmed, but coping with it all," I say, and I hear his grunt as a reply.

"Who is the girl?" I ask, looking over to see her just behind Drake and Alex.

"That's Drake's younger sister. It was demanded that she come to court with us," he says.

"Why?" I ask.

"She is of age and unmated. Very unusual for vampire females. They usually have at least one mate by now," he tells me.

"Why is it unusual? She only looks eighteen," I ask.

"She is only eighteen, and we have a low survival rate for our children. Girls rarely survive past the age of five. Drake's parents didn't expect another child after Drake, and they lived in the human world when she born. She was brought up there, and my father allowed it. She's the first vampire female not to be brought up in court, and that's only because Drake's dad used to be on the council," he says.

I rest my back against him as we speed up. "The council?"

"Yes, there are four of them, all chosen by the king and replaced every hundred years. They make the small decisions and advise the king on the big ones," he says.

"So, they are important," I ask.

"Very," he replies.

“Where are we in the world?” I ask. It’s weird to think I’m not in Wales anymore.

“France. Most of the vampire population live here,” he tells me. We don’t talk anymore as the wind gets louder and the snow starts falling. My coat is slowly getting wetter, and I’m feeling a tiny bit cold now.

"Are you mad at me?" I whisper as we pass a frozen stream of water.

"No, I'm angry at myself. I didn't protect you, and I don't deserve you," Wyatt says close to my ear. His arms wrap tighter around me.

"That's utter bullshit," I say and hear him cough, I guess he didn’t expect me to say that.

"I chose to go to the pack, and I decided not to hide. It was my choice, and I'm sorry for what happened." I say, and he kisses the top of my head.

"I'm sorry also. I didn't want to bring you here. It’s taking everything in me not to turn this horse around and run away with you," he says.

"Why don't we?" I ask.

"He will kill everyone you care about, Winter. I won't let him do that, and these are my people. I am their prince," he says, and I glance at Alex on the other horse.

"I get it," I say softly.

"Just don't wind him up," he mutters, and I nod against his chest. The rest of the trip is tiring on my thighs, I'm honestly worried how I'm going to get off this horse when my legs feel locked together.

"Welcome home, Prince," a loud voice shouts as we pass through a ward much like what the wolves have. The sick feeling is stronger, and I have to hold in a gasp.

My stomach is forgotten as I look up at the castle.

The castle is huge. I can’t even see all of it as we stop outside the massive, stone walls and a metal gate. The castle has dozens of towers and one huge one in the middle. The central part seems like five floors because of the rows of windows. The castle is made out of grey stone and towers into the grey sky. The long, stone path leads up to the main castle, it has rows of tall trees on each side. The metal gates slide open, and Wyatt rides the horse inside, with the others following. Two guards are bowing low as we pass, and I can't see anything other than their snow-dotted blond hair. We stop as we wait for the gate to close behind us, and I stare up the scary castle. My fucked up fairy-tale is about to get a lot more real.

"By the way, you're a princess here," Wyatt says, as he shakes the reins, and his horse rides off towards the castle.

25

WINTER

We ride up to the castle and toward another large metal gate, which opens to a stone courtyard with a long, grey stone path leading to another level of the castle. The tall walls of the lower part of the castle surround it, and it's quiet. Very quiet and empty. I don't know if I expected to see lots of vampires with coffins, but this wasn't what I saw. Other than the stone walls looking aged from the snow, the place looks well kept. There are three tunnels going off the courtyard, and I can see some tables inside one. Another looks onto a big, open grassy field that's covered in snow. I can't see the other one from where we are.

Getting off the horse wasn't a problem because Wyatt got off first like a pro and then picked me up from off the horse. Drake's sister jumps off her horse and brushes her long, black hair over her shoulder as her hood falls. She walks up to Alex and Drake like it's nothing. I honestly can't say that I'm not jealous of her right now. Wyatt and Drake give the reins of the horses to the two vampire guards before they come back to us. The first few steps are a little uncomfortable for my thighs as we walk up the stone path and through the middle of the large, empty, stone courtyard towards to two large, old, wooden doors. I glance back at Alex who seems to be having the same trouble as she's holding onto Drake, and she winks at me. I hope there aren't any more horse rides in the future.

Wyatt holds my hand tightly in his as we wait for the large doors to be opened. I glance behind me at Alex who nods at me; her worried face mimics mine. Who would have thought we would be here now when we were packing our bags for university only a year ago? We were happy about all the freedom we would finally have. Apparently, our freedom comes at a high price. I glance over at Drake's sister, and I see the determined look on her face, and I force myself to look as strong as she does.

The door swings open, and the first thing I see is two middle-aged men. They both have black eyes and are standing with their arms behind their backs. They're wearing all black, with a red crown stitched over their hearts. The older one with slightly grey hair steps forward and places his closed fist over his heart as he bows.

"Prince Wyatt. We welcome you and your new mate home," he says, a thick accent coming out that sounds kind of French, but it's different than I've heard in the movies. I've never been to France before, I'm taking a wild guess we won't be going to see the Eiffel Tower anytime soon.

"We don't need to be this formal do we, Harold?" Wyatt asks as the man straightens up.

"Always breaking the rules, my Prince," he chuckles slightly. Harold looks me over, and my heart must be beating a million miles a minute that he will see through Atti's spell. The necklace feels warm against my chest like it wants to remind me that it's there.

"Always. This is Winter Masters. Winter, this is Harold Livingstone, part of my father's council of four," he says.

"It's lovely to meet you," I say.

Harold bows toward me like he did Wyatt. "The pleasure is mine, Princess," he replies smoothly.

I automatically correct him before I think about it, "I'm not a princess," I blurt out.

"Yes, you are, my mate. I'm sorry, Winter is very new the supernatural world," Wyatt explains, and his thumb rubs circles on my hand in comfort.

"Understood. Your father is busy this evening and will meet you all in the morning," Harold replies, looking at me again. The man doesn't seem bad, but I have to remember he isn't human. While he looks in his forties, he's likely decades older than that.

"Fine," Wyatt replies and looks down at me. I can't read his expression, and it's gone too fast for me to figure it out.

"My son, Easton, will take you all to your rooms." Harold waves a hand towards the man who hasn't said a word. Easton has short, blond hair, slightly shorter than Wyatt and a younger looking face. He seems okay.

"Thank you, Harold," Wyatt says and Harold bows once more before leaving. I watch him move through the doors, and I see a girl about my age walking down the steps, on the side of the courtyard, from the corner of my eye. She looks like a zombie as she walks into the castle past us all. I am so busy watching her, I don't notice that Drake has been talking to Wyatt.

"Leigha is staying in the room next to yours, and I will take the other side with Alex," he says.

"That's best," Wyatt says quietly as he watches me. His gaze goes to the girl just before she turns around the corner, and he looks back at me. His expression is neutral, and yet I feel he wants to say something to me. I look away and notice that Leigha is staring at me. She is stunning now that we are closer. Her hair is pitch-black, and it suits her toned, dark-gold skin. She has her hair braided in the top half, and the rest is down. She has the dark vampire eyes, a light row of freckles over her nose, and big, pouty lips. She looks a little like a doll, but her expression tells me she's not friendly. I can see the similarities to Drake; they both have the dark hair, but Drake has a lighter skin colour.

"Winter, let me show you around my home," Wyatt says and Harold's son, Easton, comes running over.

"My prince, I was told to take you to your room first."

"You don't need to. You will follow Drake to whatever place he wants and then tell anyone that asks that you did your job. Understood?" Wyatt asks. The power surrounding his words is almost too much for me to bear. I remember feeling the pressure in my head before when he used his powers. It's just the same now.

I feel like a bug being squashed, and he isn't even using it on me. I wonder what it's like for humans to have it used on them. I remember when we first met, he tried to get me to dance with him. If I were human, I would have.

"Yes, my prince," Easton replies robotically and turns to Drake. It looks like he will wait forever for whatever Drake asks him to do. Wyatt's power is scary.

"Do you use your power a lot on humans?" I ask him.

"No. Only when I feel they're scared of me and need to relax. Most humans can sense there's something dangerous about me."

"Is that why you tried to get me to dance when we first met?" I ask. Everyone is listening to our conversation other than Drake, who is talking to Easton.

"Yes, you looked like a little mouse about to get eaten. I

wanted you to talk to me, and the way you were watching the dancers," he shrugs as I look at him. "I thought you liked dancing," he says and kisses my hand.

"I don't, I have two left feet," I say, making him smile slightly at me.

"Come with me Winter, time for me to show you my home," Wyatt says as he holds his hand in front of him, and I walk ahead. Wyatt moves an arm around my waist, and we walk into the vampire castle. The last place I want to be.

26

WINTER

The inside of the castle is just what I expected it to be. We first walk into a long corridor with large stairs on each end. The decor looks like something out of the Middle Ages; a long, red, patterned rug stretches down the hallway on wooden floors. There are no photos or paintings on the castle walls. The place just seems empty. The lack of sounds is what is, indeed, strange, there are no footsteps of people or sounds of conversation in the air.

"This way," Wyatt whispers to me, and he walks us down the left corridor and up the stairs. I see several doors down the hall, but they're all closed. There's also a staircase going down under the stairs that I see.

The room we go into is far bigger. It's a big library with many bookcases lining the three walls, they have ladders to reach the highest level. The decor is cosy with soft-brown walls and dark, wooden floors. I spot a fireplace in the corner of the room next to a few cosy chairs. There's a massive, red and brown rug in the middle of the chamber and seven sofas placed around. There are many chairs dotted around too. The place just seems comfy, and the two huge windows let in enough light without having to use electric lights. There are two large chandeliers above that look electrical, so I can guess the castle is wired up somehow.

"This is the royal library. The history of our race and all the others is in here," Wyatt tells me and walks to the window of the room. It's so tall and overlooks a massive garden that must be in the middle of the castle. The garden is bursting with different colours, it's such a contrast to the grey castle and white snow on the ground.

"The royal gardens," Wyatt fills in my unasked question.

"Lovely," I say as I look around. The roses lining the opposite wall are the main attraction, with a water fountain in front of them. There are two people sitting on the edge of the fountain.

"Much like you, Sweetheart," Wyatt says making my heart tighten as I look over at him. Wyatt watches me carefully; the haunted man I have come to know doesn't seem so haunted anymore. I wonder how much it will affect to him to know what Demi and Jaxson hid from him. Will he hate me for keeping it secret until I can tell him?

We walk around the rest of the castle. Wyatt shows me the five living areas, a corridor full of rooms which he said houses most of the council and their families. He tells me the rest of the vampires live outside the castle on the other side, that part isn't attached to the castle. Wyatt takes me to the right aspect of the castle and through a few doors until we get to a row of five rooms. I'd never be able to find my way back here, this place is like a maze.

"This is mine," Wyatt says as he opens the door in the middle. I walk in as he holds it open, and my jaw drops at the massive room. There are three large windows and one large, glass door that looks like it opens to a balcony that overlooks the forest. The room has a large, four-poster wooden bed with white sheets that look new, and they match the white walls. There are three doors in the chambers and I guess they are for wardrobes and a bathroom. The room is relatively new, it doesn't fit the old theme of the castle, but I like it.

"I don't have any clothes," I mumble as Wyatt shuts the door.

"It's all taken care of, Winter," Wyatt says as he looks around the room, his face trying to hide some pain from me. The problem is that I'm starting to know him too well, the way he clenches his fists. The vacant look his eyes have when he's thinking of something wrong. When he's thinking of Demi.

"You okay?" I ask him.

He doesn't look at me as he answers. "I haven't been back here since I took Demi. Once I realised who she was, I trashed this room. I grew up with her, just thinking she was a normal wolf until my father bragged to everyone at a party that he had the prince of the wolves' half-sister," he says and walks over to the window.

"I took her to Jaxson the next day, and my father thought that she had just escaped. I had to leave her there and come back here, I couldn't go back into this room before today, and someone has replaced everything in it."

"Wyatt."

"I stayed next to my father's side, until I found out, she was dead. I found out when her body was thrown in front of my Dad," he tells me.

I don't know how to tell him how sorry I am for his loss. I want to tell him about Freddy, but I can't find the right words to say. "Who killed her?" I ask instead.

"Talen, he's one of the council, and you've seen him

before. He came to get you for my father, the one with the red crown marked on his head," he tells me, and I suppress a shiver at the memory of the big man with the dead look in his eyes.

"He's my father's closest friend and does anything he asks. I want you to stay far away from him. If he speaks to you, tell me." Wyatt says.

"I will," I say, and we go silent for a while. "Jaxson will kill him one day," I say, more of a thought than something I wanted to say out loud. I remember the promise Jaxson made when I first started to get to know him better. Jaxson wouldn't hesitate.

"I'll help. I wanted to kill him so many times, but I couldn't. Not without leaving Jaxson's pack alone to find him. It took everything in me not to kill him when he came for you. I cared about saving you more," he admits and looks back at me.

"You stayed all that time in town to protect Jaxson?" I ask, my voice like a whisper.

"He may hate me, but he needed my help. I didn't stay for Demi, I stayed for my stubborn brother that wouldn't speak to me," Wyatt says, and I stare at him. He loves Jaxson like family, they all do. They might not show it because, well they are guys, but I can see it. I can feel the love through our strange bond when he speaks of Jaxson.

"He should know," I mumble as I move closer to him. There are a lot of things both these men need to know. I lift my hand and place it on his shoulder.

"We have other things to worry about now. Like making sure no one knows who you are and getting you out of this hell hole alive." Wyatt says.

"Should we even talk about that in here?" I ask.

"The room is warded. There's a crystal built into the wall, no one can hear what's said in here. This is the only place we can discuss private matters," Wyatt says as he walks up to me. I let him undo my coat, it drops to the floor as he pulls my damp hair off my shoulders. I breathe in his calming scent, which makes me want to rub myself all over him. That's a bizarre thought, but it's true. Since I woke up all I've wanted is to be close to him. The same feelings I have for all four of them. Wyatt's blond hair is damp from the snow, and the darkness of his black coat bounces off the great, dark eyes that are currently watching my own. The slight dimples in his cheeks appear as he smirks at me. I'm sure he knows how attracted I am to him at the moment. I want to blame it all on the prophecy, and any other reason other than me, being a normal girl attracted to an insanely hot guy. That's all it is, the prophecy may have guided them to me but that's it. The rest is us, how I feel about them all and how much I care. I should tell Wyatt about my odd dreams of the past and how Elissa mentioned a prophecy.

"I have to tell you something," I start, planning to tell him all about my weird dreams when the door is knocked upon.

The door swings open and Drake's sister walks in, shutting the door behind her. She's changed into black leggings and a short black shirt that shows off her flat stomach. There isn't even one curve, totally unfair. I could never pull that outfit off.

"My prince and his mate, I'm sorry to be rude, but I wish to speak to the princess," she says with a slight Russian accent like Drake's. I turn to see her watching me and not Wyatt. It's clear the question was for me, alone.

"Why?" Wyatt asks, and his voice doesn't sound happy at us being interrupted.

"It's okay, Wyatt. I'm kind of hungry, could you get us something to eat?" I ask.

"You hurt a hair on her head, and I will take yours off. Drake's sister or not," Wyatt warns her. He walks over to me and takes my head in his hands as he gently kisses me.

"Always teasing," I whisper.

"Could you handle more?" Wyatt whispers against my lips. I can't reply as he lets go and walks out of the room.

"We haven't met, I'm Winter." I hold out a hand to her, and she shakes it tightly.

"I'm Leigha. I want to make a deal with you," she says, getting straight to the point. The girl doesn't seem like she wastes any time on being nice.

"One Wyatt wouldn't approve of?" I ask with a smile.

"Yes. I will teach you how to fight and how to use your powers."

"How do you know I have any powers?"

"My gift is to see other gifts, I can tell what they are from one touch." She touches my shoulder. Her eyes start glowing black like I've seen Wyatt's do before she lets go.

"Well, well Princess, don't you have a few secrets?" she says without an ounce of a smile.

"If you repeat any," I warn.

"I wouldn't. I'm not stupid, and I know who you are," she tells me.

I wonder who she thinks I am, and if she knows about the prophecy. "What did you sense?" I ask her and cross my arms.

"The power to move things, perfect aim, a weird connection with animals, and something else I can't get a reading on," she tells me. She looks as annoyed as me that she can't tell me what the last one is. I guess she's right, the aim thing I learnt with Jaxson. I apparently managed to move all the guys and furniture away from me when I got mad yesterday. I've always felt close to or the need to help animals, so I guess that can be called a connection.

"You may be right," I say.

"I will help you to learn how to fight like a vampire, how to protect yourself, and you will take me with you when you leave. I don't want to be sold to a bunch of stupid, old men that I don't love. I would kill them first," She tells me plainly as she walks towards the window of the bedroom.

"Why did you come here then? Why not run?" I ask her.

"Drake means everything to me. Our parents passed away last year, and I have no other family. Drake won't leave Wyatt and his mate. I don't want to make him, so I don't have a choice."

"Why do you think I can take you with me?"

"You're a mate of the Prince. A princess here, and you're allowed one person as your defender. If you name me as yours, you can take me with you and demand I don't marry anyone," she tells me.

"A defender?" I ask.

"Or protector. Whatever you want to call it, Drake is Wyatt's," she tells me, and I sit on the edge of the bed. This is a big decision, but I feel a little sorry for her. I can't imagine what it would be like to lose your parents and then be forced to marry some men you have never met.

"Can you fight?" I ask her.

"I can show you tomorrow," she offers.

"I'll think about it. I want to help you, but I can't agree to something like this so quickly. I don't know you."

"I get it. I will help you and protect you. I only ask that you protect me, too. There's something going on in this castle," she says.

"Like what?" I ask her.

"Have you heard of mini-demons?" she asks me.

"Yes, well, kind of, once," I think back to Harris telling

me about them. He said that witches have them as familiars, and there were other types.

"Well they are pests, but some of them will talk for some decent alcohol. I'm not joking, they love to get drunk. Anyway, one of the castle towers has a problem with them. There are hundreds up there, and they see everything in the castle," she says.

"You think we should ask them?" I say as I realise what she's thinking of.

"Yes, they look a little scary until they drop their glamors, but they speak some English," she tells me.

"Why do you need me then?" I ask her.

"They are stuck-up, little fuckers," she says.

"What?" I laugh, not expecting her to say that.

"They won't speak to me. They like royalty, and I want to know what they know. Will you help?" she asks, and I think of Atti saying the king was up to something, and that's why he is coming to the court.

"Okay, but we will need a big distraction," I say, thinking what we could do.

"That's something we need to think on, and if you have an idea let me know. I'll leave you to your prince."

"When will we go?" I ask her.

"You are too watched at the moment, but, in a little while, they will get lazy and bored of seeing you," she replies before she walks past me out the door without a goodbye. I don't disagree with her.

Wyatt comes back into the room a little later as I stare out the windows. The forest looks so peaceful, like a white wonderland. It reminds me of my dreams of Elissa and how they always have snow around. I wonder if she's trying to warn me of something.

I turn as Wyatt puts a hand on my shoulder, and I look up at him.

"I found chocolate cake," he says, making my dreams come true. Who wouldn't want a hot guy who brings you a chocolate cake?

"You are amazing," I mumble as I practically run over to the tray on our bed. There are two bowls of a red-looking soup and two plates of chocolate cake.

"What flavour is the soup?"

"Just tomato. If you want blood, you only need to ask," Wyatt smirks as I look back at him.

"Where do you keep the blood bags?" I ask him, and he shifts uncomfortably.

"We have human slaves, Winter, but I don't expect you to feed on them. I don't either, but if anyone asks you, you feed on them, alright?" I nod and remember the girl I saw.

"Slaves like the zombie girl I saw outside?" I ask him. I lose my appetite for food as I remember her face.

"Yes," he says, a clear warning in his eyes. I don't think he likes me questioning him on this.

"Do they have any choice? Do they enjoy being snacked on all the time and used as a food source?" I ask, crossing my arms as my anger rises.

"My kind will feed on them here and in front of you if they want," he tells me. "I told you once that my kind isn't right. What did you think you were walking into, Sweetheart?" he asks with a hint of sarcasm.

"I don't know. How many slaves do you have here? How many humans like me?" I ask him.

"Hundreds live in the basement housing, and you are not human," he answers, his dark eyes glowing.

I want to scream at him for not feeling anything for those people. "Hundreds," I echo his words.

"My kind will feed on them in front of you. It's just their way, and you cannot show them the disgust you are showing me now," he tells me.

"It's wrong!" I shout. "How can you think it's right? They are people, and you keep them here for food. Can your kind not work out a way to feed on blood bags? It's not right, and you can't tell me how to react. If I look disgusted it's because I am, I won't change who I am to keep some selfish vampires happy," I say, my mind going fuzzy with anger.

"You're right. I can see it now, the queen you will be."

"I won't be any queen to monsters who have no humanity," I reply and hold my head up as he stares at me. The dangerous and powerful side of Wyatt is coming out in his words, and all I want is to run from him.

"Then we will change the future," he replies as he moves a step closer.

"Can we?" I ask a quiver in my words.

"For you, I would make the whole world change or let it burn down," he tells me so passionately, that I take a step back.

"Winter, your eyes. They are so striking," Wyatt says staring at me.

"I . . . ," I manage to get out as Wyatt moves closer to me. Wyatt's hand guides around my waist as he pulls me to his chest until we are so close that I can see the silver specks in his own eyes.

"There isn't anything I wouldn't do to protect you, you know that?" he whispers but doesn't want an answer as his cold, soft lips meet mine. I melt into his body, and my hands slide up his chest into his hair as he deepens the passionate kiss. I feel us moving just before my back is laid onto a soft surface and Wyatt's body covers mine. I moan slightly as he kisses down my neck, and his hands slide under my top, his thumbs brushing under my breasts. My back arches as his sharp teeth graze my lower neck, an overwhelming urge to feel him bite me is controlling my mind.

"Wyatt, please," I whisper desperately as I run my hands over his tight back.

Wyatt doesn't reply, but pleasure fills my whole body as I feel the sharp pain of his teeth going into my neck. The pain is brief and replaced by a wave of pleasure that goes to every part of my body as I press myself as close as I can to him. Wyatt's hand grabs the back of my head to keep me in place as I wriggle underneath him. Desperate for any kind relief, I scream out in pleasure as Wyatt's knee pushes in between my legs, and the simple contact is enough to finish me off.

Wyatt pulls away to look down at me, my neck feels a little sore, but I'm in a state of wonder as I look up at him. His lips have a tiny drop of my blood on them, and his face is showing a million emotions as he looks at me. Much like what I'm feeling for him.

"You taste like heaven," he says before he kisses me gently. I sigh as he pulls away from me and frowns at something next to me. I look over to see the soup has slipped out of the bowl and all over the tray but thankfully the chocolate cakes are safe in their big containers.

"Oh my god, I thought the chocolate cake was lost. That would have been terrible," I murmur as I pick up my cake and sit up on the bed. I moan as the melted chocolate centre hits my tongue. Chocolate tastes even better now than it did before.

"I feel second best to a chocolate cake right now," Wyatt says, reminding me that he's in the room.

"You are," I tell him around another bite. He laughs loudly before getting his cake and handing it to me.

"I've eaten something far better, you can have mine," he says, making me blush, but I still take the cake.

While I eat my cake, Wyatt puts the tray on the desk near the front door, and I put my empty bowls on it when I'm done. I turn around to see him pulling off his shirt, and like my personal strip tease, he pulls off his trousers, too. Wyatt looks like a God without his clothes, a sculpted chest, a six pack and a line of blond hair up his chest that I want to feel. He looks amazing, and I don't know what to say as I stare. Over his heart is the same mark as mine, it's the same size and looks just right on him. Kind of sexy if I'm being honest.

"I like the shocked look on your face," he smirks at me.

I snap out of my drooling gaze before I say, "Why are you just in your boxers, not that it isn't a beautiful sight?"

"I usually sleep naked, but for you, I'm a gentleman."

I laugh as a reply and take my clothes off as he watches. I'm not as skilled at taking clothes off and looking sexy like Wyatt does, so I end up tripping on my one legging-covered foot and face-planting the floor. He laughs as I glare at him, and I stand up with my hands on my hips, just in my panties and top. "You're not a gentleman right now."

He looks me over slowly. "Believe me, I am," he says before getting into bed as I watch.

After we're both tucked in, he pulls me close to him. The feel of all his skin next to mine is making me fuzzy-headed, so I try to distract myself.

"The prophecy says I could destroy people," I say, but it's more of a question.

"Yes, but we won't let that happen. We're your mates, and that's the only part of the prophecy that we are confident of," he says gently.

"Is that why you four like me? Just because you were

told to?" I mumble. Wyatt puts a finger under my chin and forces me to look at him.

"No. The first moment I saw you, I knew there was something different. I didn't realise how different but that's not what makes me want to be with you. Your kind, yet bossy, attitude, the way you don't care who I am, and how passionate you are about the people you care about. You care about the human strangers here, when most people would be worried about themselves. I hated that I had to force you into becoming a vampire because of what happened, but at the same time, I respect you for it. You didn't care that it was a supernatural war and you were human. You only cared about those you love, that is something rare," he tells me.

I don't know how to reply to his comment, so I just nod.

"I often wondered what it would be like to born human and have a simple life," he says.

"I did have that, and I still got here," I say as I rest my hand over his mark. The area feels warmer than the rest of him.

"A few hours after I was born, my eyes turned silver. Every vampire fell to their knees, and their eyes turned the same silver as mine as the words 'true king' was singing through their minds. The only one that didn't kneel was my father. He was livid that I had controlled his whole race, and I was only one-day-old. He tried to kill me, but my mother stopped him. She convinced him that he needed an heir, and he let me live for her."

"Jaxson told me something happened when he was born too. How is that possible?" I ask.

"The goddess."

"Harris told me once that a goddess made all the races."

"Yes, we think she did, but no one believes in her anymore. It's said her sister Elissa made up the prophecy over five hundred years ago."

"Elissa?" I question him because I can't believe it. Elissa can't be real. The woman I've been dreaming of since I was ten years old.

"Yes why?" he asks me, he turns to look at me as sit up.

"I've been dreaming of a girl called Elissa. I have been for years," I say.

Wyatt sits up in bed as he stares at me, "That's . . . ," he says, but shakes his head at me.

"I know. It means I must be the girl in the prophecy, a prophecy she apparently made for me," I say to him. The whole idea of having four mates is hard enough to process, let alone that they are princes, and I'm meant to rule. Also, the total destruction problem if I fall. I can't even think about the saviour will die part. Who the hell is my saviour?

"Don't worry about it now. Every day, we'll go the library and get every book we can find on Elissa and the goddess. I will get Alex and Drake to help you."

"Okay," I say feeling too worried to even sleep.

"What did Leigha want?" Wyatt asks me.

"Oh nothing, just to be friends," I say and look away. I've always been a terrible liar.

"So, you're not going to tell me?" he chuckles.

"No," I reply slowly.

"Lucky I like you, my little mate," he says.

"I more than like you too, Wyatt," I say before I pull him down into the bed and lie on his chest. It doesn't take long for my dreams to come and take over, it never does.

27

WINTER

"Winter," a voice sings. The female voice keeps repeating my name again and again, as I open my eyes. The sound is different from the childlike, female voice I'm used to hearing. I recognise the voice straight away as I glance over to see Elissa. Dressed in the usual white dress and this time wearing a long, white cloak. She is standing next to me, close enough for me to reach out and touch her, but I can't move my hands. She points in front of me, and I look where she is looking.

We are in a park, and a woman is walking through it, pushing a black pushchair with its hood down. There's a little toddler in it, but I can't see her, just her white trousers and her pink shoes sticking out the end of it. The woman is wearing jeans and a black coat. A man is walking next to her, his arm around her waist as he looks at her with love. The man seems so familiar too, with light-brown hair and pale-green eyes. The woman has short, brown hair, a slim build, and is about my height with bright-blue eyes. She stops at a bench and sits down, the man sits next to her. The baby is facing me, a few steps away from us, but I don't look at her as I stare at the woman. She seems so familiar to me.

"I have to tell you something," she says to the man. Her voice is so soothing, and I'm sure I've heard it somewhere before.

"Yes?" he asks.

"You know I'm different," she says gently.

"We don't speak about that, you promised not to use your powers," he replies in a heated tone.

"And, I haven't. It's not safe for our baby to be around us. You know what you are, and what I am," she replies, her tone careful and controlled.

"Where can we take her, Isa?" he asks her.

"You have to take her. I can't," she says, her face filled with tears.

"No," he whispers, reaching over to wipe them away.

"He has found me, you're human, so he won't get you with her," she says, and he shakes his head.

He looks at the baby before replying. "That's why you brought us here?" he waves a hand around the empty park. I look around, wondering what he's talking about.

"Yes, I have to go back alone," she replies, and he takes her face in his hands.

"He will kill you. I love you, Isa, I can't let you," he starts and shakes his head.

"It's me or her. Just keep her away from my kind," she tells him.

"What of the prophecy?"

"We always knew it was her," she whispers quietly.

I block out what they are saying to look at the baby. She looks around two, with dark-brown hair clinging to her heart- shaped face.

"Remember what I am showing you. You need to understand your past before you can save your future," Elissa whispers into my mind.

"Why do you always talk in riddles? What are you showing me?" I demand as I look at the little child.

"Your family," she whispers as I look back at the baby, and she opens her bright-blue eyes.

Blue eyes I've seen a million times in the mirror.

I open my eyes with a jump, as I throw my covers off

and get out of the empty bed. That couldn't have been me. My mother wasn't there, and I don't know who that guy was. I have a few photos of my father, and he doesn't look like him.

No, it's not true.

The door opens and Wyatt comes through it, shutting it behind him. "Hey, I had to check something and didn't want to wake you," he tells me. Wyatt looks at me as I run my hand through my sweat-filled hair, my whole body is still shaking.

"Bad dream?" he asks.

"I'm going to shower," I say and walk straight to the bathroom, knowing he's watching me the whole time.

Only, I open the wrong door, and it's a massive, walk-in closet with clothes lining each side. Ah well, I needed a change of clothes. I ignore all the other clothes when I see my bag on the floor and pull out some jeans and a blue top. I get some clean underwear out, too, before opening the other door and finding the bathroom. I don't even look at Wyatt, but I hear his chuckle.

"She can't go to see a king looking like she has been pulled through a bush backwards, Wyatt," Alex's voice comes through the closed bathroom door as I turn the hair dryer off after a long shower. The shower is amazing and kind of like a waterfall. There is even a dressing table in here, with everything a girl could need. I look at myself closely in the mirror, noticing again how my hair doesn't need straightening anymore. My eyelashes are so long and black now. My face just looks more refined.

"She won't!" Wyatt defends me.

I walk out with a glare at my best friend which stops when I see what she and Wyatt are wearing. She's dressed in a black dress that shows off her back and goes high up her neck at the front. It falls to the ground and looks stunning with her long, red hair. My mouth drops open when I see Wyatt dressed in a black suit. His hair is gelled to the side, and his suit stretches across his chest. When I finally meet his gaze, my body tingles in excitement at how he's looking at me. Memories of him on top of me last night flood my mind, and my face heats up.

"Always jeans," Alex says with a slight tut and draws my attention towards her. A thankful distraction from the extremely hot vampire I'm mated to.

"What am I supposed to wear then?" I ask Alex and look down at my jeans which have a small hole in the knee. I don't look that bad, but compared to them I look a little weird.

Alex just shakes her head at me and opens the wardrobe. Whoever went shopping for me went overboard. The closet is full of dresses, smart trouser suits, and little tops.

"Out of all the things in here, you chose this?" She points at my outfit.

"I like jeans," I reply dryly as she grabs my hand, and pulls me into the room. Alex shuts the door, leaving Wyatt on the other side.

"The vampires are old school here, they all dress in cocktail dresses, and the men are in suits. That's why Wyatt is in one. You don't need to stand out any more than you already are going to, Win," she tells me. I sit on the small cushioned bench in the room.

"You're right, this is just a lot to take in," I mumble. I think that's the understatement of the year.

"I get it, but Drake told me all about the prophecy last night." She stops to look at me, her face is scared–an emotion I rarely see on Alex.

"I want you alive at the end of this," she tells me and turns back to the dresses.

"I will be," I reply as Alex slides the dresses along the rail. There are around twenty different dresses, all of them long and look like designer makes. The vampires don't have a problem with money, but it makes me uncomfortable.

"You are a lucky bitch, you know that, right?" Alex says as she looks at a dark-blue dress.

"In what way?" I ask her.

"Imagine all the hot sex you're going to have with those four hot princes," she says, and it makes me laugh.

"I haven't got my head around being with any of them yet, let alone all four," I mumble out eventually, but she hears me.

"I would ride them all like a pony if I were you, have you seen them?" she replies, and I laugh.

"I know you would."

"Ah, it's a shame my heart is only made for one guy, but I know yours isn't. You already love all those men, even if you don't know it yet," she replies. I don't think on her words because I don't like how right she likely is. Well, for at least two of them. Atti and Dabriel are growing on me too.

"I have something for you," she pulls out a small vial. It's filled with a glowing, purple liquid. "It's a contraceptive herb from the angels. It will stop any little Winter's running around."

"Thanks, do I just drink it?" I ask.

"Yep. Drake gets it for me, and I asked him to get you one. You don't need to thank me, I don't want to be an auntie yet," she winks at me, and I drink the vial. It tastes like a fizzy drink.

"I had a dream last night," I mumble as she pushes the blue dress away and pulls out a long, red one.

"A bad one?" she asks and stops to look at me. She

knows how messed up I can get over my dreams. When I was thirteen, I had a terrible dream: a woman I couldn't see was being held down by big, blue men. They were just shadows, but there were two of them, they changed as I watched into men and then shadows again. The dream was terrifying as I watched them kill the woman, they pulled some white and blue light out of her. When I woke up, I was screaming at the bottom of the garden. I must have walked out of the house in my dreams, Alex ran out and pulled me inside the house. She covered for me when my mum came running down the stairs and found us in the kitchen. We were lucky my mum believed the story that I saw a mouse when I got up to get water. I couldn't sleep for days after that dream, and every time I closed my eyes I saw the brown-haired woman on the ground. The weird thing is that Isa looked like the woman from that dream. I can't remember it anymore, but there was something familiar about her.

"No, not really. I was a toddler, but I wasn't with mum or dad." I tell her, and she raises an eyebrow at me.

"What do you mean?" she asks.

"Someone else was my mother and father. I don't get it, my dreams are becoming more real. And, with everything going on, I'm worrying that they aren't just dreams anymore. Elissa said they were my family."

"Maybe they are just dreams," Alex suggests.

"Yeah, and maybe vampires don't exist," I say sarcastically, and Alex comes over to me with a simple, white dress. It has two silver rings that hold it up on the shoulders, and it looks like it stops below the knees with a slight slit because of the tight fit. It's posh and sexy at the same time. I'm a little worried this is going to show off my not so flat stomach and curves, but it looks my size.

"You know, whatever happens, your mother loves you,

and I love you. Don't worry too much about a dream you can't change," Alex tells me as she puts a hand on my shoulder.

"Thanks, and I love you too," I say, and she grins as I stand up and take the dress off her. I quickly change and do a twirl for Alex, and she nods. I glance at myself in the full-length mirror, the dress is tight around my hips, but it has slight waves. It looks good and hides the proof of my chocolate addiction. We walk out of Wyatt's room and find him with Drake in the corridor. Wyatt looks at my dress closely before taking my hand and pulling me gently to his side. Drake is dressed similarly to Wyatt, and it's the most dressed up I've ever seen him.

"You may dress Winter whenever, Alex," he says.

"I told you so," she laughs. The door to the left of ours opens, and Leigha walks out. She looks every bit the vampire in a tight, black dress, it stops mid-thigh and covers her arms. The top half is open to show her shoulders. When she turns to shut the door, I see her mark on her shoulder. Its looks a little like a bird, made up of dozens of swirls. It covers the top of her arm and over her shoulder, where the birds head rests.

"Let's hurry, I want to get this stupid thing off," Leigha crosses her arms and walks ahead of us. I glance at Alex, who is trying not to laugh.

Drake wraps a hand around Alex's waist, and they walk after Leigha. We follow them down an endless number of corridors and stairs. Weirdly, we manage not to pass anyone else. The place reminds me of a haunted castle of one of those ghost shows because the dated corridors are quiet and mainly dark, apart from the small, wall lights.

"Where is everyone?" I ask Wyatt.

"The humans use back passages, and the vampires are all called to court to meet you," he replies.

"Oh, no pressure," I respond. I have to remember to thank Alex later for dressing me. I couldn't turn up in front of hundreds of vampires wearing jeans with a hole in them. They would never take me seriously.

"None at all. They will love you," he replies. Our eyes lock together for a second before we both turn to see where we're going. I only needed that second of a glance to fill myself with a false sense of safety, a safety I only feel at Wyatt's side.

"Does the king have a mate?" I ask.

"He has turned ten female humans, but he never calls any of them a mate. They usually die when he gets bored of them and doesn't let them feed on any other vampire or himself. They may wear his mark, but he has no respect for them. That was my mother's title," Wyatt says with little emotion in his words.

"I didn't realise you could turn more than one person," I say.

"It's not advised, but yes, you could turn endless numbers. Most people see it as an insult to do that. Sometimes the turned don't survive, or they go a little mad," he tells me. It's a scary thought that his kind could just go around turning people.

We walk up to large, stone doors, with three guards standing outside looking at us. They have dark skin and black eyes that match their uniforms. The red crown is stitched over their hearts, and they put their fists to their hearts as they bow.

"Open the doors," Wyatt says, and they quickly do as he asks. I didn't feel him use his power, but he makes you want to do as he says anyway. I have to remember he is a prince here.

The doors swing open to the throne room. Hundreds of eyes stare at me from their seats on both sides of a long path towards the throne. I don't look at them as my gaze hits the famous, vampire king. He looks like Wyatt, with his light-blond hair, but his has a bit of grey on the roots. He has a big build like his son, filling out the gold throne he sits on. The king is wearing a black suit, a few buttons are undone on his shirt, and he looks casual compared to the vampires in the room. Next to him, on the left, are four vampires seated next to each other in small, gold chairs and a long, wooden table stretches out in front of them. Harold is the first I see and then an older, stern-looking woman with short, grey hair, and she gives me a slightly distasteful look as our eyes meet. The other two are familiar, the one with the red crown tattooed on his head smirks at me. The seat next to him has the common, greasy-haired man he was with when he came to get me from Wyatt months ago, who also is looking very happy. I try to ignore the three wine glasses full of a dark-red liquid. I know its blood, but I'm going to pretend its wine. Yep, it's wine.

I press closer to Wyatt as we walk, and he squeezes my hand once in support. I glance around the room, seeing all the vampires. They look like they're waiting for a supermodel contest as not one of them is bad looking. It's intimidating because they are all stick thin, pale, and mainly blonde. There are a few dark-haired people in the crowd but not many. I catch a glance of a little boy in the seats, his white hair standing out compared to the light-blondes in the room. He looks around Freddy's age, and he smiles at me. I pull my gaze away as we get to the end of the path. The massive, gold throne stands on its own at the front of the room, and it's made of solid gold by the looks of it. It's big enough to put the queen of England's throne to shame. There are four large, glazed-glass windows behind the throne; they have a red tint in them, making the room almost seem like it's glowing red.

The king stands up, his thick, red crown shining in the light from the large windows. Though, the king is difficult to look away from, I feel drawn to look at the crown. The top looks made out of smooth thorns, and has four large, red stones encased inside it. I can sense its power from where I am standing. It's like my insides are telling me there's something different about the crown.

"My son has returned and with a human mate," he says, looking happy, but it's clear it's an act. His fake eyes meet mine like he knows what I'm thinking as Wyatt stops before the three steps that separate us from where the king is standing. You wouldn't think he was evil. In fact, he almost looks like an average guy. One you would expect to pass on a street as he goes to his nine-to-five job at an office. Except he is the monster under the bed, instead.

"Father, this is Winter Masters," Wyatt says respectively and slightly bows his head.

"Winter. Come here," the king holds out his hand. Wyatt's grip tightens on my hand as I try to let go to move forward, and the king laughs.

"You are not letting me near your new mate. I don't blame you son. I only wish to greet her." He laughs, and the crowd of vampires laughs with him.

"Fine," Wyatt says and lifts my hand to place a kiss on it before he steps back next to Alex and Drake. Leigha is standing at my side, and she bows before stepping back. I walk toward the King, and he offers me a hand. I place my hand in his, and a wave of sickness fills my body. I quickly pull my hand away, and the feeling goes away.

"Winter. You look so familiar to me," he says, and he moves closer as I take a step back.

"We haven't met," I reply, making him laugh.

"I'm sure we haven't," he replies staring down at me. He is as tall as Wyatt which makes him far more intimidating as I look up to meet his eyes.

"Oops, wrong timing," Atti's voice says behind me, and I turn to see him walking down the middle of the Throne room. Atti looks every bit the prince he told me he is. Wearing a black shirt, and black trousers under a long black cloak that hits the floor. A small black crown sits on his head, and his hair has been cut shorter. It now hits his eyebrows and is a lot shorter at the sides. It suits him. I nearly trip when I see the white and black tigers that walk next to him. Atti is extremely tall, and these tigers are half his size. The white one has white and grey striped fur, a tail made of sharp looking spikes mixed in with soft fur. It has two massive teeth that make it seem like a Sabertooth tiger. The black one is a little smaller, with large eyes and bigger ears. A shiny coat covers its whole body, with large black spikes running from its neck to the end of its tail. They both have bright-grey eyes, just like Atti's grey eyes. Atti moves between Drake and Alex as they step aside. He stops next to Wyatt.

"My Queen has sent me, we have things to discuss." Atti bows slightly.

"You are welcome witch prince," the king replies with an amused look in my direction.

"Looking as hot as ever Winter. Seriously, the dirty things I'm thinking of doing to you in that dress," Atti says in my mind, and I cough to hide my shocked laugh.

I move slightly away as the king moves closer to me and takes my hand again. The sickness is overwhelming, and I can just barely stand up, as he offers my hand to Atti, "May I introduce Winter Masters? My son's new mate and our new princess."

Atti takes my hand and presses a little kiss on the back

of it before he lets go. A look of disgust fills his face for a second as he looks at me. He hides the emotion so quickly that I can't be sure it was there.

"A human mate?" he asks Wyatt, who moves closer to me and pulls me to him.

"Careful, witch," Wyatt spits out. If I didn't know better, I would be convinced these two hated each other. It's a little upsetting to see, and weird to watch. I guess they must have had years of perfecting it.

"Boys, now, now. You are starting to sound like his dead father and me," the king points at Atti, and a feral-sounding growl comes from the white tiger as Atti stands straighter than before.

"Be careful. You are not my king, and you will not speak of my father like that," Atti warns. The king just nods, a calculating look on his face as he returns to his throne. I move to stand next to Wyatt, who holds my hand.

"Come here, human," he says, and I think he means me until I see a girl around seventeen running across the room from where she was standing by the wall. Her clothes look worn and stitched in many places. Her hair is pulled up in a tight bun, her skin is pale, but she is still gorgeous, though way too thin. The king pulls her roughly onto his lap the minute she gets near and bites her neck. She moans in pleasure, but her voice withers away as the king feeds from her. I watch in horror as he feeds, my hands crawling into Wyatt's arm as he holds me to him. No one does anything as he kills the girl, and her body falls the ground.

"Does your mate need a feed?" the king asks as he steps over the body. I stare at her empty eyes, feeling my anger rising beyond control.

"Winter I know, Love, I know. Your eyes are changing, and I need you to be strong. The king is a bastard but strong with many

secrets. We can't just kill him, the vampires would avenge him, and they love him."

Atti must have noticed how upset and angry I am, as he whispers in my head, and I turn to him to see him shaking his head a little, and I close my eyes.

"No. Winter developed a new power, and we will be using the training rooms to work on it," Wyatt replies.

"Ah, what power does our princess have?" the king asks.

"My mate can move thing with her mind, a form of telekinesis. Much like my uncle had, if I remember."

"Yes, a compelling gift indeed," the king says, but I keep my eyes on the floor.

"You'd best teach our new princess how to fight and use her powers. I expect to see you at the council meetings," he tells Wyatt.

"Yes, father."

I open my eyes, just to see the king smiling at me. An evil smile.

"Miss Leigha Sokolov, what a beautiful vampire you have turned into. My council will be finding mates for you soon," he says, and Leigha steps to my side.

"As you wish, my king," she bows her head and glances at me when she turns around. The panic on her face is enough to let me know she needs this deal as much as I'm going to.

"I always expected Wyatt to take you for a mate, perhaps when he is bored of this one," the king waves a hand at me.

Wyatt doesn't say anything but squeezes my hand so tightly I'm scared it's going to snap off. Leigha's eyes meet mine, and she looks down.

I quickly put my eyes to the ground as I feel a wave of dizziness.

Wyatt turns with me by his side and walks out the throne room with Alex and Drake following us. Leigha stays near my side, and I look back at the girl's body on the floor in front of the big, gold throne. Such a waste of a short life, she is so pretty, and the king had no regard for her life. Like she didn't matter, when she did. I don't think I'll ever forget her empty, blue eyes.

"Look away, this can't be changed, Love," Atti whispers in my mind, and I turn away as Wyatt walks us out the door.

28

WINTER

We walk straight back to our rooms and get changed into something more comfortable. Wyatt tells me he has to see the council, and that Drake, Alex, and Leigha will take me to training. Wyatt doesn't bring up what happened in the throne room, and I know it's because he can't protect me from his kind and their ways.

I walk next to Alex, and yet, what I'm used to seeing doesn't happen. Every set of eyes we see is staring at me and not Alex or Leigha. I don't get it, they are far prettier than I am.

"Why are they all stopping and staring?" I ask when we walk through an archway into a massive, stone courtyard. The snow has been swept away, and despite the fact it should be freezing in my sweatpants and long-sleeved top, I'm not cold. There are boxes of weapons on one side and around twelve vampires fighting each other. Each one stops when they see me.

It's creepy.

"They're curious about their new princess. Many have

heard about you," Leigha tells me, and Drake nods next to her in agreement.

"Why are they still staring then? It's getting awkward in here," Alex says, and I hear a chuckle from one of the vampires in front of me.

"They want Winter to say hello," Leigha says to us like it should be obvious.

It isn't. "Hello!" I say and try to do a little wave as I step forward. Unfortunately, I'm way too clumsy to be princess and trip on a stone after two steps. I manage to stop myself from falling, but everyone saw.

Alex just bursts into laughter next to me. Leigha even laughs a little.

"Very princess-like Win," Alex finally says, and every one of the guards bows at me, with their one hand in a fist on their chest before straightening again. I want to stop them, but I know it's likely rude.

"Leigha will be training me," I tell Alex and Drake who look at me like I've grown two heads.

"Are you sure? Leigha is–" Drake starts, but his sister interrupts.

"Is happy to help my princess," Leigha says, and Drake narrows his eyes at her. "So, Princess, what can you do?" Leigha asks me with a dare in her eyes.

"Not sure, I managed to move things once when I got mad. I'm good with a crossbow and throwing daggers," I tell her, and she nods.

"Hand to hand combat?"

"I'm alright, I had some training but more at a human level,"

"Come," she waves a hand, and we walk through the men training, who quickly move out of Leigha's way. I'm glad it's not just me she scares. She opens a small, wooden door, and I quickly follow her. Inside is a gym, like nothing

I've seen before. It looks more like an army, training camp. There's a big structure in the middle, it's made of wood and ropes. There are several large, metal barriers. I watch as someone blows a whistle, and two vampires run down the marked track towards one of the biggest ones. The metal is tall and smooth with nowhere to put your feet to climb. The monsters jump about three feet away, one looks like he's flying as he jumps over, and the other just gets to the top but manages to pull himself over.

"This is where young vampires are trained. I did a summer here once, vampires have the speed and strength to be able to do most things, but you need to learn how to use them. Your other powers, we will work on when you find out how to complete this whole course in five minutes. That's the average time."

"That tall, metal wall?" I ask.

"Yes, and you will."

"You will see a Winter-sized shape in the wall."

"Try not to hit it then," she says with a smirk. I have a feeling she'll enjoy seeing me run into that wall. The door opens as Drake and Alex walk in. Alex's eyes widen as she looks around the army camp. Yes, I'm calling this the army camp room, or torture room. I haven't decided yet.

"Alex will be doing the same training as you, but not all of it. I will deal with her combat training," Drake says.

"You have to be joking?" Alex glares up at him.

"No, I am not joking." he says plainly, and Alex groans.

"You best have a big bath waiting for me at the end of this."

"I'll even join you," he replies, and she leans up to kiss his cheek.

I glance back at Leigha who is watching the room. "Where do we start then?" I ask her, thankful for the new trainers I'm wearing.

"Follow me," she says. Alex comes over and walks next to me as we follow Leigha up to what I'm guessing is the start of the course. The first part looks like a simple, wooden climbing frame, and thankfully, there are steps. I've never climbed anything like it in my life, so I don't know how she expects me to do this part.

"Go," Leigha waves a hand and checks the watch she's wearing. Alex and I take off for a run, and I stop when I get to the wall. I manage to pull myself up the first few without too much trouble, but it's hard. I glance at Alex who's using her strength to propel herself off each one and to the next. I guess I could try that, I push down and try to jump up to the next holder as Alex did. Except I have no control and I push down too hard. I fly up with a scream and land on top of the tower with a giant thud.

"Holy crap," I mumble. I rub my sore shoulder where I landed and crawl to look down the wall at Alex's shocked face. I wait for her and help her up the last part.

"How did you do that?" she shouts.

"Didn't mean to," I reply.

"Less chatting, that took you three minutes slow coaches," Leigha shouts from the bottom.

"I dislike the army brat," Alex says as she pushes a stray red hair out her eyes.

"She's your sister-in-law," I reply.

"Still a brat," Alex laughs, and we both stop when we look over the other side of the tower. There are five nets, I guess you have to jump from one to the other because the wood connecting them is too small to walk on. The distance between them is vast, and the wooden floor underneath is far away. Falling would hurt.

"After you," I wave a hand, and Alex just looks at me with an 'I'm not that stupid' look.

"Fine," I say and walk to the far side of the tower. I run

for it and jump, I fly through the air as everything slows down. I can see myself landing with my right foot on the net. The net bounces my foot back up, and I push harder with the next step on the net. Everything seems easy when it's so slow, and the next thing I know, I'm at the last net which is attached to another tower. I climb, using the holes until I get to the top.

"Yes!" I say and wave over at Alex on the other side, her jaw is dropped open. I wait for Alex to make it over. She does, but I cringe when she nearly misses the third net. I help her up the last part, and she collapses on the floor.

"Kill me now, I mean it. Find a stake," she breathes out.

"That was fun," I say and smile down at her.

"There is something seriously wrong with you. Stop being such a bubbly pain in my ass," she says as she dramatically sighs.

"Come on before army brat finds us," I say and offer her a hand. The next part is to the left and looks like a puzzle of small wooden pieces. They look just big enough to walk on.

"There isn't anything to hold on to," Alex says.

"I guess balance is a vampire thing,"

"Fuck me," Alex pants out. She doesn't like heights. I put a hand on her shoulder before going first. The wooden strips are thick and just big enough to put one foot on. I figure I'm going to have to move quickly, one foot after another. I make the first few steps no problem until I look down. There's a big pool under the bars that you can't see until you're walking across it. One minute I'm walking, and then I'm falling.

"Ahhh," I scream as I hit the cold, murky water. It's deep enough that I have to swim up to the top. When I get out, I hear another splash and turn to see Alex's red hair just before she comes up.

"Ten minutes, and you fell. You two are going to be training for a long, fucking time," Leigha says as she stands at the edge of the pool. Drake stands next to her with his hands on his hips, both of them looking scary as hell.

"They both seem to like the serious jackass look," Alex says to me, and I laugh as I nod.

"Apparently you both like the drowned rat look," Leigha replies and just stares at us. She doesn't give a crap.

"Did you just call me a rat?" Alex asks.

"Yes, a drowned one," she replies.

Alex looks at me, apparently agreeing we do look bad and then says, "Fair enough, then army brat."

29

WYATT

"Please, I didn't kill," the middle-aged, half-turned woman pleads in front of the council and me. I can't help her, and I doubt she killed the vampire, she is accused of. She's lucky she's even in front of the council and wasn't killed straight away. The only reason she isn't dead already is that she's beautiful and half-turned. The sun shines through the red glass and makes the woman seem like she's glowing red. The whole morning has been filled with petty things like this, I wonder how my father can just sit here and do nothing like I am. The vampires have become selfish and care only about things that don't matter instead of things that do, like a human's life. The last vampire in here was accusing her next-door-neighbour of stealing a necklace made of diamonds. I'll have to get Atti to check out Jewel's hiding places for it before the two vampires try to murder each other.

"Don't listen to her, you were caught with the sword in your room. Humans are not allowed to kill vampires, you know the rules and the punishment," Talen says, an evil gleam in his eyes. I bet the fucker put the sword in her room, the vampire that was killed was one of Talen's cousins, yet he apparently doesn't feel sorrow for his loss. No, this is all a game, and he will kill that woman. I'm sure he's wanted an excuse to kill her for a while. If I knew about this meeting before now, I could have made Atti take her to the human world, she doesn't deserve to have the death she will have. No one does.

"Take her to my suite. I'll deal with the punishment and her death," he says, and the rest of the council nods their heads. Disgust fills me when I see the two guards drag the poor, screaming woman away. I turn to stare at the empty, golden throne. The weight of the responsibility I will one day have is crushing. Winter was right when she called my kind heartless monsters because that is what most have become. They stay in this castle, separated from the human world and feeding off the humans that are born and bred here. They don't treat them any better than dogs.

"Your mate fits in well with the vampire life, must be a difficult transition for a human who knew nothing of us," Harold says as he comes to stand next to me. The rest of the council are walking out.

"It is. Winter deals well with changes," I remark. That's a little understatement, Winter has fit into my world like she always belonged in it. Maybe she always has.

"Have you spoken to the king?" he asks once the throne room is empty. The words echo around the room, a room that has only ever given me pain as I grew up. I look at the cold, wooden floor in front of the throne. Demi's ruined body is still fresh in my mind, as the last time I saw her was on that floor. Talen had removed her heart and drained her of all her blood. I doubt he made her death natural. I never did get to bury her, I just took her body back to Jaxson's pack and stayed near until a guard found her. "No, his defenders say he is busy," I reply. I've been working with the council for the last two weeks, and I only get to see Winter for a few hours a day. It's not ideal, but with my father refusing to come to the meetings, I have to be there.

"He isn't here," Harold says.

"Where is he then?" I ask. I didn't know he had left, not that he would tell me.

"With the witches and the dark queen," Harold says, and I know it's a risk for him to tell me. I trust Harold, out of all the council and most vampires, he is more human. Harold is who I get my blood bags from because he and his family don't use the servants. I know his family half live here and in the human world.

"What does he want? I know he visited the angel council and the light queen," I say, remembering my previous conversations with Atti and Dabriel.

"I'm unsure, but it doesn't bode well for us. I respect your father, but I believe in the goddess," he says and bows at me. I watch as he walks out the room. It's a risk for anyone to hear him say that, no one talks of the goddess in the castle. I didn't know he believed in her, I thought my mother was the last one who did in this place. They all thought she was crazy when she spoke of the goddess and a time of change coming. At least, from the way people talk about the last queen.

I walk out of the throne room and search the castle for Winter. I find her training with Leigha and Alex. At least she hasn't fallen in the water pond today, she must have figured out how to balance. It was a little funny to see her coming back for the first week looking like she'd been swimming in her clothes. Winter's long hair is up in a ponytail, but it's so long that it hits her lower back. The tight yoga trousers and vest top are showing her more toned body. Winter is more toned since becoming a vampire, but the training is making her curves look more seductive than I'm used to. She's always been a temptation, but now it's impossible to resist her. Drake is leaning against the wall by the door when I come in.

"Prince Wyatt, are you done with the council meeting already?" Drake asks, pulling my gaze away from my mate. I never wanted to force a mating with her, not the way it happened. I remember holding her body in my arms as I gave her my blood, pleading with the goddess to let it work. I couldn't lose her. She came back wearing my mark. The mark looks so sexy on her lower back, I only get to see it when she wears those small shorts and a vest top in bed.

"Yes. How is she doing?" I ask. I watch as Winter jumps over a medium-sized wall. I wonder if she can jump the highest yet; I jumped it when I was ten, after one year of training in here.

"Better. Leigha is good for her, doesn't give in to any whining that she can't do this. She's training Alex as well, although I don't believe it is helping them bond," Drake says.

"Leigha has said no to every vampire the council has suggested, it's now twelve she has refused," I tell Drake.

"I don't believe she needs a mate," he says.

"The king hasn't heard what she's doing yet, I can't defend her for long. Talen has never taken a mate, and I've seen how he talks about her," I say.

"He is not touching my sister," Drake warns.

"I won't let him, but taking one mate would save us a lot of trouble. Not all the guys are bad. Easton, for example, is from an influential family, and is a good man." I say referring to one of Harold's children, a good guy but a little-laid back.

"She would eat him alive," Drake laughs. Winter stops to chat with Alex before the massive wall.

"Yes, she would," I chuckle.

I listen in on Alex and Winter's conversation because I don't want to interrupt their training.

"Do you miss Jaxson?" Alex asks. I know she does.

"Yes, and Freddy. God, I miss Freddy, I love him, and it's difficult that I can't tell Wyatt about him," Winter says with a sigh. Who the fuck is Freddy? I know our relationship is based on sharing, but not with another guy I don't know. Why would she have hidden a massive secret like she is in love with someone else, from me? She hasn't told me she loves me, but I feel it in our bond. I don't know if she can feel my emotions yet, it might not happen until we finish the mating because of how different she is. The warmth she feels when she talks about this Freddy is hard to believe.

"It's hard not to be honest with him, I don't like keeping secrets from my mate."

"You should tell Wyatt soon, but I agree it's difficult. It's weird hearing you call Wyatt your mate," Alex replies, and I turn to walk out the door before I hear the response.

I don't know who Freddy is, but I won't share Winter with anyone other than my brothers. I just can't.

30

WINTER

"Hey, mum," I say when she answers my call. I've gone to call her five times this week and changed my mind. I'm not sure what's stopping me, maybe it's finding out any answers I don't want. I don't think my mum would have lied to me my whole life. She isn't that kind of person, my mum is sweet and kind. The type of person that spends her last money of the week on buying food for the homeless outside her church.

"A call a month? Is that all I'm getting now. I miss you Winter, and I'm worried," she says, sounding upset as she talks. It hurts to know I've upset her. I never meant to.

"I'm fine, mum, I just needed an escape for a while, just like Alex said," I reply.

"You think I believe that crap, Winter Masters? This is your mother you are speaking to," she says, making me feel like shrinking in my seat. Why do mothers become the scariest people on earth when they're upset?

"Mum, what was my dad like?" I ask her, changing the subject.

"What exactly do you want to know?" she asks. She isn't saying no, so that's a start.

"When did you meet? You never told me," I ask her.

"Oh, well. I first met your father in university, we were just friends for a year, but I always liked him as more. He was studying to be a doctor, and I was just finishing my art course. He was two years younger than me," she says. I hear her moving around in the background.

"So, how did you get together in the end?" I ask her.

"He moved onto my street around five years later. I took him a toffee cake over to say hello, and then we got together," she says.

"Why weren't there many pictures of him around? I can only remember seeing one of him at his graduation," I ask her because that's the only photo I've seen of him older. There are several of him as a young boy, but she has none of them together.

"He didn't like the camera, honey," she says tensely, a little too protective for me to believe her. I hate thinking she would lie to me.

"Mum, you wouldn't keep anything from me, right?" I ask her, my voice betraying me as I try to sound strong.

"I could ask you the same question. But, I don't hide anything from you unless I think it will cause you pain," she says the end part in a whisper. I know she doesn't want to tell me something, I can just hear it.

"What if I needed to know, mum?" I ask her.

"Are you okay? All these questions are worrying me more than I am already," she asks.

"I'm good, just been thinking about things," I reply. I hear someone come into the room and ask for her help.

"I have to go, Winter, I'm at work. I hope you enjoy the rest of your break and come home soon. When you need to," she says.

"I will, mum. I love you," I reply, feeling more than disheartened.

"Bye, honey, I love you more," she says and puts the phone down. Why do I feel like that conversation gave me more questions than answers? I know she is hiding something. Mum always avoided any questions about my dad. The dream with Elissa has been stuck in my mind this last month in the castle. We can't leave because the king is insisting Wyatt stay to help him with council decisions. Wyatt says they are just idiots. Last night, Wyatt told me we could leave in a month, after the royal ball the king is throwing in celebration of me. I run my hand over my hair, it's braided down my back, the braid hitting the top of my bum. My hair grows impossibly fast, and yet, the rest of me rarely need shaving. I've only shaved once in a month and my legs are still smooth. Alex said it's the same for her. Training with Leigha is getting better but nowhere near her high standards. I can make it through nearly all of the course in ten minutes now, but I can't jump the huge, metal wall. It's impossible. What's worse is when training is over, I'm nearly always alone. Drake takes Alex away, and Leigha watches me but doesn't talk much. I usually stay in my room like now or go to the library. The library is slowly becoming useless, half the books are in Latin or French, and the ones in English are so poorly written, so it takes ages to read a few sentences. Nothing is coming up on the goddess that we can use to help me.

"Why do you look so down?" Atti asks as he appears next to me, making me almost jump out of my skin. I don't want to admit that things are difficult here. I don't get to see Wyatt much, and all I do is train until I can't stand up. I miss Jaxson, Atti, and Dabriel. I miss Freddy, too.

"I miss some people," I say, choosing to look out the window again. I feel Atti move close to my side as I sit on the window seat. Three library books sit in front of me as I try to read them. One of them is purely French, so I've given up on that one.

"Like me?" he says, his voice holding a teasing quality.

"Maybe," I say with a small smile.

"Everyone misses me when I'm not around, don't worry it's natural," he says, and I roll my eyes, but the smile on my face stays there. I didn't know I needed Atti until he was here, and he can always make me feel better.

"Dabriel and I want some time alone with you. You've been all work and no play for too long, Love," Atti says and offers me a hand. I look down at my jeans with holes in them and my Batman top. It will do. Atti is wearing jeans and a tight, grey shirt that clashes with his eyes. I look at his hand before slipping mine inside it, and he pulls me to his chest.

"Smile, Love," he says, and I feel his magic flowing around me. It's only a second before my feet hit the ground. I open my eyes as Atti lets me go and standing a few steps away is Dabriel. His arms are crossed against his tight, white shirt. He looks normal in jeans and a backward cap covering his white hair. Dabriel's purple eyes seem to draw me in as I walk over to him, and he greets me with a little kiss. His hands are sliding down my back slowly as he pulls away.

"I missed you, Dab," I say, and he grins. I look over his shoulder in shock when I see the Disney castle behind him.

"Disneyland?" I turn, asking Atti who nods. He doesn't seem jealous that I kissed Dabriel, but then Atti has never tried to take our relationship further than friends.

"Where else would a princess go to chill out?" he says, and I laugh.

"I've always wanted to come here," I tell him.

"Then your dreams have come true. Please, I want to find that Thunder Mountain ride," he winks at me.

"Let's go," I say and take Atti's hand. Dabriel takes my other hand and we walk down the path, out of the small corner Atti brought us too. It feels weird holding both of their hands in public, and a few people stare. I think it has more to do with how hot Atti and Dabriel are. I wonder if humans can tell there is something different about them. I guess there's something else about me now, too.

We go on several rides on the way to the mountain ride. Atti pulls out fast track passes for us all, so we don't have to wait. When we get to the mountain ride, Atti sits next to me in the front cart, and Dab takes the seat behind us. I guess his wings need the extra space. I know he has some kind of glamour on, so the humans don't see them, but I can. Dab looks hot with his angel wings. The ride starts inside the mountain, and as it turns, I slide into Atti. When we are just coming out of the mountain, I turn to look at Atti, and he kisses me. His arm is tightly wrapped around my waist as the cart swerves around the track but all I can focus on are his sweet lips. Atti tastes like the sweetest thing in the world, and when he pulls away, his glowing grey eyes tell me that he felt affected by the kiss as much as me. I slide to the left of the cart, when it turns, and I catch a glance of Dabriel's face. I expected jealousy or anger, but instead, there is just a happy, warm look in his eyes as they meet mine.

For once, I can see this working for us all, the happiness Dabriel told me about once. The rest of the day we go on the rides, except when Dabriel and Atti have a competition in one of the shooting gun booths. I had to distract Atti when he lost, and he looked close to killing Dab who was grinning. Silly alpha males.

"The fireworks start in a minute, Minnie," Atti says

next to me as we move through the crowd outside the castle. I grin at him with my Minnie mouse ears headband on that Dabriel brought me. Dab jumps over a small bar to a bit of grass no one is standing on. I follow and stand next to Dab. Atti comes behind me and rubs my arms.

The fireworks light up the sky, shining brightly against the dark skies. This was just the day I needed, a reminder that even in darkness, a beautiful light can brighten up the world.

31

JAXSON

"My cheeky, little lad," my aunt says as she comes in with the pack. Her hundreds of wolves follow close behind her. Most are in wolf form, and the rest are in the row of twenty different cars I can see. They're all getting out of their cars as she pulls me into a tight hug. My aunt looks my age and a lot like me, with dark-brown hair and light-green eyes. She always wears bright clothes around her curvy form. While she looks like an innocent aunt to me, I know she is fucking far from it. This woman handed my ass to me when I was ten in a sword fight. She then beat me for four years before I could beat her. She is that good.

"How has my wee, little lad been?" she asks me. I hate when she calls me that. I hope she doesn't say it in front of Winter, she would wind me up for it. Just thinking of Winter makes me miss her; that girl has me wanting to fall to my knees in front of her.

"I'm coping with my new responsibilities," I say, and she gives me a brief glimmer of pain in her neutral expression. Fergus's death is like a little hole in my chest, it's always there as is my sister's, but I have to live on. My life has always been drenched in war, and there are always high prices. I see the price every day in my sister-in-law's eyes as she rubs her pregnant stomach.

Both of my siblings are dead, and I wish it were different in our lives. A lot of fucking good wishing does, no one ever responds.

"Aye, I know you are, we will hold the ceremony tonight and crown our new king," she says with a big smile.

"Yes, it's time I took my throne. I want you to meet Freddy. I know you haven't had a chance," I say, and she nods following me up to the main cabin. Harris comes out one of the cabins and walks over to us.

"Aunt Lucinda, meet my beta, Harris." I wave a hand at Harris, who nods in greeting.

"We have all the extra cabins ready for the guests, my mother is currently sorting the list out for your pack," Harris says.

"A list would be good," she replies.

"Go and help, and when you get a second, check that the guards are alert. We don't need anyone coming into the pack while we are weak. Talk through the bond if you need me," I tell him, referring to the bond I have with all the wolves in my pack since I became their alpha. I can contact any of my wolves when I need to, and because Harris is active, he can send messages to me. Not all the wolves can do that, mainly it's used for just betas and guards.

"Yes, alpha,"

"Less of the 'alpha' shit, my name is Jax to you, Harris,"

"Alright, Jax," he chuckles and runs off.

"I'm proud of you, Jaxson, if nothing else, know that, laddie," she tells me as we walk on.

Everything has been fucked up since the night I lost Fergus and nearly Winter. I had to find a witch quickly to make the pack safe, bury my brother, and look after his pack. The ceremony tonight will finally bond me with the whole pack, and I wish Winter could be here. I still have no fucking idea who killed my brother. It was someone in the pack. I'm sure of it. I was with Freddy inside the house when it happened, so I'm not sure who was missing. It pisses me off that I don't have a clue who managed to stab my brother in the heart.

I see Esta walk past the garages at the side, and she waves at me. I don't bother looking at her. Esta has been playing a fucked-up game from the beginning. I never lied to Esta or dragged her along. I told her when we were eighteen that I wouldn't mate with her. I only wanted a friend. She said to me that the prophecy must be fake, and she still wanted to wait. I let her keep telling people we would mate eventually because Fergus asked me to. He didn't want everyone to know about my friendship with the other princes, and the fact that he was aware I believed in the goddess. It's hard not to believe in someone that predicted your birth. I never wanted a relationship with the girl from the prophecy. I convinced myself I would kill her and get rid of the threat straight away. God knows, I have no love for humans.

Then Winter slammed into my life and into my heart.

I couldn't walk away, instead, I got as close as I could.

She is my queen, and I want her at my side; I knew that from the moment my lips touched hers.

I fucking hate that she's in the middle of all my enemies right now.

"I smell vampire on you, please say you haven't chosen a vampire as a mate," she says. She must be smelling Winter. Her scent does feel a little like a vampire now, but it's different, like she is. An image of her standing in the middle of her living room comes into my mind. I remember her eyes glowing silver as a blue wave flows out of her chest and hits everything in the room, including me, who flew into the wall and landed on my ass. Whatever she is now, she isn't just a vampire. She is so much more.

"No, well not exactly. We have a lot to discuss," I say eventually as I hold the front door open. The two wolves guarding it look at me briefly before focusing on something behind me. I had to replace five guards after the attack; the ones that we lost. The two new ones are Suzy and Malic. Those are the two guarding the cabin and me now, and the rest are patrolling the edges of the ward. My brother used to only let one woman in his ten guards. I chose the best at fighting, and that's Suzy. She has power to stop her enemies with one touch. Her seven mates were not happy, but they wouldn't try to stop me.

"We do," she says. The house feels a little colder without Fergus. We may not have agreed or believed the same things, but he was my brother.

"Uncle J!" Freddy runs up to me, looking flustered.

"What's going on?" I ask him.

"Frederick! Where are you, my wee one?" My great aunt from my father's side calls from the kitchen. She is a bigger woman who just loves children and smothers them. I remember her as a child, and I understand Freddy's panicked look. I used to hide when I knew she was coming over, I'm sure I still have the itchy jumper she knitted me once. She forced me to wear it all Christmas day when I was fifteen. It has a reindeer with a light-up nose–if you squeezed the fucking nose, it played a song.

Atti saw me in it when he came to get me at midnight to see the others.

He wound me up for a year, I wouldn't be surprised if he tells Winter about it. I fucking hope he doesn't.

"Save me," he pleads, and Lucinda starts laughing next to me.

"Freddy, this is my Aunt Lucinda." I introduce him.

"Why don't you go and help some of the wolves into the old cabins?" she suggests, and he grins. A grin that reminds me of Wyatt. A lot of Freddy reminds me of Wyatt as he gets older. I just hope his vampire side doesn't come out anytime soon. It's not the right time.

"Yes, I can do that, and hello!" he says before running out of the room.

"He reminds me of you as a child," Lucinda says watching him fly out the door.

"Hmm, perhaps. Let's go to my new office," I tell her, and she nods, all business now. My aunt has four brothers-in-law, all of them are bringing wolves here from their different packs. We are grouping, and they will all be here today. The first time the whole wolf population will be together in many years.

We walk into Fergus's old office, my new one, and it still faintly smells of him. I miss him, I remember holding him against the wall as he threatened Winter. I wouldn't change it, but I hate that we spent the last few months of his life arguing. The last day was the only time we had agreed that I wouldn't leave Winter, that I wanted her as a mate. When I told him that, I had already called the engagement with Esta off because I'm in love with Winter, he asked me to stay for the wedding and then go to get her.

I never expected Esta to kiss me. She'd never tried before, and I thought she fucking understood after our many talks about being friends. She told me that pretending to plan to mate with me kept her away from the other wolves' pressure to choose a partner. I understood in a way until she attacked Winter. I knew something was up then, and she hasn't come near me since the party.

"I have found the girl from the prophecy. I love her, and she will be my queen," I get straight to the point, no point fucking about.

"Where is she, then?" Lucinda asks.

"With her other mate or her other soon-to-be mates," I reply. I don't care about having to share her, I never did. Jealousy will be something we can work on, but my wolf is bonded to the guys anyway. I couldn't challenge them without expecting a bad fight. We are too evenly matched with each other.

"Which prince?" Lucinda asks me. I guess she expected this, too, because her expression isn't one of shock. My aunt always believed in the prophecy. Our culture finds it common to share, it's just unheard of between different races.

"Vampire," I reply.

"Have you lost your mind to let her go there?" she asks, her hands on her hips.

"We have little choice. Winter is stronger than she looks and a little bit vampire now," I tell her.

"Is she just human?" she asks me.

"No, when I first met her, I started training her in defence. She was very strong for a human and hits targets dead centre with no training. When she gets mad, she can move very fast. I'm not sure what she is," I reply. Lucinda doesn't say anything for a while, just looks out the small window in the room. I look where she is watching as three wolves walk with a young child on one of their backs. Two wolves in human form are following those, carrying bags, their laughter I can pick up with my hearing.

"I can look into this. We have some old books from the times the goddess and her sister were alive. They might have something in them about these kinds of powers," she finally replies and faces me.

"Thank you," I say simply.

"Your mother always wanted you to fulfill the prophecy, but it was the vampire king that killed her. He will do anything to stop it and get his way. She is not safe there. No matter who she is with," Lucinda warns.

"I trust Wyatt and Atti. They will keep her safe," I say.

"Perhaps, but she needs more protection," she shakes her head slightly.

"Yes, I'm working on it. Our world is not going to be happy about her existence," I say and lean back in the brown-leather chair.

"It's finally some proof that our goddess hasn't left us," she says.

"She never did. I have to tell you about Freddy," I say, I know I can trust her.

"What about him?" she asks.

"He is a half breed, half vampire, and half wolf. He's different, and I'm worried because his father is going to find out about him soon. I've kept him a secret for so long, to keep him safe." I say, the words feeling strange to say now that the blood bond is broken. I felt it break when Winter guessed; it was like being free.

"It's not as surprising as you think, but I'm a little surprised there is a hybrid so close to us. We must keep this to ourselves until the boy is older. Who knows what powers he might have," she says finally. I'm glad about her reaction, not everyone will feel the same way.

"Agreed. I want to assign Katy as his protector for

now," I say thinking of the young girl. Since she was shot, she has become dedicated to her training, to building on her power and maturing in general.

"I remember you telling me about that lass who was shot and recovered well, any reason why?" My aunt replies.

"Harris is going to be announced as my only beta tonight. I only trust him. Katy has an ability to hide her scent, she could protect Freddy's if need be," I say, and she nods.

"I trust your judgment, alpha,"

"It's weird hearing you call me that when I remember you chasing my ass around the pack when I drank your whisky," I say, and she laughs. I was thirteen at the time and wanted to impress the two girls my age in the pack, it didn't work.

"You were always my alpha, you only had to grow up and realise it. I'm glad some girl has given you the kick up the backside that you needed," she says, making me laugh.

"You have no idea, the woman is more stubborn and headstrong than me," I mutter.

"I can't wait to meet her," Lucinda grins.

"Soon, I swear it." I nod.

"Another thing. You know my power is to talk to the trees and plants. The earth is worried, keeps telling me about demons," she says, a slight shiver of fear passing over her eyes.

"Like what?" I ask her.

"That they are coming, the demon king is coming back," she says. As far as I know, demons are fairy tales, told to scare little children. I only know of mini-demons, but they aren't a threat. A demon king doesn't sound right.

"Back?"

"Aye. They say, he once lived on earth, but a goddess's

death locked him away. I don't understand everything they say, but they are clear. War is coming. That's why I'm here, my bonny, little prince," she says. Lucinda walks over to me and places her hand on mine on my desk. "We need a king."

32

WINTER

My eyes threaten to close as I read a chapter in the old book. The women is describing how some Lord is throwing a dance, and everyone has to attend. Nothing about the goddess in this one. I have decided I don't like the castle, most of the vampires don't speak a word of English, and the ones that might do tend to ignore me. They just bow and wait for me to go away. The humans, well normal people just run away from me or bend so low I'm sure their backs are going to break. Neither is any good for them or me. I should have realised that we are in France, so not everyone is going to speak English. Apparently, Wyatt can speak a couple of languages, who knew speaking in French is sexy? Wyatt is very hot when he talks away in French.

"Anything?" I ask Alex who shakes her head at me, her long, red hair shines from the dull strands of light coming through the library's tall windows. We are sitting on one of the sofas, both of us have books in our laps and a pile of them on the floor next to us. Leigha is watching us from a chair near the window. She won't help because, apparently, she doesn't like dust or old books. She also informed us that we wouldn't find anything other than old-wives' tales in here. I'm starting to believe she's right, but we have to try. I haven't had any dreams in a while, and I'm starting to think Elissa has left me to it. If she was Demtra, the goddess's sister, then wouldn't she have been a goddess too?

"It would help if they wrote these books better, it's like reading a child's diary," she says and closes the leather-bound book.

"And you've read a lot of those?" I chuckle as I push my own book closed, and dust flies everywhere, making me cough.

"I used to read your diaries all the time, who knew you liked Travis in year six?" she says and grins at me.

"Bitch, those aren't meant to be read by anyone, and he had lovely hair," I mutter.

"Don't worry, I never told him," she laughs as I throw one of the pencils I have near me at her, and she catches it.

I glance back at the pile of ten books I've read through in the last week on the goddess. Most of it is made up, and not one of them describe how she looks and gets it right. I've told Alex, Drake, and Wyatt about what she looks like so they can help search. Leigha listened but still just told us we're wasting time and should be doing more training.

It's been a long month with two weeks of training in the morning for three hours. I enjoy reading for the rest of the day. I haven't seen Wyatt much, other than at night and in the morning. I had to force myself to drink two mugs of blood last night because I was so hungry. I want to say it was gross, but it wasn't. It so wasn't, and it reminds me of chocolate, melted chocolate.

"Mr. sexy witch is coming your way," Alex says and nods behind me. Sure enough, Atti is walking straight towards me. I don't recognise him like this, his usual carefree face is gone and replaced with a stern look that matches his massive build. The five vampires that are in the room with us all stand to watch as he stops in front of me. I get up from my chair, so we are facing each other.

"You are requested in the prince's room, I offered to take you, so I might meet the princess properly," Atti bows slightly and winks at me as he straightens.

"Of course, let's go," I say, and he takes my hand gently and links it into his arm. I glance back at Alex to see her grin at me.

I feel Atti's magic sweep over as he moves us to God knows where. When I finally feel my feet hit the ground, I open my eyes and see the inside of Jaxson's cabin. Freddy sees Atti and me first because he jumps up and throws himself into my arms. Jaxson is sitting with a younger woman, who looks at me with curiosity.

"Whoa, hi, little wolf," I say and tighten my arms around Freddy. The soothing earth smell of the wolves calms me. I missed Freddy so much.

"I missed you, and Uncle J is miserable without you here. All he does is mope around," Freddy tells me. Freddy has gotten taller since I last saw him, he reaches my chin now. I know he's going to be taller than me when he's done growing up. I hope I get to see it.

"Does he?" I ask Freddy.

Jaxson answers, "Yes, lass. Now, come here," he demands. Part of me wants to jump into his lap, but my stubbornness takes over.

I let go of Freddy, to stand straight with my hands on my hips.

"I don't believe you asked nicely," I say, holding in the urge to smile.

Jaxson grins, "I don't ask anything nicely."

"If I say please, do I get a hug?" Atti asks next to me, a slight joking smirk on his face.

"You don't have to say please, only the jackass over there," I point a thumb in Jaxson's direction as I speak. Everyone in the room laughs as Jaxson gets up and stalks over to me. I duck behind Atti to hide, and Atti disappears on me.

"Damn witch," I mutter as Jaxson picks me up and kisses me. His lips move softly against mine like he is reminding himself I'm real. I sigh and run my hands into his hair.

"That's gross, they always do this, Aunt Lucinda. At first, it was just weird looks between them, now it's always kissing," Freddy says, and I break away from Jaxson with a grin.

"Remind me when he gets a girlfriend to be this annoying to him," Jaxson says.

"Will do," I giggle.

"Winter," Dabriel's voice comes from behind me, and I turn in time to see him walking into the cabin. I let go of Jaxson to run to Dabriel, who pulls me into a hug the moment I get close. I pull back slightly to look at him.

He is just stunning. Long, white hair is tied at the back of his head with many braids running throughout it. His purple eyes watch mine, and he's wearing the white tunic and trousers I saw him in the first time we met. It must be an angel thing to wear all white. His wings are folded at the sides, and I stare at how soft they look. All white feathers with silver strands just like his hair.

"How is the vampire castle?" he asks me, his hands sliding down my arms leaving goose bumps and butterflies in my stomach.

"Mostly boring," I reply.

"I'm glad of it," he responds and kisses my forehead. I

turn around as Jaxson comes to my side and takes my hand. Dabriel walks over to Freddy and Freddy hugs him.

"We must get on with the ceremony, the wolves are waiting, my alpha," Lucinda says as she watches me.

"I need a second alone with Winter," Jaxson tells her.

"Yes, my alpha," Lucinda bows and walks over to me. Jaxson stays close to my side. I feel like I'm going through some test.

"I am honoured to meet you, Winter. My name is Lucinda," she offers her hand to me, her strong, Scottish accent flowing through her words. She sounds a little like Jaxson, but Jaxson's accent isn't as pronounced as Lucinda's is.

I take her hand as Jaxson winds his arm around my shoulders.

"This is my aunt that I told you about once, she is like a mother to me," Jaxson says. It's clear from his words how much she means to him.

"I remember," I mumble as she stares at me.

"Atti, why do you have pictures of like a million cats on your phone?" Freddy asks, and Atti looks over from where he's sitting on the other sofa.

"They're my kitties," he replies.

"Crazy cat man," Freddy mumbles.

"Your right, I do have an addiction to puss–" Atti replies, and I glare at him before he ends that sentence.

He coughs out, "I mean I have an addiction to cats."

I think he forgets that Freddy is nine.

"You do," Freddy replies not getting the joke.

"Sorry, I meant to say cats when I realised who I was talking to," Atti says into my mind with a slight sheepish expression when he sees me glaring at him.

"Bad influence," Jaxson says to me, and I nod. I guess Atti doesn't have much experience with kids. I don't have a lot other than when I used to babysit the neighborhood kids for pocket money growing up.

Jaxson takes my hand as Atti gets told off by Lucinda. I almost want to stay to see what happens, but Jaxson pulls me into the dining room.

"I want to ask you something, but can you sit?" he asks me, looking nervous. It is the first time I've ever seen Jaxson nervous, it's just not like him.

I take the seat he pulls out, and I sit down. I watch as Jaxson falls to his knees in front of me.

"By the goddess, I ask you,

To be your mate and give me the ability always to protect you.

I will be yours, and you will be mine,

Until the end of our time.

I give you my heart and ask for yours,

Will you be my mate?" he asks on his knees. The position isn't lost on me, and it's the second time he has kneeled for me, the man who once told me he would never kneel for anyone. My heart pounds against my chest as I stare into his bright-green eyes. The amount of love in them is overwhelming. I don't need to think about it long. I know people say that distance makes the heart fonder, well it's true. Being away from Jaxson has just taught me how much I love him, that time and distance have no effect on my feelings for him.

"Yes, and I will protect you as long as I live," I whisper. Jaxson's smile could have set the earth on fire as he lifts me up and kisses me. A wave of power and promise sweeps through me, making me dizzy. The words are filled with some magic.

"The ceremony is to make me king, and I want you at my side as my new queen," he tells me.

"You're sure?" I ask in a breathless whisper.

"Yes, my mate," he says, his expression is filled with love and pride.

"We are not mated yet," I grin.

"We have exchanged blood and said the vows. We have to consummate the bond, but we are still linked either way, even if you decide to walk away or try and kill me for pissing you off."

"You could try being nice and not pissing me off," I suggest.

"It's not possible, and you like it," he says and kisses me gently.

"I like you my Wolf-man," I respond.

"I like you, my little human," he kisses me gently. A kiss full of unspoken promises.

"We must get ready, Anna has left a dress on my bed for you."

"What if I said no?" I ask at the door.

"I always get what I want, lass."

"Doesn't surprise me, Jax," I laugh and walk out of the dining room. I don't see anyone as I walk to Jaxson's room and find a long, dark-green dress on the bed. It has three slits across the ribs, and it looks tight. I put it on, and it sticks to all my curves. I'm lucky I'm getting a little more toned with all the training; my stomach is flatter than it's ever been, and my body feels lighter. It doesn't mean I've stopped eating chocolate cake every night because I haven't. No one is brave enough to refuse me chocolate.

I look in the mirror, and it doesn't look too bad, just a little slutty. Alex would be proud.

The dress hangs off both my shoulders, and I take my bra off because the dress is so well fitted, I don't need it, and don't want bra straps showing. I end up taking my underwear off too because you can see them outlined in the tight dress. I'm glad I had flat, black shoes on that are hidden under the end of the dress, anyway.

My hair is down and reaches my backside now, must be a vampire thing because it grows way too bloody fast.

I'm just smoothing my dress down when the door opens, and Katy comes in. She squeals and throws herself into my arms.

"You look so hot, like out of this world. A real queen for us," she whispers the end part.

"You look lovely, too," I replied looking at her small, green dress and black cardigan. Katy's hair is cut short, stopping near her chin and falls straight. The effect makes her look a lot older.

"I came to do your hair and makeup," she holds up a little bag and points to the only chair in the room. I pull it out a little, so she can get behind it and sit as she plugs in a hair curler.

"We'll do the makeup first, I think," she mumbles, and I stay quiet as she starts applying something to my eyes.

"So, how does it feel to be a princess of the vampires and soon to be the queen of the shifters?" she asks me.

"How did you know?" I ask her. I didn't know she knew about Wyatt and me.

"I've seen how you and Jaxson are together. There is no way that man isn't going to have you at his side. Harris told me about you being the girl from the prophecy. Just don't destroy us all," she jokes.

"Oh well, no pressure. If it helps I don't have any plans to destroy things or people," I tell her.

"That's a relief. I couldn't see you hurting anyone, Winter. You're so sweet," she tells me.

"I'm not that nice, Katy, but I'm not a monster. This whole prophecy is weird to accept," I say, and I hear her going through her makeup bag.

"What part?" she asks.

"That I'm going to have more than one mate for starters? That they are princes, and the other two princes in my life I have big crushes on," I reply.

"It's weird because you are human," she says.

"What do you mean?" I ask.

"This is our way of life, Winter. I know humans don't share, and that's fine for them, but I believe love is infinite." She brushes foundation around my face.

"I just . . . ," I reply, but I don't know how to explain it.

"You just don't know how your future is going to be?" She finishes my sentence.

"They are all princes who will be kings one day. How am I going to move between them all?" I ask.

"You believe in the goddess and her plan. You are her program, Winter," she tells me.

"Why do you think that?" I ask.

"My mother and fathers taught me about the goddess. It's said that the goddess that made the prophecy had four mates: a vampire, a shifter, an angel, and a witch. Something went wrong, and she was killed,"

"What do you think happened?"

"I don't know, no one does. It was so long ago. All we know is that all her mates were killed on the same day. That she and her sister who made all the races, died on the same day," she tells me. A memory of a dream of Elissa dying flashes in my mind.

"Where did you learn this?" I ask her and try to turn my head to see her. I open my eyes as she starts messing with my hair.

"My mother has these old books, she said they were passed down through her family. There are lots about the goddesses' sister in them, but only my mum can read them as they are in Latin," she says.

"I need those books. I've been searching for anything on the goddess. It's essential, Katy," I tell her.

"All done, and I'll get them for you. She would happily share them with our new queen and tell you anything you want to know," she says.

"When did you get so mature?" I ask, while she's curling bits of my hair. I stay quiet when she doesn't reply, and I feel her pulling parts of my hair back.

"Around the time my queen saved my life," she winks at me as she moves a few pieces of hair around my face and moves back. I stand up and stare at myself in the mirror. My hair is half up in a bun with bits braided and other parts twirling down my back. My face looks more defined like this, it's amazing.

"Wow," I mumble.

"Come on, hot stuff, I know a wolf that needs you," Katy laughs and opens the door.

We walk down the corridor and the stairs, at the bottom is a sight that makes my heart jump.

Jaxson is standing in the middle of Atti and Dabriel. Each one of them is looking like kings of some fairy tale. Jaxson is impressive with his hair styled and wearing a green shirt and black trousers. Atti has on his crown and is wearing his cloak over his black shirt and pants. Dabriel also has a crown on, smaller than a king's but still impressive. Dressed in all white, as I've gotten used to seeing. Each one of them seems in shock as I stroll down the staircase.

"Fuck me," Atti says, and Jaxson whacks him on the back of his head.

"What Atti meant was that you look beautiful, Winter," Dabriel says as he looks me over. A wave of heat is touching every part of my body where he looks.

"Yeah that," Atti mumbles, and I look over at him as he stares at me.

"My queen," Jaxson says as he steps forward and takes my hand in his.

"That's a bizarre thing to get used to being called. I've just gotten used to the term 'princess'," I tell him, and he smiles.

"It must be," Jaxson nods and walks us out the door.

My jaw drops, and I quickly remind myself to close it when I see all the wolves outside the cabin. There must be hundreds, maybe close to a thousand of them, all in wolf form with their heads touching the ground. They look like they are bowing. The driveway has been covered in little, green lights in lanterns. They hang from the trees and of hooks in the ground to make a pathway for us to walk. We walk slowly down the driveway with Atti and Dabriel following us, until the path turns left and we walk up a little hill. I smile at a few little wolves sitting next to each other as they raise their heads a little as I walk past. A little, grey one with both the tops of his ears missing nods at me before lowering his head. I wonder what happened to him, but I don't have time to think about it as we come to a large clearing at the top of the hill. The floor is made out of stone and carved with wolves in a large circle. I walk up the three steps, and Atti and Dabriel stand like guards at the sides of the steps. Lucinda is positioned in the middle with five men behind her. I see Freddy–in his wolf form–next to a few wolves, and I look away quickly as Jaxson walks us up the steps. We stop before Lucinda and she bows. When she talks, her voice echoes around the trees, like they are carrying her words as a blessing.

"We have come here today to swear our allegiance to our new king and our new queen. Jaxson is the last of our royal line, and we ask the goddess to bless our new king.

Every wolf here has sworn allegiance to you and your new queen. We will protect you as you protect us," she says, and one of the males behind her hands her a silver dagger. They are all large men, but one of them gives me a small, reassuring smile.

She cuts a line down her hand and offers the knife to Jaxson. He accepts and cuts his hand, as they hold hands, a wave of power hits us all. I fall to my knees as everything turns green, I hear a voice, but I can't make out what she is saying, only that it's a woman. When it finally stops, I open my eyes to see Jaxson glowing, actually glowing a faint green. His eyes find mine, and he reaches for me. The moment his hand touches mine, a warm feeling surrounds me. Jaxson doesn't stop as he pulls me to him in a passionate kiss. Our lips meet, and the world blurs. I don't see anything other than Jaxson, his hands on my waist, our lips pressed together, and our minds focused on each other. The wolves howl loudly, the sound echoing through the forest. When we break away from each other, Jaxson grins at me before turning to Lucinda. One of the males behind her rushes to help her up, and she smiles at us.

“The goddess has spoken, and this is your birth right," Lucinda says and accepts a box from one of the men. Lucinda opens it and pulls out a crown like no other. The green metal stretches around in dozens of twirls. There are four, dark-green, massive gemstones held by the crown. I can’t take my eyes off of the crown as I feel its power from here, so much like the crown the vampire king has. What is different about those crowns?

Jaxson gets on one knee in front of Lucinda as she moves to hold the crown over his head.

"The new king of the wolves, we welcome you," she says and places the crown on his head. All the gems glow brightly, and the wolves howl once more as Jaxson stands.

He looks so much like a king, it's hard to watch without feeling like I'm in a movie. Jaxson looks powerful as he stands watching his wolves, they rejoice with their howls. I may not be able to understand the wolves, but their joy is evident, and it makes me smile widely. When his eyes meet mine, I nod in respect. I know how much he wanted to avoid this, but it's where he is meant to be.

The rest of the night, I meet a lot of different wolves, some speak English and some only a little. I can see the difference of females to males there are at the party. Jaxson never leaves my side. Atti and Dab stay close as well, as we dance and eat some food.

"I want to take you somewhere," Jaxson says as we sway to the gentle music the band is playing.

"Should I be left alone with the new king?" I tease him.

"Yes, my Queen," he says seriously, and I can only nod. I wave at Atti and Dabriel, who laughs at something Atti says to him while they watch us. God knows what he said. Jaxson walks us off to the right of the party and through the woods. The sun is finally setting in the sky, and the forest seems so peaceful.

"What happened when you and Lucinda exchanged blood?" I ask him.

"Lucinda had exchanged blood with every wolf here, so I connected with everyone. I can feel all the nine hundred wolves that are bonded to me," he tells me.

"That's a lot of pressure," I respond.

"It's my job, I wouldn't deserve the title of a king if I couldn't protect them. My grandfather was the last king, and he was a good man. Females can't take the throne, and my mother only had me before she died. My aunt couldn't have children, so I'm all that is left. I think it was meant to be this way; the power I was given at birth and the power I just got from the wolves. It all was given to me, so I can be the king they need," he tells me.

"The goddess made a right choice then, I couldn't imagine anyone better for the throne than you," I say and stop talking when I see the cliff we're at. It seemed like years ago when we were last here, but I know it's only been a few months. No words are needed as we walk over.

Jaxson moves us onto the smooth rock as I wrap my arms around him. He rests his chin on my head as his power lifts the rock and travels us down into the cavern. When he stops, I let go and look around. Nothing has changed since I was last here and, yet, so much has. Jaxson moves behind me as I stop to put my hand in the water.

"I love you," he says in a whisper only meant for me as he kisses my neck. I arch myself into him as his hands sweep down my body. Jaxson pulls the zip on the back of my dress down until my dress falls off me slowly. Leaving me bare to him.

"Jax," I say in a breathless whisper as he turns me to face him.

"Tell me to stop, and I will," he says.

"Don't stop," I reply. Jaxson's light growl fills the cavern and my ears as he pulls me up to him. My legs wrap around his hips as he kisses me–a kiss that starts an inferno inside my body. Jaxson carefully lays me on the damp, soft floor of the cavern and leans back to pull his shirt off. The gentle, yellow light lets me see his large chest for a second before he's on top of me. Our bodies are pushing against each other as we both struggle with our passion. Jaxson kisses down my body, stopping to make me moan like crazy as he kisses my breasts. His lips move slowly down my body until he finds my core. I scream out in pleasure as he devours me, just like the wolf I know he is. There's nothing sweet about how Jaxson takes me over the edge. It's all fire and passion like he is. He moves up my body before leaning back to undo his trousers. My eyes widen at the sight of his large, thick length as he kicks his pants off.

Jaxson settles above me, and he looks down at me. "You're mine, lass," he says against my lips before kissing me deeply as he pushes inside me. My back arches in pleasure as he fits perfectly. A slight sting of pain is lost in pleasure as he kisses my lips and fills me completely. Jaxson doesn't wait, and he instantly starts thrusting away, our moans filling the cavern.

"I love you, Jaxson," I mumble again and again as we both lose ourselves.

A burning pain fills my middle back as we both finish, making me wriggle and wrestle between the pain and pleasure filling my body.

"It's just my mark, it will stop in a second, lass. I'm sorry, I forgot about it," he says as he pulls me on top of him, the pain from my back feels like it's going to burn through my whole body. When the pain finally stops, I sigh as Jaxson runs his fingers over my skin where the pain was.

"Can I see your mark? I've never seen it," I ask him after a while.

"Yes, I will never refuse you anything," he says.

"Even your brownies?" I ask.

"Well, if I have to, I'll share them with you," he says, looking worried, and I laugh. He grins at me as he sits us up. I sit on the ground as he turns so I can see his lower back. There's a wolf, made up of twirls at the bottom, and it's howling up at something. It's amazing and looks so real. I must have it on my back now, I wonder what it looks like next to Wyatt's.

"You need to go back with Atti, the necklace will hide our mating," he tells me. He doesn't look happy about it.

"I don't want to leave you, but I can't leave Wyatt," I tell him.

"Have you told him yet?" he asks.

"No, he's been busy with his father," I respond. I'm sure he is avoiding me. Every night, I'm sure he waits until I've gone to sleep to come back, and in the mornings, he's gone before I say a word to him. I see him sometimes watching me in training or the library, but he disappears if I get up. I don't know what I've done to upset him.

"I never wanted him to hate me. I never actually hated him for loving my sister. I'm glad she had a little happiness before her death." he tells me. I can't help feeling a little jealous of Demi; she had Wyatt first and gave him a child. I know it's silly, and it doesn't take away from the sorrow I feel for Freddy, Jaxson, and Wyatt.

"He did love her, he has always told me that. He stayed around this town, making sure you were safe. He may not admit it, but he loves you, too. You are like real brothers, blood or not. It never mattered, and I understand because I feel the same about Alex," I tell Jaxson.

"I kept his son from him," he says, a hint of sadness in his voice. I know he didn't want to, not really.

"You didn't have a choice, Wolfman," I tell him.

"I hope Wyatt sees it like that," Jaxson replies and pulls me to him. We kiss slowly as the sun sets in the sky, and the wolves rejoice at their new king with howls that fill the night.

33

WINTER

"Winter," the childlike voice sings into the air. The cold air chills my skin as I open my eyes. I'm in the middle of a forest. The dream is the same one I've seen many times before they started changing. Elissa is sitting in the midst of a clearing, in front of a small fire. Mumbling words I can't hear as her black hair sways in the wind. My head turns up when another woman walks over. She has a red cloak hood over her face, so I can't see her, but I'm sure it's a woman from the way she moves and the shape of her body under the cloak. She stops next to Elissa and rests her hand on her shoulder.

"The boys want to see you, sister," she says. This must be Demtra, the goddess that made all the supernaturals. It's strange to be so close to her, I've gotten used to Elissa by now. I look at her differently, now that I know she is a goddess, the one that made the prophecy about me.

"I love them, and I love him," Elissa replies, her voice sounding cracked like she has been crying.

"I understand," Demtra says, her voice sounding like velvet and like I've heard it before.

"I am pregnant," Elissa says quickly as she stands.

"Who is the father?" Demtra replies, the forest seems colder all of a sudden. Elissa doesn't say a word as she looks at the fire. Demtra follows her gaze. I can only see them both staring at the fire for a long time; the trees creaking in the wind. I look down to see I'm wearing a white dress, a dress I've never seen before, and it matches the blue one Elissa is wearing. She must not feel the cold like me.

"That child will be half goddess and half demon," Demtra says, her voice echoing in the woods.

"And still mine. I will love her regardless," Elissa says quickly, she turns to look at her sister for the first time.

"And so shall I, sister," Demtra says and slightly nods her head.

Elissa embraces her sister tightly.

"Have you seen any of the future of this child?" Demtra says as Elissa pulls away, I can only see bright-blue eyes under the red cloak.

"Yes," she says.

"And?" Demtra asks when no one says anything for a while.

"He will kill the child and me for the power. He will kill all my mates when they choose to protect the child and me," Elissa says, her sentence ending on a sob.

"No," Demtra whispers into the fire. "We will change it, I promise you this," Demtra says. The words echo in my mind just as Elissa turns to look at me with wide eyes.

"Winter Sweetheart, wake up." A hand shakes me awake from the dream, and I open my eyes to see Wyatt leaning over me in bed. His hair looks freshly showered and still slightly damp. A warm smile is on his face as his dark eyes search mine.

"Bad dream?" he asks as I relax into his bed. I remember coming back last night, and Wyatt wasn't in bed. I assume he was keeping his father busy because he knew I was gone for the evening. Atti told me that when he brought me back.

"Yes, more of Elissa and Demtra," I say feeling tired, the dream is fading from my mind even as I speak about it.

So, Elissa was pregnant and with a half-demon baby. So, did she have a demon mate? She must have, but why would she say that he would kill her and the child. What happened? I remember the dream when she died, I wonder if that was the demon king? I never did get to see his face. She said the child survived then, so is there a half demon and half goddess running around somewhere?

"Demtra, did you see what she looked like? There were ten books that referenced her, but we don't know if they are true," Wyatt asks.

"No, but I was certain who she was," I reply.

"I believe you, did you learn anything interesting?" he asks me.

"Elissa was pregnant. Demtra said the child would be half goddess and half demon," I tell him.

His eyes widen. We are just getting used to the possibility that the goddesses existed, and now demons must exist too. "That's impossible," he says.

"Clearly not," I say gently.

"You are mated to Jaxson now," Wyatt says, not a question but a simple truth. My back still tingles a little from the mark, and I haven't even seen what it looks like yet.

"Yes, I love him as much as I love you," I tell him and realise what I said a second too late.

"You love me?" Wyatt echoes in shock. I'm not taking it back because I mean it. I know it, despite my mind telling me it's wrong to be in love with two different people. It doesn't feel wrong. It feels right.

"Yes, I have for a while now," I tell him quietly, and he still doesn't respond.

"Who is Freddy?" he asks, and I'm sure my face goes pale of all colour.

"How did you find out about him?" I ask, wondering how much he knows. His face is clouded in anger.

"Find out what? I heard you tell Alex that you love Freddy. Do you tell all your guy friends that you love them? I can accept my brothers as your other mates but not anyone else. Why didn't you tell me about him?" Wyatt asks, sitting back and away from me on the bed.

"I have to explain this to you."

"Explain what?" he asks me.

"Freddy is your son," I whisper, and he looks at me in shock before he laughs.

"I don't have children. I've only ever slept with Demi, and she was a wolf. I may have fed off humans, but I never slept with them. It's the best-kept secret of the vampire prince, and not even my friends know. I'm too fucked-up to risk letting anyone close because my father would use them against me. He killed the first girl I slept with," he snarls and gets off the bed. He stands near the door like he wants to run out of it.

"Demi was pregnant when you took her to Jaxson. She made Jaxson swear not tell you or she would leave," I say, and Wyatt goes still. He doesn't move an inch as his eyes go entirely black, a pressure in my mind as he talks.

"He kept my child from me?"

"Don't use your power on me. It only hurts me, Wyatt," I say, holding my head. The pressure disappears quickly.

"Just answer, I didn't realise I was doing it, Winter," he says. That's the entire apology I'm getting from him when he is so angry. He is shaking.

"Yes, but for the right reasons, Wyatt. Think about it, if he told you, you would want to see him, and someone would have guessed. Jaxson has made sure no one thinks he is anything but a wolf."

Wyatt listens to me as his eyes glow blacker than I've

ever seen them. I flinch when he punches a hole through the wall by the door.

"My mate kept this from me as well until I found out. You didn't think I needed to know!" Wyatt shouts at me. Blood drops off his knuckles, the wound closing as I watch.

"I was trying to find the right time," I say, but Wyatt slams the door open.

"I just can't deal with you right now," he says and shuts the door behind him, the whole wall shaking with how hard he slammed it. I don't know how long I sit in bed, with silent tears falling from my eyes before I get out of it. Times like this, I need chocolate. I can only find a few packets of unopened Oreo's in the drawers, and they just remind me of Wyatt.

I go into the bathroom and take all my clothes off before looking in the mirror at the markings on my back. The wolf is just below the phoenix and the two are connected with little swirls. If only the actual two men would get along like the mark is or without trying to kill each other. The wolf reaches to the middle of my back. I can almost feel Jaxson as I touch it. I shower quickly and dress in jeans and a white shirt before leaving my room and bumping into Atti.

"I wish to speak with you and the prince," Atti says, and I nod, opening my door and letting him in.

"Wyatt isn't here," I say, but Atti cuts me off.

"When I saw how mad he was, I took him to Dabriel and Jaxson. I also told Leigha you won't be training today. She is telling people you hurt your arm or something," he says, and I hit his arm.

"Ouch, what was that for?"

"He will kill Jaxson in the mood he's in, and you need to take me to them. I love them both, and I can't let them kill each other, they won't talk," I blurt out, and Atti stops me by placing a finger on my lips.

"Dab won't let that happen. They will calm him down, this isn't your fault, Love," Atti says as I pace in front of him. I need to be there and stop anything bad happening. Can Dabriel stop them if they decide to kill each other? Can I survive the loss of either of them? No, I can't. They are everything now.

"It feels like it," I reply.

"No, this happened way before you even met them. It's their past to deal with, and they will not blame you, or I'll drop their asses in the middle of the Antarctic until they cool down." I wonder if he can take them there, it's a scary thought.

"Now, I want you to meet my familiars. I think you'll like them," he says making me smile and slightly agree with him.

"Where can we go that someone won't see and hear us? Only this room is warded." I say.

"I'm a witch, we can go wherever I want to, remember?" he teases.

"Oh, I forgot," I say, feeling silly.

"You forgot about my witchiness?" he grins.

"'Witchiness' isn't a word," I tell him as he moves closer.

"It's my new word I invented today," he chuckles and pulls me to his chest.

I close my eyes and hold my breath as Atti moves us to where ever he wants. When I open my eyes, we are in a stone room. The room has archways surrounding an altar in the middle with three steps leading up it, and it's very familiar.

"I've seen this place in a dream," I mumble and Atti looks down at me. He seems to know this and nods. I wonder if he brought me here to see if I recognised it. It's the room Elissa died in, I kneel down and place my hand on the cold, stone ground. The place where she died.

"We used to come here as kids to meet. The place is well-guarded, and my mother showed it to me. Everyone is scared to come here," Atti tells me as I stand up.

"Why?" I ask. The place is full of cobwebs and dust. The archways are falling apart, and the white floors I remember are now grey and covered in vines. I walk over to the entrance where the wind is blowing through the room from. There is a small corridor, as derelict as the rest of the place, and two door frames that go onto a balcony. The air is warm outside, and the sun is shining over three mountains that I can see. I walk to the edge of the balcony where there was once a small, stone wall, but it's falling off the edge. Once I'm close enough, I can see we are on the top of a big castle. The castle has holes everywhere, vines covering the bits of stone that have fallen. The place is destroyed. I can see stone buildings in the fields surrounding the castle, the areas are covered with weeds and trees. The place is a mess but still beautiful, untouched by the world.

"It's the old home of the goddess and her sister," Atti tells me, and I step back from the edge. I rest my head on Atti's chest, and he just lets me. I don't know why I feel such sadness being here, but I do. The place I remember in my dreams is a ruin now, and I have a feeling the demon king did this. Why would he do that to her? Elissa said she loved him. I could never hurt someone I love as he did.

I hear a slight growl behind Atti, and I look around him to see his familiars walking outside. They both stop by the door, sitting down as their big eyes meet mine. They look like tigers, just not any that I've ever seen in a zoo, and they are bigger.

"Mags and Jewels," Atti waves a hand towards them, and they both turn to look at him.

"Was the story about Jewels and Mags, true?" I ask. I remember him telling me he found Mags as a kitten in magazines, and she still likes sleeping in them. I know that much is true because I still have photos on my phone that he sent me of a cat on top of a pile of magazines sleeping. The cat was white and sort of looks a little like the white tiger, much smaller and more cat-like though.

"Yes, until we touch our familiars, they live in their glamors. They both are the cats I once sent pictures of to you, but they don't like to wear their glamors," Atti says.

"Wow," I say. He sent me a photo of Jewels once, a healthy-looking black cat with grey eyes and wearing a gold necklace. Atti said she borrowed it from his mother.

"The white one is Mags, and Jewels is styling all black," Atti waves a hand towards them.

"Is Jewels still stealing?" I ask as I take a seat on the ground, leaning back to look up at Atti.

"I'm pretty sure she has robbed half the vampire court. I had to tell her off when I caught her staring at the king's crown." He chuckles and sits next to me. Atti wraps an arm around my waist and pulls me to his side. I rest my head against his large, firm chest. Atti smells like flowers in a meadow. So very sweet.

"Where is she putting it?" I ask distracting myself.

"Under my bed, I'm just giving it to the humans to put back. Unless you want some priceless heirlooms, she managed to find a ring with a rock the size of an apple on it." Atti grins at Jewels when she turns her head our way. Jewels walk over to where we are sitting and places her head on my lap. I stroke her lovely fur with little fear. I never thought I would say that, having no fear of a giant tiger with massive teeth who purrs on my lap.

"I hate how the humans are like slaves to the vampires. They won't even look at me, and the vampires just feed on them whenever they want. I'm thankful they haven't killed any more humans in front of me, it's so wrong, and I want to kill them for it." I tell Atti who nods.

"I know. My city isn't like that. We don't have humans in our walls. Everyone is paid for work, and we believe in community. That if you help someone, they assist you back," Atti tells me.

"Tell me about your people," I ask him. I look over at the snow-topped mountains, this place is really beautiful and is so quiet. I bet it's very private, too.

"We are split. Dark witches rule one-half of the city, and light witches, like my mother, rule the other. Our people don't mix or breed with each other anymore. All witches monitor the elements but depending on what side you're born on you are more likely to control individual ones. Light witches have control over water, air, and a little earth. Dark witches control fire and spirit. They also have some weather magic," he says.

"What about you?" I ask.

"I'm special. I have high control over all of them," he tells me.

"Why are you split?" I ask.

"Their queen is persuasive, she managed to convince enough of the dark witches that my mother isn't strong enough to keep us all safe. My mother is powerful but crippled with the loss of her mate, my father," Atti says, his voice echoing with the light wind.

"How did he die?" I ask.

"My father died in the war between the angels and my kind. My mother killed Dabriel's father for killing her mate," he tells me.

"Oh, I'm sorry, Atti," I say and lean up to kiss his cheek

at the same time he turns his head. We both pause, a breath away from each other. I move slightly and brush my lips against his. A low groan escapes Atti before he responds with a gentle amount of pressure. Atti's kisses are sweet, his lips move softly on my own. It's almost like he is treasuring me, taking his own time.

A low growl escapes Jewels, reminding me that her head is still on my lap. I look down with a chuckle as I break away from Atti.

"Sorry, girl, I didn't forget you," I say and stroke her head.

"Worst wingman or wing cat ever," Atti grumbles, but it sounds playful.

"Wing cat?" I ask, and he laughs. Mags chooses this point to walk over. It's hard not to be a little scared as her long teeth shine in the dim light of the room. Mags is scary, she looks like she could rip someone to pieces in seconds.

Mags moves in between Atti and me. She nudges my spare hand with her cold, wet nose. I try to control the slight shake in my hand as I stroke the top of her head, and a loud purr fills the balcony.

Atti stands up and stares down at his familiars and me; Jewels is now snoring lightly on my lap, "They haven't let anyone but J, D, and Wyatt touch them before. Even my mother they hiss at."

"I like them, do all witches have familiars?" I ask.

"Most do, my mother has a large, white bear. The dark witch queen is rumoured to have a falcon she can fly on. The animals vary depending on if you are light or dark," he says, and I nod.

"Do you think Wyatt will be okay?" I ask looking up at him. His cloak floats in the wind, his short, blond hair lighting up his worried expression.

"I don't know, Winter. It's not every day you find out you're a dad and your best friend has brought up your child for you," he says.

"It sounds like something off that TV show, you know the dude who shouts a lot," I reply trying to remember the name.

"Jeremy Kyle?" he asks.

"Yeah that! Alex loves that show," I say, and he laughs.

"We should send Wyatt and Jaxson to the show. Could you imagine it?" Atti laughs.

"I can imagine the title now: 'Prince of the vampires wants a DNA test on the king of the werewolves' nephew'," I say and start laughing. Atti laughs with me until we are both wiping tears away.

"In all seriousness, he doesn't need a DNA. Freddy looks so much like Demi and a little like Wyatt," Atti tells me and moves to lean against the wall. His eyes never leaving mine.

"How is it possible?" I ask.

"I believe there are a lot more hybrids out there than we know. So many people have gone missing over the years. Other people could have hidden their children, just claiming they are normal. Their powers could be easily hidden," Atti says.

"Freddy is immune to silver, heals super-fast, and Jaxson says, he fights well already," I say.

"I wonder if mixing our races can cause these extra abilities. Freddy could be stronger than us all when he is older," Atti says.

"Do you think that's why the prophecy exists? It wants us all together. Any children I would have with anyone in our group would be a mix," I say, and Atti nods.

"I believe so. I don't think keeping our races apart and at war was ever the goddess's idea," he says, and I agree.

"No, I don't think she would have wanted this," I say.

"If you think about it, when she created the races, they must have bred with humans. So, isn't everyone a half-breed in a way?" he says, and I've never really thought about it like that.

"I guess you're right," I smile up at him.

"I'm getting jealous of my cats," Atti says, nodding at them both. Jewels' large head is taking over my lap and Mags is pressed against my side as I gently stroke her soft fur, avoiding the spiky tail.

"I need a favour," I ask him, remembering the mini-demons.

"Will I get a kiss from the princess if I say yes?"

"Yep." I grin, and he laughs.

"What would the princess want?" he asks.

"I need a distraction, big enough that most of the guards will go to it for around ten minutes. Oh, Wyatt has to be with you too, Drake as well, if possible."

"What will you be doing?"

"Something not dangerous, I promise."

"So you're not going to tell me?"

"You probably don't want to know," I say, knowing he'll want to come with me, and he can't be the distraction if he does that.

"Time scale?" he asks, and I grin.

"Soon," I respond, and he nods, clearly thinking about it.

"We should be going back soon. Leave Winter, guys," Atti says, and they both move slowly. Jewels lick my cheek, making me laugh before walking back to stand next to Atti. One on each side.

"Why did you cut your hair?" I ask him as I get closer.

"I felt like a change," Atti shrugs.

"You're hot either way," I reply with a slight blush, and he grins at me

"Thank you, Love," he says and pulls me closer to him. I look up as he leans down and kisses me gently. I don't notice him use his powers this time until we're in Wyatt's bedroom.

"I should go," Atti pulls away, one look suggests he doesn't want to.

"You're right, only a week or so until I can leave," I say smiling.

"I can't wait for that," Atti says and vanishes into thin air.

I wander around my room, and I jump when the door opens. Two humans come in the chamber, both dressed in rags with dark-coloured skin and dark-brown hair. They both instantly lower their heads and bow at me.

"No, don't do that. I'm not . . . I was human like you," I mumble out as I move over to them. They both lift their heads but don't say anything. I notice the trolley full of sheets outside the room, and I assume they are here to clean something.

"Are you here to clean?" I ask and they both nod.

"Can you talk to me?" I ask, as they both glance at each other.

"We are not allowed, Princess. We will change your bed sheets and clean," the taller one says.

"How about I do it?" I ask, and they look at me like I've grown two heads.

"I don't think–" the one starts, so I suggest something else.

"Could one of you get me some lunch instead? I have no idea where the kitchens are," I say. I have an idea, but this place is a maze.

"I can do that," the smaller girl says and moves quickly out of the room.

"I will clean," the other girl says, shooting a look full of worry at me before she gets sheets off the trolley.

"And I will help you," I say.

"You are a princess, they would kill me and my family for letting you do such things," she says, looking at the floor. This is so wrong.

"Then it will be our secret, how long have you lived here?" I ask her.

"I was born here," she tells me.

"Oh," I reply, and she looks at me. Her pale-blue eyes like mine, the same dark-brown hair and we could have swapped places in a second. I could have been born here and her in my place in the world. I can't imagine the life she has here, but I don't know how to help her without getting myself killed.

"Why don't you escape?" I ask after a while of silence, both of us just staring at each other.

"The same reason you don't, I have people I love here. My whole family is here, and we don't have your powers. If we are lucky, one of them might choose us as a mate," she tells me.

"Even if you don't love them?" I ask.

"Love is just fairy tales," she says.

"It's not," I reply quickly.

"Maybe not for you, Princess, but for me, it is," she says, and we clean the room in silence until the door swings open. Talen is standing there, holding the door open.

"Out, the Princess and I need to chat."

"Don't," I say, but the girl runs out of the room. Talen shuts the door and walks over to me as I drop the bed sheets on the floor.

"No protectors around? Silly mistake, little girl," he says.

"I don't need them," I respond, trying to hide my shaking hands behind my back. Talen is creepy and evil. He watches me as I keep eye contact with him. His eyes are slightly red, meaning he fed recently. Talen is wearing a black suit, a black tie and his white shirt has a drop of blood on it.

"You think you are safe?" he says and laughs. His laugh crackles around the room. He moves quickly right in front of me, and I panic. The power I've only felt once before fills my body, and I watch as a blue glow moves out of me and slams into his chest. He flies across the room and hits the wall, breaking the mirror that he hits.

"What are you?" he asks, I lift my hands as I see they are glowing blue. The door opens again, and Leigha comes in, she quickly moves next to me.

"Get out, you will be lucky if the prince doesn't kill you for this, Talen. The king cannot protect you all the time," she says calmly.

"Don't threaten me. You will soon be underneath me screaming my name. Someone needs to teach you some respect, and that you're just a woman," he spits out.

"She is my defender and protector. She will not marry anyone. Run along and tell the king that. You don't deserve any respect, Talen, from any person–woman or not." I tell him. I straighten my back and smile at him, feeling a confidence, I didn't know I had.

"You can't do that!" he shouts at me, his face slowly turning red.

"She can," Drake says walking into the room. He walks over to Talen and punches him. The force slams him into the wall again, and he slides down, unconscious with blood all over his face. Drake picks up his foot and walks out, dragging Talen behind him.

"Thanks!" I nervously shout after Drake and shut my door. I lean against it and look at Leigha.

"Thank you," I tell her.

"A servant came running to me, she told me he was in your room. I sent her to find Drake."

"I will have to thank her," I say, and Leigha nods.

"You shouldn't be alone, but well done on using your power," she says.

"I didn't mean to," I reply.

"You did. We will work on your powers tomorrow. I didn't want people seeing you use them and turning all blue. It doesn't matter now that Talen has seen you," she says, but she doesn't look that worried.

"Okay." I nod, and she walks to the door.

"I will stand guard until Wyatt returns," she says. I want to tell her that might be a long time if he hasn't got himself killed by my other mate. Worry and the urge to throw up fills my body.

"You don't have to–" I start saying and she stops me.

"Winter, you just saved me from a life not worth living. I will protect you until you release me, but I will be your friend endlessly." She says.

"Thanks," I say feeling a blush. Leigha shows me a rare smile before she shuts the door.

34

WYATT

"Atti, I'm going to fucking kill you," I shout as Atti disappears on me. I was walking down the corridor, trying to calm down when he grabbed me and brought me here. We are in a field in the middle of nowhere. What the fuck is he doing?

I sense him a moment before he comes back, with Dabriel and Jaxson at his side.

"I'm going to sort your mess out with Winter," Atti tells me and disappears, but I just stare at Jaxson.

The new king doesn't look worried as he should be.

"You fucking bastard. You kept my son from me?" I say, my voice is loud and full of anger. I go to move to hit him when Dabriel runs between us. His skin is glowing, and he's giving me a clear warning look. I respect Dabriel, but fighting an angel isn't easy. They're great warriors. Even if the dark angels are more the fighters of the angel race with their ability to cause pain with their touch, light angels aren't easy to beat. They train all their lives, and with their capacity to heal themselves and fly, a fight could go on for a while, and they would still beat your ass.

Jaxson just nods, a grim look on his face when I look over at him.

"Demi didn't want you to know. I was blood bound never to tell you, I couldn't," he tells me.

"What?" I ask feeling the painful shock of his words. When you are blood bound, it's a promise you can never break. The result would be death if broken.

"Why would you agree to that?" I ask him.

"She threatened to leave if I didn't. I had just met her, and she was scared of me, afraid of her past. She wasn't thinking right, you know how scared she was. How heart-broken that she couldn't be with you," he says.

"You brought my son up," I say, the anger fleeting away. I can't be mad at him, not now. I don't know why Demi made him do it, but I guess she was scared of my father finding out. I don't blame her, not in that sense. This whole situation is fucked-up. Winter is mated to us both, and hurting him would only hurt her.

"His name is Fredrick, but we call him Freddy. I have a photo for you, I knew it wouldn't be long before we needed to chat," he says and pulls out his wallet from his jeans. Dabriel moves out of the way, his powers disappearing now that there is no threat.

"Here," Jaxson hands me a photo of a boy around eight. His hair is brown and blond at the tips. He looks like Demi, so much that it hurts a little. His eyes are the same colour as hers, but his grin, in this photo, looks like me.

"He is nine now and a real pain in my ass," Jaxson says as he messes with his hair, watching me carefully. I expect he still thinks I'm going to try and kill him.

"His powers?" I ask.

"He is immune to silver, heals extremely fast, and is very fast. Faster than most wolves in the pack. He's training with two swords, and he's good. I think spending so much of his life in the pack makes him smell more like wolves. If you get close enough, you can feel it a little. Every wolf in my pack would protect him. I will keep him safe," he tells me. He apparently loves my son, and I bet Freddy loves him like a dad. A little jealousy fills me before I realise how stupid I'm being. I wouldn't have been any sort of dad to him, I would have kept him hidden away from me. I'm too closely watched, someone would have told my father. One look at Freddy, and he would have known who his mother and father are.

"Thank you, I owe you for keeping him safe," I say, offering my hand to him.

"You were always a brother to me. I would have done it anyway, without him being my nephew. Just for you," he says and shakes my hand. He pulls me into a hug and pats my back.

"I have missed you, my brother. You are the only one out of these idiots that can hold your drink," I say with a grin and tuck the photo into my trouser pocket.

"You know angels don't drink," Dabriel groans.

"Except you when you're mad," I smile tightly. I owe these men my life, more than once over. When I was younger, I hated my life. I was the unwanted son, my mother was dead, and I was beaten daily. My father said it would make me a stronger king. Dabriel healed me time and time again. Jaxson and Atti made life worth living. Now, they are family to me, or at least Jaxson is now that he is mated to Winter. It won't be long before Atti and Dabriel mate with her too, she loves them. It's easy to see.

"Not often," Dabriel answers tightly. I only laugh as a response. Angels are the most uptight people you will ever meet. Dabriel is a little different, but you can't change everything about where he comes from. His brothers are worse, a pair of idiots in my opinion.

"So, half of us are mated," I muse.

"And, you're a father, it has been an interesting few months," Dabriel comments.

"How are Winter's powers coming along?" Jaxson asks.

"Better, Leigha is training her well. Leigha hasn't tried her other powers because she's struggling with her normal, vampire ones. It won't be long until we can move her back to her apartment, and we can work on them more," I say.

"Have you asked if she wants to move back? She could run into the pack. You could come too and live near Freddy while we tell him," Jaxson offers.

"I'll ask her," I nod.

"I can't find anything about her kind of power," Dabriel says.

"She has dreams of the goddess and her sister. More recently she told me she had a dream about two people claiming to be her parents," I tell them. Neither of them seems that shocked.

"Let me guess, one of them wasn't her mum?" Jaxson says.

"Or her father. I don't know what's going on, but I think her mother is the next best option to get some answers," I say.

"Do you think she could be related to the goddess? That could be the reason she has such a high connection to them in her dreams?" Dabriel says.

"Perhaps, but why haven't we heard about a child of the goddess," I say.

"We can't guess this, it's too important," Dabriel says.

"There a pub over there, why don't we go for a drink? Atti will find us," Jaxson offers.

"I'd like that," I reply, and he nods. Dabriel grins as we walk over the field.

Things are finally back to normal with us, well better than normal now, because we love Winter.

35

WINTER

"Winter, you’re so lovely. My lovely, lovely Winter," a voice mumbles to me as I open my eyes in bed. Wyatt is laying on the bed next to me, a relaxed grin on his face which doesn't match the Wyatt I just saw earlier today. I stayed awake until one in the morning, but he didn't return. I had guessed he was staying away from me. The overwhelming smell of beer and spirits hit me as he moves closer.

"Are you drunk?" I ask him, and he nods, looking like a happy puppy with his blond hair all messy.

"Did you see Dabriel and Jaxson?" I ask him.

"Yes, Dabriel passed out after four drinks. Angels are such lightweights. Jax and I got into a competition with these biker men,” he says and leans his head on my shoulder.

“We ended up winning and then fighting them because they’re sore losers. So much fucking fun,” Wyatt says, I just notice the slight line of blood on his cheek and the dirt in his hair.

"Are you guys alright?" I ask.

"I had to convince them that they did it to themselves, but they're fine," he laughs.

"I asked if you were alright," I chuckle.

"I'm good, excellent. I'm a dad," he says with a smile.

"That you are," I say a little wide-eyed. I'm not sure if I like drunk Wyatt, but he is cute.

"Atti showed up, grumbled about us being irresponsible and that you need us to protect you. I mean the guy that hides my shit regularly, said I was irresponsible," he laughs.

"Yeah, totally strange," I comment, holding my hand over my mouth, so I don't laugh.

"Totally," Wyatt mumbles and lies back on the bed, I grab his arm when he nearly rolls off.

"Oh shit, I forgot the floor was there," he says.

"Yeah, easy to forget the floor," I chuckle. A moment later he's asleep, and I snuggle into his side before drifting off myself.

When I wake up, I'm alone in bed, and I can hear the shower. I dress quickly in jeans, a purple vest top, and a leather jacket I like. I get bored while I'm waiting for Wyatt, so I make the bed. The human who helped me clean up yesterday flashes through my mind as I look at the broken mirror on the floor.

Is there any way I can help them escape?

Wyatt comes out of the bathroom, fully dressed in black trousers and a white shirt. The buttons are undone at the top, and he smiles at me until he sees where I'm looking. The cracks in the wall are huge, and the broken mirror, with Talen's blood on the floor, was difficult to miss.

"Who?" Wyatt asks tensely.

"Talen. Drake and Leigha helped me deal with him. He was just trying to scare me." I say carefully.

"I'm going to kill him," Wyatt starts for the door, and I stop him by grabbing his arms.

"No, just leave it. He got what he deserved from Drake. I doubt he'll try that again. I made Leigha my defender, and he hated that. I don't think he will come after me again," I say looking into his dark-black eyes as they glow. They slowly return to the black colour with bits of silver in them.

"Leigha would be a good defender for you, I suspected that was what she was doing training you."

"So, you're not going to attempt to murder Talen?"

"It wouldn't be an attempt, but, for now, I will let him live," Wyatt quietly says as he kisses my forehead. I don't miss the 'for now' part in his sentence.

"Okay," I reply.

"Let's get some food from the kitchen, and then I want to take you somewhere," he says, and I nod.

"Hangover food?" I ask following him to the door.

"Vampires don't get hangovers, and it's harder to get drunk. I think I drank around four bottles of Jack Daniels last night and a lot of beer," he says as he shuts the door behind me.

"I like wine, myself," I say.

"I have a private collection of wines in the kitchen. Each bottle is priceless and extremely old. I can show you if you want. I may even let you try one for a kiss," he teases me. I remember the mini-demons and how we need some expensive alcohol. Maybe they will listen if I bring some costly, old wine. Wyatt is going to kill me.

I paint a sweet, innocent smile on my face as I answer,

"I would love to see them."

Wyatt just grins at me and holds my hand as we walk through the many corridors. We pass seven vampires on the way, and each one bows low as we pass. I have to hold back the urge to tell them off and make them stop doing that.

Wyatt takes me into the surprisingly small kitchen, with dozens of cabinets, several cookers, and a lot of humans running around. Each one of them stops as we walk in.

"Carry on," Wyatt tells them, and they do, but slowly, as they watch us.

Wyatt offers me a stool at one of the empty work tops and goes off to talk to one of the people. The woman moves aside, clearly in fear as he asks, "Can I help myself?"

"Ye-yes," she says, and Wyatt nods. I shoot the girl, around my age, a small smile, and she drops her head to look at the ground as she waits.

Wyatt brings over a plate of bacon, eggs, and hash browns. We eat in what would be a comfortable silence if it wasn't for the people in the room stopping to stare at us now and then. It's like they haven't ever seen Wyatt or me eat before today.

Wyatt surprises me by taking my empty plate and washing them up before we leave. We take a lot more corridors until we get to the stables.

"I should get to training soon," I say. I missed yesterday as well.

"I sent a note to Leigha, she will understand. Nonetheless, Leigha has to get ready at some point for the ball," he says.

"Not long until we can go home. I'm not a fan of dancing and dressing up, but I'm excited because I know we can leave after," I stop in my tracks as Wyatt opens the stable doors. Wyatt doesn't have time to answer as he chats with the two men in the room. They rush off to get Wyatt's horse, while I worry. I don't want any more rides in the snow, but I don't tell Wyatt that as his huge, white horse is brought out. Wyatt places me on the horse and takes the seat behind me. Every part of my back is touching him as he wraps an arm around me and takes the reins with the other.

"What's your horse's name? I didn't ask before."

"Star," he tells me.

"Simple, I like it," I say, and he kisses the top of my head.

"I'm glad I don't get cold that much anymore," I shiver a little as a cold wind hit my face. My leather jacket is doing little to stop the breeze.

"Not much further," he tells me.

We travel into the forest and take a left down a worn path. At the end is a cave entrance, two women statues are outside. I lean back to look at them when I realise that they are both familiar. They both look like Elissa.

The one looks just like my dreams with long hair circling her, and the other statue looks a little like her, but she has shorter hair and a slightly different facial expression. I've never seen her with short hair.

"I wanted to show you this," Wyatt says.

"It's Elissa," I reply, and Wyatt hums as a response. We get off the horse, well I fall off with Wyatt's help, but it's not as bad as before.

Wyatt ties the horse up before we both walk in. Inside is an altar of some kind, filled with lit candles and incense fills the air.

"There are a few of these places, people come here to worship the goddess. My father allows it to exist because my mother loved this place," he tells me. I didn't think people believed in her anymore.

"It feels tranquil," I tell him.

"It is," he says looking at the candles. They're all different, and there are twenty of them, in a circle.

"Wyatt, I'm sorry I didn't tell you about Freddy straight away. I should have," I say.

Wyatt takes my face in his large hands and rests his forehead against mine.

"I am sorry, not you. I was just shocked and possibly jealous of Jaxson's part in my son's life. I spoke with Jaxson, and considering we both love you, I want this to work between all of us," he tells me.

"I love you, too," I whisper and he kisses me. The passion overrides anything else as we wrestle with each other. Clothes disappear as we tear them away, desperate for each other. When we both are finally naked, and Wyatt settles himself over me, he doesn't wait or pause as he pushes himself inside me. I moan loudly as he holds my hip with his one hand and pulls my neck towards his mouth. Wyatt stops to look back at me, still inside me.

"There's no going back after this, you will be mine," he warns me.

"There was never any going back from the day I met you. I've always been yours, Wyatt," I whisper, and his eyes turn silver before he kisses my neck. Wyatt sinks his teeth into my neck as he starts thrusting away inside me. The pleasure is overwhelming, and we both lose ourselves. Wyatt pulls back to kiss my lips as he picks up more speed. I lean up and bite into his neck. Something changes the minute I taste his blood because the pleasure increases; every sip tastes like Wyatt, and I'm filled in every sense with him. My body explodes in pleasure, as Wyatt finishes with me, our moans filling the cavern.

"Winter, the future is uncertain, but I will keep you safe," Wyatt says passionately as he looks down at me.

"Together, we will keep us all together, and we will be safe," I say.

"Together," Wyatt whispers, a shared promise as he fills me again and makes love to me until the stars fill the skies.

36

WINTER

"Two days off, and it's like you have never been trained. Pathetic." Leigha says as I pick myself up off the floor. I just hit about three-quarters up the tallest metal wall and then slid all the way down. It's the highest I have ever gotten. Leigha is standing a few steps away, dressed in all black with a mean look on her face. Alex and Drake aren't here today because Alex is sorting our clothes out for the ball. Drake has to go with her, and he did not look happy about it. I don't blame him.

"That's not fair. I did the whole course in five minutes. Like you demanded!" I say with my hands on my hips.

"You didn't complete the course," she says with an unimpressed look.

"That's impossible," I say, and she laughs. I watch as she takes off her hoodie and walks to the start of the small path leading up the wall. She runs fast towards it and jumps. She lands perfectly on top of the metal wall and looks down at me.

"Not impossible, and you can do this." She jumps down and lands in a crouch before standing.

"One day, your life could depend on you being able to jump high and fast. When someone is chasing you, this may be the only way you can escape," she says and lowers her voice to a whisper as she adds, "Like castle walls, for example."

I know she's right, this metal wall is roughly the size of the stone walls that surround the castle, and if I needed to escape I need to be able to jump them. I give Leigha a determined look.

She smiles, "Finally."

I take a deep breath as I walk over to the start of the path towards the large wall. I can do this. I run with everything I've got and push as hard as I can into the ground. I fly up, and my heart feels stuck in my throat when I clear the wall. The downside is that I see the ground, and I know I'm going to land on my side. I close my eyes and instead of feeling the hard floor, I feel a cold wind surrounding me. I open my eyes as I'm lowered to the floor. Atti is standing by the door, his one hand stretched out. His arm and hand are glowing slightly white. He winks at me before leaving.

I hear his whisper in my mind a second later, *"Good job, Love, I knew you could do it."*

I hear Leigha clapping as she comes over from the other side of the wall. I stand up slowly.

"Time for some combat and working on your powers, let's go outside," she says and turns. I didn't expect a 'well done' from her, but I know she's proud of me. I can just tell, or maybe I'm hoping. I'm treating myself to a slice of chocolate cake tonight, okay maybe the whole cake.

We walk outside, and Leigha stops in the middle of the stone courtyard that has the weapons around it. The snow is pushed to one side, and there are two vampires practising fighting with metal swords. They stop when they see us, they bow and then go to stand at the side. Stopping to watch us.

"We'll start with that power of yours, explain what you feel when you use it. It might help," she says, standing about three steps away.

"When I'm mad or angry, I get this pressure in my body, and it just leaves. I then start glowing, and a blue wave hits everything near," I tell her.

"So, it's moving things with your mind but not quite. It's just protective at the moment," she muses.

"Yes," I say slowly.

"Try to use it on those guys and me," she says and looks at the guards.

"What?" I ask, but she ignores me.

"Come here and help your princess," Leigha calls to the guards who bow and move to where she points.

"Close your eyes and remember something that scares you or makes you angry," Leigha suggests.

"I don't think–" I start, but she cuts me off. I hate when she does that.

"Don't think, just feel," she says. I close my eyes and remember Talen as he ran towards me. The anger in his eyes, the blood on his shirt–and the fear fills me. The pressure rises, and I open my eyes as the blue wave leaves me. I have no control, but I do try to stop it.

"No," I say as Leigha and the guards go flying backward. I run over to Leigha as she gets up.

"Very good, do it again, but think about lifting me, instead. You need to plan what you want your power to do," she says.

"Are you mad?" I ask, and I see the guards get up, running away.

"Such pussies," Leigha says watching them with a mixture of disgust and humour. I can't help but chuckle.

"Use your power again," she says, and I do it and she goes flying through the air again. Leigha just gets up as I cringe, Wyatt walks into the courtyard and comes over to press a gentle kiss on my lips. We haven't been able to keep our hands off each other since we fully mated a few nights ago. It's like our relationship has changed now that we don't have any secrets. I feel closer and more in love with him than ever before. Wyatt asked me everything I knew about Freddy last night, and I showed him all the messages he used to send me.

"I have an idea," Leigha says as I break away from Wyatt.

"I'm not hurting you again, it's clear I have no control," I tell her.

"Not me. Your mate." She waves a hand towards Wyatt.

"No," I start, but Wyatt kisses me and moves a few steps away.

"I trust you, go for it Sweetheart," he grins and opens his arms. I close my eyes and find the pressure again, willing it not to hurt Wyatt. The pressure fills my mind, and I open my eyes as the blue wave leaves me. I try to stop it or control it, but it doesn't work. Wyatt goes flying as I run after him.

"Let's go again," Leigha says behind me as I kneel next to Wyatt. He looks fine, although a little shocked as he sits up.

"No, we won't," I turn a glare at her then look back at Wyatt. "You okay?" I ask him and run my hand through his blond hair.

"You're stunning," Wyatt says and kisses me. We don't train for the rest of the day because Wyatt carries me back to our room, and we do our kind of training.

37

DABRIEL

"The human from the prophecy exists," a dark angel called Lucifer from the council repeats my words as I stand in front of them all. All eight of them are giving me mixed looks of shock and fear. Four light angels and four dark angels, who rule over all of us. Each one of them is ancient and late into their extended lives. These are the angels that the rumours are made from. They healed humans once, and the people turned against them when they couldn't save everyone. Many stories were written because of that. I don't know if there is a god, but I know there once was a goddess. The witches stepped in and stopped the angels from killing thousands of humans. That's what caused a massive war between our races and why we have little of our people left. They now hate humans, the ones they used to love and sing songs about, just because they forgot about them.

"Yes," I say simply. The council all stand behind a half-moon table, each one has their family symbol sketched into the table they stand in front of. I glance at the royal marks on the back of my hands, the two angel wings. I wonder what it will look like on Winter.

"Why do you tell us this now?" Lucifer asks me once the whispering stops. Dressed in all black, and matching his pitch- black wings and black hair that is long like mine. Lucifer is the youngest of the council and the easiest to talk to.

"Is this a weak explanation as to where you have been the last few months?" Gabriel, a dark angel, asks. He would want that, he brought my two brothers up and tainted them into monsters like him.

"I tell you because I am your prince, soon to be your king. Times are changing, and I wish to know what the vampire king asked from you," I say, and each one of them goes silent.

"He wished to know where something was, something lost in the past," Michael tells me, a light angel who is usually very wise but sounds like an idiot right now. I respected him growing up, but I know he hasn't seen the future in many years.

"Did you tell him? What did he offer you, and why wasn't I told?" I demand, my skin glowing and wings spread out in anger.

"You are not king, and it has not been decided you will be. The past and future are hidden from us since your birth," Michael replies.

"Maybe because you have become so biased in your beliefs not to help anyone but yourselves, the goddess has turned her back on you," I say. His face goes red in anger, his white hair is in a short cut, and his wings are a lot smaller than mine as they spread out. A few symbols appear on his arms but nothing like mine. My symbols cover all of me.

"Humans do not deserve our help," Gabriel says, his voice cold and bitter.

"Who are you to make that choice?" I ask, and none of them say a word.

"Answer me, what did you tell him?" I say my voice echoes around the domed room we are in. The room has white and black marks all over the walls, and the ceiling is made of glass.

"We will not. Furthermore, we believe that if you mate with the human, you will bring nothing but a war to us. We have finally made a deal with the vampire king who will keep our future clear," Gabriel says. The rest of the council are silent.

"That was not your choice to make. You forget who you all are," I respond.

"You forget that you are one of three princes, there isn't a rule stating the oldest should have the throne. You are best to remember this young prince," Lucifer warns.

I laugh, my laughter filling the dome.

"I would rather destroy our whole race, than let one of my brothers rule. They have no humanity and care for little. They would walk us into a war without blinking," I say. I have seen it. Winter would be the price of such a war, and I will never let her get hurt again.

"That will be our choice, young prince," Lucifer replies.

"I saw your future," I tell him, and his eyes widen. Dark angels can only see the past of the person they touch. I want a debt with one of them, so that they can tell me Winter's past. Lucifer is the perfect dark angel for that. I only have to get him on my side.

"I saw my brother standing over your dead body, your wife's, and your teenage sons'. War was destroying the very city we have, everything was burning, and our people were screaming," I tell him.

"That could happen if you are king as well," Lucifer says, his face pale and his fists clenched. Lucifer's black marks glowing against his dark skin and his black wings are stretched out in anger. He has a lot of marks, that's how he got on the council in the first place, and I also know he isn't a bad person.

"No, it won't. My brother was wearing the crown, it was dripping with angel blood. I can stop that future," I tell him, I wait for him to nod at me before I turn and walk out of the council room as they demand me to return.

38

WINTER

"Wow, you lasted a minute longer than usual," Leigha's sarcastic tone comes through as I groan face-down on the grass.

"That's what she said," Alex shouts over.

I roll on my back as Leigha looks down at me with a smirk.

"Bitch," I pant, and she laughs.

"If you would just work on your powers, we wouldn't need to do this," she says as she offers me a hand and pulls me up. Fighting against Leigha is hard. She doesn't give me a break and happily kicks my ass every morning. She's a good teacher, she shows me how not to attack her and corrects my moves. So, I can last a minute against her now, and we have only been fighting like this for five days.

"You're not using your vampire skills, your extra speed, and strength. You're still thinking like a human," she says as she walks around me.

"I was human until recently, how do I think like a vampire?" I ask her sarcastically.

"You don't think, you are a vampire. It's inside of you, you just have to realise who you are," she tells me.

"You sound like you're going to break out in song in a minute," I say.

"I'd rather break your face, but I'm trying to be a good girl," she deadpans. I try to hold in the chuckle and fail, she just glares at me.

"Why don't Alex and I fight? Drake has trained her, and she is good, better than you," she says, and I swear I almost hear the, anyone is better than you, she wants to add on. Alex is watching us from the side as she paints her nails, Drake is with Wyatt this morning.

"Okay," I shrug. I watch as she calls Alex over, and they get into position. It's hard to watch them fight because they move so fast. I have to force myself to slow them down and watch. It's weird to see Alex move like this; she avoids nearly all of Leigha's hits and sweeps under her arm when Leigha almost gets her. Leigha is better in the end, she manages to get Alex by her shoulder and flip her over.

"You broke my nail," Alex says from her place on the ground.

"You're such a girl," Leigha stares down at Alex, who looks at her.

"You could be too," she suggests, a faint blush appears on Leigha's cheeks as an answer. I'm about to step in when a gigantic boom from a distance distracts me, and fireworks flash in the sky. What the hell? The guards, who are here training, run too quickly for my eyes to see until we are left alone.

"Get to it, love," Atti whispers in my mind.

"Finally, I thought it would take forever for Atti to come up with a distraction," I say with a big smile, as black smoke fills the air in the distance.

"Big fucking distraction, what did he set on fire?" Leigha asks as Alex gets up off the floor.

"I said to distract our guards, not the entire castle," I say, and Alex looks at us both.

"What are you guys up to? And why are we still standing around talking if we have somewhere to be?" she says.

"You're not going to like it," I mumble, and Leigha grins.

"You can go in first," she suggests to Alex, who looks ready to punch her.

"Did you get the wine?" Leigha asks me, and I nod. I run over to my bag I've been carrying everywhere and pull out two bottles of Wyatt's costly old wine.

I hope he doesn't kill me when he sees they are missing.

Leigha nods at me before running off towards the far tower. Atti made the blast as far away from the tower as possible, which is perfect for us. I don't think he meant to do it on purpose.

Alex and I follow Leigha, me moving slower because I don't want to drop the wine. We get to the tower, and Leigha kicks the door open, smashing the wooden locks.

"We aren't meant to look like we have been here," I mutter.

"Anyone would just assume the mini-demons did it," she shrugs. I suppose she has a point.

"Here," I shove the bottles of wine at her and she huffs at me.

"Mini-demons? Are you two out of your fucking minds? You know they are little devils, right?" Alex says loudly behind us.

"They just like to party, you had a lot in common with them when you were younger," I say.

"I can't remember those times," Alex waves a hand at

me, and I chuckle. We move up the dozen or so steps of the tower, avoiding broken wood, and rolls of toilet paper chewed into tiny pieces and strewn all over the place. There are dozens of bottles of beer and other drinks making the place look like a frat party gone wrong. Loud, dance music is coming from the highest room in the tower.

Leigha opens the door when we get to the top, and Alex screams. The room is full of rats, I hold in a scream as they all stop to look at us. The scene changes so quickly, it makes me feel fuzzy. The rats aren't rats at all, they are little people who glow a slight blue. They are brown, grey, and I see some with blue skin. They all have white hair and big squashed-in looking noses, their feet and hands are as large as their big stomachs. They are wearing rags over their bodies, some have little rags in their hair holding it up and they're about the size of a small rat, no wonder their glamors work so well. They don't need to change size. Leigha holds up the two bottles of wine.

"We need to talk, the princess brought you five-hundred-year-old wine from the prince's private collection, you know the one that's locked up tight, so you guys can't get in," she says, and a hiss is returned from them. I duck as something is thrown at us. I glance down at the water dripping from my leg and the condom on the floor. I glance up in horror as I see them lift dozens of condoms filled with water.

"Fuck, you little shits," Alex shouts as more of those things are thrown at us. I get soaked as we scramble out the door. I gaze behind me as Leigha is hit with a random sofa cushion and drops the wine. They roll across the floor as I get hit in the back with water,

"Stop!" I shout as three demons take the wine as Leigha tries to get up, but they are still throwing things.

Alex pulls the cushion off Leigha, while I hold up my arms to stop the incoming water condoms they are throwing.

A sharp bit of wood hits my arm when they throw a chair leg at the wall near my head, and it leaves a nasty cut.

"Out, out, out!" I shout, and Leigha and Alex don't waste any time following me out the room. I slam the door shut.

"They are nuts," Alex says, squeezing the extra water out of her hair.

"You have a condom in your hair," Alex points at Leigha. She's right, she does.

"What?" Leigha pulls out the condom and holds it in front of her in disgust before dropping it.

"They looked like they were using them as balloons, they must have stolen someone's supply," Leigha says with a slight chuckle, which makes us all laugh. We all look at each other and start giggling until reality hits.

"This was all pointless because they won't help us," I sigh.

"Hello," a small voice says from the bannister of the stairs. A mini-demon is sitting on the edge, he looks different from the others. He is slightly blue, with white hair tied with a little rag. He is thin and has big, grey eyes that watch us closely.

"Hi, I'm Winter. This is Alex and Leigha." I introduce them both with a wave, and he nods.

"I am Milo," he says and stands up. I watch as he does a tiny bow, so cute.

"Hello, Milo, we need some help," I say.

"I'll help you," he replies. His voice is small and sounds like a small child.

"We need to know what the king is doing," I say gently.

"Bad man," Milo shakes his head.

"Yes, he is," I nod.

"He is bringing king back," Milo says, he struggles to pronounce king, so it sounds a little like ring.

"I don't understand," I frown as he shakes his head at me.

"I'll help you," he nods.

"Yes, you are, but what king is he bringing back?"

"Your family," he says looking at the cut on my arm.

"My family? That makes no sense, Milo," I frown. I think of Jaxson, but it doesn't make sense.

"You will. King is coming," he says and stands up. Tiny little white wings come out his back, and he flies over to me. He lands on my shoulder and sits down.

"What are you doing?" I ask.

"You keep Milo safe, Milo helps you," he replies.

"You have a pet demon, only you, Win," Alex chuckles, and even Leigha looks shocked.

"He isn't a pet," I say, and I look at him.

"I am your friend," Milo says with a smile.

"Do you know anything about a king coming back, guys?" I ask Leigha and Alex who both shake their heads.

"We need to ask the boys and look through the books. Just be careful about it," Leigha says, and I nod, agreeing. We all leave the tower and get back to the courtyard without seeing anyone. I tell Milo to hide in my bag, and he happily does when I tell him there is chocolate in there. I guess I can share or get more.

About five minutes after we start training again, Atti and Wyatt come into the courtyard. Atti is covered in black soot, and Wyatt doesn't look any better. His blond hair is covered in it.

"What happened?" I ask innocently.

"Atti got a little fire happy when showing some human children a fireworks show." Wyatt glares at Atti.

"I was just keeping the little ones happy, I just need to work on my aim," he winks at me.

"Yeah, hitting the stables wasn't the best idea," Wyatt says dryly.

"Are the horses okay?" I ask, feeling worried.

"None were in there, thankfully it was being cleaned out. No one was hurt, but it took a while to put it out because it was magical," Wyatt glares at Atti and comes over to kiss me gently.

"How is training?" he asks. I watch as he turns my arm over and looks at the cut.

"Uneventful," I mumble as I look over at my bag. Milo chooses that moment to poke his head out covered in chocolate and grins at me before going back.

Yep, Wyatt isn't going to like our new roommate.

39

ATTICUS

"So, young prince, what brings you to my court?" the vampire king asks as he sits on his throne. Disgust fills me as I see the human people on their knees in front of him. Their empty stares across the empty room are haunting, but I know I can't help them. They won't be alive long anyway by the thin, pale looks of them. Death would be a mercy for them. "Other than destroying my stables to please a few children," he says, but he doesn't care.

"My queen sent me to discuss the proposition you gave her," I say loudly. The four members of the council are sitting on their chairs to his left, and Wyatt is standing by the window.

"She refused me. There is little to discuss. I found your dark queen more agreeable. She has helped me with the item I needed," he says, a mysterious smile appears on his face when I get angry. I'm sure my eyes are glowing.

"She is no queen," I grit out.

"Oh, but she is," the king laughs. The sound is hollow even to my ears.

"Little boy, you should run home to your queen before you find out what I gave the dark witch in return for her help," he says as he stands. I clench my fists, resisting the urge to fight him, and I turn to walk out.

I flash once I'm outside the throne room and go straight into my mother's home. When you are close to someone, you can go to wherever they are as long as it isn't warded. Not many wards keep out a witch anyway, they aren't meant for that. Our magic can easily find a gap and then open it. My mother's city has a powerful ward, but only against other races, witches can leave or return if they wish. I just think of my mother and my magic guides me to her.

I find her in her sitting room, sitting in a large, leather chair with her familiar's head on her lap. My mother's familiar is a bear. An enormous white one with the scariest, fucking eyes you've ever seen. The bear is called Bart, and I always find it funny to call him that. The Mother said he has a longer, complicated name and calling him Bart is easier. I understand that, Mags and Jewels have demon names that are very long and annoying. When you touch your familiar, their true demon name is whispered in your mind.

"Mother," I say, and she turns to face me. She looks tired, more than she usually does.

"You've finally come back to see me," she says.

"Winter was ill. I couldn't leave her, and she is in the vampire castle now. I'm sorry I haven't been back sooner," I tell her. It's not exactly unusual for me not to visit for weeks, I have my apartment in the city and don't live in the castle. I have a room, but I prefer my space where none of the witches who want my attention can find me. My mother found the place for me, she understands my need for space sometimes.

"Come closer, Atticus," my mother holds her hand out for me. I walk over and take her small hand in mine. Not that I'm stupid enough to mention it, but my mother's age is catching up with her. I know she must be close to a hundred and eighty years old by now. Her light hair is greying, and her magic seems weaker these last few years. She is still stunning, she always has been.

"With Winter at your side, you will become a real king. Whatever happens, my son, know that," she says. I kneel in front of her and push the big bear out the way. Bart grumbles but moves.

"Nothing will happen, you will be queen for many years yet, and, hopefully, if I can convince Winter to have my little ones, you will be a grandmother to them," I tell her. I'm talking at least twenty years after we have mated. I want to enjoy Winter first.

"Maybe. Maybe not. Go back to your mate, she will need you soon," she tells me but won't look at me.

"Mother, are you well?" I ask her. She seems so pale. She looks away from me at the windows of her room. The room itself is one of the best places to see the city, other than the throne room. You can see our high walls in the distance, the fields inside them where we grow our herbs, and the jewel trees glitter all around the city. The rows of homes we built that are topped with different colour roofs; a city that's never been touched by the human world. It's wonderful, much like its ruler.

"I am well, my son. Don't leave your mate alone too long. I've warned you once, and I will once more," she stops speaking to look at me finally.

"The vampire king is messing in dangerous waters. Either way, there will not be a good outcome for your mate," she tells me.

"Mother," I start but she waves a hand at me. I know

the conversation is over. I wonder what my mother was like before she lost her mate. She has never been a bad mother, just distant with me. Mother always looked at me like I'm a ghost sometimes, I know I look very much like my father.

"Go," she says, and I nod. I stroke my hand over my mother's cold hand before flashing to the training yard where Winter should be. I hear her straight away.

"I like Milo, and I'm keeping him," she shouts. Even when she shouts, it isn't that threatening.

"He is a mini-demon Winter, not a pet!" Wyatt replies loudly, and I hold in the laugh as I stop on the top floor that overlooks the training yard. Winter is standing with her hands on her hips looking furious, as Wyatt stands opposite her. Wyatt is holding a tiny, blue demon, whose face is covered in black and white stuff.

"You're just mad because he ate your Oreos," Winter replies. Yep, the demon is done for.

"We are not keeping him," Wyatt shouts louder, and I laugh. I tune out their argument as I look down the corridor. Watching Winter and Wyatt is one the council members. I don't know what his name is, but Wyatt told me he was the one that threatened Winter when she was alone. He has the royal vampire crown tattooed on his shaved head, but that's all that's special about him. I flash straight behind him and wrap my hand around his throat. I call my fire powers, so my hand is slowly burning him. Not enough to kill him, but it's painful and burning his throat enough that he can't speak. I can tell from the way he holds back a scream, and he tries to move my hand away that it hurts. Luckily I'm bigger than he is and a lot fucking stronger.

"If I catch you watching her again, I will find ways to make you wish you never saw her," I say in a deathly whisper and let him go. He drops to his knees gasping as he turns to glare up at me. "Cat got your tongue?" I laugh. "Don't worry, I don't need an answer, but my cats will have your tongue if you don't heed my warning, vampire," I tell him and walk away as he is still gasping for air. His vampire healing will heal him, eventually.

40

WINTER

"I can't breathe," I gasp out.

"Just a little more," Alex says as she finally ties the last part of the corset to the massive dress I'm wearing. It's dark red, tight at the top where the corset pulls in my chest and stomach. The skirt flows in layers down to the floor and hides my lovely, silver heels. The skirt is filled with little, sparkling gems, so when I move, the dress sparkles. I look like a bloody princess for once; I'm not sure I like it.

Wyatt had it made for me, with Alex's help for styling and getting the size right. I've never been a girly girl like Alex, but I love it.

"Go and have a look at my work. You finally look like a princess and not my jeans-loving sister," she playfully says.

I smile at Alex and pull her into a hug before letting go.

I walk over to the mirror in the bathroom, and I don't recognise myself. My hair is straight, and the top part is up in some fancy bun. My makeup is perfect and makes my blue eyes look bigger. I know that they look brown to everyone else, but it's still amazing. My necklace is tucked between my breasts on a longer chain we found in the wardrobe, the crystal reminding me of Atti. I wonder what he and the others will think of the dress.

The dress does make me look like a princess, straight out of a fairy-tale book.

It's weird and beautiful at the same time.

"You look stunning, Sweetheart," Wyatt says behind me, and I turn as he walks into the bathroom. A wave of desire fills me when I see him in his tux. He looks amazing, and part of me just wants to rip it off him to find the impressive body underneath. I smile when I see he is wearing a red bow tie that matches my dress. I'm sure it was done on purpose.

"You look so sexy," I blurt out way too quickly, and he laughs. I have no idea why hot guys like me. I can be seriously uncool.

"We can't be late, let's go, and I can bring you back and take off that dress. I prefer what's underneath," he says seriously as he takes my hand and we walk out. Wyatt has the right idea for later tonight, butterflies fill my stomach at the notion. Alex must have left to get ready, and I didn't even hear the door shut.

We pass a few vampires, dressed in tuxedos and lovely dresses that look strange in the dark corridors. Most of the women are wearing red, it must be out of some love for the throne. Every person stops to bow at us we walk past.

When we get to the throne room, Wyatt takes a left down the corridor I haven't been down. At least, I don't think I have, they all look so similar.

At the end, there are two massive, dark wooden doors and four vampire guards standing outside. They each bow with their fists over their hearts before two of them open the doors. We walk in together, to a gigantic room full of vampires. The mix of people in coloured dresses and beautiful decorations is amazing. There is a huge chandelier in the middle of the room, it looks like it has thousands of tiny light bulbs on it. The two walls are lined with mirrors, and at the front is a massive band. Music plays softly, and I look over to see one huge piano in the middle of the band being played by a lovely woman and various other instruments are being played beautifully in tune with her. The front half of the room is filled with couples swaying to the soft tone of the music and others are gathered around a long table filled with food. Wyatt tugs my arm in his, and we walk through the people. Many stop to bow, and smile at us. Most look at Wyatt and me in wonder.

We eventually make our way to the left side, where the king is standing with his council. The king is laughing, looking a lot like Wyatt, but the vibe they both give off is so different. The only thing they seem to have in common is that they look like they have a lot of power, a power you can't miss.

Wyatt's power is pure and the king's is, well, evil.

"Wyatt, we were just discussing you," the king turns, dressed to perfection in a suit like Wyatt's.

"Oh?" he says.

"Talen, here, has never heard you play the piano. I was telling him how wonderful you are at it," he says, his voice might come across as a proud parent if it wasn't for the calculating look he gives me.

"Yes, I am," Wyatt responds. His arm slides around my waist as he talks.

"Talen was never interested in music. If I remember right, he used to annoy our home teacher by playing so poorly," Wyatt says.

"I do enjoy music now, Wyatt," Talen replies tensely, as he shoots daggers at Wyatt.

"Why don't you play a song for us? I will keep your mate safe," the king suggests, but it doesn't sound like a suggestion. More like a demand.

"As you wish," Wyatt says, but his eyes look down at me. I can see the worry, and I nod, trying to reassure him. As Wyatt walks off, I glance over the crowd and spot Alex standing with Leigha and Drake. Alex is handing pieces of what look like Oreos into her handbag. I know for a fact that Milo is in there. I did tell him to stay in my room, but he wouldn't have it. Alex said she would sort him out. Clearly, this is what happened. I smile as I remember how Wyatt found Milo in his bedside drawer, eating all his Oreos and he went mad. It took a whole day to convince him that we can't get rid of him. Milo did promise to stop eating his Oreos, apparently, that promise didn't mean he couldn't get other people to get them for him.

"Would you dance with me?" The king offers, just as Wyatt starts playing a haunting tune on the piano. I look over to see him staring over at me as his fingers move expertly across the piano. He is excellent. I nod and accept the king's hand, and the same disgust fills me. I'm thankful that he keeps a respectable distance between us as Wyatt plays a song I've never heard. The music speaks to me, filling me with dread with every note.

I don't have to look up to know Wyatt has seen me with his father. The song is proof enough.

"My son is very enamoured with you," the king says, his gaze looking at something over my head. The feeling of sickness is sliding up my throat, threatening me with throwing up all over the king's suit.

"I am his mate," I respond, keeping my eyes on his perfect tux instead of looking up.

"Isn't it strange to you? To be in such a world, a world you know nothing about?" the king asks.

"In a way," I respond. The song gets a little faster, and the king moves me quicker in the dance for it. The sick feeling is overwhelming.

"Ah the innocence you give off is sweet, such a shame for you to lose it," he says, a slight laugh in his words.

"Why does that sound like a threat?" I ask him, regretting that I look up when I do.

"Because it is," he says, his eyes turning slowly red.

"Can I interrupt? I was promised a dance with the new princess," Atti says next to me, his hand on my shoulder and stopping our dance. The king nods slightly at Atti behind me before walking off. The second his hand lets go of mine, the sickness goes, and I can finally breathe normally. What is with that feeling when the king touches me? It's like my body just wants to scream.

Atti turns me around and pulls me closely into his arms, our bodies pressed together as I look up at him. Atti is dressed in a suit under his long, black cloak. The small crown sits on his short, dark-blond hair. The song changes, still as beautiful but slower and romantic. The song tells a story only love could understand, as I dance with Atti and stare into his grey eyes. I can understand it, I understand the story Wyatt is telling with the music.

Warmth fills me as Atti speaks into my mind, *"You're still so pale. Whatever the king said, please ignore it. You are safe, always."*

We dance until the song ends, Atti never says a word until he lets me go.

"A perfect dance," he says in a whisper. Wyatt jumps off the stage and walks over to me as Atti walks away.

A cold, metal blade is pressed against my neck, as I watch a look of horror pass over Wyatt's face. The blade cuts through the necklace and a large hand throws it across the floor. The blade is pressed back close to my throat.

"I have an announcement," the king shouts behind me and presses the blade closer to my neck. Wyatt stops next to Atti as Talen and the greasy black-haired man, from the council, walk in front of me and the king.

"One more step and she dies," the king laughs and the blade nips my throat. A line of my warm blood drips down my neck as I bite my lip from the sting. I try to pull for my power, but it doesn't work. I don't feel anything other than panic.

"Let her go," Wyatt demands, his power spreading over me and hurting my head, but the king just laughs.

"Won't work on me, boy," the king says. "Atticus, if you try to flash over here or do anything else, I will kill her," the king promises, and Atti's stormy eyes glow a bright-grey.

41

WINTER

I watch in fear as Wyatt is held by Talen and his friend. He lets Talen inject something into his neck that looks like a thick, silver liquid. Wyatt falls to the ground as Atti is shackled by a pair of handcuffs by two other vampires. They are white and glow yellow when they are locked around both of Atti's wrists. They both kneel, still watching me but in pain. I can see it in their faces. The vampires are slowly running out of the room, and the king grabs me by my arm, removing the blade from my neck. A few of the vampires are standing at the side, watching us.

"Did you think I wouldn't know who she is?" he asks, looking directly at Wyatt, who doesn't reply. He just stares at me. I see Alex, Leigha, and Drake from the corner of my eye. They are moving slowly around the food table on the one side. Using it to hide.

"The prophecy girl," the king says and laughs.

"You don't even know who you are. Who your little family is?" the king says close to my ear. I see Wyatt try to move closer, but Talen kicks him in the chest, and he falls to the ground.

"Time to learn some secrets, little princess; a princess I will make sure is never queen," he says and pulls me in front of him, I trip on my dress and nearly fall over. The king catches me by my arm, his grip is painful.

"Stop!" Wyatt roars, trying to fight his way out, but whatever that injection is doing is making him weak. Talen only has to punch him once, and he falls the ground.

"You're a coward, you can't even fight your son without the use of silver," Atti shouts. The king doesn't respond to him, and I just stare up at the king's empty, black eyes.

The king doesn't even look his way as he holds the silver dagger in his one arm and pulls my hand towards him. He cuts a deep cut from the middle of my palm up my wrist. I scream with pain, and the room goes fuzzy as blood pours out of my arm.

Everything seems to slow as the king pulls out a large, blue stone from his pocket. The stone is inside a silver circle, and it hovers inside. The king pulls my arm above it, and my blood drops on to the rock. The stone falls out of the silver circle and onto the floor. The king throws me to the side, and I land harshly on my side near Atti.

"Winter," Atti says breathlessly. I couldn't see it before, but I can now.

I groan, holding my arm as I watch the blue stone glow, the glow gets bigger until it's the size of a large car in width and as tall as a tree. It stretches to the ceiling of the massive room.

Only a second later, a blurred, blue figure walks out of it. The shape looks vaguely human, but it's not. It's too tall, too broad.

"Demon king," Wyatt's father, bows his head, and the shadow laughs deeply.

"Your body will do nicely," it says, its voice sounding like nails being grated on stone.

"No, my son is for you," he points at Wyatt, but the demon king doesn't listen and moves towards the vampire king.

"I have the human and vampire army you need under the castle, and we can work together. I kept my son alive all these years, so you can use him. He is younger and a waste of existence, anyway," the king screams. I glance over as Wyatt watches his father, pain stretched all over his face.

"I help," Milo's voice comes from next to me and sees him walk right up to my face as I lie on the floor. I've never been so glad to see the Oreo-covered little demon.

"Help Atti, he needs the cuffs off to get us out of here," I whisper, and Milo nods. I sit up painfully as he walks around me, and I grab the dagger that's fallen to the floor with my good arm. Blood is dripping all over me, but I can't give up. I stand, just as the demon's shadow floats into the vampire king's body as he tries to run away. His body shakes, but he doesn't make a sound as a light-blue glow surrounds his body. An eerie silence fills the room as we all stare at the back of the new demon king. Talen and his greasy-haired friend run out of the chamber, apparently giving up on their king rather quickly. Unfortunately, there are still two guards standing next to Atti.

A grunting noise breaks my gaze from watching them running away. I turn to see Leigha and Drake fighting the vampires that were holding Atti. Alex is helping Wyatt up, while I turn to see Milo glowing blue on top of Atti's handcuffs. He glows like I do when I use my powers, how odd.

"Finally, we meet," a crackly, deep voice says, and I turn to see the demon king watching me. I wouldn't know he took over Wyatt's father's body if his voice hadn't changed. The new king looks the same, but as I look closer, I can see that his skin is greyer than usual, and his eyes are glowing red like he's just fed. The king's body is glowing a faint blue.

"Who are you?" I ask.

"King of the demons, and you are my granddaughter," the crackly voice says as a grin spreads across his face.

"What?" I stumble back, dropping the dagger.

"See, when your great aunt killed herself and locked me back in my dimension, the stupid goddess cast a curse. Only one of her blood line could break it," he waves towards the blue stone on the floor. The glowing, blue wall shimmers a little as five shadows like the demon kings come out of it, and just stand like ghosts waiting to be ordered to do something. What has the vampire king done?

"Winter," Atti shouts, and I see him standing in line with all my friends. Atti has an arm wrapped around Wyatt, who is struggling to stand. Alex is holding Milo with Drake and Leigha next to her. They are all holding hands, and Drake's hand is on Wyatt's shoulder. I realise they are waiting for me to get close, so Atti can get us out of here.

I run over, ignoring my blood on the floor and the wave of dizziness I feel. I grab Atti's outstretched hand.

Just before we disappear from the room, I hear the crackly voice of the king, "You will come to me, just like your mother did before she died."

42

WINTER

We crash into Jaxson's lounge in one big puddle. I recognise its Jaxson's place by the glass fireplace and brown sofas. Atti pulls me close as he turns my arm over.

"Dabriel, Jaxson!" he shouts and not long after, they come running into the room. Dabriel picks me up off the ground as he starts to glow and holds my arm in his hand. Jaxson places a hand over my hair. Atti holds a hand on my foot rubbing circles. Wyatt stands, a little shaky, and completes the box of males around me by taking my free hand.

"What happened?" Jaxson finally asks as Dabriel moves me away from them all, and the pain from my arm slowly disappears as he glows. Atti and Wyatt still look pale as they sit on the floor. Alex sits on Drake's lap, with Milo sitting on her head watching me. That's what Milo meant when he said, 'my family', when I asked him about the king. The demon king is my grandfather. I don't think I'll be joining him for family dinners. Now, the demon king has hundreds of vampires and humans his little friends can possess like he did the king. A ready-made army and a castle full of weapons.

Leigha moves to lean on the wall by the door, just as Esta walks into the room. I haven't seen the wolf since I last saw her with Jaxson. She looks tired and stressed, but I feel no sympathy for her. Jaxson has told me enough about her to know she kissed him to hurt me. Jealousy or not, it's not acceptable.

"Out," Leigha says, moving in front of Esta.

"I came to help, I was visiting Anna," she says, and Leigha just glares at her. Alex walks over from the sofa as I watch. Milo slides down off her head to sit on her shoulder.

"Was it you that attacked Winter?" Alex asks.

"She was going after–" Esta starts saying.

"I don't care, you little, wolf bitch. Get the fuck out of this house before I make you," Alex says. Milo is standing on her shoulder with his hands on his hips, and the sight is funny.

"Leave, Esta. You are not welcome in this house. Anna can visit you at yours," Jaxson says from next to me but doesn't bother looking at her. I watch as she turns and leaves.

"Now explain what–" Jaxson asks, but before he can finish a woman appears right in front of Atti. She looks in her fifties with long, grey hair, and she is wearing a black cloak. The front is stained with blood. The bottom is covered with dirt and leaves.

"Mother, what happened to you?" Atti starts to ask, as his mother collapses in his arms. I try to move, but I must have lost more blood than I thought, because I feel dizzy.

"Take Winter," Dabriel passes me to Jaxson and moves over to Atti. His hands glow as he puts them on her stomach over her black dress.

"It's too late. The dark queen has taken over the city and has my crown," Atti's mother says.

"It's not working Atti, something is blocking me from healing her," Dabriel leans back.

"No!" Atti says as he holds his mother to his chest. I try to move to him, but Jaxson holds me tighter.

"Take back the crown and take the throne. I love you, son," she says as she rests a hand on his cheek. Her hand drops as Atti watches his mother. He closes her eyes with his fingers and pulls the cloak around her body.

I watch as Atti gently lays her body on the ground.

His tear-filled eyes meet mine, with such a mix of grief and anger. "I will kill the dark queen for this," he says, every word drills into my mind.

The demons and the witches have just made a lot of enemies and started a war that could destroy us all.

How can we win?

WINTER'S PROMISE

War is coming.

The prophecy is coming true.

When the world is close to falling, and all those she loves are in danger, what can Winter do to save everyone?

Winter finally has the answers to who she is, but everything else in her life is in question.

How much of her past can control her future?

Can Winter make the decisions she needs to save the future?

Follow Winter in the third instalment in Her Guardians series.

Reverse Harem Series

43

WINTER

"Winter knows, Winter knows," The childlike voice sings around the frozen field, and as usual, I can't find the singer, but Elissa is here. I can feel her next to me before I even turn to look at her.

"I have a lot of questions," I say, as I look around the cold world we are standing in. The song plays over and over in the background, stuck like an old record.

Elissa is standing completely still as the cold wind whips around her, as if she isn't really here. I want to reach out and shake her, but I can't. Elissa's long, black hair flies in the cold wind, mixing with her swaying white dress. Her blue eyes watch me closely, not saying a word.

"I'm related to you, aren't I?" I ask when she doesn't respond to me. I don't need her answer because I'm sure I already know. I just don't want to know.

"You are my only granddaughter," she says.

It's all real, what the demon king said about me, and it makes me feel like my world is crashing down. My mother lied to me; she can't be my mother when this woman's daughter must be.

"The demon king wasn't lying," I say.

Pain haunts her face as she speaks. "Every word he says is usually a lie but not this time. I loved him and had a child with him many years ago," she says the words slowly. Her eyes are glazed with unshed tears. I want to comfort her, but I can't. I don't really know her; she is still a stranger to me.

"My mother?" I ask, and she nods.

"She was half demon and half goddess. You have a lot of her in you, but what's important is the human side you got from your father," she says and moves closer. I hold my breath as she goes to rest a hand on my shoulder but changes her mind at the last second.

"Why is it important?" I ask her.

"Every little thing is important in the end," she whispers and steps back.

"Riddles again," I mutter, trying to move forward, but it's no use. The cold wind gets stronger and blows into my face as I hear her speak.

"You call my spirit into your dreams, but I cannot tell you everything. Look into the past, and you will find the future."

"That makes no sense, Elissa. None of this does, everything is going wrong! The demons are taking over, and he is back!" I shout. I have to hold my hands in front of my face, as the wind gets stronger. I can't see Elissa anymore.

"It's not too late. The past, Winter, find the past!" she shouts at me over the wind, and everything goes blurry as I feel myself falling.

"Win, babe, wake up," Alex's voice comes through the haze as I open my eyes. The bed is empty where I'm sleeping, Jaxson no longer in it. His shirt is stuck to me with sweat, and my hair is all over my face. I push it out of the way as I sit up.

Alex looks stunning as usual; her red hair is up high in a ponytail, and her makeup is done to perfection. Not that she needs it.

"Where's Jax?" I ask her, rubbing my eyes. I glance at

the clock on Jaxson's bedside table; it says it's only seven in the morning. What happened to sleeping in?

"Jax is with Dabriel and Atti. Wyatt is helping Jax's aunt with the last of the funeral arrangements," she says.

"It's today," I mumble, suddenly remembering we are burying Atti's mother today. The days are mixing together with my guilt over letting the demon king free and my worrying about how we are going to survive this. Atti is distant with me; well, he won't even speak to me. Jaxson says it's just his way of coping, and it isn't anything to do with me. I don't believe that.

"Has Atti spoken to you yet?" Alex asks.

"No, he won't let me close, I'm worried he's going to do something stupid like go straight to the witch queen and try to kill her," I say, watching as Alex looks at me closely.

"Why would that be bad? That bitch totally needs a kick up the ass," Alex says, and I just notice that she's dressed in all white. I'm really not with it, that dream with Elissa is stuck in my mind. What did she mean about my past?

I know I need to speak to my mum, but how can I just ask her. How can I even look at her without feeling so angry that she has lied to me? I'm sure she had a reason, but doesn't everyone deserve to know who their parents are?

I eye the white dress on the end of the bed.

"Not black?" I ask.

"No, light witches wear white to their funerals. Drake said it's a tradition of theirs. Atti can't bury his mother where she deserves, so the funeral needs to be as close as it can to a witch's funeral," she explains.

"Oh right, I guess that makes a lot of sense," I say quietly.

"I still think he should go and kill the queen."

"It would be a bad idea. He can't just kill the new queen. Not only has she been messing with the demons, but she is also going to be very powerful. The people respect her, she won the crown. Atti could kill her, but he wouldn't win the people that way. Atti is a light witch, the dark witches will not follow him, and the city would be at war."

"I still think Atti could take her," Alex huffs. I know how she feels; I want to kill the stupid queen for hurting Atti that way.

"You haven't met her," I say with a small smile.

"I'm just saying that guy is built like a tank," she says and winks at me.

"I haven't noticed," I mumble.

"Don't go holding back on me now. How is werewolf sex?" she asks.

I go bright red, "Err."

"Does he prefer doggy style?" she asks, making me laugh. I go to tell her to mind her own business when the door is slammed open.

"Milo ate all the good food in the house," Freddy says as he comes in the room. Milo, my own little sub-demon, comes flying in behind him and lands on my lap. Alex bought some doll clothes for him, so he doesn't have to wear those rags we found him in. Now, he looks a little like a sailor, with white shorts and a blue shirt with an anchor in the middle. He has his blue hair tied with a little, blue headband. Overall, he looks like a little Smurf, a really cute one with light-silver wings.

"Milo, not the chocolate," I say, and he nods; the melted chocolate all over his face is a good giveaway.

"He ate it all, Winter, and every bit of junk food he could find. Uncle J is going to go ape when he sees his chocolate brownies are gone," Freddy says in annoyance. I smile over at him, seeing he is dressed in white trousers and a crinkle-free, white shirt. I slide out of bed and put Milo on the dresser.

"Freddy your tie is a little crooked, come here," I wave him over, and he lets me straighten it up before I kiss the top of his head as he hugs me. Wyatt chooses that moment to walk into the bedroom, seeing me hugging his son. Wyatt and Freddy haven't said two words to each other since Jaxson introduced them. Freddy just said he didn't like vampires and stormed off. Wyatt is just as stubborn and won't talk about it. They are way too similar. I don't think Wyatt has any plans to tell Freddy who he is any time soon. It wasn't a good father and son meeting. It doesn't help that Freddy has no idea who Wyatt is to him. Or the fact he is half vampire, half wolf in the first place.

I guess Wyatt has a lot of problems at the moment to deal with, like the fact no one can get near the vampire castle. There's a massive, red barrier that's appeared around it. Jaxson sent wolves out to find any survivors, and Wyatt went with them a week ago. That's when he saw the barrier. We haven't been able to find anyone. Not a single human or vampire that had escaped.

"I'm happy you're here, can we watch Harry Potter again? You're the only one that likes it," Freddy says.

"Didn't you watch it with Dabriel last night?" I ask.

"Yes, but he kept pausing the first film to ask me questions. I'm not watching any more with him," he says.

"Hi, Wyatt," I say, and Freddy turns around quickly. Wyatt has a white shirt on and it's tucked into smart white trousers. His blonde hair has been cut since I saw him yesterday and now it's just an inch short all over his head. It's styled to the left away from his eyes–eyes that are watching me. A feeling of warmth and love flows over me from him through our bond. I can tell it's him because of how it feels; it's different from my own emotions.

"When are you leaving, vampire?" Freddy asks tensely, a slight growl coming out with his words. Freddy may not know who he is, but Wyatt gets a response out of him every time they're in the same room. Jaxson thinks it Freddy's wolf that's sensing who Wyatt is, but Freddy won't listen. He's too young to truly understand.

"That's not nice," I tell Freddy, but he doesn't respond as he stares down Wyatt. His skin is shaking, and I'm sure he's close to shifting.

"My name is Wyatt, and I am the prince of the vampires. I will not be leaving, and you would do wise to learn some respect," Wyatt says.

Oh god, he's going all dad-mode already. It's really bad that I think it's hot.

"Whatever," Freddy says and storms out of the room, slamming the door shut and making the whole wall shake.

"He is already acting like a teenager, holy smokes, you two will have your hands full," Alex comments, and we both glare at her. She holds her hands up.

"I'll take Milo for a bath," she says and picks him up. He smiles at me with a cheeky grin and tries to move closer to Alex as she holds him with one hand.

"Don't try to hug me, I'm wearing white, you little demon," she says, and I hear Milo laughing as they walk out. Wyatt closes the door and turns to face me.

"How's Atti?" I ask him.

"He needs you, but he doesn't know how to talk to you," he tells me as he moves to stand close to me. He smooths a hand down my hip and watches me. Every touch with Wyatt feels like pleasure, even when Jaxson's shirt is in the way.

"Oh," I say a little breathless.

"Winter," Wyatt says and he turns away from me. I place my hand on his back as he stares up at Jaxson's sword on the wall.

"I called myself a prince, but I'm not really anymore. My people are likely all dead or demons by now," he says quietly.

"You couldn't save them," I say. There was nothing we could have done, and it's not Wyatt's fault. It's mine; it was my blood that opened that hellhole in the first place.

"Isn't that what a king is meant to do?" he asks.

"What? Die for no reason?" I move around him, glancing up at his glowing, dark eyes, and watching as his teeth grow in anger. I feel my teeth respond without my control. I'm sure my eyes are glowing silver now.

"Yes, kings die for their people. I ran like a coward," Wyatt says, his power slipping into his words and making my head hurt.

"You didn't have a choice, you had no weapons and were weakened. If you stayed, I would have died." I know the words are true. I grab his head and try to turn him to look at me, but he just stares at the sword.

"We would both be dead or worse," I tell him angrily. My hands start glowing blue as I hold them around his face, and he finally looks down at me.

"I failed them, my people. How do you know I won't fail you?" he asks me. Every word is filled with desperation. I know his worst fear is to lose me; I don't need to feel the fear in our bond to know that. Wyatt looks at the ground, like he can't hear my answer.

"Because I believe in you," I tell him, lifting his head with my hands. I press my lips gently to his, and he kisses me back. I feel his relief and strength in our bond; it's enough to make me know I've gotten through to him. Being around Freddy is so much more difficult than he can tell me. Wyatt told me one day that he looks so much like Demi. I break away from the kiss when Wyatt's hands start raising Jaxson's shirt, knowing this can't go any further right now.

"I'm going to get dressed," I tell him, and he nods with a little smirk. I glance over my shoulder as I grab the dress and some new underwear, then go into Jaxson's bathroom. Wyatt is standing where I left him, a predatory look in his eyes, a look full of promise for our future.

44

WINTER

"I like you in white," Wyatt says, once I come out of the bathroom fully clothed in the long, white dress. It reminds me of the dress I wear in my dreams, but Alex wouldn't have known that when she brought it to me. I left my long, brown hair down, and it circles around my arms as it stops at my waist. It's perfectly straight and frizz free, someone needs to learn how to sell this vampire hair shit. They would make a fortune.

We both walk out of Jaxson's room and through the house. Lucinda, Jaxson, and Freddy are in the kitchen when we walk in.

"Lovely as always, lass," Jaxson says and stops cutting up sandwiches to come over to me. He kisses me gently then moves away.

"Blood sucker," Freddy mutters and goes back to playing with his phone. I hold in a chuckle when Wyatt glares at him.

"That's very rude, young laddie. It's like calling us a dog, we don't like that," Lucinda tells him off and takes his phone from him.

“Give it back,” he says.

“No. Prince Wyatt, here you go. When my nephew decides to be nice, you may give it back,” Lucinda says, and Wyatt takes the phone. He holds it up with a smirk and slides it into his shirt pocket.

“So unfair,” Freddy complains.

I give him a warning look as he looks at me. I’m not helping him, no matter how cute he is. "Where's Atti?" I ask while stealing one of the sandwiches Jaxson is cutting up. Jaxson laughs as I quickly move out of the way when he tries to take the sandwich I took back. A girl has to eat. I move next to Wyatt as he stands the near the door.

"With Dabriel, Freddy can take you to them," Jaxson replies, and Freddy jumps up.

"Let’s go, Winter," Freddy says and grins at me. Waving goodbye to everyone, Freddy and I head outside.

I follow Freddy past the training cabin, which looks full of wolves fighting in both their human and wolf forms. It’s interesting to see. We pass several wolves, all of them bowing to me, and I have to remember they see me as their queen now. All of them are in white, and some are tying white ribbons around the trees.

“Is that Leigha and Harris fighting?” I ask Freddy, when we come around the other side of one the cabins. There are several wolves watching as Harris and Leigha fight with swords. They’re both good as they circle each other and keep coming back for blow after blow. Harris knocks Leigha’s legs out from under her and somehow gets her on her back with him kneeling over her. His sword is pressed against hers over her neck.

I never thought I’d see anyone beat the warrior princess. Neither moves as they stare each other down.

“They’ve been fighting every day; I think he likes the vampire. Gross,” Freddy says.

"You do realise I'm part vampire, right?" I ask Freddy. Harris helps Leigha up, and they both talk quietly as the wolves who were watching walk away.

"Yeah, but you're different."

"No I'm not. Wyatt isn't that bad, and I love him Freddy. I know you don't trust him, but do you trust me?" I ask, and he watches me carefully with his bright blue eyes.

"Yes."

"Then give him a break. Not everything is as it seems," I say, and he hugs me. I press a kiss on his forehead.

"Come on, they don't seem to have noticed that we're here," I say as he lets go. I watch as Harris lays a hand on Leigha's arm, and she blushes. Actually blushes. Holy crap, the warrior princess has a crush on a wolf. I have to admit that Harris is hot. He has that sexy, wavy, blond hair and massive build you expect to see on a surfer. I know he did well with girls at the university we went to. The girls would all talk about the hot guy that sometimes came to parties. Even Alex had her eye on Harris before she met Drake.

Freddy walks us through the woods until we see Dabriel and Atti in a clearing.

Dabriel is talking quietly to Atti, who is on his knees in front of a white casket. It's decorated beautifully in lots of white flowers and little lights. Dabriel places his hand on Atti's shoulder, and they both stare at the coffin. My heart breaks for Atti.

"Freddy, go back, and thanks for bringing me," I say.

"Sure," he says and hugs me before running off.

I walk over, and Dabriel lifts his head as I get closer. Atti goes tense, but he doesn't face me. They're both dressed in white. Dabriel's large wings are resting close to his back. Now that I'm so near, I can see the slits in the back of his shirt that make room for them. Dabriel's unusually bright-purple eyes watch me; sadness is written all over him, "Winter."

I rest my hand on his arm as I get close. "Can I speak with Atti alone?" I ask. I glance down at Atti, his hair is a mess, and he has a beard now. The effect suits him; his clothes are in better condition than how I've seen him in the last two weeks. Atti has been drinking himself silly and passing out. The guys have taken turns watching him. I tried at the start to be there for him, but he just disappeared on me every time I got close. I don't think he could stand me being near him. It wasn't my fault his mother died, but if he wasn't looking after me, he could have saved his mum. At least, that's what I think.

"Okay, Winter," Dabriel says and steps away after kissing my forehead. I watch as he spreads his large, white wings and flies away. I've never seen him fly before; it's pretty cool. I wait until he's just a white line in the trees before I look back at Atti.

I go to my knees next to Atti and slide my hand over the one on his knee. "Atti," I say gently.

When he finally turns to look at me, his face is filled with pain and grief. I place my other hand on his cheek, and he leans into it. We don't talk as we stare at each other like this, I want to be there for him in any way I can.

"*The last time I spoke to her, she told me to be with you. I think she knew her death was coming,*" Atti says gently into my mind. I wish I could talk back into his mind, so I don't have to break the strange silence that has happened between us.

"Tell me about her," I whisper as quietly as I can.

"My mother was strong. So strong. She told me once that she slapped my father when they first spoke. He was a rude king, and she didn't want anything to do with him. The rest of the women at the court would do anything for him, but she wouldn't. She told me that my dad said he fell in love with her the moment she slapped him." he says out loud, his voice still quiet.

I chuckle, and he continues,

"My mother said they were so happy when I was born. The castle shook that day, and when it stopped, the castle was full of flowers. They were everywhere, and every witch said the castle glowed like a rainbow."

"The war was still happening, and my mother won it. It was at the cost of her mate, my dad. Most people would have given up, but she didn't. Oh no, she won her throne in the arena and brought me up. She was a great mum, even with her responsibility to the city."

"She sounds like a strong woman."

"The strongest I've ever known. Sometimes acting normal is the hardest thing to do, and she did it well. I always knew she was sad."

"I am sorry, Atti."

"I know," he whispers and pulls me onto his lap. I rest my head on his shoulder and wrap my arms around him as he holds me.

We don't move for a long time. He's silent, and I just don't know what to say anymore.

I watch as Jaxson, Dabriel, and Wyatt walk over to us from the trees. They stand behind us, and I see Alex, Drake, Leigha, and Freddy standing near as they come over. The rest of the wolves stand in the trees, holding little white lanterns and bowing their heads. They're bowing for a queen they didn't know, a queen that wasn't even theirs. It's a sign that one day we can work together, all of us.

"It's time," Atti says. I get up, and offer him my hand to help him up. He accepts and kisses my cheek before he moves away from me. Atti walks up slowly and places his hand on the wooden coffin. The coffin is wrapped in white cloth and flowers are spread all around. The top of the coffin is a crown made out of wood. I have a feeling Jaxson made it for Atti.

"May the true light guide your way. May you find your home. And, may you always know peace," Atti says the words slowly, every word filled with pain and hope.

He steps back and raises both his hands. The coffin bursts into a slow fire, the fire turns white as we watch, and little white lights fly out of it into the sky. We all watch as they fill the sky. The wolves start howling quietly, the noise filling the sad day.

I move forward and hold Atti's hand as silent tears run down his face.

"Goodbye, my strong mother, I will avenge you," Atti's voice whispers in my mind. The resounding howls tell me he told everyone that thought.

I hope the dark-witch queen heard it, too.

45

WINTER

I run my fingers over Atti's cheek as I'm lying on top of him on the sofa, and he's fast asleep. I slide off him and cover him with a spare blanket. He grumbles a little, but I think he hasn't slept in a while. He stayed quiet after the funeral, wanting to just watch movies, and we all just stayed with him. I told the guys to go to bed after the film, and they did. I walk out of the lounge and through the kitchen to the back door. I open it quietly and nod at the wolf sitting outside. The wolf nods its head, and I walk past.

I open the training room door and flick the light on.

The training room looks different these days. There are more weapons around because of all the training going on and the sheer number of wolves they have here. Jaxson has to deal with fights over the female wolves, guys thinking they are the stronger wolf, or simple arguments because they don't like each other every day. It's not easy to have so many wolves in one place. His aunt Lucinda and her mates help with a lot of the problems, so Jaxson can focus on training the pack. I smile as fond memories of my time with Jaxson come rushing back as I look over the room. There on the floor is the first place he kissed me, even if he was a dick afterwards. I run my hand over the crossbow on the wall, and think how things were different before.

"You should never run from a wolf. I will always find you," a deep voice says behind me. I glance over, seeing Jaxson stand with his arms crossed at the door to the training room. He has no shirt on, showing off the impressive chest from all the training. His jeans are hanging low on his hips, and I bet he hasn't got any boxers on.

"I wasn't running," I say with red cheeks and turn fully to face Jaxson. He smiles as he walks over to me.

"A shame, I like to chase you," he says.

"You always catch me in the end," I whisper as he smirks.

"Yes, I always will, lass," Jaxson says and slides his hand into my hair. I let him pull my head to his and press his slightly warm lips to mine. I run my hand up his chest, loving being so close to him.

"How are you?" he asks when we both break away. I stay in his arms as we talk.

"I'm fine," I say.

He looks at me, "I'm calling bullshit on that, lass." I shrug. "I know you've been focused on Atti, but you just found out about your true family."

"I'll be better when I find the strength to talk to my mum about this all," I say.

"There's no rush, I have ten wolves watching her constantly, and Dabriel has a light angel watching her, too. She's safe for now. If anything happens, we'll bring her here and explain everything," he tells me.

"She's not my biological mother. I doubt I have any relation to her at all. My mother was a half goddess and half demon. What the hell does that make me?" I say, hating every word, but it's all true. She can't be. The demon king's last words to me are running through my mind. Did he kill my real mother? His daughter? It makes no sense.

"I know," Jaxson replies.

"I'm quarter goddess, quarter demon, and what human side I had, is now vampire," I say. I'm sure he came to the same conclusion as me.

He nods, "I agree, the human half of you was turned, but the rest of you couldn't, because it's too strong."

I'm half vampire in a way, but I'm more than that. I guess I have always been strange. I never got sick as a child. Not even a cold. That should have told me that something was up. It's funny how you make excuses about weird shit in your life until you have to face the problem. I think I've always done it. My mother doesn't like the winter months, but she named her daughter after them? The dreams; I should have guessed from those alone. "I'm complicated," I mumble, and Jaxson laughs.

"That sums you up, lass," he smirks down at me. "Harris and his mother wish to speak to you as soon as possible. I'm not sure what it's about, but she is a good woman.

"It's about some books on the goddess. Katy told me her mother knows some things."

"Anything we can learn could help us," Jaxson says.

"Can we go and see my mother tomorrow? Atti might take us, or we'll drive," I say. I know I have to get this over with.

"I'll take you," Atti says, stepping out of the shadows of the doorway and walking over to us.

"You alright, man?" Jaxson asks. Atti shakes his head, his eyes never leaving mine.

"I'll take you to your mother, and then we'll make a plan to take my throne back," he says. The challenge is clear in his eyes; he wants to know if I'm on his side.

"I'm at your side, always." I say, and he nods sternly before he disappears. "Atti has changed," I mumble as I watch the doorway where he once was.

"Don't think too much on his grief. I can understand it, and he will be okay in time," Jaxson says, reminding me that his mother and father are dead, too. That he also lost his sister and brother. When will the men I love stop losing people? "You need to feed," Jaxson says. I guess he's right, I haven't fed in a week, and my teeth keep coming out. Normal food starts tasting bland after a while.

"Yes," I say, watching his neck, and he pulls me close to him. I don't refuse his offer when he turns his head to the side. I bite into his neck, and he holds me close as he groans.

"Winter," he says, and I feel him pull my dress up as I hold his neck close. My underwear is ripped away, and his jeans fall to his feet just before he slides inside me. I let go of his neck to kiss him, and he kisses me back as he pounds into me.

"I've always wanted to have you in this room," Jaxson says gruffly, and I smile for a second as he lays me down on the cold floor and shows me everything he ever wanted to do to me in this room.

46

WINTER

Atti holds me close as we appear outside my mother's house, my old home. All day I've been fretting about coming here. About seeing her. Alex finally told me I needed to do this, and I asked Atti to bring me.

I only want Atti with me, and the others seem to understand that. I didn't think about how this might hurt him, seeing my mother when he just lost his, but he didn't refuse. I breathe in his flower-like scent for a second before turning in his tight arms to look at the house on the empty street. I first spot the car parked in front; it's not one I recognise. The two wolves sitting in it, I do.

"That is not inconspicuous," Atti whispers in my mind, as he must be thinking the same thing as me.

The three-bedroom, beach house looms over me as I finally look at it. Everything looks the same about the house I grew up in, the same white, painted, wooden decking surrounding the house. The same blue-panel, wooden walls look like my mum has painted them recently. The grey slate roof and the small, green garden at the front of the house look just like they did when I was a child. The back of the house has a large decking that leads onto a long path towards the beach. The beach is a little rocky, but it's nice to watch the ocean from.

Everything about this house is as homely as my mum. Yet it feels like a lie, and I feel like a stranger as I stand outside. I remember pulling my suitcase out to my car with my mum and Alex at my side. We both hugged mum goodbye and left with tear-filled eyes. She cried the day we moved out, she cried at every one of my plays at school. My mother does care about me, I know that, but I can't help the anger I feel.

A flash of light from the bright sun hits a car as it drives by. It's a nice day; the sea air fills my senses.

"I'm glad the whole vampire and sunlight thing is a fake rumour," I tell Atti, and he smiles.

"I think the garlic rumour is the worst one. I once filled Wyatt's bedroom with garlic as a joke. He chased my ass around for a month after that. He got me back when he cut my hair off when I passed out drunk with the guys one night," he says with a slight smile.

"Did you have long hair then?" I ask.

"Yes, it used to be as long as D's. I was growing it out when I met you but–" he stops as I look at him, his grey eyes swirling like an oncoming storm. I've never seen his eyes like this; it's a reminder of how powerful he is.

"But what?" I ask as he stares down at me.

"Winter?" My mum's voice comes from the house stopping Atti's reply. I see her drop her bag and run to me, leaving the front door open. My mum has aged well, and she doesn't have a wrinkle on her face like most women her age. Her blonde hair is cut short in a bob; she has little grey for her fifty-year old self. My mum has on three-quarter length jeans and a white top. She pulls me into a hug the minute she can. Her homey smell hits me, it's like I can smell the home-cooked food and sweet perfume she has always worn. I hold her closer; I need this second of normalcy.

"You look different," she says as she pulls back.

"Not that much," I laugh and she looks at me closely, too closely. I forgot about the changes in my appearance. At a distance, I look the same, but my mum is too close. She knows my hair wouldn't behave this well, or my eyes don't shine so brightly. I best make sure she doesn't see my marks; she'd have a heart attack thinking they were tattoos. I remember when Alex got one done by her short-term boyfriend when she was sixteen. It's an infinity symbol on her hip. It wasn't a bad tattoo, luckily, considering she let her boyfriend choose it. Mum went crazy when she saw it; Alex was grounded for two months and had a list of stuff to clean every weekend.

"Who's your friend?" Mum says looking at Atti and snapping me out of the thoughts of the past. I can't be lost in them anymore.

"I'm Atticus Lynx, the boyfriend," Atti introduces himself, and I realise I didn't know his last name. In fact, I only know Wyatt's last name. I make a mental note to ask them all later.

"A boyfriend? You didn't tell me about this handsome one," my mom scolds me.

"There have been a lot of changes that we need to talk about, mum," I say. We both stare at each other, me watching her dark-blue eyes and eventually she nods.

"You best come in then," she says and walks in the house. Atti links his hand with mine as we follow.

The inside of the house is a large open-plan kitchen to the left and the lounge has big French doors, so you can see the sea. There's a white, modern fireplace with a white sofa in front of it. Two white armchairs are next to the sofa, and there's a white dresser with a mirror by the start of the corridor to the upstairs three bedrooms.

"Would you like some tea?" she asks us.

"No thanks, mum," I answer.

"Two sugars, no milk. Thanks Winter's mum," Atti says, and I smile.

"Oh, call me Daniella," she waves a hand at Atti, who nods. I sit on the sofa with Atti, while mum makes tea. She comes in and gives him his then sits in the armchair with her own.

"What brings you home?" she asks. It's best to get straight to the point, I'm too angry not to. I'm twenty years old, and I've only just found out who my parents are. I should have known before. Especially because in the world I'm from, not knowing information like this could get me killed.

"I'm not your biological daughter, am I?" I ask, and she turns white. Her hand shakes as she puts the cup on the small, white wooden table next to her.

"How did you find out?" she asks, a quiver in her voice that I hate hearing.

"Doesn't matter, but I need to know where I came from, it's important now," I tell her.

She looks down at her hands. "I told you once that I knew your father from university, you remember?" she asks, and I nod remembering the conversation at the castle when had I called her.

"When he moved onto my street a few years later, he had a two-year-old daughter. You," she says quietly, but I hear every word.

"I helped him with you at the start because he couldn't find decent childcare. After that, I fell in love with him all over again and you as well. He never felt that way for me.

Your father was in love with your mother, he talked of her all the time. Her name was Isa," she says.

"He never told me where she went, and he wouldn't tell me anything other than stories of how they met, how you were born. Your father's name was Joey Bloom, and your mother was Isa Bloom."

"How was I born?" I ask her bluntly.

"Joey said it was in the middle of winter, in Scotland. The coldest winter in years, and they were trapped in their house. That's why they named you Winter," she says, and I nod, unable to respond.

"Everything was quiet for two years, and then the car accident happened. I was looking after you, and Joey had left you in my care if anything happened to him," she says, looking down at the ground.

"So, you adopted me?" I ask.

"Yes. I'm sorry I didn't tell you, but I just didn't know how. It was easier not to tell you the truth," she admits with a slight sob.

"Didn't you think I had a right to know?" I ask, getting angry.

"Yes," she whispers and runs out of the room in tears. I hear her bedroom door slam shut.

"At least I know," I say to Atti. Neither of us says anything for a while. I angrily wipe away my tears.

"Go after her and tell her you love her, Winter. That woman brought up a child who wasn't hers, for a man who never loved her back. It would be a mistake for us to leave now," he says, and I nod, knowing he's right.

I go up the stairs, passing my old room as I go. I glance at the pink walls and the shelf full of trophies I won at singing competitions over the years. The awards in self-defence sit next to them. I push the door open and smile at the pictures of Alex and me all over the mirror. I was so happy growing up here; she was never a bad mum to me. I can't imagine the position she must have been put in. I close the door and go to my mum's room and knock.

"Mum." She doesn't answer, but I go in when I hear her moving. She has pulled a few boxes out of the cupboard and picks a smaller, black box out of it. Her room is simple with a small, double bed, with blue sheets and matching blue curtains. The room smells like her, and it comforts me, despite the reasons we are here.

"Joey was a good man, but he would tell me all these stories; of witches, werewolves, angels, and vampires. He even believed goddesses and demons existed," she says and sits on the end of her bed. I don't say a word as I sit next to her.

"I thought he was mad, but he was so sure they existed. In his will, he wrote me this letter," she hands me a blue envelope. I pull out a letter; it's old and slightly yellowed. The ends are creased like it's been read a few times. I start reading, realising that this is my dad's handwriting:

Dearest Daniella,

When we met in university, I knew you would be a great friend to me. Winter is so very young as I come back into your life, and I know if you're reading this that our past has caught up to us.

Winter is half human; her mother was half demon and half goddess. Isa could do amazing things: control animals and make people do what she wanted with only words. She saw little of the future but enough to keep herself safe over the years. Isa could also call people into her dreams; she used to bring me into hers all the time just to see me. Even as I write this, and she is miles away from me, she visited me last night. I know she wants to visit Winter, but she won't, she misses her too much, and she is still so young.

Isa told me her mother was a goddess, and she created animals. She could see the future of her line, and the humans worshipped her. She said a true goddess can live for thousands of years, and Isa was five hundred years old when we met. I know you won't believe me, but trust me on this. Winter needs to be trained, taught some self-defence for her future, and when the time is right, please show her this letter.

My sweet little Winter, the little girl who I just tucked into bed after reading The Princess and the Pea *to for the millionth time, I love you.*

I love you so much, Winter Isa Bloom.

The moment I saw your beautiful face in your mother's arms, I knew I would do anything for you.

Your mother loved you dearly, but I was scared of her power. I'm sure you will be as powerful as she was, and she would have done anything to be with you. You look so much like her.

Isa spent her whole life on the run from her father, and never really got close to anyone because of him. We were blessed with you five years after we met, and your mother was so happy. Your middle name is her name. Her name is also like her mother's, Elissa. She thought it was nice to keep the name. She never knew her mother, as she died three years after she was born. Her protector was also killed many years later, but she escaped.

Isa said she loved me from the first time we met, and I knocked her over in a park. It's also the last place I saw your mother, when I had to run with you and give you a chance for a normal human life.

Isa once told me a prophecy about you, a very old one that her mother said. She said every supernatural heard the prophecy when she spoke it, and now everyone is fearful of it.

They shouldn't be.

You will raise them all up and keep them safe.

I love you, my sweet little girl.

Goodbye,

Dad.

I wipe my tears away as I put the letter down, and my mum hands me a black box. It's smooth and deep; it's also a little heavy.

"I could never open it, it had a note on it saying only you could," she says. I pull the lid up and it lets me, easily.

Inside is a crown, a massive white gem is held in the middle and the rest is a soft, silver colour. There are four little gems inside the twirls holding the main gem up. There are red, green, white and black. The crown is powerful, I can feel it, and it wants me to hold it. It's like it's connected to me.

The crown glows blue as I touch it, the power spreading over me, and I quickly move my hand away and snap the box shut.

"A crown," my mum whispers, watching me as I look over at her. I look at my hand; hell, my whole body is glowing blue. I guess the cat's out of the bag, or more the glowing Smurf in my case.

"Why did you change my middle name as well as my last?" I ask because I never had a middle name.

"It was part of your father's demands, so I could have custody of you. I think it was another way of keeping you safe," she says sadly.

"Thank you," I say and put the box down. I move closer to my mum and hug her, she doesn't move to respond for a while, but then she slips her arms around me.

"What for?" she eventually mumbles.

"Being my mum, not leaving me when most people would have. You're always going to be my mum; blood does not matter to me." I tell her. It's true, it doesn't.

"Oh, Winter," she sobs. I hold her close for what seems like a long time. When we break apart, I notice Atti by the door. Atti looks at the box on the bed and back at me, a slight crease appearing in his forehead. I wonder if he can feel the power of that crown, too.

"The things your father talked about are true, aren't

they?" she asks, looking at Atti and then back at me. I simply nod.

"It's hard to believe that all those things exist," she says quietly, and Atti chuckles as he walks into the room. He stops at the pot of flowers near mum's bed. Atti's hand glows a little green as he touches the flowers and they start growing fast. He stops when the plant, which had one flower, now has dozens.

"What are you?" my mom asks. She isn't scared, no her face is just wondrous.

"A witch," he says and does a little bow.

"Okay," my mum says and grips my hand tightly. We don't say anything as she stares at me; she read the letter and knows what I am, too.

"Can you both stay for some lunch?" my mum asks after an uncomfortable silence.

"Yes," Atti answers, and I nod.

"Keep the box and letter. They were always yours, Winter," she says, and I pick them both up. The worn letter being the last thing I had from my father and the crown from my mother.

"What's in the box?" Atti asks as we walk out, and he goes to put his hand on the box, but I pull it away.

"An heirloom I won't be using for a while," I respond and look down at the black box. It feels like my future is inside it and already made up before I have chosen anything.

It's a crown for a queen, and a queen is what I am.

47

WYATT

"Wyatt, there has been news," Jaxson says stomping into the room, where I was sitting with Winter quietly. Winter looks up with a smile at Jaxson. The quiet is ruined because Jaxson doesn't know the meaning of it; he never sits fucking still for more than a second. It used to drive me mad as a kid, it still pisses me off now.

"Yes?" I ask him.

"Two of my wolves who watch the old castle say there are vampires in it. They have just returned to the pack to tell me."

"Where's Atti?" I ask standing up. Winter holds my hand and smiles up at me. She is just as happy as I am that there are survivors.

"Coming," Jaxson says, and the door slams open as Atti walks in the bedroom.

"Come on, then, let's go and check it out. Here," Atti throws a sword to me and one to Jaxson. We both hold them at our sides as we walk over to Atti.

"I'm coming," Winter says with her hands on her hips

as she stares us down.

"No, Sweetheart, we don't know what we are walking into," I tell her and she glares at me and her golden skin starts glowing blue, like it always does when she gets mad these days. Her beautiful eyes grow even more stunning as they glow a soft silver. Winter is stunning.

"Not happening, lass."

"Atti?" she pleads after she gives a death look to Jaxson.

"We need you here, someone to protect the pack and Freddy. Who better than their queen?" Atti says. Who knew he was the smart one? Jaxson and I glance at each other, both of us wondering how he outsmarted us with Winter.

"Okay, you're right," Winter says, and the glow slowly disappears.

"Be back soon, love," Atti says and claps a hand on my and Jaxson's shoulders. When we arrive at the castle, Atti makes us appear just outside. Big pieces of stone lay crumbled on the old staircase up to the castle doors. What once were two massive doors is now just an empty archway, with the doors covered in dust and laying on the ground. Fond memories of escaping here as a child sweep through me, this was the only place I can remember being happy. It's clear someone has been here, the footprints on the ground an obvious sign, and the smell of blood is another. Jaxson gives me a nod as he moves behind me. He smells something. I hold my sword close as we move into the castle.

The first room is empty, other than the massive heaps of dust and destroyed walls. I hear a tiny noise up the stairs. I jump over the five missing, bottom steps and onto the landing. I land silently, feeling Atti and Jaxson following me closely. They have my back; they always will.

I stop when a little boy comes out of an archway, his eyes widen when he sees me, and he starts crying. I move closer, and I know he is a vampire, I can sense him. His mother comes running out and picks him up. When she turns and sees us all, she falls to her knees with her child sobbing into her neck. Both of them look terrible–wearing old, torn clothes–and they are both pale enough that I know they need to feed. Children can go around two weeks without needing a little amount of blood, but adults can't do that. I turn my head when Harold, a member of my father's council, and his son Easton come out of the room. I really hope Talen, another council member, is alive, so I can fucking kill him for what he did at the castle. Injecting me with silver is a coward's move, and could have killed me. I will rip his head off for that one.

"Prince, I hoped you would find us here," Harold says as he bows.

"How many of you are here, my friend?" I ask and move closer to the woman. I offer her a hand, and she stands up. I ruffle the little kid's hair, and he smiles shyly at me.

"Four hundred of us escaped, but the rest were lost," he says, and I nod. It was my job to protect them, and I didn't. I would understand if they hated me. Whoever is left is going to have my protection and help. I don't need to be their king or even their prince; I'm just going to help.

"How are you feeding?" I ask.

"The local hospital in town, which is only half an hour away," he says as the woman moves next to Easton, and he takes her hand as the kid hides behind her.

"It's not nearly enough, and the people are noticing all the blood going missing. Most of us don't believe it's safe to leave this castle and have so little knowledge of the human world that it isn't safe to go and find food," he tells me. To say they have no idea, is a vast understatement; they have no fucking clue. Most haven't left the castle in their entire lives because they didn't want to. They have always had everything spoon-fed to them. Time for a huge fucking change; like calling humans food for one. They have got to stop that shit.

"How did you know of this place?" I ask, as not many do. This is the old home of the goddess, and it's well hidden in the middle of the Lake District in England. There's a huge glamor that makes it impossible to find unless you know it's there and even then, no one ever finds it. The only reason we know of it is because Atti's mother showed it to him. He then brought us here, and we used to come every week, no matter what. Jaxson had wolves watching the place just in case anyone ever found it.

"Those that believe in the goddess can always find her home. Your mother once told me of this place–a story really, my prince. I knew it was a risk, but we didn't have anywhere else to go," he tells me.

I nod, ignoring the pain from him speaking about my mother. I wish she was here to guide me, and maybe she could have stopped my father's death. I don't feel grief for my father, not when I know every moment of kindness he showed me growing up was a lie. The only reason he kept me alive was for the demon king, and I fell straight into his trap with Winter at my side. It was fucking stupid and won't be happening again.

"How many women and young are there?" Atti asks, and I glance at him. *"This ruin of a castle is no place for young children, look at the boy,"* Atti whispers into my mind.

I nod at Harold, who finally speaks. I'll give him credit; he hasn't backed down in front of all these princes. "There are ten children and eight women. The rest are the guards and men that I could get out. I had an escape plan made up for weeks. Your father never told us what he was up to, but I am no idiot. I will not lose my family," he says firmly.

"I offer you my pack and help," Jaxson says making Harold's eyes widen in shock; I turn to Jaxson, ignoring the whispers I can hear down the corridor. A few still get through to my ears, and most are in shock that the princes seem like friends.

"We need to make this place liveable and sort out a delivery of blood to come here," I tell Atti and Jaxson.

"My prince," Harold interrupts.

"Yes?" I turn to him as he comes to my side.

"You are our king. Tell us what you wish us to do," Harold says and lowers himself to one knee, his head bent. I walk over and put my hand on his shoulder.

"We work together." I say and Harold nods. I glance back at Atti who smiles like a dickhead at me, while Jaxson smirks.

The next two days, I stay at the castle and help set my people up. Atti took me into town, so I could convince the local hospital to order in a regular delivery of the blood we need. I made a generous donation to the hospital for it, and now every week someone will bring the blood to a meeting point away from the castle. Jaxson helped using his earth powers to clean the place up, with Atti using his gifts as well.

Alex and Drake have taken over the running of the castle, while I've been ordering beds, clothes, and human food to be delivered to us. I also used my power on a local building company; they're working at the castle for the next couple of weeks. That cost me a fortune. I'm lucky we have a lot of money saved up.

"This place is looking great," Alex says walking into the bedroom with Winter. I stop to smile at her. As always, she looks happy and beautiful. She must have been at training because she's wearing tight, black leggings and a small, black top that stretches across her chest. I have to divert my gaze away from Winter when Alex clears her throat. I'm helping two guys sort their room out, and the beds are finally done. I've done twenty of the stupid, flat, pack beds today, Ikea does not make those things easy to put together.

"Hey," Winter says looking me over. I'm sure I look like a fucking disaster, with dust in my hair and dirt all over my clothes. I lift the spare wood over my shoulder to take outside and both the girls sigh deeply, making me look at them.

"You totally rock the hot builder look," Alex says, and Winter playfully hits her arm.

"That's my mate you're talking about," Winter says.

Alex shrugs, "Just saying. I'm off to find Drake, and then we are going to the furniture store to pick up another delivery of stuff."

I'm thankful for all her help, I can't stand talking to the humans in town more than I have to. One of them spent twenty minutes telling me there was a difference in two red colours of paint. I didn't see a difference.

"Bye," Winter says, and Alex whispers something to her. I don't listen in, but the red cheeks on Winter's face tell me that I should have.

"Thank you for your help," a teenage boy says as he sits putting together a bedside unit. This is a huge change for the older vampires, not many of them are happy about it. They have gotten used to living like kings for years, trapped inside a castle with no communication to the outside world. The teenagers and children are coping a little better. They love the iPhones I brought everyone, and I explained what the Internet is and how to use it.

"No trouble," I say and hand him the bag full of bed sheets. I walk out holding Winter's hand, and she looks around. Jaxson's two wolves, which have a talent for building, managed to get plumbing and electric fitted throughout the castle yesterday.

"We found something in one of the towers," I say to Winter and walk her towards the left tower. We only just got into it yesterday because it had a powerful ward surrounding it. Atti finally managed to get in after a lot of work. The vampires stop to bow at us as we walk past, Winter blushes every time.

"What's in there?" Winter asks when we get to the door of the tower. It radiates a certain power; I can feel it now that the ward is down, and I'm not surprised that Winter can too.

"Come," I say, and she nods. I love that she trusts me completely. I open the door and walk through the new ward with Winter. It only accepts Winter, me, Dabriel, and Jaxson now. Atti doesn't need to be accepted as he created the ward and can just walk in. The stairs are high, and when we finally get to the top, Winter stops to stare.

A massive, blue crystal glows in the empty room; there are no lights other than the crystal as there are no windows. A change I will make because it doesn't seem right. The light should be able to be seen from afar; the tall tower as a beacon of hope to any supernatural who needs it. I can see this castle being the home we need to unite our people and live in peace with Winter. The outside of the crystal is like glass, and the inside filled with thousands of tiny blue lights that move in a swirl. Atti has never seen anything like it; he says it's what protects the castle and the grounds.

Winter doesn't say a word, but she moves closer. I go to stop her, but I'm too late as she places both of her hands on the stone. The stone threw Atti at the wall when he touched it, and it did the same for me. Winter just starts glowing the same blue as the crystal, the little lights inside the crystal moving faster into a whirlwind. The air in the room seems lost as it's hard to breathe, yet Winter looks fine.

"Winter?" I ask her, and she turns to smile at me.

"It knows me. It sings," she says just before she collapses to the ground. I move quickly and catch her before she hits the ground. I hold her close as the crystal returns to normal, and she stops glowing. I move down the stairs, holding her in my arms.

Atti is coming up them with a frown. "I felt something strange," Atti says and stops talking when he sees Winter, "Winter, is she alright?" he runs up and places a hand on her forehead.

"Yes, I think so. The crystal let her touch it, and I think it spoke to her. She just passed out," I say, and Atti strokes her cheek.

"I'll take you both to the pack," Atti says, placing a hand on my shoulder. He moves us, and we reappear in the kitchen of the house.

Anna is standing, washing up. "I will not get used to that," she starts, and then she sees Winter in my arms. "Is Winter okay?" she asks, and I nod.

"I'll return and keep the work going," Atti says and squeezes my shoulder before he leaves. I watch him closely. The usual dickhead I have to put up with is gone, and instead he's serious all the time. It's not like him. He hasn't been in my room once to move my shit around.

I move Winter up to the room I've been using here; it's simple with a double bed and one dresser. I lay her on the bed, smoothing her long hair out of her eyes.

She is so innocent and beautiful. Not just on the outside but in her heart as well.

My beautiful mate.

48

WINTER

"Winter, Winter, Winter needs to run. Run fast child of winter, for the storm comes," the childlike voice sings in my mind, repeating the same sentence again and again until I want to scream. I blink my eyes open and see myself standing before the very crystal I just saw with Wyatt. I think I passed out. I watch as Elissa comes into the room, heavily pregnant and with a man whose face is hidden beneath a cloak. The man is huge in his build; the cloak is split down the middle, showing off his golden chest. Elissa is wearing a purple cloak and a crown on her head, but it's not the one I've seen before. This one is white.

"Elissa, you shouldn't be up here," the man says, his voice sounding deep and strong.

"Henrick, I wanted to check the barrier. I felt the need to. Our time is running low," Elissa says and moves to place a hand on the crystal. She stops just before she touches it and moves back.

"We still have time. The demon bastard won't get us. We have our own army now; the castle is protected and hidden," the man says, and lowers his hood. His grey eyes are the first things I see; they look so much like Atti's eyes. They even have the same build and some of the same facial features. This man is far sterner with two long scars

on both sides of his cheeks. They look very old. I would guess the man is in his late forties, but, being a supernatural, he could be hundreds of years old.

"Elissa, my sweet mate, you must rest. The baby is coming soon," he says, and she turns to him. I can't see her expression, but I imagine her smiling.

"Very soon. My water went about an hour ago," she says, and his eyes widen in shock. He stomps over to her and swoops her up in his arms.

"Oh, Elissa, you do love your games," he says, and she laughs. They both disappear and I'm just standing staring at the crystal until I close my eyes.

I shoot up, awake in the dark room I'm in, the curtains blocking out the dim light, but I can see through them. Wyatt moves next to me; his deep breaths tell me he's still sleeping. I glance at myself; I'm just wearing the tank top from yesterday and some knickers. Wyatt must have stripped me of everything else after I passed out. I'm not as sweaty as before, but I still need a shower after this latest weird dream. Henrick must have been Atti's ancestor, another man who was clearly in love with Elissa.

I slide out of bed, pulling on the jeans that I find folded on the dresser, along with my boots. I pick the boots up and slide out of the room to find a shower. I knock on Jaxson's door before I go in. The room is empty, so I quickly shower and dress in a long, blue top that says, 'I'm the queen' on it. Alex thought it was a funny top, but it's the only thing clean at the moment. All my clothes are at the vampire castle, so I'm not getting them back. I find some new leggings and some socks in a bag by the door. After slipping my boots on and plaiting my hair, I leave the room to find some food. I bump into Dabriel as he walks out of the kitchen. I laugh as I nearly fall over, and he picks me up. He looks normal, well as much as he can be when he is seriously hot. His white hair is down, shaping his face. It stops near his shoulders. He's wearing jeans and a tight, black shirt; the black stands out against his large, white wings. They look white, but if you get closer, you can see the silver shiny strands in the feathers. His hair has a little of the silver in it too, like highlights.

"Hey, you," he smiles at me. I gasp when he kisses me before I can say anything, his hand sliding behind my neck as he pulls me closer.

"So gross," Freddy's voice comes from behind me, and I giggle as Dabriel leans back with me still in his arms.

"You'll like girls one day," Dabriel says, and I turn in time to see Freddy roll his eyes.

"That's what bedrooms with locked doors are for," he says, and I feel like I'm about to get a lecture from a nine-year-old. Should he even know about this stuff?

"Yes, locking you in your room alone sounds like a brilliant plan," Dabriel mutters. I chuckle and shake my head.

"I'm a wolf, I'll just break the door," Freddy says with a smirk. A smirk much like his father's when he is being an asshole.

"We could tie him up and gag him," Jaxson says coming into the corridor and ruffling Freddy's hair. Jaxson has just jeans on again, foregoing a shirt, so his chest is on full display. I swear these men are trying to kill me by setting my hormones on fire.

"You wouldn't," Freddy glares at him and shoves his hand away.

"I will if you don't go and tidy that room like I asked you to last week. I want your washing downstairs in ten minutes as well, or I'll start your training an hour early, for a week," Jaxson says, crossing his arms. If I thought dad mode was hot on Wyatt, Jaxson gives him competition.

"I don't want to," Freddy growls.

"Two weeks?" Jaxson says, growling far louder and scarier.

"Fine," Freddy says and stomps out of the room. Dabriel and I can't help the laughs that escape. Jaxson just smiles at us both.

"Let me cook for you, lass," Jaxson says.

"I have already cooked, I was just coming to find Winter when she found me," Dabriel says and turns me towards the door. I walk in and see that he has cooked pancakes and has lots of different fruits spread around the table.

"Thank you," I say as I lean up to kiss his cheek and walk over to the table.

"Where are Atti and Anna today?" I ask.

"Anna is out on a walk. The pack loves to see pregnant wolves. There aren't many. They are all saying that the goddess is blessing us again as there have been more pregnancies," Jaxson tells me. When I widen my eyes in disbelief, Jaxson continues. "There have been seven newly pregnant wolves in the last two months, far more than there have ever been," Jaxson piles a plate full of pancakes. I get two and some strawberries.

"That could be just luck," I say.

"No, lass, it's not. You're the goddess's granddaughter; people always believe the two goddess sisters brought luck to the people. She did create them after all. The pregnancies and Marie's safe birth are a blessing," Jaxson says. All this talk of the goddess just reminds me of the dream last night. Elissa was pregnant with a half demon baby, that couldn't be good luck for her considering the demon king wanted to kill her.

"It's true. Wyatt said there were four more pregnancies confirmed in the months following you coming into our lives. We all believe you bring the supernatural race some form of good luck." Dabriel says.

"I don't agree, but I am not going to argue about it when there is chocolate sauce for my pancakes. Some things have to come first," I say with a grin, and Jaxson grabs the chocolate sauce before I get it. He holds it up and smirks at me.

"I'm not saying 'please', you jackass," I say with an angry glare.

"I want a kiss this time," he laughs, and I shake my head.

"I don't believe you deserve one. No one should come in between a woman and her chocolate. No matter how hot they are," I tell him, standing with my hands on my hips.

"How about I take this chocolate sauce to our bedroom and find out how it tastes on your sweet body?" Jaxson asks, making me go red.

"Err," I stumble out. Dabriel and Jaxson laugh as I stare at my plate. Damn sexy men.

"Harris and Katy's mother is expecting you over there this morning. I can't go with you," Jaxson says.

I look towards Dabriel, who nods at me.

"I'm interested in these books she has." Dabriel says.

"All sorted then, lass. I have to go, and Harris is off duty today, so I have to deal with the small pack stuff. Come to me tonight," Jaxson says and holds up the chocolate sauce. He walks out with the sauce, and I laugh.

Dabriel and I clean up after we eat our breakfast. On the way to Katy and Harris's house, we have to stop to ask a few people the way, but I eventually recognise Harris's car outside a large cabin. It's two floors and has seven or so cars parked around the sides. I walk up and knock on the wooden door. Dabriel holds my hand in his.

Katy slams open the door, pulling me into a bone-crushing hug.

"I wanted to come and see you, but everything is hectic," she says, and I hug her just as tightly. Everything we went through when we saved each other's lives has given us a bond. Plus, I just like Katy, she reminds me of Alex. I have a feeling they would get on really well, like 'someone would end up hurt, and I would have to break them up', kind of well.

"I missed you as well," I say.

"And, you brought eye candy with you," Katy whispers, and I laugh as I pull away.

"I'm here to see your mum," I say.

"Oh, I know. She had me and my dad cleaning the entire house because the queen was coming. She even baked you chocolate chip cookies, because she heard you like chocolate." Katy says and rolls her eyes. "Come on in, so I can finally eat one of the cookies," she says.

We walk into a small corridor with wooden stairs going up. The cabin is mainly wooden floors and soft-cream walls. The corridor wall is full of pictures; of a young woman and several men. There are photos of Katy and Harris as children on a man's shoulders. They look so content. Katy walks us down to the end of the corridor and through a large kitchen to a dining room. The dining room has a wooden, round table in the middle, and there are eight chairs spread around it. There is a lovely bunch of flowers in the window and big French doors that are slightly open. A middle-aged woman is sitting talking to a dark-skinned man who looks near enough the same age. They both turn when I walk in and instantly stand to bow at me.

"My queen," they say together. It's still really weird to see them do that.

"It's nice to meet you, err–" I stop talking when I realise I don't know their names.

"My name is Roger, and this is my mate, Angela," the man introduces them and holds out a hand. I shake his hand, and Angela pulls a chair out for me. I don't want to be rude, so I sit down. The minute I sit, she offers me a cookie from a plate of them. I take one, as does Dabriel, who sits next to me.

"Can I finally have one?" Katy groans from the doorway. This is a girl after my own heart, and I grin at her with a mouthful of cookie. Damn, these cookies are good. Angela gives her the plate.

"Make sure to share them with your brother," she says.

"No way in hell, mum. He has a girl over, so they are all mine. I'm going to watch some human TV," Katy says with a disgusted wrinkle of her nose and walks out, a cookie already shoved in her mouth.

"I'm sorry about Katy, she can be–" Angela starts to say.

"A little bonkers?" I finish her sentence, and she laughs with a nod.

"I like her, she reminds me of my best friend," I add, and she smiles at me. I can see the resemblance to Katy; they have the same brown hair and large eyes.

"Here you go; these are the four books that have been passed down through my family. They are the diaries of my great something grandmother. She was a maid to the goddesses, and a friend of theirs. Her great grandfather was mated to the goddess," she tells me.

"I don't understand." I say. If her great grandfather was mated to the goddess, then wouldn't she be related to her, too?

"Oh. I'll start from the beginning, it should answer most of your questions," she says, and I nod.

"So, a long time ago, when the goddess was in trouble and dying from silver, a human saved her life. The man was dying as well, and he used the last of his strength to pull Demtra into his home and stitch up her wound. Demtra had the power to do almost anything, but she could not save someone from a silver wound. Silver is the only thing that could ever hurt her, and she couldn't heal others from it," Angela says.

"The man died," Dabriel adds in, and Angela nods.

"Yes, and he asked Demtra for her blessing for his children. My ancestor said that Demtra promised to give them long lives and treat them as her own children. The problem was, Demtra had trouble finding them, because they had moved, and she had never met them.

She eventually found two of the sons in an old hut in the middle of nowhere. The two twin sons were not as she hoped to find them; one had passed away from an illness and another was gravely injured. The one son had only just died, so she breathed life into the man, and he came back as what are known as vampires. The other son, she pushed earthly powers into and he became a wolf as he healed," she says; this is a far better telling of the story than what Harris said.

"I know that part from Harris," I tell her, and she nods.

"I am not aware what happened to the other two sons, but–" Angela stops when Dabriel holds a hand up.

"Please allow me to tell that story. I know that part."

"May I write this down later on? I would love to add it to the books for our future generations," Angela asks, her eyes lighting up when Dabriel nods.

"The other two sons had travelled over the seas for work. When the goddess turned up with their other brothers, neither wished for her help. My ancestor was happily married and had a child. Demtra stayed near when the other sons returned home. Later, a fire raged through my ancestor's house. The man screamed for her help when his child and wife were stuck on the highest level, and no one could get close. Demtra gave him wings and the power to heal his wife and child."

"Amazing, and the witch ancestor?" Angela asks gently.

"Time went on, and the final, youngest son found his own wife. She was told to be very beautiful, and many men in the small village were in love with her. There was one man who would watch her every move and was mad about her. The man snuck into their house and took the wife when the youngest son was at work," Dabriel says and glances at me.

"The youngest son went to ask for Demtra's help when he couldn't find her or the man. She gave him the power to move anywhere he wished, including to be able to go to someone close to him and control over all the elements to serve punishment to the man who took his wife. When he found his wife, she was already long gone, and the youngest son ripped the island away from the rest of the earth with his power in anger. Demtra blessed the earth where the wife's body was buried, and the first jewel tree grew there. The youngest son killed the man who took his wife, but he was lost in sadness. The goddess gave him a final gift, the power to make a barrier around the island and keep it for himself. I don't know anymore," Dabriel says and reaches over to hold my hand.

"How terrible, but it makes a lot of sense," Angela says.

"How so?" I ask.

"Well, it is said that Demtra didn't always have a sister. Not at the start and not when she met the sons. The goddess' sister was born many years later, no one really knows where the goddess's parents are from, or if they had any other children," she says and opens the book. She moves a few pages of the worn book and stops, "Ah here," she says and starts reading.

"Elissa is a grown woman now, no longer the young baby Demtra brought back to the castle and told us was her sister. Elissa has fallen in love with the original sons, all four of them, after her heart was broken."

"So, she mated with all the originals?" I ask.

"Yes. They all must have had several, or at least one child over the hundred or so years before they met Elissa. The book tells of a gathering where Demtra asked them all to come and see her. That's when they first met. There's another part which is interesting," Angela says and flicks through the book carefully.

"Elissa was very much in love with the king of demons. Demtra told me he thought himself a god, but he was not. Only Demtra is a true goddess, Elissa is a goddess but with a tiny amount of power. The demon king had eyes for more than just Elissa, and cheated on her. Elissa found out and left. Demtra was very upset," she says.

"In my dreams, I see Elissa, my grandmother," I tell Angela and Roger. Both of them look at me in shock.

"One time, she was talking to your ancestor, Dabriel. He had long white wings with black tips and hair like yours. The point is, he said that the demon king could not be trusted, and he had Elissa's heart first. Elissa said she loved the demon king and all her mates the same," I say to them all.

Dabriel watches me in fascination, "You saw my ancestor and he had both black and white wings?"

"Yes," I answer.

"I heard people say that he had twins, one born dark and one born light," Dabriel tells me.

"There is one more thing that is said," Angela adds in. "Demtra gave the originals and all the descendants that stayed to fight in the castle new powers, so they had a chance of survival against an army of demons. The witches were given weather magic, the wolves given a bundle of different abilities from being able to turn invisible to talking to the earth. The angels were given a power to cause pain with a touch, and to see the past and future. The vampires were given the ability to share their life with their human mates. The vampires were also given some special powers by accident; the goddess was growing weak as she protected her sister. The goddess said it was all she could do to protect the future; she said the past was lost. I will fight to protect her, she is my goddess, and Elissa is my queen," she stops and smiles sadly at me.

"So, do you know any more?" I ask her.

"One more part, and it is a sad ending," she says and moves a few pages in the book.

"Elissa and her mates are dead, much like the rest of the castle as I write this. Demtra has a stone, which she says her blood can control and is using it to lock away the demon king. I will not survive much longer, but many have. Demtra saved many today. May the goddess never die."

"Why would he kill her and them? He loved her, or must have had feelings for her to mate with her?" I shake my head.

"Is there anything else?" Dabriel asks as I swallow the sadness I feel for Elissa and Demtra.

"No, I'm afraid not," she says and closes the book.

"I have an idea. A dark angel owes me a reading because I told him his future. If he touches you, he can show you your past," Dabriel says to me.

"Is it safe? "I ask.

"Very. I will always protect what is mine," Dabriel says and lifts my hand to press a kiss to my knuckles.

"Ah, young love," Angela says, and I smile at her with a little blush.

"Thank you for all your help; I really needed to know about this. About my family," I say.

"Oh, don't thank me; you have helped me as well. Finally, I know how all the supernaturals were created," Angela says. I smile, and she comes around the table. After she hugs Dabriel and me, we walk out.

When the door shuts behind us I hear, "One time, it was a one-night stand, Harris. It did not mean anything," Leigha shouts. I look at Dabriel who winks and places a finger to his lips as he pulls me closer. I hold in a scream when Dabriel spreads his large wings and flies up in the air. He lands us silently on the other side of the roof. We can both look down to where Leigha and Harris stand very close at the back of the house, both of them looking angry.

"The fuck it didn't, Leigha." Harris says.

"I'm sure you will get over it," Leigha says and pats his cheek. Harris grabs her hand and pulls her closer; they both kiss each other in an explosive passion that makes me look away.

"No," Leigha says, and I look back to see her push him away. She stomps off into the woods.

"When you drop the cold-hearted act, come find me." Harris shouts and storms into the house.

"He's an idiot," I groan.

"Why?" Dabriel asks me.

"He called her cold-hearted. I mean; I know she comes across like that sometimes, but I don't think she really is. She just doesn't let people close. If Harris wants her, he has to prove it. Leigha will never be with someone weak, someone who lets her walk away," I say.

Dabriel nods, "I believe I agree. To give up, just means

you didn't love the person as much as you thought." I lean back as his wings spread out again.

"Are we going flying?" I ask a little nervously.

"Would you like to?" he asks me.

"Maybe a little?" I ask, and he holds me closer to him. I wrap my legs around his waist as he lifts me, my mouth near his, and he speaks gently, "You only have to ask."

I scream into his neck as he flies us into the sky, and he holds me closer.

49

ATTICUS

"Paris is controlled by the demon king," I say in disgusted horror as I watch the news. The newswoman goes on about how last night; a red ward-like wall appeared around Paris. The woman says the government is taking blame and saying it's for protection purposes. What a load of bullshit.

What I don't get is, why Paris? Why hasn't he attacked the witches or us here? From what I've heard, the new, fake queen has taken control of the city and killed all the light witches that opposed her. Now, she has complete control, and I know she was helping the vampire king, to open the portal for the demons to come through. She must have gotten some power boost to be able to kill my mother and control the city. All I want to do is fucking kill her.

"What's in Paris that he needs?" Dabriel asks, but he knows none of us know the answer. I glance around the room; Winter is sitting close to Dabriel's side, his arm around her shoulder and her hand on his knee. They look mated already; they are so close to each other. Winter looks gorgeous just wearing a long, purple dress that sticks to her body and makes me want to run my hands all over her. I have pushed Winter away, not because of anything she did, but because I don't want anyone close to me. Winter, especially, because her blue eyes see straight through me.

"I need to return to my city, we need an army to stop this. I need to sort my shit out," I say angrily. All I feel is anger recently. I should have been with my mother; I knew something was wrong the last time I saw her.

"The angels might help in the war, I'll go to them after we take back your throne, Atti," Dabriel says, and I nod. "I'm staying here with the wolves and Winter," Dabriel tells us all, and I agree silently. He needs to be close to Winter. He can heal her if the demon king attacks or he can fly her away.

"I'm going with Atti," Winter says. I snap around my head to look at her, and she stands up.

"No, don't even try to dissuade me from this," she says to me, her hands on her hips.

"You know I like it when you get mad, love, but they're right. I won't be welcomed back," I tell her. She needs to realise it's going to be a fight from the start. The fake witch queen is fucking crazy if she thinks I'll just let her rule. I fucking wish I could get Wyatt to use his power on the witches and make them do what we want. If only Wyatt's power actually worked on witches. They're the only race he really struggles with. He can't convince me to do anything. I know he can't convince Winter to do anything, and I'm hoping that's her goddess side, not her demon side. It would be useful if he could control the demon king. I have a feeling the fake queen will be powerful. The throne is mine, and the role of queen belongs to Winter. I'll die to make sure Winter gets to where she needs to be and is protected.

"So? I should be there. I'm not a damsel in distress.

Don't even try saying because I'm a girl, I should stay home," she says, pulling out the sexist card. I can't say anything. I was brought up around women, and I know when not to talk. This would be one of those instances.

"I will come as well, as your protector, so I can defend you," Leigha says coming into the room. She doesn't even fucking look a little sorry that she was eavesdropping, again. Leigha is dressed in a full leather outfit, has daggers all over her, and is carrying a big-ass sword on her back. She looks ready to fight at a moment's notice.

"I don't think this is a good idea," Leigha says to Winter, and she raises her eyebrows at her.

"Okay army brat, your opinion has been registered," she nods.

"I can't wait to start your training again, this was only a temporary break," Leigha says, and Winter goes a little pale.

"I'm good," Winter coughs out and Leigha walks out of the room with a laugh.

"Brat," Winter mumbles under her breath, making both Dabriel and I laugh.

She turns to me, a serious look in her eyes as she smiles gently. "I have to do this with you. I'm at your side, always," she says, her words meaning far more than she has to say. The tension stretches between us as I look at her gorgeous face. She walks up to me and places a hand on my chest.

"Fine, but I don't like it," I finally say.

She leans up and kisses me. "I know," she says against my lips and moves away.

I sit on one side, and she holds my hand as she rests her head on Dabriel's shoulder. Dabriel switches the TV on and we watch a show about a big group of friends. It's funny, and I wish it could take my mind of the future to come.

It doesn't.

50

WINTER

"Be safe lass, I don't want to have to kick Atti or Dabriel's ass for letting you get hurt," Jaxson says with a slight growl. The growl sends shivers down my spine as he holds me close to his side.

"You could try, and I'll leave you on the stage at a strip club, again," Atti says.

"That wasn't fucking funny," Jaxson says loudly as Dabriel and Atti laugh.

"You nearly got eaten alive by those women on their hen night," Atti says with a chuckle.

"You're such a little fucker, Atti," Jaxson moves forward, but I stop him with a kiss. These guys argue all the time about the small things, in a way it's nice to see how close they are to each other.

"I think we should be going," I say.

"Be safe," Jaxson says with a nod and lifts my chin with his one finger. He kisses me once more before I move away. I already said goodbye to Wyatt at the castle. His people need him right now, and I can't expect him to come with me. The same can be said of Jaxson.

Atti holds his hand out for me as I walk away from Jaxson. My crossbow is in my one hand, and my arrows are in a drawstring bag, tied to my back. Leigha has two small, silver swords strapped to her back and daggers strapped to her leather-covered thighs. She looks like a warrior princess whereas I, I'm sure, don't look half as good as she does. Atti doesn't need weapons; he's a weapon himself, a very attractive one to boot. Atti has his long, black cloak wrapped around him, the hood is pulled up, and I can only see his bright-grey eyes as they slightly glow from what's to come. Once Atti explained it to me, I finally understood why they use cloaks with large hoods. It's because the cloak is woven with magic and blocks other witches from speaking into your mind when you have the hood up. I glance over at Dabriel; he's wearing all white again, his wings folded tightly at his sides, and a long, silver sword is attached to his waist with a belt. The sword is black at the end, with swirls carved all the way up it.

"That's an impressive sword, almost as big as Jaxson's," I say to Dabriel, and the guys start laughing.

"I don't think so, lass," Jaxson gets out with a laugh.

"It's really how you use it that matters," Atti says in between laughs.

"I really don't want to sit here and compare your dick sizes, can we go?" Leigha snaps. She is in a really bad mood recently. I know why, but I'm a little scared to try and talk to her.

Her dark eyes meet mine as I giggle a little, "I didn't mean," I trail off when Atti pulls me close to him.

"We know, love," he says, and I blush. Atti lets me go so I can move in between him and Dabriel.

They both take my hand, and I see Atti place a hand on Leigha's shoulder before his magic moves us. The first thing I see is a large room with high, gold walls and smooth, silver-panelled floors. The room has massive, ceiling-high windows that overlook a vibrant city with mountains in the background. The mountains look like they surround the city, or very large town, with dozens of sparkling trees in the middle. The houses all have different-coloured roofs; the whole city is filled with colour. It's like nothing I have ever seen. The witches' hidden city; it's so beautiful and alive. I don't have time to look much more before a massive gush of wind knocks me off my feet, and I go flying across the room. A warm arm snakes around my waist, and I slam into a hard body. I look behind me to see Dabriel flying while holding me in the air. His sword is out at his side and he's holding me with one arm like I weigh nothing. This could be good for my ego if it was a different situation.

A bang draws my attention back to Atti, and he's glowing with a lot of different colours. His hands are on fire up to his elbows and around ten people are on the ground, burning and screaming as he moves a whirlwind of air around them in a circle. Most of the witches aren't fighting back anymore; they're passing out or holding their throats. Atti doesn't seem to notice as he continues to use his power.

"Atti!" I shout, and Dabriel flies us over to him. I glance over at Leigha by one of the windows, just as she hits a witch on the head with the back of her sword, and he falls into the pile of three other knocked out people near her feet.

"Atti, we didn't come here to kill your own people. They are only doing their job," I say loudly when we get near him. The heat from the fire on his arms is catching my skin, causing little burns as I try to get his attention.

"Atti, please," I beg, and he finally looks at me. Atti's

eyes are grey and swirling like an oncoming storm. He looks at me like he doesn't recognise me.

"I'm safe," I say gently, his eyes don't lose the stormy swirl, but his arm stops setting people on fire.

Atti looks away and waves his arm, which shines a white colour. Cold air shoots through the room, and the flames on the burning people are extinguished. All of them look unconscious, but I don't think any of them are dead.

"You could have just knocked, Atticus," A sweet-sounding woman says walking into the room.

The woman is stunning, with long, black hair that hits the floor, and it looks shiny and perfectly straight. Perfect, strong facial features make her look like a doll I used to play with when I was a child. On top of her head is a black crown with large, black stones imbedded in twirls. It draws me in and reeks of power. She has a long, black dress on that reveals way too much, and a black cloak that slides across the floor as she walks. Her heels are clicking on the stone floors with every step she makes. Two more witches walk next to her, they stop on either side of her like a practised routine. They both must be witches, but I can't see anything else about them as their hoods are large and stop halfway down their faces.

"You dare to wear my mother's crown?" Atti says, his voice booming around the room. I feel Leigha come to stand behind me, her hand presses on my shoulder once to let me know she has my back. Atti's hands are still slightly shining with a variety of different colours. The woman, who I'm guessing is the new queen, watches Atti with far too much interest. I move closer to his side and rest my hand on his arm. That doesn't impress her; every part of her skin starts glowing a little blacker; her dark eyes watching my hand on Atti's arm.

"I have a deal for you," she finally says, breaking the

tension slightly. I don't think the offer is for me as she stares at Atti; he looks at me once before looking at the fake queen.

"You can be king, and I shall be queen. We only need to mate and unite our kingdoms," she offers, and she watches Atti for his reaction, obviously not caring about me at his side.

"That is never going to happen," Atti says with a small, dark chuckle.

"The demon king is going to wage war on our city when he finds us, and we need to be united," she replies her eyes narrowed at Atti's reaction. She looks pissed.

Atti laughs deeply. His laugh is spreading around the large room.

"No," he says simply and moves to step forward.

The queen starts shaking in anger, black smoke flittering out of her fingers. "I do not wish to fight you. The battle for the throne was won in the arena. I did nothing wrong," she says.

"Then let's go to the arena. Call all of the witches, and we will see who fairly deserves the throne," Atti replies.

"No, because I am not taking your throne from you. You can still be king," she opens her arms as she speaks.

"Not with you as my queen. You will die for what you did to my mother," Atti says darkly. There's a glimpse of fear on the queen's features before she schools her expression.

"Yet, I am queen," she says with a raised eyebrow.

"What if I offer you something else?" I say, stepping in front of Atti before he kills her. I know he is seconds away from doing just that.

"The human from the prophecy finally speaks," she says.

"My name is Winter," I say, and she nods. A little of

what I believe is happiness in her face as she looks at me. Why do I have a feeling that I've just walked straight into her trap?

"Queen Taliana," she introduces herself.

"A fair fight in the arena for the throne? I will fight you for the right to be queen," I say, remembering what Atti said about his mother. Apparently witches approve of fighting in this arena. I have no idea if I can beat her, but I will train every night and day to try and win for Atti.

"No," Atti pulls me back by my arm, but I shrug him away. He clearly lets me because he could stop me if he wanted too.

"To become queen, I had five fights chosen by the old queen. I won every one, and, in the last, I killed the queen. Well, nearly did, but she fled." Taliana waves a hand like it's not important.

"You fucking bitch," Atti says moving forward, and Dabriel grabs both his arms to hold him back.

"I will fight three fights of your choice in the arena, and, when I win, you give me my crown and get out of my city," I say strongly.

"Three fights won of my choice, and I will hand you the crown," she says. A sardonic smirk on her face suggests that she isn't going to make it easy for me.

"I will fight them," Atti says, shrugging Dabriel away.

Taliana laughs. "The offer isn't for you. Winter, the offer is yours alone. The crown will be yours to give back to Atti or mate with him and rule," she says with a smile. She clearly doesn't think I have a chance. I probably don't, but I'm not giving up. I have to try. I'm no coward, and I won't run.

"No, she would never survive a fight in the witch arena," Atti says angrily.

"Deal, only if you swear on a blood bind," I say.

Atti shouts, "*No Winter, you will die,"* in my mind.

"We don't have a choice; you can't kill her *and* every witch in the city that believes in her. We need an army to fight the demon king, not a dead one, and those who are left at war with their own king," I say to him. Watching me, he stalks over, neither of us saying a word, the swirling storm of his eyes drawing me in and making me want to be close to him. Atti has never looked this powerful or frightening to me.

"I won't let you die, but I support you," Atti whispers in my mind.

Taliana waves me over, and Atti stays close to my side, his hand in mine.

She pulls a silver dagger out of the side of her dress and cuts her hand.

"I swear on my blood to give the crown to Winter, if she wins the three fights I choose in the arena. She will rule," she says, and I feel the magic like a vice around my neck. It should shock me, but the feeling is not all that different from when Atti uses his magic to move us.

"One more thing," I say.

"Yes?" she asks impatiently.

"You swear to let us live safely in the city," I tell her. She gives me a disgusted look. Like I would be mad to think she would try to attack me or send someone to. I'm not mad, I bet under those supermodel looks, she is just as conniving.

"Fine," she says and swears the words I asked for over the cut.

"All done, now leave, demon child. Atticus, you are always welcome to change your mind," Taliana says, her eyes watching Atti.

Atti glares at her but lets me pull him away. Once we get to Dabriel and Leigha, Atti flashes us away quickly.

We reappear inside an apartment I've not been to before. There are four black-leather sofas spread around and a massive TV that takes up one wall, a white rug sits in the middle of the sofas with a small glass coffee table on it.

There are two doors in the room, and one swings open, looking like it leads to a kitchen. A large, familiar black cat walks in. I recognise her as Jewels. Jewels looks at us and walks past us to the sofa where she stretches out. She puts her head on her paws watching us, I'm really expecting her to go and find some kitty popcorn or something.

The tension is high when I finally get the courage to look at Atti.

He is furious.

"Atti–" I start.

He waves me away. He moves to the glass windows and looks out, his back to me, so I can't see his expression.

"I will stay close and heal you, Winter. Atti and Leigha can teach you how to fight witches or anything else they put in the arena. It's not going to be easy, but I think you're right. This is the only way the witches will see you as a queen. The wolves have accepted you, and the vampires have as well."

"The angels respect warriors, they are more likely to accept you as their queen if you can do this," Dabriel says. He doesn't look happy about the idea, but he isn't going to stop me. Jaxson, Wyatt, and Atti are going to be a completely different story. I don't even want to be the one to tell Alex.

"I don't know what happened back there, everything somehow got out of control," I say quietly, but I know they all hear me.

"Your ass is not dying in that arena. I will make sure you are ready." Leigha offers. Despite her, sometimes, cold demeanour towards me, I know she cares in her own way. Harris is right; she does have a heart.

"Thanks, Leigha, I think I can do this," I say.

"No, Winter, you were only human a few months ago, and you're not invincible!" Atti roars and turns to glare at me, his hood falling away. He looks so angry. Not calling me 'love' is a big sign that he is pissed. Atti rarely calls me by my name.

"I'm not human; I have never just been human. I know it won't be easy, but life is not easy. I can't walk away from this, from everything, because that's what you want me to do," I say to him. It's true, I have to fight or walk away. I won't ever walk away from my guys. I know Atti isn't mine yet, and I had trouble planning us all together in my mind at the start, but it's changed now. I want our future, a life for us all at the end of this. We won't get that if I take the easy route and just let Atti kill half the city, starting with the queen. He would never forgive himself, and we still wouldn't have anyone's respect. You don't get respect from taking the easy route; it's the hard route in life that will give you it.

"She planned all this, killing you in the arena will be the best way to prove you aren't the one meant to be queen," Atti says, his tone dark and lost.

"No pressure then," I say quietly, and Atti disappears, his stormy, hurt eyes embedded in my mind.

"Atti is just grieving, don't take his words to heart, my little wildfire. He's worried he will lose you so soon after losing his mother. I'll explain to him that we won't lose you. I would never let that happen, and I believe the goddess will protect you. You are meant for better things than dying in an arena. Let me show you the spare room in Atti's home," Dabriel says and comes over to me. I'm still staring at the space where Atti was, and his words snap my attention to him. He gently slides his hand down my arm and entwines our fingers.

“You can sleep with me in the one room. Leigha, there's a room for you as well," he says and looks at her.

"I’ll sleep on the sofa.” Leigha waves a hand at the sofas; only frowning briefly when Jewels huffs. Clearly Jewels has no plans on sharing with her.

“I think we should take turns standing guard. I don’t trust that witch’s word, anyone could attack us, despite it. Winter should not be alone while we are here. I’ll start now," Leigha says, all business in her tone, and I know she is right. The queen may not attack us, but I don’t trust her not to find a way around the blood bond.

"Jewels, will you help Leigha guard the house?" I ask Jewels who stretches out her huge paws, the leather sofa creaking as she moves. I take it as a ‘yes’ when she jumps off the sofa and comes over to me. She presses her head against my stomach gently and follows Leigha through the door to the kitchen.

Dabriel takes my hand and leads me through the other door into a small corridor with some stairs at the end. We go up the stairs, and there are four doors, two on each side. One is slightly open and Dab takes me into it. It's a small, double bedroom, there's a bed with a pile of folded blue sheets on the end and a small wardrobe made of wood. There's a small window, and I go over to look out. We’re in a small street with a grey road in the middle. The houses are average and detached. Each one has a brightly coloured roof that matches the flowers outside their homes. I wonder if there’s a reason the houses are painted in such a way. I can see from here that the mountains do surround the city. I open the window, only hearing children’s laughter in the wind and catching a very flowery scent that reminds me of how Atti smells.

The city is lovely and so unusual.

"The secret city, humans refer to it as the lost city of Atlantis," Dabriel says as he sits on the bed, then lies on his back. I wonder for a second if it's uncomfortable for his wings to have his body lay on them, but he doesn't look uncomfortable. In fact, he looks at home; he takes up nearly all the double bed. I wonder how I'm going to sleep later, most likely on top of him. I glance at the firm muscles I can see from where his shirt has risen up, and a blush fills my cheeks.

"This is Atlantis, like the movie?" I ask, changing the subject, and I'm actually interested. I liked that film; the Disney one was the best.

"Yes. When the goddess was alive, the city wasn't hidden, and humans were welcomed if they managed to travel over the sea. I'm unsure why the city was hidden, but I'm guessing the times when they started burning witches didn't help. You remember what I told you about the witch ancestor?" he asks me, and I nod.

"This was the part of the land he ripped apart. The jewel trees in the middle are where she was apparently buried, and the trees appeared to remember her. They are as beautiful as she was said to be," Dabriel says. I can't see the trees from here, but I remember the ring filled with the shiny trees from the castle.

"Where is the city exactly?" I ask, as I know it's not on any globe I saw growing up.

"In the middle of the Atlantic Ocean," Dabriel smirks, like it should be obvious. I shake my head with a small smile.

"How do human scanners not find it? With all our technology and boats, someone must know about this place," I say.

"The higher-ups in government know of its existence,

much like they know how angels have a massive town in America that humans aren't welcome in. They are aware of the supernatural world, and cover up many of our secrets," he tells me.

"So, apparently Google Earth isn't as good as it seems," I say. I never really saw the point of Google Earth anyway; all I ever did was Google my own house. I guess I must be a little lame.

"No, it's not," he laughs. Turning slightly to face him, I watch as he gets off the bed and comes to stand close to me.

"Can I survive this?" I ask, while he looks down at me.

"I won't let you die in that arena. I'll stop it if I think you can't do it, but I believe in you," he tells me. Dabriel always believes in me, I've noticed. He's always on my side. My protector.

"Why?" I ask quietly.

"You are far stronger than you look, Winter," he says, and he leans down to kiss me.

I pull back when he stops moving, and I frown up at him as he straightens.

His eyes are completely white, and he's shaking slightly.

"Dabriel?" I ask him, I shake his arm, but he doesn't move. He just looks in a trance. Did my kiss break him?

"Atti, Leigha!" I shout, not knowing what to do.

Atti rushes into the room a minute later while I'm still shaking Dabriel, and he takes one look at him and sighs. "I thought something was wrong," he relaxes against the door.

"It is, look at him," I wave a hand at Dab.

"It's normal. He's having a vision," Atti says and sits on the bed, his huge form taking up all of the bed as he lies back and rests his head on his arms. I don't know how I didn't notice before, but Atti's shirt is missing, and his hair is messy like he has been running his fingers through it. I get a glance at his tight stomach and pecs, the little blonde hairline that stops at his jeans.

"Winter," Dabriel says, snapping my attention to him. His eyes are back to the normal purple I love, and he looks worried.

"The first fight is with a Dentanus," Dabriel says, and Atti sits up straight in bed.

"You have got to be fucking kidding me?" Atti roars, he smacks the bed as he stands up and paces by the door. Muttering something rude about a witch and murdering a city.

"No, I only saw Winter and a Dentanus in the arena. I don't know how it ends," Dabriel says with a worried look in my direction as he crosses his arms. He looks two seconds away from flying my ass back to somewhere safe, and keeping me there.

"What's a Dentanus?" I ask quietly. I know I'm not going to like the answer.

"A Dentanus is a dragon that's thought to be a demon. When faced alone, it can cause its victim to be consumed with everlasting terror, a vicious cycle that renders them helpless. The last one I know being on earth was when I was a baby. It took twenty witches and my parents to kill it. They nearly didn't," Atti answers me, but he doesn't stop his pacing by the door.

"This one was young, not half the size of its adult form. Winter may have a chance," Dabriel says, yet his eyes give away his lie when he looks at me. I know he doesn't want to say it, but fucking hell, it's a dragon, and I'm well, me. I might as well walk into its mouth.

"Demons are immune to silver! That includes the

dragon; the only way the last one was beaten was to remove its head," Atti says and looks at me.

"Winter loves animals, unless she plans to charm the dragon into some tea and biscuits, we are screwed," Atti says sarcastically.

"My mother could control animals, and my grandmother created a lot of them. Maybe I might be able to at least calm it down. I used to be able to calm any animal growing up; I loved them. I was training to be a vet for a reason," I say.

"A dragon is a big step up from a cat, Winter," Dabriel says gently.

"This is not happening," Atti says shaking his head.

"Dabriel already saw me there, so it is. We need to find out what weapons work on it and fast. If not, I'm going to work on my blue power and running away fast," I say to them both. They glance at each other.

"Demons aren't weak to silver or anything I know of. This is a major concern, considering your demon grandfather likely has a large army full of demons, and we have little ways to kill them," Dabriel says.

"Then we have a week to find out anything we can. I can ask Milo. He might know," I say.

"If you can understand anything he says, other than 'more food'," Atti says, and it makes me smile a little.

"To be fair, I understood when he told me about seeing you in the shower. I believe he described your thingy bob as a large stick," I say causing Atti to laugh with Dabriel and me.

"I think the mini-demon has a crush on me," Atti says, and I nod with a grin.

"Oh, I know he does. You do realise he has been sleeping in your bed every night?"

"That's not at all creepy," Atti shivers.

“Milo tells me all about you when he comes to wake me up in the morning. Jaxson and Wyatt think it’s funny. They both said I shouldn’t tell you,” I laugh when Atti groans.

“Didn’t know he was your type, brother,” Dabriel says, and Atti chuckles.

“Nope he isn’t. We share the same type,” Atti says and winks at me.

"You could die," Atti says quietly after a moment’s silence. His words are spoken slowly as he moves to stand in front of me. Atti moves his whole body close to mine, until we’re touching, and I’m forced to tilt my head up to meet his eyes.

"I will destroy the whole city if you die. I will destroy the world if I lose you Winter," he says, each word filled with an image of my fun-loving Atti losing it. It reminds me of his ancestor; how he lost his wife and literally tore the earth apart. I could never put Atti through that pain; I care for him too much. I vaguely hear the door being shut behind Dabriel as Atti and I stare at each other. Atti’s sweet scent fills my senses, and I breathe him in.

"You won't lose me. We can do this; we can take back what is ours and do what is right. We will always do what is right," I say, each word a quiet whisper, but my words are powerful enough to be considered a warning to our enemies.

Atti lowers his head and brushes his lips against mine, once and then twice until all I can focus on is his sweet lips. He always kisses me like he is savouring his favourite dessert, every kiss slow and leisured, making me desperate for him–more than I can admit. I’m sure my body is telling him everything I’m thinking as I tighten my hands that have found their way into his hair. He groans as his hands slide slowly down my back, until his large hands squeeze my bum.

He lifts me, and I wrap my legs around him, as he deepens the kiss.

"Winter we can't, not yet," he says and breaks away from me after putting me down. It hurts to see him say no, and I don't really understand why.

"Why?" I ask quietly.

"Winter," he groans and pulls me to his chest. "I want nothing more than to strip every little piece of clothing off you and show you how much I care about you. We can't because it wouldn't be just sex; I want to mate with you. Our first time, I'm going to mate with you, and make you mine," he says. I understand. The urge to be with him is hitting me strongly too. I never imagined being with more than one person for the rest of my life, but it seems impossible to imagine a life without all of them at my side. My life is a lot longer now too, longer than I know how to deal with.

"I want to show you something. I know we have a lot of crap to deal with, and you might hate witches after this, but let me show you our city," he says and kisses my cheek. "The city and people are not all evil. I know you haven't had the best introduction to dark witches or light, but I swear that some of the kindest people I know are witches. We survived a war much like the wolves' and vampire's war, so I want to show you what we fought for," he tells me.

"I would love that," I smile, and he grins at me.

"Come on then, love," he holds out his hand, and I take it happily.

We find Dabriel in the kitchen with Mags–Atti's other familiar. Dabriel is currently feeding Mags, in her normal form, pieces of chocolate but stops when he sees us. She lifts her big white head to stare at Dabriel until he gives her another piece.

"Not chocolate, man, she gets pissy if I don't feed it to her," Atti groans, she doesn't even look at him. I don't blame her.

"Mags loves chocolate," Dabriel shrugs.

"More than anything else, including me. She will stomp and try to eat me if I don't give it to her when you leave."

"I think I've found my spirit animal," I say, staring at Mags with love.

"It was only a little," Dabriel chuckles and puts the bar back into the fridge. The kitchen is more modern than I thought it would be. It looks brand new with black counters and white drawers. There are all the appliances you would expect, and a large coffee maker. Atti must be a coffee man. In the one corner, are two massive pet bowls, both pink and have his familiar's names on them. I have to admit, that's cute.

"We're going out, I want to show Winter the city." Atti pats Dabriel on the shoulder.

"Count me in," Dabriel says.

"I think Leigha is coming too," I tell them both.

"No, she can stay and watch the house. You'll be safe with us both," Dabriel replies.

"You're telling her then," I say, and Dabriel gives me a shrug like he doesn't see the problem. He really doesn't know the warrior princess.

"Sure," he says and walks out the front door. It takes two seconds before Leigha is shouting her rejection of his idea and threatening to kick his ass.

Atti looks at me, and we both burst into laughter.

51

WINTER

After what felt like forever, Dab and I finally manage to convince Leigha to stay at the house. Atti said Leigha scares him and stands a distance away letting us handle her. I will admit she scares me a little, too, but I know Atti is just being a dick. Leigha takes protecting me really seriously and demands I at least take her dagger with me. I think she feels like she will fail in some way if she isn't there to protect me. At least with the pack, I was safe, and she didn't need to worry, here is a different matter. Atti walks with me close to his side, his arm around my waist. I glance up at him, he's wearing his black cloak, and the hood is up. Dabriel is close behind, also wearing a cloak, to hide his wings and hair. It makes him look massive, with oddly-shaped shoulders, so it's not too obvious he's an angel. We walk down the quiet street; it's strange because there are no cars. Other than the one time we went camping, I've been used to the noise of roads and cars. This place is so peaceful. Dabriel moves to my other side when the path opens up. The city is slightly cold, with a hint of a sea breeze in the air. I pull my leather coat closer around me, as the wind blows a little.

"Do you like the witch city?" I ask Dabriel, as we turn around a corner.

"The island and city are called Atlantis," Atti adds in before Dabriel can answer.

"Yeah, but I just think of the film every time I think of the real name, so 'witch city' it is for me," I say to Atti who chuckles, and I look at Dabriel to answer my earlier question.

"I've never been around the city. I visited Atti's house a few times, but we didn't risk coming out," Dabriel replies.

"Ah, I forgot people don't know you grew up as close friends," I reply. I glance at the house as I go past; the front garden is filled with different flowers. Some I recognise, like the roses, but some are so different from anything I've ever seen with a range of multi-colours and strange shapes.

"No, they don't; I believe Taliana was shocked to see me at Atti's side. She will take into consideration that I'll heal you after the fights," Dabriel says, and I look away from the garden at him. We move out of the way when a few witches walk past us, their hoods up, so I can't see them.

"Less talk of the fights for now, I want to be a normal tourist for a bit," I say, and Dab laughs.

"Normal is not a word I would ever use to describe you," he says, and I whack his chest with my hand. Unfortunately for me, it just makes him laugh and hurts my hand because his chest is like a rock.

I stop in my tracks when we get to the end of the street because the sight is striking. There's a paddock of hundreds of different-coloured trees with sparkling jewels hanging from them. Each one is tall, built like an oak tree in shape, and they have little crystals hanging from them instead of acorns. There are so many; more than I can see, and a grey road, which looks like it goes around the paddock of trees. In front of the grey gates, that keep the jewel trees in, are dozens of stalls. It looks like a flea market, like the one my mum used to take Alex and me to sometimes. The only thing that is a lot different is that the witches walk down the streets with a mixture of different animals next to them. A woman walks past with a huge snake wrapped around her arm and neck. Another witch has a polar bear walking next to them; a small child is riding on the polar bear's back and pointing at things. All the witches have their hoods up, it looks like I'm nearly the only one that doesn't. The closest stall to us looks like it sells the crystals from the trees in different types of jewellery. The stall next to it is selling different coloured powers.

"This is so amazing," I say in wonder, and Atti chuckles.

"Those are the trees I told you of once, and this is the market. People sell and buy everything here. I told you once our people live equally, and money isn't a thing here," he tells me.

"So, what do you trade?" I ask.

"We trade our magic using the stones or we trade for work," he tells me and pulls out a clear-purple stone; it looks blue inside with dozens of little sparkling magic things. I miss the old necklace Atti gave me, even if it was just used to hide my appearance. I liked that it was from him.

"Here, this will buy you anything you want," he tells me and places the stone into my jeans' back pocket. His hand slides out slowly, and being a typical man, he gives my bum a little squeeze.

"This place is so different, is it like this with the

angels?" I ask Dabriel, who is looking around, and several people are stopping to stare at us now. Well at me, being as I'm dressed weird–in jeans and a leather coat. At least I ditched the crossbow and arrows before we came out. The dagger is out on my hip though, so I still look strange.

"No. The angels live a little differently from humans, but we aren't as hidden from the world. They prefer to just watch humans from a near distance," Dabriel says.

"Things are changing for all of the supernaturals," I say, thinking of the vampires in the new castle.

"Your Majesty, I am sorry for the loss of your mother. She was a true queen," a man says, and he bows at Atti. I'm surprised anyone recognised him under his hood, but this man clearly does. He is the only man I can see; the rest are shaped like women.

"Thank you," Atti replies with a small nod and lowers his hood.

Several other people suddenly start to notice Atti, and they bow, removing their hoods. I hear '*true king*' whispered in my mind as people look at us.

"Why are there so many women, and only one man that I've seen?" I ask Dabriel. Atti is watching the women with a blank expression; giving me the feeling he's talking in their minds.

"Males are rare here, the very opposite to the wolves. Many women decide to dedicate their lives to magic instead. The women here are amazing fighters," Dabriel moves closer as he speaks. "Just what we need in the times ahead," he whispers close to my ears.

Atti takes my hand as Dabriel leans away. We walk away from the women; more and more stop to stare at us, but Atti puts his hood up. I guess he's done with talking. Dabriel moves behind us as we walk through the many stalls. I stop when I see a stall full of wands. Actual witch wands, Freddy would love one. I nod my head, and the guys follow me as I walk over to the stall. They stop on the path as I approach it.

"Charming lady, how may I help you?" the woman behind the counter asks as I look at the wands. I glance up at her, she looks around thirty, but looks can mean nothing when supernaturals have a longer live span. Her hair is wrapped in purple cloth, which matches her purple dress that has a corset at the top and fans out underneath into a dress. Atti lied, witches do wear corsets, and now she just needs a spiky hat.

"Do they do anything special?" I ask when I snap out of my own thoughts.

"They are used for directing and holding magic, the colours of the wands are a representation of the element they help. For example, the blue wand is for water and the green for earth." She waves a hand over the green and blue wands.

"This one?" I ask as I point at a white one.

"Spirit," she says, and I nod as I pull out the stone Atti gave me and offer it to her.

"Is this stone okay payment for the spirit wand?" I ask.

"A deal, thank you very much, my lady," the woman nods and takes the stone from me. I pick the wand up, and she offers me a paper bag for it. I accept and look back at Atti and Dabriel who are watching me curiously.

"Ah, to win one prince's heart is a gift, to win two is a true prize. I'm sure the queen who wins all four shall be the truest winner of all," the woman says, and I look at her quizzically.

"Thanks," I utter as she offers me the bag.

"My future queen," she bows. I quickly make my way back to the guys, wondering about the woman's strange words.

"A wand?" Atti asks with a small smile as I reach him.

"For Freddy. He loves Harry Potter, and I thought he'd like it," I say.

"Here, give it to me a sec," Atti holds out a hand. I take the wand out of the paper bag and hand it over. He holds it in both his hands, and it glows white until I can't look at it anymore. I blink, looking up at Atti when he is finished doing whatever, and he holds out the wand to me.

"I added some magic, usually it would allow someone to see a close family spirit, but that is very rare and old magic. Freddy will just be able to shoot white, harmless sparks out of it for a while," Atti says with a grin.

"Awesome," I say and put the wand away in the bag.

"That's nice of you, but is it safe to give to a child?" Dabriel asks.

"It's harmless, D," Atti laughs.

"Can I see the trees?" I ask Atti, and he nods as he takes my hand. Dabriel takes the wand from me and slides it into one of his pockets inside the cloak.

"Wyatt and Freddy aren't getting along," Atti notes as we walk towards the gates to the trees.

"It must be difficult for them both. Freddy hates vampires; they killed his mum and his uncle. They have constantly battled with them, and now one is living in his house, talking to him all the time. Wyatt and Jaxson don't believe it's best to tell him anything yet," I say.

"Poor kid," Dabriel shakes his head.

"It's a fucked up world." Atti says, and I squeeze his hand.

"I think Freddy is lucky in some ways. He doesn't know it, but he has a father who would die for him and three uncles who would protect him at any cost. I love Freddy and would do anything for him as well," I say.

"Not many people have that many people in their lives that love them," Dabriel agrees with me.

"You're kind of his stepmother now that you're mated to Wyatt and his aunt-in-law to boot." Dabriel tells me.

"You're a MILF," Atti chuckles, and I laugh. Only Atti would call me that.

"Do I want to know what that means?" Dabriel says.

"It means mother I'd like to fu–" Atti goes to say,

Dabriel whacks him on the back of the head, "Changed my mind."

"That hurt, fucker," Atti mumbles, rubbing his head.

"You should learn to be polite around a lady, then," Dabriel says. I may not be able to see his face, but I know he's smiling.

"I'm sorry, my lady, might I kiss the back of your hand as a sweet apology?" Atti says in an over-the-top, posh accent.

"Nope," I say, and they both laugh with me.

We stop at the gates; it's white and has flowers and vines shaped into the metal work. Thoughts of Freddy and everything else float away when Dabriel pushes the gates open, and I walk behind him.

A warm feeling fills me, just before I hear the singing. The song is sweet and light as the childlike voice sings of peace. The voice reminds me of the one I hear in my dreams; it could be the same person. I look around, but no one else is in here, and the singing is getting louder.

"Do you hear the singing? So lovely," I say in a daze, and they both look at me like I'm nuts.

"No, it's quiet, Winter," Dabriel eventually says.

I ignore their questioning stares and walk to the nearest tree as the singing gets louder. I place my palm on the wood, and the voice sings in my mind.

I sing the words, like I've known them my whole life:

Peace is coming, like war shall rise. Winter months will see the change.

Winter shall make the princes fall,
For Winter is the peace of all.
Shall the princess who will be queen bring us peace?
The trees welcome the ancient one's child,
We welcome you,
We welcome you,
You, my goddess, we have waited a while.

I sing all the words, my eyes closed, and when I finally open them I see I have a crowd of people watching me. All the witches have their hoods down, and they look shocked. I look back at my hand on the tree. The tree is glowing blue where I'm touching it, and I feel like it's alive.

"Our queen!" one woman shouts, and I look over at her as she falls to her knees and bows. The rest of the crowd fall to their knees like a wave until only Atti, Dabriel, and I are standing.

"My queen," Dabriel says and kneels in front of me. I watch as he undoes his cloak, and it falls to the ground letting his wings stretch out. A few gasps can be heard in the crowd, but no one says anything about the prince of the angels in the witch's city.

"My queen," Atti echoes loudly as he falls to his knees next to Dabriel.

"No, you are both my equals," I say to Atti and Dabriel. They both stand and move to either side of me. The crowd whispers the word '*true queen*' around in my mind until I can't hear how many people say it.

The trees express their happiness, and it fills me with joy as I watch everyone.

This is my future, with my men at my side.

52

WINTER

"You need to get this right, Winter, again!" Leigha shouts at me as she pins me on the floor for the seventh time today. She jumps off me and stands.

"I can't beat you," I wheeze and roll over to push myself up. I'm glad we came back to the pack to train because I'm sure the witches would lose any respect for me when they see army brat kicking my ass.

"You're the daughter of a half goddess. You are part demon, and you are also part vampire. You can do this," Leigha tells me. I know she's right, but I just want to throw things at her. The past week has been like hell. Leigha demands me for training in the pack at five in the morning, every morning, then, she doesn't give me even a water break until ten.

"Yes, but I can't," I pant out.

"Stop whining. Do you think your enemies are going give you a chance to whine about your problems?" she says while charging towards me with her sword. I have just enough time to deflect her blow with my own sword as I pull it off the floor. My arm shakes as our swords clash, she's circling me, and landing hit after hit with her fast speed. My part vampire side is slowing her down in my mind, so I can, at least, see her attacks. My forehead is lined with sweat, and my power builds up like an inferno inside me. I try to stop it knowing Leigha wouldn't really hurt me, but my power doesn't listen. My body glows blue just before the blue wave escapes. It goes in all directions, looking like a wave of blue smoke as it hits everything in its way. Leigha goes flying, smashing through the training room door, breaking it off the frame, and disappearing from my sight. I quickly drop my sword and run into the room. Harris is pulling Leigha up, both of them staring at each other like there isn't anyone else around, not noticing the ten people in room. Luckily for Harris and Leigha they aren't looking at them, they are all looking at me. I raise my hand to see I'm still glowing.

"Let's try something else," Leigha says coming over to me.

"You okay?" I ask, and she waves a hand at me. I see the slight cut on her forehead, and I wince. I didn't mean to do that. My power keeps attacking her, and anyone nearby us. That's why we were training outside in the first place.

"Nice to see you, Winter," Harris comes over and gives me a hug. I watch in fascination when I see Freddy fighting another boy his age. Freddy has two long swords that look too big for him to hold; yet he does and fights well with them. The other boy has long, blond hair that stops around his shoulders and he is just using one large sword to fight against Freddy's two. They circle each other, hitting hard and moving even faster. They don't take their eyes off each other as they fight.

"They are both very impressive. The other boy is called Mich, he's the only person around their age who can keep up with Freddy." Harris tells me. Mich jumps into the air and somersaults over Freddy's head; he lands perfectly and places his sword at Freddy's neck.

"That was incredible."

"Yes. They will both be strong wolves when they are older." Harris says. Freddy and Mich shake hands. When Freddy spots us watching him, he puts his swords down and runs over.

"Hey, little wolf, awesome job in the fight," I say as he gives me a hug. I hug him back and notice that Mich has followed him over to us. The boy has really strange eyes; I tilt my head to the side to look at him. His eyes look like someone has swirled blue and grey paint together, and it hasn't mixed. It's really nice.

"Hello Mich, your fighting was really good," I say over Freddy's shoulder. Freddy lets me go and grins at me.

"Mich doesn't speak. He's deaf, but he understands you." Freddy says and taps his head.

"How?" I ask but Mich answers.

"I can speak inside minds, like witches do. Thank you for your words," he says, his voice deeper than I expect from a boy his age.

"Oh, well that's a cool power." I say, and Mich nods.

"Let's go for a run," Freddy nudges Mich's shoulder, and they both run towards the doorway, where there used to be door. I watch them both chuck their tops off and shift, ripping their trousers. Mich is a grey wolf, the one I saw before when Jaxson was crowned. Both the tops of his ears are missing. Freddy's wolf is much bigger than the last time I saw him, at least half the size of me now. They both quickly run off out of sight.

"Everyone, your queen needs your help," Leigha says loudly next to us as Harris moves to her side. I see his hand gently brush hers. It's so sweet, and I have the urge to help them be together. I know it's not accepted, but isn't Freddy proof enough that two races can be together?

The wolves all stop what they are doing to come over and bow at me.

"Please stand in a line by that wall," Leigha says and I glance at her with a 'what the fuck' expression. Harris joins the others until they are all lined up, around a metre apart.

Leigha walks off and grabs a belt that has a line of throwing stars on it. She hands it to me, and I slip it over my head. I know where this is going, and she is bloody mad.

"I want you to throw one star at each person, just above their heads," she says, confirming my thoughts.

"Are you crazy?" I whisper harshly, and she just looks at me with a blank, unimpressed face.

"No. Just do it, Winter," she says and steps away. The distance I'm standing is at least ten metres away and every one of the wolves looks nervous. I try to give the first guy a reassuring smile, if anything he looks more nervous afterwards. I pull a star out of the belt; it's light and made of black metal in the middle. Each end of the five star points are silver and look very sharp.

I pull my arm back and try to calm myself. I close my eyes and open them just as I throw the star. The star hits perfectly, just above the man's head with a little of his hair caught around it. Harris starts clapping and grins at me.

"Again," Leigha says. I move down the row of men, throwing star after star until I run out. I turn and Leigha smiles at me as the men clap with Harris.

"That is a power of yours. Proof that you are strong and in control. If you weren't, you would have killed one of them. When we are fighting, you need to let your senses and mind take over. Stop thinking about how to beat me, and trust that you will. Like you trust your power to make those hits perfectly." Leigha says. She chucks a sword at me from off of the wall as I put back the star belt. I think about her words, I need to trust my powers.

"Come on then, Princess," Leigha says with a nod, and we face each other on one of the mats. I watch her closely, knowing when she is going to attack, and I move to deflect her. I pull the calm feeling to me that I used when I threw the stars. I feel myself move–faster than I thought I could–and I finally understand what Leigha means. I can't think about every move or plan the fight. I have to feel it and trust myself. I move quickly towards Leigha as we battle. She pushes me back step-by-step with each hit. I feel myself getting close to the wall, so I throw a hard hit to her sword. I turn and run towards the wall, Leigha quickly following me. I jump, using the wall for momentum to push off, and land behind Leigha; kind of like how I saw Mich go over Freddy's head. I pull my sword up and point it at her back, not enough to cut her, but enough, so she knows I've won.

"About time," Leigha turns and bats my sword away. I lower it with a grin and wipe the sweat off my forehead.

"I won't say this again, but you were right," I tell Leigha. She simply smirks.

"Why do I never hear you tell me that?" Jaxson says behind me, and I grin, turning to see him walk through the doorway. He glances at the door on the floor and back at me.

"Guys are never right, man, best learn that quickly," Harris says walking over to us. "Can I have a word?" Harris asks Leigha.

"Outside," she says and walks away with Harris following her. I walk over as Jaxson picks up the door. It's really hot to watch him carry the door like it's a bag of potatoes to the doorway and rest it near the wall. He goes into the cupboard and brings out a large toolbox.

"I'll fix this, lass, Dabriel wants to see you in the main cabin," he says while I watch him as he slowly pulls his shirt off; like a teenager discovering her hormones for the first time. I've seen him without his shirt plenty of times, but hot damn; he gets me all flustered every time.

"Err yeah, I'll get to that," I blurt out. Jaxson merely smirks at me and slaps my ass as I pass by him. I find Dabriel in the dining room, books all over the table he's sitting at. Just the top of his white wings and white hair can be seen as he leans over a massive book. I walk around the table and rest my hand on his shoulder. He takes my hand in his and kisses the tips of my fingers as he speaks.

"I missed you this last week," he whispers.

Dabriel went back to the angels to find a way to kill demons or anything that can be used on them. The angels apparently have a large library and many records, if anything could be found, it would be there.

"Me too," I sigh. Dabriel pushes the chair back with his large legs, his wings hanging over the back and spread slightly out. He wraps an arm around my waist and pulls me onto his lap. I wrap my arms around his neck, resting my head on his shoulder. We don't say a word for a while; just enjoy being near each other.

"Did you find anything?" I eventually ask as he runs his large fingers up and down my back. The effect is soothing.

"No, well not really," he says.

"Not really?" I ask.

He sighs. "There was one book, about a bundle of weapons that could kill demons. The writer says they were Fray touched," Dabriel says, his voice sounding annoyed.

"Fray?" I ask, having no clue what that is.

"Fairies. The writer believed that fairies exist, and that

they can place their magic in weapons. These weapons can kill demons," he answers, but his tone is laced with frustration, suggesting he doesn't believe it.

"Do fairies exist?" I ask.

"No, my little wildfire. I don't think they do," he says, and I stay in his arms for a long time. If only I knew how to speak to a fairy.

53

WINTER

"Hello," I shout through the trees that greeted me when I opened my eyes. This place is nothing like I've ever seen. Large, purple trees stretch into the bright-blue skies, and the grass is a yellow colour instead of green. This place is spectacular. I watch as a butterfly the size of a cat flies past me, the wings filled with bright colours. This is a dream, but I don't see Elissa anywhere, or anyone for that matter. There is nothing but the purple trees and yellow grass.

"You called me?" a woman asks with a little laugh as she walks out of the trees to my left. She stops dead in her tracks when she sees me, giving me time to look at her.

She has on a long, purple dress that is split in the middle showing off her stomach and the flower tattoos that cover it. The tattoos look like marks as they slightly move; they are lilies, I think, on blue vines. They also cover all of her arms and her shoulders as well. In the middle of her forehead is a weird symbol that looks like a half moon inside a circle. Her long, strawberry-blonde hair is braided and hanging over her shoulder. Bright-yellow eyes meet mine; they remind me of a cat.

"You look just like your mother. I never would have guessed you

inherited her ability to dream-call," the woman says, her voice is soothing and sweet.

"You knew my mother? And what is a dream-call?" I ask her. I try to move forward, but I can't, my feet are rooted to the spot.

"Yes, I knew her very well. She would call me often after we met," the woman says, speaking fondly of my mother. "Dream-calling is rare. It's the ability to call people you want into your dreams or travel into theirs. Have you not had strange dreams before?" she asks me.

"Of my dead grandmother and her sister," I reply.

"You can call your family spirits? It must be easy for you. Have you called your mother yet?" she asks me.

"I didn't know she existed until recently," I tell her, and she nods.

"Isa will come if you call," she tells me. I'm not exactly sure I want to do that. I didn't even know that I had wanted to call Elissa and see her past. I guess in a way, now I did, but not at the start. So how did that happen?

"I don't even know how I called you," I tell her. "Wait, who are you?" I ask quickly before she can answer.

"My name is Lily, or at least my shortened name that you may use is. I am a fray or fairy as you like to call us in your human words," she tells me. I fell asleep with Dabriel thinking of fairies and how I wanted to know if they were real. I guess I got my wish.

"Fairies exist?" I ask her. I realise how silly a question it is when she giggles. Her laugh sounds perfect.

"Demons have invaded your realm, and you question if fairies exist, child?" she laughs.

"Well," I say, and she laughs more. "Why would I call you?" I ask her.

"You need my help, and you wish for a promise," she tells me.

"How can you help me?" I ask her.

"The question is, will I help you?" she says and laughs.

"Forget it," I mutter and try to pinch my arm. It only hurts, and I still don't wake up.

"Demons can be killed with fairy-touched weapons," she tells me. The stories Dabriel found must be true. I snap my eyes to her yellow ones as she smiles.

"When you realise how much you need me, only call and we shall make a promise," she says.

"Wait," I say when I see her walk away.

"Goodbye, Winter, daughter of my friend," she says, and the world goes black as I fall backwards onto the yellow grass.

"She's awake," Dabriel's voice flutters through my mind as I open my eyes. He is leaning over me while I lie on a bed. I sit up, feeling slightly dizzy. I'm not in a bedroom that I've seen before; it's modern with black and white dressers. The curtains are grey and open, so I can see the mountains outside. It's Atti's house, and I think this is his room. The bed is huge, with a black headboard that I move back to and lean on. Atti and Wyatt are leaning by the wall and staring at me, both of them look angry. I feel my hair being tugged and look up. I see Milo sitting next to my head on the headboard.

He flies over to my shoulder and kisses my cheek.

"No dream-call so far," he says.

"What?" I ask croakily and sit up. Dabriel brings me a glass of water, and the room is silent as I sip it. I feel like I'm starving. The dizziness is from me needing blood, but I just fed yesterday, at least I think I did. Everything seems fuzzy.

"So, you want to explain where you've been the last two weeks?" Wyatt snaps. I raise my eyes to his and put the drink down on the black side unit. Wyatt's hair looks like he has just woken up, his skin is pale, and he seems angry. Our bond tells me he's worried.

"In bed?" I ask nervously, and he groans.

"You've been sleeping for two weeks, Winter. The first trial is today, and I thought . . . ," Atti says, and his words drift off. Atti runs his hands through his hair and comes to sit on the end of the bed. He rests a hand on my knee.

"*We were all scared. It's no fun being this powerless around you,"* Atti whispers in my mind.

"The sleeping beauty act is getting old, and I'm going to get grey hairs at this rate," Alex says as she walks in the room. She jumps on my bed and gives me a side hug.

"Sorry. It's not like I asked to sleep for so long. I feel worn out," I say honestly.

"Milo told us you where dream walking, and we figured out the rest. Milo and Dab were sure that nothing bad was happening to you," Alex says. She's dressed in tight jeans and a white cardigan over her vest top. Her long hair is up in a messy bun.

"I saw a fairy, or dream-called her. She knew my real mother," I say. Alex winces a little; it's weird knowing that our mum kept this from us. Alex grew up at my side, and the same woman adopted us both.

"Apparently, I've been calling Elissa into my dreams for years. It's a power of mine," I say.

"Leigha picked up on it and understood it when Milo explained," Alex tells me. I forgot that Leigha could touch people and find out their powers.

"Did you know Leigha and Harris are getting jiggy with it?" Alex whispers to me, not caring that there are three large, scary men glaring at her.

"Jiggy with it?" Milo asks, and we both start laughing.

"That's not a sentence you need to know. Wait maybe you do, mini-demons must make new demons somehow," Alex says.

"Fire born," Milo huffs.

"We have a bigger fucking problem that includes my mate fighting for her life in two hours," Wyatt cuts in, and our laughter dies away.

“I woke up just in time, then,” I say.

“You haven’t trained, and we have no weapons that you can use on the Dentanus,” Dabriel says shaking his head.

"I best get showered and dressed," I say quietly into the tense room.

"I need a second with Winter," Atti says, and everyone nods. Dabriel kisses me gently, whispering in my ear, "I will heal anything that happens today, but I know you can do this. Remember, I’m here for you," before walking out of the room. Wyatt just gives me a look, a look that promises that we are going to talk later, and leaves.

"There's a leather outfit in the bathroom. Before you say ‘no’ to wearing it, you need to, it’s easy to move in, and you need to look strong out there. Jeans will not do that for you. There are also daggers that Jaxson made for you. He says good luck, and he loves you," Alex says, and I nod, feeling a rush of warmth at her words. She leaves; taking Milo with her, and Atti shuts the door.

"Don't do this; not for me," Atti says, I can only see his back as he faces the door. I don’t need him to turn to know how angry and stressed he is.

"Atti, I can't walk away from this," I say gently, and he turns to look at me. The grey, playful eyes I'm used to are now stormy and dangerous looking. At times, Atti can seem big and scary, yes, but dangerous, no. Now, he seems more dangerous by the day. Atti looks close to losing it, and I don’t want to see the after effects of that happening. I never realised how dangerous it is to fall in love, let alone with four powerful princes. Princes that will be kings; princes that could destroy the world if they lost me.

"Not for this, for me. I love you, and I cannot lose you!" he shouts, his fists tightly clenched together. Atti’s hair is curled around his face, looking wild and unkempt.

"And, I love you, so I will fight for you!" I shout back, and he stomps over to me. I expected a fast and punishing kiss. Instead, his lips move over mine slowly, embracing me with every brush of his soft lips against my own.

"Mine," Atti says as he pulls away to kiss down my neck, his hand holding the back of my neck as he steers the kiss exactly where he wants it.

"Atti," I moan when his other hand slides slowly down my body, grazing my breasts. We kiss for a long time, with me sliding my hands around his chest and into his soft hair. My neck straining to meet every kiss because of how tall he is compared to me.

"Soon," Atti says suddenly and pulls back. We lie close, both of us breathless and staring at each other.

"I love you," I say quietly, and he smiles a little.

"I will always love you, Winter. I did from the moment I saw you. The moment you told me about those kitten knickers, I was a lost man," he says making me a chuckle a little. "I won't let you lose this, no matter what." Atti says, straightening out with a stern look replacing the carefree one I just saw.

"Where has my playful Atti gone?" I ask, smoothing my hand down his cheek.

"Not gone, just suspended," he replies gently.

"Like you've been naughty in school?" I tease him.

"I bet you were a naughty girl in school," Atti chuckles, and I grin.

"Shame I didn't have you around to spank me," I reply as I wink at him, and he laughs.

"I'm sure you are going to give me plenty of reasons to spank your pretty ass in the future," he tells me.

"Perhaps I will," I giggle as Atti laughs. I walk around him, knowing he's likely looking at my ass as I go to the door. I open the door and laugh as Alex falls on her butt.

"Eavesdropping?" I ask, and she glares up at me.

"She was," Milo offers and flies up off the floor to land on my shoulder.

"I made you Choco Pops cereal this morning and then gave you a bath after you swam in it. Yet, you still snitch on me," Alex says.

Milo just shrugs a tiny shoulder at her as she gets up.

"You can take your pet back, he is a pest," Alex says, and I hear Milo laugh. He clearly doesn't care about her insults.

"You love Milo anyway," I say, and she looks at me with raised eyebrows as Atti walks past us all and goes downstairs.

"I'm glad you and witch boy are happy again," she says when he has gone.

"Thanks," I say with a slight blush.

"I've said it once or twice before, but you are a lucky bitch," she says with a small grin, and I laugh. She isn't wrong.

"If you take photos of all those guys topless and put them in one of those calendars, we would make a killing," Alex winks.

"It reminds me of that time we were in the university entrance, waiting for someone to show us around on our first day, and there was that hot guy," I say, and she laughs,

"Ah I remember, I tried to take a sneaky picture," she says.

"It was so funny when the flash went off and you shouted shit, dropped the phone, and then told him he was hot," I laugh.

"I did get his number, though," Alex grins. That she did.

"That's the bathroom," Alex says and points at the

door next to Atti's bedroom. She looks at me for a second, her face instantly sobering.

"I'll be okay," I say, and she nods.

"Atti told me what your mum said," Alex says quietly. I didn't want to tell her, so I'm glad Atti did. I know she already guessed, everyone did, but it was only me that needed to hear it from the horse's mouth, so to speak.

"Mum told me a lot. There's a box at Jaxson's with a letter from my father. I want you to read it, okay? Ask Jaxson, he'll give you it," I tell her, and she nods.

"Alright, but you are not mad at mum, right?" she asks.

"No," I say, and she smiles slightly.

"I don't care about the rules of this stupid fight, but I'll personally pour water all over that witch if she hurts you," Alex says and hugs me gently.

"Water?" I ask quizzically.

"You know, that's how they do it in the Wizard of Oz. It might be a trick for the wicked witch," she says making me chuckle.

"She kind of looks like the wicked witch," I say, thinking of the witch in question.

"Shower and then get your game on. You have a dragon to beat," Alex tells me.

"Any ideas how I'm going to do that?" I ask her.

"No," Alex says softly.

"It's alright, I'll think of something," I say.

"I love you, Win," she says before she pulls me into a hug.

"I know. I love you as well; you're my sister and my best friend," I say. Alex pulls away and pats her shoulder with a look at Milo.

"You bleed, demon stop," Milo tells me.

"What? That doesn't make much sense," I reply.

"You blood work," he says.

"You know we need to work on your English or at least how to make sentences," Alex tells him and pats her shoulder again.

"You work on food for me," Milo tells Alex, and I hold a hand over my mouth to stop the laugh from escaping.

"Cheeky, little demon," Alex says, and I wander into the bathroom, listening as she tells Milo off. There's a pile of black-leather clothes and a belt with two daggers on each side. The daggers are silver and sharp. There's a small note on top with a J on it. I open it, knowing it's from Jaxson.

"*Fight this and come home*," he says. Short and simple, yet it fills me with strength.

I pull my shirt and underwear off before getting in the shower.

How can I possibly think I can beat a dragon?

This isn't a video game I can ask Freddy for tips on.

After my mini-freak out in the shower, I get out and dry off. I French plait my hair and twist it into a bun. I use the clips I find on the vanity and a headband, so it's held up tightly. I don't need my hair getting burnt off.

The clothes are unbelievably tight but soft and easy to move in. They, unfortunately, show off my hips, but it doesn't look too bad now after weeks of training have changed me. I feel an ache in my teeth before they slide out, reminding me I need to feed. I glance at myself in the mirror. Everything about me looks different. Even if you look past the slight blue glow and the silver eyes I have going on, I still look strange. I don't look human any more, my hair is too straight, and my face is too smooth.

The door is opened behind me, and Dabriel comes in. He shuts the door and glances at me.

"Wyatt said he felt your need to feed. Angel blood will

make you the strongest you can be," he says. I'm a little shocked and nervous at his offer.

"You sure?" I ask as he sits on the toilet. His legs spread widely, and he beckons me over.

"Yes, I want this," he tells me. I hear *I want you* in my head instead of his words. Dabriel watches me closely, his wings hanging near his hips and gently fluttering.

I move over him, hooking my leg over his as he helps me get comfy on his lap, our mouths a breath away, just before he presses his lips to mine. I let him control the kiss until the need to feed becomes overwhelming. I move my lips away and kiss down his jaw as his hands tighten on my hips.

I lick his neck before sinking my teeth into it. I don't know what heaven tastes like, I thought I'd came close to it by eating chocolate, but I was wrong. Dabriel tastes like I'd just drunk a glass of holy water right from heaven itself. He pulls me close as I feed, his hands pulling my core over the large bulge in his lap. The rocking sensation is overwhelming, and he doesn't have to do it more than a couple of times before I go over the edge. I break away to whisper his name, the pleasure taking over me.

"I can't wait to have you do that again when I'm inside of you. I've waited for what seems like forever to mate to you, Winter," he says and kisses me.

"Dab," I whisper, realising this was exactly what I needed: this release and peacefulness before the storm of the fight; one that has a high chance of me dying.

"Winter, my blood will make you stronger. Or at least your vampire side," he tells me and kisses my lips softly again.

"Thank you," I say, and he chuckles.

"Don't thank me. I belong to you, I always have," he says and kisses me before he lifts me up as he stands. I slide down his body, feeling every hard and toned part before I step away in a daze.

"Time to fight a dragon," I say, and he cocks his head to the side.

"You're scared," he says, and I nod.

He runs his hands down my arms. "Didn't I already tell you that nothing will happen to you from now on? I will always protect you, Winter," he says. There is not a slight bit of doubt in his words.

"I can't," I start and Dabriel puts a finger against my lips.

"You are never alone, Winter. Don't be scared," he says, his words don't expect an answer as he presses his lips to mine.

54

WINTER

Atti flashes us all over to the arena when we are ready, and, by this point, I would be lying if I said I wasn't terrified. Atti holds my hand, and Milo is on my shoulder as we walk across the massive arena.

It looks like something out of Greece, with its sandy dirt floor. Hell, this place could be the copy of the arena they have there. It's made out of stone, and rises high in the sky with thousands of seats. The stands are full to the rim with witches, all the light witches on one side and the dark on the other. It's easy to tell with their cloaks. There's a clear line between them of empty seats and it's weird. The contrast of light and dark on each side is chilling. There are very few witches without their hoods up; they are such an antisocial bunch.

There's a large, metal gate on one side–big enough to let a dragon out, I suppose. Right above it, are a few raised platforms, one in which the queen sits. There are two witches, one on each side–both look like they want to kill me–with their hoods down. The one to the left has short, shaved, black hair, marks all over her neck, which look like spikes, and a small green snake curled around her arm as she leans on the throne. The other woman is just as pretty as the queen. She has an innocent look about her, but as I meet her dark-grey eyes, I know she is far from it. There's just something off about her. Her long, white hair reaches the floor, and her pale-grey eyes remind me of Atti. She must be a light witch, and she also has her white cloak down. The queen isn't wearing a cloak at all. No, she has decided to wear a transparent, black-net dress, which shows off her perfect body, barely covering her private parts. She has a disinterested expression until she sees Atti. It's clear how interested she is in him from one look as she runs her eyes all over his body. I glance at my hands when I see them glowing blue because I want to throw her off a high-rise building for looking at my Atti like that. Hell, my Atti? Screw it, he *is* mine.

Atti looks over at me, and the slight widening of his eyes is all he does before looking away. Dabriel and Wyatt are on either side of me. Alex and Leigha stay behind us.

"I didn't think you would be truly foolish enough to come here. I've always thought humans were cowards," the queen says when we stop in front of her. Dabriel moves to stand next to Wyatt, letting Atti come to my side; Atti rests his hand on my shoulder.

"Said the witch wearing a crown she stole, and who is sitting on a throne that doesn't belong to her," I say loudly. The silence is echoing as she stares at me.

"Let's hope you die quickly rather than having a prolonged death," she says, but her sneer gives her away. She hopes I have a long death.

"That's the only death you will get," Atti says, and she narrows her eyes.

"The angel prince and the vampire prince standing

side-by-side. You should have introduced yourself to me at the castle. I would have made you very welcome," she says, every word is a suggestion. Atti slides an arm around my waist when I step forward, stopping me from going closer. I have to close my eyes and beg my power to calm down.

"We are here with the true king and queen," Wyatt replies. Dabriel doesn't look her way as he steps in front of me.

"Good luck," Dabriel says, and Wyatt nods at me before he turns to walk away with Dabriel following. Alex and Leigha give me brief looks of worry before following the guys. Atti brings our entwined hands to his lips and places a long, sweet kiss on them. He moves back and bows to me.

"My true queen," he says loudly and winks at me before he turns to follow the others to where they are standing.

"Let's start," I hear Taliana say, and I look at her. Her pale complexion is slowly going red, and I smirk at her. They are mine, and I'm here to fight for them, she needs to get that.

The jealously is clear all over her face as she leans back into her large, black throne. The metal gates screeching open make me look down, and I take a step back when a burst of bright-blue fire shoots out from the dark door. A large thud shakes the ground as the dragon shoots out of the door and lands a few metres away from me. It's huge, nearly as big as a house with blue scales covering every part of his body, except for some yellows ones that make a pattern down its back to its tail. Two large wings spread out and his bright-blue eyes lock onto mine. His face is slim, stretching down to his large mouth full of sharp teeth.

If this is his size when he's young, I don't want to see him fully grown.

"*Meal,*" is hissed into my mind by a gravelly voice, and it takes me a second to realise it's the dragon who spoke to me.

"Nope, I'm so not a happy meal for you," I say as the dragon's big wings flap once, twice, and he takes off into the sky. I look up, and I'm glad I do as he shoots a line of blue fire at me.

"Shit," I say and run out of the way. The fire manages to catch my arm, lightly burning, but not badly. I'm too worried about the shadow on the ground I can see; it means the dragon is following me. The dragon swoops low and its massive claws wrap around my stomach, lifting me off the ground. Pressure fills my body. I embrace it, and when I can release it, I beg it to hit the dragon in my mind. I open my eyes as the blue wave hits the dragon's stomach, and he screeches in pain. His claw scratches down my arm as he lets go. I'm glad to be free but not so much when I see how high we are. I fall to the ground with an alarming speed. I manage to use my vampire speed to slow everything down and roll as I land. The crowd is shouting, screaming my name and other things I don't understand.

The dragon lands with a thud in front of me, and I slip the dagger out of my belt. I know it won't work, and I don't think I can hurt him anyway; I feel sorry for him, he's just hungry. The dragon stares at me, his very intelligent eyes go to the dagger, and I throw it into the ground in between us.

"*Princesss*," the dragon hisses in my mind. I hold my hands up not needing the dagger.

"I don't want to hurt you, but I have no choice if you hurt me again," I say. The crowds are screaming at this point, I have no idea if they can hear me. I don't even know if they want me dead or alive at this point.

"*Need food. Not hurt family of king*," he hisses in my mind. His eyes go to my arm, and I look down at it, seeing it covered in my blood. Milo's words come back to me.

Why didn't I think of it before? I'm quarter demon and of the demon king's family. I might be able to get out of this by demanding him not to hurt me. There must be at least one benefit of having messed up family members.

"Fly away," I say, and he steps closer.

"*Cannot. The witches block the top*," the dragon hisses, and I look up to see a faint, white movement over the arena. I didn't notice it before, but, of course, they have a strong barrier up. The dragon moves another step closer.

"*Winter, what are you doing? Run!*" Atti says in my mind.

"No!" I turn around and shout. I take the other dagger out of my belt and throw it at the queen. I aim it just in front of her throne, at her feet. She starts glowing black as she stands. A large falcon flies from out the skies and lands on her shoulder. The falcon is the size of a cat, with beady eyes, a large beak, and is all black in colour. I have a feeling it's using a glamor. It must be her familiar.

The arena goes quiet as I walk up to the dragon, my insides screaming to stop this and walk away. Another part of me, the dark part, loves this creature and recognises it as my own. Just like I did with Milo.

I place my shaky hand on its large nose; the scales are warmer than I expected them to be. Enough that it's likely that he is burning my hand; I don't move my hand away, though.

"What's your name?" I ask him.

"*Demon name is long*," he hisses in my mind.

"Well, blue dragon, I'm Winter," I say.

"*Princesss*," he hisses in my mind.

"What are you doing?" is shouted across the arena by Taliana. I smile gently at the dragon, his eyes watching me, and then I turn to face her.

"Winning with peace and not death!" I shout back, my words echoing around the arena.

"That's not our way, and you cannot win unless you kill it. It's a demon," she spits out.

"Isn't the falcon sitting on your arm a demon as well?" I respond.

She doesn't answer, but her angry eyes watch me as I address the crowd.

"You expect everything to be won with death!" I shout. Silence is all I get from the witches sitting with their cloaks up.

"I am no witch. I am no human, not anymore. This is my way, and this creature does not deserve death any more than the familiars you have next to you," I say, and I see a few people remove their hoods and stand.

"The goddess wouldn't want this death. The dragon should be free," I shout. I feel the power in my words, a power I don't recognise as it takes over me. My arms start glowing blue as I lock eyes with Taliana. She is glowing black; her hands have black smoke flowing out of them onto the floor.

"*Freedom*," I hear someone whisper in my mind, and another person says it, and another.

The witches all start dropping their cloaks as they shout the word in my mind and in everyone else's. It becomes deafening, but I stand still as I look back at the queen.

"You win this," Taliana spits out and storms off.

Atti walks over to me and pulls me into a kiss. The crowd cheers loudly, and I pull away with a little blush.

"I believe I have a dragon to return home," he tells me.

"Where is your home?" I ask, turning to meet the dragon's eyes.

"*Let me fly to where I choose*," he hisses in my mind.

"He wants you to lower the wards up there," I say, and Atti nods. I watch as he disappears, and not long after the ward goes. The dragon lowers its head and then takes off into the sky.

"*Debt will be repaid, Princess*," he hisses into my mind as he disappears from view.

55

WINTER

"Let's look at your arm, I saw it cut," Dabriel says. I pull my top off, since I have a vest top on underneath it, and show Dabriel my arm. We left the arena quickly after the dragon flew away; the witches all disappeared as well. Atti said he was proud of me, and that I did the right thing, even if I scared him. We're in the spare bedroom, I'm not sure why, but it's where Dabriel took me once we got back to Atti's house. I look down when he wipes the dry blood away, and he frowns as he turns my arm over. The skin is clean and the burn I got on the top of my arm is nearly all gone too.

"How? You're healing like an angel," Dabriel says, and he leans back.

"Don't vampires heal like this?" I ask.

"Not from a magic fire or a cut that deep. It would take at least a day. My people can make natural healing herbs and put magic into them, but even that wouldn't heal a magic burn that fast," he tells me.

"Must have been your blood," I comment, and he shakes his head.

"No, vampires have had angel blood before and all it does is make them a little stronger," he says quietly and watches me.

"So, this is weird?" I ask, and he nods.

"What's wrong? I can feel your worry through the bond," Wyatt says coming into the small bedroom, and Atti follows, he closes the door behind him.

"She healed herself," Dabriel says as he links his hands with mine, and Wyatt walks over to me. He kneels in front of me and takes my now healed arm, so he can look at it.

"I've been thinking about something," Wyatt says, and he stands up.

"When Winter shared blood with Jaxson, she developed the power to aim perfectly. After a chat with Alex, it's clear she didn't always have that power," he says.

"Then when I gave her my blood, that blue power developed," Wyatt says.

"You think I'm somehow gaining more powers when I take your blood?" I ask. It makes a lot of sense. Maybe that's my power from my goddess side as well as the animal connection or maybe the dream-calling is.

"I'll get Leigha, she'll tell us if you have a new power," Wyatt says and walks out.

"I think the connection with animals is a goddess gift of mine and dream-calling a demon power, perhaps. I'm not sure what this one is," I say, and Atti comes to sit next to me.

"I wonder what you will get when you feed on me," Atti says and takes my hand in his.

"No idea, I don't seem to be getting the same powers as you," I comment.

"Well, Jaxson does have a deadly aim, but it certainly isn't like yours," Atti tells me.

“Yeah, and I’m pretty sure I haven’t seen Wyatt glowing blue recently,” I add, and Atti smirks.

“I think your demon half has some effect on that power,” Dabriel says, and I turn to him.

“Why?” I ask him.

“Most demons glow a shade of blue, and I can see their auras as well. They are blue like yours, but yours is lighter,” he tells me.

"Let’s have at it then," Leigha comes into the room with Wyatt following. I hold my hand out, and she takes it, a few seconds later she breaks away.

"New healing power, as well as the others," she says, and I nod. I knew she was going to say that.

"I guess the new power will help," I say.

"You were impressive in the arena," Atti says, and I smile slightly. I only did what felt natural.

"I can’t see the next task," Dabriel says, and he looks down at me with worry.

“Faster, pony,” I hear and glance towards the open doorway just in time to see Milo riding on Jewel’s back. Milo even has a ribbon, and he’s swinging it around in the air.

We all burst into laughter, even Leigha. That’s not something you see every day.

56

WINTER

"Get up, and let's go out, you look bored," Atti says as he walks into his lounge. He's dressed more casually than usual, in jeans and a tight, black shirt. I wouldn't say I'm bored, I'm just seeing how many of my chocolate biscuits I can balance on Mags' head as she sleeps on my lap in her glamor. I get to seven before Atti speaks, and she moves her head. The biscuits fall to the ground as Mags looks up at me. She gets off my lap and walks out, pushing her body against Atti's leg as she goes.

"I'm not bored, exactly," I say, and Atti just smiles as he comes over and pulls me up to his chest. He wraps his arms around me and gently leans down to press a simple kiss to my lips.

We disappear as he pulls away from the kiss. When I open my eyes I see that we are at the pack.

"Thought you might miss a broody fucker that lives here," Atti shrugs, and I laugh.

"I hope she does," Jaxson says, coming out of the front door and walking over to me. Jaxson is just wearing jeans and a grey shirt, but he somehow manages to look every bit the dangerous and sexy Wolf-man I love. His hair is newly shaved at the sides; the top part is shorter letting me see his bright-green eyes. Jaxson doesn't care that I am standing next to Atti, as his hand goes into my hair and his lips meet mine. I moan as the taste of him fills my senses; I underestimated how much I missed him.

"This is strangely turning me on," Atti says, and I break away from Jaxson with a small smile.

"I really didn't need to know that, witch," Leigha says as she walks past us all. I can't help the small laugh that escapes when Atti winks at me.

"Anna's in labour, I was close to calling for you." Jaxson says, and I lean back, shocked.

"Me?" I ask nervously. Why the hell would she want me at the birth of her child?

"She wants you here," Jaxson confirms my worries.

"Okay, let's go," I say, because I can't say no when I hear a scream come from the house. Jaxson grabs my arm gently as I walk past.

"Esta is up there, she's a midwife," he says, and I nod.

"You're my mate. We don't have to argue or hate each other anymore. It's the past," I say. I can't say I like her, but she hasn't actively tried to go after Jaxson for months. He told me she is mated with another wolf she met when the packs joined. She's moved on, and the past is the past. It's not like I don't have enough enemies as it is.

"You're too nice, love," Atti says, and I wink at him. I turn and walk into the house, leaving the guys to catch up. The two wolves at the door lower their heads when they see me, and I look back to see my guys watching me as I open the wooden doors. They look so strong standing next to one another. Atti is slightly taller than Jaxson, but Jaxson is a little wider in his shoulders and arms. I close the door behind me, and a scream directs my attention upstairs. I follow the noise until I find Anna's room. I knock before coming in, and Anna is on her side in her large bed. There's a wooden cot on one side, and a changing unit filled with things for the baby.

Esta stands at the side; her back going rigid when she senses me. She turns to stare at me, I don't know why I feel threatened around her, but I do. I don't get it.

"Winter!" Anna shouts, and I look down to see myself going blue.

"Shit, sorry Anna, I can't control the glowing," I say. *I didn't even notice I was doing it.*

"Come here," she says before she screams again. I run over and pull a chair close to her bed. I hold her hand, her other is holding her stomach.

"Here, wipe her face, while I see what's going on," Esta hands a cold, wet hand towel to me, and I nod as I take it. I do as Esta says, and Anna rolls onto her back with Esta's help. She checks her over.

"So close, I can see your baby's head," Esta says, and I give her a shocked look. She just looks at me like I'm an idiot.

"Push for me when you get the next contraction, Anna," she says, and Anna squeezes my hand tight as she screams. I don't dare move in the next few minutes until we hear a baby cry. I choke back tears as Esta passes a small baby wrapped in a white towel to Anna.

"A girl," Esta says, and I look in shock at the little one. Girls are so rare for wolves, and this girl is a child of an alpha to boot. She has a little blonde hair on her head, and she opens her eyes. They're blue, just like Fergus's. Anna bursts into tears, and I kiss her forehead.

"She looks just like her dad," I say, and Anna nods watching her baby.

"Her name is Marie, after my mother. Her middle name is Winter after you. The queen that will give her a future," Anna says, she meets my eyes, and I nod. It's the first time I realise that I'm not just fighting for a future for me; I am fighting for a future for all of the children. If that's not a reason to fight, then I don't know what is.

"Thank you," I say, and she goes back to staring at her little baby.

"Why don't you go and tell everyone?" Esta says. It's not rude because I know she has to clean up Anna.

"Okay. Is that alright?" I ask Anna, and she nods still staring at her little one.

I walk out and down the stairs. Everyone is sitting in the lounge, and Freddy runs up to me.

"Is the baby okay? We heard a cry," Freddy says.

"Yes, you have a new cousin. A girl called Marie Winter," I say, and everyone starts clapping. Jaxson meets my eyes, and his smile is so wide, I can't help but grin back. Wyatt nods at me, his gaze watching Freddy closely. It must be strange to talk of babies when he missed Freddy being that young.

Wyatt looks as hot as always, I notice his hair looks a mess, like he's been running his fingers through it. I kind of like it. He's a hot mess. He's dressed in jeans and a white shirt, so casual compared to what I'm used to seeing him in.

"The first girl born in two years for the packs. The first alpha girl in fifty years," Lucinda says coming into the room, and she comes over to me. I give her a hug when Freddy moves away, and she smiles.

"I'll go and see if I can help," she says and walks up the stairs. Freddy pulls my hand and leads me to the sofa.

"Wyatt, how are the vampires?" I ask him.

"Stupid vampires," Freddy mutters under his breath, and I glare at him.

"Settling in at the castle. Others have been turning up, but it's a slow build to get the place suitable for the people. Jaxson's been helping us," he says. Jaxson nods his agreement.

"That's good. I was wondering what all your last names are, what's the baby's?" I ask Jaxson.

"Jaxson Ulrika, but we don't use last names often. The baby's last name will be the same," he tells me.

"I know Atti's is Lynx, Wyatt?" I ask him.

"It's simple, Wyatt Reynolds. Like Jaxson said we don't use last names often," he says.

"And Dabriel?"

"Dabriel Demetri. The royal name is as close as they can get to Demtra," Atti explains.

"Mine was Bloom. My real last name that is," I tell them all. It's weird because it's a connection to a father I don't remember. I don't feel connected to the name, because I don't feel connected to my father, I guess.

"Winter Bloom. That's kind of strange, like your full name is a representation of the cold month and the spring month in one. They're opposites of each other," Dabriel says.

"It sounds like a randomly generated name you would get on *The Sims*," Freddy says, and I grin at him,

"That's true. They come up with some weird names," I say.

57

WINTER

"So sweet," I say to little Marie as I hold her in my arms at the pack house. Marie's blonde hair is the same colour as Anna's, but everything else is from her father. Anna is sitting next to me, watching as I hold little Marie's hand. Her tiny fingers squeezing my thumb as hard as she can.

"Do you want children?" Anna randomly asks. I look up at her, thinking on her words. Anna has her dressing gown on, and she looks so tired.

"I don't know, maybe?" I say.

She nods, "I never wanted children, not in this world. It was Fergus who wanted a child."

"Anna–" I start.

She shakes her head. "I couldn't imagine my life without her now. She is the image of Fergus," she says, looking at her daughter with love. I couldn't imagine bringing up a child after losing their father; it must be so hard.

"She is," I say. I stare at the door when I hear something; something loud, and then the ground starts shaking.

"Jaxson just sent out a message using the bond. There are demons attacking," Anna says. I pass her Marie carefully as she rushes to me. The fear in her eyes is clear, and she holds Marie close.

"Go upstairs and hide," I tell her. She steps away from me when I start glowing, not in fear but shock.

"You're coming, too," she says. The earth shakes harder, making me sway a little. Anna leans on the wall to stay standing. Something is really wrong.

"No. I can't, and as queen I'm telling you to go upstairs and hide. Please," I say, and she nods finally. I run towards the door and outside. The wolves are running in one direction, so it's easy to follow them using my increased speed.

When I break into a clearing of broken trees, Jaxson is right in the middle, looking every bit the powerful king with his green, glowing crown on his head. He's glowing green as he holds a sword in his hand, and he swings it down onto the neck of a man. The man's head rolls off, and he disappears into a dark-blue dust. Jaxson's eyes meet mine across all the wolves fighting with the men. I see his eyebrows crease together with worry, but two more of those men jump in front of him, and he has to fight. The ground is still lightly shaking, and a hand goes around my throat. I try to pull the hand away as I manage to turn to see who is holding me. The demon man has glowing, blue eyes that remind me of me when I glow blue. The man is grey, and his face is covered in blue veins, giving him a scary look. There is no emotion on his face, not happiness or fear, just blank. The hand is burning hot enough to leave a mark, and I feel for my own power as he tightens his grip and lifts me off the ground. I start glowing just before my power sends the man at my back flying in the air. He isn't the only one that goes flying, so do lots of wolves and all the demon men they were fighting as well.

Whoops.

The wolves use it to their advantage and rip the heads off of the men on the ground. I fall to my knees when the ground shakes harder than before. I look up to see Jaxson, his sword in the ground at his feet, and his hand is glowing green as he holds the handle. Hell, his whole body is glowing a bright-green. I can't stand up as I watch the earth split open from his sword, causing a massive crack that spreads towards the herd of demon men running towards him. They don't even notice as they fall into the hole, no screams or anything leaves their mouths as they fall. The wolves make quick work of killing the last of the demons, and Jaxson closes the hole he created. When the shaking stops, I walk over to Jaxson. He's still staring at the place where the hole was, and he's still glowing. I put my hand over his on the sword, and he seems to snap out of wherever he had been.

"Eight," he says to me. I frown, not understanding until I hear a cry and then the pain-filled screams. I turn to see Angela holding a brown wolf to her chest, Katy is behind her and crying silently.

"We lost eight," I say, and Jaxson nods. I watch as he walks over to Angela and places his hand on her shoulder. He speaks quietly to her, and I walk over to Katy. She lets me hug her, and we stay quiet for a long time.

"I need to redo the ward, they shouldn't have been able to break through," Atti says. I didn't even realise he was here. His eyes meet mine, but he only nods. I forgot he was coming to take me back to his house for a movie night today. I've been at the pack for a few days, and I spent a few days with Wyatt at the castle, too. The castle is improving slowly, Wyatt thinks that one quarter of the six hundred bedrooms are finally done. It's a big job, and there is only so much they can do in a short amount of time. The kitchens and bathrooms are done, which is a big improvement. Wyatt showed me the ten buildings outside of the castle. He thinks they used to be where the humans lived because they have about ten rooms in each of them and their own kitchens.

"No, we are moving." Jaxson's says suddenly, snapping me out of my thoughts.

"What, J?" Atti asks.

"The castle has the best ward. They just walked through our ward like it was nothing and started killing. They could attack us at any time here," Jaxson says.

"The castle is safer," Atti agrees. The wolves standing around us start speaking quietly.

"What do you think?" Jaxson asks me. I glance around at the wolves; most are covered in blood and blue dust. I see two men covering a black wolf with a large coat.

"It's smart for us all to be together," I say quietly. There are several wolves around us, and I blink when I see Harris push them out of the way. He comes over and drops to his knees in front of his mother and the dead wolf.

"No," he says and places his hand on the wolf's back.

"Harris," I say gently as Jaxson stands. He moves next to Atti.

"Go and get Dabriel. We have many that need healing," Jaxson tells Atti, and he nods. He disappears a second later.

"I couldn't get here in time; they attacked near the other cabins but not as many. The weapons don't work on them, you could stab them, and they just carried on. We had to cut the heads off, and I couldn't leave them," Harris mumbles.

"No one expected you to, my boy," Roger, one of Angela's mates, says coming out the trees with three other men following closely. They all fall to their knees around

Angela and place a hand on the wolf. All of her mates band together to mourn the one they lost.

"We move tonight after we bury our lost wolves. We are at war!" Jaxson shouts, his voice vibrating around the trees. They seem to carry his message along with the fear that follows his words.

We are at war.

58

WINTER

Once again, I find myself in the middle of the arena, a little scared, but more determined to make a better future for the children like Marie. Her sweet face flashes through my mind, I have to do this. I have to win. I have no idea what I'm up against, and Dabriel has tried desperately to see any part of this future. He says a blue wall is blocking his vision, and we suspect Taliana has found a way to block visions like the vampire king did before his death. Atti has tried finding out by asking around the witches he trusts, but no one is talking. Everything we *are* hearing is just rumours.

The queen smiles down at me, her black cloak wrapped around her head today as she sits alone on her throne. She's wearing a long, green dress that I can see through and a black cloak. Atti, Dabriel, and Leigha are at the sides watching me. Wyatt is helping move all of Jaxson's pack into the castle. There's space, but it's cramped. It doesn't help when the werewolves and vampires don't get along. There have been many fights, but

Wyatt and Jaxson end them quickly. Alex and Drake are working closely with Harris to keep the guard up on the castle. They run twenty-four-hour watches around the castle grounds and in the local village. We haven't sent any people to check out Paris yet. There's little point, the red wall is impossible to see through, and our magic won't work on it. The humans say technology can't get near it without exploding. So, what little photos they have are from a distance. That's good in a way, but people are angry they can't get in touch with their loved ones, and I fear that the demon king has them possessed to make an army.

I glance back at the queen when she claps her hands, and the arena goes silent. I look around, noticing that many witches have their cloaks down today, and many smile at me as I meet their eyes.

"Witches have the ultimate control over the elements. The next challenge is to see if the human can defend herself, or if she will die when the elements are used against her. Any true queen would be able to survive this," the queen's voice surrounds the arena; her sarcastic tone isn't lost on me. The crowd cheers, and the metal gates open. I look down as four witches come out. Two light witches and two dark. There seems to be one male and one female for each side. They all stop in a line a few steps away from the gate and a good distance from me. I can't see what they look like as they have large cloaks covering their bodies, the only reason I know what side they are on is because of the colour of their cloaks.

One of the dark witches, wearing a black cloak, steps forward and holds his hands high in the air.

"*Fire*," he says into my mind, and a stream of fire leaves his hand and surrounds me in a circle. The heat warms my skin but not enough to burn. The second dark witch steps forward, she bows her head slightly at me.

"*Earth*," she says, and the ground underneath me rises. I fall to my knees, unable to stand, as the loud sounds of the earth cracking fill my ears. The ground rises around ten feet in the air before it stops. I stand up and move as close as I can to the edge. The fire rises higher until I can't see the witches anymore, only the tops of the arena.

"*Air*," a man speaks into my mind. The fire mixes with the air and twirls up into a whirlwind tornado of fire. The tornado stretches high into the air, leaving only a small hole of sky when I look up.

"*Water*," the last witch says, and the ground shakes roughly making me fall backwards onto it. I crawl towards the edge, pulling my head over to look down just as a section all around the raised ground falls in. It's instantly filled with deep water that shoots up; I move out of the way just in time and watch as it shoots into the sky. Mixing with the fire and air tornado.

Holy shit, I'm completely trapped. I can't see the sky anymore when I look up, and it's getting harder to breathe. Or even think.

"Winter, use your power, stop this," Atti says in my head. Everything starts to blur as I call for my power. The pressure builds as fear for my life takes over, the hot water starting to scald my skin as it falls from the top of the tornado. Death by suffocation is not a good way to go. The edges of my vision are going black. The pressure of my power is building, but I can't think straight because of the fear.

"*Winter, I'm coming love, hold on*!" Atti shouts in my mind, his voice frantic but muffled to me.

My head snaps up as pressure I'm not used to takes over, filling my body, and the blue wave shoots out of me. My feet leave the ground as a blue wave of my power hits the tornado, pushing it away. The water falls away–as does the fire and wind—as I take in a deep breath, and open my arms. My feet are slightly floating off the ground, and my blue waves are still leaving me. The last thing I see before everything goes black is the queen's shocked and fearful face.

59

WINTER

"Winter, Winter, Winter," Is sung by the child-like voice. I open my eyes slowly, not seeing the child that's singing but, instead, the back of a large man standing in front of me. The song drifts away as the man walks forward towards a bed. When he moves to the side, I can see Elissa. She is sitting in the middle of the bed, covers wrapped around her. A small bassinet made out of vines is by the bed. It's the same room she died in. I glance at the man as he leans over the bassinet. He looks about forty with blond hair that's cut short. He's only wearing black trousers, and it leaves his pale chest in full view. There's a mark–a phoenix very much like Wyatt's–on the middle of his chest. I can't really see his face from this angle as he looks down, but I'm guessing this is Wyatt's ancestor, the first vampire.

"She looks just like you, my beloved," the man says in a gruff voice. It takes me a second to realise that the baby is Elissa's, and that the baby must be my mother.

"You say that every time you see her, Athan," Elissa says with a sigh. She looks very tired.

"And, every time it's because it's true. She is the image of you," he says in return and smiles at her. I look over just as Elissa starts

glowing white. Every part of her skin glows, and Athan falls to the ground, his hand clutching his head in pain.

Elissa says nothing aloud, but I hear her make the prophecy in my mind.

The blue-sided human will choose a side.
When four princes are born, on the same day, they will rule true.
Her saviour will die when the choice is made.
If she chooses wrong, she will fall.
If she chooses right, then she will rule.
Only her mates can stop her from the destruction of all.
If the fates allow, no one need fall.
For the true kings only hold her fate, and they will be her mates.

After she speaks the final word, she closes her eyes. Athan shakes his head as he gets off the floor. He checks on the baby just as a woman in a long, red cloak comes into the room. I can't see her face or anything other than the ends of the white dress under her red cloak.

"Every person for miles just heard that, the demon king will find us," she says, her voice worried rather than angry.

"Then it's time, Demtra," Athan replies sadly and looks at Elissa.

"My poor sister," the goddess says, and she turns her head to where I stand.

"Winter, love," Atti says, and I blink my eyes open. I'm in Atti's arms as he holds me close. Dabriel has his glowing hands on my head, and he lets go when he sees I'm awake.

We're still in the arena; it must only be moments since I blacked out. Yet, it seemed like a long time in the dream-call. I didn't even mean to see that, so why did I?

So, it was Elissa making the prophecy that let the demon king know where she was and where his child was.

My mother.

Elissa must have hidden her not long after that dream, and I know she died in that room. I've seen all her mates now, Athan the vampire, Henrick the witch, Nicolas the angel, and Leo the wolf. She had mates just like me, but she had the demon king as a mate too.

I sit up slowly as Atti helps me stand on the rock we're on. I see Leigha seconds before she runs and jumps onto the rock. Warrior princess makes that look easy.

"A win," Taliana's voice drifts over to me as I stand. I turn to see her watching me as Atti grabs my arm, Dabriel holds my hand, and Leigha puts a hand on Atti's shoulder. We disappear while I smile at her, a smile proving that I can do this.

When we reappear, we are just outside the goddess's castle. I smile at a few wolves who bow when they see us, and I look around. The outside is quiet, with just the two wolves sitting outside. The castle looks so much bigger from here as I look up at it. It's made of smooth, grey stone, the parts that were destroyed are fixed, and it doesn't look like anything has ever happened to the castle. The four towers stretch into the sky, and right in the middle is the huge balcony that I spent time with Atti on. Someone has a row of flowers on the small wall that has been newly built, yet still looks like the rest of the castle.

"Let's go and find the others," Atti says. I see Harris come out of the castle and stop, not looking at us but at Leigha. I turn a little to see her staring at him as well, a mixture of emotions written across her face, but her stubbornness wins out when she turns and walks away. Harris's growl fills my ears, and I turn just in time to see him shift into a large, brown wolf. He jumps down the steps and goes chasing after Leigha.

"Never run from a wolf," Dabriel says gently.

"That's something Jaxson said once, she will be okay, right?" I ask him and Atti.

"You should be asking if Harris will be okay, Leigha is the scariest woman I've ever met," Atti says, and then chuckles to himself. "Well, other than you when I try to steal your chocolate," Atti jokes. Well, I hope he's joking. I'm not that bad.

"Very true," Dabriel nods, and I glare at him.

"You are meant to be on my side," I cross my arms.

"You nearly bit my finger off when I tried to taste that chocolate ice cream just last week," Dabriel crossing his arms in mimic of me.

"Ben and Jerry's?" Atti asks me, while I wince at Dabriel.

"Yes, the chocolate brownie flavour. Jaxson bought it for me," I say.

"Then, bro, you had it coming," Atti pats Dabriel on the shoulder with a laugh. I smile at them both as I feel hands slide around my waist, and I'm pulled back against a large body as cold lips kiss my neck.

"I missed you," Wyatt says into my ear.

"Me too," I say. I laugh as Wyatt picks me up and we move quickly away from the other guys. I take a deep breath when he stops and lets me go.

"Wanted me alone?" I ask him, and he grins as he lightly kisses me.

"Yes," he says, no other explanation needed. I glance around to see we are on the balcony I was just looking up at. There's a blanket on the floor, with a selection of food and some roses in a vase. I smile up at Wyatt with a big grin.

"I want to show you something first and maybe get you some more clothes," he glances down at my leather outfit. I nod and pull my wet hair out of the bun, and undo the plait. It falls in waves as he just watches me.

"You're beautiful, Winter," he says, making my heart pound in my chest. Then he walks away to the new doors. Someone has replaced the stone ones that were destroyed with large, glass doors. I like it. We go into the newly painted, white hallway; the floors are still the old stone but smoothed down. There are new lights on the walls, and the archways to Elissa's bedroom have new, wooden doors. There used to be white curtains in the past, but the light-wooden doors suit it better. They are shaped perfectly to the archway, and Wyatt pushes the door open. I walk in, and my first thought is that the room has changed so much. Where there once was a raised stone alter and stone floors, there is now an even, cream-carpeted floor. The new, arched windows are massive and letting lots of light into the room. There's a beautiful, wooden fireplace on one side and two small, white doors on each side of it. The main thing in the room is the huge bed in the middle, with a large, white headboard; it looks like it could fit at least five people. The bed sheets are white to match the white fur rug in front of the fireplace.

"We will get other things for the room, but this is all yours," he tells me, and my jaw drops.

"The four rooms next door are for each of us, they're just down the corridor, but I'm sure we'll take turns sleeping with you," he says making my cheeks go red at the thought.

"We could live together, all of us," I say in a whisper.

"When we have peace, we will." Wyatt says to me and comes over to kiss my forehead.

"Then we will fight for peace," I say, my words feeling like a promise.

60

DABRIEL

I smile at the old council member who goes on about how he is going to support me, if only I was stupid enough to not know he wants a price for the support.

"The older brother returns," the sarcastic voice of my younger brother says behind me.

"Excuse me," I say to the angel from the council whom I was speaking to. I turn to see my two younger brothers standing right behind me. Both of them are dressed in white, looking like twins when they're not. Their hair is more blonde than white, and its cut short, not like most angels who keep their hair long. Zadkiel is the one that spoke; his light-purple eyes make his narrow face seem cruel. Or maybe it's because I know how fucking cruel he can be.

"I have never truly left," I reply, crossing my arms.

"The council feels otherwise," he smirks.

"A council you are not on nor have any control over, Zadkiel," I say. His fists tighten as the few symbols he has start glowing on his arms. I resist the urge to smirk at the weak show of power. Govad, my other brother just watches us with distaste. Govad has white hair that stops at his shoulders; he looks more like me than my other brother. He's only a few inches shorter than me, and his eyes are darker than Zadkiel's. He hasn't spoken a word to me since I stopped him from killing another angel over a female. The fight was not needed and unfair, seeing as the other angel was not aware the female had been promised to my brother. My brother did mate with her in the end, and I offered the other man my protection. He was lucky he didn't sleep with her and make a bond; Govad would have had a real excuse to kill him then. Govad only speaks to my brother and is just as cruel. The only reason I can put up with him is because he doesn't want the throne. Zadkiel's thirst for power will be his undoing in the end, and it makes a problem for me.

"I will when I am king," he replies eventually.

"No," I say with a smirk, my skin lights up with my all my symbols. A little fear shines in his eyes, but he is quick to turn around and walk out of the room. Govad follows close behind him, and he doesn't meet my eyes. I look up at the old painting on the wall in the entrance hall to the council. It's of my father, and it's gigantic. My father has grey hair in this painting, a sign of how long he lived before he died a natural death. The narrow face and light-purple eyes are just like Zadkiel's, and I look very little like him. I look like my mother, with all my father's power.

"The council will now see you, prince Dabriel," a young, female angel says. She bows to me as I walk past and into the dome room the council sit in. They all watch me from their seats, each looking older than the next. The only one who is young is Lucifer, and he nods to me. He still owes me a favour for his future. I wouldn't say I like the dark angel, but I wish him to be on my side. I need a dark angel to sway the council with me.

"Why was I called?" I ask, getting to the point, so I can return to Winter. I don't wish to be away from her for long anymore. I've fallen for her, and the threats against her life are too high.

"The demons have been attacking our people, prince," Gabriel snaps out. I look over at him; he looks stressed and angry. Gabriel's hair is nearly all grey, and he sneers at me. He will never be on my side, as he supports Zadkiel.

"We can't see any attacks made by demons. We can't see them coming, and the witches' wards aren't working," Gabriel snaps out. It doesn't surprise me; I'm more surprised that more angels haven't died from the attacks. If I can't see any part of the demons' future or anything about the king, then they would not be able to see them coming. This is a shock for the angels, so used to seeing any attack before it comes to their doorsteps.

"I am aware of the issue. The vampires and werewolves are now living in a protected castle. The castle is the old home of the goddess," I tell them, each of them stare at me with mixed looks of shock and disgust.

"Impossible!" Gabriel spits out.

"No, it is not. The castle has a large ward, much stronger than any witch can give us, and the prince of the witches has used his magic to hold it. It also has its own ancient magic," I inform them.

"What are you telling us this for?" Lucifer asks me.

"We should move our people there," I say, and they all go silent. Not one of them says a word as I meet each of their eyes.

"Our people are at war. It is now the time to come together and fight. We can win if we are all together," I tell them.

"It's only a month until we choose a king. Is this truly the conversation you wish to have with us?" Raziel asks me, and I nod at the dark angel. Raziel has always been impartial, and I hope he does side with me on taking the throne.

"Yes. I care not for a throne if all my subjects are dead or turned into demons," I tell them.

They whisper quietly amongst themselves for a long time before Gabriel speaks, "We will not work with the vampires or werewolves. The war can be won on our side," he says. I knew what they would say, but I'd hoped they would be smarter than this.

"You are all old fools who will get our people killed!" I shout out.

"Zadkiel believes that we should fight, they can be killed, but it takes a few angels to take down one. We would like it if you stayed and fought with us," Gabriel smiles at me.

"He is wrong, and our people will pay for the mistakes of my brother's bloodthirsty nature," I spit out.

"I do not believe we should make a decision now. There is much to be discussed and a war on the way which we must defend ourselves from," Lucifer says, and his eyes meet mine for a second, knowing he is giving me time to save the angels from themselves.

"Agreed," is repeated around the council. I turn to walk out, but I hear, "Do you have any visions, prince Dabriel? Your brother does not," Lucifer says, and I stop in my tracks.

"Yes, but none are certain or of any use. I can't see anything other than blood and death in our future. I believe that we can work together to change this." I say, and I don't look at them as I walk through the doors, slamming them open. My wings spread open, and I take off out of the front doors, into the sky. I fly for a while before I see the old house I used to meet Atti at when he came to get me as a child. The house is in ruins, but it's away from humans and angels. I land just seconds before I'm knocked to the ground. I swing around and punch the person in the stomach, using my wings to fly into the sky. Zadkiel's eyes meet mine as he shoots into the air, and heads straight for me.

My younger brother was always the stupid one. My symbols kick in, and I fly down to meet him. I'm bigger than Zadkiel, so it's easy to slam him into the side of the house. Bricks fall all over the ground and around our heads as I wrap my hands around his throat. He tries to fight me off, but he has seriously underestimated me. I've always been abnormally strong.

"D, what the fuck?" Atti's voice comes from behind me, and a hand is slapped on my shoulder. I don't see anything other than Zadkiel's gasping and panicked eyes. His hands clawing my arms as I hold him down. If I kill him now, there won't be any competition for the throne. My people would have to listen to me.

"Fuck, he isn't worth this." Atti says as I look down at my brother. The guilt wouldn't be worth it, and I don't want to take the throne this way. I let go, listening to Atti's words and stand up slowly, taking a few steps back.

"I will have the throne," Zadkiel laughs and coughs out. I laugh humourlessly, myself, as I step forward, and Atti appears in front of me, blocking my gaze from Zadkiel and his fucking laugh.

"He is an idiot, D, don't waste your time," Atti says as he places his hands on my shoulders.

"I can just about fucking see you when you're glowing like a torch man, let's go," Atti says, it's hard not to smile.

"Fine," I say and Atti moves us. His magic feels like being on one of those human roller coasters Atti convinced me to go to once. I didn't see the point, but Atti kissed

Winter for the first time on one, and Winter loved it. Atti is good for Winter. More than he realises because they are very alike. They both like to see the humour in life when times are getting bad. I don't know how to do that, but she still seems to like me.

"Why are we here?" I ask Atti when I see he has brought us to his house. Winter isn't here; she's at the castle seeing Alex and Leigha for the night. She expressed that she missed them and wanted some time alone.

"Boy's night," he says, and I just don't know how to reply to him.

"Pardon?" I ask, and he laughs.

"Atti means we need to chill out for one night, and Winter is safe with her friends," Jaxson comes into the lounge with two beers in his hand. He hands me one just as Wyatt comes in.

"Fucking hell, is that what you brought me here for?" Wyatt asks and takes a sip of his beer. I watch in humour as Mags follows Wyatt and jumps on the sofa next to him as he sits. Mags jumps into his lap, and he holds his hands in the air.

"You just stroke her, or do I need to explain to you about how to deal with a girl on your lap?" Jaxson says with a laugh.

"I would have said pussy," Atti jokes and laughs. Jaxson smirks at Atti and sits next to Wyatt. Mags gets up and sits on his lap as he strokes her.

"I'm not a cat person," Wyatt glares at Jaxson and moves away.

"So, we are discussing cats all night?" I ask, because I don't wish do that. Mags is a lovely cat, but it's pointless when we have much more pressing issues.

"No. I got Avengers on DVD and beers. I'll go and get

pizza from New York in a bit. You can't beat that shit," Atti says, and I laugh as I take a seat.

"Boy's night it is," I groan out.

"You guys are such fucking losers, I swear I have no idea why we are friends," Wyatt grumbles.

"Because you love my ass," Atti says with a big laugh, and Wyatt throws a book at him. "I'm just joking, fucker, chill," Atti laughs as he stops the book in the air with a wave of his hand, and a gust of air throws it across the room.

"Such a dick," Wyatt says, but he relaxes in the seat and drinks his beer.

It was a good night.

61

WINTER

"So, who is this guy we are waiting for?" I ask Dabriel. Atti brought us to a little café in the middle of town near the university I used to go to. The café is empty other than the waitress who brought us two teas over. I drink a little of my tea, it's nice and normal. I could be on a normal date with a hot guy, you know, if he didn't have wings. I know the waitress can't see the wings, or she would have run out screaming. I know this dark angel we're meeting is meant to be able to see my past, but I don't know who he is. Atti is picking us up here in a few hours, as it's not safe to go back to my apartment or to pack lands anymore.

"His name is Lucifer," Dabriel answers.

"Like the fallen angel out of the bible?" I ask, but it's not Dabriel who answers me.

"Yes human, that was me."

I glance up at the man, or angel, who spoke. He is the very opposite to Dabriel. He has long, black hair with dark-brown skin. His eyes are a dark-purple, and his wings are full of black feathers instead of the bright-white of Dabriel's.

"I'm not sure I can class myself as human anymore," I tell him; he tilts his head to the side to look at me.

"Perhaps," Lucifer says and takes the seat opposite us at the small table. The bubbly waitress with blonde hair comes running over. Lucifer orders a cup of tea. It's so normal, that it's weird.

"You don't look like much," Lucifer tells me.

"Let's get on with this," Dabriel growls out, his tone is pissed off and goes with the scowl he's aiming across the table at Lucifer.

Lucifer laughs and offers me his hand over the table. I hesitate a little when I see the glowing symbol in the middle. It glows grey against his dark skin and looks like a half moon with an arrow going through the middle of it.

"I would never offer my power to anyone, let alone a human who is now a vampire. I owe my children's lives to Dabriel. That debt will be repaid, as I do not wish to have it over my head," Lucifer says.

I look at Dabriel, seeing his reassuring smile before I slide my hand into Lucifer's cold one and watch as his eyes glow black.

"So little, how I wish I could protect you." Isa, my mother, says to me. She is crying as she holds me in her arms. I'm only a toddler in this vision, with the little bit of brown hair that I have up in pigtails. I'm standing in front of her as my mother sways me from side to side. My little, yellow dress matches the yellow top my mother's wearing. I don't know why I'm focused on that and not how my mother looks at me with such love that it hurts.

I guess because it hurts to admit I miss her. I miss a mother I can't remember.

The vision changes quickly, and I'm in an empty street that looks familiar.

"We could just kill her; he won't know, and her power will keep us on earth," a crackly voice says behind me. I turn, seeing Isa on the ground. She's bleeding from her mouth, her clothes are torn, and she's watching the sky as two blue shadows stand over her. They keep flickering between real men in black clothes and the blue shadows.

"Do it," Isa whispers. The shadows hold her down, their hands over her chest, and she screams. I scream along with Isa as she dies. I recognise this dream; I had it when I was ten.

The vision flashes again.

This time Isa is with my father, Joey. I recognise him from the dream I had before. His brown hair is like mine, and I have his nose. They're both looking at the little baby in their arms, wrapped in a knitted, pink blanket. The room is bright with a raging fire in the fireplace, and the windows to the little house are covered in snow.

"Winter, her name is Winter, and she will save them all," Isa says gently.

"I like it," Joey says and kisses her. The baby cries, and they both smile down at her; at me.

I blink when I realise we are back in the cafe. The waitress stands, holding the mug of tea, and stares at us. I attempt to pull my hand back, but Lucifer holds on.

"Put it down, thank you," Dabriel tells the woman. She shakes a little as she puts the tea next to Lucifer and runs off.

Lucifer finally releases my hand, and I sit back in my seat. His eyes are completely black when he finally looks up at me. They slowly turn back to purple as I watch. It's the opposite of the way Dabriel's go white when he sees the future.

"I saw other bits, but those are the only important things I will show you. The rest is small," he tells me.

"To you, perhaps, it's all I have of my birth parents. Thank you," I say, my voice a little cracked. It hurts in my chest; the feeling of those memories, of parents I never knew, but I just saw how much they loved me.

"I am sorry for your loss." Lucifer says, and he stands. "My debt is repaid my prince," he looks towards Dabriel.

"It is," Dabriel answers. Lucifer goes to walk away, but Dabriel stops him. "I saw another child, a young one with dark wings and dark eyes. This one will need to move soon before the war takes him. You know whom I speak of, and I know the decision you will make. It's the only way," Dabriel says. I don't understand what he's saying, but, apparently, Lucifer does because he turns to face him with fully black eyes. Lucifer comes back over to the table and stands at the end. He joins his hands together, grey symbols appearing all over his skin. He has as many as Dabriel, well maybe a few less, but it's impressive. I watch as he rests his bent head on his hands.

"Latus vero regi," he says, his words deep, and I see the waitress drop a mug on the floor and run out of the shop. Yep, this freaked her out.

Dabriel gets up and places his hand on Lucifer's head. Lucifer raises his head and nods at me before he leaves. I watch him go outside the shop and just fly into the air. A few people passing by stop what they are doing, looking shocked.

"Does he not care if humans know about him?" I ask Dabriel who is pulling money out of his wallet and putting it on the table. It's a hell of a lot more than our drinks cost, but I don't say anything.

"Angels don't like humans, nor care if they see us. Not all are like that, but most are," he says. I hold his hand as we walk out of the cafe.

"What did he say to you? What happened back there?" I ask him.

"An old magic-filled promise. I will explain one day, my

little wildfire," he says. The street is quiet, as it's Friday and in the middle of the day. I spot the bowling alley across the street, and I look back at Dabriel.

"Let's go bowling," I say suddenly.

"The human sport of throwing balls at non-moving objects?" Dabriel asks with a slight frown.

"Yep. Scared I'm going to beat you?" I ask him, and he laughs.

"No, let's go," he starts walking towards the bowling alley. Guys can't stand their ego being threatened, supernatural or not.

I catch up and slip my hand in his.

"We are safe for a short amount of time, right?" I ask him.

"You are always safe next to me, I would fly you away if there's a problem," he says like there isn't an issue.

I don't reply. I just squeeze his hand as we walk across the road to the bowling alley. The male attendant looks half asleep as Dabriel pays for our games and shoes to rent.

"What size?" the man asks with a yawn.

"Seven," I say.

Dabriel says, "Thirteen."

The man nods and looks under the counter at the rack full of shoes.

"Those are big feet, dude; I'll have to go check in the back room. Two minutes," the man shouts, and I look at Dabriel.

"What?" he asks when he sees my big smile.

"Just thinking of all the big feet jokes Alex and Atti would come up with if they were here," I laugh.

"I don't get it," he says looking at me like I'm strange. I forget that he didn't grow up around humans.

"Oh, it's a human rumour that if you have big feet, you

have a big–" I stop talking when the man walks back up with the shoes.

"Big what?" Dabriel asks as he takes the shoes.

I grab mine and shake my head. "Never mind," I laugh. I'm not answering that.

He tilts my chin up with his hand and smiles down at me.

"I know the saying, and one day you will know if the rumour is true," he says in a deeply seductive tone. I blink in shock, and he laughs as he walks over to the benches to change his shoes. Did Dabriel just trick me? I didn't know he had it in him. *It's damn sexy*, I think as I watch him bend over to put his shoes on, and I get a good view of his sexy butt in those jeans he wears when he's acting human. I like him dressed like this: he has a baseball cap on backwards, and a white shirt and boots that he just took off. I only move when he looks back at me, and I snap out of my staring contest with his ass.

I go first when we start bowling, and I knock all the pins down. I completely forgot about my perfect aim thing. There is no way I can lose this.

Dabriel is just as good as me, and we both end with perfect scores. The place is empty other than the staff and us.

"We didn't think this through," Dabriel laughs.

"Nope, but it was fun, normal. I feel like I don't get enough of that anymore," I say, and he pulls me to his chest.

"How about I buy you lunch? I might treat you to one of those massive milkshakes I saw a photo of on the wall," he says. I can't see anything other than his chest, but I hear the smile.

"That sounds very boyfriend-like."

"Being the good boyfriend that I am, I'll find out if

they have a chocolate-flavoured milkshake," he says, and I laugh.

"You are a good boyfriend, no, an awesome one," I say and lean back to look up at him. He presses his lips to mine gently before he increases the pressure. My mouth parts, and Dabriel takes over the kiss.

We do eventually get to have milkshakes and lunch, but we spend a lot of time kissing first.

62

WINTER

"No one can get into Paris. Many people are questioning the government's excuse that it is a chemical explosion, and they have sectioned off Paris to make sure the chemicals aren't spread into the air. It all sounds made up," a middle-aged man in a suit talks on, on some morning TV show. I know I shouldn't be sitting here watching this, I should be training or doing anything else, but I can't.

"This is what we are being told, but what the people are speaking of is demons and an invisible ward," he says. The humans can't see the red wall like we can, just a red blur.

"Yet, there is no proof. If demons did take over Paris, wouldn't they want to take over other cities? Demons do not exist, and what people are saying is just nonsense. There is no video evidence," the other man says. He's much older; around sixty, with a bald head and a smart suit.

"That's because everything electronic turns off when

you get near. People are furious and want to hear from their families who are in the city," the man says in return.

"The government will open the city when it is safe," the older man says.

Dabriel turns Atti's TV off and kneels in front of me.

"What's going through that mind, my little wildfire?" he asks me.

I glance at him. Dabriel is dressed in a white top that stretches across his chest. His muscular arms are on display, and the huge, white wings rest against his sides. His hair is braided at both sides and pulled back to the bottom of his head, and his purple eyes watch me closely. He is very handsome, that I've always known. Dabriel could have anyone he wanted because he looks like he fell straight out of heaven.

I'm sure that's out of a song somewhere. Or it should be. I'm glad I didn't say that out loud, that would have been a cheesy line.

"Winter?" he asks and cocks his head to the side.

"Everything is being destroyed because of me. I opened that portal and let him out. The goddess died to stop him. Yet, I still let him out. I feel like I have all this pressure from that prophecy and who my parents were. My mother believed I would save people. She actually said that to me when I was a baby, and yet, I've saved no one. Paris is literally gone, and I know my dear granddad is killing the people there, or he already has, I just–" I blurt out.

Dabriel rests his finger against my lips to stop my rant. He stands and offers me a hand to get up. No words, just a hand.

I slide my hand into his and he moves us into the kitchen where Atti is cooking Mags and Jewels chicken breasts.

"Take us to my town, to the pool, Atti," Dabriel says as he walks in. Atti takes one look at me and nods.

"Be back in a second to sort your food out, guys," he tells them both. They both are in their normal cat forms making me think they prefer their glamors.

Atti links his hand with mine and presses a kiss to my forehead as he moves us to where he was asked. I have no idea where he means. We appear just outside a long pool inside a white building. The sun shines down on the glass skylight above the pool. The water is clear and brilliantly blue; blue enough that I know it's not normal water. The tiles look like real gold and feel cold under my bare feet.

"I'll come back in a couple of hours for Winter's training," Atti says and kisses me gently before disappearing.

"Where is this, and why did you bring me here?" I ask Dabriel, and I watch as he steps back and pulls his shirt off. I didn't see the slits before; they are down the sides of his shirt, and they come apart when he pulls. It makes it easy for it to come off. I'm about to comment about how cool that is when I see his chest. Men's chests can be works of art, but Dabriel's is something else.

He has hard pecs that lead to an eight pack that dips to his white trousers. There is also a long scar across his chest, it's pale and looks old. I wonder how that happened.

He undoes the top button on his trousers as I watch, and he turns around. My eyes widen when I see his firm ass as his trousers fall to the ground. He kicks them off with his shoes and jumps into the pool with one long dive. I move away when the water splashes me.

I move close to the edge as he rises in the middle of the pool. His white hair comes around his shoulders as the band is loosened, and his wings are spread out, dripping sparkling water.

"The reason I brought you here is because this is my favourite place, and it's mine. Growing up, I was alone a lot. I had a lot of pressure on me at a young age, and I hated that," he tells me. I watch in wonder, as white symbols appear all over his body, there isn't a space that doesn't have one. They're hard to look at, to see what they are other than the outline shape. They look like a mixture of lines–some are like crosses, and others look like swirls. I wonder what they mean.

"My mother went into early labour. I wasn't expected for a month, and she was out in the human world. She was helping a young, human child with cancer and had just healed him. She had me in a park in the middle of Indiana, and she didn't survive it. Angel births are difficult, and mothers rarely survive," he says gently.

"I'm so sorry," I say.

"No one was around, but I started glowing. Glowing so bright that the angels couldn't help but come to me. They all had a vision and had to come to me, no matter what and . . . ," he says.

"They found you," I finish his sentence.

"Yes, and my body was covered in white symbols as my dead mother held onto me. My father never truly cared for her. The bastard had gotten someone else pregnant, while my mother was still pregnant with me. I knew he never cared for my mother growing up, but I learnt how much he despised me with every glance he gave me. I don't remember him much as he died when I was very young, but what I do remember is being ignored," he says and takes a breath.

"The angels took me home, and when the news came that the other princes were born, they worshipped me; the prince that was so strong that the goddess had sent him. Then my two younger brothers were born, and my father was devoted to them. I think I threatened his power even as a baby," he says.

"Do your people like your brothers like your father did?" I ask.

"Yes. They are cruel and don't hesitate in killing someone." Dabriel says, his symbols glowing brighter. "I always let my opponent go. I won't kill without reason, or prove myself to anyone," Dabriel says softly. I just nod.

"You don't have to prove yourself to anyone because of a prophecy. What happened was not your fault, and what we do in our future is up to us," he tells me.

"Still, many people have died," I say thinking of Paris. I was there with Atti and Dabriel recently, enjoying Disneyland with all the other normal people. I wonder what's left of the place where I shared my first kiss with Atti.

"And, many more will, that is just the way things are. But, if we fight–if you fight–we can make a future worth living in," he says.

"Together?" I ask him.

"Yes, because I love you, Winter. I will love you until I take my last breath and even after my life ends," Dabriel says, and my breath catches.

I don't say anything as I pull my shirt off. I slowly take all my clothes off as he watches me. Both of us are silent, and he swims close to the edge in front of me. When all my clothes are gone, I sit down on the edge, and his warm hands go to my hips. He lifts me into the warm water, our bodies pressed together and our lips seconds apart.

"Cor meum tibi, quod tuum est meum in sempiternum," he whispers. Before I can ask what he means, he kisses me. My back is pushed carefully against the pool wall as I hook my legs around his waist. Dabriel takes his time, stroking my body with his hands until I can't think straight. When I stroke him and guide him inside me, he starts glowing brighter. White symbols cover every part of his body as he pushes himself fully inside me. He kisses my lips before grabbing hold of my hips and drawing out every thrust, making me scream out in pleasure with every movement. He glows so brightly, all I can see is white.

"Dabriel, I love you," I whisper again and again as we both find our finish. A slight burning fills the middle of the top of my back where my shoulder blades meet making me wince.

"My mark," Dabriel says and kisses my forehead. He pulls me lower in the pool until the cold water stops the burning.

"That feels great," I say, and he laughs.

"I hope so, my little wildfire."

"Why do you call me that?" I ask him.

"Because you have the power to destroy everything in your path. Even if it's taking their hearts or making them bow to you. It's who you are, you stole every part of me from the first moment we met," he says. I don't know how he does it, but his words make me fall in love with him a little bit more.

"When you took my seat in the restaurant," I mumble.

He laughs, "Yes."

"What were the words you said to me? I didn't recognise the language," I mumble. I also wonder what the new mark looks like.

"The ancient mating words in Latin," Dabriel says and kisses me before he tells me the sweetest and truest words he has ever said to me,

"My heart is yours forever."

63

JAXSON

"Freddy, turn that music down!" I shout across the hall of the castle. Freddy's room is at the very end of the corridor, which has the guys' rooms and Winter's in the middle. I want him close to us.

"He is acting like a teenager already," Wyatt says coming to stand next to me.

"I'm just glad Anna has taken Marie to visit her parents for the day, and they're on other side of the castle," I tell him. I did offer Anna a room in this corridor, but she decided to stay in the block of rooms the wolves are taking over. She says it's nice to have the help all the time. Marie looks so much like Fergus, it's haunting. I wish I could have saved him.

"Winter is coming soon," Wyatt replies, and I nod, swallowing my grief at both my brother and sister being gone.

"She has mated to Dabriel," I tell Wyatt. I'm not surprised he felt the change too, yesterday. I felt when she mated to Wyatt as well. It's like Winter is a link between us all. There has always been a link, a reason we all got along, but it's stronger now. I would die for any of them, to protect them.

"So, you think I should tell him?" Wyatt asks me. I know what he's referring to.

"Yes. We both had shit fathers. Freddy deserves to know he has a good fucking one," I say, and Wyatt pats me on the shoulder.

"Thank you. Come train with me. I've missed kicking your ass," he says, and I laugh.

"I could do with some sword training," I say and walk out the door. We go to the training room, which is outside the castle and actually just a huge room inside a stone building. The room is full of wolves and a few vampires. None of them are fighting together, and there's a clear divide. Every one of them bows when they see us both. At least they do that together. The amount of fucking fights we've had is unreal. I know they hate each other, but all of them are hiding here. Many of the wolves look at Wyatt with distrust. I feel their worry in my bond, and I try to send calm to them.

"A fight between the vampire king and wolf king. Should be interesting to watch," I shout, and a few wolves cheer. The vampires stop what they are doing to watch. I grab two heavy swords and chuck one at Wyatt, who catches it perfectly. The wolves move away to make a large circle in the middle of the room. I stand a distance away from Wyatt and hold my sword up.

"Come on then, vampire," I grin, and he laughs before he charges with his own sword. I swerve to avoid him and swing around, but he is as quick as I am, and he meets my swing.

We fight for ages, neither one of us giving up and both of us dripping with sweat.

"Hey," Winter says, making me turn, and I feel the sword pressed against my neck a second later.

"Unfair distraction," I say.

"Never be distracted," Wyatt shrugs and drops his sword.

"Fucker," I mutter and walk over to Winter, who smiles.

"Did Atti bring you?" I ask as I kiss her.

"Yes, and Milo came too, but he went to hang out with Freddy," she says. She treats Milo like her own child and not a mini-demon. I'm thankful Milo is nothing like the rest of his alcoholic kind, but it's still strange how well-trained she has him. They are way too alike; both of them eat my food and adore chocolate.

"Hey, sweetheart," Wyatt says as he comes over, and he leans down to kiss her. I always hated the idea of sharing her. Fucking hated it, but I don't anymore. It seems right.

"Hey, how's everything going?" she asks us both.

"Good, the castle isn't far from being done, and the wolves are settling a little better with the vampires. Freddy and his friend Mich have made friends with a vampire child their age. It's a start," I tell her. Wyatt seems to like this information as he smirks a little.

"That's great," she grins.

"I have a present for Freddy," she holds up a paper bag.

"Let's go, then," I say and link my hand with hers. Wyatt walks behind us as we go to the castle. The few wolves we cross bow to us, the vampires do the same. The music is still loud outside Freddy's room, and I knock loudly.

"A girl is about to come into that mess of a room you call a bedroom."

I hear the music being turned off before Freddy opens the door. His hair is all over the place, and his crinkled clothes are the same he slept in.

"Hey, Winter," his little face lights up.

"I got you something, can I come in?" she asks, and he opens the door. It's not too bad, but I still have to pick some clothes off the floor and bed. I chuck them in the basket by the door and close it. Wyatt leans on the wall by the dresser, and Freddy glares at him.

Winter sits on the end of his bed, and Milo flies over to her shoulder as Freddy sits next to her and opens the bag.

"Wow, it's a wand," Freddy holds it up.

"It's made from a witch stone. It's a spirit wand, I thought it looked Harry Potter-like," Winter says and he nods. The wand starts glowing and Winter tries to pull it out of his hand as Freddy's eyes roll back, going fully white.

"Freddy!" Winter shouts as I move in front of him. I hold his head in my hands. He doesn't respond. Wyatt pulls the wand with Winter, but it's stuck in his grip, and I shake his head a little.

"Freddy!" I shout, holding his chin up, and he finally snaps out of it. The wand stops glowing, and Freddy lets it fall to the ground. Standing, Freddy pulls away from me.

"You're my father," Freddy says with a glare at Wyatt. Wyatt backs up a little, but doesn't take his eyes off Freddy. Fucking hell, what did the light-up stick tell him? How the hell did it tell him that?

"Yes," Wyatt answers simply.

"You didn't tell me?" Freddy looks at me with anger and a slight bit of fear. I can't tell him being a half wolf and half vampire is safe. I have no idea what he will become when he gets older. When wolves are around sixteen, they go through a change. Their wolves change size, some are smaller, but most become bigger. This is also the time they get extra abilities. Freddy already has a few: fast healing, immunity to silver, and he is so fast for his age.

"I was sworn not to tell you by your mother, she didn't

want you to know until she could tell you, but that didn't happen. After that, it was safer for you not to know. I wanted you to have the most normal upbringing I could give you," I tell him. His blue eyes, so much like Demi's watch me. The boy has already been through so much at such a young age. I really didn't give him that much of a fucking normal upbringing like I wanted to.

"How did you know?" I ask him, and Freddy stands up.

"That wand showed me my mother. She was standing right next to me, and she told me who he is to me. She said she loved me and loved you," Freddy points at Wyatt. Winter looks down, and Wyatt's jaw is ticking as he watches Freddy.

"You saw Demi's ghost?" Wyatt asks, a hint of the love in his voice he had for my sister. I glance at Winter, but she doesn't seem to be upset about it. If anything, she just looks worried as she glances between Freddy and Wyatt.

Freddy starts shaking, his whole body getting close to shifting in anger.

"Freddy, listen to me." I say, adding a little alpha power, and I draw his gaze away from Wyatt.

"This, changes nothing. I'm still here for you, and so is Winter. Wyatt is your father and a good man; one of the best men I know, and I would trust him with my life. I grew up with Wyatt, he might be a stubborn, little git, but he is my brother. Give him a chance. I'm not telling as your alpha or commanding you. I'm asking as your uncle and your friend," I say. Freddy looks at Wyatt for a long time, the stubbornness in his jaw reminds me of his dad.

"Tell me about my mother and you," Freddy says, the shaking stops, and he looks calm. I see Wyatt nod from the corner of my eye. Winter gives me a relieved look, and I smile. Fucking hell that could have gone badly.

"Let's go for a walk, Freddy," Wyatt says, and he opens

the door. He doesn't wait as he walks out, but he glances at Winter. I see her nod at him before he turns.

Freddy follows but stops in front of me, "Wyatt brought my mum to you, didn't he?" he asks.

"Yes, and he stayed to protect her. Even after she died, he stayed around and protected the pack. Even you."

"Okay," Freddy says, and he hugs me. I wrap my arms around him, remembering the late nights where he would wake up crying from his fear of lightning as a baby, and the first time we played basketball together. I knew he was never mine, but I treated him like he was. He has always been more than my nephew to me; he is a son to me. Freddy lets go and walks out.

"Smart boy," Winter comments, watching the doorway. She sits on the end of Freddy's bed. She picks the wand up.

"Atti put some magic into it. He said it would just shoot white sparks," Winter admits.

"I'll have a word about giving real magic toys to a kid later," I say with a groan. I should have known Atti would have something to do with this.

"Sorry Wolf-man, I should have–" she starts.

I wave a hand to cut her off. "I know. Don't worry. No harm was really done, but Atti is a strong enough witch to know what magic he is fucking with," I say and sit by her on the bed.

"Family good," Milo says making Winter jump. Even I forgot the little shit was here.

"Do you have family, Milo?" Winter asks him as he flies into her hand in her lap.

"Yes, but like drink," he says sadly. Winter and Alex have been working on his speech. It isn't great, but I doubt he had much time to learn when he was with the others. Massive parties where they wreck shit aren't good for learning. I didn't know they could speak more than two words before I met Milo.

"Why don't you drink and party like them?" I ask him, and he turns to look at me. I don't know how he managed to get the weird, pink, tutu dress thing he is wearing, but fuck he looks weird. I thought he was a guy?

"We used to be different," he says, and I nod.

"You know you're family to me now, Milo," Winter says, and Milo flies to her cheek, he presses a little kiss to her.

"Same," he says and Winter's whole face lights up. The little thing may be annoying, but if he can make Winter happy then, fuck it, we're keeping him.

"If you stay away from my fucking chocolate brownies and don't make a bed out of them. I'll keep you around," I say, and Winter snorts in laughter.

"They nice, and I eat bed," Milo shrugs.

That little fucker.

"Can't be as bad as the bowl he filled with Atti's chocolate milkshake and lay in it naked. Atti said he would never get the image out of his head," Winter tells me.

"Yummy," Milo says, and I laugh.

"I've changed my mind, I like him," I say, and Winter grins.

64

WYATT

"How long did you know my mother for?" Freddy asks me. My son is looking at me like he's seeing me for the first time. In a way, he is. This is fucked up, and yet, I'm glad he knows. I felt like a weird stalker following him around the castle. I did learn that he is strong and good with a sword but fights like Jaxson. I can fix that. I know he's smart, smarter than others seem to realise.

"I knew Demi my whole life. I remember her always being around. Her human foster mother was my maid, and she brought Demi with her to learn how to clean," I tell Freddy. We stop talking when he sees a bench and sits down. I sit next to him and just look at him. He looks like me a little, but so much like Demi.

"So, she was your slave," Freddy deduces.

"For a time, but, honestly, she was the worst one and just told me point-blank to get over myself. Demi was real when the rest of my people were not. Most people were scared of me or wanted to get close because I would be king. Demi just wanted a friend, and that's what we were at the start," I tell him. When he doesn't respond, I keep talking.

"Then things changed one night. After that, we kept our relationship a secret. We didn't have a choice, and I wanted to get her out."

"Why didn't you just run away with her?" Freddy asks me.

"Part of me–back then–loved my father, and I didn't want to run away. I loved Demi, but she wouldn't ask me to do that," I say. It's true, I used to look up to him. I'm not sure why I did, but when he had Demi killed that ended any feelings I had for him.

"Two months later, my father bragged about how he had the half-sister to the werewolf prince. I knew he meant Demi because she was the only wolf in the castle. I took her to Jaxson the next day. She wanted me to stay, but I knew we could never work. It was better for her to have Jaxson look after her and find a wolf to have a life with," I say.

"So, you walked away?" Freddy growls out.

"No. I stayed in town. I stayed close because I couldn't walk away," I tell him, and he doesn't look at me.

"Where were you when she died?" he asks and looks over at the castle.

"My father planned it all. He called me back to the castle; said it was urgent, and I was needed. I shouldn't have gone," I admit to him, it was a stupid move.

"Why did you fall in love with my mother, when you knew Winter would come into your life?" Freddy asks, seeming older than he is.

"Falling in love is never a choice. It's something that takes over you and knocks you on your ass when you least expect it. It happened to me both with Demi and Winter. Just because I'm with Winter, I haven't forgotten your mum," I tell him and place my hand on his shoulder. It's the first time he has let me touch him, and I know it's a big step, when he doesn't move.

"I wish I remembered her," he says sadly.

"I always wish the same with my mother, too. I never had anyone around to tell what she was really like, only rumours. You have that with me; I will tell you anything you want about Demi," I say, and he looks over at me. One nod and then he stands up, and I move my hand away.

"Jaxson is a dad to me. Don't expect me to start calling you dad, I don't even call him that," Freddy warns, making me smirk.

"No problem, son," I lean back on the bench.

"You can't call me that," Freddy says, and he crosses his arms and looks at me like he wants to kill me. There's my son.

"I'll do whatever I want, and you *are* my son. If you don't want to call me dad, that's fine, but I am going to be a dad to you," I tell him honestly. I'm not hiding him anymore; people are going to know that half-breeds exist, and that Freddy is my heir. That makes him a prince, whether he likes it or not.

"I don't want that," he says angrily, his whole body shaking with anger.

"I know," I reply, and I watch as he storms off.

Drake and Alex walk over to me, coming out of the trees near the edge of the castle. Alex still has twigs in her hair, and Drake has a big grin as he kisses her. Both of them are dressed for training, the camp we have set up is on the other side of the castle. It's good for the werewolves and vampires to train together. Not that they do, but it's progress that they aren't trying to kill each other.

"I figured out what's in Paris," Drake says as he stops in front of me, his voice going stern and losing whatever happiness he had with Alex mere seconds ago. She clings onto his arm, and I have a feeling it's not going to be a good answer.

"Well?" I ask.

"Silver weapons. The biggest collection in the world is on display in a museum in Paris. He wants the people and the weapons," Alex says, her voice high and panicked.

"That's fucking perfect," I grit out. I stand up and run my fingers through my hair as I pace. How can we tell our people and Winter about this?

"There's another thing we need to tell you about," Alex adds in, and I turn to meet her eyes, but it's Drake that replies.

"Humans are posting online about groups of demons walking around. They are always in groups of ten. Some are recognising them as the missing people that are in Paris. The government is struggling to keep this a secret."

"Most of the humans just think they are strange people wearing odd makeup, but I looked at the videos on YouTube. They are demons, and the groups are everywhere. Not attacking, just walking from town to town. They don't respond when people talk to them, they just keep walking–" Alex says.

"He's sending out patrols to find us," I cut her off. It's smart.

"Why? Winter said he has been at this castle. He killed Elissa here, so he knows where we are," Alex says, reminding me of Winter's dream.

"Maybe it's hidden from him, I'm not sure," I say.

"We need to be sure. We have so many young here," Alex says.

I nod at her. "I am well aware of our issues, but don't tell Winter about this. Not until she wins these fights. She doesn't need any more worry," I say, and they both nod in agreement. "Go and have the day off. I will train the men and women today," I say.

They both look happy at the idea. Drake picks Alex up and throws her over his shoulder as she squeals. "Thank you, prince," Drake chuckles when Alex tries to wriggle free.

I want that peace with Winter one day. Hopefully, one day soon.

65

WINTER

"Wow," Atti says, and then clears his throat as he looks at me. I should be the one saying 'wow' when Atti is dressed like a hot pirate. He has a loose, white shirt on that dips to show off his impressive chest. He has a white cloak on, stretched around his large shoulders and tight, black trousers. Honestly, I expect him to throw me over his shoulder and take me to his ship.

"This looks okay?" I ask, glancing down at the white, lacy dress I'm wearing. Tonight is the summer solstice, and witches all go to the trees to dance and celebrate. Atti wants to take me; Leigha is watching the house, and Dabriel had to visit the pack to heal a few people after a fight broke out. The wolves and vampires are still having trouble mixing. I was left to Alex and her fashion do over.

"You look amazing, no hot, no wait I can think of a good word," he mumbles out, making me chuckle.

"So, what happens tonight?" I ask him.

"A big party and . . . ," Atti stops and shakes his head.

He takes my hand and pulls me close, "I'd rather just show you," he says, and we float away with his power.

When we reappear, we are in the middle of a crowd. A few people stare at us and bow their heads. Other witches look on in worry or just walk away from us. It takes me a second to recognise them as witches because they all have their hoods down. Most of them have black or dark-blonde hair like Atti. There are a few with silver hair, which makes me wonder which side they are from. They have a mix of skin tones as well, but most have a gold complexion like Atti's. Sun-kissed skin. I glance up at the stars in the sky; they are so bright here.

There's a long table full of different food spread down the middle of the trees. Children and parents spin in circles as music plays fast, merry tunes.

The trees have yellow bunting hanging between them, and I can hear the trees singing to the music. They're happy.

I smile up at Atti who takes my hand and leads me through the crowds to the dancers. He spins us around, and we hold hands as we dance around in circles like the others. I laugh as he pulls me close and spins me out. We dance close, my big smile matching his; our hips sway to the music, and my head is tucked into his chest.

The song ends, and I clap with everyone else to the small band–just a few witches playing a variety of different instruments with one singer. People are still staring, but it isn't too bad. I kind of got used to it at the vampire castle.

"Will you dance with me?" A little girl asks Atti. She looks around five with her white hair in two plaits, and a little, yellow dress. It reminds me of the yellow dress I saw myself wearing as a toddler with my mother. It's hard not to feel the pain with the memory–the tears running down my mother's face.

Her mother, I guess, comes running over and lowers into a bow.

"I am so sorry for my daughter, she doesn't realise who you are," the blonde woman says. She stands up; she has on a simple, white corset dress that falls to the ground.

"I'm just a witch like her. I would love to have this dance with you, my lady," Atti says and does a bow at the girl, who giggles.

Atti holds a hand out, and she takes it. I move back next to the woman and watch as Atti picks the girl up and dances around with her.

"He will make a good father, my lady," the woman says, and I nod watching him. I can't imagine a life where I would feel safe enough to have a baby. The world we live in isn't safe and yet, I could see a little girl with my hair and maybe Atti's eyes. I could imagine having a child with any of my guys.

"Agreed. I'm Winter," I hold out my hand to her, and she accepts it.

"I sincerely hope you win the last fight. I have always believed in the goddess," she tells me. Her light-grey eyes are large on her bold-looking face. There's a slight scar by her eye that stands out in her perfect face.

"Thank you," I nod, and she smiles.

"I'm going to try the food; could you tell Atti where I am?" I ask.

"Of course, my lady," she bows again, and I move away towards the food.

"This is a message from the queen," a woman I recognise steps in front of me. The woman is one of the two I usually see with the queen. She is the pretty one, with the long, blonde hair, and is a light witch. I wonder why she is on Taliana's side and not Atti's.

"What is it?" I ask, and she smirks before answering.

"The next fight is the last, and you are allowed two women to fight with you. This fight will be the end, the queen is done with the games as we have a war to fight," she says, her voice echoing, and everyone stops to stare at us. The music cuts off a second before I feel Atti appear next to me and slip his hand around my waist.

"Fine," I reply. The woman disappears. The witches all go back to whatever they were doing, but a lot of them are still watching us.

"Who are you choosing?" Atti immediately asks me.

"Leigha and Alex. I don't know any others to help me," I say.

"Two vampires are not a good idea. Leigha, yes, but Alex is still so untrained," he says. I guess he is right; Alex wouldn't be a good choice. Also, I would be way too distracted trying to protect her.

"Who would you suggest?" I ask.

"Katy or maybe Lucinda," he tells me. I didn't realise he knew her.

"Why?"

"They are both strong, and Jaxson has made Katy a guard. Lucinda is an alpha of strong blood. I believe one of them would be the ideal person to have at your side."

"I will ask Jaxson. She's only sixteen, and Lucinda has a lot of responsibilities," I say.

"And, you are only twenty. Age is just a number for us, we don't have the pleasure of being innocent for so long. Our children don't know a time without death and war," Atti says, his eyes watching the dancers.

"Twenty-one in two months," I say, and Atti smiles.

"We will have to celebrate," he winks.

"Only if the whole world isn't destroyed, you mean," I joke a little too loudly. Several people look my way. Okay, maybe a bad joke.

"I'm going to feed you, so you stop talking. I have better ways to keep you quiet, but we can't do those in public," Atti winks at me, and I laugh with warm cheeks. He walks us closer to the table of food, his arm tight around my waist.

"Oh, chocolate cake!" I point at a large chocolate cake, and he walks us over. He cuts me a big piece and then gets me a fork.

"I would try the whole romantic, feeding you thing, but I'm honestly scared you would try to eat me and not in the good way," he laughs.

"What's the good way?" I innocently ask him, and he smirks.

"The same good way I would enjoy eating you," he winks, and I blush, my mouth closed around a piece of chocolate cake.

"And baby," Atti says as he moves his head close to my ear, "I can be as slow or fast as you like," he whispers, I nearly choke on my chocolate cake at his seductive words. I was wrong; fucking hell, Atti can flirt like the best of them. I miss this side to Atti, the less serious side.

"What was it like growing up around here?" I ask him as we eat.

"I didn't get out much. My mother was protective to say the least; she couldn't cope with me being far from her until I was stronger and able to protect myself," he says.

"So, you were lonely?" I ask.

"No, just bored. You forget I used to sneak out and see the others. When I first started seeing Wyatt, he was an angry kid. It was fun to wind him up. We both came up with this great idea to see the other princes. Jax was cool, but Dabriel tried to kill us. He was a serious one with a stick up his butt," Atti says, and I laugh at his choice of words.

"Anyway, my mother finally caught on about my disappearing acts. Witches usually can't use the power to move until they hit sixteen, so she didn't know I could do it. She showed me the castle and told me it was safe to play there." His words are hinted in sadness.

"The rest of my childhood was council meetings, fighting in the arena, and learning everything I could about ruling," he tells me.

"You will make a good king," I say.

He looks down at me. "With you at my side, I will," he whispers and kisses me. "You had a little chocolate on your lips," he smirks.

"You don't need an excuse to kiss me, Atti," I grin.

"I know," he smiles and wraps an arm around me. We both watch the dancers for a while, lost in our thoughts.

"Here, my lady, I brought you a drink. They're made from the grapes I grew in my garden," a woman says with long, black hair as she stops in front of us; a dark witch. She hands Atti and me two glasses.

"Thank you," I say, and drink some as she moves into the crowd. The grape juice is soft and sweet. It's really nice.

I eat a few more bites of cake before I start feeling hot.

"Winter," I hear, and I try to respond, but nothing comes out.

66

ATTICUS

"Dabriel," I shout as I hold Winter to my chest, while I pull on my magic to find him. I reappear just inches away from him.

"What happened?" Dabriel instantly asks as he takes Winter from me. She isn't awake, and she's barely breathing. I don't feel myself move as I watch Dabriel glow white all over, to the point that I can't see Winter anymore. I don't look at anything other than the light. I feel Jaxson move next to me and put his hand on my shoulder, but I don't respond. What feels like years later, but is probably only moments, Dabriel dials down the glowing, so I can see Winter. She looks pale and is still sleeping, but Dabriel nods. That nod is all I need, and I rest my hands on my knees as I take a deep breath. Jaxson goes over and strokes Winter's hair away from her eyes.

"What the fucking hell happened to her, and why isn't she awake?" Jaxson snaps as he faces me.

"A witch gave her a drink, it was poisoned," I say as I straighten up. I thought I'd fucking lost her; I can't lose her. Winter means everything to me.

"D, why isn't she awake?" I ask, but the door slamming open again behind makes me turn to look. I notice for the first time that we are in the castle, in the kitchens. Dabriel was cooking when I came here, I realize as I spot the stuff on the sides. Wyatt, with Milo on his shoulder, storms into the room.

"Oreos?" Milo asks as he flies towards the cupboards. Wyatt storms over to us, his eyes completely silver in anger and leans over Winter when Jaxson moves out the way.

"Why is she sleeping?" he asks.

"She is–" Dabriel starts, but Milo interrupts as he chews on an Oreo.

"Dream-calling," he muffles out.

"Again?" Wyatt asks sharply, none of us reply.

"I'll take Winter back to her room, we will wait for her to wake up," Dabriel suggests. We nod, and he walks out with her. I clench my fists, cracking my knuckles as I look at my friends.

"We have a witch to find, and I know exactly where to find her," I say. Words are not needed as Wyatt and Jax put their hands on my shoulders. I move us to my city, straight into the castle. The guards rush forward, and I raise my arm, using my air power to swipe them across the hallway, and they slam into the wall.

"No fun," Wyatt smirks. I walk forward and slam the door to my mother's old room open. I don't expect it to be empty and completely ruined. Someone has set the place on fire; the windows are smashed and there's nothing left. I can only hope her familiar was buried. Familiars die with us, their lives linked to ours. I have to ignore the painful lump in my throat as I look at the room my mother loved. It increases my anger as I walk out of the room and down the corridor. The next two guards we come across rush at us when they should be running away. Two female, dark witches call on fire and try to throw it at us. I blow it away with my air and hold the two witches in the air. Their hoods fall back as they try to escape.

"Where the fuck is Taliana?" I shout. Neither answers, loyal to their fake queen. I'm about to try different, harsher actions to get an answer when the bitch in question walks in.

"If you wanted time alone with me, you only had to ask, Atticus," she purrs out.

"Not even in your dreams, Taliana," I sneer and drop the witches. I stalk over to her and stand inches away as I speak.

"Where is the witch who poisoned Winter tonight?" I shout.

"I do not know who you are talking of. I swore not to hurt her," she smiles, a seductive tone in her voice as she moves closer. The scent of whatever perfume she's wearing hits me and makes me feel sick. She makes me feel sick.

"Let's go and discuss this privately. I can make you much happier than the human ever will," she suggests and goes to place her hand on my chest.

"Do you think I would ever look twice at you? You killed my mother, and I am in love with a woman who is a million times fucking better than you. Find the witch who attacked her, or I swear I will kill you and anyone that gets in my way. I am not playing fucking games anymore," I say, and I grab her hand to push her away.

"Fine, the witch is dead. I didn't kill her, but someone else did. They used demon powers, destroying her home. I believe she was killed moments after she returned home," Taliana says.

"I want to see," I demand.

"I will take you," she holds out a hand.

“No, just the address. I know my city like the back of my hand,” I say, and her face tightens in anger. I’m glad I’m finally pissing her off.

“Fine, but you will be mine, Atticus,” she says and tells me the address. I walk back to Jaxson and Wyatt who nod, clearly hearing all of the conversation. My brothers always have my back.

“How did you kill my mother? Dabriel couldn’t heal her,” I say and look back to meet her cold eyes.

“Demon-touched weapons can’t be healed, and I will kill Winter with one as well,” she says and Jaxson’s growl fills the room. Dabriel starts glowing brightly, and I debate whether it’s worth killing her.

“I will enjoy watching my queen kill you,” I say, and call on my power to get us out of here.

I move us to the street that Taliana said. It’s close to my own home, and we walk down the quiet street until we find the home we need. A few witches in light hoods bow as we walk past. When we get to number seven, the house where the witch lived, it’s easy to see the evil that’s happened here. I wonder what Dabriel would see when he looks at a demon and reads their aura.

I walk in, as the door is open, and the wards are down. The living room is destroyed, blood covering the walls and floors. Crystal powder is all over the floor, what a waste.

“I smell demon,” Jaxson says.

“Why would a demon do this?” Wyatt asks as he looks around the room in disgust.

“How did they get in the city is another important question,” I say.

“The witch is dead; she would have had an easier death if we found her first. She clearly suffered,” Jaxson gestures around the room. I take one more look at the room before we leave, Jaxson is right; there is nothing we can do here anymore.

I'll wait until Winter wakes up, and then we will plan a way to make the city safe.

67

WINTER

"Have you come to make a promise?" a sweet voice asks. The voice is familiar, and I struggle to open my eyes. My body feels tired, and I'm not sure why. When I see the purple trees, and look down at my feet in the yellow grass, I know why I'm tired.

Shoot, I've dream-called the fairy again. I turn slightly to see her standing at the line of trees a few feet away.

Lily stands looking over at me, in a black dress with a cut-out in the middle. She isn't wearing a cloak today, so I can see how she has a perfect body to go with her beauty. All supernaturals have this perfect-looking thing sorted.

Her long, strawberry-blonde hair flutters in the warm breeze. The air even smells nice here; it tastes like sweets as I breathe it in.

"For your help?" I ask turning to fully face her, I go to take a step forward, but I can't move. I brush my hands down the white dress I'm wearing and look at her.

"The demon king will demand the world, and only I can help you. What I ask for in return isn't terrible," she says with a slight giggle.

"So, explain exactly what the offer is," I say. I can't say we don't

need the help. I saw first-hand how weapons are useless, and it took two wolves to take down one of them. The witches' powers aren't going to be useful against demons unless they have weapons that work. The vampires could team up, but we don't have the numbers anymore. There just aren't enough of us if he has turned even a quarter of Paris. That doesn't even include the vampires and humans that were in the castle. The angels won't help, not unless they're sure they'll win. Well, that's what Dabriel thinks. The dark angel's power to cause pain when they touch someone won't help kill the demons when they look like emotionless zombies. We don't have a big enough army with the low birth rate and deaths that have happened because of the wars between the supernatural people. The witches and angels fought for years and killed each other. Then, the werewolves and vampires declared war, and did the same. This is the most vulnerable time for them, for us all and we now have the biggest threat on our doorstep. The demons can't be killed by silver, but we can.

"I offer you this for a single promise. I swear to send five thousand of my fray army to your world. They will carry four weapons each, and you may keep three of each of their weapons for your own men and women. When the war is won, they will all leave and not come back," she says.

"How will they get here?" I ask.

"The war will happen on the Winter solstice, we can travel through the dimensions on that day only. The earth is weak on that day, and that's why the demon king needs to use it."

"What will you ask in return?" I ask her, I cross my arms, and she smiles.

"In your world, there is a half-fray child. I wish for you to send her to me when you meet her," she smiles.

"How do you know I will?" I ask.

"Your mother told me," she says, and I look away. I don't know why it bothers me that she had such a good relationship with my mother. I guess I could almost be jealous that I didn't get that time with her.

"How would I send the child back?" I ask.

"When you make the promise, you will only have to touch her, and the portal will open. Ancient magic will take her to me," she says.

"Why can't you just find her?" I ask.

"I can't risk being in your world long, my soldiers will only stay a day to win the war. Fray do not belong in the human world, and half children are rare gifts," she tells me.

"Do you believe in the goddesses?" I ask.

"Not yours. We have our own," she replies, she looks up to the sky and then lowers her creepy, yellow eyes on me.

"Why do you want the child?" I ask. I can't send any child to someone if they plan to hurt her. Not that I have a clue if Lily is lying to me as she replies.

"She is royalty. There is little of the Royal fray left," she answers. I watch her closely, but she looks like she's being honest. I feel my back warming up, like it's burning.

"Make the promise, your mates are calling," she says.

"I promise," I say, and feel a snap around my wrists like shackles. When I look at my wrists, there are two white lilies in the middle of both of them.

"I promise my side. Thank you, queen Winter," she says.

"You never told me your full name."

"Queen Lily. Queen of all the fray," she says, and my eyes widen. She is a queen here.

"One more thing, queen Winter, the portal to the demon dimension must be closed with the king on the other side. The only way to close it is a death. Not just any death, only one with goddess's blood may close the portal. I am truly sorry." She lowers her head to me. Does that mean I will have to die?

"No," I shake my head; no one can die to close the portal anyway, it's in the middle of the vampire castle. How would I even get close enough?

"Her saviour will die when the choice is made," Lily says gently as I feel myself falling.

I blink my eyes as I open them, I'm lying on top of Atti, and he's gently snoring.

"Atti," I whisper, wondering how long I fell asleep for this time. The last time was two weeks. Lily's final words come rushing back to me. The prophecy said my saviour would die and someone has to die to close the portal. Only I have goddess blood, so surely, I would die?

Who the hell is my saviour?

In a way, I've been saved by a lot of people I care about. I won't let any of them die for me, no way in hell. I'll send my grandfather back to the demon dimension myself and make that choice. It's me that has to pay the price; it was me that opened the portal in the first place. My heart tightens at the thought, but what choice do I have?

"You're awake, thank god." Atti says, and sits up with me. He kisses me gently.

"What the hell is this?" he asks when he sees my wrists. I glance down and see the Lily marks on both my wrists. The dream was real, and it snaps to me what I've done and the choices I have to make in the future.

"I made a promise with the Fray queen. She will send help when we need it. I have to send someone to her, a child that is half-Fray. Lily said a portal will open when I touch the child," I tell him. His eyes widen, and he shakes his head.

"I don't know anything about Fray, but how can we know to trust a promise from her?" he asks.

"You shouldn't make a promise with Fray," Jaxson says coming into the room. He sits next to Atti and me. I turn slightly to look at him as he takes my hand in his warm one.

"What do you mean?" I ask.

"I don't know, lass, but Lucinda talks to plants remember?" he asks, and I nod. I once saw Lucinda on pack lands, with both her hands on a tree and she was glowing slightly yellow. Jaxson was with me and explained about her power to talk to trees and most plants. I was shocked that they spoke at all, I know after everything I've seen I shouldn't be shocked but I was. It was only a few weeks later that the jewel trees sang with me. Weird shit happens.

"I told her you had been dream-calling a Fray, and that's what the plants told her when she asked them for me. Not to make a promise with a Fray," he says, and a cold sweat fills me. That can't be a good sign. Why do I feel like I've just made a huge mistake?

"I made one with the queen," I say quietly. Jaxson looks up at the ceiling, his jaw ticking and his grip on my hand tightens.

"We will work it out," Jaxson finally says.

"The last fight is today," Atti says.

"I don't even remember going to bed, we were dancing at the summer solstice and then . . ." I drift off when I realise I don't have a clue what happened. I vaguely remember the queen's friend speaking to me about the fight, and then that's it.

"Then you were poisoned," Jaxson finishes, and I can't remember it. Is that why I feel so tired? I felt tired before I went to fairyland, but now every part of my body is aching like I've been working out with Leigha for a week.

"The grape juice had poison in it, only yours. Dabriel saved you," Atti says. His voice is tense and full of anger. I bet the guys had to stop him from killing someone for poisoning me.

"Where is he, so I can thank him?" I ask.

"With Wyatt at the castle. A few vampires were attacked last night by demons in the next town. They just walked into the bar and went straight for them. The humans ran away, and there were only ten demons, but everyone has been called to the castle. Dabriel needs to heal them. They lost five vampires. Only three survived and just barely. They said the demons were too strong," Jaxson says, and I know why I feel so worried and sad. I'm picking up on Wyatt's emotions even from this distance away.

"Oh no," I say quietly.

"You need to eat and get ready; I'm here to be a snack. I'm the only one you haven't fed on, and you need any help you can get in the fight," Atti says.

Jaxson stands. "I'll get you some normal food, too, have fun," he smirks at my shocked face and walks out.

"You sure?" I ask as I look at Atti, and he laughs. Atti pulls me onto his lap and turns his head to the side.

"Are you kidding me? I've been fucking waiting for this for months," he says, and I laugh. My laughter drifts off as I smell him. He smells so sweet, and I'm powerless to stop myself as I bite into his neck. He tastes better than anything I could think of, and he groans, pulling me closer with every second. I moan when Atti's hand slides down my stomach and even lower to my core, as I feed on him. The pressure is crazy, and I let him take me over the edge as he slowly moves his hand against me. When I stop and pull away, he removes his hand and smiles at me. I wipe the little bit of blood off my lips as he watches. It used to freak me out, drinking blood, but it doesn't anymore.

"Winter, all I want to do is lie you down and make love to you," he says making me turn bright red. I'm such a dork.

"I want that too, I feel incomplete without you," I tell him honestly.

"Soon," he whispers and kisses me.

We eventually leave the bedroom, and I shower. I find

my leather outfit and my daggers folded up with a chocolate bar on top of them. That has Alex all over it, and it makes me smile. I decide to plait my hair into the same bun as last time.

When I'm all dressed I come down the stairs and nearly walk into Jaxson's back when I see Esta by the door.

"What the bloody hell is she doing here?" I ask a little harshly. Esta is dressed to fight, wearing tight, black leggings and a short leather top that looks like it's trying to replace her skin. There are guns strapped to her arms and thighs. She also has a large, silver sword on her back. Jaxson told me that a lot of supernaturals don't use guns because the bullets are so small and only a tiny amount of silver. The only good thing is that if you fire enough, it will slow them down and give you time to make a final kill with a sword or something else. Esta doesn't bother looking at me as she speaks.

"I may not like you, my queen, but I have amends to make. Anna is a sister to me and begged me to help you. Katy is too young and Lucinda too old, so here I am; I have the power to move extremely fast, so fast you can't see me. I will help you in the fight for Anna, but I can't shift. I can't move as fast as a wolf, and it's useless to you anyway," she says, and I turn to look at Jaxson.

"If I could help you I would," he says quickly, and hands me a plate with a sandwich on it. I eat it quickly.

"I don't know, you are a big enough girl to maybe trick the queen into letting you fight," Atti says, and Jaxson turns to glare at him.

"Fucking asshole," Jaxson says, and Atti laughs.

"You have us confused, bro," he says, and I snort a little in laughter. Atti isn't wrong. Leigha comes into the room, dressed like a leather-loving, warrior princess. Two swords on her back and a load of daggers all over her outfit.

It's a wonder how she doesn't manage to stab herself when she sits down or hell, just moves.

I would.

"Time to leave," she says, and I look over at Atti. *It's time to win this for him.*

68

WINTER

Leigha and Esta are standing on either sides of me as we face the empty queen's stand. When we first got here, the crowds of witches were going crazy. Screaming my name and Taliana's into the slightly cold air. I glance up just as a few snowflakes fall from the sky.

It's been a long time with us just standing here waiting. Leigha is tapping her foot, and my guys are sending me worried glances. The large, metal gate slowly opens, creaking as it does.

The queen walks out like she hasn't got a care in the world. She is dressed in a long, black dress; it sticks to her small body as she moves and has two massive slits on the side. I guess it's for easy movement. The main difference is that she has the black crown on her head. I haven't seen it since the first day, and its power calls to me. Taliana looks paler than she usually does. I wonder why she doesn't wear the crown all the time. It's so powerful–like Jaxson's and the vampire king's that I've seen. The two witches I usually see with her are at her side, walking close to her under their large cloaks. I haven't discussed it with the guys, but I knew she would fight me. Dabriel couldn't have seen anything, as he would have told the others or me. The guys wouldn't want me fighting her, but this is personal for her. She wants Atti. I'm the only thing in her way of taking Atti and the throne. She will get everything she has ever wanted, and I bet she doesn't want to risk me winning this fight. Taliana stops around five feet in front us, the two witches at her sides undo their cloaks and let them all fall to the ground. I guess it's three against three. At least the odds are fair.

"Let the best queen win," Taliana says, and she flashes straight in front of me. She throws a punch straight into my face, but I'm trained enough to duck. Thank god for my power as a blue wave slams out of me and straight into her. I watch her fly across the stadium and hit the wall hard by the gate.

No one is taking Atti from me.

My hands glow blue as I walk towards her, she stands up and flashes again, this time I don't see her as she appears at my side and slams a kick into my stomach. I fly across the arena and hit my side as I land on the dusty ground.

Air leaves my chest as she raises her hand, and a cold wave of wind pushes into me. I roll onto the ground, dust getting into my mouth and mixing with my blood. I hear a loud scream and turn to see Leigha just as she kills the light witch by shoving a dagger into her throat. I stand up a little shakily as my eyes meet Leigha's, and she drops the witches' body and runs towards me.

"No!" The queen screams in anger and flashes to me again, this time behind me, her hand slides over my mouth as her arm holds me tightly. I feel like I'm drowning, water filling my lungs.

"*Winter,*" Atti shouts in my head, seconds before

Taliana's hand is removed, and I fall to the ground. I cough up the water after falling to my knees. I turn to see Leigha fighting with the queen, both of them just as good as the other, as they throw hit after hit.

"Bye, wolfy," I hear near me and snap my head over to see Esta fall to the ground. Her stomach ripped open and blood is everywhere. Her eyes meet mine, and I know she can't heal from this. An uncontrollable anger fills me when I see the witch standing over her. The dark witch turns to me with a smirk and raises her arms. I pull a dagger out of my belt and rush over, the witch cracks the earth I'm running on, and I see her dark-grey eyes glowing. Unfortunately for her, I just jump over the crack and kick her chest as hard as I can as I land. She falls backwards onto the ground. I follow, not feeling my feet on the ground as I walk slowly to her, seeing only my revenge. The fear in her eyes is clear as she watches me.

"My pack," I say, my voice louder than before, and it echoes around the silent arena. I don't think about the witch who pleads for her life as I slam my dagger into her heart. I watch the life leave her eyes before I turn and run to Esta. I pull her head into my lap, and she gazes up at me, blood is pouring out of her mouth. I can hear Leigha fighting with Taliana in the background. I have to give Esta these last moments; no one deserves to die alone.

"Ask the goddess to forgive me," she coughs out. I barely understand her words.

"Why?" I say quietly to her.

"It was me; I killed Fergus and let the vampires in. I wanted them to kill you, and then I would have Jaxson as my mate. I love him," she says. I watch in shock as she dies in my arms. I'm not sure I know how to give her the forgiveness she wanted now that she is dead. Her blood feels warm against my hands as I hold her, and yet, she feels empty. Anna would hate her for this.

"I forgive you, and your life was payment for that mistake," I say, and look up to catch Jaxson's eyes across the arena. I know he heard every word by the angry look he's giving me. I don't think he's angry with me, but with Esta. I can't believe she did it. I let her body fall gently to the ground and glance over at Leigha as she fights Taliana. *I've had enough.*

I'm covered in blood as I walk over to both of them, my hands glowing, and my power rising. Taliana gets the best of Leigha when she sends a blast of wind at her. Leigha flies across the arena. Taliana flashes to me. Just when she reappears in front of me, I pull for my power. It comes out in a wave as she grabs my arm, this time we both go flying together. She slams into the wall, my body driving hers further into the wall, as her grip on my arm loosens enough for me to pull away.

I wipe the blood off my lip, standing at the same time she does. She smirks before throwing a stream of fire at me. With no time to save myself, and being so close to her, the blue fire consumes me.

"*No!*" I hear Atti scream in my mind. The ground shakes, and I have no doubt that it's Jaxson's power. The fire doesn't hurt my skin; in fact, it feels good.

I walk forward, my clothes burning away as I pull the dagger out of my belt and hold it at my side. The handle is burning hot but doesn't hurt anymore. This must be what I got from Atti. I can't see the queen, but I don't need to. I know she's close to me, I can see her hand. I throw the dagger, and the fire disappears.

The crowd is silent as they watch their dark queen hold a hand over the dagger in her heart.

Taliana dies, my silver eyes reflecting back at me in her

own dark ones, and the crown rolls off her head as she falls. I look at her dead body, feeling a little sadness. I didn't want to have to kill her, but there wasn't much choice. *When did I become this person that just killed two people and didn't feel anything doing it?*

I glance over as Atti appears next to me, he wraps his cloak around my naked body, which I'm suddenly very grateful for. I don't know how I forgot I'm naked. Bloody hell, Alex is going to love this story if I don't tell her the whole part about me nearly getting killed. I glance at Atti, knowing I would do anything for him. I would do anything for any of my men. I reach down and pick the crown up, feeling its power rush over me. That's why Taliana was so powerful; it's the crown.

Atti keeps his hand on my back as I turn in his arms; I lift the crown with both my glowing blue hands.

"My king," I say loudly, and the witches cheer, their support shouted in our minds and the sound of their clapping hands.

Atti lowers his head, and I put the crown on his head. He straightens up and winks at me.

King Atticus Lynx of the witches has finally taken his rightful place.

69

ATTICUS

"Does it feel weird to be king?" Winter asks as we sit in the high council rooms together. The council rooms take over the entire bottom floor of the castle; it's where all witches can come to have their grievances heard and where we enforce our laws. Our laws are not that different from human ones, and witches rarely break them. The room we are sitting in now has a long, gold table; our seats are in the middle. The rest of the council sits on our sides, four light witches and four dark witches. The room is split like that also, with half the walls white and the other half black. The floor is the same with a gold line in the middle leading up to our seats. The witches have always been divided, but things are changing. I'll make them. Mags and Jewels were happy to get back to the castle; it's much bigger for them, and they like the massive waterfall in the royal garden. They drink out of it like it's their personal water bowl; it used to drive my mother crazy. The council all stare at us with worry and fear. They all rushed to put together a meeting the second Winter put the crown on my head. The power from the crown floats through me, making me feel like I can do anything with it on my head. It's fucking strong.

What Winter did was crazy, powerful, and a sign of who she really is. I glance down at her as she watches me for a response; she is so lovely. I know she doesn't even realise it, but she is something else to look at. Every time she walks into a room, she demands attention with her beauty and strength. No matter what happens from today, she will always be known as a powerful woman. The prophecy is still bugging me, there's a lot in it that makes little sense. Winter is dressed like a queen today, thanks to her friend's help. She has on a long, white dress, which tightens in the middle and flares out at her sexy hips. Her long, dark-brown hair is straight with just the top part up in some plaits.

When I saw her being covered in fire by Taliana, my fucking mind exploded. I tried to flash to her, but Taliana had cast a watertight ward around the arena, and she had two witches keeping it up. I knocked them both out with Jaxson's help and then blasted the ward, but I only got through once Winter had killed Taliana. She must have gotten the power of immunity to fire from me. It's actually a power I have; most witches do. Winter hasn't said much about killing two witches today, she just told me she was okay. I hope the guilt doesn't get to her, but if it does, I'll be at her side. I love her.

"Yes, very weird. I know what my mother warned me about now. The power boost from the crown is strange and a little overwhelming. We need to get you a crown now," I say.

She looks away. "I have one, but I can't, not yet Atti," she says. I get how nervous she is. Putting on this crown is accepting my destiny, which I'm meant to be. I never really thought I'd have to take the throne for many years, my mother's death was not expected. I look around at the familiar faces of the council, the ones who stood at my mother's side for years. It hurts that she isn't at my side to guide me, I'm fucking clueless, but I'm going to do my best for her memory. For Winter.

"In time," I whisper and lift her hand. Her sparkling, blue eyes lock with mine as I kiss the back of her hand.

"My King and Queen. I wish to thank you for my place on the high council."

The words come from the first male on the witch council in hundreds of years. One of the queen's friends had been a council member, so there was a space when Winter killed her, and I think we need this change.

"It was the right choice," I say, and he lowers his head.

"In fact, I want to show My Queen the castle, so goodbye," I say and hold onto Winter's arm as I move us before they say anything. Winter and I have been stuck in meeting after meeting following the fight. The city was out of control, with the dark witches not wanting me on the throne. They are currently locked up until they calm down. Taliana's parents were devastated, which I understand, but I did not condone their decision to try to burn the castle down. Thank god, I was close enough to pull water from the waterfall in the garden and flood that part of the castle. No one was hurt, but I had to lock her parents up. The council believes that they will calm down when things settle down. What we didn't know is how the city has been attacked by demons in the last few weeks. Only groups of ten or so, but they are killing and walking through wards like they aren't there. Thirty witches have been killed in the last two weeks. We have some serious problems, and I've called the witch guard to come here in the morning. The witch guard is a hundred witches who protect our city, and I want to know how they let the demons in. Not one of the witches who died was in the guard. It shouldn't be that way.

"This is my room, well the one I stay in when I have to be here," I say as we appear in the lounge of the rooms I have. It overlooks the whole city from where we stand; it's similar to the rooms my mother had. They're gone; Taliana destroyed them all. I wish she was alive, so I could fucking kill her again.

"Wow, what a view," Winter says, moving away from me and standing close to the window. She turns her head to look back at me, a small smile on her sweet lips. Winter doesn't even know what she does to me.

"It is," I say looking only at her. She seems to realise this as she smirks at me.

"I'm surprised you didn't show me your bedroom first," she says with a little wink.

"That's next," I laugh as I walk over to her and take her head into my hands, and I kiss her. Winter tastes like every sweet you wanted as a child but couldn't have. I move us to my bedroom and rip her clothes off as she pulls my belt open.

I've waited too long for this, for her, and I know she feels the same way.

I love her so much, and I want her to be mine.

When our clothes are gone, I explore every part of her sweet, little body with my lips and hands. Loving the little moans she does, and the way she wriggles when I do certain things. I kiss up her soft stomach until we are perfectly aligned.

"I love you, Atti," she whispers as I fill her, and she arches her back. Every part of me demands for my magic to mark her as mine, and I don't hold back as I move inside her, she feels too good. I pull out and roll her onto her knees before entering her again. She seems to understand, or my magic is already affecting her.

She moans as I pick up my pace, and when I know she's close, I rest my hands on her back and push my magic into her. The magic I've never let out, but have always known, blasts around the room as we both scream out each other's names in pleasure. The mating magic is designed for just one person, and I have always known it, in the back of my mind. It's meant to guide us to who we are meant to be with. Mine always knew it was Winter.

When I can finally open my eyes, Winter is lying on her stomach, her head tilted to look at me with a happy smile. I glance at her back and grin at what I see.

Winter's back is covered in marks. My mark is a tree with large roots. The tree is made of swirls that match the other guys' marks. Winter hasn't seen my mark as it's on my back, but it looks so much better on her. The tree takes over my whole back, but it fits just right on hers.

Jaxson's wolf is near her lovely bottom and there are twirls that rise to join with the phoenix in the middle. The two angel wings are just below her neck. My tree is in the middle and they are all connected with swirls. The mark moves gently, like it's alive.

"What does it look like?" she asks me. My lips part with no words as I run my hand over the marks, feeling the slight power from each of them. We are finally all together, like it's always meant to be.

"Complete," I say and I lean down to kiss her. I spend the night with my queen and 'complete' is the only word to describe it.

70

WINTER

"Winter, my baby girl," I open my eyes to a frozen field, there's a large willow tree on top of the hill, its long branches blowing in the cold wind. Elissa is standing next to a woman I know, but it's still a big shock.

My mother stands in front of me, in the same white dress as Elissa. Her long, brown hair sways in the cold wind like Elissa's black hair does. When they are next to each other, I can see the similarities. They look so alike, but my mother's gaze is filled with love and tears. I want to run to her, but I can't. My heart pounds against my chest as I meet her blue eyes, just like mine.

"It's not safe, and he'll do what he did to me. You need to wake up and run," she pleads with me, her words desperate.

"You're dead?" I ask, and she nods. I knew it, but I had to hear it.

"Yes, many years ago, when my father called me to him. My father can call his own blood, it's like your dream-calling power, but he can control you. He didn't expect his demons to want to feed on me when he sent them to take me through a portal. They did and killed me, but that was a blessing because he couldn't find you. My father

has to be close to you for him to have control, you have to run," she says. The wind blows snow against my cheeks, and I blink the cold away as I focus on her words.

She steps close to me.

"How can I call the dead?" I ask.

"Because our spirits never left you. I will never leave you my child. War is coming, and your heart will break, I only wish I could hold you as it does," she says, making me worry; her words can't be true. I refuse to believe them.

I realise she can't touch me when she hovers her impossibly pale hand over my shoulder; we are exactly the same height as she stands so close to me.

"I dream-called your friend, Lily, she is going to help me win the war," I say, looking over every detail of her face. How she has freckles, but I don't. How her nose is slightly different from mine, but we have the same lips.

"She is no friend; that was a grave mistake, Winter. The price is too high for the promise," she tells me, and I feel sick. What have I done?

"I don't–" I say, and my mother cuts me off.

"You can fight him; your mates can save you."

"Only her mates can stop her from the destruction of all," Elissa says as she moves next to my mother. Her bright-blue eyes meet mine.

"Remember that, remember the words," Elissa says, and the sky turns black slowly as I turn my head to watch. The cold air becomes painful to breathe in as my mother and Elissa disappear. I can't see their faces as the cold wind pushes me over into the snow. I stand up shakily and watch as the demon king walks over the hill.

"Thank you for accepting my call," he says and laughs.

I wake up and jump in the bed, nearly falling off the side.

I glance at the empty bed, and I wonder where Atti is. A shaking fills the castle, and the bed slides on the floor.

The window blasts open near the bed. I scream and pull the sheets closer around myself.

What's happening?

I didn't expect to wake up from finally mating with Atti to this. I blush when I think of the night with Atti, but the shaking castle soon snaps me back to reality.

I need to find Atti and tell him about the dream; I need to make sure he's alright. I get up in the dark bedroom and pull Atti's shirt off the floor and over my head, it hits my knees with how large it is. The castle shakes again, and I fall to the ground. I think a witch or several must be using their earth powers. Jaxson went back to the pack with Wyatt after the fight.

The door is slammed open, and I scramble back as the demon king walks in. He smirks down at me, a look of pure evil on his pale face. The demon king's face is covered in blue veins but they are nothing on his glowing, dark-red eyes. They're nothing like mine when they glow; no, they are scary. The demon king has a long, black cloak over his clothes and the vampire crown on his head. He looks so much like Wyatt's father, but everything is harder and lost because of the demon controlling his body.

"Time to come with me, my princess," he says and holds out a hand. I hold my throat as something takes over me. I can't move, and I fall to my knees as pain takes over my body in a wave.

Suddenly, I feel nothing.

My mind screams 'no' as my body ignores me and stands up. I walk over to the demon king and place my hand in his with a large smile spreading over my face. *Why am I smiling?*

The demon king leads me over to an older witch with long, black hair. The dark witch bows, and looks at the demon king with clear desire. I try to scream in my head, I try to move my body as I feel darkness slipping over my mind.

"Time to destroy the world, my princess," the demon king laughs. I don't refuse him as the witch takes us away, and darkness turns everything black.

WINTER'S WAR

The blue-sided human will choose a side.
When four princes are born on the same day, they will rule true.
Her saviour will die when the choice is made.
If she chooses wrong, she will fall.
If she chooses right, then she will rule.
Only her mates can stop her from the destruction of all.
If the fates allow, no one need fall.
For only the true kings hold her fate, and they will be her mates.

The prophecy is true, the war is here, and her saviour will die.

Reverse harem series

71

ATTICUS

Wake her up, wake her up, new king. For the crown will fall, the crown will fall. The crown will fall . . . .

The shaking of the ground wakes me up from my deep sleep and the strange dream. I can't remember anything other than words about waking someone up and the child-like voice that sang them. I glance over at Winter, who is pressed to my side, her arms wrapped around a pillow. The room is still dark, the stars lighting up the sky outside, and it's cold. Colder than I remember it being when we fell asleep. Winter moves slightly, rolling onto her stomach and her soft, dark hair spreading across the pillow. *My mate.*

I smile when I see the marks on her back, a beautiful reminder of last night. I've waited so long to be mated to her, to my Winter. We finally have everything, and even with her grandfather causing issues, I know we will make it through this. I didn't wait this long to mate with her, only to lose her. That is never happening.

The room shakes again, and this time I know it's not a dream that woke me up. I sit up and pull myself out of bed, careful not to wake Winter up. The room shakes again as I throw on some jeans and a shirt. *What the fuck is going on?*

I storm out of the bedroom, and there's a dark witch outside, her head covered by her cloak hood, so I can't speak into her mind. When she lowers her hood, I see that she is an older woman I don't know, but she bows to me. *Where are the guards?*

"Watch Winter, and do not let anyone in this room. If she wakes up, tell her to stay inside," I say, knowing full well Winter wouldn't stay inside, but I hope that she doesn't wake up. At least, this witch will be able to tell her where I am. The witch straightens up, and her dark-grey eyes watch me closely, before looking at the door behind me.

"Yes, your highness," she says in my mind. I pull on my power to lead me to the throne room and hope I can find some answers there, if nowhere else. The room is in chaos when I appear in the middle of it. There are at least fifty demons in the room attacking my witches. One runs straight at me, with a large, silver sword and an emotionless look in his eyes. The demons look worse than the last time I saw any of them; the grey skin is peeling off their faces in places, and the smell from them is overwhelming. They smell like death. I quickly pull on my fire power and throw a line of fire towards him with my hand. The demon-possessed man doesn't even move out of the way as the flames head towards him and burn him into nothing. There was no scream, and that's the weird part. It's like he didn't feel anything. *How can you fight against demons that don't care if you hurt them?* A loud growl gets my attention, and I look over to see my familiars, Mags and Jewels, jumping onto demons and using their large teeth to rip the heads

right off them. I kill more demons as I make my way over to them.

"They want the queen," a witch runs over to me. I cover her from the two demons following her by using my wind power to throw them through the glass windows, smashing the windows to pieces Witches with the air gift start to copy what I did and start throwing them through the windows rather than trying to kill them in here. I look over at the witch, who has a deep cut down her face and black ash covering her, mixed with blue dust from the dead demons.

"How do you know that?" I ask, lowering my hands a little but keeping an eye on the enemies around us. The castle shakes once more, followed by a loud howl that I recognise as Jaxson's. I forgot he was staying at the castle tonight. Everyone else went back to the Goddess' castle.

"The king let Taliana's parents out from the dungeons. I was there, and the demon king said he wants Winter," the woman pleads. She looks familiar, but I don't know her. She clearly cares about Winter, and that's enough for me to believe her. I pull on my power to try and find her, it doesn't work. I can't feel her, only darkness. *No.*

I use my power to take me to my bedroom and find our bed empty, a feeling of dread fills my stomach. I pull the door open to find the older, dark witch is gone. The castle shakes again, and I use my power to find Jaxson. There isn't a witch strong enough to move the ground like this, and knowing Jaxson, he would be outside. The whole castle is shaking as I disappear, and I know it's lucky the castle doesn't fall. I appear in the gardens. What was once a beautiful place is a disaster. The trees are on fire, and a dead witch looks up at the sky from beside my feet. My mind goes to Winter when I look down at the dark witch's hair, which is only a little darker than my Winter's. I cannot lose her. I stand straighter when two demons run at me, their grey skin giving them away, as well as the empty look in their eyes. They have big, silver swords raised at their sides, and I use wind to divert the fire in the trees towards them. They don't stop running as they burn, the awful smell filling the night, but I bet they are better dead than having a demon in their bodies. I lean down and close the witch's eyes. She is so young, and it's a shame her life ended like this. A growl gets my attention, and I look to my right, seeing Jaxson.

Jaxson has split a hole down the middle of the royal gardens that you can't miss, and it's smart, as my witches are pushing demons into the hole. Jaxson is in wolf from, and is ripping the heads off demons as he runs past. He is massive like this, taller than a human and at the right level to kill them easily. His black fur is covered in blood and blue dust, and I know he must have been fighting since the start of the attack. Two witches run up to me, and I use my air power to push three demons following them into the hole.

"There are too many, Your Highness," one witch says, and she must only be sixteen by her looks.

"Go to the Goddess' castle," I tell them both and send an image of the castle into their minds.

"Thank you," she says and disappears with her silent friend. I look over to see some are using wind and most using fire, I'm proud of how they are working together. I try to find Winter again, finding I can't. There's nothing, but I'm not giving up. *I will find her.*

"Jaxson!" I roar into his mind when a demon runs at him from behind with a large, silver sword aimed at his head. I pull my power and lift the demon off the ground, throwing him into the hole, but it gets Jaxson's attention as

his glowing, green eyes lock onto mine across the fire and death that surrounds us.

"Winter is gone!"

Even over the witches' screams, the distance between us, and the noise from the shaking ground, Jaxson's threatening growl fills the night; a growl that speaks of pain, revenge, and a promise. We will find our queen.

72

JAXSON

"Where is she?" I growl out when Atti gets to me through the demons he kills on the way. A demon runs at me, and I grab him by the neck, lifting him up in the air and watch as he dies. The clothes he was wearing fall to the ground, and I look down. I shake the blue dust off the jeans he was wearing and pull them on, thankful they fit at all. Atti stops walking toward me to throw a demon into the hole. I pick up a silver sword off the ground by the leather handle and quickly run, swinging it down on the head of a demon that leans over a dead witch. Atti lifts his hands, using air to throw two more demons into the hole and then ducking when another witch does the same and throws a demon over his head. I woke up to this madness when five demons came into my room. They got a shock when I shifted and killed them all, or would have if they didn't fight like emotionless zombies. It took me a long time to even get to the gardens, killing countless demons that I came across. I tried to help the witches in the gardens, but there were, and still are, so many demons here. So, I made a hole for them to throw the demons in. Otherwise, the ones without the fire power had no defence and no weapons. If there are this many in the castle, then the screams I can hear from the city tell me there are just as many out there. They are dying, and all I can think of is what Atti said, that Winter is gone. *He has to be wrong.*

"I can't find her, I can't sense her Jax," he says, his words filling me with panic. She can't be dead, I would know. Our mate isn't dead. Yet, I can't feel her like I would usually be able to. I can't sense her around, and Atti wouldn't just say this.

A demon runs at us, and Atti shoots a fireball at him, burning a hole in his chest, and the demon collapses into blue dust. I stomp over to a demon who is holding a young witch on the ground. She is struggling to hold him off with her air power.

"The whole city is under attack. Atti, you're their king. You need to tell them to go to the castle!" I shout as I pull the demon off the witch on the ground, throwing him into the hole. Winter would never forgive us if we let our feelings cloud our minds over the responsibility we have to these witches. We can't just leave them. Atti closes his eyes, his body glowing a yellow colour as he tells the whole city to leave,

"Everyone leave and go to the Goddess' castle. It's safe. I'm showing you the image now. Everyone go, leave the city, and you will be safe."

I hear the same thing as the witches do, and they start disappearing. Atti stumbles a little, his hands going to his knees as he takes a deep breath. *That must have been a fucking lot of power.* I grab Atti's arm, shaking him a little, and he nods at me. This isn't the time to give up. We need to find Winter, and we can't do that here. He straightens up and flashes us back to the Goddess' castle, straight to Wyatt and Dabriel, who are pacing Winter's bedroom.

"Winter feels gone, where is she?" Wyatt shouts walking over to us, and Dabriel follows. They both look as panicked as we feel. A feeling of sickness is spreading all over me, and I don't know what to do. I can't fucking do anything.

"I can't feel her," Dabriel says, and I nod, feeling the same. I feel empty, the place inside me where she was is hollow, now. *I can't sense her.*

Fucking hell, she'd best be alive, or I'm going to destroy the world until I find her or kill myself doing so. There isn't a life without Winter. I can't lose her, not now. The only person that could have taken her is her grandfather—the demon king. It wouldn't surprise me because I have a feeling he needs her for something.

"The demon king has her, doesn't he?" I ask, and there's silence from all of them.

"You remember that witch, the one that poisoned Winter and a demon killed her?" I ask them all.

Dabriel replies, "I remember. You think the demon king was protecting her?"

"Yes. He needs her for something, so that means he won't kill her. We would all know if she was dead."

"We have to find her. Whatever he wants her for, is nothing good," Wyatt says and then mutters a string of curses to the room. We all feel the same way.

"Wait, I feel her," Atti says and grabs our arms.

I feel a flicker of something; just before Atti takes us to Winter. To our mate.

73

WYATT

"Winter," I breathe out when Atti bring us near her, but there's a massive, blue barrier between us. She is standing next to the huge crystal that keeps the witches' island protected from the world. There are dozens of little cracks in the crystal that shouldn't be there, and the shaking ground is making more sense now. He is trying to drop the ward on the city, but why? It makes no sense as his demons can clearly walk straight through wards. I guess it would make the witches vulnerable, but we were right, he has her.

The demon king is standing next to her, his hand on her shoulder. I don't look at him for more than a second as Winter ignores us. I've never seen her look like this, the way she looks at me. Her eyes are silver, completely silver, as she rests her hands on the crystal, and she is glowing blue, the way she does when she uses her power, but it's darker. The blue almost looks unnatural compared to the light colour it usually is. The way she looks at us all, makes me wonder if she recognises us at all.

"Winter," Atti shouts, moving forward and banging his

hands on the blue barrier which is stopping us getting to her. Atti's hands glow white as he tries to break the barrier, but it doesn't work. I can tell that nothing happens after a minute. If Atti could break this, he would have by now.

"She is mine, now," the demon king laughs as the crystal cracks in half. Both pieces fall to the ground, and the cave shakes. The screams from the city get louder, just as I hear a loud roar. *What the hell is that?* Winter lowers her hands almost robotically, still staring at us with an empty look. A witch appears next to the demon king, placing her hand on his shoulder, and he smiles down at her.

"You betraying, little bitch, I will kill you for this!" Atti shouts at the witch, and she shrugs a shoulder.

"You let my daughter die. Taliana should have lived and been your queen!" the witch shouts back, and everything makes a little more sense.

"Trust me; when I get my hands on you, you will beg for the same death as your daughter," Atti promises, and the witch pales a little.

"Winter, Winter snap out of it," Jaxson shouts, banging on the barrier, and he growls loudly. Winter doesn't move, she doesn't even blink as she stares at us. For a second, I think I see a flicker of blue in her eyes, but it's gone the moment the demon king steps next to her. We need to get him away from her as he must have some way of controlling her. I'm surprised we didn't think of it before. She is his blood.

"You are no kings, you can't even protect your queen," the demon king laughs, and Jaxson growls as I step forward.

"You will die, and I will kill you," I say the words slowly, and the demon looks at me with a smirk that reminds me of my father. I know it's not my father, but it's his body still, it's him still.

"I enjoyed killing your ancestor, he was always the best fighter. Vampires have speed but rarely brains, I believe you have neither. Ah, but children do dream, don't they?" He laughs.

"Things have changed in the years you were locked away," Dabriel says in a clipped tone, his eyes never leaving Winter.

"And, your ancestor. I liked him . . . but he was stupid as well. He tried to kill me and save Elissa," the demon king tells Dabriel.

"You killed your mate, how could you do that?"

"She stole my child, my child!" the demon king spits out. "But, it doesn't matter. I have Winter, my grandchild, which is even better," he says with a dark laugh and nods at the dark witch. I watch as he disappears, taking Winter and the witch with him.

"Winter!" Atti shouts, but it's no use. The barrier falls, and the city shakes harder as the ward falls. Screams fill the night as I look at my friends, my brothers.

"We need to save our people and then Winter. She will never forgive us if she comes back to everyone dead or if we kill ourselves trying to get her, now," Dabriel tells us all, and we nod, not liking the idea but knowing he is right as we listen to more screams.

"He won't hurt her, he needs her," I tell Jaxson who looks close to shifting. Jaxson looks over at me and nods. "Let's save the city," I say and walk out of the cave, with my brothers. Each one of us are broken but willing to fight. First, the city, and then, we will save our mate.

74

DABRIEL

"Is that everyone?" I shout after healing a little girl, and her mum nods at me as she holds her close. A bundle of crystal is at her side, and I think back to the crystal trees that the demons burnt down. That's all we have left of the most beautiful, and magical trees in the world, just those crystals. I don't hear anyone shout out after a few minutes, but I take the time to look around the infirmary at the witches here. There is only a fraction of the ten thousand that lived in the witches' city. Thousands have died today, and when the barrier dropped, the demon king sent two dragons to kill the rest of the witches and burn the island. It makes sense that he would have creatures like dragons, but knowing of them and seeing them is another matter. We just managed to pull a couple hundred injured witches out of the fires before we had to leave. By now, there will be nothing left of Atlantis. I walk out of the room and look over as two wolves carry a dead witch wrapped in sheets out of the room. *So much death.* The castle is out of control with witches being brought in, and surprisingly the vampires and wolves are trying to help.

There aren't that many, not compared to the ten thousand we knew lived on Atlantis.

"How many?" I ask Wyatt as I walk into the entrance hall where he is talking to a vampire who doesn't look impressed. They are talking in French, which I don't understand a word of, and Wyatt changes the conversation to English when I stop next to them.

"The witches need help, and as your king, I'm saying you will help them. They are mainly women and children, are you that heartless?" Wyatt shouts, and there is silence as the old vampire bows his head and walks away. I'm surprised he didn't use his power to command them, but then he has never been that kind of vampire. Or king.

"Atti called," Wyatt taps the side of his head, not answering my question, but I can tell from the little witches that are here that it is bad. The demons must have killed thousands today, and Winter is gone. How did a day of celebration of Atti becoming the king we knew he was meant to be and mating with Winter, become a day we, and the witches, will never forget? I follow Wyatt up the stairs, stepping over the witches sitting huddled up and watch as they bow their heads to us as we pass. They shouldn't bow to us, we have done nothing but let the demon king take our queen. Plus, their city has been destroyed. We go up the four flights of stairs until we get to our rooms that are on one long corridor. Wyatt walks straight to Winter's room, and I shut the doors behind us. Jaxson is sitting on the bed speaking quietly to Freddy, who looks over at Wyatt and nods at him.

"I can't be long as more people need to be healed," I tell Atti who turns to face us with Milo on his shoulder. Milo has some strange, green outfit on that looks made of leather. I bet some doll, somewhere, is missing an outfit.

Milo almost makes me smile until I look at his blue hair and memories of winter come to me.

"We have a way to get Winter back. Well, Milo does," Jaxson says.

"Me," Milo replies and points at his chest.

"Freddy and Milo were talking about the ward around the vampire castle," Atti says, and relief fills me as I see Atti's nod. The annoying little creature who eats Wyatt's Oreos is a demon after all, he might be able to help us. We haven't been able to think of any way to get her back at all. It's seeming hopeless, as we can't fight the demon king as he hides behind his army and the ward.

"Tell me how," I ask Atti.

"I can walk through my blood ward," Milo says and then flies over to sit on my shoulder. He's not making much sense, as he hasn't quite learnt how to put sentences together right yet.

"What Milo means, is that he can pull one person through the ward around the vampire castle," Jaxson says, standing up and walking over with Freddy following.

"Who and what's the point? We can't fight the demon king and his army on our own. He could hold a knife to Winter's throat, and we would put our weapons down for her," I say and groan when I realise Freddy is young to be hearing this about someone he loves.

"Winter is going to be okay, right, uncle J?" Freddy asks Jaxson who puts a hand on his shoulder.

"We are going to get her back, we love her as much as you do. Why don't you go and watch some movies?" Jaxson suggests.

"I'm not a kid, I'm not watching movies when everything is going wrong," Freddy snaps, pushing Jaxson away.

"No, you're not a kid. No kid should have to live what

you have gone through already at such a young age. Jaxson only wants to protect you," Wyatt says to him.

"I don't need advice or sympathy from you," Freddy growls out, and Wyatt steps closer, not one bit fazed by his show of aggression.

"Look, Harris and the others are going to need some help sorting out the witches and finding them rooms. Why don't you go and help the beta?" Wyatt suggests, and I see Jaxson nod.

"I will send a message to him. They need help," Jaxson says, and Freddy looks down at the ground before meeting Wyatt's gaze.

"Fine, but save her. I won't forgive you if you don't," he says and walks out of the room.

"The kid is growing up and getting balls to speak to all of us like that," Atti says, making us laugh a little despite the situation.

"Balls? Do humans have balls?" Milo asks, and Atti laughs.

"One day I will explain that, but not now," I tell Milo, who nods with an innocent face. I bet the little demon is winding us up.

"Right I have an idea for Winter. I'm going; as her mate, I can try to push my magic into her, and hopefully it will snap her out of it. It's the best chance we have, but I'm going to need a distraction," Atti says, making it clear it will be him that goes in after her. I want to suggest I should, but I know it's not what's best for Winter. I have no way of getting her out of his control, whereas Atti does, and I trust him to save her.

"I suggest we take fifty wolves and vampires, and attack the castle," Wyatt says, and we all nod. It's the best way to make a distraction, hopefully the demon king won't take Winter with him.

"I can get fifty witches to appear and take everyone back to the castle after twenty minutes," Atti offers.

"If we time it right, that should be all you and Milo will need to get Winter and get out," Jaxson says, pacing the room.

"She might not come willingly, and you might need to knock her out and bring her here," I say, remembering how she looked at us, how she reacted. She is under his control, and it's going to be a fight. I can't even think about what the demon king might be getting her to do, even in the one day he has had her. If we attack tomorrow, that's two days she will be alone with him and completely under his control. The thought just makes me want to kill him.

"I will save her," Atti promises, his words strong, and I know he will.

"I should go and see the angels; see if they will come here to be safe. I have a feeling the demons will attack them next," I say, but it's more than a feeling. I haven't had any visions; the future seems blocked to me. The last one I had was just a storm. A tornado in a storm, and there was so much fire. I don't know what I was seeing, but I don't want to be around to see that in real life. I still hold on to the vision of Winter and all of us by that lake in the future, but it seems so far away, and I know the future can change in a second, making my visions useless.

"They won't come," Wyatt warns, knowing my race are stubborn, and nothing will make them leave their precious home. They wouldn't want to live with other races, as they see them as inferior.

"Well, at least, I can get some of the healing herbs and bring them here as I can't keep healing everyone," I say, knowing that my old room there has a wall full of jars of herbs laced with my magic.

"Go, brother, and we will plan the attack for tomorrow morning," Jaxson says and pats my shoulder.

"A lift, Atti?" I ask, holding out a hand as Milo flies off my shoulder and goes to sit on top of Winter's bed. Atti grabs my arm and moves us instantly, and when I open my eyes I'm outside the council. The large, white building is so different from the normal houses that line the streets of the village. No humans live in this village, but they do drive past it, believing it's just a field thanks to a witch's ward.

"I'll wait," Atti says and goes to sit on the seats outside as everyone stops moving to stare at us. I'm sure we look a sight with our burnt clothes, and both of us covered in blood and blue dust. I don't care what they think, this is their future if they don't leave. There aren't many angels left to begin with, being that the war with the witches killed so many of us. The idea of even asking the angels to now come and live with those very same witches, seems like a disaster, but I won't let them die because I don't want to ask.

"How dare you bring a witch into the council?" Zadkiel says as he walks down the stairs and smirks at us. Zadkiel's hair is completely shaved off now, and he has decided to wear a royal cloak that I believe our father used to wear. I don't even know where he got it from. At least, he isn't wearing the royal crown, I don't think I would hesitate to kill him if he was.

"I suggest you shut up, brother, before I lose what little control I have and kill you," I tell him. He doesn't move or speak as I open the doors to the council and walk in. My brother was always the coward. My marks appear on my skin without me calling them, because I've been awake so long, and I'm tired. I want my mate safe and need to rest. I don't know how many witches I've healed, or demons I've killed, in the last day. The council is speaking to each other when I walk in, and only one of them is missing. They might actually listen to me when there are so many of them here.

"The witches' city has fallen. Queen Winter of the witches, wolves, and vampires has been kidnapped, and I'm begging you to move our people to the Goddess' castle. It's the only place that is safe and our only chance," I say loudly, and the room goes silent. I look around at the aged angels, seeing the sympathetic look on Lucifer's and Gabriel's faces but not many others seem that upset about the loss. Thousands of witches and people have died, and they almost look pleased.

"Dabriel, I am sorry for your loss and the loss of the witches' city," Veja says; a dark angel who is old but one of the kinder ones.

"How many died?" Gabriel asks me.

"Thousands, there aren't any more than two thousand witches who escaped," I say, and there's silence around the room. They know how many witches were on that island, they know how a loss like this would be told in history, and that what they say here will be remembered. If the demons killed that many witches, who are powerful, in their own city, the angels will struggle. We don't have the numbers that the witches did, and at least twenty percent of our population are old. We lost a lot of our younger generation in the war.

"Then, many demons would have died, and the demon king's army will be smaller. I feel we are safe here," Gabriel says, and dread fills me. They can't be serious. The demon army will be bigger than ever, because he wouldn't have just killed the witches, he would have taken some of them back to the castle and turned them.

"No," I reply, and there's a hushed silence around the room.

"You are thinking with your emotions for your lost mate and not what is best for our people. We have four thousand angels that would not be easy to move without a reason."

"Isn't the death of an entire city reason enough? The witches had ten thousand!" I shout, and it's Melan who speaks.

"Not our city," he says. He must be the oldest angel here, a light angel who has scars from the war, from losing his four sons when the witches killed them. I understand why he would never feel sympathetic to the witches, but this isn't about him and his own desires, this is about the fate of the angels. I don't want my entire race to be destroyed.

"You are all fools," I spit out.

Lucifer stands up. "I side with Dabriel, and I'm taking my family to the Goddess' castle. I suggest you do the same and stop being fools," he says and walks around the council and out the doors, nodding at me before he walks out.

"I side with Dabriel. I may believe the demon king army is smaller, but I'm no fool to know we will not win the fight here. I sincerely hope you choose to follow the rightful king," Gabriel says, shocking me a little, but he nods at me before walking out.

"We will discuss this and wish to have you come back here tomorrow at midnight," Veja says, and I give him a look of shock. I had hoped he would be another to side with me on this, he has a young family.

"It will be too late," I say, knowing if we get Winter back, the demon king will attack the next place he can. I can't tell them we are going after Winter because I cannot trust any of them. They could be working with the demon king, and I wouldn't even know. I won't risk our rescue plan for Winter for anything.

"When our people look back at the history of the biggest war of supernaturals, this will be remembered. It will be remembered how you sat in your chairs and made the biggest mistake that cost lives," I tell them, but not one replies as I turn and walk out of the room. When I get outside the council building, every single angel outside stops and bows their head to me. Atti stands up and walks over, wordlessly placing his hand on my shoulder.

We have our Queen to save.

75

WINTER

Darkness and snow. Darkness and Winter. Darkness and love. Darkness and life. Which one saves the queen? Which life will end for the queen?

The child-like voice sings through my mind, the sentence keeps repeating and getting louder and louder. I want to scream for it to stop, to stop the song but everything feels cold, and words don't seem to leave my lips when I think them. I blink my eyes open, and there's nothing but blackness. An endless, black smoke that fills an empty place. Emptiness and darkness, and I don't know why I'm trying to escape. What is out there in the darkness?

"Wake up, Winter. Winter, you must wake up and wear the crown."

"What crown?" I whisper to the female voice I barely recognise. It's Elissa, my grandmother.

"Your inheritance. The crown is yours, and you are stronger than him," Elissa says, her voice urgent.

"Who?" I ask.

"You're only a quarter demon, Winter. Your humanity is what will save you," the voice says. Demon?

"Time to wake up, little princess, I want to talk," a voice says, waking me up from a strange dream that I struggle to remember. Something about humanity and demons. I open my eyes to see a pair of dark-red ones watching me; they almost glow in the dimly lit room. *Demon.* The demon king. Everything comes rushing back to me as I lean back in the seat I'm in and try to swallow the fear that climbs up my throat. I glance around the dining room we are sitting in and see the faces of three other people with us. The dining room is a room I've never seen, but the massive windows overlook the vampire gardens, and the library can be seen on the other side through the windows. At least, I know where I am. I look back at the betraying idiots that are sitting at the table. Damn, I'm in trouble. One is an older witch with long, black hair and a grin that is creepy as she watches me too closely. The other two are angels with white wings and look familiar. They both have light-purple eyes and cruel expressions. The older one of the two, has short hair, whereas the other one has longer hair. I glance down at my hands, one is holding a wine glass, and I don't remember picking it up. I quickly pull my hand away as I look at the table which is set with food and a half-eaten plate in front of me. I rest my hand over one of the knives on the table and the other on my lap. I nearly jump when I see the long dress I'm wearing. It's a corset at the top and has an old-fashioned, lacy skirt. *Damn, the dress is a nightmare on its own.*

"Don't think about it, my princess. I will put you back in your mental cage before you even get a chance to touch me with that knife," the demon king warns. I refuse to even think of him as a relative of mine. We may share blood, but he means nothing to me after what he has done. I turn and look at him, sitting at the top of the table and looking every bit the king he is pretending to be.

"My name is Winter, not Princess," I spit out.

"But, you are my princess," he tells me.

"I'm not your anything. I am the queen of three races and soon to be four. When my kings come for me, and they will, you will regret this," I warn him, and his dark laugh fills the room.

"Silly words from a murderer," the witch opposite me says, spitting out the words as I stare into the dark-red eyes of the demon king. Other than the slight, grey shade to his gold skin, he still reminds me of Wyatt, as he wears the old vampire king's body. I look up at the crown, the crown which belongs to Wyatt and not him.

"Everyone I have killed, has deserved their fate," I turn my gaze away and meet the angry face of the witch.

"My daughter did not deserve you to kill her! She was the queen, you stupid little–" the witch stops shouting as a dagger lands in her neck and blood sprays all over the table. I look away in disgust as her head slams onto the table, and the demon king simply smiles at me.

"No one will insult my princess," he tells me, suggesting he just killed the witch for me. I look back at the witch, her dead eyes facing the windows, and I gather that Taliana must have been her daughter. I understand her anger, her pain, and she died because of it.

"She didn't deserve this," I mutter, and the angel with no hair replies.

"Yes, she did, beautiful one," he says, and I glare at him.

"Does your king know you're here?" I ask, and he slams his hand on the table, making me jump.

"I will be king," he says, and I just laugh.

"You will regret this, being here," I say to the angel

who looks seconds away from trying to kill me before looking at the dead witch's body out of the corner of his eye.

"Do you know your father said those words as one of my demons killed him?" The demon king tells me.

"What?" I ask quietly, shock shaking me to my core. My father died in a car accident or that's what I was told happened. I doubt my mum would have lied to me about that.

"Your father said those last words as my demons tortured him to death. It was a shame he wouldn't speak a word about where you were. He died protecting you from me and yet, here you are," he says, leaning toward me and resting his head on his joined hands.

"It was a car accident," I spit out, not believing a word that comes from him. He only chuckles and leans back in his seat, linking his hands together.

"No, it wasn't, but he was only a silly human that my daughter thought would be safe to love," he says.

"He was not a silly human. He was my father and a brave man," I say, standing up and calling my power. The second it leaves me and releases a blue wave, the angels in the room go flying with the table and everything else on it. Including the dead witch body, which I almost regret doing. The demon king just watches me as I look at him, the blue wave not bothering him one bit as he lifts a hand and makes his own ward.

"They say you were once human and innocent. I see that is no longer true of you," the angel with shaved hair says after he flies over, landing next to me. I lift the knife off the table and hold it in front of me as I push the chair out of the way, walking backwards.

"So, beautiful, I know why my brother liked you now. I know why he is going to die for you," the angel comments as he reaches a hand out to me, I whack it away with the knife, cutting him and turn, running for the door. Dabriel's brother is here, and it makes sense why the angel looks familiar. My mind runs over the fact it means the angels must be working with the demon king. *I need to escape.* Just as I open the massive, hall doors, a haunting, dark laugh fills my ears. Blackness fills my eyes as everything disappears, and I feel myself drop the knife.

"And, I only wanted a nice family dinner, what a shame," I hear the demon king taunt as blackness takes over my eyes.

76

WINTER

"Elissa, run," a man roars as I open my eyes and see the entrance hall to the castle. Pieces of stone and dust fall from the ceiling near me, but I can see the destruction surrounding me. I turn and just see the back of Elissa, running up the steps of the castle. The castle is old, and in ruins as one wall is on fire and another is in crumbles. The smoke in the room just floats around the white dress I'm wearing, the sparks coming off the wall of fire should burn me, but they don't. I can't even feel the heat from the room, if anything, it still feels cold.

"You and me then, boy," the familiar voice of the demon king says, and I turn to see the voice coming from an attractive, middle-aged man. The man has a long, black cloak on and dark-black hair. He stands holding a sword at his side, and at his feet is the dead body of Atti's ancestor, the first witch. I watch as he holds the blood covered sword up at his side, blood dripping onto the stone floor.

"Whatever happens here today, she is safe. She will live, and her child will finish this war. She will finish you," the voice of the first vampire, Wyatt's ancestor, says as he holds his own sword in the air. They don't say any more words as the demon king rushes forward and attacks him, their swords clashing together and the force nearly springing

them both backwards. I try to move as they fight, as I know the ending to this vision already, he will die. Both are fast, but the demon king is better, it's clear with every hit and swing of his sword. The demon king hits the vampire ancestor in his side, and he falls a little, giving the demon king the second he needs to shove his sword straight through his heart.

"No," I breathe out, but no sound comes from my lips, and the world is silent for a second before the vampire ancestor's pale face has black lines crawling over it, and he collapses on the floor.

"All but children in a game I've played for many, many years," the demon king says, his tone almost soft as he speaks to the two bodies on the floor. He steps over the witch and walks up the stairs, going after Elissa. I turn slightly to the left and see a woman walk in, her long, white cloak dotted with blood. She lowers the hood, and shock fills me when, for a second, I think it's Elissa, but it's not. It's Demtra, but they look so alike, the only difference is the hair and eyes. I met her once, when I died, and I thought it was Elissa, but it never was. Demtra looks straight at me, her green eyes staring straight through me.

"They did not fall so that you would fall, Queen Winter. Only you can stop this, you and your mates. Their last children if this is not stopped. Win the war, Queen Winter, win the war, win the war . . .," Demtra says in my mind, and the sentence repeats again and again in my mind as she walks up the stairs.

I shoot up in bed, feeling a hand shaking my shoulder, and open my eyes to see Atti leaning over me, relief spread across his handsome face before he takes my face in his hands and kisses me. I throw myself into the kiss, letting him pull me closer. I break away and just stare up at him, seeing his stormy, grey eyes that almost glow. He has a cloak on, his hood up, so I can't see his blonde hair, but I lift my hand and place it on his cheek under the hood.

"Atti," I whisper, seeing him close his eyes and pull me close. The bond between us is clear when I'm in his arms, my back almost tingles, reminding me of my marks and Atti's, which I haven't seen yet.

"We have to leave," Milo's voice comes from near us, and I break away from Atti to look over at the door, where Milo is hovering in the air. Milo has a strange, green outfit on and a green sash holding his blue hair up. It's such a relief to see them both, but as I look around, I have a feeling we aren't out of danger yet.

"Milo, Atti how are you here?" I ask, looking around the bedroom I'm in and down at the black dress I'm still wearing. I'm still in the vampire castle, how am I not under his control, and where is he?

"Milo can pull people through demon wards, now we have to go. The distraction isn't going to be long," Atti tells me and pulls me off the bed. A wave of dizziness hits me as I stand up, and I can feel the demon king in my mind, only a little bit. It's like a dark stain.

"Wait . . . how did you?" I ask Atti, pulling his hand to stop us walking across the room.

"Make you not, well controlled? I just flooded your system with my magic, mates can do that. You might feel a little–" Atti says, and I interrupt him.

"Dizzy?" I ask, resting on his shoulder, and he nods.

"Can you run?" he asks me. I stand straighter and remember everything I have to fight for. This isn't the time to be weak, I don't have time for that.

"Yes," I reply, and Atti links our hands as we run out of the room. Milo lands on my shoulder. I smile at him, and he rests his head next to mine as we stop at the end of the corridor, and Atti looks around it before we start running down the next one.

"Glad you safe," Milo says quietly and lightly kisses the side of my head.

"Me too, and thank you for saving me. I will always be thankful," I tell him quietly, and Atti smiles at me before we stop at the end of another corridor. Atti places a finger on his lips as he looks around the edge of the wall and then nods at me, tugging on my hand. We run down familiar-looking corridors, and Atti has to catch me when I trip on the lacy dress, ripping it. I pick some of the dress up as we get outside, and I hear the sound of screaming in the background. When the ground shakes, and the blast is strong enough to shake the castle, I know Jaxson is near. Worry fills me from the idea of him fighting the demon king, but I trust my mates to have made a plan.

"Jaxson?" I ask Atti as we run down the main court area and towards the large walls that enclose the castle. It's surprising how there isn't anyone here, not a single person or demon around. I think back to the humans that used to live here, how they never really had a chance to truly live, to be free and are most likely dead or demons now. I'm not sure which fate would have been better for them. An awful, groaning noise comes from next to us as we run, and I look to the left of Atti to see two demons running at us. They look horrible, their grey skin falling off their faces, and the smell from them can't be missed.

"Jaxson is making the distraction," Atti tells me and pushes me behind him as he raises his hands, and a large stream of fire leaves his hands. I look around him to see two piles of blue dust, and then we are running again before I can look at or say anything. In some ways, killing them is putting them to rest. Or, that's what I have to keep telling myself.

"We need to jump; can you do that?" Atti asks me, and I look up at the big wall and the blue ward that is just on the other side. Milo starts flying up as I watch and take a few steps back.

"Yes," I say remembering my training with Leigha. She would kick my ass if I don't jump this. All that training is finally becoming useful, and I could just see her smirking at me if I told her she was right.

"One, two, three . . .," Atti says, and I run next to him, jumping at the same time and pushing as much as I can to make the jump. I fly through the air and just manage to hit the top, catching my hands on the stone and hanging off the edge. My hands scrape across the sharp stone, and it cuts my fingers; my blood making it harder to hold on as the cold wind pushes me to the side. I look up, just as it starts to snow, it's falling thickly from the sky. I try to pull myself up, but the stupid dress catches on the stone and stops me from using my legs to help. These old dresses are not meant for climbing. Atti lands after me, pulling himself up and reaches down to lift me up only a minute later. He pulls me to his chest and I gently press my lips to his.

"My mate," I say softly, and he presses his forehead into mine. Atti lifts my cut hands and wipes his thumb across the cuts, which are slowly healing on their own. My teeth extend, but I don't feel hungry, which only makes me feel sick. I must have been fed or fed on someone while I was here. It's the only thing that makes sense.

"Hey, don't leave me and disappear into your thoughts. I missed you, and whatever it is you're worried about, we will sort it," he tells me, and I look up at him.

"I missed you, too," I whisper, and he kisses my forehead before he steps away, our moment gone as we both walk over to the dark-blue ward. The ward is thick, almost stopping you from seeing the other side and the forest behind it.

"You touch and push," Milo tells me as he flies over and Atti holds out his hand to Milo.

"You think I can walk through the ward?" I ask Milo, who nods his little head, making his hair bounce up and down.

"Demon, you," he tells me, and I nod back, understanding what he means. I should be able to do this because it's part of who I am. If the demon king can use that small part of me to control me, then I should be able to use it, too. I step forward at the same time Milo pulls Atti through the ward. I push my hands against it, feeling it pushing back like a sponge, but the more I push the further I can walk. I push and hold my breath, closing my eyes as I step through the ward. I gasp for air when I finally break through the other side, and I hear a loud shout.

"No!" the demon king's roar seems to echo around my mind, and I hold my hands over my ears as darkness starts spreading in my eyes. My power starts rising, and I scream as I push it away, refusing to let it hurt anyone. Especially not my mate.

"Atti," I whisper, feeling his hands picking me up and then the feeling of us moving, seconds before everything disappears into a familiar darkness.

77

WINTER

"Winter," a familiar voice says as a hand strokes my cheek, and I open my eyes to see my angel leaning over me. Dabriel watches me closely, his hair falling around his face and his marks glowing ever so slightly all over his skin. I've never spent a lot of time looking over each mark, seeing how they all resemble shapes, and they are difficult to look at for too long as it hurts your eyes. It's kind of like looking at the sun. Dabriel has a white shirt on, and jeans, but they are crinkled, and he looks tired. I look down to see I'm wearing the stupid black dress still, and I'm lying on top of the covers of my bed at the Goddess' castle. The bedroom is such a comfort to see, as much as being with one of my mates.

"Dab," I say, sitting up, and he pulls me to him with a contented groan. I wrap my arms around his neck and kiss his cheek, waiting only a second for him to turn his head and fully kiss me. I moan as he slides his hands into my hair, and his tongue gently wrestles with my own. This is everything, being here with him and being safe.

"You're awake, lass," Jaxson says from somewhere nearby, and Dabriel breaks away from the kiss, leaning back, so I can see Jaxson as he walks into the room. Jaxson looks tired, but so determined, as he walks over to me and leans down, pulling me off the bed and into a hug. I wrap my legs around his waist as he kisses me fast, then breaks away.

"I fucking missed you, don't do that again. I can't keep losing you like this," he tells me. I run my hand over his beard that needs shaving and the messy hair that falls slightly into his face. He looks tired but still has the wild side to him, the side that makes him the very wolf I know he is.

"It's not like I chose a family reunion, Jaxson," I say, wriggling out of his arms, and he sighs as he lets me go. "How did the distraction go?" I ask him, looking him over for any injuries but not seeing any.

"I decided the best way to get his attention was to destroy half the castle, so I caused an earthquake and brought down the left side of the castle," Jaxson says with a shrug like it was nothing when I bet that was some hell of a show of power. "The demons attacked, and we held them off, until the demon king got there. I went to fight him when he realised you had gone, and then the witches came and used their power to portal everyone out," Jaxson tells me. I bet the demon king was mad.

"What happened to you? How could he take power over you, make you almost a zombie?" he asks me gently.

"He controlled me somehow; he got into my head and made everything go black."

"Do you know about the witches?" Dabriel asks me gently, and I shake my head. I only remember the witch the demon king killed at that messed-up dinner. There isn't anything else, just blackness and every time I try to think about it, it seems to slip away from my thoughts.

"Winter, he used you to destroy the crystal ward that protected the witches' city. Then he brought his dragons in, and the island is destroyed,"

"Dragons? He used me?" I ask, shock making me feel sick.

"Yes, but it wasn't your fault."

"How many witches survived the attack?" I ask, and Jaxson hesitates before he tells me.

"About three thousand, maybe less as a lot are injured still," he says, and I know that means thousands died in the witches' city. A city full of people I'm meant to protect as I'm their queen, and instead, I let the demon king use me to destroy the ward that protected them.

"It's not your fault, you know that?" Dabriel asks me, and I just look away. There's silence between us all as I guess they don't know what to say to me. It is my fault no matter what they say. I should have done something, fought more or tried to wake myself up. If I hadn't been stupid in the first place, the demon king wouldn't have even escaped.

"What do you remember, Winter? Anything you could tell us could help at this point?" Dabriel asks me, trying to give me a way to be useful.

"I don't remember much, only bits. I remember a dinner, and two angels were there with a witch," I say but turn to talk to Dabriel more. I hate that I have to tell him about his brothers. No matter the fact I know he doesn't get along with them, this is more than just sibling fights. No, this means his family betrayed him, and I know he will never forgive them for it.

"What angels?" Dabriel asks me, sliding off the bed and his wings gently fluttering at the side of him.

"They were your brothers, they told me," I tell him

gently, and he frowns, standing up off the bed. I won't tell him what else they said to me or about him dying, I would never let that happen. I would never let any one of my mates die for me.

"And, he is working with the demon king. It wouldn't surprise me to know the whole council is," he says, coming over and kissing my forehead. I wrap an arm around his waist, feeling his one wing almost holding me to him. I wonder if he even notices he is doing it. I can't help but gently guide my hand over his wing, and I feel him gently shiver.

"I'm happy you're safe and here, but I must go and speak with Lucifer. If the angels are working with them, we are not as safe as I would like," he tells me, and I nod. I get it, being the royals we are means we don't have a lot of time to celebrate them saving me. Dabriel walks out the door, holding it open as Freddy runs in and tackles me in a hug. I take a deep breath as the kid almost suffocates me with his strong arms.

"You're back," he says, happily squeezing me, and I hold him close.

"I am, where is Wyatt?" I ask Jaxson over Freddy's head.

"We are having problems with the witches and Vampires, there is a fight going on, or he would be here. He saw you before Atti, and he had to go and deal with the problems," he says, and it's not surprising knowing that my mates would have brought the surviving witches here. Now, we are trying make vampires, witches, and wolves live together after hating each other for so long. There is always going to be arguments, but I know this is the best thing for us. This castle is the safest place.

"Let's go then," I say, letting go of Freddy and letting Jaxson take my hand as he leads us out of the bedroom.

"Go and find Katy and Harris will you, Freds? They will want to know Winter is back," Jaxson asks Freddy when we get outside my bedroom. Freddy gives Jaxson a grumpy look before sighing.

"Fine," Freddy says and runs down the corridor in the opposite direction. I look up at Jaxson as he leads us out of the corridor that has our rooms, and I hear the shouting the moment we get to the top of the stairs. I listen to the arguments as we walk down the four flights of stairs and past many witches, wolves, and vampires that are leaning over the bannister and watching. Many turn and look at me with wide eyes that have a range of respect, kindness and what's worse is fear.

" Ils ne restent pas ici, ni les sorcières," I hear some man shout, his French words I don't understand making me guess he is one of the vampires.

"I don't want to be around stupid old vampires anyway. At least us witches aren't cruel, evil people" I hear shouted back to whatever the man shouted in French. I come down the stairs just in time to see Atti hold a witch against the wall by his neck, while Wyatt lifts another older-looking vampire off the ground by his coat, his feet hanging off the ground.

"What the hell is going on?" I ask, and the room goes silent. Wyatt drops the vampire at the same time that Atti lets go of his man, they both smile over at me. *Atti and Wyatt both look stressed even with the smiles.* That's the only thought that comes to mind as I rest my eyes on them. Atti has his cloak on, the black contrasts against his wavy, blonde hair and his grey eyes light up as I smile at him. Wyatt draws my attention the most right now, it feels like forever since I've seen him. I let my eyes drop down his body, seeing the tight trousers and button down white shirt he has on, that show off his impressive body. His dark, almost bottomless, brown eyes watch me, and I think he is feeling the same as me. The urge to be close to my mate is hard to resist, even with the number of eyes on us. It's almost funny the looks of happiness they give me, like they weren't just stopping a fight or Wyatt wasn't holding a vampire up by his neck. The vampire on the floor coughs and moves away but I'm kind of proud of Wyatt, he could have just used his compulsion on the vampire and made him stop. Instead, he was trying to be reasonable, well as reasonable as a vampire prince who just got his mate back can get that is.

"Nothing we can't deal with," Wyatt says, his eyes drifting over me and finally landing on my eyes. I take a step closer to him and trip, almost falling, but Jaxson slides an arm around my waist and stops me. I clear my throat and look down, seeing nothing. I just tripped on air in front of lots of people, damn it.

"Supernaturals are not meant to live together, this is wrong," the witch with light-blond hair, who Atti was holding, says as he stands up and shakes his head at me. Jaxson's loud growl is enough to make him stay quiet and not comment on whatever he is thinking. I know I don't have many fans with the witches, not after what I did to their city. They don't seem to look at me with hate, like I expected them to. No, they seem to only have fear in their eyes as they stare at the vampires and wolves. I glance around at the five female witches with their hoods down, bundled together on one side and then to the ten or so vampires huddled closely together. The wolves are bundled together by door. The space in-between them is huge.

"Everyone listen." I shout, and the crowd of witches, vampires, and wolves turn to look at me. I take a deep breath, knowing I need to say this and then spend time figuring out everything else.

"The demon king has an army; a massive army. I saw them. He has thousands and thousands of soldiers that will kill anything in their way, and they have the weapons to kill us. He won't stop until we are all dead; witch, vampire, wolf, or angel. It doesn't matter to him," I tell them, the fear shining in their eyes as they watch me.

"Isn't he your grandfather? You brought down the ward and let the dragons in!" a female witch says and steps forward.

"You're right, he is. He has also killed all my blood relatives other than himself. He has killed because he is insane, and his thirst for power is out of control. I can only say I'm truly sorry for the ward, for letting him take control of my mind and not figuring out he has that power."

"How do we know you won't flip and start attacking us?" an older, French vampire asks, watching me with his hand on a sword strapped to his side.

"If you attack her, if anyone attacks my queen, I will personally rip you to pieces," Jaxson growls out and the vampire looks down. I place my hand on Jaxson's shoulder and step away from him.

"The demon king can't come here, and he can only control me when he is close. I understand your fear, I feel it, too. I have family here, and you are my people. I won't stop until he is back in hell, where he belongs. You may not trust me, or some of you may hate me for everything I've done. It doesn't matter, at the end of the day, war is coming. In war, you will see I side with you. I was human once, but I never felt right. I felt lost and being here is home," I say, and several of the supernaturals all look at each other.

"Our queen is right, we are at war, and squabbling like children over race is not going to win us a war that will save our children. Save our mates," Atti shouts into the room and then walk over to my side.

"There has never been a threat like this, there has never been a war like this. We will all die if we don't work together, our children will die. There isn't a choice here. We fight or we die. You make your choice and spread the word. Those who want to fight, meet me and the other kings in the training rooms in the morning. Those who don't or won't, stay out of our way, or I will kill you, myself," Wyatt shouts, and his voice echoes around the room as whispers follow. I watch as he walks over to me, sliding his hands over my cheeks and kissing me.

"We will win this for you," he tells me, and lets go, dropping to his one knee in front of me and bowing his head. Jaxson and Atti mimic his actions, and so do all the other people in the room, each one of them kneeling and bowing their heads. I look over to see Alex standing near the door, her arms crossed, and she winks at me before bowing herself.

"We will win this war, and I will kill the demon king. It's what I'm destined to do. It's what my grandmother, my great aunt, her mates, and my parents died for. I will fight for us all," I say, my words echoing as I leave out the most important part of the prophecy, that someone will die, and I'm going to make sure it's me. No one else is dying for me.

78

WINTER

"What the hell are you wearing?" Alex asks as she walks over to me when everyone walks away other than my mates. She pulls me into a tight hug and I just don't move except to hold her back. It feels like a long time since I hugged my best friend.

"Other than looking like a weird, goth princess, are you okay?" she whispers to me, the words only meant for me to hear.

"I'm good, just it was like sleeping and having no control. I don't remember much, and it's best I don't," I tell her quietly, and she lets go. Memories of thousands of dead, demon soldiers, the smell of death, and the demon king's glowing, red eyes will haunt me for years. I have trouble pushing them out of my mind as I try to focus on my best friend. Alex looks amazing as usual, with her red hair down and wearing some kind of leather leggings that stick to her and a baggy white top that hangs off of one shoulder.

"I have something I need to talk to you about," she tells me, and I frown wondering what when I see Harris and

Katy running into the room, followed by Anna holding baby Marie in her arms. Marie looks so much older, which I know babies grow quick, but it's still a sight to see. It's Anna's haunted eyes that hold my attention as I watch them come closer.

"Winter!" Katy shouts and hugs me. "What on earth are you wearing? I want to say you look good but err . . .," Katy says as she lets go.

"I know, right? It's awful, that dress should have burnt in the eighteen hundreds and never made it this far," Alex says, both of them eying my awful dress up. *Hey, it's not like I disagree with them.*

"Win, shit I was worried about you," Harris says, and he wraps his giant arms around me.

"I'm good," I say as he moves away.

He nods, "I let you down, My Queen, and—"

"Don't start that stuff, or I will start feeling guilty, too," Leigha's sharp voice comes from behind me, and I turn to see her push her way through my mates, and she gives me a small smile.

"Back from the demon den, then?"

"Did you miss me, army brat?"

"In training I did," she smirks, and Harris walks over to her, wrapping an arm around her waist and kissing the side of her head. Her red cheeks and small smile she gives him is enough proof to me that she loves him. And, the fact that no one seems shocked by their actions.

"I heard what happened with Esta. What she did," Anna says softly next to me, and I turn to look at her. Despite her soft tone, her eyes have anger in them. Anna's pale complexion matches her blonde hair, which is up in a bun, and the casual clothes she has on. Marie has a Babygro on and the wavy, blonde hair is all I can see as Anna holds Marie on her shoulder.

"Esta," Anna says her name in anger, and the silence in response to her words is enough to know everyone has spoken about it. Someone has told her, and in a way, I'm glad it's not me that has to.

"She told me she killed Fergus, just before she died," I reply, and she nods, knowing this.

"And, you gave her forgiveness," Anna says, her tone filled with judgement.

"I had little choice. I gave her my forgiveness, not yours, not the pack's, and not Jaxson's. I showed kindness in front of thousands of witches that watched me as I took their throne. The one I took from a cruel witch, and they needed to see I'm different. I couldn't be cruel to someone who died for me, not in their last moment. What she did, was because of her love for Jaxson and her need to be with him. In the end, I felt sorry for her," I tell Anna, and there's silence as we stare at each other.

"You're my queen, my friend, but she took my mate. I do understand your decision, and it's your kindness that led you to that choice. I hate her for what she did, that she was at the birth of Fergus's child, and that she pretended to be my friend. I hate her and hope she rots in hell for her crimes. I wish she was still alive, so I could kill her, myself," Anna spits out, and her eyes start glowing, and only stops as Marie cries a little. She hushes Marie gently and pats her back.

"Do you hate me?" I ask quietly, and she looks down at her baby and back to me.

"No. I understand. Winter . . . win this war for us, for Marie, and honour Fergus' memory that way," she says firmly and waits for my nod before she walks away. Leigha pats my shoulder as she passes with Harris and Katy following her. I wait until they all walk away before I look up at Jaxson who walks to my side.

"I understand what you did, Winter. You're a better person than me, I would have told her to rot in hell before killing the bitch, myself. But, she was still pack, and you acted like a shifter queen who lost a pack mate, no matter the circumstances," Jaxson tells me, his voice dripping with anger as I look up at him.

"Thank you." I nod, and he pulls me into his arms.

"Queen Winter, King Jaxson, King Wyatt, and King Atticus." He paused for a moment, looking at Alex. "I don't know who you are," Lucifer says, walking over to us and bowing low.

Alex and I share a look, there are way too many attractive men in this room, and I know she is thinking the same thing.

"Just Alex. I don't need all that fuss, hot stuff," Alex says, and I laugh a little as Lucifer gives her a strange look.

"Hot stuff? Am I on fire?" he asks and pats down his black shirt making Alex laugh.

"No, it's a human saying."

"A very strange one, indeed," Lucifer says and looks at me, "Queen Winter–" he starts to say, and I interrupt him.

"Lucifer, you supported my mate when little others did and showed me memories I will remember forever as they are all I have of my parents, so we are friends. Just Winter please, I'm your friend first," I say, and he nods with a small smile.

"I wish to look into your mind, Queen Winter, I can see your past these last few days and then convince the angels that Zadkiel is working with our enemy. I doubt the council truly knows, and I want to give the angels, my people, the best chance I can," Lucifer says and holds out a hand as Dabriel comes into the room with another angel I've never seen. He nods at me as he continues speaking to the angel as they walk over. I slide my hand into Lucifer's and watch as he glows with his black symbols. I expect him to show me, but he doesn't, I watch as his black eyes disappear back to normal, purple ones. I'm glad he doesn't show me when I think about it, I don't need any more memories to have nightmares about.

"I could see the meal with Zadkiel and Govan, and little bits of the army he has," Lucifer says, reminding me of the brief image I have of Paris and the dead army he has inside it. It's like a ticking time bomb, waiting to destroy the world. They could so easily. A memory flitters though my mind of the demon king shouting that the humans keep dying as the demons try to take over them. That thousands are dying all the time, and thousands of humans keep hiding from him in the city.

"We should go to the angels, all of us. A united front," I say, and there's silence as Dabriel walks over to me.

"No fucking way," Jaxson snaps out.

"You may be my mate, but you don't control me. Don't speak to me like that, Jax," I snap back, and he growls lightly.

"I lost you, I fucking lost you, and you expect me to let you go anywhere near him again?" Jaxson says, and my anger disappears when I realise his reaction is pure fear of losing me again, nothing more.

"Jax, I'm here now, and what happened before, won't happen again. He chose a time when we were celebrating winning the crown and mating to Atti because we were all distracted. Nothing is going to distract us again," I say and look over at Wyatt and Atti as they step closer.

"I'm not taking you out of this castle, Winter. The demon king could take control of you again, and we can't risk him using you to get here. The winter solstice is in two weeks, Winter. He is coming, then, and we have no way of preventing him from taking over your mind," Dabriel says gently, making me turn to look at him as he slides a comforting hand down my arm.

"How about we go, and I stay next to Atti the whole time? He can pull me away the second anything happens, but it's unlikely the demon king will be there. I know it's a risk, but I feel like I need to be there," I try to reason.

"Atti?" I ask when no one responds, and he looks down at me as he moves in front of me. Atti places his hand on my cheek, and I rest my head into it.

"You don't leave my side?" he asks almost in a whisper, fear coating his eyes, and I nod.

"Fine, we will go tonight," he says.

"Someone needs to go and get my mum. The wolves protecting her won't be enough if the demon king finds her. He must be furious I'm gone. I need her here," I tell them all.

"I will send a witch, Leigha, and Drake to get her. Between them, they will be able to safely get her here," Atti says and kisses my cheek before walking off.

79

WINTER

"I should go and get changed. Alex?" I ask her, and she walks over, linking her arm in mine as we walk away from them all, feeling them watching me. My back almost tingles with the knowledge that all my mates are watching me, and I turn my head to see them. They look every bit as powerful as I know they are, as they watch me. But, there's more than that, I feel nothing but love as I meet each of their eyes and give them a little smile. I haven't even seen what my new mark looks like since I mated with Atti, and all I want is to see it. We walk up the stairs and instead of walking to my corridor, I walk down the opposite one.

"Where are we going?" Alex asks me.

"To see the crystal, I need to know something," I tell her, and she nods.

"Why didn't you tell your mates?"

"I need to speak with it alone. They won't let me touch it after last time, and I can't really explain this feeling I have. I think the crystal is somehow in my dreams, the child-like voice I always hear; I think it is the crystal," I tell her as we stop and open the doors to the tower. I'm surprised no one is guarding it like they should be, but I make a mental note to sort something out later. I shut the doors behind us and stop on the bottom step of the stairs.

"Can I be alone?" I ask her, and she looks behind me up the stairs and meets my eyes.

"I trust you," she says simply, and I know there isn't much more that is needed to be said. I climb up the dozens of stairs of the tower and feel the crystal calling to me before I even see it. The crystal is as huge as I remember it being, it lightly glows, and I look around the room to see someone has drawn on the walls and there are tools on the floor. It looks like they planned to put windows in here and the very thought makes me happy. People should be able to see the beautiful light from the crystal. I walk over, whispering quietly,

"Hello. I know this may seem weird. Okay, it is weird that I'm talking to a giant crystal, but I know you're alive in here. I feel it. You sing to me, just like the crystal trees in the witches' city. You have been in my dreams and helping me, is that true?"

I place my hands on the crystal, seeing the millions of little lights inside swirl around and then rush at the place my hands are, before the light shines so brightly that I can't see anything for a second.

"Winter," the child-like voice says as I open my eyes, and the little lights from the crystal have formed into a ball in the middle, I look only for a second before the loud, sorrow-filled song fills my mind.

"Child of Winter . . . .

Child of demons . . . .

Child of the ancient ones. A child planned to rule, a child planned to save. For all children grow to love, to mourn, but only the child of death will pay the ultimate price. A price for love, for the

world. Death and sorrow, death and love, death and wishes for change will never be sought. The prophecy tells the truth, as much as time will pass. Blood will fall, blood will fall, blood will fall . . . ."

The song drifts off as my hands start to burn on the crystal, but I don't move my hands away.

"I understand, I know it's my life that must be given to save everyone," I whisper and only a small whisper responds to me,

"*You will understand at the final choice.*"

I pull my hands away, the ball of light breaking into millions of little lights inside the crystal, and the power I felt in the room seems to have disappeared. I look down at my slightly burnt hands as they heal and then back to the crystal, feeling like I'm missing something. Like it knows something that I don't.

I shut the door to my room after leaving with Alex, and she hasn't said a word, the confused look on my face likely says it all. I instantly start pulling the dress off, and when it falls to the ground, I look at my back in the mirror. Despite my underwear being in the way a little, it's one hell of a massive mark all down my back. The strong phoenix at the bottom, the brave wolf next, then Atti's beautiful tree is in the middle of the delicate wings. My heart hurts when I think of the trees in the witches' city, how they are lost to us for the time being. I hope when we get the city back, and we will, we can re-grow them. Their beautiful songs play through my head a million times as I just stare at my reflection. So much has been lost, and so much more is going to be lost. How can I be strong enough to save everyone? To do what I need to?

"Here," Alex says, coming over and handing me some jeans and a black top, snapping me out of my thoughts.

"Your mating marks are beautiful," she tells me as I pull the clothes on.

"Thank you. They are." I reply as I pick the awful dress up and walk over to the fireplace. I chuck it in and look around until I find some matches, before setting the damn thing on fire.

"It looks better on fire." Alex chuckles as she stands next to me, and we watch the fire burn the black material. Even the awful smell from the burning fabric doesn't make me move. I want to watch it burn.

"What did the crystal say?"

"Nothing I didn't already know, I think it's alive," I reply.

"That's . . . well, I would say crazy, but we live in a crazy world."

"A crazy, dangerous world," I reply, and she nods at me before sitting on the end of my bed and looking down at the ground. Alex never makes much sound as she cries, I know her too well. Alex never cries, it's just not her way, but the rare times I've seen her cry, it's been for a bad reason, and worry fills me. Nothing else can be wrong, not with my best friend, too.

"What's wrong?" I ask, keeping the fear out my voice as I walk over and sit next to her.

"I know it's the worst timing, the worst thing that could have happened right now, and I swear we were being safe, but it happened," she whispers after a long silence. Confusion fills me as I look at her, I have no idea where she is going with this.

"What happened? Whatever it is, I'll cover for you. If it's hiding a body or helping you kill someone, I will, no questions asked," I say, making her laugh a little as she shakes her head at me. I watch her closely as I take her hand. She shocks me to my core as she places her other hand on her stomach, and I figure out what is going on before she even says it.

"I'm pregnant," she whispers, and I sit back in shock, keeping hold of her hand. Alex is pregnant.

"Oh, wow. I didn't expect that," I mutter, my eyes going from her face to her stomach and back again.

"I know, but it happened, and I couldn't be more scared. Every time I close my eyes, fear just fills me. I can't shake the powerless feeling I have," she admits.

"Why are you scared? You will make a wonderful mother," I ask her, knowing for certain she will.

"We are at war Winter. We could die, and anything that happens to me, happens to my baby. I love her or him already, I know it's early to feel this way, but I do. I would do anything to save my baby."

"No, we won't die. You will not die, and you will have this baby. He will not win this time. I will fight for our freedom, our lives. The lives of our future," I say and nod my head towards her stomach. Any doubt I had about winning this war, about giving my life up slips away as I think about Alex's baby.

"I want to be at your side, fighting, but Drake won't have it, and I can't help but agree with him. Vampire pregnancies are so rare, and everyone I've asked says they are difficult to carry for half-turned like me," she says, and it's not surprising. I know about the low birth rate all supernaturals have.

"Someone will need to be with the women and children who can't fight. Someone needs to be helping the injured and that's where you're going to be," I say, and she hugs me. Neither of us move for a long time, just holding each other and my mind running over the idea of Alex and a baby.

"I can't wait to meet her or him," I whisper to her in the quiet room, only the sound of the fire crackling in the background to listen to.

"Winter, come now," Leigha bursts into the room, blood pouring down the side of her head. Her clothes are ripped in various places, and when I see the blue dust on her, panic fills me.

"Leigha what happened?" I ask, standing up.

At the same time Alex asks, "Where's Drake? Where's our mum?"

"We'd just got to your mum, and demons came. There were so many, we barely got away. I think they were waiting for us, for anyone to come. Drake and your mum are badly injured," Leigha tells us as we run down the corridor and down the stairs. Alex makes a strangled sound, and everything goes blurry as I run after Leigha.

"No, no, no," Alex mutters, wiping her eyes as we follow Leigha through the castle and run past many people, who stop and stare. Leigha slams the door of a room open, it's full of beds, and I see Dabriel first as he is glowing.

"Winter," I hear someone say, but everything seems slow as I walk over to Dabriel and see my mum on the bed in front of him. There are three long cuts in the front of her top, and there is blood everywhere as Dabriel tries to heal her. I look over at the two silver swords at the side of the bed, covered in blood and back to my mum.

"Mum?" I ask, taking her hand, but she is unconscious. I look over to see another light angel I don't know glowing lighter than Dabriel and watch as he pulls two daggers out of Drake's stomach as Alex leans over him. Next to him is a female light witch, three daggers in her arm, and she winces as she pulls them out.

"Winter, I can't. I'm sorry, but the cuts are laced with the same poison that killed Atti's mother, and your mother is too human to survive this," Dabriel says quietly, his purple eyes locking on mine as he gives me the news I knew from the moment I saw my mum. I can't lose her, too. This cannot be happening. I'm so stupid, I should have demanded she come here, no matter what she wanted.

"No!" I shout, pushing him out of the way as he removes his hands, and my mum looks up at me as her eyes slowly open. I push her grey hair out of her face, wincing when I leave a trail of blood on her cheek from my hands.

"Alex, come and say goodbye," I hear Dabriel say, and the sound of Alex's crying fills the room.

"Go say goodbye to your mother. I'm okay, Alex," I hear Drake say, and then I hear her move closer as I stare into my mum's eyes. I don't look away.

"I love you both, you know that?" she whispers out, her breaths sounding slower and slower as I brush some hair out of her eyes.

"I love you, too, mum, please don't leave me," Alex begs as she grips her hand.

"Sing for me Winter, I love your singing," she mumbles and I nod, wiping my eyes. I don't know what to sing as I open my mouth, and then a song fills my mind. A song she used to sing to me as a child.

"Blue, blue rose dancing in the snow. Oh blue, blue rose you have come to say Winter has finally come. Winter brings the cold but the warmth along, too. I can hear the snow falling, I can hear the foxes sleeping, and I can hear the sun setting as Winter comes . . . as the snow falls, and all is clear . . . "

"Winter, save us. Save us all, and I'm so proud of you

both," she says as I stop singing. Blood flows out of her mouth, before her hand drops out of mine, and her eyes close. I can't say a word as I watch her die, every part of me feeling as cold and distant as the very song she used to sing to me.

"Mum, mum don't," Alex whines. Everything seems surreal as I feel Dabriel pull me into his arms and whispers what I'm sure are comforting things. All I can hear is Alex's cries and the echo of my mum's last words: *Save us all.*

80

WINTER

"What are you doing?" Jaxson asks me as I throw my dagger, and it lands perfectly in the next target. It's been a day since my mum died, and I don't know what I'm doing. Dabriel decided to put off seeing the angels until tonight, and I haven't spoken to any of them. I can't speak about it because it will make it more real. It will make it more heart-breaking that my parents have been killed by my grandfather. That my entire family is dead except for him. Him. The evil son of a bitch that hides in his castle and gets his demons to do his handiwork. Everything he has taken from me just continues to add up, he was destroying my life before I was even born. He was destroying everything before the prophecy was even spoken from my grandmother's lips.

"Do you need me to answer that?" I ask sarcastically, and he glares at me. I ignore him and pick up two more daggers, throwing them into the target and landing them perfectly on either side of the first dagger. I imagine the evil, red eyes as I walks over to the target and pull out the daggers. I see the eyes of everyone who is training in the room on me, but I ignore them. I can't deal with being their queen right now; being the reasonable one. Death, just more death, and what else will be left, in the end, if I don't kill him?

"Out, everyone, now," he shouts in the training room, and the twenty or so wolves, witches, and vampires quickly run out the door at Jaxson's growly words.

"You didn't need to do that," I mutter, and he chuckles as I put the daggers down on the bench and turn my back to him.

"Fight me, like we used to," he tells me, and I look over my shoulder, only seconds before he charges at me. I move at the last second, dodging his attack and spin around, running at his back. He turns and blocks my hit, and I slam my leg into his side. He grabs my hip and slams me onto the floor, and I knock his legs out from under him. He slams onto the floor next to me, and I roll onto him, holding his arms down.

"I've always liked you on top," he says as we both breathe heavily, and I lean down, kissing him. Jaxson groans slightly and flips us over as he deepens the kiss, pressing himself into me.

"No sex, we need to talk, lass," he tells me as he breaks away but keeps me trapped under him.

"I don't want to talk," I say, looking to the side, and he grabs my chin, gently pulling my face to look at him.

"I get it. You want to fuck and kill and do anything to forget what happened. We are far more alike than I want to admit, lass. I know you feel guilty, you feel like everyone you love has died, and you have lost that last part of your parents," he says, his tone growing gentler with each word.

"I lost my mum, my sister, and my brother, and I wanted to destroy everything because of that. But I didn't, you know why?"

"Why?" I ask quietly.

"Because I had family left to fight for. You have us; your mates. And Alex, who is like a sister to you. You have so much to fight for. We will be at your side; there to make sure we don't lose anyone else," he tells me, and his words crack some kind of barrier I've held onto since my mum died. I burst into tears, and he sits up, pulling me onto his lap.

"You cry now and let it out. Then you are going to hold your head high and walk out that door, and be their queen. They are all scared and need their queen to be strong," he whispers to me.

"With you at my side," I whisper.

"I will always be at your side, Winter," he tells me, and gently kisses my forehead.

"Everything okay?" Wyatt asks as he walks into my bedroom where I'm putting my belt full of daggers on. Wyatt's blonde hair is as long as when we first met, and his jaw is freshly shaven. Somehow, just dressed in smart, black trousers and a white shirt that is slightly undone, he couldn't look more powerful with the massive sword strapped to his hip. He couldn't look more like the vampire king he is meant to be.

"I'm sorry I shut you out, after mum," I say, my voice cracking a little.

"Winter, you can shut me out, throw those daggers at me, or, in general, just ignore me, and I will still be here for you," he tells me, and I chuckle.

"You would catch the daggers anyway."

"True," he smirks.

"We have angels to go see," I say and walk over, leaning up to kiss him gently.

"I'm proud of you," he tells me, and I nod, letting myself have this moment with him before pulling away. Wyatt takes my hand as he leads us down the corridor. The door at the end opens, and Freddy walks out, followed by a boy I've not seen before. He has wavy, black hair, with what looks like red tips in his fringe. I can't tell what he is, but he seems almost familiar to me. I spend way too long meeting the boy's eyes before pulling my own eyes away.

"Winter," Freddy says when he notices me and runs over.

I hug him, and I'm a little surprised when Wyatt says, "Son, who's your friend?" I know Freddy is his son, yet it's still strange to hear him say that.

"Josh, come here," Lucifer says as he walks down the corridor towards us.

"Is Josh your son?" I ask Lucifer when he places a hand on Josh's shoulder and Josh looks over at me. The bright-blue eyes are so familiar and clash against the tips of red in his hair.

"Yes," he replies tensely.

"So, you're an angel? Sorry, for a second I thought you might be something else," I tell Josh who just crosses his arms and looks at his dad. Josh looks a lot like his dad, I can tell he is going to break some hearts when he's older, much like I can see Freddy doing. The two of them should be locked away from girls.

"Yeah, Dad, why is that?" Josh asks, his voice dripping with sarcasm. Josh and Lucifer seem to share a look before looking back at us again.

"Angels do not get their wings until their sixteenth birthday, and that is why," Lucifer answers, but Josh surprises me by laughing loudly.

"Any kind are welcome here, you don't need to hide anything from us," I tell Lucifer.

"Nah, it's more the issue that my step mum and half-brothers wouldn't be happy with anyone knowing my secrets, right Dad?" Josh says.

"Let's go," Lucifer demands, and I watch as they both walk away.

"Your friend is odd."

"He's a half," Freddy tells me, shocking me a little bit, but some part of me knows the truth in his words as I look over at Josh before he walks out of the corridor.

"Half what?" I ask, knowing I was right, and there is something strange about that boy.

"He doesn't know. His dad won't tell him, but he was living with humans until recently," Freddy tells me.

"I'm going to find Mich," Freddy says, reminding me of the deaf wolf that Freddy made friends with. Seems they are still friends.

"Is Mich a half, too?" I ask Freddy, just having a feeling.

"Yes. His dad was a witch, how did you know?"

"A feeling," I say, and Freddy hugs me before walking away.

"Keep an eye on who you make friends with, son," Wyatt tells him, and he turns around at the end of the corridor.

"Careful, you're starting to sound nice, vamp," Freddy laughs before walking away, and I look up at Wyatt who is trying not to laugh as he watches where Freddy was. They are very alike.

"It's weird you have a child, a child that's not mine," I blurt out my thoughts, and then cough realising what I just said.

"Does it bother you?"

"Sometimes, I'm jealous of Demi, that she had your love first. That she had your children first, and then I realise I'm jealous of someone who is dead. I just can't help how I feel," I admit; what I've never really said to him. He takes my hand and leads us out onto the balcony, and shuts the glass doors behind us. I look over the woods from the balcony, the very place that reminds me of my first date with Atti and loving the pots of flowers someone has placed out here.

"What I felt for Demi . . . well, I never want to admit it to Freddy, but it wasn't love. I know that now, but back then, I didn't. It was lust and tiredness of everyone in my home that was so fake towards me. The countless vampires my father tried to make me mate to. The countless humans and vampires I watched him kill. It was just a chance to be happy. I know this because I never felt for her, an ounce of what I feel for you. Nothing in my life compares to how I feel for you, you're so much more, Winter," he says gently, his dark eyes willing me to believe him.

"I don't want you to just say that," I whisper.

"I'm not. You will understand one day soon that I love you so much that I would die for you. I would do anything to keep you safe," he tells me and looks away, watching something out in the skies. I know how he feels because I would do the same for him, but more. I would do anything to just have a life with him, with my other mates. I feel like every one of them ran away with my heart the moment we met, and I wouldn't ever chase them for it. It's theirs.

"You won't have to die for me, no one will," I say firmly.

"You mean the prophecy?" he asks, and I nod as he steps in front of me, then I look up at him.

"Someone might die, Winter, and you need to accept

that, but it won't be you," he says and tilts my chin with his finger and gently kisses me.

"The last sentence of the prophecy was '*Her saviour will die when the choice is made*'. I don't have an idea who that is, but it can't come true. There has been too much loss," I whisper the end part.

"Then we will make sure that part doesn't come true, but we have an entire race of angels to win over first, My Queen," he tells me and gently kisses my forehead as he pulls me to him. I rest my head on his chest, and relax in the safety of his arms, the cold wind blowing around us, but it doesn't matter as everything feels safe in his arms.

"Before the war I will, and I will announce Freddy as my heir. He is already heir to the wolf throne, but it will give him extra protection. Is that okay with you?" he asks, and I love him more for asking me. Not that he needs to, I would do anything to keep Freddy safe.

"Yes. I see him as family. I hope one day he sees me like that, too," I reply.

"He already does, Winter. It's how he looks at you, you two were drawn to each other from the very start," he says and lets me go. He walks over and opens the door. I look back at the sun setting over the sky, and the way it sends oranges and reds across the sky. It's so beautiful, like the peace before the storm.

81

WINTER

"Remember to stay close, no matter what happens," Atti tells me as I slide my hand into his, and my other hand is held tightly in Dabriel's grip. I can feel the worry through our bond from all my mates. They all don't like this, and I have to admit I don't, either, but we can't leave the angels alone until the council knows everything. Apparently, Lucifer can show the council members if they won't let me show them my memories. The guys decided to all come today with three angels as well as Leigha who demanded to protect me when she heard what we were doing.

"Time to see my home, Winter," Dabriel says gently, and I nod, squeezing his hand and keeping my eyes locked on his as Atti moves us all with his power. When we get there, the first thing I notice is the loud noise, a ringing noise that makes me want to put my hands on my ears, but both my hands are held in the tight grip of my mates. When I look away from Dabriel, I almost wish I hadn't when I see all the bodies on the ground in front of me and the destroyed building we are standing in. Two demons run at us, not stopping once as they kick the angel's bodies out of the way. Atti lifts his hand, calling his fire and destroying them before they even get close. There are bodies everywhere, of all ages, and sickness fills my mouth.

"Over there," Lucifer says, getting our attention, and we look up to see a bunch of angels in the air, avoiding the arrows the demons on the ground are shooting at them. Most of them are holding children and trying to fly away. This place must have once been beautiful as I look around at the small houses, but all there is now is blood and more death. The demon king didn't send his army here to help them or work with them, he came to kill them all.

"We need to save them, stay here," Dabriel says and lets my hand go, flying over with three angels that came with us. I glance over as Leigha and Wyatt come to my side, and Atti keeps me close as we look around. What once must have been a beautiful building is now just pieces of rock, and I see a painting on the floor under the rubble, only the head of a handsome angel with a white crown can be seen. I take a guess that that was Dabriel's father, the old king.

"We need to help them," I tell Atti, who looks over at the angels fighting and back to me.

"Stay close, I don't think the demon king is here now, but he could come back," Atti tells me. I know the demon king isn't here, this is just a game to him, and he wouldn't waste his time. I doubt he would leave the portal now, knowing that's the only way to keep himself safe.

"I'm going to shift, makes it easier to kill them," Jaxson tells me, and hands his sword to Wyatt before his clothes shred away, and he shifts into his giant, black wolf. Jaxson's wolf presses against my side just before we all start walking. I pull one of my daggers out of my belt, holding it at my side and my other hand is in Atti's as we approach the massive group of demons. There are so many angel bodies at their feet, and just behind them are a big group holding off the demons, with what looks like women and children behind them. They are all a mix of white and black wings as they fight, holding each other off.

"I have an idea," I say and step in front of Atti, pulling my power and sending it out like a shockwave towards the group of demons. My blue wave of power hits them one by one, and they disappear into blue dust. It even pushes some of the demons that escape the wave into the angels. The angels make quick work of killing the remaining demons as Jaxson rushes forward and starts helping them by ripping the demons to shreds with his paws and teeth.

"Your power works against them," Atti whispers.

"I can't do it again, it takes too much," I tell him breathlessly, as I glance over at the twenty or so demons that are still left, but Jaxson is making a good go at killing the demons brave enough to come near us.

"That's what your kings are for," Wyatt says and lifts both his swords, and runs towards the demons. Jaxson runs over at his side and Leigha smirks at me before following them, throwing knifes at the demons that get close. I glance up to see Dabriel fighting with an angel, and I catch a glance at his face, recognising him from the meal.

"What's Dabriel's brother's name?" I ask Atti, who is looking up as well.

"Zadkiel," Atti tells me, just as Dabriel tackles Zadkiel to the ground right in front of us. They both get up quickly, both of them weapon-less from the fall.

"You got them all killed, thousands of them must have died because of you. You are their prince, and you betrayed them all. I always knew you were a selfish bastard, but this . . . this is unbelievable even for you!" Dabriel shouts as he holds Zadkiel up by his white shirt and throws him across the field.

"No! Govan did!" Zadkiel shouts back as he stands up, and Dabriel shakes his head, the cuts on his face disappearing.

"Where is Govan? What do you mean?" Dabriel asks, but his tone is so sharp, I doubt that he believes a word his brother says, and I don't blame him.

"Dead. I killed him when he told the demon king where we lived. I never told him that, I just wanted an alliance for my people," Zadkiel says and glances at me. The fear in his eyes when he sees me is clear, and it almost makes me want to attempt to kill him myself. I don't know if his words are true, but he knew the demon king couldn't be trusted. You should never make a deal with the devil. I grew up knowing that and even most humans wouldn't be stupid enough to make the decisions he did.

"They are not your people, and they will never be."

"You're not going to kill me, brother," Zadkiel laughs.

"I am, and then I'm taking my throne. I'm going to kill you for treason. I'm going to kill you because I don't believe a damn word that comes out of your mouth. I hope the Goddess forgives you when you die," Dabriel says, his words echoing around.

"It wasn't me!" Zadkiel protests, his worried eyes glancing between Dabriel and me.

"As a child, you always blamed Govad for your mistakes, and it seems like nothing has changed. You want the throne, then fight me for it!" Dabriel shouts, and calls his marks, which glow on his skin so brightly that I can barely look at him. I glance behind them both to see the battle is over, and Wyatt is walking back to us, unharmed and throws a sword each to Dabriel and Zadkiel.

"Good luck, my brother," Wyatt says as Dabriel lifts

Jaxson's green, metal sword and swings it around his hand a few times. He clearly knows how to use it.

"What is left of the angels is here to witness this fight. Whoever wins takes the throne, and as a member of the council, I decree it," Lucifer says after he flies down and lands next to me. The rest of the hundred, or so, angels stand behind Wyatt, Jaxson, and Leigha on the other side of the fight.

"Don't, you can't interfere. Believe in your mate," Atti whispers when I try to take a step forward as Dabriel smiles at me. He mouths "I love you," and I do the same. I watch as both Dabriel and Zadkiel bow low and then lift their swords.

"I remember beating you in sword lessons, you never had that skill, Dabriel," Zadkiel taunts and does some complicated show with his sword before dropping into an attack position.

"No, I just refused to kill innocent angels for fighting practise, like you did. Always trying to prove something to someone, Zadkiel. What were you looking for in the demon king?" Dabriel asks, and I watch as Zadkiel's face tightens in anger.

"Do I get your pretty, little, demon bitch to fuck when I become king? Does she come with the throne?" Zadkiel asks, and Dabriel charges at him as I hear Jaxson's wolf growl and feel Atti tighten his grip on my hand. I watch as Dabriel strikes hit after hit on Zadkiel who is only defending from the hits and not getting any of his own in. Dabriel slashes a cut across Zadkiel's leg. I watch as fear fills Zadkiel's eyes, and he tries to fly away, but Dabriel grabs his injured leg and slams him onto the ground. I watch as Dabriel lifts his sword and swings it down on Zadkiel who doesn't move as his head is cut off. The fight is quick, and it wasn't even a fight at all. There was no chance for Zadkiel; Dabriel would never have let him get away with speaking to me like that.

"King Dabriel wins," Lucifer shouts out, and Dabriel stands straighter, throwing his sword on the floor and walking over to me. Dabriel pulls me into a kiss the moment he can, and there's silence as he breaks away from me, linking our hands.

"We have a place that is safe, and we will bring back witches to bring you there. War is coming, and we need angels to help win this. We will never win this apart, now what do you say?"

"May the queen and her kings rule true," a male angel shouts out, and then the rest of the angels repeat the words.

"My Queen," Dabriel says to me gently before he kisses me once more.

82

WINTER

"You are no God," Demtra's cold-sounding voice flitters through my mind as I open my eyes and see my own bedroom, but it's from the past, when it was my grandmother's bedroom. Elissa's body is on the ground where I have a rug now, blood pouring out of her mouth and stomach. I look up to see Demtra and the demon king standing close together, just outside the door. The demon king has some kind of white ward wrapped around his body, so he can't move, and only his head is visible.

"Does it matter? Your poor, little sister is dead, all her mates are dead, and I'm going to find my daughter," the demon king sneers, and Demtra laughs.

"It does matter," she says and lifts the silver circle that opened the portal and drops it on the floor between them. The demon screams as Demtra slams a dagger into her stomach and falls to the ground, her blood slowly making its way to the silver circle. When it touches it, the blue portal opens, spreading and pulling the demon king into it as he screams but he can't move because of the white ward. There's silence as the blue portal sinks back into the silver circle, and Demtra picks it up. I try to move closer, but as usual, I can't do anything but watch.

"Only one of my blood can open it. Only my blood can close it, it

can only be closed with a death," she says, her hand glowing white over the silver ring, and it's clear that her words are a spell of some kind. That they are meant to stop anyone using it to bring the demon king back, but it's too late for that. There's only one person who can die to close it now, and that's me. There isn't anyone else with her blood left.

"No," I shout, watching as she dies, and her lifeless eyes meet mine. I glance between Elissa and Demtra, seeing them both dead and knowing all of the ancestors are dead in this castle too. So much death, and for what? For me to just open the portal and let him back in, it feels like I'm repeating the same mistakes that my family did before me. As the silence of the castle, and the death around me hits me, all I want to do is wake up, but I can't. I watch as a girl runs into the room, her brown hair is curly, and I would guess she is a vampire from how pale she is.

"Demtra, Elissa . . .," the woman says, walking slowly into the room with tears falling down her face.

"It's too late, I'm too late," the woman whispers, falling to her knees and taking the silver circle off Demtra.

"Erina," a man with curly, blond hair says as he runs into the room and stops at the sight of the bodies and Erina on her knees. I watch as she closes Demtra's eyes and stands up, holding a hand up to stop the man from walking over to her.

"We have her child, and we will keep her safe, you knew we wouldn't be able to save her Erina."

"Let's go back to Isa and your mates, it's too late." I hear them talking about my mother, as everything goes black.

"Sleepy head, time to wake up," Dabriel whispers in my ear, and I snuggle myself further into his side. For a moment, I forget everything we have to worry about and just lie with my mate, after a long night of settling angels into the castle. But, that doesn't last long as the memories of the war that is coming and the dream haunts my mind. I know it's me that has to die to stop this, there isn't any other way. How am I going to get close enough to the portal and get the demon king through it? I can't use my power like Demtra did and bind him.

"How are we going to survive this?" I whisper, looking up at Dabriel as he leans over me. The morning light casts a light around his body, and his white hair seems almost too bright to look at. He is amazing to look at, I could spend hours looking at him.

"Together. We will make it," he tells me and kisses my forehead. I push him back on the bed and climb over him as I kiss him. He groans when I deepen the kiss, and his hands slide up my back, before he shifts us on the bed until I'm underneath him, and I push down his trousers, feeling that he has nothing else on. Dabriel rips my long shirt off me and starts kissing down my neck, to my breasts and spends his time running his hands all over me before kissing me again and sliding inside me.

"Dabriel," I moan out when he moves fast, every thrust getting me closer to the edge and Dabriel shocks me by rolling us, until I'm on top. He lets me take control as I lean up and he runs his hands over me, pushing me closer. When I speed up, and he groans, I know he is close, and he rolls us once more, taking over and we finish seconds after each other only a few moments later.

"I love you, Winter," Dabriel says gently as we both get our breaths back.

"I love you too Dab, I always will."

"You sound like you're going somewhere, when there is no chance I'm letting you go," Dabriel says, and I wrap my arms around his chest as he pulls me to his side. He has no idea, I don't want to go, but I know only a death will win this war, and I won't let the past repeat itself. *My mates won't die for me.*

"Good morning, lass," Jaxson says when I walk out of the bedroom after having a long shower with Dabriel. Dabriel kisses my cheek as he shuts my bedroom door and walks down the surprisingly quiet corridor.

"Morning to you, too," I laugh as Jaxson pulls me close and kisses me.

"You're glowing a little this morning," he says.

"I had a good sleep, wolfman," I tell him, avoiding saying the wakeup call was better, and he laughs.

"I heard," he says and nods his head towards his own room which is next door to mine. I don't reply, only blush. I don't know why the thought of him hearing me and Dabriel makes me blush, but it does. *Damn, these hot mates of mine.*

"Any more dreams, lass?" Jaxson asks me, thankfully changing the subject.

"No. Nothing unusual," I reply, remembering the dream I had before the demon king took me and what my mum said about Lily, the fray queen. I need to tell everyone that they might not be helping us at all, and we need to plan for that. I know it was stupid to make that deal and I was played by that damn fairy. She used my need for a connection to my birth mum to make her seem like a friend to me, when she wasn't. It was smart, but I need to be smarter now. I have four races of people and family I want alive after this war.

"I need to speak to you, and everyone important to the

war. I have things about the war I need to tell you all," I tell him, he briefly frowns but nods.

"Come on then, there's a conference room that we use to talk," Jaxson says and links our fingers as we walk down the corridor. We pass a lot of people, and all of them bow their heads to us as we pass. It used to be weird for me, but I've grown to accept who I am now, I'm not that normal girl who wanted to be a vet. I can't be her anymore, it just isn't in my future. As we pass the different kinds of people, it's strange to see how they have adapted to living together, how they walk past each other like they would pass any normal person in the street. I think every wolf, witch, angel, and vampire here have lost a lot, and that binds people together, any kind of people. Jaxson leads me through the castle and towards the back, which I've not been to before, and we get to a set of three doors. There's a door that leads outside, but Jaxson opens one of the doors for me, and I walk in.

"I will go and get people, be right back," Jaxson says and leaves me in the massive room. The room has a giant, round table in the middle, made out of a dark wood. There are three large windows that overlook the forest, and there is a big whiteboard on the one wall. I look at the dozens of seats around the table, and the only thought that goes through my mind is the old fairy tale my mum used to tell me about Arthur and the round table. Except this isn't a fairy tale, and my mum isn't here to tell me that story anymore. A loud purr grabs my attention, and I look over to see both Jewels and Mags sitting near the windows. These two used to scare me in their real forms, with no glamours to make them look like normal house cats, but now I know they wouldn't hurt me. There's also the fact that there are far scarier things out there than two cats who love shiny things and magazines. I walk over and try not to laugh at Jewels who has one large paw on top of a familiar box. *My crown.*

"Are you keeping it safe for me?" I ask, and Jewels gives me a look that suggests I'm not getting it back. Mags walks over and pushes herself against me, and I stroke her head. Atti loves these two, they are part of him in a way. Or, that's what he has tried to explain to me. Not many familiars survived the attacks on the witches' city, or I haven't seen many around the castle. There was a polar bear that I walked past yesterday and tried not jump. Just a random polar bear walking past me, no big deal.

"After everything happens, he will need you." I tell them both, and they seem to understand as they both stare at me. I wonder how intelligent they both are as I look at them, they almost seem sad. I turn and look out the window, watching the breeze move the dozens of different trees in the forest, and the mountains you can see in the background. I don't know how far the trees go on for. They seem to stretch on and on, making them seem endless and beautiful. I look down when I hear some shuffling to see Jewels pick up the box in her large mouth and bring it over to me, dropping the box gently on my feet.

"It's time I wore this, huh?" I ask Jewels, who tilts her head to the side. I lean down and pick the box up, hearing the door open slightly, and I turn to see Milo fly into the room. Milo lands on top of the box and looks up at me.

"Hey, Milo, you look nice today. Very Robin Hood," I chuckle, seeing the strange, green leather outfit, and he even has a fake bow on his back. I will admit it's likely the cutest thing I've seen, but he has a serious face which is unusual for him.

"Crown keep you safe from blood."

"From blood? Do you mean my demon blood? Safe from the king?" I ask him, and he nods his head with a big smile replacing the frown. I wonder if it's true, but why wouldn't my mum have used it to keep herself safe? I don't have to think of the answer long because I know, but it hurts to even think it. She didn't use the crown because she gave it to my dad, for me. She let herself be taken, to keep me safe. My mum didn't want him to know about the crown because she knew it could keep me safe one day. I lift the lid and stare down at the crown; the large white crystal in the middle and the four crystals encased around it in silver. Red for the vampires, green for the wolves, black for the witches, and the white stone for the angels. I lift the crown, feeling the power spreading through me, and I hear the door open, but I can't look away from the crown as it lightly glows. It's meant for me.

"Winter," I hear someone say, but I close my eyes and place the crown on my head, feeling the power spread through me. When I open my eyes, the room is full of people. Every one of them bows their heads, except my mates who stand strong in a line by the door. They never need to bow to me, they are my equals, as I am theirs. Damn, this crown is so powerful that it floods my mind, making me want to destroy things. I glance down at my hand, seeing it glowing blue slightly and feel for my power, knowing it feels stronger for the extra boost the crown gives me.

"*Winter, we don't wear our crowns all the time because they are powerful, meant to be worn in war. They are meant to boost our powers and help us,*" Atti says gently in my mind, using his gift to appear next to me. I don't move as he takes the crown off me, and the power boost drifts away. I nod at Atti, just as he puts the crown into the box and closes it. Jewels slides between us as everyone comes further into the room and waits for me to say something.

After taking a deep breath, I say, "The crown makes

sure the demon king can't control me. I can fight him now, and I can win. My family hid this crown for me, the demon king doesn't know of its existence. It was hidden with my human mother for years and only someone of my blood could open the box. We finally have a way to win, a way to beat him."

The looks of relief around the room are clear. This has been a losing battle until now, we were just hoping for luck to win the war, but this is something else. *This gives us a chance.*

"You can't fight him alone," Atti says gently, looking down at me. I look at him before meeting everyone else's eyes in the room.

"I won't, but this is what I called you here for. Our first meeting of all the supernaturals, the first time we plan anything together. War is coming, and we need a united plan to win. There isn't any other option, so sit or leave," I say, and everyone takes a seat.

83

WINTER

"What was the reason you called us here today, Queen Winter? I have a feeling the revelation about the crown is new to you," Harold asks as everyone finally sits down, and I stand up from my seat. I look around the room at the mixture of supernaturals in here, all of them sitting side by side to plan a fight. Harold, Drake, and Leigha are here for the vampires, today. Lucinda, a man I recognise as one of her mates, and Harris are here for the shifters. Then there are three witches, one man and two older women I do not know, but I'm sure they look familiar to me. For the angels, are Gabriel, Lucifer, and a female angel with long, dark hair and black wings; she also wears a stern expression as she watches me for the answer. I clear my throat before I speak, having the eyes of so many powerful people on me is a little daunting.

"Do any of you know about the fray? The fairies? Some call them Fey," I ask, and no one says anything until one of the witches I didn't recognise puts her hand up.

"I'm sorry, I do not know your name," I say, and she stands up, bowing before she speaks.

"My name is Duzella. I was on the council for Atticus' mother, and she was a true queen, as well as loyal friend. I was kept in the dungeons until Atticus took the throne, like he always should have. My loyalty is to our king, the rightful heir and the rightful new Queen."

"Thank you, Duzella, my mother spoke kindly of you often," Atti says with a sad smile directed at Duzella.

"I've heard stories of the fray, the ones who live in a dimension next to ours. They say the fray cross over when the wards between worlds are weak, to cause havoc. There were many books on the fray in the royal libraries of the witches. Unfortunately, I only read a few, but I will ask around the surviving witches and see if anyone read more than I did. I only saw them as fairy tales, I'm afraid," Duzella tells me.

"Thank you, that would be highly appreciated. Let it be known, the fray are a very real race, with a very real world," I reply.

"The plants tell me the fray are not to be trusted, that they only bring sorrow. Their world is connected to ours, with portals only fray can see. The plants told me about the portals but nothing else," Lucinda tells me. I nod at her and give her a friendly smile. I haven't had time to speak to Lucinda, but I did watch her in training the other day. She was teaching sword skills to some teenagers, they looked terrified of her by the end of the day. Well, except Freddy, Josh and Mich, who loved it. They are all amazing fighters, and it's clear they have been training since they were little, with the way they fought. A clearing of someone's throat makes me come back to the present and remember what I was going to say.

"I apparently can dream call, a demon power I have.

It's a variation of the demon king's power to control his own blood. My mother was rumoured to be able to control people, but I can only control bringing blood relatives into my dreams. I dream called the Queen of the fray by accident, her name is Lily, or that's what she told me. But, it seems like she played me for a fool by making me believe she was friends with my mother," I say, and Wyatt frowns as I look down at him.

"Just before I was taken and controlled by the demon king, I had a dream. In this dream, my mother, Elissa, and Demtra were there." There's hushed whispers following my words. "They told me about how Lily is no friend of my mother's like I was told, and how she cannot be trusted."

"How does that affect us all, Queen Winter?" Lucinda asks me.

"It's just Winter, no need for the title every time we speak. We have a lot of discussions to be made," I say, and my mates chuckle a little. I hold in the urge to kick one of them under the table.

"I made a promise with the Queen of Fray. I promised to hand over a half-fray child that is in this world, in exchange for soldiers and weapons on the day of war," I say, and there are more whispers around the room following my words. I wait for someone to say something, knowing that all my mates know of this already, so it's no shock to them. It is a shock that the fray has tricked me, and the anger written all over each of their faces says it to me. They are as mad as I am.

"It sounds like an easy enough promise, and I don't see how she will get herself out of it," Lucifer says.

"But, I disagree, mate. The child part is easy, the offer she made is not. There is always a way around what you promise in a deal. If the fray are not be trusted, then we can expect them to betray us," the woman next to Lucifer says.

"I don't trust her. I have no idea if those soldiers will betray us, but I know we need to be prepared if they do," I say, and there's silence around the room for a long time as we think about it. I don't know how she is going to betray me, but I just remember my mother's panicked look when I told her I had made a deal with Lily. She wouldn't have wasted her time warning me otherwise.

"Right we need a plan, no more waiting around and training," Wyatt says, and there's quiet agreements around the room.

"How are we going to win this war?" Jaxson asks no one specifically, but all of us.

"How many of us are there for starters? Let's talk numbers." Atti asks as he stands up and goes over to the white board. I watch as he gets a marker off the side and opens it.

"We did a head count, and not including women and children, we have nine thousand and twelve," the vampire who spoke before says, and I feel a sharp pain at the thought of how many have died to get us here. So, so many are lost.

"We have to take into account that it takes at least two of us to kill one. We can get lucky, but we don't have the weapons we know the demon king's army has."

"What is the weapon count? The pack doesn't need weapons, remember that," Jaxson asks, reminding us how the wolves are weapons themselves.

"Neither do witches, not really. Most witches have element powers enough to fight," Atti says. His point is true.

"Okay . . . we have no idea how big his army is, but I'm guessing he has at least ten thousand, if not more, turned humans from Paris, alone. We know he has two dragons, and they will be able to fly in," Atti says and writes this on the board.

"Why can they fly in? In the witches' city, the ward had to be broken to let them in."

"I figured this out last night," Atti gives me a worried look, "the wards are always weaker on a solstice. It interferes with them somehow, and I forgot about it. It means the dragons might be able to get through easily."

"Dragon," Milo says, flying off from the window and sitting on the table.

"Dragons. There will be two of them. How do we kill them?" Atti asks Milo.

"Yes, dragon Milo," Jaxson says.

"I will call dragon," Milo says and flies off towards the door. I shake my head at him, having no idea what he is going on about. We really need to work on making full sentences with him some time.

"We need help, and I doubt the humans will help us with this war, not after Paris," I finally say into the silent room.

"I know a place with supernatural people who may help us because the demons will be after them, too, but a warning, My Queen," Lucifer says, "They might just as easily betray us, this is why I never wanted to tell anyone about them."

"Who?" I ask him.

"My son is half angel, and they came to me once, asking if I wanted to give my son to them to protect. They claimed to have thousands of refugees and half's that are hidden," Lucifer says.

"We cannot trust a load of halflings, my Queen and Kings. I've heard of these people, and they will betray you all," Gabriel says.

"Be careful, my son is a half, and I will rip your throat out if you say another word about them," Wyatt snaps, his sentence followed by the wolves' light, warning growls. I place a hand on Wyatt's shoulder.

"We need help, or it doesn't matter whose blood we have. It doesn't matter if we are halfs, if we are full bloods, or even human, we will all die the same way. The demon king doesn't care what blood we have, to him we are all dead already, and this is just a game. I suggest we stop acting like children and win the big game," I tell the room of supernaturals, who watch me with fear and hope in their eyes.

"Wise words, My Queen, I am sorry for speaking out of turn," Gabriel says and bows his head.

"Our Queen is right. It doesn't matter anymore. We all have family and children we want to keep safe and alive, and we need help to do that," Dabriel says, his sentence hanging around the now silent room.

"Where can we find these people?" Atti asks, leaning over me on the table, his chest brushing against my back. I have to resist the urge to lean back into him with all the eyes of the people in here on us.

"They said you call for them in your mind, they have a witch who listens out for calls about halfs. I can get Josh to call for them, and then I will explain," Lucifer says.

"That must be one hell of a powerful witch," Atti comments, and he has a point. I've never seen even Atti use that amount of power.

"The man and woman who came to see me, were very powerful. They put a ward around us while we spoke and then just disappeared," Lucifer says.

"Like how witches move?" I ask.

"No. With witches you can see them, a glimmer or something. Supernaturals can always tell when a witch uses their power. This was different, and the people that I saw, I believed were an angel and a vampire, anyway," he says. I can't tell much, but that might be because I never really look.

"Freddy, my nephew, is powerful. Far more than I've ever seen any child," Jaxson says.

"I believe mixing our blood makes us more powerful, stronger," Dabriel comments, and a few people nod. My eyes meet with Leigha's across the room, but she only looks at me for a second before looking at Harris. The look says everything, she wants it to be okay for wolves and vampires to mix. She loves him.

"Call for them, tell them the new kings and queen want to make a deal for help. We want to meet," I tell Lucifer, who nods.

"I can't call from here, but I can from the local town. I will go there now with Josh."

"I will take you and protect you," Atti says before I can even offer to send someone to go. I don't like the idea of Lucifer or Josh going outside the castle right now.

"I'm coming, too. Freddy wouldn't forgive me if his new best friend got hurt," Wyatt says, standing up as well.

"I should come," I say, and both Atti and Wyatt shake their heads.

"No, the crowning for Dabriel is in two days, and important. I know Alex has a dress she needs you to try on," Atti says, and I groan, looking around for Alex but not seeing her. I dread to know what kind of dress she has planned.

"We will meet the day after the crowning to plan for war. Every person who is going to fight, needs to be training. Working together," Atti says firmly and walks out with Lucifer and Wyatt following.

"Soon you will be my Queen, officially," Dabriel says once everyone other than Jaxson has left.

"Erm . . . I want to say I'm looking forward to it, but I don't want to know what dress Alex has planned," I say, and he laughs.

"Dabriel, I need a word," Harris says, poking his head around the door.

"Hey Harris," I say, and he smiles.

"Hey, Win, but I'm serious, two of your angels are fighting, and it's not good. We have stopped them, but they are talking about the laws of females or something," Harris says with a worried look, and then we hear a loud bang outside the room, followed by the sound of glass smashing.

"Be right back," Dabriel says and kisses me gently before walking out. I look down at Jaxson, who pats his lap, and I move so I'm sitting on him.

"That right there, was a Queen I'm extremely proud of," he tells me, and I laugh.

"I thought I was being a little too bossy," I say, hoping I wasn't, but I know they need to get over their silly traditions and hate for halfs. Things have to change now.

"It was a major turn on, if you want to know," Jax says, leaning closer and trailing his lips down my jaw.

"Oh yeah, I can tell," I say, moving a little on his lap and feeling how hard he is. Jaxson laughs before he picks me up and lays me down on the table, kissing me, pressing his body into mine. Jaxson seems to have as much urgency as me, as we quickly remove all our clothes and he thrusts into me, capturing my moans with a kiss.

"Best be quiet, lass, we wouldn't want someone to walk in," Jaxson says with a slight growl before he does everything he can to make sure I can't stay quiet.

84

WINTER

"What's this?" I ask as I walk into my bedroom after a long day of training and then helping some of the angels move into their new rooms. It's been difficult to move them in, but surprisingly, the witches, wolves, and even the older vampires helped. They seemed to have some kind of change when we turned up with the thousand, or so, angels and told everyone they were moving in.

"Girls night. Everything is so serious, and well, I think we could use a relaxing night in," Alex says as I look around to see her, Katy, and Leigha sitting in front of the fire which is lit. There is a movie on pause on the TV, and I try not to laugh as I see Milo sat on my bed, a selection of chocolate surrounding him. The little demon looks more than happy, and his green outfit has been exchanged for some duck pyjamas. I have no idea where he is getting these clothes.

"And Milo? Milo isn't a girl," I say as I slip my shoes off and walk over, sitting in between Alex and Katy.

"Milo is, well, Milo. He saw the snacks, and here we

are," Katy says as she picks up the bowl of popcorn and hands me it.

"I do not blame him one bit," I say, and we all look over at Milo who burps loudly and grins at us all with a chocolate-covered face. We all can't help but laugh, but Milo doesn't notice as he continues eating away.

"The demon is cute, but where does he get the outfits from?" Leigha comments, thinking exactly what I am.

"I don't know," Alex shrugs.

"Milo come here a sec," I shout over, and he looks between me and the chocolate. I can see it's a difficult choice, but he does get up and fly over. Milo lands on my lap, and I try to wipe some of the chocolate off his clothes.

"We wondered where you got your outfits from." I ask him, and he nods.

"Prime," he says, and I frown at him. *Prime?*

"Oh my God, it makes so much sense now." Alex says, and I look over at her in confusion as she glares at Milo. He looks down, but I see the little smirk.

"Okay, so I have Amazon Prime, and my account kept saying I was buying Build a Bear outfits. Dozens of outfits. Now, I haven't had time to think about it but . . .," she drifts off as we both look at Milo and start laughing.

"Man delivers to woods," Milo says proudly, and I just don't want to think about the poor person who delivered packages to the woods. Or, if Milo actually accepted the package. I can just imagine the poor man's face when a tiny demon with blue hair appears out of the woods to sign for the delivery. I bet the man dropped the packages and ran off.

"You even bought a Minions outfit, I mean what?" Alex says, looking up from her phone.

"Yellow?" Milo asks and then flies off back to my bed and the safety of the food. We all chuckle as we watch him start eating, and Alex mumbles about closing her Amazon account somehow and wondering how he got the password in the first place.

"The demon is lovely, I like him and want to see him in the minion outfit," Katy laughs around a small cake bar she is eating.

"He is, well, compared to the rest of his race," I say.

"Well, come on, you're part demon and pretty lovely, Win," Alex knocks my shoulder, and I drop some popcorn on the floor.

"Look what you did," I laugh and pick a piece up and throw it at her. She only laughs and catches it before eating it.

"Where are all the guys, then?" I ask her.

"Wyatt wanted to talk to them all anyway, so it was easy to convince them to leave us for a night," Alex shrugs.

"So, what are we watching?" I ask.

"It's called *Bad Mom*, it's brilliant," Alex says, and I smirk at her as I glance at her stomach.

"I seriously hope you're not watching this movie for tips?" Leigha says, but there's a small smile as she leans back.

"You're pregnant?" Katy asks in shock, and we all look at her.

"You didn't know?"

"Nope, I missed that memo," Katy laughs, "But, congratulations, you'll make an awesome mum."

"Thank you," she says with a smile, sliding her hand into mine and squeezing it before pressing play.

"Shh," I whisper to Leigha as she stands up, and we look down at Alex and Katy who are sleeping on the rug after falling asleep during the film. Milo is sleeping on Katy's stomach, and I gently walk towards the door with Leigha. I get why they are all tired, with the training and the stress at the moment, they aren't the only ones tired these days.

"Can I have a word?" Leigha asks as I open the door for her. I knew she wouldn't want to sleep here when she got up after the movie. She is at training stupidly early in the morning these days. I quietly shut the door behind me, and we walk down the corridor and away from the rooms. We come out of the corridor to the main level, and it's empty. Leigha stops near the bannister to the stairs, and you can see all the way down.

"What's up?" I ask her, and she frowns at me, pushing her long hair over her shoulder.

"He is coming any minute now," she says, and I just lift my hands in the air as a response just as I see Wyatt coming up the stairs with Freddy and a familiar, older vampire.

"Hey," I say as Wyatt gets to me and gently kisses me.

"Winter, you remember Harold?" Wyatt introduces me as Harold and Freddy come over. Freddy hugs me and moves away as I offer a hand out to Harold to shake.

"Queen Winter, it is lovely to see you again and looking so well," Harold says and bows his head as he shakes my hand.

"It's good to see you too, but what's going on here?" I ask, because it's a little suspicious us all meeting in the middle of the night like this.

"We are crowning Wyatt tonight and Freddy as heir, in secret. There is a lot of disruption in the castle and with our people, I believe it would make more sense to have the crowning private, and we do not have the crown to give Wyatt anyway," Leigha tells me as she walks over.

"What about Jaxson, Atti, and Dabriel?" I turn and ask Wyatt. I do agree with him in a way. The angel crowning is coming up, and there is already enough worry throughout the castle. Wyatt being crowned isn't the issue, it's the fact the vampire crown is on the head of the demon king, and Wyatt is naming a half breed as his heir. There are rules, I'm sure, and it makes everything easier to do in secret.

"They are setting it up," he tells me, but I already guessed he wouldn't keep this from my other mates. They are like brothers to him and, really, the only people we need there.

"Drake?" I ask as Wyatt places his hand on my back, and Freddy takes my other hand as we walk down the stairs.

"There too, but no one else. Leigha, Drake, and Harold are my new council of the vampires and the only ones I need there today."

"Aren't there usually four on the council?"

"Yes, I'm naming Freddy as the fourth."

"You can't do that," Freddy protests, and the statement echoes around the stairs. Leigha glares back at us and places a finger on her lips to suggest we all be quiet.

"I can, and I will. You are the prince of the vampires and heir to the throne. A seat in the council will teach you what you need to rule one day."

"I might not even rule, if Winter has a child, they will be heir to all the races," Freddy says, and Wyatt glances at me with a strange look. He almost looks sad, and it confuses me. *Why would he be sad about the idea of us having a child in the future?*

"No one knows the future, son. For now, will you do

this?" he asks. Freddy doesn't say a word as we walk down the final set of stairs. We follow Leigha and Harold down one of the corridors, and they open a door, walking in when Freddy stops.

"I will do this, but it means nothing," Freddy says, not looking us in the eyes as he walks in the room. Wyatt catches my arm as I go to walk in and pulls me to him. I gladly slide my hands around his neck, and he gently kisses me.

"I remembered that I never asked if you want to be my queen?" he says, and I chuckle a little.

"Wyatt, I chose you the moment you kissed me, all the way back then. It's me and you," I tell him, and he nods, resting our heads together for a while as we look into each other eyes.

"I'm lucky to have met you, Winter, to be part of your life," he whispers and then steps away from me as I hear footsteps next to us. I look up to see Jaxson leaning against the door and watching us.

"Are you coming in?" he asks with a smirk, and I roll my eyes at him.

"Coming, wolfman, so impatient," I reply, making him laugh as Wyatt slides his hand into mine, and we walk into the room. The room is a pretty basic one, with some chairs around the room, and it's been recently painted by the smell in here. Harold is standing at the front of the room with Freddy, Leigha, and Drake at his sides. Jaxson joins my mates who are standing near the back of the room, and I smile at them all as Wyatt walks us in. We stop in front of Harold.

"I usually speak the Latin or French version of this, but this time I will use English for the new queen," Harold says gently, and I give him a grateful smile. It would make no sense to me otherwise, and I could be swearing to protect a race of pumpkins and not know it.

"Please bow as I say the ancient words," Harold says, and I copy Wyatt as he kneels and bows his head.

"The council has been chosen, and the chosen have come here to crown their new king and his queen. Royal vampire council crowns the new king. Only death shall break the vow you will now make. Your souls are now joined and here to protect the vampire race. May the vampires also protect their new king and queen."

"I vow to protect," Wyatt says, and there's silence until someone clears their throat. Crap, I think I'm meant to say that too.

"I vow to protect," I say and there's silence until I feel a finger under my chin and I lift my head to see Wyatt standing in front of me.

"This ancient book has the blood of every king and queen that has ruled. You must cut your finger and place your finger on the book," Harold explains as he comes over with a very old-looking book. *It's a weird thing, but who am I to judge?*

"Okay," I say and watch as Wyatt pulls a dagger out of his suit jacket and cuts his finger quickly. Harold opens the book; one page has two bloody finger prints on it and another language written around the prints. I would guess it's Wyatt's parent's names and their blood. I watch as Wyatt presses his finger on the book and then hands me the dagger. I shake my head and push the dagger into his hand.

"I trust you to do it," I say and hold out my hand for him. Wyatt keeps eye contact with me as he takes my hand, only looking down for a second as he cuts my finger, and I try not to wince at the sharp pain. I quickly place my finger next to where Wyatt had placed his, and Wyatt takes my hand off the book, putting my cut finger into his mouth. I have to admit it's pretty sexy, despite the room full of people watching us.

"Later," I mouth silently as he lets my finger go, and he winks at me in response.

85

WINTER

"I seriously doubt you could have chosen a bigger dress, Alex," I say, and she chuckles as she looks at me. The dress has a massive, black skirt at the bottom, with a white, frost pattern laced down the dress on one side, and the top part is all white lace. Alex put my hair into a bun that is on one side, and there is a little curled bit left out that shapes my makeup-filled face. I don't usually wear this much, but the smoky eyes and pale lipstick does look pretty. The thoughts of my long night with Wyatt flash through my mind; the things he whispered in my ear as he was inside me. The way he held me in his arms all night afterwards, last night was perfect. Only when I left Wyatt's room this morning to get dressed in my own, I didn't expect to walk into the selection of dresses and madness that Alex had turned my bedroom into. The dress is every bit perfect for the crowning of the angel king and queen, well me and Dabriel. Alex couldn't have chosen a better dress for me to wear, and even being in it is giving me some confidence about today. The black represents the dark angels and the white lace, the light angels. I want us all to be united, and this dress shows off that. I love that I didn't even have to tell Alex this, she just knew.

"This one isn't as tight as the red one I made you wear last time," she says, reminding me of the night I was stupid enough to let the vampire king use me to open that portal. The dress was amazing, though. I look over at Alex as she straightens her long, red hair, and memories of growing up with Alex flash through my mind. I remember the first time I met her and sharing my ice cream. I remember holding her as her parents hadn't fed her in two days and giving her my lunch before taking her back to my house for the first time. Once I told my mum, she adored and looked after Alex as much as I did. Alex was always more of a sister to me, and despite the fact the demon king has killed all my family, I still have Alex. I will fight to the very end to see her live through this war.

"You're my best friend, you know that?" I tell her and walk over, giving her a hug. Alex has on a simple, white dress with little, black flowers up the sides. *Simple, but stunning.* Her red hair brings that little bit of colour to her outfit, as well as the red, jewelled necklace she has on. I don't recognise it, but it's lovely.

"Yes, I think so, although I miss the days where we planned our nights out and not how to survive a war," she replies.

"I miss those, too, but I think this was always planned for us. All of it," I say and place my hand on her still small stomach.

"What did Drake say?" I ask her, and she smiles at me. I haven't had much time to speak to her alone about everyone's reactions to the pregnancy. I know everyone knows but not how she told them.

"He was over the moon and told everyone. I've never seen him this happy," she tells me with a bright, happy smile. Alex is almost glowing recently, with what I'm sure are pregnancy hormones.

"Want to know what the army brat said?" Alex asks me, referring to Leigha.

"Something about locking you somewhere safe, I bet," I reply, knowing what Leigha is like.

"Yep. She insists on training some poor girl to protect me and locking me away," Alex says. *It doesn't surprise me one bit.*

"My mates all say she is amazing at training, that all the people respect and listen to her. Jaxson thinks it's best to let her and Harris work together permantly to train everyone. They are both very good," I say.

"Only because they are scared of her and too scared to say anything about her in case either Harris or Drake hear them. Both of them are seriously protective of Leigha," Alex chuckles, and I remember Leigha training me, I was scared of her, too.

"I think Harris is good for Leigha. He has that playfulness that is good for her. She is too serious on her own," I reply.

"Like how your mates are good for you. Each one of them. I don't know, it's like they make you complete and happy."

"It's because I love them. It's that simple." I say gently, thinking of them as I smooth my dress down, and there's a knock at the bedroom door.

"Come in," I shout.

"It's time," Lucifer says as he walks in. Lucifer has a long, black cloak on, with dark-black clothes on underneath, and there is a clip with double wings holding the cloak together near his neck. His large, black wings fold in on themselves, so I can only see the tips of them as he stands waiting for us. There is only him and Gabriel left from the council, and it's custom for a council member to walk the new queen to the soon to be crowned king. This was explained last night by Dabriel before he left me with Wyatt and went off to play cards and have a few drinks with the other guys.

"Good luck, but you don't need it. You're every bit the queen they need, you're kind, strong, powerful, and most of all, you're meant for this," Alex tells me and walks out as I take a deep breath. She is right, but it's hard to convince myself of it.

"Let's go," I tell Lucifer as I walk over, and he offers his elbow, so I link my arm in his.

"I wouldn't have chosen a better queen for us, even if you are no angel. Only angels have sat on the throne for many years. But, times are changing, we as supernaturals are never going to forget this war or the fact it's brought us all together," Lucifer says, and I laugh a little.

"Have I ever told you that the Goddess shows me the past in my dreams sometimes?" I ask him.

"No, you have not,"

"In the past, all supernaturals lived together in the castle. In peace," I say, knowing that this has worked for the supernaturals in the past, and it will work again. We just need to put our differences aside and work towards our future.

"Can I ask you a favour?" he asks as we walk down the corridor, and he stops us at the top of the stairs. The stairs are lined with flowers, all white, and have been tied to the bannister. Someone has even tied fairy lights around the bannister in-between the flowers and the effect is amazingly beautiful.

"You can ask, but I can't guarantee I will be able to help," I reply, knowing as a queen my word is not something I can just hand out to anyone. I've come a long way since I first met everyone, and since then, there is a lot of responsibility resting with me.

"My son Josh, is a half and what he is . . . well I don't want anyone ever knowing. Especially, not him," Lucifer tells me, and I look up at him.

"Why not?" I ask, because I don't believe in anyone not knowing who they are, what they are. My own past and who I am was kept from me, and that nearly killed a lot of people.

"Because it would destroy him," he tells me, his dark eyes watching me, and I don't know what to say to him.

"Did you love his mother?" I finally ask.

"No, my sister loved his father," he tells me, and it starts to make some sense now. I know angels only mate to one person, so having a child with another would have to have happened after he was mated. I know this does happen because of what Dabriel told me of his father and his siblings.

"So, he isn't yours?" I ask gently.

"No, but no one can ever know that. My mate, well she dislikes Josh but won't ever tell the secret of where he came from. She was bound by my sister before my sister died in childbirth. Angel births are difficult to survive, and with who his father is . . .," his sentence drifts off when some witches in cloaks walk past us, stopping to bow at me before going down the stairs.

"What is it you wish from me?" I ask him gently when they are gone, understanding that this is big for him to tell me. I have the feeling he never told anyone other than his mate this.

"If I die in this war, protect him as your own. Tell him that his parents are both alive but in a place no one can return from. That they could only be together that way."

"But, you said his mother died?"

"She did," he tells me, and I just don't understand what he is saying. If she is dead, how is she with her partner?

"That doesn't make sense," I say.

"I can't, I can't tell you anymore . . .," he says firmly, but the slight quiver in his tone suggests he wants to tell me more.

"You're blood bound," I say, realising straight away why he can't tell me. This must have been what it was like for Jaxson not to say anything about Freddy.

"I will protect him, if I can," I tell Lucifer, who takes a deep breath at my words.

"And, I will protect you on the battlefield and your mates, My Queen," he says and nods his head at me before starting to walk us down the stairs. When we get to the bottom, there is a mixture of people standing around, all in white or black with their heads bowed. Some in cloaks, and some are in wolf form. The very presence of all these supernaturals, standing together to crown the angel king and queen is amazing. We walk down the path way in the middle of them, which is sprinkled with white rose petals on the floor, as I look around the entrance hall. We eventually get outside, where I see my mates all standing together, one after the other next to an archway of white and black roses. My eyes run over all of them. Wyatt, Jaxson, and Atti have black shirts and black trousers on, with white roses pinned on the pockets. Dab has a white shirt and black trousers, with a black rose pinned on him. They all look extremely handsome as they stand there and all I can think of is how good they look without their clothes, too. After getting my hormones in check, we walk down the pathway and Lucifer lets go of my arm, handing it to Dabriel.

Dabriel pulls me close to him, whispering as he brushes his lips against my ear, "You look so beautiful, Winter."

I blush, and he smiles as he pulls away from me to face the old angel standing under the arch. I walk forward with Dabriel, remembering this angel is called Gabriel and the last light angel on the council to survive the battle. I haven't spoken to him much, just a little with Dabriel, but he comes across as firm. The angel has long, grey hair, which I'm sure was white when he was younger and large wings, much like Dabriel's. His light-purple eyes watch me and he smiles as he starts to speak.

"Thank you to everyone that came here today to witness the crowning of the King of the Angels, and his Queen. I never expected to crown a king like this, with not only angels, but witches, wolves, and vampires to watch. I feel this is how we will survive from now on, united together against a war that threatens us all. We need our royals to win this, for it's what the prophecy told us, and the only way I feel we will win," he says, and cheers follow his words through the crowd. Gabriel walks over and picks a crown out of a box that a male angel holds behind the arch before walking back over. Dabriel lets go of my hand to kneel down and lower his head.

"I crown King Dabriel, King of the Angels."

The cheers that follow Dabriel being crowned are so loud I'm sure the world can hear them and seem to go on for a long time as Dabriel stands up, his purple eyes glowing. The crown is just as powerful as the others, with white, almost silver stones inside the silver swirls. I pull my gaze away when Dabriel links our hands and holds them up in the air.

"Queen Winter!" Dabriel shouts, and then everyone shouts my name back, the sound filling the outside. The angel ceremony is far simpler than the vampire one, the crown seems to be important to them. I look over to see Jaxson and Atti with their crowns on and the absence of Wyatt's crown is noticeable. I don't feel you need a crown to rule, you can rule on your own.

"We will win this," Dabriel whispers as he lowers our hands and slides his other hand onto the back of my head, kissing me. I hope he will win this too, and that the price isn't too high to do so.

86

WINTER

"I should come," I hear Freddy say, a slight growl slipping in with the words. I walk around the corner, and see Freddy arguing with both Jaxson and Wyatt. I have to admire Freddy, he is standing up to both of them, holding his ground. There isn't a lot of people who would do that at his age, but also, he is going to be a handful when he is older.

"It's not safe for you," Wyatt responds firmly, his hands on his hips as he stares down his son.

"It's not safe for Winter, but she gets to go. You need me there; I'm a half, and they might actually talk to you if they know you look after me and don't care," Freddy points out, making a valid point. I don't want to take him with us. It will be dangerous, but I know we could easily protect him with all of us there. Not to mention he can look after himself, too. We need to convince these people, we will need them to save everyone and stand a chance.

"He has a point," I say walking over, and they both look down at me. I hate being short sometimes, next to all these tall guys. Freddy is even growing and is now about my height.

"Not happening, lass," Jaxson says, shaking his head. *Stubborn wolf.*

"I will protect him, so will you and Wyatt. Atti and two other witches are coming as well," I point out. It only takes seconds for any of the three witches coming to bounce Freddy out of there.

"I'm not using my nephew as bait," Jaxson says, shaking his head at me.

"I wouldn't ever do that, Jaxson." I snap back, and his face drops,

"Sorry. I just can't lose him, not after everything, and my wolf doesn't like it," Jaxson says. I walk over to him and rest my head on his shoulder. I get it, everything is beyond stressful at the moment.

"I'm suggesting that I've seen Freddy fight, and all of you are very powerful. There is no way we would let anything happen to him, but we need these halfs to talk to us. Freddy may be the best chance. No offense, but all of you guys are scary and intimidating. Bringing Freddy may just help us," I tell him, and he looks at Freddy, who has a long sword strapped to his back and the same determination on his face that his dad and uncle always have. I don't want to take him, but I don't think we have much of a choice. The war is five days away, only five. Every time I go to sleep, I beg for a dream, or for my family to come to me, but it's not working. I haven't spoken to Elissa or my mum since the dream before I was taken. I need to talk to them because I know the prophecy is coming true, and the price is my life. I need to be certain it's me that is paying this price. I feel more than ever, like I'm missing something.

"Fine, but you stay by a witch and my side the whole time," Wyatt says, with Jaxson nodding in agreement.

"Awesome," Freddy says with a big grin aimed at me, before running over to Atti and the two witches chatting by the door.

"You ready for this?" Wyatt asks as he comes closer and holds my hand. I look over at him, seeing the vampire I love, but he looks beyond hot today with his sword on his back and the suit he has on.

"To try and convince a load of people that have hidden from us, for years, to fight for me? Yeah sure. It's just like convincing Alex that salad is a real food," I say, making him and Jaxson laugh. I've never actually seen Alex eat a salad, she doesn't need to, apparently. I know if I didn't force myself to eat a salad at times, I would be huge.

"I heard you're going to be an auntie," Wyatt says gently.

"So are you, you know Drake sees you as a brother," I remind him.

"Maybe," Wyatt says, but a flash of pain flies over his face. It's gone quickly when he blanks his expression. I go to ask him what happened there when Atti distracts me.

"Time to leave," Atti says as he walks over and wraps his arms around my waist, kissing my cheek. I laugh as I feel him use his power and move us. When we reappear, it's at an old building in the middle of a forest I've never been to. Atti lets me go slightly when Jaxson and Wyatt appear with one witch and Freddy with another. The witches have their hoods up, so I don't know who they are.

"Why here?" I ask again as I look around. Atti said the halfs never came to meet them when Josh called them. They placed a message asking to meet and an address in their minds. It really bothered Atti because he couldn't see where they were. I think he is just curious about how powerful these halfs are.

"It was part of their agreement. We couldn't exactly

say no, as it would be a sign that we don't trust them," Atti tells me, and I agree. He has a point, but I still don't like where they have chosen to meet us. I jump when a ward appears around us and the house. It's white and large enough to spread up to the trees, but I can't see who is making it. My mates move closer to me, just before the door to the house is opened.

"You are right not to trust strangers, witch King," a voice says, and I watch as three people come out from inside the house. One is an angel, with dyed-blonde hair and large, black wings. She has on a mini, black top and worn jeans, showing off her stomach. She is extremely beautiful, but the slightly cruel smirk on her lips suggests I shouldn't trust her. The other two are sisters, I would guess, with brown hair and matching, blue eyes. Atti told us that someone called Mila and Soobeen would be meeting us, they told them the names in the brief conversation they had. I couldn't tell the twins apart, not as I look between them. They both have worn tops on, and leggings underneath. The main thing I can see is how thin they are. It's not a natural thinness either, their cheeks are too hollow, and I have a feeling they aren't well.

"I'm guessing one of you is Soobeen and the other Mila?" Jaxson asks, stepping closer to Freddy when all three of them ignore us to stare at him. Freddy holds his head high, meeting each one of their gazes and doesn't show any fear. It's really good to see him so strong with everything that is planned for us.

"The rumours are true, sister, they really do have a half in the royal family," one of the sisters says, and the other one nods. It's extremely difficult to tell them apart at this point.

"I'm Soobeen, and this is my sister Mila. This is Chesca," Soobeen introduces her, and her eyes lock with mine for a moment before she looks back at Freddy. I glance at the angel called Chesca, who gives me a small smirk as she tilts her head to the side and then looks at my mates. When she winks at Jaxson, my power automatically comes out, and I step forward without realising I've done so.

"Please ignore Chesca, she is half succubus demon, and flirting is in her blood. She won't touch your mates, Queen Winter," Mila tells me firmly, a worried look crossing her face. It doesn't surprise me that the angel is a demon of some sorts.

"Winter, it's okay," Atti whispers and puts an arm around my waist as I try to calm my powers and myself down. All I can think about is ripping the angel's wings out for flirting with my mate.

"Behave," Soobeen tells Chesca who sighs but looks away from us all to look at her nails.

"I will speak to the Queen and the half boy, alone," Soobeen says, and Jaxson's growl is all that needs to be said on the matter.

"Give us a minute," I say loudly, and Soobeen nods at me, understanding that I need to talk to them about this. We all walk back off into the woods a little, close to the ward.

Jaxson says, "There is no fucking way I'm letting you and Freddy go in there alone."

"We don't have much choice. I don't want to, but I'm not weak, and I saw the fear in their eyes when my powers came out. I don't think we are a threat to them. Look at how they are dressed, how thin they all are. I think they need our help as much as we need theirs."

"I will protect her, too," Freddy says and comes to stand next to my side.

"They have fifteen minutes, and then I'm coming to get

you." Atti pulls me closer to him, kissing my cheek. "Until then, I can speak in your mind," Atti whispers the end part just for me.

"I don't like it," Jaxson says.

"Neither do I, but I trust Winter and Freddy. I've seen them both fight and know they can do this," Wyatt says, and I see Freddy give him a strange look. It almost looked respectful.

"At the end of the day, if they kill me, the demon king wins, and they will never be safe because you would all kill them. The demon king doesn't want me dead, so even if they are working for him, they won't kill me. I will shout in my mind for you if I sense the demon king, but I don't think he is stupid enough to fight you all out in the open like this," I say, knowing it's true.

"I would love to fight the bastard," Atti says.

"That's the point, he won't fight you alone. He is a coward that hides behind his army. If he wanted to fight you, he could have done so easily in the castle, but he didn't, he came for me when I was alone," I say, and Jaxson pulls me into a hug when I step away from Atti.

"Fifteen minutes," he says and kisses me gently. Wyatt and Atti nod at me as I hold Freddy's hand and walk over to the sisters and Chesca. The closer I get to them, the more I feel like I can trust them for some reason. I don't get why it is, and it's not something I can explain to my mates. *There's just something.*

"You have fifteen minutes," I tell them, and Mila nods at me in response. They all look between each other for a second, but I see it.

"Sure," she says and walks into the old ruined house. The house looks like it could be blown away any minute, and the inside isn't any better. There is nothing inside, other than a burnt-out fireplace and a massive, red rug that's covered in dirt and burnt in places. It stinks of smoke in here, making me wonder if there was a fire recently. I watch as Soobeen pushes the old rug across the floor, and Mila opens a hidden door in the floor. The loud creaking of the door is the only sound, and it's eerily quiet.

"This place looks like the Shrieking Shack," Freddy whispers.

"It does," I whisper back, wondering why the place looked familiar to me.

"This isn't a book about witches, little boy," Chesca snaps before walking down the steps in the trap door.

"I know," Freddy says but smirks at me. I try not to laugh at his attitude.

"Come," Mila says and walks down the steps, with Soobeen holding the door open. I walk in first, making Freddy walk behind me, and take the steps down to the dark room below. The steps are lit up by small fires in sconces on the walls, and the steps are pure stone. There isn't anything to hold on to as I take each deep step, and it takes everything in me not to trip up. I could just imagine tripping over and crashing into Chesca in front of me. I doubt she would take it well.

"Everything okay?" Atti asks in my mind, almost making me jump and fall down the steps like I was thinking about.

"Dammit," I mutter out loud.

"Be careful, Queen Winter. The steps are difficult down here until you know how to walk down," I hear Chesca say, and the sarcasm in her voice is overwhelming.

"So far, so good," I think, but know he can't hear me, and I feel a little stupid until I remember he actually asked me a question, so it's natural to answer.

"I can hear you when you project your thoughts like that, it's a witch mating thing," Atti says, with almost a laugh.

"Then we are walking down a creepy, underground staircase, and

I'm trying not to pull the annoying angel's hair out," I tell him, and I can hear his laughter in my head for a little while as I concentrate on walking down. I feel Freddy place his hand on my back a few times, the steps are just as large for him to walk down, and it's comforting to know he is okay despite me not really being able to see him.

"Be careful," I hear Atti say, his tone gentle.

"Love you," I say back, and then there is silence, but I know he heard me, and that's enough. I bet he is telling the others about what I said. I look forward as we get to the end of the stairs from hell, and there is a clear ward. I can't see anything through the ward, despite it being clear.

"You must walk through the ward. It will not interfere with your bond and your mate hearing you," Soobeen says behind me, and I can't see her in the dark, but I feel Freddy place his hand into mine.

"If this is a trap, I will destroy you and everything else," I warn her, before turning and walking through the ward, pulling Freddy with me. When we get through, it's nothing like I would have expected. The ward is hiding a whole town underground, with lights strung across the ceiling and dozens of tents on the ground. Various people stop to stare at us and me at them. They are very different, and I can tell from one glance around that they are mainly halfs here. Some angels have white and black mixed wings, some witches' hair is mixed, too. One teenage boy stops and stares at us. His black hair has bright-blue tips that match his blue eyes. The boy looks at Freddy for a long time before smirking and running off.

"This is no trap, we want something as well, and we need to show you our life. The ward is blessed, it will only let those who mean us no direct harm through," Soobeen says as she stops next to me, and the silence of all the people who stare at us, seems to carry her words. The underground cave is amazing to look at, it is really something. I love how the lights are hung on the roof of the cave, and in the walls, there are carved steps and little caves. The only things that concern me are the tents and the amount of people that must live down here. There is no sunlight, no running water that I can see, and no plants. It isn't a great way for anyone to live.

"Then, show me," I respond, smiling kindly at her.

"We will be fine from here," Soobeen tells her sister and Chesca, who bow at us before walking away. These three must be the current leaders of the halfs. People start to move away from us when they leave, and noise seems to return to how it was before we came here.

"For too many years, we have hidden underground and away from both humans and supernaturals," she tells me. "Please let us walk as we talk," Soobeen asks me, and I nod, putting my hand on Freddy's back to lead him away from whatever he is staring at.

"Why hide from humans?" I ask her as she walks next to me. We make our way to a long path in the middle of the tents and some little make shift shops by the looks of them. I pass a group of children playing. The children can't be older than seven, and they are running around a stick in the ground. Their laughter is sweet, even to my ears.

"The humans are just as bad as supernaturals. We do have some humans here, with their half children. But then, we have a lot of half humans whose parents didn't want an unnatural child."

"'Unnatural' is not a word I would use to describe anyone half human," I say, feeling defensive because I was half human and lucky enough that my mum didn't care.

"Yes, I agree. You say this because of who you are but then everyone knows your story, Queen Winter. You were fortunate not to have powers as a child, no outward appearances that give you away. Most of our people are not so lucky and 'unnatural' is a word we hear far too often," she tells me, just as a man walks past, and I almost stop walking. The man has his mark on his face, the vines of a flower all over his forehead and also, he has fur on his arms. I don't know what he is, but he nods at us both before walking on.

"I understand," I tell Soobeen.

"Safe still?" Atti asks in my head.

"Yes, and you won't believe what is down here," I reply and follow Soobeen as she gets to a large tent. She slides inside through a flap, and I hold it open for Freddy before following myself.

"Please sit," Soobeen offers and waves a hand at three old-looking chairs seated near a fire. There isn't much in the room to look at, not that I expected much. The bed looks years old, and the furniture is the same.

"You know what we want, what we need," I start to say, and Soobeen holds a hand up.

"You should know your grandfather came to us, only a day ago," she tells me, and my blood runs cold as I stand up off the seat. Freddy pulls his sword out and moves closer to me.

"I don't see him here, now, and that's lucky for you," I respond, and she laughs.

"I wouldn't bring you here if that was so. Now, boy, put the sword away and both of you should sit down," she suggests, and I place my hand on Freddy's arm.

"It's okay," I say, sitting first, and Freddy keeps eye contact with Soobeen as he puts his sword away and sits down.

"He gave us two days to make a decision, fight with him or die. He could walk through our wards like they didn't exist, and I don't believe it was because he wished us no harm. The army of demons he brought with him told me he was never here to discuss peace."

"Not much of a decision. Knowing the demon king, he will kill you, anyway. The same deal was made with two of the angel princes, now both of them are dead and thousands of their people," I respond, and she nods. She must have known about what happened to the angels.

"We have three thousand men and women, who are strong and can fight. Mixing our blood makes some of our abilities extremely strong," she tells me.

"How many children and people that cannot fight do you have?" I ask her.

"Five hundred." She responds, and I nod. I look around the tent that has holes in it, the fire that is made from old wood and little else, they don't have much but they have been on the run so long.

"I have a suggestion," Soobeen says, and I nod, wanting to hear it.

"You will have our support, our alliance, and we will fight on your side. I will bow to you as Queen, and all your mates as our Kings." She tells me just what I wanted her to say. This is what we need.

"But?" I ask, knowing that every deal comes with a price, and she smiles.

"You make a law, a law that bans any aggression against halfs. A law that recognises halfs as a breed, and we become part of the council for supernaturals."

"How do you know about the council?"

"We know many things here. We know you have three representatives from each race. We want three on your council, it would be me, Chesca, and Mila," she tells me.

"Why don't you take your people and run? Let us deal with the war. You haven't come to us before this, and I'm confused why you have invited us now," I ask because they have been hiding throughout the supernatural wars that have already happened.

"We don't want to live like this, I don't want my people to live underground and hidden for the rest of their lives because of who they are," she tells me.

"Freddy is a half, and heir to both the shifter and vampire throne. Freddy is on the wolf council and will be attending meetings when he turns sixteen. He will also be heir to the angel and witches, unless I have a child, but then that child would be a half, anyway. I will never let the mere fact that he is a half be used against him. Things are changing already, and I feel I would be offering you little in return for your army and help. This is already going to happen, halfs will be accepted," I say firmly. I don't want to make a deal with her for something that is going to happen, anyway. That's lying to her and not how I want to be. I'm not a queen built on lies.

"You are a smart Queen and said the words I needed to hear," Soobeen says, leaning forward and tilting her head at me.

"That was a test?" I ask with a small smile. It's a smart move on her end, too.

"Yes. If there was any way you wouldn't accept your own step son, then there is no way I could trust you," she tells me. I look over at Freddy, who grins. I've never heard anyone refer to him as my step son, but I do like him being called it. I would be proud to be any kind of mum to Freddy.

"So . . . we have a deal?"

"You still want a deal for those things, despite the fact that most would happen anyway?" I ask, and she nods, holding her hand out for me.

"Winter, it's been fifteen minutes, do you need us?" Atti says.

"*No. We are making a deal now, and they can help us. I'm fine,*" I say back and feel relief down my bond with them all only a minute later. I lean forward and shake her hand.

"I will give you the places on the council and a safe home in the castle for your people. There are a lot of us living there now, but many houses in the woods. So, we will find room," I tell her, and she looks relieved as she lets go of my hand and sits back.

"Thank you, My Queen. I will move our people to your castle tonight, I hear it's the only place safe now?" she asks me.

"Until the Winter solstice. That is when the war is coming. I will be honest with you, the demon king will send his army to destroy us. It's going to be one hell of a fight," I tell her, and she nods, standing up.

"Our people have lost a lot, but there is finally hope with you on the throne. A half human, quarter demon, and quarter Goddess. Any child you may have would be more than a half could ever be. You are our hope."

"I have one more question before we leave," I ask, not standing up with her.

"Yes?" she asks me, sitting down once more when she sees the serious look I'm giving her. I know there's a chance the royal half fray child is here, and I can't be anywhere near the child. I need to make sure that part of my promise never comes true.

"Are there any half fray children here?" I ask.

"You know about fray?" she asks me, and I nod.

"One boy," she tells me, with a nervous expression.

"I need to meet him," I tell her.

"Why?" she says, and I can't miss the hostility in her tone this time. The boy must be close to her.

"I made a promise with the Queen of Fray, for her help in the war. I know I've made a mistake, but I promised to send a half fray child over to her, a royal that she said she cannot find here on earth." I tell her the whole truth, there is no point clouding the truth when it's clear the half fray boy means something to her.

"My son is the only half fray here, and he is no royal as his father told me he was a guard, but you may meet him to make sure," she says.

"I will call my sister to bring him here," she tells me, before her eyes glow white and she is silent for a little while. When her eyes return to normal, I wait a little before saying anything.

"What do you know about the fray?" I ask her, knowing that she might be able to tell us something about the help they will bring.

"I met my son's father only once, and it was a one-night stand. I don't know much about their kind, but my son has control over storms and water. I'm a vampire mixed with an angel, so that is not from me, and no, I didn't get wings when I received my powers. The fray I met had dark-blue hair and strange, blue flower-like marks down his arms. My son doesn't have those marks yet, but he is only fourteen," she tells me, knowing that most super-naturals don't get their marks until they turn sixteen. They also get their extra powers. I glance at Freddy, wondering what he will get then, if any. He is already so strong, with his immunity to silver and fast healing.

"Thank you for telling me that," I tell her, and she nods.

"I was young and foolish, he was gone before I even woke up the next day. I remember him saying something about it being the summer solstice," she tells me. It makes sense that the fray had come through the wards then.

"Did he tell you what he was?" I ask her.

"I have a gift, I can tell what someone is from simply

looking at them. When I walked into the night club, I saw him straight away. I had never seen a fray before, and he told me that he came from the Winter court of the Fray," she tells me.

"Winter court?" Freddy asks, curious like I am.

"Yes, he told me there are four courts, but not much else." I wonder if they are all seasonal. Like Winter, Autumn, Spring and Summer courts.

"Anything you can think of, I would appreciate the knowledge," I tell her. I feel like I should never have made that promise to Lily when I'm clearly blind to their world and everything in it. I shouldn't have, I should have just woken up and tried to deal with this fight on my own.

"I will send someone to bring your mates and witches in here," she tells me, and I nod at her, watching as her eyes turn that white again.

"Atti, they are sending someone to bring you all in here, we have a deal," I shout out in my mind for him to hear.

"What did you offer them?" Atti asks me.

"Nothing that I wouldn't have given them freely," I say back.

Atti chuckles in my mind as he speaks. "*That sounds like I need more of a description in a while. I love you, Winter.*"

I look over to see the flap of the tent being opened and a teenage boy coming in. It's the same boy I saw when I first passed through the ward, his blue tipped hair is easy to remember. It matches his unusual, bright-blue eyes.

"Nathaniel, this is Queen Winter and her step son, Freddy," Soobeen says standing up and walking over to the boy who watches us all. I wouldn't say he is nervous, but there is something there. I don't feel any old magic or anything as I walk over and offer the boy my hand to shake.

"Just Winter, no need for all that," I say, and he smiles.

"You don't look like a queen," he points out straight

away, and I look down at my leather outfit and daggers on my waist.

"Nathaniel, that was rude," his mum scolds, and Freddy laughs as he comes over.

"You're right, I look like I'm some kind of assassin or something," I say, and he chuckles.

"I'm Freddy," Freddy introduces himself as he steps next to us.

"Nice sword," Nathaniel says, and Freddy pulls it off his back.

"Here," he hands the sword over, and they start speaking. I walk off with Soobeen as we both watch them and wait for my mates to come here.

"They say halfs are drawn to each other, much like all supernaturals feel more comfortable around their own kind," she tells me, and I completely agree with her as I watch them talk.

"It makes some sense if you really think about it, nature's way of getting people to stay close to who are like," I say.

"Are you and Freddy close?" she asks me.

"I like to think we are, I would do anything for that boy," I say, thinking of how we first met and how protective I was over him at the start. There was always something that drew me to protecting him far more than I should have really. I've always liked kids, but with Freddy it was an instant bond. A need to look after him.

"It's because you're a half like him, and there is always that draw to each other," she tells me.

"Like how I feel safe here?" I ask because it's true. I've felt a sense of safety from the moment I passed through that ward and felt no threat from these people.

"Yes, in a way. I want to be completely honest with you," she says, turning to look at me.

"Okay?" I ask her.

"Some of the people we have here are exiled from the supernaturals. Some for crimes, others have done things in their pasts and are known by everyone at the castle, but have changed as they live here" she says.

"They get one chance, that's it. Make it known that I won't have anyone betray me. I get that not all of your people will want to live in the castle permantly, but here is the deal: if they fight for us, then they are free to leave, and we won't punish them for their past. That deal has no reflection on anything they do after war, though," I say, and she bows her head at me before looking up once more.

"A fair deal," she replies. I look over at Freddy and Nathaniel, the future we are fighting for is always going to come with repercussions, but it is worth it. We have to make sure everything here is worth it.

87

WINTER

I swing my fist down on Leigha's arm as she slides to the left of me, and I jump over her leg that she aims at my feet. She jumps away when I catch her, but I don't pause as I follow her, swinging my own leg at her stomach and sending her flying across the training room.

"Fuck, princess . . . you beat me," Leigha says as I offer her a hand up.

"Never thought you'd see the day?" I ask as I laugh a little and get my breath back. This is what training day and night for the past two weeks has done to me. I was close to beating her before, but I needed to do this.

"No, I knew it was in there, just needed a little push," she chuckles.

"Yeah, there is pushing and then there's whipping my ass since we met," I laugh out.

"Hey, I still let you eat chocolate," she tells me.

"Only because I would have attempted to kill you if you stopped me," I laugh, but it dies off as I look around the training room. There are so many of us training in here, and I spot Jaxson just as his wolf lands on another wolf. He lets the other wolf go and shifts back, completely naked and explains what the other wolf did wrong. I let my eyes run down his back, and his wolf mark on it.

"Wolves have literally no worries about nudity, do they?" Leigha asks, and I laugh.

"Not one little bit, but you should know that, you know with Harris," I say, and she whacks my arm.

"We actually spend time, not naked, together," she says with red cheeks.

"You love him?" I ask her, and she nods.

"I'm worried about losing him. The war is two days away," she says, reminding me what I already know. It only took us a day to move in the halfs and everyone else, but the amount of fights my mates and everyone had to break up was crazy. The people seemed to forget about winning the war to make enemies with the new race that moved in. It took a lot of work and arguments in council meetings to get everyone on board with the new plan. The other council members had mixed views on bringing halfs into the meeting and giving them their rightful places, but no one had to the guts to say anything after Jaxson punched one of them. They shouldn't have said anything rude about halfs in the first place, so I didn't exactly disagree with Jaxson.

"I can't tell you that you won't lose him, but make the most of the time we have, while things aren't certain," I tell her gently, knowing that's all I want to do. I want to spend time with my mates and the people I care about, but here I am in training.

"You should take your own advice, too," Leigha says and nods towards Dabriel and Atti who are speaking to each other by the doors to the training room.

"Later, army brat," I say, and she laughs as I walk off.

Dabriel and Atti stop talking when I get close, and Atti pulls me into his side, kissing the top of my head.

"How's training going?" he asks.

"I beat her, can you believe it. I don't think I've ever been as happy to knock her on her ass," I say, and Atti laughs.

"That angel is crazy," I point out, watching as Chesca picks up two knives off the side and then throws them in the air, catching them perfectly. Unfortunately, she is wearing even less clothing than the first time I saw her. Now, there are just tight mini shorts and an even smaller black top.

"She kills the people she sleeps with, so no matter what she looks like, she is evil."

"Chesca does what to her lovers?" I ask, because I'm sure I didn't hear him right.

"She kills them," Dabriel says.

"Why?" I ask as I look over at the dark angel with dyed-blonde hair. She is very beautiful, and a few guys are staring at her, you can't blame them.

"I've heard it's because she gets jealous," Dabriel shrugs, and Chesca chooses that moment to look over at me. She winks.

"How do you know that about her?" I ask Dabriel.

"She was exiled from the angels after her trial five years ago. I remember it well because she was a half. The angels kept her as baby, and the council raised her, not knowing for sure what she was but that her mother was angel. She killed two of her lovers, both angels and then tried to run away with her newborn son. The child was taken off her, and she killed another angel trying to get to the child, before she was forced to leave."

"Why would they take the child off her?" Atti asks.

"She couldn't be trusted with a child, after her killing

spree. The council said they had proof she had killed more than just the two we knew about. Her only excuse in the trial was that those men had used her for sex, and she didn't want them to be with anyone else," Dabriel answers.

"And the child? Is he here?" I ask.

"No idea," Dabriel answers with a sad look. We both know how many angels died in the attack, so she could have very well lost her child. I watch as Chesca walks away into the castle and then look around at the army of training soldiers.

"How is the training going? How are the halfs doing today?" I ask, wanting to change the subject.

"Training is going as well as can be expected at this point," Dabriel answers.

"The half's are something to be admired. Their power is amazing, and I feel more confident than ever about winning the war," Atti says, and nods his head over to the left. I follow his direction to see a man sitting on the ground with his hands in the dirt. All around him, three small trees are growing slowly from the ground.

"Good, but I'm going back to my room, want to join?" I ask. I would try to make my tone more seductive, but I know I'd end up just sounding weird. I also don't know which one of them I'm even asking. I know they both won't come with me, but I just want to be alone with them.

"Let's all go," Atti says, shocking me when Dabriel nods, placing his hand on Atti's shoulder and Atti uses his power to move us. I'm not surprised when I see it's my bedroom, they don't seem to use their own very often.

"Let us," Atti says, leaning down and kissing me. I never thought much of the idea of being with more than one of them at a time, but as I feel Dabriel step behind me and start kissing the side of my neck, it doesn't seem like a bad idea. Dabriel rips my shirt and training bra off, the ripped material falling to the floor as his hands slide between me and Atti to roll his finger around my nipples. I moan and break away from Atti's kissing to lay my head back on Dabriel's shoulder. Atti kisses down my chest and my stomach before he pulls my jogging pants down and my knickers with them. Atti doesn't wait as he kisses my core and lifts one of my legs onto his shoulder. The mixture of Atti's tongue and Dabriel's kisses on my neck as his hands slide around my breasts, makes me lose control in seconds. Just before I'm about to finish, Atti stops and looks up at me with a grin.

"Not yet, we have only just started," he says, and they both spend the rest of the day showing me that that was only the start of a long night of pleasure.

88

WINTER

"Elissa, this is the four men I told you about. The wolf, witch, angel, and vampire." Demtra's voice drifts through my mind, and it takes me a few tries to open my eyes and see the massive ballroom we are in where Elissa, the ancestors, and Demtra are all standing together. I recognise the ballroom as the training room now, but it once was amazing. The wall is a shiny gold that matches the glossy, gold floors. There are five crystal chandeliers, lit up with hundreds of candles, the light touching everywhere around the room which is heavily decorated in green flowers. There are hundreds of different supernaturals, dancing in unusual dress to the loud, unfamiliar music being played. The female supernaturals all have white and black Greek-style dresses on, and the men just have togas that cover their lower halves. Their marks are visible as they sway to the music, and I find myself admiring the different animals that are also in the room. There are three large, purple birds I've never seen before sitting on a branch by the window, and there are large cats, wolves, bears, and even a horse. The horse is pure white, and as I look closer, I see the horn in the middle of its head. Oh my god, it's a unicorn. I can't believe it.

"May I have a dance with the Goddess' sister?" the witch

ancestor asks, getting my attention from the unicorn in the room, just in time to see Elissa as she blushes and nods. They walk off and start dancing as I stand and watch. I look over to see all the ancestors watching them, they loved her from the start. It's clear to see in the way they look at her. Demtra walks slowly towards me, and stops so close, I almost imagine she can see me.

"War is coming, the past won't help you, now," Demtra says, but her words aren't for me, they are for the demon king who sits at a table behind me. I turn to see the demon king simply smile in a cruel way. Despite the fact he is in the vampire king's body now, he has the same smirk and evil quality in his eyes. It's his soul that screams evil more than anything else.

"The past always controls the future," he replies.

"No, it doesn't, and you won't control her," Demtra says, her voice calm despite her harsh words.

"Gods control all," he sneers before walking away, and I close my eyes as I'm pulled back to sleep.

I blink my eyes open, remembering the dream and how it all started, how my grandmother fell in love with the ancestors, and they loved her. How the demon king was always around, always ruining what could have been special. I guess I should be thankful in a way that he did, because my mum would never have been born if the demon king and Elissa hadn't been together all those years ago. But then, I have to die anyway, so it will all be for nothing. All this death over many years, will be ended with my death.

"Such a serious face when you first wake up," Dabriel whispers, and I turn my head to see him lying on the bed next to me. I place my hand on his warm, naked chest, tracing my finger around.

"Dreams and war have a way of making me serious," I comment.

"Didn't we help you forget that a little last night?" Atti asks, sliding his hands around my stomach from behind, and I feel how naked he is as he pulls me against him.

"Yes, but we have to plan today, make the hardest decisions for tomorrow," I say, reminding them both of the meeting planned today. I have an idea to tell them, and half my mates are going to hate me for it.

"Then we best get up and be the royals we need to be," Dabriel says and kisses my forehead.

"How are we going to get into the vampire castle and win a fight there?" Lucinda asks, through the noise of everyone trying to shout their ideas into the room. There are sixteen of us in here: the council we have made up to try and win this war. They are a mix of every race and the halfs. To say they didn't take it well when Chesca, Soobeen, and Mila walked into the room despite me warning them this would happen, would be putting it lightly. There was a fight, and Chesca punched one of the witches, it just didn't go well. Luckily, Atti stopped them, and as the shouting gets louder, I know another fight is not far away.

"Enough!" I shout, slamming my hand on the table, and I look down to see my hand glowing blue. I must be glowing like a Smurf again.

"I have an idea," I say and stand up, walking to the whiteboard. I pick up a pen and start drawing while they silently watch me.

"So, you all know that demons can go through the demon ward around the vampire castle. It's how I got out, and it's how I will get in once more. I spoke with Milo, and he will take one person into the castle, and I believe I can pull one person through the ward as well," I say.

"I will go to the vampire castle with Wyatt because he knows it best, and Jaxson because his wolf can smell demons nearby. The rest of the kings and people will stay and fight here," I say, and my mates give me mixed looks of shock and anger.

"No way, Winter," Atti says, his voice dripping with anger.

"I need to close the portal, only me. The demon king is not going to come here and fight. I don't remember much from my time there, but he never left the castle for long because the portal is his weak point. With my crown on, I can fight him, push him in the portal, and close it. This is what I'm meant to do, and I need to," I tell everyone in the room, and there's silence for a long time as they think over my words. I know I don't stand much chance of beating him, but I stand a chance of getting him through that portal, and that's all that matters.

"He could kill you," Dabriel points out.

"I want you all with me, but his demons are going to kill the people here. Our people," I tell Dabriel, who tightens his jaw but nods. I look over to see Atti finally nod in agreement with me.

"We will take a hundred mixed supernaturals with us, just in case. They can wait outside the castle and, hopefully, kill the rest of the demons he will keep with him when the ward drops. Also, we might need to fight our way to the ward in the first place, if the demon king has any of his demons outside," Jaxson says.

"It's not a bad plan," I comment, agreeing with him.

"Then, I will be at your side," Jaxson nods but the

slight glowing of his green eyes is telling me his wolf isn't happy with everything.

"You know my answer," Wyatt says, and I smile at him with relief. I look around the room.

"The fray are bringing weapons and their army to fight for us, but we cannot trust them. I would suggest placing all the women and children into the castle basement. The rest of you spread out around the castle for the fight," I say.

"We can plan for a war here, My Queen," Lucifer says.

"Then, we have our plans. There is a lot still to be done," Soobeen says, and there's agreements said around the room.

"Winter, you need to see this," Freddy says running into the room, holding his iPad.

"Freddy, what is it?" I ask, knowing he wouldn't rush in here with just anything. He puts the iPad down on the table, and we all gather around it.

"The wall around Paris has fallen, and whatever happened in there, is not good. I'm fairly sure we are looking at a mass killing of thousands, with thousands still missing. Many were killed in their homes–" the news woman says as she is recorded speaking in front of what is left of Paris. They must be just inside the city, in the streets as some of the houses are on fire and there are what look like bodies behind her on the street.

"We have a survivor," a woman shouts out, and the camera shakes as they run over the road. A little girl about ten looks into the camera and then at the camera woman.

"Can you tell us who did this?" the woman asks, sliding her arm around the little girl.

"Magic people," she says quietly, but I hear it.

"We are hearing many reports of wolves and witches. Things we only believed existed in fairy tales, but it seems they are real," the camera woman says, and there is silence around the room.

"The government won't hide this, us. This is a mass killing of one of their capitals. They will blame the supernaturals, and humans will hunt us for this," Lucinda says, and I nod my agreement. I don't need to say anything about the humans, as I listen to them rant on about the evil supernaturals. They will never see us as the good guys now.

"You had a witch that can hear for halfs and then find them?" I ask Soobeen.

"Yes," Soobeen answers.

"I want you to ask her to put a call out for any supernaturals, tell them that here is safe. When we win the war, we will get Atlantis back, and then we will have two safe havens for supernaturals. Including the pack lands at some point," I say, and she nods.

"Yes, My Queen."

"Many supernaturals hide with humans, maybe they will be safe," Atti comments.

"I hope so," I say and look down at the iPad as video recordings of destroyed Paris appear.

Paris is gone.

89

WINTER

"W*inter. Winter. Winter!" the child-like voice screams in my mind, sounding in pain and making me place my hands on my ears before I even open my eyes. The voice is still screaming as I take in the white, snow-filled field and the one tree in the field that sways in the breeze.*

"So little time left, so much left to fight for," Elissa's kind voice says as she and Demtra walk towards me from behind the tree. Despite her being quite far away, I can hear every word she says. They look like they always do, in white dresses, and when I look down, I see I'm wearing the same. If I dream call them, why am I dressed like this?

"And, it's only you that can win this," Demtra says, her bright eyes locking with mine, and I nod. I know it's only me that can do this, I've known from the second I heard the prophecy. I have a feeling I've known I'm meant for something my whole life, but I wonder if everyone feels that way?

"When you need us, call us. The power is inside you," *my mother says stepping out from behind the tree. Her words are spoken in my mind. I watch in silence as I look between them all, all three of them watching me as the snow gets heavier, and I struggle to keep my eyes open.*

"I will win this for you all," I say, my words lost in the cold wind.

"The prophecy was never for anyone other than you, Winter. Only you." Elissa says, and everything turns to white as the snow causes me to close my eyes.

"We need the queen and all of you; the fray leader is demanding to see the queen and kings," Harris's voice drifts over to me, and I sit up in the empty bed to see Jaxson holding the door open. It's the war today, and when I pull Jaxson's phone off the side to see if we slept in, it's only five in the morning. I groan as I sit up in bed, pulling the sheets closer around myself.

"Fine. Tell the fairy we will be there soon," Jaxson snaps. He is not a morning person, and neither of us got much sleep last night. Both of us are worried about today—the war. It's finally here, and in some ways, I'm glad it is; it means I finally finish this. The prophecy leads us all up to this point, and I don't regret a moment of it. I have my mates because of it, even if my death is the price I have to pay. I would pay it a thousand times for the short time I got with my mates.

"Maybe, don't call him a fairy when we meet the leader of the fray army," I say, laughing a little with Harris before Jaxson slams the door shut.

"They are fairies," Jaxson points out, before rubbing his face. Surprisingly, Jaxson actually put boxers on today, I didn't know he had any here with how often I see his naked butt. Not that I'm complaining, the memory of said butt is kept like a treasure in my mind.

"No fairies are cute, little things meant for children, with pink, sparkling wings. The fray queen didn't have wings, and I highly doubt they are all nice and cute," I tell him as he climbs onto the bed and pulls me onto his lap. I press my head into his neck, breathing in his forest-like scent. I love how it makes me feel calm.

"I don't want you to fight him. Every part of me is telling me not to let you go with me. I just can't lose you," Jaxson says gently, kissing his way down my cheek, and I turn my head to meet his lips. Jaxson rolls me onto my back and lowers his body over mine. He kicks his boxers off, pressing himself into me and making me moan slightly.

"You will be at my side," I whisper, breaking away from the kiss.

"I love you, lass. Everything that makes me–well, me–loves you. I don't do romantic words or love poems, but fuck, I would do anything to have a life with you. I was beyond lost until you came into my life. The very thought of letting you fight someone that could kill you–" he says, his voice cracking, and I lean up, kissing him gently again.

"I never did anything, Jaxson. The amazing, strong, and kind man was always there. You never needed me, I was just lucky to have you love me," I say, and he smirks down at me.

"So, I didn't put you off with being an idiot at the start?" he asks, and I laugh.

"No, you had me with that first kiss and the jackass behaviour . . . well you're a hot asshole, so I'll forgive you for it," I say, and he grins.

"You're mine, and I'll always be here for you, Winter. No matter what happens today and tonight," he says, resting a hand on my cheek.

"Always," I respond, and he kisses me.

"Sorry to interrupt, but I need to chat with Winter," Wyatt says as he walks into the room and closes the door behind him. Jaxson groans but rolls off me before walking over to the bathroom, naked.

"Clothes, brother," Wyatt says, looking away, and I laugh.

"I'm a wolf, we don't like clothes," Jaxson replies.

"Yes, but the rest of us don't want to see your ass and everything else first thing in the fucking morning," Wyatt shouts as Jaxson shuts the bathroom door, and I laugh even more.

"I like to see you laughing," Wyatt says, and I stand up off the bed. I pull a dressing gown on slowly, watching as his eyes roll over my naked body, and I wish we had more time to explore whatever thoughts are blazing in his dark eyes.

"Morning," I say, walking over, and he kisses me slowly.

"Not that I'm not happy to see you, but I thought you had to meet with the council this morning," I say, knowing they are all meeting very soon, while I'm helping move the women and children to somewhere safe.

"I think we should feed on each other, make us both as strong as we can be. Blood bags are not a good idea when we are going to fight," Wyatt says gently, and I nod, knowing I need to feed, anyway.

"Okay," I say, and he tilts my head to the side, before gently kissing my neck and then biting me. The bite is painful, but only for a second, before nothing but pleasure fills me. I try to keep the moan in by biting my lip, but my teeth are growing sharp in my mouth, so I can't do that. Wyatt licks my neck as he pulls away and then tilts his head to the side. I don't have much control as I lean forward and bite him gently, loving how he tastes like chocolate. His hands tighten on my hips.

When I eventually pull away, he whispers, "We could kick the wolf out and have some fun. I don't have to go to the council meeting straight away,"

"The fray are here, or I would. We have to meet them, and you have to deal with the council before we can all do that," I say, and he groans as he steps away from me.

"I'll meet you later, but I need a minute to calm down," he says, and I see the outline of how turned on he is through his trousers.

"Well, I'm about to strip, so I doubt that will help," I say, and he groans before walking out. I take my time dressing in the leather outfit I have worn to all my fights. It's easy to move in and has places for all my daggers. I leave half my hair down and put the top half up in some plaits. Nothing complicated, but it looks good. When I'm done, Jaxson walks out of the bathroom, fully dressed in jeans and a normal shirt that has a belt around his chest which will hold his sword.

"I'm going to get my weapons," Jaxson says nothing else as he walks out, and leaves the door open. I know that our moment in bed together is over now, and we have to be the royals our people need. They need us to be strong and deal with the fray. I go over to the box by the side of my bed, and open it up. The crown calls to me as I pick it up and put it on my head. I walk over to the mirror, seeing myself with the crown on for the first time. I'm slightly glowing blue, and my eyes are brighter than they ever normally are. They have a slight silver quality to them, suggesting they might turn silver at any moment. The crown's power is hard to ignore, but I know I need to.

"My Queen," Atti says as he leans against the wall outside my room. Atti has his own crown on, and his black cloak is covering his clothes. The cloak has silver tree marks stitched down the parting, and he is crossing his arms as he watches me, making his shirt tight on his chest. Atti has shaved his hair on the side of his head, but left the top part long, with his fringe just falling on his forehead. His stormy, grey eyes take their time looking me over.

When he finally gets to my eyes, I say, "My King," with a little bow, and he laughs.

"We sound so formal when all I can think of is shutting this door and fucking you until you scream my name," he tells me. I don't think it's a bad idea at all, and my mark warms on my back as he watches me.

"I don't think we have time," I say with red cheeks and he chuckles as he walks over to me, pushing my body against the door with his own.

"It's a plan for the future, then," he tells me gently before kissing me. Atti moves his lips slowly against mine, and the kiss feels like it's over way too quickly.

"They are waiting, and a fair warning, they are stuck up, rainbow-hair-coloured assholes," Atti says, and I can't help the laugh that escapes my lips.

"'Rainbow-hair-coloured assholes'?" I ask through my laughs, but unfortunately, the door at the bottom of the corridor opens, and one of the said assholes walks over. The man is taller than me, but I'm short so that's easy, and has dark-blue hair. His eyes match his hair, and I can see flower tattoo-like marks on his neck, which are some kind of blue flower. He has blue eyes that slightly glow, and there's a strange feeling to him that gives him away as a fray. Another thing, is he is extremely hard to look at, he is stunning. Every part of him is extremely beautiful, but in a fake way. It feels like when you eat a chocolate cake that is too rich, and you can't eat all of it.

"I got tired of waiting," he says, his sharp tone means he heard every word. *Way to make alliances, Winter.*

"You should bow," Atti snaps, stopping us from walking closer and puts his arm around me.

"You are not my queen or king," the fray man snaps out.

"And, you are in our home. Sent here to fight for us, so you should show some respect," I say, my tone sharp, and the man's eyes widen as he stares at me, even taking a step back. I glance down to see myself glowing brighter. *Damn, I'm scaring the fairy by glowing like a damn fairy.*

"Are you the leader?" Atti asks with an annoyed sigh as he strokes a hand down my arm, and the man shakes his head. It seems like the fray man is annoying him.

"Yes. I'm the second in the royal court of the fray. The queen will not step foot into this world as it makes her weak," the man says, but there's a quiver in his voice.

"Shame. I wanted to speak to Lily," I say, and leave out the fact I want to punch her for tricking me.

"Queen Lilyanne sends her kindness and asked me to say hello to you," he tells me, but I highly doubt she said it nicely, or she isn't as smart as I know she is.

"I'm sure she did," I arch an eyebrow as I speak, and the man nods.

"Why would it make your queen weak to come here?" Atti asks.

"Full-blooded fray cannot stay in the human world for more than a day, or we start to lose our powers."

"You are being very honest despite working for a queen that is no longer a friend to any of our thrones," Atti replies, tilting his head to the side as he looks at the man.

"What's your name?" I ask him, before the door behind him is opened, and Dabriel comes storming down the corridor. He picks the man up by his neck and slams him into the corridor wall making cracks appear down the newly painted wall. The man squirms, and lightning appears on his fingertips.

"Your people killed one of my angels in a fight. I suggest you deal with them before I start mass killing of fray," Dabriel says, his marks glowing brightly, and his wings are moving slightly, making him seem like he is floating.

"Y-yes," the man blurts out, and Dabriel lets him drop to the floor.

"Dab?" I ask, and he looks over at me with a kinder smile, but tension is written all over his face.

"The army they promised you is full of untrained soldiers who have no idea what they are doing. The weapons they promised can only be used by people with fray blood, and most of the soldiers are just picking fights. We had to put a few hundred of them in the dungeons underground, and our supernaturals teamed up to kill a few who flat out wouldn't play nice," Dabriel tells me, shooting a disgusted look at the fray on the floor.

"What?" I ask, looking down at the man who only stares at the floor.

"The weapons are things like sword handles, which have silver swords come out of them when a fray touches them. There are strange bracelets and other things I have no clue how to use," Dabriel says.

"Why shouldn't we kill you, send a message back to your queen about how we don't like to be tricked?" Atti says walking over to stand next to Dabriel, and I wait for the man's answer.

"The army she sent are all prisoners of the fray war, some may be able to fight, but most are too weak from being kept in the dungeons for years. The queen would never risk her royal army, and she doesn't care about a single fray here," the man says, his words aimed at the floor as he doesn't look up at us. "Just kill me now if you wish."

"There is a war in fray?" I ask, ignoring his offer.

"Yes, and there has been for a long time. Ten years ago, Lilyanne made an army. She hunted down every royal fray and killed them. There is only her left, now. We have no choice. My family are being held captive, I have no choice but to do as she asks. When I return to fray within twenty-four hours, if any of the fray here come with me, she will kill them all," he tells me, only looking up at me for a second, and the guilt is written all over his face. I believe him when I can see the pain in his eyes, and in some ways, I know Lily is smart enough to do this.

"I believe you, and I won't kill you for telling me the truth. Lily is the only one I want dead right now," I say.

"You say all the royal Fray are dead?" Dabriel asks.

"Yes. I don't know every detail of how the war started as I once was a simple man that lived in the city and worked as a jewel miner. There were once four families for the four royal courts. The autumn court, Lily, is the only one left now," he says.

"Lily made a promise with me, she told me she needed a half-royal fray that lives in our world,"

"Then, there is hope," the man breathes out, and for the first time, there's relief all over his face. "You must never touch the royal fray, no matter what. She is not safe in my world, but I will return. If the royal ever comes back, I will be there at Lily's side. She needs me to control the miners in the city," he says.

"I will never touch the royal, I never want to make good on my promise," I tell him honestly.

"You may never want to, but magic of the old Gods will make the promise come to pass. Promises are always fulfilled," he says, and I just look away from him. I know they have their own Gods and their own magic, the lily marks on my wrists are proof of that.

"So, we have thousands of refugees, instead of an army?" I muse, looking through the glass windows just as the sun rises up in the sky.

"Yes," he says.

"Get everyone in front of the castle, so they can see the balcony. All the fray and supernaturals," I tell the man, who nods and scrambles off the floor, running out as Dabriel still glares at him. I don't see him as a threat to me, but I'm not stupid, I'm going to be careful.

"I will call my witches and ask them to bring everyone as well. I hope you have a plan, or we all need to come up with something quickly," Atti says and presses a kiss against my forehead before he steps away. Dabriel walks over, and I wrap my arms around him.

"I'm sorry about the angels who were killed," I mumble quietly.

"What's the plan?" he asks gently as he pulls me as close as he can to his chest.

"I need to do what I was born for, I need to be a queen," I say, resting my head on his chest.

90

WINTER

I look down at the thousands of people on the ground watching me. It's strange to think how many different races there are down there, mixed races, and yes, they all may have differences, but we are here together. All of them are dressed for war, even the women and children are standing with weapons in their hands and determined looks. There are so many people that they stretch out into the forest edges as they wait for me to speak. I try not to remember the human woman who would have laughed if I told her she would be doing this in a year. I'm not her anymore; I'm the queen of four races of people who need my help. They need to see me strong, to remember me like this. Remember me leading them into war for one thing: for peace. For a life for our children. I glance to the side of the balcony, where Freddy is standing, dressed every bit the prince he is, and the small crown on his head reflecting the sunlight. The sun is high in the sky as everyone looks up at me and my mates. I glance behind me once more to see all four of them standing next to each other, each one looking every bit like the kings they are. Wyatt is the only one without a crown, but he doesn't need it; he commands power on his own, like they all do. The crown is nothing without the powerful king that wears it. *I believe that.* I turn back to the people; the silence is only broken by the cold wind as it blows against the castle. The fray are standing to the left of the supernaturals, a clear gap between them, and no one seems to want to move. The fray all have strange, bright-coloured hair and old, ragged clothes, and they clutch weapons in their hands. They honestly look terrible, and over half of them must be teenagers or women. There are even some children dotted around, and one woman holding a baby in her arms. Right at the front of the castle, is a group of fray, all big men with determined eyes as they look up at me. A ward is around them, and I know they must be the fray that started the fights and killed the angels. Not the best way, but then if they have been kept in dungeons for years it's likely their families have been too. I know I would do anything to keep my family safe, and I bet they think coming here is just Lily's way of killing them.

"Thank you for coming. For those who do not know who I am, I'm Queen Winter. These are my mates, King Jaxson, King Wyatt, King Dabriel, and King Atticus." I introduce them, and there is silence as I look back at the people. I want to say they can call me Winter and not be formal, but I doubt it's a good idea when I'm trying to get their alliance.

"I have heard that the fray are at war, a war very much like the one that comes for us today. I'm not going to stand here and ask people who have been kept in dungeons for years to fight for me, for supernaturals who they don't know, and frankly, don't give a damn about. I'm no fool to ask that of you," I say, my words seeming to be carried by the wind.

"This castle was my grandmother's and my great aunt's. They were Goddesses, and my aunt made the first witch, vampire, wolf, and angel. They all lived together in peace in this castle until my grandmother fell in love with a demon. She loved him blindly, and my mother was the only good thing that came from that love. The demon king destroyed this castle, murdered her other mates, and has murdered every blood relative of mine," I say and pause as some of the people start whispering.

"I know the queen of the fray must have killed some of your family, killed people you love." I tell this to the fray and then look to the supernaturals.

"The same way the demon king has killed many of our loved ones in this war."

There are mumbles of agreement through the crowd as I wait for them to be a little quieter, so everyone hears my words.

"I'm not going to demand you fight for me, or ask. I only stand here and tell you that I will fight for you. For every single one of you, and the fight is for freedom. No more wars, no more death, and a life for our children!" I shout, and cheers follow my words. I wait for them to calm down before I shout.

"I will kill the demon king and make sure that you are safe. Many of the fray here may not want to fight, and if you don't, we will keep you safe, regardless, because we are not evil. We are not the bad guy here. We want peace and a safe place for all kinds. It's that or death, and I hope everyone here agrees with me that I choose to fight."

"But, if any of you can fight, please join us," I direct that at the men in the ward, and a few of them nod at me.

"I'm not asking for me, I'm asking for a chance of freedom here. I will welcome you to live here and your children will be taught alongside ours," I say, and I wait for them to say anything. A man steps forward and bows his head, and then another. The rest of the fray follow and so do the supernaturals.

"Freedom!" Wyatt shouts as he moves next to me,

"For Queen Winter," Dabriel says as he steps forward.

"For those we lost," Jaxson says as he stands next to me, and his hand finds mine.

"And, for the future," Atti finally says and steps forward. We all hold hands as the people cheer and for the first time we watch as they actually help each other. The first step in creating peace. Now, we need to win the war.

~

"Be safe," I tell Dabriel, and he gently kisses my nose, making me giggle. Dabriel doesn't need to say any words as we look at each other, all the love he feels for me is written in his eyes. Dabriel only nods before walking away and out the doors of the castle, to his angels to be at their side in the war. I wouldn't expect him to be anywhere else, but worry still fills me when I watch him walk out.

"Queen Winter?" a small, familiar voice says behind me, and I turn to see the half fray child, Nathaniel.

"Nathaniel, right?" I ask, looking down at him a little. Nathaniel pulls out a dagger from his cloak, the blade is glowing purple and there's silence around the room as several people stop to stare.

"I can make weapons more powerful than fray touched, and I made this for you. I'm not that strong, yet, and this took me days. I want you to win," Nathaniel says, and I pick the dagger up from him as Soobeen walks over to us. The dagger feels powerful, I can tell. I slide it into a space on my dagger belt.

"Thank you. I won't forget this, and it will help me win," I tell Nathaniel, who shyly nods.

"Nathaniel, we must go," Soobeen says as she wraps an arm around her son.

"You have an amazing son, you must be proud," I say, and Soobeen looks down at her son.

"Very proud," Soobeen says and walks off with her son as I watch.

"Winter?" I hear Alex say, and I look behind me to see her with Drake and Atti. Drake is dressed for war, there is literally no other way to describe him. He has weapons on every single part of his body and some of them I'm not sure I would even know how to use. They just look like sharp things. A small sob comes from Alex, who wipes her eyes with the men's jumper she has on over her leather leggings.

"You okay?" I ask her, and she nods quickly, putting on a brave smile. I know that smile because it's all I've done all day when I've spoken to anyone. Act brave, or that's what I kept telling myself.

"I can't lose you," she says, and I hug her. I can't give her words of encouragement, not when I know I have to die to close that portal. There isn't another way. I hate that I won't get to meet her little one, but at least I know her child will live. Since Atti saved me, I've tried to swallow the fear and guilt of leaving my mates behind, but I know it's no use. It's me or the rest of the world, and as I pull away and look at Alex, I know she has to survive this. Her baby needs to be born into a good world.

"You go and kill him," Drake says to me, and I nod. Alex kisses my cheek before walking off with Drake. I smile at Harris as he pulls Leigha into a deep kiss by the door. I know they will look after each other.

"Be right back," Atti says and walks a few steps away

from me to talk to a couple of witches who seem to be arguing.

"Winter!" I hear Freddy shout and turn to see him running over to me from the stairs. I hold him close as he nearly knocks me over when he gets to me. I pull back when I see his swords strapped to his back, and the reality that he is going to be protecting the women and children with Alex sets in. It's strange that the kids of this war are needed to help, and what childhood Freddy could have had is lost in war. The poor boy has lost so much, and I don't want him to lose anyone else. *I don't want to leave him.*

"You do as Dabriel and Atti ask, okay? I need you to be safe, Freddy," I whisper to him and pull him closer one more time. I don't want anyone else to hear my words.

"I will," he whispers back, and I pull back and look down at him.

"Why do you have your swords on your back, then?" I ask, and he grins.

"Just in case they come near the women and children. I might need to kick some demon–"

"Don't finish that sentence," I say with a laugh, and he grins.

"I'm not a kid, anymore. I haven't been just a kid for a long time," he tells me, and I know he is right, but it doesn't make the situation any sadder. I hope after all this is done, he can have some part of a childhood again, but I doubt it. He is on the vampire council, and he will be the heir to all of the thrones when I finish this war.

"Just think, this all started with me finding you in that parking lot, another time where you didn't do as you were told," I murmur, and he smiles at me.

"I'm glad you saved me, Winter," he says.

"Me too, Freddy, me too," I say and hug him once more before letting go and having to wipe my eyes a little.

"You can do this, I know it," Freddy tells me, and his bright-blue eyes stare up at me.

"I will try," I tell him, and he nods. I look away for a second as I feel Milo come and sit on my shoulder, and I can't help the chuckle that slips out of my lips when I see Milo's war outfit.

"Dude, we need to work on your fashion sense, I don't even have words for that," Freddy says, and I agree with him as I take in the strange, pink, glittery jumpsuit he has on. There is no way to miss Milo with that outfit and the pink headband in his hair to match.

"You know what?" Freddy tells me.

"What?" I ask.

"You're an awesome step-mum," he says with a cheeky grin and runs off as I laugh. My laugh is cut off when a scream, followed by a loud bang comes from outside. I feel Milo hold onto my neck as I step backwards as the castle shakes a little. There's more sounds of screams, and all the people in here run outside. I look over as Wyatt and Jaxson run down the stairs, both of them have their swords strapped on their backs and are wearing tight clothes in black. Jaxson's crown makes him seem like he is lightly glowing, and Wyatt is oozing power as they run over to me.

"It's time to go," Atti says walking to my side, and he links his fingers with mine as Wyatt and Jaxson run over to us. I duck as a demon comes flying through the door, and lands in the entrance hall. I pull a dagger out of my belt and throw it at his head, watching as it hits, and the demon disappears into blue dust. I hear a scream and turn to see Leigha fighting three demons who must have snuck in somehow, with Alex behind her. I go to step forward when Harris runs past me.

"Wait, we need the hundred people we are meant to be taking with us," I say to Atti, and he shakes his head.

"They came too early, we need to go now. We can't afford to wait, Winter," he says, and I look back at Alex, Leigha, and Freddy, wanting to help them.

"Go, I will sort them," Harris shouts at us as he runs towards Alex, and Leigha follows him, with a small nod at me as she passes. I feel Atti's magic pulling us away only a second later.

91

WINTER

"We're here," Wyatt says as I open my eyes to the vampire castle. It's snowing, and the large flakes of snow land on my face as the cold wind blows it around us. It's almost fitting that it's winter, and there is so much snow. Like my namesake being Winter, I've always loved the cold and the snow. I wonder if that's why there is always snow in my dreams with my family, because I subconsciously chose it. We walk in silence towards the castle, listening for any sounds, but there is nothing. It's eerily quiet here.

"Come Vampire," Milo says, and I look up as the blue ward surrounding the vampire castle comes into view. No one says anything about the fact the demon has moved it beyond the wall, and I hope it's not because he has demons just waiting for us behind it. Milo flies off my shoulder and lands on Wyatt's shoulder. I look up at Atti, who leans down and kisses me.

"Go and kill him," he tells me firmly.

"Save our people and know I love you so much," I tell

him, trying to keep my voice stronger, and he pulls me into a deep kiss before breaking away. I watch as he disappears. I love that he believes in me, there wasn't a bit of doubt in his voice, and that kiss was what I want to remember as I walk into this castle. As I, literally, try to send a demon back to hell.

"Lass?" Jaxson says gently, and I wipe some of the snow out my eyes as I look up at him.

"Let's go," I say and link my hands with Jaxson's as we walk up to the ward. The ward is as deep as I remember it being, but there's something strange about it, like it's weaker. I walk straight through it and pull Jaxson with me. It's easier to travel through the second time, than it was the first, even pulling Jaxson with me. My spare hand goes to one of my daggers as I take in the imposing wall and wipe more of the snow out of my eyes with the back of my hand. There're no demons around, and Jaxson nods down at me, he can't sense any either. I wait as Milo leads Wyatt through after us only moments later, and Wyatt looks around.

"We need to jump," I say, wondering how Jaxson will make that jump. I know Atti used his air power to help boost him, and Wyatt won't have an issue because of him being a vampire.

"No, we don't. I know a way in," Wyatt tells us. "Come on, we'd better get inside in case there is a patrol."

We follow Wyatt as he walks next to the wall for about ten minutes before he stops and holds his hand up. Wyatt pushes against what looks like the rest of the castle wall, but it moves inwards at his push. The wall slides to the left, and Wyatt walks into the dark room. *That's a cool secret door.* When I step forward, I notice it's not a room at all, it's a corridor. The dark corridor is impossible to see down, and the strong smell of damp fills my senses. Wyatt gets his phone out, using the light, so we can see down the now creepy, cobweb-filled corridor.

"I won't shift unless we need to fight, I can use my sword if there are only a few," Jaxson whispers gently.

"You should try not to use your power inside, the castle is old and won't last through an earthquake," Wyatt warns Jaxson, who nods. He has a point; the castle is ancient and made out of stone.

"Okay, but can you smell any coming near us in your human from?" I ask Jaxson.

"Yes, they smell like death. It's not hard to miss," Jaxson says.

"Milo, you need to stay here. You can't come with us here."

"Live, you family," Milo tells me, making me want to cry, but I put on a brave face as he kisses my cheek and then flies to sit on a ledge just inside the corridor. I know any demons won't hurt him if they find him, he is part demon after all. Wyatt looks back at us for a second before he keeps walking down the long corridor. I remember what they smell like, and how the dead bodies they inhabit seem to be dying, anyway. *I wonder how long it would take for the bodies they have to die? Do they just find a new body until all the people on earth are dead or demons?*

"This opens up just outside the throne room, where the ball was held, and the portal is open. That's why I chose this one," Wyatt tells us as we keep walking, and the corridor takes a left.

"Hopefully he is there."

"The portal is weak today, just like the castle ward. All ward and portal magic is weak today," Jaxson tells me, and I don't question how he knows. Everyone has been researching and finding out all they could to help us. I'm sure someone found this out for him. It seems like forever that we walk in silence, with the dripping water, and our breaths, being the only sounds.

"I can smell some close," Jaxson tells us, and Wyatt stops at the same time I do. I don't think they are close, but there is a faint smell of death.

"The door is right there," Wyatt says and points up with his light. There's a small hole and a long ladder to climb up. Wyatt pulls the creaky old ladder down quietly with the long handle, and then we wait for a second to see if anyone heard us. When nothing happens, we all take a deep breath. This whole plan banks on the demon king not being ready for us. If he caught us down here, we would have a disadvantage.

"Hold the light," Wyatt says, and hands me his phone. He pulls his sword out from its holder and starts climbing the ladder. Jaxson follows after him, and I hold the light until Wyatt opens the door. The light from the door fills the tunnel, and I quickly drop Wyatt's phone into one of my pockets and start climbing. I hear Jaxson's growl, and then the castle shakes slightly, making me nearly fall off the ladder, but I manage to hold on. When I finally get to the top, Wyatt and Jaxson are fighting dozens of demons. Wyatt is using both his swords to fight and behead demon after demon. Jaxson is doing the same with his large sword, both of them glancing over at me. I don't have time to look again as three demons run at me with silver swords. I pull my power and send them flying, both of them disappearing into dust, and I pull a dagger out of my belt, throwing it at a demon at Jaxson's back. The whole corridor is full of demons, there are far too many for us. I pull another dagger out and throw it at a demon running at me, and the moment it hits its head, it disappears into dust. The demon king was waiting for us.

"All fun, isn't it?" the demon king's laugh comes from behind me, and I turn to see him leaning against the entrance to the throne room. He has a long cloak on as well as the vampire crown that belongs to Wyatt, and his red eyes meet mine. In so many ways I hate that I'm related to him, that I share his blood, and that I have to be the one to fight him. I hate that he tricked the vampire king into bringing him back, I hate everything about this man.

"Why?" he asks, tilting his head to the side as I walk over to him. I keep my eyes on him as I call my power and kill two demons with a wave as they run at me.

"Family treasures. Seems you don't know everything, demon," I respond drily.

"Well, well . . . my princess isn't stupid after all," he says, looking at my crown and then he turns and walks back into the throne room. I run after him, surprised that no demons try to attack me as they seem to let me pass. The demon king is standing in the middle of the throne room when I run in, the portal is still open and takes up the entire side wall now. It's getting bigger, and it's hard to take my eyes off it. It almost calls to me, as I can feel its power from here.

"Let me guess, you came to put me back in the demon realm forever?" he laughs as he speaks, "Your dead great-aunt tricked me once, but I am done being tricked."

"Yes, but it will be no trick. You will die in that realm, in hell, where you belong," I respond. I don't need to look down as I feel my crown's power stretch though my body.

"You're not strong enough." He laughs, and the castle shakes hard, knocking us both to the floor with a bang. I look up as I roll across the floor, seeing the large cracks going up the ceiling, and the ground keeps shaking. I call my power, using the crown's power to make it stronger and stand up on the shaky ground. The demon king is just standing up, an annoyed look on his face.

"Stupid wolf," he says with anger, walking away from me and towards the door to my mates. I won't let that happen.

"Then, fight me and see who wins. See who deserves to rule and who truly has the blood of a Goddess," I shout, knowing from my dreams that he believes he is truly one when he is not. He turns to face me with a slow smirk.

"Don't cry when I kill you, at least die like a real demon princess," he says, and I don't waste time listening to him as I shoot a wave of my blue power at him as the ground shakes harder, and the room seems to almost tilt to the side. I look up to see him walking over to me as he avoids pieces of stone that fall from the cracked ceiling He sends his own wave of red power towards my wave as he walks, and when the waves meet, it sends a shock wave that sends me flying across the room. I manage to land on my side and quickly get up, calling my power again, and he does the same, shooting a long stream of power at me. I copy what he does, trying to hold my power against his, but it doesn't work for long. Another shockwave fills the room, and I scream as pieces of stone fall from the ceiling and one hits my shoulder. This time, I fly into the wall and my head bangs against it. I pick the fray-touched dagger out of my belt, but the demon king leans down, taking it out of my hand before I can throw it. He looks at the dagger and laughs, before sliding it into his pocket as I try to get up, and everything goes blurry.

"Silly princess to think you could kill me. You know, I

never wanted to kill you, I wanted you to rule at my side. My only family left, and you betray me. I'm four times more powerful than you are, and all I have to do is get that silly crown off you and then order you to go and kill your mates," he says and leans down to touch the crown.

"Winter!" I hear Wyatt shout.

92

ATTICUS

"Watch out!" I shout as three demons run at an angel who is picking a woman up off the floor. I call my fire, but I'm too late to stop one ofthe demons running a silver sword through the back of the angel. He screams out in pain, the scream mixing with everyone else's on the battlefield outside the castle, and I kill the demons with my fire. The angel I recognise as Chesca flies down from the sky and stands in front of the woman on the floor, and nods at me. She is going to protect the Angel I turn and look around the battlefield outside the castle, which is littered with supernaturals bodies, demons running around with silver weapons, and angels are flying in the skies overhead.

"No!" I scream as a demon rips the head off a wolf with his bare hands, and another, smaller, female wolf runs towards the demon. I pull my air power and hold the demon in place as the female wolf jumps and rips the head off the demon and lands on the ground. I don't have long to see if she is okay as a ball of fire flies past me, and I jump out of the way.

"Atti!" I hear shouted behind me, but when I turn around in a circle, I can't see who shouted at me. I turn just in time to see a fray lift his hands in the air, and, to my shock, a tornado appears in his hand. The fray, with green hair, throws the tornado towards the demons running towards us, and it gets bigger as they run straight into it. Another fray woman runs up next to me and puts her hands into the air. Rain pours down on us as dark clouds fill the skies. I watch as she redirects some of the rain, turning it into sharp icicles and shoots them into five demons necks in one go.

"Weather magic, that's what you can do?" I ask her, and she nods. A loud roar fills the night as I feel a big intrusion to the ward. The demons can just walk straight through it. It must be something to do with the Winter solstice. But, I doubt we will ever know. A loud roar fills the night, and a lot of people stop, but not for long as the demons don't seem to notice. The tornado is pulling the air from the ground, and it feels like I'm being suffocated as I look up into the dark skies.

"Demon," the woman screams next to me and points up to the sky. The dragon that Winter set free flies across the woods and shoots blue fire into the tornados. It suddenly comes back to me what Milo said about dragons. He must have called the Dragon here.

"Dragons, Milo, seriously?" I mutter, knowing tornadoes mixed with dragons is just as dangerous to us, as well as the demons. I glance over to see Dabriel fighting with four demons, and I know I need to help, now. I run over and use my air to send two of the demons flying away into the tornado. By the time I get to Dabriel, he has killed the other two, and all that is left is dust.

"That is not helping us," Dabriel points at the dragon, which is setting half the woods on fire and randomly flying down and picking demons up, throwing them into the fire.

"Freddy!" Dabriel shouts, and I turn to see where he is looking. Freddy and a silver wolf are surrounded by at least ten demons, the wolf is injured, and Freddy is protecting him.

"No!" I shout when the demons block my view of Freddy, and I run over to them. I burn all the demons in my path, and see Dabriel flying ahead towards Freddy. Winter could never live with herself if she lost Freddy, none of us could. The little shit is family to us, and he needs to live, so I can kill him myself for being out here fighting.

"Duck," I shout at Freddy when I get through the demons and see Freddy is fighting with one. Freddy does as I ask, and I lift both my hands, calling air and lifting all the demons around me into the air. Dabriel flies around and kills each one before landing next to Freddy.

"I'm fine," Freddy says, holding his arm that is bleeding.

"What the fuck are you doing out here?" I shout at him, picking up the sword he had dropped and giving it to him.

"Mich needed me," he nods towards the injured wolf.

"Get inside," I say, and he nods. I go to take him and Mich back when the dragon roars loudly, and I look up just in time to feel two more large things pass through the ward that is connected to my magic. Even now, the crystal is trying to fight for us. I watch the skies and two more dragons appear in the distance. The dragons roar at each other, and the tornadoes are making it difficult to see them, but the fire they shoot is killing everyone on the ground.

"They will destroy everything in this fight," I shout at Dabriel and hear a scream behind me. I turn around to see

Lucifer holding his chest, a sword in the middle of his chest and he falls the ground. The demon behind him pulls the sword out of Lucifer's chest, and I shoot my fire at him, burning the demon to pieces as we all run over.

"Lucifer," Dabriel says as he pulls Lucifer's shirt up and tries to heal him.

"Tell Josh–" Lucifer says but doesn't finish his sentence as he coughs on blood and his head drops to the side. Dabriel just stares down at him, his hands still on his chest.

"Dabriel . . . he is gone," I say, shaking his shoulder and needing him to get out of his shock. Dabriel stands up and nods, lifting his sword and standing in front of Freddy and Mich's wolf.

"Get everyone inside the castle, now," I shout and use my powers to send the message to all the witches.

I wrap an arm around Freddy and Mich, and Dabriel puts his hand on my shoulder before I move us all inside the castle. The castle shakes as we get inside, and I run back to the door with Dabriel at my side. The dragons' roars are loud enough to shake the castle, let alone their fight. I only hope Winter's dragon is strong enough to kill the others and take the demons with him.

"We fight together, brother, and save as many as we can," Dabriel says.

"Together," I say, and we run out into the battle as our people run inside.

93

WYATT

I swing one of my swords down over the head of the final demon in front of me as the castle shakes. I turn to see Jaxson has killed his demons but destroyed the castle as he has been using his power. The castle shakes, and all of us go flying into the side of the corridor, the remaining demons that are running towards us flying through one of the doors in the room. A loud scream makes me stand up as quick as I can.

"Winter," I shout when I hear her scream again, and this time it sounds more desperate than before. I run into the throne room with Jaxson following to see Winter on the ground, holding the crown in her hands as the demon king tries to pull it off her. I know if he gets that crown off her, he will control her, but I won't let that happen again.

"I will cut your hands off, little princess," the demon king warns, and I run over to him as he turns to see me.

"Ah the vampire comes to save little Winter," he laughs, letting go of the crown, and Winter falls to the ground. I look her over quickly, seeing the blood on her head and the cut that is healing but, otherwise, she looks okay. She is alive, at least.

"I've come for my queen and my crown," I nod my head towards the crown he is wearing that belongs to me. That crown has always been worn by the king of the vampires and, despite hating my father and the royal family I was born into, the crown is mine.

"You vampires are always fun to kill." He laughs. I chuck one of my swords over to him, and he catches it.

"Fair fight," I say, and he nods with a smirk. Jaxson runs into the room and over to Winter, and I see him from the corner of my eye, but I don't take my eyes off the demon king as he looks over at Winter.

"Wolfy has come to die, too? I have to say; your ancestor was the best one to kill. So easy," he says, and Jaxson's growl fills the room as well as another shake of the castle which almost makes me fall over. I hold my ground like the demon king does as he turns his evil, red eyes on me.

"I'm a demon, I don't play fair, so don't expect it, boy," he shrugs, looking every bit like my father as he does.

"Good thing I don't either," I say and use my vampire speed to rush at him, catching him off guard a little and cutting his side. He swings around, and I block with my own sword as he throws hit after hit, and I block him. He shocks me by using a red wave of his power, but my sword blocks it, cutting through the wave. His eyes widen as he takes in my fray touched sword, one that Freddy had his friend make for me. I manage to get him back across the room towards the portal with the fifth hit. He knows it by the evil smirk he gives me as our swords clash, and he throws wave after wave of red power between the hits. I look over to see Jaxson holding Winter as she screams for him to let her go and to help me. Her blue eyes meet mine, filled with worry, but I look away before I can feel any guilt for not spending more time with her. For not telling her what I planned today. I focus back on the demon king, his red eyes bright with power as he hits my sword again with a big bang and I twist, so my back is towards the portal. The coldness of the portal hits my back as I'm pushed against it with every hit of our swords. I hit him once more, but this time jump off the ground, catapulting over him and slam my legs into his back He looks on in shock as I send him flying against the ground in front of the portal, and his sword falls into the portal. I run after him and pick him up, pushing him into the blue portal with both my hands. I pull the crown off his head quickly with one hand, as he struggles to hold onto my other hand that is pushing him further into the portal. I edge my feet closer, knowing he could easily pull me in with him at this point.

"If I'm going, then so are you," he says as he struggles against me, and I push once more and let go, as I feel a sharp pain through my heart. The demon king laughs as he disappears into the portal, and I look down at the silver dagger in my heart.

"No, it can't be that," Dabriel says, standing up from the chair he is sitting on in the meeting room. Atti and Jaxson look at me in shock, not expecting me to tell them this when I asked to speak to them all before the war tomorrow. I called this meeting because Winter has to survive, nothing else matters to me, and I know they feel the same way. I never expected to fall for her, to love her more than myself.

"Listen to the prophecy: the words. I know it's me. I saved her, I brought her back to life. I'm her saviour," I tell Jaxson. I don't need to convince them what I already know.

"It's bullshit and doesn't mean anything. I'm not losing you because of some old prophecy, not after everything we have been through," Atti snaps out.

"The blue-sided human will choose a side.
When four princes are born on the same day, they will rule true.
Her saviour will die when the choice is made.
If she chooses wrong, she will fall.
If she chooses right, then she will rule.
Only her mates can stop her from the destruction of all.
If the fates allow, no one need fall.
For only the true kings hold her fate, and they will be her mates." I repeat the prophecy to them all, and they silently watch me.

"Every part of the prophecy has already come true. We were born on the same day, she chose right and rules all races. We as her mates stopped her from destroying everything with the demon king . . .," I say and clear my throat. "To close the portal, someone of her blood must die. I can feed on her and have her blood. I'm her saviour, and I will die for her." I finish my sentence, and Jaxson punches the wall next to him. Atti looks up at the ceiling, and Dabriel looks down at the ground. There aren't many words that can be said, nothing will change what has to happen. It will be me or her, and I'm going to make sure it's me. I just hope she knows the strength of my love for her, it's everything to me.

"Did you always know?" Atti asks me quietly, a look of shock on his face as he meets my gaze. His voice sounds like he has given up all hope, and he finally understands how I've been feeling for a long time.

"No. Not at first. I realised when she came back to life, and I had saved her," I tell him. I remember when I walked into the bedroom and saw her awake on my bed. I remember kissing her as I realised that I saved her and what that meant. Every part of me wanted to run away until she woke up, and then I knew, I knew I'd never leave her. If it meant death, then that was the price I'd willingly pay for my time with her. I never had true happiness, not with anyone, until her.

"That's a long time to know," Jaxson practically growls and starts pacing the room.

"The prophecy still says, 'If the fates allow, no one need fall,'"

Dabriel says. I know that part of the prophecy, but I doubt fate can save me now.

"Tomorrow, you need to get Winter out of the way," I tell Jaxson, who stops pacing and rubs his face with his hands.

"She will hate me for not stopping you. She will hate us all for knowing. We have to tell her," Jaxson says.

"If you tell her, she will never let me in the castle. She would die to save us all."

"I think that's been her plan all along," Atti says quietly.

"I want her alive, but this is too much, what you're asking for," Dabriel says, shaking his head.

"Let's put this simply, if any of you could die to save her, would you?" I ask them, and they don't say anything, which is the answer I needed.

"She will be alive, that's all that matters to me. Let me do this," I say. Jaxson's simple nod is all I need as an answer from him.

"Fine," Atti responds.

"The fates will stop this, no one is cruel enough to do this," Dabriel says, but I know from how he looks at me that he won't say anything. Winter is everything to us all, and we won't risk her life.

"NO!" Winter screams behind me, but I watch as my blood mixed with Winter's drops onto the portal, and it cracks. The portal slowly disappears as I fall to my knees, nothing else matters now. *I saved her.*

94

WINTER

"Let me go, Jaxson," I struggle against him as he holds me close, and I watch Wyatt push the demon king into the portal. The demon king says something to him, just as he falls into the portal and is too far inside to get out. *He did it.* I need to put my blood on the portal now and close it, ending this all. I have to die, or it can be opened again. All these thoughts rush through my mind as I continue to struggle in Jaxson's arms, and then I see the dagger. The demon king slides a dagger straight into Wyatt's chest and then falls into the portal. The portal cracks and closes when it hits me. Wyatt is my saviour and he fed on me, he has my blood. His death will close the portal.

"NO!" I shout, and Jaxson lets me go as the portal disappears completely, and Wyatt falls to his knees. I run over the broken stone all over the floor and avoid the bits that are still falling as the castle shakes, and I catch him just as he falls back, laying his head on my lap.

"Don't do this, please, God, no!" I scream, holding my hand over the dagger and pulling it out. I look at the blood-covered dagger, seeing it's the one Nathaniel made me. The dagger I tried to use on the demon king and he used to hurt Wyatt instead. I drop the dagger in shock. I place my hand on his chest and look over to Jaxson who kneels on the other side of Wyatt.

"DO SOMETHING!" I shout at him with tears running down my face, "Please," I beg, and he shakes his head as he bows his head.

"Nothing I can do, lass. I would save my brother if I could," he says, and I shake my head.

"Winter," Wyatt groans my name, his word mixed with pain as I look down at him.

"You cannot die . . . I love you so much. We have years left together, and children. I want my life with you," I say, my voice catching as I start crying harder.

"Dad!" I hear Freddy scream behind me, and I turn my head to see him running over with Dabriel and Atti following. They fall to their knees around Wyatt as I gently push a piece of his hair off his forehead with shaky hands.

"Heal him," I beg Dabriel, and he puts his hands on Wyatt's chest. Dabriel glows brightly for a few minutes before he takes his hands away and shakes his head.

"No, no, no, no," I mumble and hold Wyatt as close as I can.

"Thank you for being in my life, for saving Freddy, and for letting me love you. I would die over and over for you, Winter," he says as black lines crawl up his neck and cover his face. His dark eyes close, and I can't control the half sob and scream that escapes my lips.

"DEMTRA! ELISSA! MOTHER!" I scream their names again and again into the silent room as pain fills my body, and I close my eyes, resting my head on Wyatt's cold one. I can feel the emptiness of his loss, and the pain is overwhelming in my chest as waves of pain crash through me. They can't let it end like this, not like this. I don't want to live without him, not when he died for me. My mate. My saviour. My love.

"Come to me, help me now. I need you, I need my family to help me now and will never call you again," I whisper, and that's when I feel it. A coldness and stillness to the room that makes me look up. The castle has stopped shaking, and the room is still as snow falls through the hole in the ceiling onto us. Jaxson's wide eyes meet mine as I look around, and he nods behind me. I look behind me to see three, white, ghost-like figures, which gradually come into view as Elissa, Demtra, and my mother. All three of them have the white dresses on from my dreams, and it's Demtra that moves close to me.

"Do you know another name for a Goddess?" Demtra asks me, her voice is gentle and kind as my heart begins to fill with hope.

"No," I whisper as the others move away, so Demtra can kneel where Jaxson once was. They all look at her in shock before bowing their heads, even Freddy does as he shifts into a wolf, losing whatever control he had over his emotions.

"Fates," she says.

"If the fates allow, no one need fall," Atti whispers the line of the prophecy for all of us to hear and Freddy's wolf howls into the night. The howl is full of hope, much like what is filling my chest as I watch my family. I don't take my eyes off Demtra as my mother and Elissa move to her side. They both place a hand on her shoulders.

"The vampires have the mark of a phoenix for a reason, sweet Winter. Phoenix's are reborn," Demtra says and places both her hands on Wyatt's stomach. The black lines slowly disappear before he takes a deep breath, and his dark eyes open, locking onto mine.

"Wyatt . . . Wyatt, oh my God," I sob out in between tears as he sits up and pulls me into his arms. I look over Wyatt's shoulder to see all three of them standing close together and watching us.

"It's our time to rest and your time to rule, this is your fate, Queen Winter," Elissa says gently before she and Demtra disappear into the snow that fills the room. I lock eyes with my mother, and I know this is the last time I'm going to see her.

"Thank you, and I love you, Mum," I say in a whisper, but her whole face lights up.

"We are so proud of you, our Winter," my mother whispers as she disappears too, and my breath catches in my throat. I feel my other mates kneel next to us. None of us move for a long time.

"We won," Atti finally says into the silence of the snow-filled destroyed room.

Yes, we did.

"Is the castle safe?" I ask as Freddy's wolf comes and places his head on Wyatt's lap. Wyatt strokes his head as Freddy whines.

"Yes, your dragon turned up, and the fray created some tornados . . . ."

"Tornadoes and dragons . . . is anyone else alive?"

"Yes, we saved a lot of people, and the demons are dead. Harris is leading some fighters to check the rest, and the angels are now healing everyone. We won," Dabriel answers for me. I don't respond as Wyatt gently tilts my face to his, and brushes his lips against mine. I feel nothing but relief and happiness through my bond from all of them.

"It's over," I whisper, and everyone hears my words.

EPILOGUE

Winter

"Where was I?" I ask as I finish feeding the baby in my arms her bottle of milk. I place the bottle on the bench next to me and carry on my story.

"We won the battle against the bad king of demons, and the big dragon that lives in the mountains now, killed the other bad dragons and demons here. There were many brave people lost in the war, but they will never be forgotten. Now, we live in peace, with cute little babies everywhere like you," I tell Ella, as I rock her in my arms, and she looks up at me. Not that she understands a single word I'm saying, as she is two months old. I glance up at my home, the Goddess' castle and see how it looks far better since the war. The dragons destroyed a lot of it, so we had to build again, but it didn't matter to us. The only thing that mattered was the fact that most of the supernaturals got inside the castle and to the underground dungeons before the massive, dragon fight. I wish I could say thank you to my dragon that won. He lives in one of the mountains around the castle, and we see him fly over the castle at times. He is like our protector now. The castle has been made more modern while we did the fixes it needed. There is a lot we had to deal with, like the humans who now hunt our kind or anything that seems supernatural since the war. The governments have an order to kill any supernaturals they find, but our witches send out messages to any stray supernaturals, to come here and we will keep them safe. I hate that our people can't be safe everywhere anymore, but it's not something I can change. We have the witches' city back, after a long time of building new wards around it and safely removing the humans who found the island.

"I doubt the stories of how the war was won are the best kind of baby story to help my daughter sleep," Alex says as she walks over to me. I glance up at my best friend as she laughs at me.

"I didn't know what to say to a baby. Everyone keeps handing me babies and expecting me to know what to do." I laugh as I hand over her daughter to her.

"Well, auntie Winter, maybe try fairy tales next time," she says. I guess that makes sense.

"Like the big bad wolf?" I joke, and she laughs.

"Speaking of wolves, your mates want you. They're waiting outside the castle," she says, and I stand up from the bench I was sitting on.

"Alright." I say and kiss her cheek before walking back through the newly planted trees that lead to the castle. My mates are sitting on the bottom steps, Wyatt is laughing with Jaxson over something, and Dabriel is looking at something on Atti's phone. For the first few months after nearly losing Wyatt, I never let him out my sight. I kept all my mates close as we rebuilt everything we lost in the war. I wasn't happy that Wyatt died for me and that my other mates knew, but then, I was prepared to do the same sacrifice for him. In the end, we all love each other that much that we want to make sure we all live. I don't see how that can be considered a bad thing. I look over to see Dabriel straighten up, his eyes going white like he does when he has a vision. I run over and stop in front of him, all of us silent as we wait for him to come back from the vision. When his purple eyes come into focus, he looks down at me and I take his hand in mine.

"Adelaide," he whispers, and I frown at him.

"Who is that?" I ask, considering it's an unusual name, and I think I would remember it.

"The fray you will meet. I saw you shaking hands with her and someone else saying 'this is Adelaide,' and then what looked like a portal opened," he tells me.

"How did you know she is the fray child?" I ask him, hoping for any way to get out of this vision being right.

"I could see her aura, it was so red and bright. It looked just like a fray's, and I doubt a portal would open for anyone other than the royal," he tells me, and I nod, letting him pull me into his arms. I feel sick at the idea of Lily being anywhere near Adelaide, even if I don't know her. I have spoken to many of the fray that survived the wars, and they all speak only of her cruelness. They say she is an insane queen that is touched by the God of Death, but I don't understand their Gods enough to make sense of that. All the fray are slowly losing their powers, now, and they say it is what they want, but I still feel sorry for them.

"We will worry about the promise another day, we can't do anything about it now," I say after a long pause, and he sighs.

"That is true," he leans down and gently kisses me.

"I heard you all wanted me?" I ask, and he smiles.

"We found something and want to show you," Atti says

and links my other hand in his. We walk around the castle, where we pass the outside training area. Freddy and Nathaniel are training, both of them circling each other with swords. Mich and Josh are watching from the sides and drinking water. It's good to see them all together, all friends. It's like what my mates had with each other growing up.

"They have gotten close since the war. Freddy told me that Mich, Josh, and Nath saved him, and that's how Mich ended up getting hurt in the war," Wyatt tells us. Wyatt and Freddy have gotten closer, too, and I couldn't be happier to see that change come about. Freddy actually calls him Dad since the war. I think losing Wyatt for that brief time made Freddy realise how much he actually loves Wyatt, but he wouldn't admit that out loud to us. Stroppy, teenage hormones and all that. Josh waves as we walk past, and I wave back. I was sad to learn of Lucifer's death in the war, and I'm keeping my promise to bring Josh up. I moved him into Freddy's room, and now he is part of my family, despite the fact Josh doesn't speak to us much, and I have no idea what he is.

"So, why are we going into the woods?" I ask, trying to distract myself as we take a path into the woods to the left of the castle, where I have never been before.

"It's a surprise," Atti laughs.

"You know I don't like surprises, unless they are chocolate-covered," I say, making them all laugh, but I'm being deadly serious. A chocolate surprise is always a good one. We walk around the woods for a little while before we get to a lake that is hidden within the trees. You couldn't see it from the castle before, but now that some of the trees were burnt down, the sun is shining down on the lake, and it's really beautiful here. I think it's the calmness of the water and the way it feels like you're away from the world here.

"It's beautiful here," I comment, looking up as Dabriel pulls me to his chest.

"You remember that vision I had of us all by a lake, and Freddy was much older? The one I told you about once," Dabriel asks me.

"I remember. Was it here?" I ask, knowing that Dabriel said he felt complete in the vision. Much like I do now with all my mates when war isn't chasing us, and we have our lives to enjoy.

"Yes, and I didn't tell you something about that vision," he says, and I pull away a little to look up at him.

"What was it?"

"You. You were pregnant in that vision, Winter," he tells me, and I lean up and kiss him, knowing we will have our future we fought for. *It was worth all this.* I lean back and catch a glance of three figures in white dresses floating in the middle of the lake, feeling their love from here.

This was my fate and my future, with all my mates.

The End.

ALSO BY G. BAILEY

The King Brothers Series-

Izzy's Beginning (Book one)

Sebastian's Chance (Book two)

Elliot's Secret (Book three)

Harley's Fall (Book Four)

Luke's Revenge (Coming soon)

Her Guardians Series-

Winter's Guardian (Book one)

Winter's Kiss (Book two)

Winter's Promise (Book three)

Winter's War (Book Four)

Her Fate Series-

(Her Guardians Series spinoff)

Adelaide's Fate (Coming soon)

Adelaide's Trust (Coming soon)

Adelaide's Storm (Coming soon)

Saved by Pirates Series-

Escape the sea (Book One)

Love the sea (Book Two)

Save the sea (Coming soon)

Only one night series-

Strip for me (Book one)

Live for Me (Coming soon)

The Marked Series (Co-written with Cece Rose)-

Marked by Power (Book one)

Marked by Pain (Book two)

Snow and Seduction anthology-

Triple Kisses

The Forest Pack series-

Run Little Wolf- (Coming soon)

Protected by Dragons series-

Wings of Ice- (Coming Soon)

LINKS

Here are all my links (I love to be stalked so if you have some free time...)-

🖤Join my FB Group?🖤-

https://www.facebook.com/groups/BaileysPack/

🖤Like my FB Page?🖤-

https://www.facebook.com/gbaileyauthor/

💖Be my FB friend?💖-

https://www.facebook.com/AuthorG.Bailey

💛Add me on Twitter?💛-

https:twitter.com/gbaileyauthor

💘Check out my website?💘-

www.gbaileyauthor.com

🤍Follow me on Amazon?🤍-

http://amzn.to/2oV9PF5

🖤Sign up for my Newsletter?🖤-

https://landing.mailerlite.com/webforms/landing/a1f2v0

BONUS EPILOGUE SCENES

"Ella! Get back here right now!" I hear Alex shout nearby, and I get up off my desk after signing another letter of acceptance to the castle school. I look over to my bed, seeing Milo snoring on the pillow, empty Oreo packets all around him and crumbs everywhere. *Wyatt is going to try and kill him, again.* I walk to the door with a chuckle, holding it open just as Alex stomps past me, her hands on her hips and long red hair moving around her like it's alive. *Or just as angry as she looks.*

"What has your daughter done now?" I ask, trying not to chuckle as Alex stops, throws her hands up in the air dramatically, and groans.

"You don't even want to know. That girl is ten, and acts like she is a teenager already!" she exclaims, locking her eyes with mine. "Plus, her vampire speed is ridiculous. We can never catch her, she's faster than everyone!"

"Why don't I find our daughter, and have a word with her?" Drake says as he walks to us, pulling Alex to his side and kissing the top of her head. She smiles up at him, still as in love with each other as they have always been.

"We should both go, team work and all that," Alex says, patting his chest and he laughs. Fatherhood suits Drake, it makes him more like a human, less cold. Even though he is still definitely an old vampire, and still acts that way sometimes

"Good luck with that, I'll see you later," I say with a low chuckle. Still shaking my head, I walk past them and down the corridor. A few teenage witches and a wolf are scrambling down the hall, but stop to bow to me. Pulling my black jumper tighter around myself, I smile and nod at them before continuing on my way. It's freezing today, and I have a feeling snow is coming soon. I've gotten sort of used to the bowing, but it's still a little weird for me. At least I don't do the awkward wave anymore. I walk past an open balcony, seeing Atti standing there, staring out while the wind blows his shoulder length blonde hair around him. We're on the witches' island where the castle is still being re-built, and the royal supernatural school for all has just opened. It's been a long road to get the witches' island back, and get a good ward up to protect the island and its inhabitants. I walk over, stopping next to him, and he wraps a giant arm around my waist, pulling me to his side.

"Everything is so peaceful here, you wouldn't know all the troubles that plague our people by just looking from up here," he comments, and I follow his gaze to the island. Half the land is covered in tents, and small trees have been planted across the island. Many witches and shifters need to be close to nature, so the trees were beneficial for them. The other side of the island is fully built, with multi-coloured houses. It looks almost exactly like it did before it was destroyed, but with one major difference. All races live here now, and as well at the goddesses' castle. There is no species divide, and several hundred new half borns have been born over the years. Including my godson Zane,

Harris and Leigha's oldest son. They have three children now, and it doesn't seem like they are going to stop having children anytime soon. Leigha is an amazing mother, and Harris has never looked so happy.

"The hunters are continuing to get stronger and more aggressive. Perhaps it's time we find a permanent solution for dealing with them, before they become even more of a threat to us. I'm getting worried. I don't like that we had to leave the pack lands because of their attacks," I say. I hate the reports of the hunters' assaults, but the bodies that keep being brought to me and my mates are heartbreaking and unacceptable. Human hunters have become a strong, destructive force since the war. They were initially created after the destruction in Paris. The humans demanded their governments took action and wanted to make sure supernaturals were controlled. At first, they would just arrest supernaturals, and we would break them out, bringing them to the castle. But now, they are out of control, indiscriminately killing any supernatural they find without a second thought.

"We should make a plan with the council. Freddy, Josh, Nath, and Mich are more connected with the human world than we are now. It is probably best we ask their advice, and try to find a solution that doesn't bring about a war with the hunters," Atti comments, lifting my hand and gently kissing the back of it. The moment his lips touch my skin, a blinding flash of white fills my mind, and I feel myself falling without any control and Atti shouts my name.

"Josh, are you in here?" I ask, walking into his room after knocking, but not hearing any reply. Josh is sat on the floor, his head in his hands. Everything in the room is burnt to a crisp. Only the burn

patterns, outlines of where furniture stood can be seen. All that is left of the wardrobe and bed are piles of dust.

"Josh…" I utter quietly, wondering what the hell happened in here. Eventually it dawns on me–it might have been his change. He turned sixteen today, and we have all been expecting some kind of change to happen soon. Freddy and the rest of his friends all developed their powers recently. He doesn't move when I speak, but a large pair of wings spread out from his back, hovering in the air. They are striking, almost a glossy black colour, and they match perfectly with his black messy hair.

"Stunning, they are just stunning Josh," I breathe as I try to step closer, but he holds up a shaky hand.

"Don't. I don't want to hurt you and I'm worried I will. I can't control the blue fire," he begs me, his voice cracking and anxious. I shake my head, ignoring his warning, walking further into the room. I kneel down on the floor in front of him, not touching him, but still close enough that he knows I'm there for him. He needs me, and I won't run away, that's not who I am.

"Look at me Josh," I tell him firmly. He looks up, his glowing blue eyes meeting mine. I suddenly realise what he is, and I think he knows too by his nervous expression.

"You're half demon, and half dark angel," I say, needing to make sure he understands.

"I'm a monster," he mutters, and I frown. I pull him into a hug, holding him close even when he stiffens and doesn't return the hug.

"If you're a monster, then so am I. Whatever part of us that is demon, doesn't control us or make us evil. You have a choice, you get to decide. I'm here to help you," I say, meaning every word. The demon side of me never made me evil, never changed who I am, and it won't for him either. Not with me and my mates to guide him.

"I never really had a mum, not one I can remember anyway. Can I call you mum?" he asks, his voice so quiet and unusual for him. Josh is a cocky little arsehole according to Jaxson, Freddy, and well, everyone at the castle. Yet I know there is this different side to him, an

uncertain and kind side that he doesn't reveal to everyone. It's all a front, to make sure he doesn't get hurt again. He lost his mum, his dad and his half siblings hate him, so he protects himself in the only way he knows how.

"I've been your mum for the last four years, even when you argue with me, even when you eat my chocolate, and that will never change," I say honestly. It's been the same with Freddy. "Now let's get out of here, and go to celebrate your change."

"Celebrate?"

"Yes, celebrate. Besides, you know I will kick anyone's ass if they dare say a bad word about my son," I say, and he laughs.

"Okay, mum."

"Winter? Winter come back to us," Dabriel's voice quietly urges me. I manage to blink my eyes open, feeling cold and exhausted. *Really exhausted.*

"What happened?" I ask with a croaky voice, and Dabriel slides an arm around my waist, helping sit me up. Atti doesn't say a word, just sits silently at my other side looking stressed. Jaxson and Wyatt storm into the room, slamming the door open so hard it falls off the hinges, and crashes to the floor.

"What the fuck happened, lass?" Jaxson demands. Every word is a growl, but I know it's only from worry. He storms to my side with Wyatt going to the other, placing his hand on my leg, comforting me by just being here.

"Dab? We heard Winter passed out and was glowing, but nothing else," Wyatt asks him.

"We, I, don't know. Why don't you tell us what happened in your mind, Winter, and then we can try to figure it out?" he asks me, and all of them stare at me expectantly.

"Couldn't you just heal me, and find out?" I blurt out. I don't really have a clue what just happened.

"I tried, but until you woke up, a blue ward was surrounding your body. It was blocking me from healing you. I was powerless, and I don't like it," Dabriel explains to me. "Now what happened?"

"It was a memory from years ago, when Josh first got his demon powers and his wings. It was like I was me, back then, reliving it. I had no control over what was happening. It wasn't like my dreams I used to have before the war. Those were always like I was watching from the outside," I explain, making them all look confused.

"Dab, check her over. Something weird is going on, and it's too random for Winter to just have new powers appear," Jaxson says.

"Lie back please," Dabriel asks me gently, and I do as requested. I keep still as he starts glowing white and hovering his hands over my body, starting from my head and moving downward. When he gets to my stomach, his face scrunches up, just as a blue light blasts out of me, sending all the guys flying back from me. The light came from my stomach, and I sit up, holding it as I look around at my mates, speechless.

"Is everyone okay?" I ask nervously as I start to panic. Jaxson gets up first, shaking his head, and dust falling all around him.

"I'm good lass, you?" he asks, stepping over the bed collapsed in front of him.

"I'm fine. Wake the others, they all look passed out," I say, turning on the bed and a wave of dizziness hits me, making me not want to move again. Jaxson walks over, lifting a table off Wyatt and slapping his face.

"Wake up," he says bluntly. Wyatt comes around, sitting up and searching the room for me.

"I'm okay," I say, seeing the question on his lips before he even asks it. Atti lifts himself off the floor, and uses his power to disappear and re-appear right next to me, his hand going straight to my head.

"You're hot," he says, and I laugh.

"Why thank you," I joke, making him rolls his eyes at me. I look over to see Jaxson holding up a dazed looking Dabriel until he can stand on his own. I could have really hurt them, and I don't know how I even did it. I thought I mastered control over my powers years ago. They have never acted like that before. Dabriel walks straight over to me, falling to his knees next to the bed and placing his hands on my stomach.

"You're pregnant, Winter," he says, the word pregnant seems to echo around the room. None of us say a word for a few moments, stunned into silence. I slide my hands over Dabriel's, knowing my baby is in there and look up to Jaxson who kneels on his other side, placing his hand over mine. Atti sits on the bed next to me, and Wyatt on the other side, both of them sliding a hand over Dabriel's, cradling my stomach as well.

"A baby," I whisper, tears falling down my cheeks as the words catch in my throat.

"Thank you for choosing us," Atti says, tears leaving his own eyes, like all my mates. I meet each one of their eyes, seeing their love, their happiness, and I know I have everything.

BONUS EPILOGUE SCENES

SEVEN MONTHS LATER.

"Alex!" I shout, and she comes into the room, her hands on her hips with Leigha waddling in after her.

"How are you a month behind me and still bigger?" Leigha comments, smoothing her hand over her small bump.

"Because every time you get pregnant, you still look like a supermodel, and yet, I look like an elephant with swollen feet?" I snap, making her laugh.

"And hormonal, don't forget that one," she replies.

"Sorry, I'm just frustrated, and no amount of chocolate or sex is fixing it," I groan.

"It gets like that towards the end, it's not long now," Leigha says placatingly. She is trying to be nice, which is so unlike her, and really shows how pitiful I must be, "I have to go to collect the kids from daycare." Leigha sighs, before walking out of the room. Alex walks over to me, patting my shoulder as she rests against the chair.

"Can't get out of the chair again?" she asks, with a chuckle that makes me want to throw something at her. I look down at my gigantic bump, that is growing out of control, making it impossible to get up without help now.

"Nope, my huge ass is stuck," I grumble, and she shakes her head at me. She keeps insisting I look beautiful and that I'm glowing, but I don't believe it. Not the last few months anyway. Jaxson walks into the room, shaking his head at me with a smirk on his lips.

"I've got this, Alex," he says. Alex kisses my cheek before she gets up and starts to walk out of the room. She pauses when she passes Jaxon, and whispers a low, "Good luck."

"I heard that!" I shout as she darts out the door. I can hear her laughing as she goes down the hall.

"Lass, you look so tired, why don't I take you to bed?" Jaxson suggests, his own tired eyes watching mine. He picks me up off the chair like I weigh nothing, and holds me close to him. I breathe in his scent that I love so much; it always reminds me of the forest and home. It is particularly strong right now, letting me know he must have shifted and gone for a run recently.

"I can walk," I protest, making him grin.

"No, you can't. You waddle. Trust me there is a big difference," he says, but when he sees my glare, he quickly follows with "but you look beautiful either way. Now, let's get you to bed."

"I'm going to ignore that comment about my *walking*, but you know I can't sleep. The baby kicks all night, and during the day…the visions happen if I try to sleep," I tell him, but he already knows. He just doesn't know how to make it better for me, none of my mates do. They feel helpless. They're not used to the feeling, and they hate it. Jaxson kisses my forehead, and carries me across the hallway, pushing the door open with his shoulder. We all know the baby is Dabriel's, because I regularly see visions of the past and the future. Only angels have that power, but we are all confused as to how I'm seeing both the past and the future. Angels only get one power, never the ability to see both. Unfortunately, the baby won't let anyone check on her or him. We have tried everything we can think of to examine the baby, but the baby won't let us. We even attempted human scanners and putting me to sleep, but the baby always tries to protect the both of us by throwing everything around us back with its powers. It got to the point when I told everyone to stop trying because they were getting hurt. I could feel the baby kicking me, so we knew it was safe and alive.

"Winter," I hear Dabriel say with a yawn. Jaxson turns us so I can see Dabriel as he sits up from the bed he was resting on. All of my mates look as exhausted as I feel at the moment. We're waiting for me to go into labour, and they insist on being with me day and night. I want them to rest, but with the danger that the hunters pose and everything we have going on, it's just not happening.

"We shouldn't have woken you up," I say, feeling guilty. Jaxon puts me down on the bed next to him, and Dabriel immediately places a hand on my stomach.

"Yes, you should have. I slept well, so do not worry," he chastises softly. The baby starts to kick, making Dabriel's whole face light up. I look across the room at the nursery that is all set up. Jaxson made a crib from scratch, with our marks engraved all around it. There are protection crystals in the sides of the crib, from the crystal trees that are finally starting to grow back on the island. Everyone wanted the baby to have the first crystals. I have to admit I burst into tears when the witches who grew the trees handed me the crystals. Jaxson meets my gaze, an equal look of both concern and love in his eyes. Over the years, I never thought I could love them more but it seems each year I do. Our past troubles, our years of relative peace, and now our surprise on the way have just brought us all that much closer.

"Jaxson, the baby is kicking," I say, and he kneels down, putting his hand next to Dabriel's on my stomach. The thin blue vest top does little to hide the foot that you can see kick my stomach and disappear again. The baby must be so big and strong now.

"Have you decided on a name yet?" Jaxson asks me, and I shake my head.

"Erm, no. I still don't think you can choose someone's name before they are born. So, I'm waiting until I see the baby's eyes and beautiful face," I say, and they both grin at me. We all sit in contented silence for a while, just enjoying the peaceful moment and each other's company. At least, until my stomach starts rumbling, and my thoughts immediately turn to chocolate. If I thought I was addicted to chocolate before I was pregnant, I'm one hundred per cent a true addict now. *And ice cream, I need all the ice cream.*

"I'm going to the kitchen. I'm hungry," I suddenly say, trying to get up before Dabriel wraps an arm around my shoulders.

"I will go and get your chocolate box from the kitchen, you rest," he says, his hand rubbing my shoulder and making me moan a little from his expert fingers. *He could do that all day.*

"I'm pregnant, not suffering from broken legs or something. You stay here, and I will go," I demand and they both look between each other, likely sorting out which is brave enough to tell me no

"Nothing you can say will make me stay in this room, so just get over that now. I need fresh air," I state before either of them can try and talk me out of it.

"Fine, but we will both come with you," Jaxson says, offering me a hand and lifting me up.

"I can deal with hot escorts, but not jailers," I say, and they both chuckle.

"I thought you liked being tied up, at least you did that last time, lass," Jaxson remarks with a smirk, making my cheeks burn red. I choose to ignore his comment and push past him to walk out of the room. *That was a good night.*

I walk past Freddy and Josh's room at the end of the empty corridor.

"I miss them. I can't help but worry they need me somehow, and I'm stuck here, pregnant and unable to help them," I say, placing my hand on the door.

"They would call for us if they needed our help," Dabriel says, picking up my hand, and kissing my knuckles before linking our fingers.

"I know, but my un-rational side thinks something is wrong with them and Adelaide," I say, remembering the red-haired girl that has my sons completely enamored with her. I like her, but I wish I'd actually had a chance to get to know her better.

"There is nothing for you to worry about, other than having this baby, and staying well," Jaxson says and something in his tone gives me pause. I look over to him, only to see him avoiding my gaze. I've been with them for nearly eleven years now, and I know when they're lying to me. They all do this, they avoid looking directly at me. Every damn time, it's because they believe they are protecting me from something. Men and their overprotective bullshit are annoying as hell. *And maybe a little bit sexy, but that's not the point.*

"What are you hiding from me?" I demand, crossing my arms.

"Nothing," they both say in unison. *Right.*

"You're both lying to me. I know it, and you know it. Now, out with whatever you're keeping from me," I insist, and Dabriel sighs, moving next to Jaxson. I know they would have only kept something from me to prevent me from worrying, but that doesn't mean it's ok and that I'm not mad

"I had a vision. They will be in trouble soon, but even if we sent help…I don't think we can help them," Dabriel says sadly.

"No!" I shout, shaking my head and my hands start glowing blue as I panic.

"They aren't going to die, Winter. We would tell you of that and help no matter what. It's just complicated, and none of us can leave while you're like this," Jaxson points at my stomach.

"How long until they need you?" I ask, ignoring the mild discomfort I start to feel in my back.

"A week," Jaxson says. Suddenly a sharp pain shoots through the bottom of my stomach, nearly causing me to fall over but Jaxson and Dabriel are at my sides in seconds, catching my arms. I look down as water pours down my legs, soaking the floor and my boots.

"Seems like you will be helping Adelaide and the rest of our family soon, as the baby is coming," I say, breathless as another pain shoots through my stomach.

"One problem at a time," Jaxson soothes as he lifts me up into his arms.

"Getting closer now," I breath out between contractions, and Alex holds my hand tightly. The guys have been at my side for the last eight hours, and Alex has taken over for a little bit so they can sit down. Long labours are normal for supernaturals, so this was expected.

"Do you want me to get you anything?" she asks me, and I shake my head.

"My mum, I want my mum here, but I know that's impossible," I say, and Alex wipes a tear from my cheek as I try not to sob. I wish she was here, to help, to hold my baby when she or he is born. This is something your mother should be there for, and mine can't be. *I just miss her.*

"She is here, even if you can't see her, Win," she says, and the two midwives in the room come over to me with gloves on.

"Let's have a look then Queen Winter," the witch midwife with black hair says and I nod.

"Can we do anything?" Atti asks, from where he, Jaxson, Dabriel and Wyatt are all sat near the window with panic all over their faces.

"Nothing other than sit and wait, your highnesses," the midwife says, and looks under the blanket as I bend my knees. She looks back up at me, and smiles.

"I can almost see the head, it's time to push and meet your baby," she says. I wait for the next contraction before doing just that.

"Keep pushing!" the midwife shouts and I scream, keeping my head down. I feel like I'm being ripped apart from the pain, but I refuse to give up. *I will do this*. A bright blue light fills the room, blinding us all as I feel the pressure wane and seconds later we all hear a cry as the light disappears. It's a baby's cry, and it's the sweetest noise I've ever heard.

"Congratulations, a little baby girl," the midwife says, lifting the baby and placing her on my chest as she cuts the cord and ties it. I look down into my baby's blue eyes, see her puff of white hair, and I instantly fall in love. *She is perfect.*

"A girl," Jaxson says, and I look over, joyfully laughing as I see all my mates on the one side of my bed, watching us. They look just as in love as I do.

"Our girl," I correct, and then have to hold my stomach with my other hand as another contraction shoots through me, making me cry out in pain. The baby cries a little, and I try to comfort her as I wait for the contraction to pass.

"Queen Winter?" the midwife asks, feeling my stomach with her hands and frowning.

"Contractions again," I mutter, holding back the scream as another one hits me. The two midwives talk quietly to each other, and Alex brings a blanket over, helping me wrap our baby girl up.

"She is stunning, just like her mum," Alex says, "and auntie." I laugh, knowing Alex isn't actually related to me, so that's impossible. The pain in my stomach returns, and the laugh turns into a pain filled moan.

"The pain, please hold her," I try to say quietly, but end up screaming. Atti lifts our baby girl up off me, holding her close as she cries.

"What is wrong with my mate? Someone do something!" Wyatt demands as Jaxson and Alex hold my hand. Dabriel goes to the midwife's side, talking quietly, before coming around to me.

"It's twins. There's another baby, but we couldn't tell because we couldn't scan you," he explains and I groan, leaning my head back.

"I can't do that again," I almost cry. Everything is so sore, and the idea of pushing out another baby seems impossible.

"You can, because you are the strongest person in the

world. You do this for our children, Winter," Atti tells me, "we all love you and want to meet our children."

"And we are right here with you," Jaxson says firmly. I squeeze Jaxson and Wyatt's hands as I push again, the midwife's words guiding me. Wyatt and Atti stand near me, with Wyatt stroking our baby girls face, as Atti rocks her until she stops crying. Another much darker blue light fills the room as our second baby is born through my screams. The sweet sound of my baby's cries makes me burst into tears, and Jaxson kisses my forehead. The midwife lifts our little baby into my arms, cutting the cord as I hold the baby close and see that he is a boy. He has my dark hair, but Dabriel's purple eyes, that are almost glowing, and little dimples on his cheeks that are so cute.

"A boy, one of each," I say. Alex brings us another blanket, wrapping my little boy up, and Atti passes me back our girl.

"Congratulations," Alex says quietly to all of us. We don't move for a while as the midwife helps me with the after birth. My natural healing kicks in, making me feel much better.

"Names?" Jaxson asks, holding our son's little hand, which squeezes his finger tightly. Dabriel is holding our girl, with Atti and Wyatt looking over at her and waiting for their turns to hold the babies. These babies are never being put down, that's for sure.

"I don't know," I blurt out, and they all chuckle.

"What do you think about Alina for our daughter's name?" Atti asks quietly, lifting his head so his grey eyes lock with mine.

"Your mother's name?" I ask, remembering from the many times we have talked about her, "I would love that, if that's okay with everyone else?" I look around to see all my mates nod, and Atti walks over, kissing my forehead.

"Thank you, it means everything to me," he says, making me cry again.

"Alina Isa?" Jaxson says, knowing I wanted to carry on my middle name if we had a girl, and I wipe my tears away, trying not to cry anymore.

"And the boy, any ideas?" I ask as Wyatt hands me a tissue. I flash him a thankful smile.

"Alina means light and so does Lucian," Wyatt comments as Dabriel hands him Alina. I look down at my little boy, knowing it's perfect.

"They were both born in light, so it's fitting it's their names. Princess Alina and Prince Lucian," I say, loving how their names fit them so perfectly.

"Our future," Jaxson comments quietly, and I know that our future is now complete.

Made in the USA
Coppell, TX
17 January 2022

71767632R10446